# BORN OF
# LEGEND

# BORN OF LEGEND

## SHERRILYN KENYON

ST. MARTIN'S PRESS  New York

BORN OF LEGEND. Copyright © 2016 by Sherrilyn Kenyon. All rights reserved.
Printed in the United States of America. For information, address St. Martin's Press,
175 Fifth Avenue, New York, N.Y. 10010.

www.stmartins.com

The Library of Congress Cataloging-in-Publication Data is available upon request.

ISBN 978-1-250-08274-9 (hardcover)
ISBN 978-1-250-08282-4 (e-book)

Our books may be purchased in bulk for promotional, educational, or business use.
Please contact your local bookseller or the Macmillan Corporate and
Premium Sales Department at 1-800-221-7945, extension 5442, or by e-mail
at MacmillanSpecialMarkets@macmillan.com.

First Edition: June 2016

10  9  8  7  6  5  4  3  2  1

For my big brother, who taught me to read and was my first fan and who always believed in The League series. I miss you more every day, and I would have given anything if you could have seen just one of my books in print.

For every underdog who's been misunderstood and felt out of place, and who's been knocked down so hard the blows staggered them. Who had a dream, saw it crushed, got back up, and kept going anyway. As my brother always said, there's no guarantee in life, except that you will always fail whatever task you never undertake. And you're never defeated until you decide to quit.

To my boys and husband who are my life, and who have seen me through untold heartaches. For my readers, who are family, and to my friends for keeping me sane. Thank you all for being part of my life.

And as always, to Monique, Alex, Robert, John, Eric, Ervin, Mark, Nancy, Angie, Jen, and everyone at St. Martin's and Trident who work so incredibly hard on the books to make them a reality. And The MB Staff: Kim, Paco, Lisa, and Carl, and all the volunteers who keep things running smoothly! You guys are the best!

Hunger only for a taste of justice
'Cause all that you have is your soul
—Tracy Chapman, *All That You Have Is Your Soul*

# BORN OF LEGEND

# AN ANCIENT
# ANDARION LEGEND

In all the worlds, in all the legends, and in all the myths, there is only one that can make the stoutest Andarion warrior tremble like a newborn child. Only one that breathes unholy terror into his intrepid heart.

For there is only one beast we know who is truly unstoppable.

The merciless *Dagger Ixur*.

Said to be among the oldest legends of our race, the Dagger Ixur was born to the goddess of evil magic, Samari, and pure unrestrained evil she was. With her sons Duffarrar (malevolence), Fain (violence), and Arixur (darkness), she cut a trail of brutal slaughter across the lands of Andaria, laying waste to all, and taking pity upon no one.

Yet for all her heartless cruelty she loved her sons dearly.

*All* of them.

And none more so than the winged god, Koriłon, who was named for the turbulent fire he breathed. He, the darkest god of our pantheon, would hunt down the souls of the damned for his mother, and cast them into the barbarous pits of Tophet, where those who'd committed the worst acts of cowardice, and crimes against others would spend eternity in torment, forever denied the honor of reincarnation, or any comfort or solace from their suffering. Because of his pitiless brutality that could never be bargained with or daunted, Koriłon was the one child Samari held closest to her heart.

Until the day came when Saint Sarn began civilizing the Andarion races—unifying the tribes and bringing peace to our warring lands. It is said that on the very hour of the First Plenum, when the mighty Dancer War Hauk gave up the throne of Andaria to the lesser Anatole so that his Hauk bloodline could reign as the first warrior clan, Samari's sons turned against their parents for allowing such a travesty to stand.

In their great warriors' eyes, it weakened our world to have a lesser bloodline rule our races and not a true warrior on the throne.

It weakened our Warrior pantheon.

In a vengeful fury, the war gods struck down their lesser, weak parents, and when Koriłon's winged Warsword plunged deep into the womb of his mother, her heart burst apart, into a dozen blackened shards over his betrayal. With her final breath, she gave life to those fragments and cursed her four sons to die in brutal agony at the end of every day at the hands of those new children—to mark when her four traitorous spawn had ruthlessly struck her down.

*The Dagger Ixur*—they were created from those broken shards—the remnants of her shattered heart.

Her final vengeance on this world.

At the light of each dawn, Samari's four original sons arise, restored to attend their godly duties, but come the twilight shadows when Samari's dark breath again kisses the Andarion landscape, the Dagger Ixur emerge from their mother's kiss as unstoppable phantoms to seek their vengeance, first on the immortal *Petguar* who betrayed their goddess mother, and then on any child who has broken his mother's heart.

And so it goes, even now. Samari's vengeance continues and with the falling of every evening, the Dagger Ixur are released. As silent wraiths, they stalk the shadows in search of those who have made their mothers regret their births. Those who have brought shame to their lineages.

No one can escape their wrath or their justice.

For their fury is all-consuming and their aim is ever true. After all, Dagger Ixur is the Andarion term for a dark blade through the heart. And if there is a son who has made his mother weep for his birth, who has betrayed her love and returned it with hatred, they will destroy him and lay him in his grave. This is their sacred covenant with the goddess Samari. It is one they will never break.

All a mother has to do is invoke their name to seek their aid in punishing her misbegotten child.

That sacred pact is what every male with a drop of Andarion blood fears most about nightfall, and why even the stoutest heart casts a sheepish eye toward every shadowy corner. That fear alone is the one thing no other Andarion would dare mock him for. Because you never know when the Dagger Ixur will be coming next to claim your soul.

But the one thing you do know for sure.

When it comes for you, there is no escape. There is no quarter. There is no hope.

There is only pain and death. And it waits with arms wide open to welcome you in should you ever turn a coward's side in battle, betray a friend, or shame your blood with your actions. For the gods see all.

They know all.

And the shadows of the Dagger Ixur own the night.

# CHAPTER 1

This looked like a damn good place to die. And at least it wasn't blistering hot.

Grimacing in pain, Dagger Ixur pressed his hand against the wound that was slowly killing him and stepped inside the dive hole where some of the worst vermin of the Nine Worlds had crawled to find refuge from the blistering binary suns of Steradore.

His breathing labored, he hid his agony behind a mask of steeled boredom and made his way to a back table where he sat down, making sure to keep his wound concealed. Like rabid animals, the creatures here would attack en masse should they suspect for even the hair of a nanosecond he was incapable of defending himself.

Especially given the massive bounty on his head.

Hell, if he had a brain, he'd turn himself in for *that* amount of cred. At least it would get him a good meal for the first time in four years.

But then, he couldn't spend it if he was dead.

"There's a thirty crona minimum to occupy this space. You got thirty cronas, slag?"

Dagger sneered at the smug purple-skinned humanoid waitress. She had no idea that she was talking to a former prince who'd once been heir to two of the largest fortunes in the universe.

But that was years ago.

Today, he was heir of shit and shit's second cousin. And if he wasn't on the brink of death, he wouldn't have thirty cronas to waste on the watered-down, fifth-rate, synthetic hooch they no doubt served here.

Reaching into his pocket, he pulled out the coins and tossed them on the table. "Tondarion Fire."

She swept the creds into her palm and examined them to make sure they weren't counterfeit. Then without a word, she went to fetch his drink.

Adjusting his dark red-tinted glasses to make sure they kept his betraying eyes concealed, Dagger expelled an exhausted breath, hoping he lived long enough to taste the knock-off garbage he'd just ordered. At the rate he was bleeding . . .

*It won't hurt much longer.*

Sadly, he didn't know what burned his blackened soul more. The poisoned knife wound or the raw fact that as he sat here bleeding out, he had no one to call and say a final goodbye to. No one who would give a single shit that he would be dead in less than half an hour.

A scuffle to his right drew his attention.

Immediately on alert, he reached with his left hand for his blaster, expecting it to be more enforcers or assassins after him.

He relaxed as he saw nothing more than two filthy humans and an alien hauling a scraggly boy in chains. From the looks of it, the kid was probably a crew member being punished or a prisoner being transferred.

No more than fifteen or sixteen, the boy with white-blond hair jerked away from a much larger and older male. Hissing, he exposed a set of fangs in a specific, insulting manner that was known as *fanging* someone. Dagger frowned at that particular defiant and aggressive gesture.

The boy was Andarion with *that* hair color?

For a full minute, Dagger thought he was hallucinating from blood loss as he saw in his mind not the child in front of him, but his own fraternal twin brother, Nykyrian. Though there were legends of other blond Andarions who had existed at one time, Nykyrian was the only whitehaired Andarion Dagger had ever seen in the flesh. The rest of that breed had been brutally put to death long before he and his brother had been born. Hunted down and exterminated for that trait and any other ability or skill their grandmother had deemed an inherent threat to her reign and authority.

Because yeah, really, she was that insecure a bitch.

The larger alien slugged the boy.

"Don't bruise my merchandise!" the buyer snarled. "I'll only pay half the creds he's worth if he's damaged."

Dagger winced at those harsh words. Slavers out to make a quick profit off the poor kid's innocence and beauty.

Like the other occupants who didn't seem to care at all, he started to stay out of it. But then, he'd lived his whole life in selfish fear surrounded by those who were only out for themselves. And what had it gotten him?

An early death on a backwater planet, bleeding out alone.

No friends. No family.

Once he was dead and gone, these maggots would raid his corpse for his meager creds, weapons, and ring, and dump his remains like forgotten garbage.

He was going to die. That was a given.

But he did have a choice in whether he went quietly . . .

Or fighting his way to the gods, doing some good for a scared child who might have a future out of this. A boy who needed to be at home with his family and friends. Not in the hands of these callous, money-grubbing bastards.

Four years ago when Dagger had finally faced the truth in a broken mirror of a filthy bathroom, and stood sober for the first time in over a decade, he'd seen what a piece of shit he really was. In that instant, he'd forever buried the selfish, terrified prince who'd been bullied and cowed by everyone around him, and been reborn that night as the fearless survivor Dagger Ixur who was done taking orders and trying to please his worthless, back-stabbing family.

Someone who wasn't a total scabbing bastard.

While the chemically-numbed Jullien eton Anatole would have walked away and not cared what happened to the boy, the stone-cold killer Dagger damn sure wouldn't.

Rising to his feet, Dagger slowly slid his coat back, and moved his hand to his blaster grip to show them clearly that the clock on their lives had begun to click down. The only way to stop it now was for them to make the right decision. "Let the kid go."

The larger thug who was planning to buy the boy, turned to sneer at him. "Well . . . what have we here? Aren't you a fancy one?"

Dagger arched a brow. "What? Because I bathed a week ago? Really?" He was filthy, sweating and bleeding, and wearing clothes that should have been burned a year ago, at least. He smelled like the back end of something dead and rotten. Disgusting truthfully. Even *he* was offended by his stench. How in the universe would anyone consider *this* fancy?

Then again, if one considered the source . . .

Yeah, he was rather fancy, after all.

"Just shoot him, Eben, and get it over with."

When Eben moved to comply with his accomplice, Dagger drew his blaster lightning fast and shot first. The blast landed right between the man's eyes with unerring aim.

While Dagger might not be the trained League assassin his brother was, he'd always been an incredibly accurate shot—thanks to too many years of a VR shooter gaming addiction, and a need to feed his obsessive paranoia that one day one of his many obloquious cousins would find the nerve to take aim for his back.

Chaos erupted as patrons screamed and ran, and the owner and bouncers moved in to control them, and disarm Dagger.

Yeah, like that would happen so long as he was alive.

Ducking, he shot three more of them.

The other human attacked. Dagger caught the man and kicked him sideways at the same time their alien rodent-shaped friend came for his back. He knocked him away and quickly unshackled the boy.

Dagger took a second to make sure the kid wasn't hurt before he handed him his link, and wallet that contained his royal Andarion signet ring. It was the only thing of monetary value he had left from his past. The only thing he hadn't pawned or outright sold. He had no idea why he'd kept it—honestly, he wasn't sentimental. Yet he hadn't been able to part with it for some unknown reason.

Until now.

Lastly, he reached to the holster at the small of his back and gave the kid the one thing he owned that meant anything to him.

His fully charged reserve blaster.

The boy scowled as Dagger closed the kid's hands around the items. He released the biolock on the blaster's trigger so the boy could shoot it if he had to.

Dagger inclined his head to him. "There's enough in there to get you home to your parents. Make sure you call and let them know you're safe. Shoot anyone who tries to hurt or stop you. *Anyone.* You get home, *chizzi.* Whatever it takes. Conscience be damned. I mean it. Don't stop for anything. Let no one do you harm."

He saw the others rising to come for them. "Run!" he snapped at the kid before he grabbed a chair and swung it at the smelly rodent.

The boy didn't go far. Rather, he doubled back and grabbed Dagger's coat. "You better follow me or they'll have you for sure."

"What do you mean?"

The boy leaned in to whisper. "I know who you are . . . *tiziran*."

Dagger stepped back out of habit, then caught himself. Why he bothered, he had no idea. There was nothing more the boy could do to him. He couldn't believe he was still alive. Especially given the way his heart was pounding poison through his body and how profusely he kept bleeding.

As they neared the door, another group of outlaws came in, armed and ready for war.

By their gear, they were Tavali pirates. *Shit* . . .

Bad timing and bad luck were still courting him like the last male on an all-matron planet. The Tavali were only about profit. They would gut him even faster than the derelicts in this bar. And there was no telling what they'd do to the *chizzi*.

Dagger pulled the boy behind him, ready to fight them to the bitter end to keep the kid safe. Even though he doubted he had another charge left on his main blaster, he angled it for their female leader, who took aim at his head.

"Stop! Don't shoot!" Before Dagger could prevent it, the boy ran out from behind him and put himself between them. "He saved me, Mum."

The targeting dot lowered to hover over Dagger's heart, unwavering. "What?"

"It's true." The boy gestured at the bodies on the ground. "He freed me and was helping me escape."

His legs suddenly weak, Dagger tried to stay steady as a loud buzzing began in his ears, but he couldn't. Anymore than he could continue to hold his blaster that had instantly gained a hundred pounds and aim it. Instead, he focused on the only thing that mattered to him. "Are you safe from harm, *akam*?"

"Yes."

Nodding, he lowered his arm, dropped his blaster, then sank to the floor before everything went dark.

Relieved to find her son alive, Ushara blinked back tears and holstered her blaster as she saw the huge, muscled Andarion male go down without a fight. She visually checked the remaining threat level, which was currently minimal.

But that wouldn't last. They'd violated too many laws in her quest to find her only child and it could get hot in here fast. Not that she'd cared. Her boy had been threatened—for Vasili's life, she'd violate any law, any where, any time.

And raze this entire planet to a crisp.

Her baby had been all that had mattered to her. And it was still her priority. Vasili's tracker had been on its last bar. Another five minutes and they'd have lost him completely. Had his kidnappers moved him one more time, she'd have never found him.

Tears and panic filled her and threatened to overwhelm her as she realized how close she'd come to never seeing her baby boy again. She still couldn't breathe for it.

But they had to get out of here before they were all taken and jailed. She'd tremble and fall apart later. Right now she had to secure everyone's safety. "Vas! We need to go. Now!"

Her son knelt by the male's side. "Not without him."

"Vas!"

Her stubborn little progeny had the audacity to jut his chin out and defy her. "He saved me, Mum. Risked his own life to do it. For no reason at all. We help those who help us. That's what you've always told me, isn't it?"

"Don't you dare throw my words in my face. Not right now."

"It's not enough that we voice good intentions. We must back them with action."

She growled at her child and his stubborn defiance. He had far too much of his father in his blood.

Worse? He had far too much of *her* in him. A fact brought home as her brother, who stood at her back, dared to laugh at Vasili's defiant stubbornness.

"Fine!" Growling, she gestured at the lump on the floor and ordered her brother to claim it as part of their clean up of this very bad situation. "Drag him to the ship and be quick about it. We don't want to be here when any authorities arrive."

They'd moved so fast to get to this backwoods rock to find her baby, they still wore Tavali markings and gear. As well as had stolen cargo on board the fastest ship that had been docked in their station. When word had come that Vasili had been kidnapped by slavers, she'd recklessly commandeered that ship for this venture. And if they were caught, they could all be executed for it.

For that matter, it wasn't even *her* ship or crew. Rather, they were a united force of stray Tavali consisting of volunteers from her brothers', cousin's, and sisters' crews and any pirate willing to help rescue her child.

They were far from Tavali friendly territory, and flying with no allies or backup. What the lot of them had done was all kinds of stupid. They hadn't even done preliminary or safety checks on the ship to ensure it was space-worthy before taking off. All they'd known was that Vas was in trouble and they had a sort-of location for him, and a very limited amount of time to find him before he was lost forever.

*Yeah, in retrospect, bad idea.*

Trajen was right. When it came to her son, she had no common sense.

"Hey!" the owner called as they started for the door. "What about the mess in my bar?"

Ushara turned on the man with a glower, aghast at his indignation. "You allowed those scabs to use your establishment as a place to sell *my* child, and you think I owe you payment for what happened during his rescue?" She glanced back to her precious blond-haired baby. Barely thirteen, he looked older to those who didn't know better.

Just a child that they had planned to rob of his innocence. Sell for things that enraged her to a level she couldn't even begin to calm down from.

"You're right. I do owe you." She shot him where his heart should have been, then followed after her crew.

Zellen met her at the door with a fierce grimace. "That was unwise."

"Don't you dare lecture me, Gondarion. In the mood I'm in, I'll shoot you, too. Besides, killing anyone who'd sell a child is a public service. I should get a medal."

Her adjutant wisely held his hands up and stepped out of her path. Which wasn't something he did lightly or often. In his late forties, the bald human male was still ripped and physically able to outmaneuver or outfight most anyone half his age—yet not even he wanted to tangle with Ushara when she was this angry and it involved the well-being of her one, sacred child.

The only reason Zellen was grounded these days came from an injury he'd sustained a decade ago that had severely limited his peripheral vision. That single injury kept him from flying. But not from fighting, or being one of her most valued staff members.

Without a word, Zellen followed her back to the bay and on board the ship where Vasili was waiting.

While the crew quickly prepared the launch and stowed the Andarion male in the infirmary, she examined her boy, to make sure no one had harmed him. She hugged him close, then cupped his chin in her palm. "Did they hurt you?"

"Mum, stop! Not a baby. I'm fine. Really. Thanks to the male who saved me. Where is he?"

"Where you don't need to worry about him. You've caused enough stress and problems for one lifetime. Harness yourself in for the launch."

"But, Mom—"

"Don't *Mom* me, Vas. Get in your seat."

Rolling his eyes, Vasili obeyed while mumbling a complaint under his breath.

Ushara fanged her child behind his back so that he wouldn't know exactly how upset she was at him right now for the dangerous position he'd put them all in.

It was a good thing she'd struggled to birth him, otherwise the urge to strangle him would be enough that she might give in to it. This was the second time she'd almost lost him in his lifetime. The second time her world had tilted on its axis and left her feeling out of control. And she knew for a fact that if something had happened to Vasili, she wouldn't survive it.

As strong as she liked to think she was, she knew the bitter truth. It would emotionally kill her to stand over the grave of her child. Vasili was everything to her. The mere thought of losing him left her in a state of hysteria that terrified her to unspeakable levels.

She was still shaking from the news that Vas had been taken. Honestly, she didn't know if she'd ever stop at this point. She was so glad to have him safe with her again. To know they'd gotten here in time.

Thanks to that unknown Andarion male they now had possession of. A few minutes more and the auction for her son would have been completed—then Vas would have been lost to her forever.

But now to bring a stranger back home with them . . .

*Trajen's going to kill me.*

Her boss didn't like unknown variables of any kind and dragging a *guest* into any of their bases or territory was definitely a variable that would piss him off to no uncertain end. While necessity and high bounties had taught them all to be extremely xenophobic, Trajen made the rest of them look downright reckless in comparison to his extreme paranoia.

"Admiral? We need you on deck. They're being pissy with us about granting launch clearance."

Of course they were. Not like she and her crew weren't here on forged papers, in a stolen ship, with stolen cargo and hadn't just blasted their way into a bar and killed its owner. Gee? You'd think they'd give them the key to the city. Right?

Bitterly amused, she double checked Vas's harness, then looked to Zellen. "Make sure he stays put."

Zellen buckled himself in beside Vas and glowered at him. "He's not moving, Admiral."

Satisfied her child was quelled and secure, she went to deal with the next round of *fun.*

As she stepped onto the flight deck, she tapped her earlink. "This is Vice Admiral Ushara Altaan. May I ask why we haven't been given clearance?"

"Um . . . Admiral, we were told that you took a fugitive on board your ship without proper clearance or warrants."

Oh wait, this was a new, unexpected twist. Ushara glared at the man on the monitor in front of her. "Don't be ridiculous. My son——"

"Not your son, Admiral. The Andarion prince."

Oh, okay. The comptroller was obviously high.

She laughed at the absurdity. "I didn't bring any prince on board. Are you out of your mind?"

The comptroller shot a photo up on her screen of a much cleaner and rotund version of the scrappy vagabond who'd just saved her son's life from the slavers. "Jullien eton Anatole. Andarion tiziran and former heir. Has an outstanding League bounty. Thrill-Kill termination warrant." Then he showed footage of them in the bar. "Is this not the same male you carried on board your ship?"

Of course it was. 'Cause the gods had had it out for her since the day she was born.

But as she stared at the photo on her screen of a tall arrogant prince full of regal snobbery, all she could think about was the way the determined male had looked as he stood ready to defend her child with his last breath. His words to Vas——*are you safe, boy*——before he allowed himself to surrender to his injuries.

*Don't be stupid, Shara. He's a prince of the family that destroyed your race.*

*Hand him over and be done with it. Give him what he deserves. What all Ana-*
*toles deserve. A brutal death, in the worst way imaginable.*

*They should all be put to death, in screaming agony.* That was what they
did to everyone else.

It was what she should do.

She glanced to the monitor that showed Vas biting nervously at his
nails as he held a small stack of items in his lap.

*To be rather than to seem.* That was the motto her husband had lived
by. The words he'd wanted her to impart to their son.

Worse, she heard her own father's words in her head.

*We do not repay mercy with murder. Kindness grows kindness, and you will*
*reap the harvest of whatever seeds you sow.*

*Damn it.*

Hitting mute, she turned her back to the screen so that she could
speak to her crew. "Buckle up. Admiral at the helm."

All around her, her crew exploded into acts of defiant protests, and
with making quick religious gestures.

"Holy gods!"

"Sacred Mother preserve us!"

"Sacred Father save us!"

"Saints have mercy!"

"I didn't sign up for this shit!"

"Open the hatch! I want to surrender!"

"Mommy!"

Ushara rolled her eyes as they continued whining like small children.
"Oh bite it, you big bunch of nancies. You're supposed to be hardened
pirates. Act like it."

Even her brother was whimpering.

Her cousin, Gavin, who was actually the one who'd stolen this ship
on his most recent Tavali raid, took up the guns. "We are, but damn,
Shara . . . just damn."

The only one who was smiling was her child. Through the monitor,
she saw Vasili in his seat, grinning ear to ear as Ushara assumed the controls, while the comptroller continued to demand she release the prince
to their custody.

Popping open the channel, Ushara cleared her throat. "Sorry, I was intentionally ignoring you as we armed up and took launch positions. Now,

let me explain what's going to happen. You will clear the way for us, or we're blasting out and taking a shit-ton of your people with us as we go."

"I don't think you understand. We have canons aimed at you."

"You mean, you did. They are now deactivated." She continued to plow through their system as they tried to lock her out. Smiling, she shook her head. "Who programmed your security? An infant? My son was creating tougher protocols as a toddler." She opened the door. "Back your patrols down. I don't want to kill anyone for doing their jobs, but I will if they try to stop us."

Ushara launched to the sound of her crew screaming in dire protest.

Ignoring them, she focused on the fighters that descended on them with ion canons, locked and loaded. She bolstered the shields and flew straight up, knowing the fighters would have a hard time matching the escape velocity of her much more nimble ship. Still, they fired. She rolled and dipped, then rose again and cut a sharp left before she came out of the spiral.

Gavin and his gunners returned fire while her engineers kept the power flowing through their engines without interruption. By the time they hit open space and she was able to release the hyperdrive, half her crew had broken into sweats.

Or passed out.

Irritated, she smirked at them. "Really?"

Gavin drew a ragged breath. "Here's the problem, Star Skream. You say, *Look at me, I'm a professional. You can trust me. I won't screw up and slam you into anything or get you blown into atoms.* But . . . if one of *us* dared to fly like you just did, you'd bust our asses to slag for it."

Folding her arms over her chest, she arched a brow at him. "Your point?"

"No point. Just letting you know I need stain remover for both my paints and the seat."

Ushara hated the fact that she actually laughed at him. "I don't find you charming, Captain. Take your helm."

"Gladly." As he resumed his seat—by crawling to it in an overly exaggerated manner—there was a raucous cheer and applause that went through the crew that he'd relieved her.

"I hear all of you!" she called out.

"We know!"

Ushara shook her head. She'd be more offended if she didn't consider them her family. With an aggravated sigh, she went to check on Vasili who was still buckled in next to Zellen. "Any complaints you want to file?"

Vas shook his head. "Proud of you, Ma. Thank you for not surrendering."

She brushed the white-blond hair back from his forehead and placed a kiss there. "No problem. Now stay here and let me see about our guest."

"Go easy on him, okay?"

"Why?"

Vasili handed her the stack on his lap. "When he freed me, he gave me these and told me to use them to get home. He said that I was to call my parents and tell you that I was safe so you wouldn't worry. And that I wasn't to stop. No matter what." Vas handed her the blaster. "He gave up his weapon to me, Ma . . . while surrounded by enemies. Who does that for someone they don't know?"

That level of thoughtfulness and sacrifice stunned her. It wasn't often anything caught her off guard. But *that* did. She wouldn't have credited an eton Anatole capable of such feelings for anyone other than themselves.

Unable to believe it, she took the items from his hand.

First she checked the blaster. It had a biolock that had been deactivated. Fully charged. Unlike the one they'd picked up that the prince had aimed at her. That one had been drained completely. No shots in it whatsoever. He'd left himself defenseless and given her son a fully charged blaster for *his* protection.

Ballsy, and for that, she could forgive the prince a lot of sin. Any male who would willingly sacrifice his own life to protect a child he didn't know . . .

It said a lot about him.

Curious, she turned the link on, expecting it to be locked, yet it wasn't. But then, there was no need as there were no numbers programmed into it. According to the log, no one had called the prince.

Ever.

Neither friend, nor family. The only outgoing transmissions had been for random information. Impersonal calls. Mostly hunting for work or transportation. Very cheap places to stay. The kind of dives that served the homeless and charity cases.

She paused as she noticed the link's background photo. Clicking to the album, she realized it was the only picture in it. And it was the last thing she would have expected. Rather than being of the prince or a female of his, it was of a much younger Tadara Cairistiona of Andaria and Emperor Aros of Triosa—the tiziran's parents when they were young. Teenagers, in fact. Embracing, the two of them were staring into each other's eyes. It was actually a very touching couples photo.

Strange that he'd carry this one picture, and no other photos at all. Music, either. There was nothing personal in the link. It was cold and sterile.

Turning the link off, she opened his wallet. Like the link, it was basically bare. Less than twenty credits. No cards or identification of any sort. Only a strange bump in the coin area. She opened it to find a royal Andarion signet ring. Her jaw dropped at the sight of something worth a fortune. "He gave this to you?"

Vasili nodded. "He said there would be enough inside it to see me home to my parents."

The antique ring was more than enough. In fact, it could probably buy a small planet. The joke of it said the ring was worth the tiziran's weight in gold, and given what Jullien eton Anatole was reported to weigh . . . that was a *lot* of creds.

Stunned past rational thought, she closed it and carefully put them in her pocket. "Stay here, Vas. I'll be right back."

"Okay."

Not sure what she'd find, she headed for the infirmary where Marshal was cleaning up from having tended the prince. He glanced at her as she entered the room.

"How's your patient?"

"Now that Gavin's flying us, much better."

She rolled her eyes at him. "Not you, too."

He grinned before he answered her question. "He took a bad knife wound. Poisoned blade. Luckily, it was an indy strike and not a League assassin. Had we not found him, he wouldn't have made it another half hour before the poison finished off shutting down his vitals."

"Now?"

"Should pull through. I think I got it all cleaned out." He left her.

Alone with the tiziran, Ushara headed to the bed where Jullien lay unconscious. For the first time, she allowed herself to see his features. He was much better looking than he'd been in the old royal photo they'd shown her on screen, and more so than she'd realized in the bar where they'd met.

Of course, then she'd been more focused on her son and those out to harm him. Jullien had been the last thing on her mind.

Now, however . . .

He was exquisite. Tall, but lean from too many missed meals, the former tiziran was incredibly ripped. Every part of his tawny flesh was cut and defined. Every single muscle in his entire body was sculpted and honed like an athlete in training. Yet that being said, he was riddled with vicious, intersecting scars . . . knives, blaster wounds, claws—even bite marks. It appeared as if every type of creature imaginable had done its best to end him.

Sympathy choked her hard as she realized that he'd been forced to fight hard for his life.

Often.

Before she could stop herself, she stepped closer and touched the deepest jagged scar that ran so close to his heart it was a miracle that it'd missed it. There was another that ran along his collarbone, and a series of faint, faded smaller ones across his right rib cage. They were unlike any she'd ever seen before and she couldn't imagine what had caused them.

How peculiar for a tiziran to be so marred when Andarions valued physical beauty above all else. Indeed, this much damage could cause an Andarion son to be disinherited, shunned, and ridiculed.

And he had definitely been disowned. There was no missing the marks that crisscrossed his shoulders in a distinctive pattern where his mother had slashed his lineage and marked him Outcast. A harsh punishment for his kind that forever severed him from his birthright and exiled him from any Andarion territory or outpost.

"Ouch," she breathed as more sympathy for him choked her. No matter what he'd done, she couldn't imagine how any mother could be so cruel to her own child as to cast him out of his lineage and banish him from his home and family.

From everything he'd ever known.

Curious about this enigma before her, she dropped her hand to his and examined it. Like the rest of his body, his knuckles were scarred and bruised from fights. His claws torn and ragged, not the manicured hands of a spoiled aristocrat. Rather he had rough calluses and healing scuffs that said he'd been doing hard labor for some time now. Living hand-to-mouth like a savage animal.

On the inside of his left forearm, from wrist to elbow, was a tattoo of a sword piercing a bleeding heart, flanked with wings. The blood appeared to drip down his arm to his wrist. At the bottom of the heart was a rocker banner with a single Andarion word. *Indurari. I endure* or *I am strengthened*, depending on context. It was an ancient warrior's symbol that had once decorated the battleshields and war helms of the mighty War Hauk family. That word signified that through hardship and conflict, their warriors were honed for battle and made better and stronger. Forever strengthened by adversity. Ironic that he'd choose such a symbol given that the Hauks were the mortal enemies of the Anatoles, and had been since the beginning of Andarion civilized history. Even though the two families were related, the Hauk lineage hated Jullien's bloodline even more than hers did.

Not to mention tattoos were profaned by the darkheart Andarions unless they were done to pay tribute to or honor your own family.

For a darkheart tiziran to have one . . .

His royal family must have *loved* that.

Bemused, Ushara returned his hand to the mattress and checked the bandage to see how he'd been wounded. It'd been a low strike, near his hip and close to his groin. From the downward angle of it, she'd guess the assassin had been going for his femoral artery when the tiziran had countered his assault.

"If you want to move your hand over a bit more to the left and lower, I won't protest."

Heat scalded her cheeks as she realized that there was a sudden large bulge under the sheet *very* close to her hand and in the exact location he'd described. Gasping, she looked up to meet a pair of suspicious yet eerie hazel brownish-green eyes, rimmed with red.

Those weren't Andarion eyes.

They were human in appearance. No wonder he'd worn dark red sunglasses to conceal them. But what stunned her most was how much unexpected and unwanted heat those eyes sent through her body. . . .

Dagger started to smile at the beautiful blonde angel until he realized how many weapons were strapped to her black *battle*suit.

Shit. Dressed like that, she was either an assassin or bounty hunter.

Out of habit, he reached for his own blaster, only to find bare skin under the sheet. He started off the bed, but she grabbed him and gently pushed him back.

"It's all right. You don't need to move with that wound."

Yeah, uh-huh. Yet if she was taking him in, why was he still alive? Why bother? They would pay just as much for his dead body as they would for his living one.

More, in fact.

Calming down a degree to a milder paranoia, he narrowed his eyes on her. "I'm not in custody?"

She shook her head. "Do you remember what happened?"

Vaguely. There was only one thing he could recall with any clarity . . .

"The kid. Did he make it out?"

"My son. Yes. Is that all you remember?"

Dagger scowled as he tried to think of other details. But all he could recall was the pain. Same pain he felt right now. Looking down, he saw the blood that was quickly saturating his bandage.

The female Andarion glanced down and cursed. "You've pulled your sutures open. Lie back."

"I need to go. Where are my clothes?"

"There's nowhere for you to go. We've already launched."

"Launched?"

She pointed to the metal walls. "You're on board our ship."

Fury burned through him as he gathered the sheet around his waist and sprang from the bed. "I won't let you hand me over to The League," he growled.

Ushara stepped back as she saw the feral, determined fury in his eyes that reminded her of a beast about to attack. She'd dealt with enough desperate beings in her life to recognize how dangerous the tiziran was in this state. Holding her hands up, she tried to reassure him. "That's not my intent. If it was, I'd have surrendered you to the authorities before we left when they demanded I do so."

Confusion furrowed his brow. "Pardon?"

She moved slowly toward the wall monitor. "Here. I'll show you." She called up the feed to replay what he'd missed while he'd been unconscious.

As he watched it, his jaw went slack. By the look on his face, it was obvious he wasn't used to anyone standing up for him. He turned to stare at her in disbelief. "Why would you risk your crew for me?"

"Why did you save my son?"

"I didn't think anyone else would. I just wanted to make sure he got home safely."

The honesty of his unexpected answer floored her. "Well, you have yourself to thank for not being in custody or dead. That decision is the only reason you're here. You saved him and we saved you. We'll drop you off at the nearest station, then——"

"If you don't mind, I'd rather you just jettison me somewhere unpopulated. I only ask that it has a breathable atmosphere."

"Seriously?"

He nodded and wiped at the perspiration on his brow. His tanned skin had a sudden grayish tint to it.

Concern furrowed her brow. "You need to get back in bed and rest."

He shook it off. "I'll be fine. I just need my clothes."

Like her husband, he was a stubborn Andarion male. Knowing she couldn't win against him, Ushara went to the cabinet to retrieve his gear. She hesitated as she saw the poor, threadbare condition it was in. His boots were worn so thin, the left one had a hole in the toe of it that was packed with taped-in plastic to keep it watertight. Though he kept his clothes meticulously clean, his pants were patched and faded. The once black, now dark grayish shirt was stretched out from overuse and age.

Feeling bad for him, she held them out so that he could take them from her. "Can I get you anything else?"

He gathered his clothes and glanced about sheepishly. "Might I ask a favor, Ger Tarra?"

"It's mu tara," she corrected the Andarion term, letting him know that she wasn't married. Though why she did so, she wasn't exactly sure. "What?"

"Is there a shower on board that I may use?"

She gestured toward the door on her right. "Through there. You'll find soaps, razor, and towels as well."

He gave her a very regal bow. "Thank you." The sincere gratitude in those words was startling as he headed for the bathroom. He left his boots, weapons, and coat on the bed.

Ushara took a moment to reexamine them, especially the numerous bloodstains on the worn dark brown coat that Jullien had attempted to clean off and yet the stains stubbornly remained as bitter reminders of how many had tried to kill him.

Repeatedly. Their grim determination was a testament to his own resolute will to stay alive in spite of their best efforts.

The leather showed remnants of dozens of burn marks left behind from blaster wounds, as well as slashes from knives and other weapons where he'd repaired the leather with patches and jagged stitches as best he could.

"Damn," she breathed. Did he not have anyone in the universe who cared about him?

For that matter, who'd issued the death warrant? His mother was the tadara of the Andarion empire. His father ruled the Triosans, which meant Jullien would have cousins in power, ruling other empires and governments throughout the universe, as well. He would have to be related to most emperors, and have ties to the rest. His twin brother, Nykyrian Quiakides, was one of the leaders of The Sentella, a military organization that rivaled The League for power. Not to mention, he was married to the only child of the Gourish president.

Tahrs Nykyrian's political ties were terrifying. Princess Kiara's even more so.

Surely one of *them* could rescind a kill warrant for Jullien. After all, Emperor Aros had forced The League to pull the one they'd had issued for years against Nykyrian, and Nykyrian had gone Rogue on The League—a cardinal sin in their eyes. If that could be done, why could they not repeal the one for Jullien?

Unless his parents had condoned it. Or gods forbid, they were the ones who'd actually issued the warrant against his life.

Was it possible?

They had disinherited him for some reason . . .

Extremely curious, she pulled up the warrant on her link to see. Many Thrill-Kill contracts were done anonymously—which was honestly what she'd expected to find. But when the file loaded and she saw the name of the issuer, she gasped audibly.

*Eriadne eton Anatole.*

His own grandmother?

For real?

And both his parents and brother had allowed it to stand? *Dear gods . . . why?*

The answer was at the bottom of the warrant, written in plain Universal.

*Jullien eton Anatole.*

*Wanted dead, violated, desecrated, and in pieces. Thrill-Kill warrant.*

*Acts: Murder. Kidnapping. Conspiracy. Attempted murder. Theft. High trea-son against the Andarion empire and race.*

*Bounty to be paid by former tadara upon delivery of his head to Her Former Majesty. Bonus to be paid for delivery of his heart and Andarion signet ring.*

Suddenly, a shadow fell over her. Looking up, she saw the dark, deadly glower on Jullien's face as he caught a glimpse of what she'd been reading.

He pulled the link from her hand and clicked it off before he casually returned it to her. His expression was completely stoic and unreadable. "To answer your unspoken question, mu tara. Yes, I deserve it. And yes, I'm that big an asshole."

# CHAPTER 2

The fresh clean scent of Jullien's skin hit her hard as Ushara met those tormented hazel eyes that were rimmed by a thin outline of red. A mixture of human and Andarion. His thick, jet black hair was slicked back from his incredibly handsome face, and he'd taken a moment to trim his unruly beard to a sexy masculine shadow that now barely dusted his sculpted jawbone.

He was simply devastating. Lethal. Raw and masculine. And yet at the same time there was an air of regal refinement as ingrained and natural to his state of being as breathing. She'd never been around anyone so compelling.

And at the same time, anyone deadlier.

Like a savage lorina in the wild. A majestic creature of ultimate grace and beauty you couldn't stop watching in breathless appreciation. One you wanted desperately to reach out and pet, and yet you knew if you tried, it would tear your arm off and rip out your throat. That was exactly what it felt like to be near him.

Without a word, Jullien stepped away to buckle the holster around his lean hips and tie the blaster to his left thigh. He secured the rest of his weapons to his body and positioned the reserve blaster at the small of his back. Then he shrugged his coat on.

"Who did you kill?"

Jullien sighed wearily as he picked up his boots and moved to a chair so that he could pull them on. "What does it matter? You want me to tell you he deserved it to assuage us both. Whether he did or not, the ones who loved him grieve his passing regardless of his sins. And it changes nothing. I still made a harsh decision to take a life that I have to live with, and one day die for."

Bracing his elbows on his knees, he paused to look up at her. "You think I don't know your thoughts, *mu tara* . . . Tahrs Jullien eton Anatole. Royal prick. Arrogant asshole. I was born without feelings or compassion, and despised from the moment I stupidly drew my first breath and didn't have the good sense to immediately expel it and die. Unlovable and disgusting. Spoiled, rich, and blessed beyond the wildest imaginings of the most creative novelist. Believe me, that ball-shriveling hatred from your eyes doesn't faze me at all. There was a time when such condemnation from strangers and family seared me to the core of my pitiless soul and sent me sniveling into corners, but I've long grown past it."

She glared at him. "Do you know what your family did to mine?"

"Slaughtered them."

His nonchalant, unrepentant tone infuriated her.

Unperturbed by her anger, he returned her glower with a cold, blank stare. "You think they spared each other?" He pushed himself back and lifted his shirt to point to the scar by his heart that she'd touched earlier. "Present from my grandmother. She moves incredibly fast for an old bitch." He dropped his hand to the horizontal scar bisecting his eight pack, next to his navel. "Age eleven. Cousin Chrisen tried to gut me. Said it was an accident, but I saw the look in his eyes when we went for it. Only accidental part about it was that he didn't leave me sterile or dead."

Then he dropped the hem of his shirt, leaned his head to the side to indicate the scar along his collarbone. "Cousin Merrell did this one four years ago. He tried to cut my throat, but I cold cocked him and got away." He lifted his hair to show another on his forehead. "My mother gave me this precious memento when I was six and made the mistake of trying to soothe her while she was crying. And I would show you the one Cousin Nyran left me with, but it's in a place that you'd have me arrested for exposing. So given everything my family has done to each other for centuries, I can only imagine what they've done to those they're not related to."

Ushara had no idea what to say to that. "Why would your mother scar you?"

With a regal grace that was at odds with his shabby clothes, he pulled a pair of ragged fingerless gloves out of his pockets and put them on. "My grandmother had brutally murdered my twin brother. So on the day of his funeral when I went to comfort my mother and to seek some comfort myself that I wasn't about to join him in that grave—that my mother might actually protect *me*, my mother decided it was somehow all my fault he was dead and threw a gift I'd made for her on her birthday earlier that year. Taught me to never make another gift out of pottery or baked clay. After that, I stuck to paper and lightweight jewelry."

Leaning back in the chair, he hitched his thumbs in his holster, crossed his ankles and gave her a tired, emotionless stare. "Look, *mu tara*, I don't want your sympathy or pity, and I damn sure don't want your anger and hatred. I'm not going to defend my family—they've never protected me, as that lovely death warrant clearly demonstrates. And I'm not into making excuses for the actions I was forced to take while trying to stay alive in an extremely hostile environment, where every breath I drew was likely to be my last, and everyone around me was plotting my death, dismemberment, and betrayal. If you want to kill me, do it. You're in luck. I'm in too much pain today to fight for a life I never really wanted, anyway."

And with that, he folded his arms over his chest and closed his eyes.

A part of her was extremely ticked at his curt, arrogant dismissal. So much so that she was tempted to kick him.

But another part realized it for what it was. His own defense mechanism. If he was telling her the truth, his family hadn't spared him their brutality.

At all.

And given what she'd seen on that warrant and what it detailed for how they wanted him killed, and the scars on his body, there was no need to doubt him.

His own family had issued a brutal death warrant not just to kill him, but to have him brutalized, tortured, and dismembered.

Thrill-Kill. It was the most horrific warrant anyone could have issued against their life.

*By his own grandmother.* And his parents had stood by and allowed her to do it to him. Neither one had bothered to protect or shelter their own child.

Unable to believe the coldness of that single act, she left him alone to rest and heal.

Dagger opened his eyes as he heard the door close. He didn't know why, but he felt her absence like a physical ache.

*'Cause you're a minsid idiot.*

There was that. And some of it was that he hadn't had anyone talk to him in a long time. In fact, he couldn't even remember the last time he'd had an actual conversation with anyone. For the last four years, he'd lived like a rabid animal, constantly on the run. Saying as little as possible and avoiding any and everyone for fear of having to kill them should they recognize him, and decide that they wanted to become an overnight millionaire by turning him in or killing him.

Now, he was so tired of running. Tired of starving. Tired of battling for a life that just didn't seem worth the trouble.

He wiggled his toe through the hole in his boot and sighed. Wouldn't his brother laugh to see him now?

For that matter, his aunt Tylie would double over in smug satisfaction. Her favorite thing had always been to remind him of how unimportant he was. How little he mattered to anyone, especially his own mother.

Not that he needed the reminder. All he had to do was try to call his father or see his mother and it became apparent real fast that Nykyrian was the only son they loved.

He was just the one they'd gotten stuck with.

Refusing to think about it and reopen old mental wounds, he pulled his link out and checked their coordinates. If he could avoid League and Sentella forces, he should be able to pick up some tech work on an outpost. Maybe medical or mechanical. They were usually desperate enough to overlook the fact that he had no papers or a degree that he could prove.

Though it was hard to hide the fact that he was a hybrid. That tended to cost him a lot as humans hated Andarions and Andarions despised humans. Centuries of war between the two races caused them to be highly suspicious of each other.

The only thing worse to those two species was a hybrid piece of shit that reminded them they were genetically related close enough to breed.

*Thanks Mom and Dad for getting busy and not drowning me at birth.*

*Oh for the want of one effing condom . . .*

*Selfish, careless bastards.*

He looked up as the door opened to show Ushara returning with a tray in her hands. The scent of something warm and delicious hit him like a fist.

"I thought you might be hungry."

His throat instantly dry, he couldn't speak. Not when he was this close to what smelled like a real meal. Unable to resist it, he went to the tray stand where she placed it. Oh yeah . . . that *was* food.

For once, he wasn't hallucinating and he didn't even care if it was poisoned, pissed on, or spit in. He'd take whatever, and bear out the consequences later. Anything to stop the gnawing hunger. . . .

Ushara barely got the lid and her fingers clear of the plate before Jullien literally attacked the food. With his bare hands, he shoved it into his mouth with a ravenous frenzy. A little afraid of him, she stepped back, wide-eyed.

After a few seconds, he glanced up and must have caught the horrified expression on her face. He slowed down and licked at his fingers.

Biting her lip sheepishly, she held the cutlery out to him. "Would you like a knife and fork? Napkin?"

With an adorable blush, he reached for them. "Sorry. It's been a while since . . ." He went back to eating.

"You had food or company?" She finished for him.

"Either." This time his manners were flawless. Refined.

"I'm not judging you, *Alteske*. Please." She gestured at the food. "Had I realized how hungry you were, I'd have brought more."

He didn't speak as he returned to inhaling the food, then he swallowed the drink so fast she was surprised it didn't come back up. Or that he didn't belch. But he did blush again as he realized how he'd behaved.

In a move filled with complete incongruity for his earlier zest, he placed the cutlery and napkin primly by the plate and covered the dish.

"Admiral? We have a matter on deck."

She glanced to the monitor where Gavin was paging her. "Can you patch it through?"

Gavin glanced to Jullien. "It's a transmission we're picking up, but none of us can translate it, and the ship's translation software can't ID the language. We're concerned The League or another force might be tracking us."

"Patch it to me."

Finally, he played it.

Ushara scowled. It was pretty, but . . . "No idea. Pull back and—"

"Gyron Force code," Jullien said without hesitation. "Nothing to do with you. They have troops heading to Aluran C for training. They're getting ready to start some crap with their neighbors soon. It's a routine transmission from command to their leader, with orders for mission parameters."

They both gaped at Jullien.

"What?" he asked defensively. "I had cousins who were Gyron Force. One a major. The other a captain. Their uncle was the commander general before he murdered them all in a coup, and took his brother's place as emperor . . . and my chickenshit father refused to retaliate. Anyway, when we were kids, Barnabas used to take me out on maneuvers to quote—*whip me into shape*—every time I dared breathe his airspace. Personally, I think he was attempting to send me into cardiac arrest. But whatever. I grew up on that military code crap. It still sends me into PTSD whenever I hear it."

Ushara snorted at his dry, sarcastic tone. "Well, there you go, Captain. Nothing to worry about, then."

"You trust him?"

"Since he has more to fear than we do should we run into the authorities, I think so."

The screen went blank.

She turned toward Jullien with an arched brow. "Is that the truth?"

"Want me to show you more scars?" He reached to undo his pants.

Laughing, Ushara quickly stopped him. "You are so not what I expected from a tiziran."

He scoffed. "Trust me, we don't hold the market share on asshole. There's plenty of that to go 'round."

Sadly, he was right about that. Ushara moved so that she could pick up the tray. "Are you still hungry?"

"Want the polite answer or the truth?"

"Truth."

"I haven't eaten in almost five days. Where do you think the hole in my boot came from? Notice it's the same size and shape as my fangs?"

Smiling at his flippant answer, she didn't want to be charmed by him. Yet . . .

"Come with me."

As they left the infirmary, she almost collided with Vasili who was walking briskly toward her. He backed up sheepishly.

"Vas . . . what are you doing?"

"I, um . . . um. . . ." Her precious baby glanced around as if searching for an answer she'd buy.

She loved whenever he tried to lie. He was so bad at it.

Vasili looked up at Jullien. "Are you all right, *Alteske*?"

"Call me Dagger, and I'm fine. How 'bout you, *luden*? They didn't hurt you, did they?"

"Nah. But Mum almost killed me with her flying. Were you awake when we escaped?"

"No, I missed that."

"Be grateful. Half the crew is still upchucking from it."

Ushara rolled her eyes.

"But Ma, you should have seen the tiziran fight. It was awesome! He kicks more butt than you do."

She arched her brow. "Gyron Force, you said?"

"Uh, no. Their prepubescent sister, actually. I got rather tired of her flushing my head in the toilets whenever she visited. Worst part about living in a palace? Turbo flush. Toilets so powerful, you fear they're going to suck out a kidney if you're still on them when you pull the handle. Quite certain I lost a few brain cells before I learned to beat her off me."

His delivery was so dry and deadpan that she wasn't quite sure if he was serious or not.

"Joking?"

He arched a regal brow. "Would one ever joke about turbo flush, commode shampoos, missing brain cells, or Amazonian cousins? What kind of beings do you typically associate with?"

"Normal ones."

"Really? Lot of normal sign on with The Tavali, do they?"

She went cold at his question. "Who said anything about The Tavali?"

He gave her the most arrogant cock of his head. "No one. Certainly not me."

Damn, he was perceptive. Unnerved by it, she led him to the galley where she set the tray down on the counter.

Jullien pulled back to shadow the doorway as he saw that the room was occupied.

Ushara inclined her head at the cook. Short and round with blue skin and bright green eyes, Daryn had been a member of Gavin's crew for a number of years. "Daryn. How's it going?"

He wiped his hands on his apron before he took the tray. "Better with Gavin at the helm."

"Would you stop?" She turned toward Jullien. "What would you like?"

All friendliness and teasing were now gone. His handsome features stern and deadly, Jullien lingered his hand on his blaster as he eyed the cook warily. "I'm good. Thank you." With his back to the wall, he drifted into the hallway.

Confused by his sudden turn around, Ushara left Vasili in the galley to follow after the prince, who was already halfway to the infirmary. "Jullien?"

He slowed his long stride. "Yes?"

"I thought you were hungry?"

"I can make do. Thank you, though, *mu tara*. How much longer till you jettison me?"

"Why are you so nervous?"

"Not nervous. Circumspect." He handed her his link with the bounty sheet on it again. "For that amount cred, I'm lucky I can trust myself not to shoot me in the back. Therefore, I prefer to stay in areas where I don't tempt others."

"You have a point."

"Yes. And it's not just the one on top of my head." Without so much as a whisper of a boot click, he drifted into the shadows and returned to the infirmary.

Ushara couldn't believe that she actually felt sorry for a member of the aristocracy. The *Andarion* aristocracy, no less. She'd been raised to hate them with everything she had.

And yet . . .

She couldn't get the sight of his scars out of her mind. His shoddy, bedraggled clothes. The tired resignation and torment in his hazel eyes. Or his quirky humor that kept catching her off guard.

"Mum?"

She turned at the sound of Vasili's voice. "You need something?"

"Where did the tiziran go?"

"He wasn't feeling well."

"Oh. Should I take him some food?"

She frowned at the uncharacteristic question. It wasn't like Vasili to care about a stranger. While her son was a good boy, he was normally very cautious and fearful around others.

Ever since his father's death, he'd been withdrawn from the world. A shadow of the vibrant child who'd worshiped every breath Chaz had drawn. They had been so close that after Chaz's death, Vas hadn't spoken for almost a year. He'd been so traumatized and forlorn by the event that she'd begun to fear she'd never see her son again.

Now, after one encounter with the prince, Vasili was almost the boy she remembered.

How strange that Jullien had sparked something inside him and brought back his trust . . .

"Sure. And can I ask a question?"

Vasili scratched at his nose. "Okay."

"Why are you so attached to the tiziran?"

Shrugging, Vasili screwed up his face. "He had no reason to care, Mum. And he did. He gave me his link, blaster, and wallet to go home to you and then was willing to die so that I could get away. I don't know. It just meant something to me the way he did it. No one but you has ever stood and fought for me like that before. He was like a real-life hero. Like the War Hauks you used to read to me about."

And that meant everything to her. Smiling, she drew Vasili into her arms and kissed his head. "You're getting so tall. Soon I'll be looking up at you."

"God, I hope so. I'd hate to be this short as a grown-up. You think I'll be as tall as Basha Dimitri?"

"Taller."

He smiled. "I'll go get the tiziran some food."

"Okay, and Vas?"

He paused to look back at her.

"You probably shouldn't keep calling him that. It could get him into trouble. Just call him Dagger like he said, okay?"

Nodding, he headed for the galley while she went to the infirmary to check on their guest.

As she opened the door, she caught Jullien with his shirt pulled up, examining his wound. "Is everything all right?"

He jerked the shirt over it. "Fine."

She didn't believe that for an instant. "How bad is it?" She crossed the room and reached to see for herself.

He stepped out of her way. "It's fine."

"Let me see what you've done."

"I'd rather you not."

"Why?"

With an irritated growl, Jullien turned her to face the small mirror over the sink. The anguished pain in his eyes was searing as he met her gaze. "I have enough reminders of things I can't have. The last thing I need or want is to feel the hands of a beautiful female touching me when I know how repugnant I am to you, especially *that* intimately. I'd rather bleed to death first." He glanced down at her hair with such bitter longing that it actually brought a lump to her throat before he stepped back and looked away.

Sitting down, he pulled out his link and stared at it. "Just let me know when it's time to leave."

"You're not repugnant."

He snorted a rude contradiction.

"What's that about?"

"It means I don't believe you, *mu tara*. I have much evidence to the contrary, including the way your lip involuntarily curls every time you glance in my general direction, as if I'm a pile of flaming excrement someone has lit on fire and placed on your doorstep."

Ushara hated how much those words made her ache for him. Worse? She hated the fact that she'd done that to him, at all. And here she'd thought she'd been hiding her distaste for his birthright and family. Apparently, she was as bad as everyone else, and just as quick to judge.

She swept her gaze over his long, lean body. Over his clean, shoddy clothes that were so old and torn, and yet he wore them with masculine swagger and wounded pride.

Only he could carry off something that shabby and still make it look sexy and lethal.

"When was the last time you slept in an actual bed?"

The fact he had to stop and consider it broke her heart. But not as much as the answer. "I don't know."

"A month?"

He sighed before he answered. "Longer. . . . at least."

She winced at his whispered words. And before she could stop herself, her sympathy spoke for her. "Then how about you come back with us?"

He scowled up at her. "Back where?"

"To our base. You can find work there. Safe housing where no one will hunt you. Do you have any skills?"

He gave her a cocky grin. "I'm particularly skilled at pissing off everyone around me. Quite exceptional at it, point of fact. Been known to do so by merely entering a room."

She laughed. "Anything more marketable?"

"Yeah. Engineering and mechanics. If it has a motherboard, or electronics, I can run it, design it, or repair it."

Impressive. If he wasn't lying. "We can always use those skills. Ever worked on ships?"

"Custom-built my first fighter from the ground up."

She gaped at him. "Seriously?"

He slid his link into his pocket and gave her a bemused stare. "Given how many individuals passionately hate my guts, most of them very close relatives in line for my throne, you honestly think I'd trust anyone to touch something with mechanical moving parts and fuel injection systems that could horrendously explode with me trapped inside it, and it look like an easy accident where I'm burned beyond all recognition? Really?"

"Paranoid much?"

With an arrogant arch of his brow, he snorted derisively. "Second most hated being on all of Andaria. Most hated prince in the *entire* history of the Triosan empire—that's not my boasting, they actually took polls and wrote articles about it. I won. Hands down. No contest. Ten years straight on Andaria. And let me reiterate that my own grandmother murdered my grandfather during a PMS hissy fit, the majority of her family, my twin brother when we were only five—or at least tried to, and my mother slaughtered a number of her own siblings, including my doppelgänger . . . Paranoia, insomnia, and an overly high degree of extreme flexibility and peripheral vision are the only reasons I'm still breathing. Go me." His tone was drier than the Oksanan desert.

But it left her with one question. "What did you do to the Triosans that they would hate you so much?"

He sighed wearily. "I have the grave misfortunate of being born to an Andarion mother."

Yeah, right. "Seriously, what did you do to them?"

"I have an Andarion birth mother," he repeated in a slow, steady tone. "Seriously. They embrace Nykyrian because he looks like our father and somehow that allows them to see past his fangs. I have dark hair and favor no one they know. Just enough red in my eyes that it throws them. Somehow that makes all the difference to remind them that I'm Andarion, and therefore am unfit to be part of the Triosan royal family."

"And your father?"

He lifted his head to pin her with an irritated smirk. "Is this my therapy session? Yes, Dr. Tavali, I have father issues. And mother issues. I didn't bond with either parent during my formative years. Brace yourself. I had no positive role models growing up, and therefore I react badly in most situations. Tend to act out in extreme, self-destructive ways. In short, I'm an abrasive, unlovable asshole with antisocial tendencies. It's all my fault that I ended up like this. I accept it fully. I don't blame my parents for how I turned out. There's no need. Since they weren't there during my childhood, I don't see how they're responsible for my adulthood. I'm the one who raised me and I sucked at it. Never could keep a pet for long either. They always bonded to someone else and left me. Even my pet fish jumped from their bowls to commit suicide rather than suffer my boorish company."

Vasili opened the door and brought in another tray.

Instantly, Jullien's entire demeanor changed. And for the first time, she realized that he always buried his stern glower whenever Vasili was around. He softened his features to a much kinder expression. Brotherly and tolerant.

"I brought you some food, *Alte* . . . J-J-Jullien?"

He smiled. "Jullien's fine. Thanks, *luden*. You shouldn't have troubled yourself."

"No trouble. Do you like cookies?"

Jullien sat up. "Are you kidding? They're the best. You're going to share them with me, though, right?"

"Um, sure." Vasili sat beside him and picked up a cookie from the tray.

Ushara took a moment to watch the two of them. Jullien was far kinder with Vasili than anyone else. Though there was still a trace of the regal tiziran in his movements, he was much more approachable.

"So are you interested in the job?" she asked, turning their conversation back to her offer.

Vasili glanced up with wide eyes. "Job?"

"I offered the tiziran work at the base."

Jullien hesitated as he ate. Swallowing, he reached for his drink.

"I have to be paid in hard notes or cronas. Nothing traceable. Same for housing."

"Understood."

Vasili blinked with a hopeful expression. "Please come work for us! You'll love it there!"

Jullien gave him an adorable grin. "Okay. I'll try it."

"Good. Let me tell Gavin to change our course. You two stay out of trouble." On her way out the door, Ushara didn't miss the sight of Jullien handing the last cookie off to Vasili for him to eat. Even though she knew Jullien was starving, he still gave it to her son who had no idea how ragged the male's clothes were. How long the tiziran had gone without anything to eat.

Mystified and touched by Jullien's unexpected kindness toward her child, she headed for the bridge to tell them.

While she expected some resistance from her cousin, the all-out anger from him was rather unwarranted.

"Are you out of your mind, Shara? Do you know he is?"

"I know."

"No, I don't think you do." Gavin pulled Jullien's warrant file up on the monitor.

"I already saw it."

"Did you see *this*?" He showed her Jullien's Andarion criminal court records. And she had to admit, it was quite a lengthy file. "He's been in and out of lock-up since he was ten years old. Only reason he hasn't done time is his last name. Apparently, Mummy spent a lot of time pulling strings and dragging his entitled ass out of trouble."

Ushara scrolled through the charges and Jullien's old mugshots. She barely recognized the young tiziran as the same grown male in her infirmary. Ignoring the fact that he'd been extremely overweight back then, his face was battered in most of them. Black eyes. Busted nose and lips. Scratches. His skin sallow, and eyes sunken. While he stood with an arrogant pride, the boy in those pictures appeared haunted, soul-weary, and bitterly angry.

And though he apparently had liked to brawl at a very early age, this was not the lethal, wary male who'd cut through trained killers while wounded to save her son.

As for the arrests . . . most were for fighting and public intoxication, but the rest were possession, destruction of public property, perjury, breaking-and-entering into government buildings, vandalism—he'd once defaced his grandmother's image on the capitol building at Eris—resisting arrest, misuse of public vehicles, indecency, and one charge for urinating on law enforcement equipment. *That* she could almost respect, depending on the events that had led up to it. "You know, your juvenile records are worse than this."

"Yeah, but I didn't graduate to murder, treason, espionage, and kidnapping."

She noticed Gavin made no mention of his own theft charges. But then, they *were* pirates.

Frowning, she read through the file until she saw the specifics of his current warrant.

Damn. Jullien had aided in the kidnapping of his sister-in-law. That was also part of his treason charge. He'd murdered a cousin and several Andarion guards while escaping custody. Had given out information on the former queen that had led to her arrest and overthrow so that his mother could take the throne, hence the rest of the treason and espionage charges. Ratted out some cousins named Merrell, Chrisen, and Nyran to the rebels and Sentella, and had helped another named Parisa escape. Then he'd set her up to be captured by the new regime.

Yeah, it was all rather bad. None of it made him particularly sympathetic or trustworthy.

Ushara winced as she saw that his aunt Tylie, as acting tadara, was the one who'd signed the orders for him to be arrested originally on Andaria and exiled from their territory, and that his grandmother was the one who'd sent the orders to The League with a request for an execution warrant and bounty. As well as the orders for his Outcast status.

But the form that made her sickest of all was the one his Triosan attorneys had filed on his behalf, requesting political asylum and protection from his father anywhere within the Triosan empire.

*Anywhere.* Even on one of their colonial outposts.

One word, in bold red letters from his father's personal royal office, carrying the emperor's royal seal.

Denied.

Tears stung her throat as she tried to imagine how badly that had to have burned for his father to refuse any semblance of safety. There were more denials from other family members in other empires, including Kirovar. Not one single aunt, uncle, or cousin would allow him shelter.

No one.

She scrolled back to the pictures of Jullien as a battered child and remembered what he'd said to her about his parents not being there, and how they had failed to raise him.

No, his family hadn't spared him a moment of their cruelty. From the looks of it, he'd been in the center of their backbiting madness, and their uncaring depravity had been his normal everyday routine and diet. An unprotected child left to fend for himself, while no one gave a single shit about him at all.

*"Are you safe from harm,* akam?"

No wonder he'd been so adamant to ensure Vasili's welfare before he passed out. Why he'd given the last cookie to her son, even while he starved. Because he knew the cost of it all. How much it hurt to be alone in the universe, without friend or family. With no one willing to look out for you when you had no one else who cared.

And in that moment, her mind was set.

"Jullien stays."

A solid tic started in Gavin's jaw. "Trajen will have a shit-fit when he hears of this. You'll be lucky if he doesn't strip your Canting over it."

"I'll deal with Trajen."

"And what are you going to do when that royal viper prick strikes us all down?"

"You're being ridiculous."

"Am I? The entire history of our race has been written in the blood feuds of the Anatole family. Their insatiable quest for power and their willingness to cut the throat of anyone who got in their way. They chased us at blasterpoint to the farthest corners of the universe and now you dare bring one of them into our last place of refuge? Forget Trajen, it'll be the Fyrebloods who skin you alive for it."

Now *that* . . . that was a very real possibility.

And her own father would most likely be the one who led the lynch mob for her throat.

# CHAPTER 3

"You don't have to be afraid of me, *mi tana*," Jullien said softly to the boy beside him. The kid was so nervous, he was practically shaking in his chair. He half expected him to wet his seat at any moment. "You know I'd never hurt you, right?"

Grimacing, Vasili scratched at his nose. "You're really gigantic. Are all darkhearts as big as you?"

Jullien cleared his throat at the innocent question. Darkheart was a nasty little dig against his breed that the humans had started using centuries ago. It stemmed from humanity's disdain and condemnation of Andarion culture. Because Andarions were a warrior species, they used to carve the hearts from their enemies and dry them out to keep as strung trophies for decoration in their homes and for their weapons. The process they used for it would turn the hearts black and leathery—hence the term darkhearts.

And once Eriadne had begun her Purging against the winged and blond Andarions, it became applied solely to his specific subspecies as a vile insult for them, meaning they were soulless and cruel.

However, the boy, unlike the others who used the term to demean his kind, meant no offense to him and Jullien didn't take any from it.

"I'm larger than a lot of Ixurianir, but there are some bigger than me. Yet that being said, none of us can breathe fire like the Pavakahir. So that gives you a distinct advantage over us, no matter how big we are."

Vasili gasped. "You know about that?"

"The blond hair gives you away."

"If you knew I was a Fyreblood, why did you help me? I thought all darkhearts hunted and killed us."

Jullien handed him the last bit of cookie Vas had dropped. "Can I let you in on a secret?"

"Sure."

"I have a fraternal twin brother. He has white-blond hair, just like yours." At the mere mention and thought of his brother, grief and guilt racked him so hard that for a moment, it stole his breath. God, how he regretted much of his life. But nothing as much as he regretted what he'd done to his brother.

Nyk alone was the one sin that forever haunted him.

The one sin he'd never forgive himself for.

Suppressing the past as best he could and hating himself with every breath he took, Jullien cleared his throat. "When I was a boy, I was awakened one night to the sounds of my mother screaming that my brother had been killed."

He blinked back the tears that always choked him whenever he remembered that godforsaken night that had shattered his childhood innocence and any semblance of safety he might have ever known.

"I cannot tell you the misery I felt in that moment. And I pray to the gods that you never know such pain, *chizzi*. I came into the world with my brother, and had never been alone in it, until then. When I saw you today, all I could think about was that you would have a mother at home as devastated as mine was that night. That your father would be inconsolable, and that your brother or sister would feel as lost as I did when I heard my mother screaming. And I knew that I couldn't leave your family as splintered as mine had been. Not if I could stop it."

"That's why you gave me your wallet to get home?"

He nodded. "I wanted to make sure you got back to your family."

"Thank you, *Alteske*."

Jullien playfully brushed his hand through the boy's hair as Vasili continued to insist on calling him *Highness*. "Dagger or Jullien. There's no tiziran here, Vas. Just a worn-out male who's fought a lot of battles."

He smiled up at him. "Jullien. Are you sure? 'Cause that seems rather disrespectful."

"It's not. Besides, you saved *my* life. If anyone owes respect, I owe it to you for being so noble and brave, given the odds against you. Unlike me, you weren't trained. There aren't many who would run back into danger to save another, especially at your age. You might only be a boy yet, Vas, but you have the heart of a warrior in you. Fearless. Mark my words, you will grow into a *žumi* to be reckoned with. I consider it my highest honor to have saved your life, for I know that you will go on to be a far better male than any I've ever known, and certainly far better than I could ever strive to be. So don't you ever think that one as noble as you could ever disrespect someone as lowly as I." He winked at him. "And I will never breathe fire, either."

Vas snorted. "I can't breathe fire yet." He screwed his face up in frustration. "I keep trying. Mum says I should be able to any day now. But it hasn't come in." He let out a fierce breath, then started coughing.

Jullien arched a brow at the wheezing sound. "Are you all right?"

Nodding, he yawned. "See? It's so irritating."

"Be patient, my young Fyreblood. I'm sure your mother's right."

Vasili tucked his legs under him and handed Jullien his link. "So, *Alte*—Jullien. Would you like to play a game? I have a bunch."

He smiled at the boy and his innocent enthusiasm. He couldn't remember a time in his life when he'd been so open with a stranger. Royal treachery and court politics had never allowed for such. As far back as he could remember, everyone had wanted something from him—usually blood. And they'd all been quick to sell him out for favors. Every word spoken had to be carefully weighed and considered for double meanings and how it could be twisted and used against him for harm by those who pretended to be his friends. There had been entire weeks and months spent in mute silence because it'd been easier than risking the fall-out of self-serving cruelty and double-dealing bullshit.

No one in his past had ever been as pure of heart as this innocent child by his side. And it'd been a long time since anyone had actually wanted to be around him for no reason at all.

Come to think of it, it was a completely novel experience that anyone wanted to be in his company without currying a favor of some sort, or trying to get closer to one of his relatives. Most had treated him like a registered plague carrier.

This was completely alien terrain for him. "Sure, Vas. What's your pleasure?"

Vasili turned his link on. "War!"


By the time they reached the Gorturnum Cyperian StarStation, Ushara was beginning to have major doubts about her decision to bring Jullien here. Maybe this *was* a bad idea. Gavin was right. A large percentage of The Tavali who came through Cyperian were Fyreblood Andarions and if they recognized Jullien, there would be hell to pay. Or at least the blood and hide of one high profile, extremely valuable Andarion tiziran who had a bounty on his head that would make anyone an instant millionaire.

There wasn't a single Fyreblood left who wouldn't gut him on sight. Without question or hesitation.

But then, he wasn't exactly recognizable in his current state. His hazel eyes were the only thing that betrayed his birth status. Humans had eyes like his. Andarions had eyes like hers. White or silvery-white, usually with a rim of red. A handful of Andarion males had fully red eyes that were called stralen. But they were an extremely rare genetic abnormality. And she'd never heard of the Anatoles carrying that gene. Legend claimed there were only three bloodlines that had it.

Two darkheart lineages and one Fyreblood.

As she opened the door to the infirmary, she froze at the sight of Jullien and Vasili. Her son must have talked the tiziran into a gaming session, and at some point, the two of them had fallen asleep. The game continued on an infinite music loop while they lay cuddled side-by-side, sound asleep on the floor. Like two little, snuggly puppies. Or her brothers when they'd been . . . then again, her brothers *still* did that whenever they got together, and they were full-grown with sons of their own.

What was it about males that they all innately napped in a nest?

She smiled as warmth rushed through her. They were adorable in that position. Hating to disturb them, she quietly closed the distance and gently nudged Vasili awake.

He opened his eyes with a gasp.

Jullien shot up and drew his blaster. It took him a second to realize she wasn't a threat. His breathing ragged, he clicked the release back into place and holstered his weapon. "Sorry." Grimacing, he pressed his hand to his wound and reclined with a deep hiss. "Are we at the station?"

"We are."

He scratched at his whiskered cheek in a gesture that was almost childlike and somehow endearing. With a gentle smile, he handed the link to Vasili. "Looks like you won, champ."

"Only 'cause you fell asleep in the middle of your level."

"Yeah, sorry about that. Next rematch, I promise I'll bring my best game."

"You're on." Vasili held his hand out.

After shaking it, Jullien rose to his feet and took a minute to pull a ragged scarf from his pocket. He wrapped it around his neck to disguise his identifiable scars, then covered his eyes with a pair of opaque sunglasses so that no one could tell they were human. Raking his hands through his hair, he smoothed it down and caught her looking at him. "You think I don't know about my eyes? They've been causing me grief since the moment I opened them at birth."

"I think they're a beautiful shade of green."

"For a human. Maybe. Sucks if you happen to have a set of Andarion fangs and height. And they seriously blow if you're trying to blend on Andaria." He pulled his jacket back and secured it so that he could reach his weapons should he need them. "When I first started this fun vacation, I had contacts to disguise them for awhile, but I couldn't afford to keep getting new ones. And couldn't find an optometrist willing to work with me off record. They always want to pull and post medical files. For that matter, I'd kill for the creds to buy a new pair of prescription glasses. I really miss being able to see clearly."

Ushara had the hardest time believing that. His mother and father were two of the richest beings alive, who controlled two of the wealthiest empires in the Nine Worlds. "Your parents really cut you off?"

"Don't know, honestly. Last time I tried to access my accounts, I was told they were frozen by the authorities—which would be my parents' governments, and before I could clear the building where I was staying, five assassins were on me. I barely got out alive. Decided it wasn't worth another try."

"I'm sorry."

"Don't be. We all have problems. As my father said, I made my bed and since my favorite pastime was wallowing in my sheets, he hoped I enjoyed the ones I'd picked out. . . . For the record? They really chafe. Especially my tender places. And don't even ask about the super wedgie they give me when I walk."

She let out a short laugh. "How can you make light of it?"

He shrugged. "What good is crying? I tried it once. Made my throat sore and gave me a head cold. Pissed off my grandmother to no end who decided there was never any real reason to cry unless she personally gave me one. After that precious, life-altering ass-beating, I decided it was easier to hold it in."

Someone knocked on the door before they slid it open. "Admiral? Are you leaving?"

Ushara nodded at Letia. "We're right behind you." She turned back toward Jullien. Shabby elegance. She'd heard that term her entire life, but she'd never fully understood it.

Until now.

He was the epitome of the term. A luscious, evocative, walking contradiction. Ruggedly masculine and yet at the same time refined and educated. His smooth, lilting accent and perfectly chiseled features didn't mesh with his worn-out clothing.

Human eyes with Andarion features. Gallows, facetious humor, and charming mannerisms . . .

"You ready?"

"Lead me to the flaying, *mu tara*."

Gods, she hoped he was still joking and not psychic. Taking Vasili's hand, she led them from the ship and into the landing bay. Luckily, it was the middle of night here so there weren't many about.

Of course, being pirates, activity would pick up in about another hour. Most of them tended to work in the wee hours of the morning. But it was still a bit early before her brethren did their best work.

She headed for the main office. There were only a handful of workers there. All lower-ranking Tavali who saluted her as she entered.

Ushara returned the gesture. "Where's the DCP?" Chief pits were the officers in charge of the hangars, and the independent maintenance crews who worked in them, and each shift had a designated CP who took responsibility while on duty.

A human female gestured toward the break room. "Gunnar's in back, taking his lunch."

Relieved it was the CP she liked best, Ushara headed there with Jullien and Vas in tow.

Large and friendly, Gunnar had gray hair and the build of a mountain. He was eating a sandwich and flipping through his reports as she entered. "Hey, Lady VA, glad you made it back with your evil spawn." Cocking his head, he eyed Jullien suspiciously. "Where'd you dig that up?"

"He saved Vasili. Appears he's really good in a fight and knows his way around ships and systems. So I offered him work in appreciation of services rendered."

Gunnar took a slow drink as he passed a less than flattering glower over Jullien's body. "You got a name, Andarion?"

"Dagger Ixur."

She was impressed with how fast and easy that alias rolled off Jullien's tongue. He must have been using it for a while. And again with the sarcasm given that the Dagger Ixur was also the name of an Andarion boogeyman said to have been caused by an Andarion goddess when her son broke her heart with his treachery against her.

Jullien truly possessed a morbid sense of humor and irony.

Gunnar wiped his mouth. "Experience?"

"Lots."

He rolled his eyes. "Recent?"

"Yes."

With an irritated expression, Gunnar let out a long suffering sigh. "You need to understand, boy, we got a rough crowd that comes through here. You screw up and they're likely to mount your head on the wall."

"I can handle it. And I won't screw up. If I do, I'm told my right side is the better profile . . . just for future mounting reference."

The CP passed her a droll stare, but didn't comment. "See that you don't fuck up. You ever worked on freighters?"

"Fighters mostly. Some EVs and AUs. An engine's an engine. If I can't figure it out, I can always do some research. They tell me that these little doodad symbol things represent letters that when you put them together, they make cohesive words and form complex sentences. Those sentences form comprehensible paragraphs that can then explain how those ships and engines work, and miraculously tell you all kinds of things you don't know. And that each one of those large, flying objects around us have these incredible items you can access called service manuals that will actually tell you how they operate, and how to repair them when they don't. It's all dark, soul-sucking magic, really."

Gunnar laughed. "Well hell, that makes you smarter than about half my crew. Welcome aboard. But stow that attitude, as it's likely to cause me to throw something heavy at your head. Report in tomorrow morning. I'll stick you on first rotation."

"Thanks, Gunnar."

He winked at Ushara. "For you, Admiral, anything."

She inclined her head to him. "Do you have any housing he can use in the meantime?"

He sucked his breath in sharply. "We got in a bunch of Stitches and Rogues not long after you left. They took up most of the available housing. All's I got left is slag quarters."

She cringed at the thought. Slag quarters were only slightly better than a jail cell.

"As long as it's a dry bed with nothing crawling in it, I can make do," Jullien said.

Gunnar got up and went to his main office where he kept the key cards. He came back a few minutes later and handed one to Jullien.

When he called for one of his assistants, Ushara stopped the girl.

"If she can take Vasili home, I'll show . . ." Ushara paused before she spoke the wrong name, "Dagger to his."

"Yes, ma'am."

Jullien didn't speak as Ushara led him through a rear door, out of the offices, and down a back, narrow corridor with a walk that he was pretty sure had been outlawed in a few systems. Most of all, he tried to focus on anything other than how perfectly shaped her ass was. How long it'd been since he last had a female touch him.

Not that one had ever really touched him kindly. Even when he paid for their services.

Still, she was being nicer to him than anyone ever had, and it made him feel almost normal. Like he wasn't a total hybrid freak.

*Stop it.* He knew better than to have these thoughts. If he couldn't contract affection as a prince or tiziran, there was no way in hell he could expect anything except utter hatred and disdain as an Outcast. Especially from a female like her. She was honorable and high-ranking.

Beautiful and accomplished. *Way* out of his league.

All wanting did was make him hurt from the steady flow of unending disappointment. That was what his parents had taught him from the cradle. *Don't have desires or goals, and nothing aches. Just survive like the animal you are.*

Life was easier that way.

*Focus, Julie.*

Looking around, he refused to allow her to tempt him. Rather, he made himself learn about his new home. He'd heard a lot of rumors about Tavali stations, but he'd never been in one before. They were too secretive and cautious to let in outsiders carelessly. And he was stunned that she'd opened the doors to him.

After all, his reputation wasn't exactly one extolled for loyalty. He had basically sold out all but three members of his family.

He'd even sold his own soul.

Trying not to think about that, he glanced around the station. It was a lot cleaner than he'd have thought. More modern.

For that, he was grateful.

Hell, he was grateful just to have some place relatively safe to sleep again. A locking door was a major bonus.

Ushara stopped at the end of the long steel alley and waved the card over a reader. "These are really crappy quarters. I'll see about getting you moved once the others clear out."

"It's fine. Really." *Better than trash like me deserves.*

"You say that, but you haven't seen it." She turned the lights on.

Jullien swept his gaze around the small, spartan room, which took about a second and a half. "Well, it's definitely not the palace I grew up in. But hey, it's not the sewer I bled in last night, either. If the toilet and shower work, I swear I'm in *Eweyne*."

Skeptical, she handed him the card.

Jullien froze as his fingers accidentally brushed against hers. It'd been so long since he had any physical contact with a female . . .

He could barely remember what sex with someone else felt like. And he'd never had it with someone who actually *liked* him. Only females out to use him or the ones he'd contracted for it—which was the only thing he really missed most about Andaria. The sociably acceptable paid companions that had been a sweet bonus for his otherwise shitty life.

As tahrs, he'd been allowed a standard two-year contract with any agency he wanted. And while he'd craved a permanent relationship with someone, not even their paid females would stay with him. No matter how hard he tried to negotiate a longer term with a companion or what he promised them, they always left as soon as their contracts expired.

As his cousins were so quick to point out, he was nothing more than a hideous, corpulent, mongrel dog in their world. Yes, he'd been the crowned prince and heir. But not even the coveted title of Andarion tahrs could buy him affection, or mask the fact that his blood was tainted by the weaker human genetic code of his father.

*Great gods, Julie, your own mother can't love you, or even stand to look at your repugnant form. You think anyone else can?*

His aunt Tylie had been right. No one wanted anything to do with him.

They never had.

And never would the gods allow him a female as beautiful or accomplished as Ushara on his arm. Someone so incredibly kind and soft. Delicate.

She smelled like a warm summer afternoon.

Her pale hair picked up every light, even in the dimness of the station, and beckoned him to touch it. It was so compelling . . . but he'd seen enough females cringe and recoil from him that he had no desire to watch her do the same. He was through reaching for things that weren't his to have, and getting bitch-slapped for the effort.

"Thanks," he mumbled, moving away her.

She gently took his arm and pulled him to a stop.

Baffled, he scowled as she reached into his pocket and pulled out his link. Then she programmed a number into it before she slid it back into his coat. "In case you need something. It's my number."

"Really?"

She looked as shocked as he'd sounded. "That surprises you?"

"Little bit."

Smiling, she reached up and brushed the hair back from his forehead.

Jullien closed his eyes and savored the tenderness of that single action that probably meant nothing to her. Yet it meant a lot to him and sent chills all over his body. No one had ever touched him with that amount of affection before. But the worst part was the scent of her skin that made him so hard, it was painful.

Her fingers lingered on the scar that bisected his left eyebrow and it was nothing compared to what it'd done to the mark it'd left on his soul. "Do I want to know what caused this?" she asked as she removed his glasses.

"Probably not." 'Cause the gods knew he didn't want to recall the event.

Her gaze went to his pupils where she studied his eyes for several seconds before she spoke again. "Are you still using Popivul?"

He laughed bitterly as he realized what she'd been doing. While most Andarions had a degree of light sensitivity and pupils that didn't dilate the same way human eyes did, his years of drug abuse had left his with a permanent enlarged pupil that was easily detectable to those educated about such things. "Looked up my personal file, did you?"

She nodded.

Pulling his collar back, he showed her his neck and the old, faded scars from his misspent years of severe drug addiction that had required him to keep his hair much longer to conceal it. If he were still using, the area would be severely discolored and bruised. "I've been sober for a long time now. No creds for it."

She screwed her face up at the lingering horrendous marks that he always made sure to hide with clothing. "Why did you ever start that?"

"Didn't. My cousin Merrell held me down while his mother injected me. He and his brothers and mother found that I was much more pliant to their schemes whenever I was high. After a few times of them forcing it in me, I didn't want to be sober anymore. It was easier to deal with my family while numb to it all."

Ushara couldn't imagine a family like he described. It was as foreign to her as loving kindness would be to him. "How long have you been sober?"

"Since the night my brother threw me across a table in a crowded restaurant and threatened to paint the wall behind me with my brain matter. It sobered me fast. Not to mention the way my parents looked at me . . . like I was the vilest piece of shit who had ever breathed. My mother actually told me that if she lost my brother over my actions she would hand seal me in my coffin, and listen to me scream while I died in it. And my father told me that he'd never forgive me. That I was dead to him. If you saw my files, then you know he meant every word of that. We haven't spoken since, as he quickly blocked my calls and severed all access to him and his empire."

"Because of your sister-in-law?"

He nodded.

"Why did you kidnap her?"

Jullien let out a bitter laugh. "I didn't kidnap her. . . . Aksel Bredeh was my brother's adoptive brother. That's who I gave her to, and he'd sworn to me that he wasn't going to hurt her, only use her to get Nyk out of my life again and get my grandmother off my back before she killed me—which she'd promised to do. And it wasn't like he was a stranger to me, or her or Nyk, either, for that matter. We'd all gone to school together. He was the stepfather of Nyk's daughter. I'd known Aksel for years. And Kiara, too, and no offense, but she was always a snotty bitch to me. Every time I tried to be nice to her, she'd curl her lip and sneer like I wasn't fit to breathe her air."

His eyes tormented, he raked a hand through his hair. "Have I told you I was extremely high that night? I wasn't thinking straight. My entire world was crashing down around me faster than I could make sense of it all. My parents were blaming me for Nykyrian's death and absence like I was the one who'd orchestrated it. And I was a fucking child when it all happened. Five years old, to be precise. While I like to think I'm intelligent, I have to say, that level of evil was quite beyond my abilities at that time. Then, while all that shit was breaking loose with my parents and brother—the Andarion citizens began rioting in the streets to kill us all. If that wasn't enough, my grandmother went out of her mind, threatening to kill me *and* my mother if I didn't help her kill Nykyrian. Add to that, cousins Merrell, Chrisen, and Nyran who used that time to come after all of us so that they could take the throne during the riots . . . Yeah, fun memories. I tried to talk to my father about it and ask for his help, and he brushed me off, saying he was disgusted with me and didn't have time for it. In fact, his entire consulate was trying to get me disinherited. My aunt Tylie was threatening to see me imprisoned. Galene Batur had threatened to gut me. I'd been poisoned by my own guards. My cousins were being systematically hunted down and executed . . . and were trying to save their own asses by telling lies on me. Yeah, I made some really bad decisions. But my entire family had turned on me, I had no allies or friends, and I was trying to stay alive in the middle of an extremely violent political coup. So sue me that I panicked when I had no one at all to trust or turn to."

The anguish in his eyes scorched her. "Here, let me give you the exact sequence of events." He counted them off on his fingers. "My cousins Chrisen, Merrell, and Nyran had decided that it was time to put me down, and were plotting to have me and my mother killed. I didn't realize what they were doing until they had set up a guy named Talyn Batur whose mother was my mother's best friend and her head bodyguard, and had me take the fall for it. Now, I fully admit I'm not innocent. I played right into their hands, like a fool. I did just what they wanted. And it cost me. Which scared me because I knew I'd screwed up with my mother to the point she'd never forgive me for it. She's always thought more of Galene than she has of me. For that matter, she loves Talyn more. It's why I let Chrisen and them manipulate me. I hated Galene and Talyn for the fact that I couldn't get near my mother for any reason, yet Talyn was allowed to visit her like a beloved son. *Him*, she rocked to sleep and petted. He got to do homework in her lap. Me, she wouldn't look at. Not for anything. Not without slapping me or attacking me. And then when Nyk turned up with a pregnant wife and . . ." He closed his eyes and flinched. "I overheard my mother and aunt talking."

Glancing away, he ground his teeth. "The harsh things they said about me cut to the bone. It wasn't like I had any delusions where I fell in my mother's affections, but damn. It's another thing to actually hear her hatred of me spoken out loud to someone else. To hear her planning to put me back in prison when I'd just gotten out. I couldn't take it. And I lashed out in a bad way."

He drew a ragged breath. "So to answer your question, I don't know why I did it. Jealousy. Fear. Pain. Hatred. Rage. A part of me wanted to hurt all of them as much as they'd hurt me. There are a thousand reasons that don't make sense when you step back and look at them, and I admit it. It just didn't seem right that Nyk showed up after all those years, and took what little I had from me. That he had the beautiful wife and child, after both of my fiancées had killed themselves rather than become engaged to me. That he was a paid ruthless killer, *an assassin* who had murdered his own adoptive father and over a thousand innocent League victims, male and female, and yet our parents respected *him*, were proud to call *him* son, and were disgusted by me when they'd never even bothered to learn the most basic thing about me. That no one could love me for *any* reason. In the end, I realized that fair has nothing to do with anything. Life just is pain and it hates us all equally."

"And sometimes it surprises you."

"Yeah," he scoffed. "But never in a good way."

"Never?" She arched her brow.

"Not in my experience."

Ushara narrowed her gaze at him. "Well maybe it's time for your experiences to change."

"How so?"

"By your actions, it went to hell. Maybe by your actions, it'll get better."

Jullien snorted bitterly. "Doubtful."

"Never say never."

"Never," he said stubbornly.

Impishly, and to prove her point, Ushara leaned in and pulled his head down to kiss those beguiling lips.

Jullien growled at the unexpected taste as her tongue swept against his. Heat coursed through him at the first kiss he'd ever been given freely. Unable to believe it, he was completely stunned as his head spun.

Pulling back, she nipped his chin and smiled up at him as she pressed his glasses into his hand. "As I said, it's time for your luck to change."

And with that, she left him hard and horny.

Breathless and stunned, Jullien followed her to the door and watched that sexy, seductive walk until she vanished from his sight.

He bit his lip as he imagined what it would be like to actually make love to a female like her.

*Don't even go there.*

But he couldn't help it. All he'd ever wanted was a single loving hand to touch him.

Just once in his worthless, godforsaken life.

It was why he kept the old photo of his parents on his link. To remind himself that while his parents had raised him with only scorn, hatred, and distaste in their eyes whenever they looked at him that he had at least been conceived in love. In the very beginning, before his birth, he'd been wanted by them both.

*"It should have been you who died! Why my Nykyrian? Why not you!"*

*"Since the moment of your birth, you've been nothing but a bitter disappointment to me. How I wish you'd been stillborn or had died rather than see you grown into the disgrace you are. No wonder your mother lies in a drugged stupor. I hope she never comes out to face the reality of what she birthed."*

Wincing, Jullien rubbed at the scar on his forehead and tried to blot out the memory of his parents' hatred.

*"You're a hard bastard to kill. What the fuck is wrong with you? Why can't you die already?"*

Just like his mother screaming at him that he should have died in Nyk's place when he was a small boy, he'd never forget the look on Merrell's face when Jullien had survived his cousins' vicious attack on him as an adult.

As the tattoo on his arm said, he was born to suffer. He knew that as sure as he was standing here.

And the gods had no intention of allowing death to spare him a single moment of it. The best he could hope for was to endure this misery and learn from it all. There would never be peace for him.

Sighing at a single truth he could never escape, he locked the door and turned around to inspect his new home.

"Well, at least there's not much to clean." He shrugged his coat and scarf off, and looked for a place to put them. Opening the door on his left, he found the small bathroom with a toilet and shower. While it was the size of a closet, it wasn't the closet. The kitchen was a tiny area behind him with a small rectangular table and four plain white chairs that must have been made for a young girl's playhouse.

He went to the kitchen where another closet seemed to be.

Nope. Skinny pantry.

There definitely wasn't a closet in the small living room in front of him. All it contained was a monitor on the wall and a minuscule glass table below it. A couch and desk were cut into the wall opposite it with a narrow ladder to a loft above.

Jullien tossed his coat and scarf over his shoulder and climbed to the loft where he had to hunch over or risk a head injury. There, a very short bed awaited him with the promise of an extremely uncomfortable sleeping position. But at least it was clean and it had a pillow and blanket. The closet for the room turned out to be sliding cabinets along the side of the bed. He folded his coat and saw that there was another small stand up here with a monitor and lamp.

"Home sweet home," he breathed as he sat on the bed, toed his boots off, then emptied his pockets.

Not the way he'd expected his day to end, by a longshot. He was still alive.

Merrell had been right. He was a hard bastard to kill.

Jullien disrobed and slid into bed, with his pants still on in case he had to run for his life later. He reached for the remote and turned off the lights before he armed the security. Out of habit, he put his blaster beneath his pillow and kept his hand on it.

Closing his eyes, he listened to the silence.

When he'd lived in the palace, he'd always slept to music. But the necessity of having to stay vigilant for assassins and bounty hunters had caused him to give that up years ago. He hadn't listened to music for pleasure since the day his parents had disinherited him.

Against his will, he remembered the last time he'd tried to see his mother and brother. To apologize and try to make some kind of amends for it.

Sickened over what Aksel had done to them and for his own part in it, Jullien had gone to the palace the day Nykyrian had been released from the hospital.

Tylie and her girlfriend had met him in the foyer with that ever-same look of ball-shriveling hatred burning in her eyes. "What are *you* doing here?"

"I need to see my matarra."

His ever regal, beautiful Andarion aunt had stepped in front of him, cutting off his path to the family wing. With that haughty, smug sneer, she'd shaken her head. "You've done enough harm to your mother and this empire. She doesn't want to see you after what you did to your brother. I told you to go stay with your father."

But his father hadn't wanted him. Because of the turmoil on Andaria and their fear of bringing war to their empire, the Triosans had refused him landing privileges. They wouldn't even put his calls through to his father. He still didn't know if the government had issued those orders or his father.

All Jullien knew to this day was that his father had never once called to check on him during the coup. Not even to see if he'd lived through the bloody rioting and royal arrests and executions.

Weary, wounded, and aching, and suffering horribly from his unsupervised detox, Jullien had only wanted to see his mother. Just one last time before he died.

For one single minute.

He'd tried to step past his hateful aunt. "I don't want to fight with you, Tylie."

She'd shoved him back so forcefully that he'd been tempted to hit her, but he'd refrained. "Then leave, or I'll call the guards on you and have the arrest warrant I've already signed for you executed. And you should know, Galene Batur is now the prime commander of the armada and Talyn Batur has been promoted to lieutenant commander. I'm sure they'd just *love* to have *you* in their custody after what you did to them."

That threat had hit home. Out of his own stupid fear and jealousy, Jullien had only meant to intimidate and insult Talyn while Talyn had been assigned to his guard. But things had escalated fast and skidded out of control when Chrisen and Merrell had gotten involved, and Talyn had gone on a killing quest for their throats.

Jullien had arrested Talyn—with the intent to release the boy, after he'd been roughed up to teach him a lesson. But because of his personal hatred for Talyn's father, Merrell had seriously screwed Talyn over and marked him as a disinherited traitor before his brother Chrisen had broken Talyn's legs and shaved his head. The two of them had deported Talyn to Onoria and left him there to die.

To his eternal shame, Jullien had done nothing to stop it. Worse, he'd helped them to cover it up. Like a mindless idiot and too afraid to stand up to his older cousins who had already tried to kill him, too, Jullien had gone along with their plans for Talyn, hoping he could survive their treachery before he became their next victim.

If either Galene or Talyn ever laid hands on Jullien, they'd gut him for his part in what had happened. Just like Talyn had done to his cousins.

Talyn had brutally slaughtered both Merrell and Chrisen. Even though he'd faced them in the Ring that was supposed to house a *fair* fight, they hadn't stood a chance against the Andarion champion fighter.

And unlike Galene who ferociously protected her son, Jullien's mother wouldn't stop it from happening.

Jullien's second lesson in life had been that he was on his own. When the wolves came rushing for his throat, his family ran to save their own asses and left him locked outside with the wolves, to fend for himself.

He had no one at his back. His side or anywhere near him. Hell, he was lucky if they weren't throwing anchors on his body and tying raw meat to this throat.

But Tylie hadn't been through with him. She'd smiled coldly in his face with a gleam of sickening satisfaction in her white eyes. "You should also know that you've been removed from succession. You're no longer tahrs. Nykyrian is now the crowned prince and heir of Andaria and Triosa."

Those words had gutted him. Not because he'd been disinherited, he'd expected as much, but because his mother hadn't had the decency to tell him herself.

Or his father, either, for that matter. They'd done it without a single word to him.

He'd lifted his chin with as much pride as he could muster. Another thing his family had taught him early on was to never show how much pain his enemies wrung from him. Even when those enemies were close blood relatives. "I see. I'll just get my things, and——"

"There's nothing here for you. Why don't you do us all a favor and go? Don't you understand that the very sight of you sickens us? Or is that what you want? To cause us all as much pain as you can?"

No, that was the last thing he'd wanted.

As he'd turned to leave, Tylie had stopped him. "Aren't you forgetting something?"

What? His dignity? That, they'd shredded long ago. So he'd simply stared at her.

Aggravated, she'd frisked him until she dug out his link. "This is Andarion royal property. You're not entitled to it or anything else anymore." She'd stepped back and gestured at the guards. "Escort him from the premises and make sure his access is cleared from all accounts. He is not to return here again. For anything."

With that, they'd followed him all the way to the outer gates.

He could still hear the slamming of the doors behind him as Tylie had him locked out of the only home he'd ever known. Furious and past rational thought, he'd finally started back in, when Kelsei, Tylie's girlfriend, had shot him and driven him off the premises.

None of them had ever called him after that to see if he'd even survived the blaster wound. He wasn't even a passing afterthought to his own parents.

*I'm nothing to anyone.*

Rolling to his side, Jullien growled under his breath as he tried to forget everything in the past.

But he couldn't.

Every night, he went through this. Regret after regret. All the things he wished he could have done differently. All the ones he'd hurt that he shouldn't have.

He should have been a better son. But every time he'd ever tried to see his mother, he'd been shoved away. Either by Tylie or Galene, or one of the ever-revolving doctors who'd monitored his mother's health.

"Your presence upsets her. It's best for her delicate state if you just stay away from the tizirah."

"She doesn't want to see you, Jullien. She only wants Nykyrian. And you're not your brother."

Since he was five years old that was all he'd been told. And on the rare occasions he'd actually seen his mother, she'd looked past him or shoved him aside. "Have you seen Nykyrian? Where's your brother? I know he's here. Why are you keeping him from me? Nykyrian!" Then she would either attack him for daring to be alive while Nykyrian wasn't, or show him a picture of his brother that she wore over her heart.

Never his photo.

Only Nykyrian's.

Or worse, she'd mistake him for his uncle who'd tried to murder her when she was a girl, and go into hysterics where she'd try to kill him and they'd have to sedate her while he tried to make her understand that he wasn't Eadvard, and that he meant her no harm.

That he just wanted to love her.

Between his mother's insanity, his father's neglect, his aunt's cruelty, and his own insecurities and fears, his grandmother had gotten into his head and mind-fucked him to the point he hadn't known which end was up. Every which way Jullien had turned, he'd been used at best, abused at worst. If he ever made the mistake of trusting someone, they betrayed him or were murdered.

Or worse, they were psychotic . . .

*"I killed your brother. Don't think for one minute I won't kill you, too, if you don't do exactly as I say. You may be the only grandson I have, but you're not the last of the Anatole bloodline, and at least the others are full-blooded Andarions, not sniveling human byblows. You're weak and pathetic. Just like your worthless human father. A disgrace to our mighty Andarion lineage."*

Cursing, Jullien got up from the bed and dressed again. There was no need to try and sleep. His demons were out in full force tonight, and they were flogging him. Guilt over what he'd done to his brother rode him hard.

Yes, he'd wanted Nykyrian dead as much as his grandmother had. His whole life had been made miserable because of him. But that wasn't Nykyrian's fault. Anymore than it was his.

Both of them had been screwed over by their family. Yet what he'd done to Nykyrian because of their grandmother and her hatred for the human race was unforgivable and he knew it.

*I am my father's son.*

More human than Andarion.

Leaving his new home, Jullien followed the alley back to the hangar and found a Tavali crewman. "Where's a bar?"

The Tavali curled his lip in repugnance of Jullien's ragged, outdated clothes before he answered with directions.

Thanking him, Jullien headed for it, determined to drown the demons in something potent.

It didn't take long to find the dive on the station. Apparently, it was a common destination for Tavali, as it was near the hangar, and crowded with humans and aliens, even at this hour.

Which was good for someone who didn't want to be noticed.

Jullien headed to the dimly lit bar in the rear corner and ordered a bottle of Tondarian A-Grade Hellfire—the strongest of their hard liquors and a small fortified beer to bomb it with. After he paid for it, he debated going back to his new home, but honestly, he didn't want be alone with the voices in his head. So he carried his drink to the back of the bar and had to wait a few minutes for one of the small standing tables to clear.

With his spine to the wall, he poured a drink and knocked it back. As he set up the next round, a short orange-fleshed Oksanan approached him.

He gave Jullien a speculative once-over. "You come in on a crew?"

"Maybe."

"Tavali?"

Jullien hesitated. But he knew better than to claim citizenship. The Tavali would kill anyone who tried to pass themselves off as one of them. Their citizenship was something you earned, and you better be a full-standing member when you proclaimed it, or you wouldn't live for long. "No."

His beady eyes narrowed on Jullien's neck.

Too late, he realized he'd left his scarf behind so his evidence of hard drug use was plain to see. But at least he'd remembered his sunglasses.

"You interested in some Bliss?"

Jullien pulled his collar up, over his scars. "Can't afford it."

"We could work out a payment plan. First hit on me."

Yeah, that was the last thing he needed. And that wasn't what he'd meant. Even if he'd had the money, he couldn't afford to have his senses dulled with that. Not with the number of beings out to end him. "It's all right. I'll pass." He indicated his bottles with his glass. "This is all I need."

"You sure? What about a companion? I can hook you up with whatever you're craving." He snapped his fingers and an extremely attractive brunette walked over. "Delisa here has skills that are unrivaled."

She cut a salacious smile at Jullien. "Hi, handsome. Need some company?" Sidling over to him, she slid her hand down to cup him in a firm, soothing grip.

Jullien couldn't breathe as the blood rushed from his brain, straight to his groin. He almost came instantly. But he'd had enough of bored females who watched the time while they pleasured him with disinterested hands.

Pulling her palm away, he sighed regretfully. "Sorry, love. I'm sure you're very good at what you do, and you are extremely beautiful, but I don't feel like treating another sentient creature as a commodity to be bought and sold. I've got enough sin on my soul. I'm not looking to add anymore tonight."

"Pity." She walked away to find someone else.

The alien tsked. "If you change your mind, I'm always here. Ask for Rrisk."

Jullien saluted him with the bottle before he poured another drink.

"Have to say, I'm impressed. Not many males can turn Delisa away."

Jullien scowled at the deeply accented voice that spoke way too near to his back. How had the bastard gotten that close to him without his knowing it? Had he been an assassin, Jullien would be dead.

Unnerved, he studied the tall, dark-haired human. There was something about him that seemed familiar. As if they'd met before, but he couldn't peg him. And while he wore Tavali gear and Canting, there was an air of regal refinement that clung to him denoting a fellow aristocrat. Had they met on the street, in regular clothes, Jullien would assume him another prince.

The male held his hand out toward him. "Name's Tray. You are . . . ?"

"Dagger." He shook the proffered hand.

"Join me for a drink?"

"Why?"

Tray laughed. "I have a private booth and you don't."

"Well, in that case . . ." Jullien picked up his bottles and followed him.

As soon as they were seated, a waitress came immediately with a glass of Tondarian ale and assorted snacks.

Jullien arched a brow. "Take it, you're here a lot."

"Yeah. I don't sleep much. You?"

Jullien knocked back a shot of his drink and sighed. "Sometimes I wrestle with my demons. Other times, we just snuggle."

Snorting, he pushed the bowls toward Jullien. "You look like you could use some food."

Jullien took a handful of nuts.

"So, given the demons comment, why did you pass on the drugs?"

Jullien watched the way Tray poured his drink. "I'll answer your question if you answer mine."

"And that is?"

"Does anyone else here know that the high admiral of the Gorturnum Nation is a dethroned Trisani prince?"

# CHAPTER 4

All friendliness died instantly on Trajen Scalera's face. For a moment, Jullien feared he'd crossed the line and was about to have his brain melted by the man's superhuman psionic powers.

But after a long minute, Trajen leaned back and narrowed his dark eyes on him. "How the hell do you know that?"

"Which part?"

"Start from the top."

"When we crossed to the booths, everyone skittered out of your way as if terrified of catching your attention, and no offense, you're no taller than I am, and not as muscular. And *you're* not the one who's fanged. Being more obviously Andarion, I'm the one who usually freaks the humans out." He jerked his chin toward the waitstaff. "Only one who's approached you was the waitress, who knew *exactly* what you wanted, and it's the really good and expensive shit—not this watered-down swill I'm drinking. And she didn't ask for payment on delivery, which means you're more important than the owner of this less than refined establishment."

Jullien spread his hands out to indicate the food between them. "The booth magically vacated for you the moment you appeared, and no one else went for it . . . and not just any table. The only one that has a clear view of every entrance and exit from where you're sitting, which you check as much as I do. There are two guards on each door, who keep eye-balling me and deferring to you for any cues on what to do. Your uniform, while understated is custom and made from the best materials to be found. As are your weapons and boots. And while I don't know your Canting, I do know the Gorturnum flag when I see it. Something you're not afraid to openly flaunt. There are plenty of creatures in this bar for you to waste time with much better looking and far more entertaining than I am, yet you honed in on the one stray Ushara just dragged in and planted here to grill tonight. Put it together, it makes you head badass of the Gorturnum Nation, wanting to see if you should allow me to stay or jettison my sorry ass out the nearest airlock."

Trajen nodded with an irritated grimace. "Impressive. What makes you think I'm Trisani?"

"You don't have the typical eyes of one, which means you have mastered the absolute shit out of your powers and can camouflage all traces of your heritage—kudos on that, by the way. I don't even want to know what that cost you mentally and physically. But I'm guessing it's why the ancient Trisani word *Thaumarturgus,* or warlock, is stitched above your Canting. While you have buried the accent nicely, it slips every now and again on certain words and phrases. And like you, I'm a fallen prince. No matter how hard we try, we can't shake the mannerisms and decorum that were beaten in to us from the cradle. I swear to the gods, I think it's a genetic defect at times."

"Minsid hell. You always this astute?"

"You grow up with everyone around you plotting to set you up for embarrassment, punishment, or death, you learn fast to pay attention to small details."

"You must be hell at Squerin, then."

"Not really. I only played for the snacks."

Trajen laughed. "You didn't answer my question."

"You didn't answer mine."

He tilted his ale at Jullien. "As I said, you're a sharp one. And no. Only my VA knows who and what I am. It's something I suggest you keep to yourself."

"No worries. Keeping secrets is what I do best."

"And now it's your turn. I know you were a user and that you were tempted."

"True." Jullien reached for more nuts. "I had a moment when the Koriłon whispered in my ear."

"And?"

"Luckily, I lost all hearing in that ear when my brother slapped me upside my head years ago. Didn't hear a thing."

Trajen snorted. "That's not an answer."

Jullien sighed. "Truth is, it took me too long to get away from it. I have no interest in going back down that dusty, dead-end road. I didn't like the gutter-hole where I ended up on it. Never really cared for waking up, covered in vomit anyway."

Nodding, Trajen folded his arms across his chest. "Tell you what . . . *Dagger.* You stay clean and out of trouble, keep a good a record at work for the next year, and I'll sponsor you for citizenship candidacy."

That offer stunned him. "Don't fuck with me and make false promises."

"I'm not your grandmother, Andarion. I don't play those games with others. While I am not without my sins, insincerity isn't one of them. Like you said, we're fallen princes. I know what it's like to be without friend, family, or country. Hunted and alone. Hated and hurting. Checking every exit and entrance, knowing the next one through it could be an assassin who's gunning for me. . . . Sucks."

Jullien twisted the glass in his hand, as he debated Trajen's offer.

Not like he had a plethora of them to choose from.

Or any, really.

Trajen snorted. "You know I hear your thoughts, right?"

"Do you?"

"Yeah. You're wondering why I would care or even want to help you when no one ever has. Honestly? I have no idea. I don't really care. I just understand. A long time ago, a Tavali helped me out of a bad situation, and I still have no idea why he bothered to pull me out of the slag-mire when I wasn't worth it. But had he not done it, I'd be dead now. Either by my own hand or someone else's. You have him to thank for this, and yourself. Because as I sit here, looking at you, I keep thinking about him and what he did for me when a sane man would have walked away and left me to rot. . . . And the fact that you helped my VA when you had no reason to, and every reason to stay out of it. For that single selfless act, you bought yourself a chance to make something out of your life again."

Trajen manifested a Tavali Gorturnum cock badge from the thin air and pushed it toward Jullien. "The one thing about being Tavali, we are equal in our Nation. The only limits here are what you put on yourself. You rise and fall on your own merit and loyalty. No one else's. From this moment on, your slate is wiped clean. You have no past that matters. Anyone fucks with you, they answer to me. I'm not your grandmother. I don't work on hearsay or rumors. I will trust you until *you* give me a reason not to. Just don't abuse my trust, because I won't give you a second chance, and your life is what I will take when you break it. Understood?"

"Understood."

"You accept my terms?"

Jullien nodded. "Thank you."

Trajen inclined his head to him. "Don't thank me. Like I said, I'm paying forward a kindness that was once done for me. And you earned this by what you did for Vasili and Ushara. Keep making the right decisions and you'll go far in the Gorturnum Nation. Do wrong and I'll bury you."

With those words spoken, Trajen got up and left him alone with the badge.

Jullien pulled it toward him and swallowed. The black patch had the ghostly image of a screaming skull. Legend said the Canting symbol was originally chosen by the Snitches who founded The Tavalian League to represent the sound their souls had made when they learned their daughter and her crew had been wrongfully seized and slaughtered by a corrupt government who'd wanted their cargo.

He knew that sound. His own soul had made it when he'd awakened to the shrieks of his mother. Drowsy and confused, he'd left his room, desperate to find out what was wrong.

"Matarra? What's happened?"

Screaming with hysteria, she'd turned on him with a vengeance. "My precious Nykyrian is dead! It should have been you who died, but you're too stupid to have gone to school with him. You couldn't even get in! God help this empire with *you* as emperor!"

Stunned, he'd stood there as a mere, innocent child, trying to process those words and the heartbreaking grief in his heart, while his mother had continued to rail against him.

His twin was dead?

Bitter agony had stolen his tongue as his soul screamed out for his brother. Nykyrian couldn't be dead. They were twins. They were supposed to live out their lives together. Forever. That was what twins did.

Wouldn't he know if something had happened to his brother? Weren't they supposed to be so close that he'd feel it in his bones if his brother died?

Then Tylie had turned her own wroth on him. She'd slapped him so hard, he could still feel the sting of her hand. "Where are your tears for your brother? Do you feel *nothing* for him? He was your twin!"

Still, he couldn't move. Couldn't breathe. It was as if all the breath had been violently sucked out his body.

Hissing, Tylie had wrenched him by the arm to drag him from the room.

"Matarra!" he'd cried, trying to reach his mother.

She'd turned her back on him as Tylie had shoved him into the hallway and slammed the door in his face, and locked it.

Then the tears had come. Fast and furious until he was sick from them. He'd wanted to go to school with Nykyrian. But as his mother had said, he was too stupid to get in. Even though he'd studied and taken the admissions test three times, he hadn't been good enough. He'd never been as good as Nykyrian, at anything. No matter how hard he'd tried. He'd always been lacking. Always second best.

"Don't you dare cry for that hybrid bastard!"

Jullien had shrank away as his grandmother and cousin Parisa had neared him. Knowing better than to let her see his weakness, he'd wiped his tears and drawn a ragged breath. "M-m-my brother's dead."

"I know. Who do you think killed him?"

Eyes wide with cold-blooded terror, he'd looked from his grandmother to Parisa and back again.

"That's right," his grandmother had said without any feeling whatsoever. "And if you don't behave and do just what I say, it'll be Parisa's son I see on my throne. Do you understand?"

"Yes, *mu tadara.*" Horrified past any rational thought other than survival, he'd started for his room.

"And Jullien?"

He'd paused to look back at her.

"You breathe one word of this to either Tylie or Cairistiona and I will see you buried in the crypt beside Nykyrian. And your death won't be nearly as painless. That I promise you. You will die in pieces, screaming in agony."

Wincing at the memory, Jullien took another drink as he tried to put his grandmother and her never-ending threats out of his mind.

Ironically, he'd never wanted that minsid throne. All he'd wanted was his parents' time, and to stay alive.

He'd gotten half that wish. Though in retrospect, he should have just let them have his life, too. It didn't seem worth the pain of it most days.

His thoughts drifting, he glanced down at the tattoo on his arm.

*Indurari. Through blood misery we conquer and endure. Out of the bad, comes the good. By our challenges, we are strengthened. Ever strong. Forever onward.* That was the War Hauk legend and family motto, which was certainly better than his family's—*lie and murder your way to the top. Take whatever you can grab. Fuck everyone who gets in your way.*

And as he stared at the patch, another image came to his mind. For once, it wasn't the horrors of his past. It was the image of a beautiful blond angel with silvery-white eyes and lips that tasted sweeter than honied nectar. One with hair of the softest silk. Even though he knew there could never be anything between them, that he wasn't worthy of someone so untainted and beautiful, it didn't stop his fantasies from torturing him with a dream he knew could never be.

Females like Ushara always chose males like his brother. Celebrated heroes who were respected. Those who'd been wanted and treasured by the world.

Everyone followed Nykyrian. They listened to him when he spoke. Jullien was too scarred and broken. Too screwed in the head by his psychotic family—he always had been. No one had ever listened to him. And his past sins were far too grievous to be forgiven. The stories for his kind were always the same.

Horrible life. Bad decisions. Grisly demise at an early age.

Unforgiven by everyone around him.

Creatures like him were never allowed a way out. They always died horribly.

*A dog returns to its vomit.* That was what his grandmother had quoted and used to justify her evil against others. Why she never gave anyone a second chance.

Why she'd always been so hard on him.

*You're just a worthless, half-human byblow.*

Still, he wanted to change. He was sober now. No longer a pawn or a victim of Merrell and Chrisen, or Nyran. He'd broken away from his grandmother's stranglehold.

For the first time, his life was his own.

*Yeah and you've done such a* stellar *job with it. Homeless. Broke. Wandering and lost. Starving.*

He reached for the bottle, then stopped himself. Any more and he'd be loaded. He knew from experience that would lead him to a fight and lock-up.

Belligerent when sober, he became *obnoxiously* belligerent while drunk. Worse, he tended to turn his self-hatred into acts of violence against those charged with enforcement roles, or anyone with an ounce of authority.

*Make the right decision for once.*

Jullien capped the bottle, got up, and put the badge in his pocket. With one last, longing glance at the alcohol, he headed back to his meager accommodations and went to bed so that he could get up early and clean his only set of clothes for his new job.

Dripping wet, Jullien froze as he heard a knock on his door. He drew his weapon from the counter by his side before it dawned on him that assassins didn't knock. They just attacked.

Still . . .

No one ever *visited* him. That would require him to actually make and have a friend. What the hell?

Convinced it was a mistake, he ignored it and finished rinsing off.

Until they knocked again.

"Jullien?"

His heart sped up at the lilting sound of Ushara's sultry voice though the door. And it sent the blood crashing to his groin.

Damn. He was so hard, it was painful. Growling at the aggravation, he got out of the shower and pulled on his clothes, then double-checked that his erection wasn't too obvious before he went to the front door and opened it. Then wished he hadn't as the sight of her beautiful face in the hallway light only made him even harder and hornier. Something he wouldn't have thought possible.

"Hi." Holding a large bag in her arms like a small child, she smiled up at him.

It took a second for enough blood to return to his brain that he could answer such an unexpected, friendly greeting. "Morning." He frowned at her. "What are you doing here?"

She held the bag toward him. "I thought you might like some fresh clothes to wear when you start your new job. I guessed your size, but if they don't fit, the clerk assured me there wouldn't be any problem exchanging them."

Stunned by her gift, Jullien sputtered. He wasn't used to anyone giving him anything, other than a hard time. "You didn't have to do that."

"I know. Brace yourself, Jullien . . . that's the whole point of a gift. You don't do it because you *have* to. You do it because you *want* to."

Yeah and that was why he couldn't believe this was happening. No one had ever wanted to do anything for him before. Except kick his ass and insult him.

Ushara hesitated at the sincerely shocked expression on his handsome face as he continued to stare at her in utter disbelief. Cocking her head, she frowned. "Gracious, you act as if you've never been given a present before."

"I haven't. At least . . . not like this." His hand actually trembled as he took the bag and true appreciation shone in his eyes. "Thank you, Admiral."

"Ushara."

Suddenly bashful, he cradled the bag awkwardly to his chest and inclined his head to her.

She glanced around his cramped quarters. While clean, it was so paltry and meager. And though he was thin from starvation, he was still a large Andarion male. It had to be hard for him to move around in such a small living space.

Even so, he didn't say a word of complaint. If anything, he really did appear grateful for it.

"Have you had any breakfast?"

"Um . . . no. I just got out of the shower."

She gestured toward the door. "I was headed that way before my shift. Would you care to join me? I can show you where the dining areas and shops are in the mall district."

Suspicion furrowed his brow. "Why are you being nice to me when there's nothing to gain from it? You've more than repaid whatever debt you think you might owe for what I did for your son."

Ushara snorted at his tone. "Am I not supposed to like you?"

Wow, that baffled look on his face was something else. How could anyone be so stunned that someone liked them?

"You'd be the first in history to do so."

She laughed, until she realized he was quite serious. "C'mon, Jullien. You have friends and family who like you . . . right?"

He rubbed at his ear in a gesture of discomfort. "Then I must have been taught the wrong definition for that word. 'Cause I always thought it meant that you had a fondness for something."

Sobering, she wasn't sure what to make of that. Surely, he was teasing. "No one has any fondness for you, at all? Seriously?"

"Well, they all liked one thing about me."

"And that is?"

"My absence."

Ushara started to force him to deny it until she remembered that he had no record of any calls on his link.

None. And that his own family had issued a death warrant on him and abandoned him to it. He truly had no one in the entire universe who cared about him.

Leaning forward, she whispered in his ear. "I have fondness for you, Jullien. Come and join me for breakfast. I'll wait for you outside."

Jullien couldn't breathe as he watched her withdraw from his small quarters and close the door.

*I have fondness for you . . .*

Those words sent a shiver over him. It was the first time anyone had said something like that to him before. Definitely no one who possessed female body parts.

Baffled and amazed, and harder than he'd ever been before, he opened the bag to find two pairs of black pants and gray shirts and a new pair of socks. He quickly tried the clothes on. They were a little baggy on him—something new for him over the last couple of years since he'd been on the run.

As far back as he could remember, he'd always been overweight. And had been mocked relentlessly for it.

By everyone.

Even his father. He'd tried to lose weight to get them off his back. But the starvation diets invariably ended with him eating twice as much, and gaining more. A vicious circle of physical and psychological abuse that still left him cringing anytime he neared a mirror of any kind.

For that matter, dull pots and spoons, or anything with a reflective surface gave him hives.

Jullien reached into his coat pocket and pulled out his broken comb for his damp hair. Unlike other Andarions, he'd never been allowed to braid his. As a despised hybrid and bastard child, he was forbidden from joining their military. It didn't matter that he'd been prince or heir.

And since he couldn't be a warrior like his mother, his grandmother had insisted he keep his hair cut shorter than other males—just below his collar—another way to embarrass him for his mother's crime of screwing a human male. Another way to segregate Jullien from his peers and to remind them all that Jullien wasn't like them.

As if they'd ever let him forget the fact that he was half human.

Sighing, he slid the comb back into his pocket and belted his blaster to his hips. He shrugged the coat on and left the small condo to find Ushara waiting for him just outside the door.

Ushara froze at the sight of Jullien in fresh clothes. Damn, he was edible. With sharp, patrician features, he had a quiet elegance to him. And at the same time, a boyish quality. A beguiling dichotomy of arrogant bashfulness. Confident insecurity. Her large male was a walking contradiction.

And she found him completely irresistible.

Before she could stop herself, she stepped forward to straighten his oversized coat around his body.

An adorable blush stained his dark cheeks. "Am I acceptable now, Matarra?"

She laughed at the Andarion word for mother. "Sorry. I can't help it. Vasili does the same thing. He always shrugs his coat on sideways, and leaves part of the collar up, part of it tucked under . . . just like you." Her smiled faded as she accidentally brushed her hand against his chest and the hardness of his muscles there. She was completely unprepared for the sudden and overwhelming jolt of desire it sent through her entire body. Clearing her throat, she stamped *that* down immediately. "The clothes are a bit large. Sorry about that."

"Don't be. I'm extremely grateful to have something fresh and new to wear. It's been a long time since I've had anything that didn't come out of a charity donation bin."

Because a regular store would want an ID for purchase, and they'd have cameras and imprints that could be used by assassins to trace him. Things she didn't have to think about. But they could end his life.

"How have you survived so long on your own?"

He shrugged. "Carefully, and with a great deal of skill."

She rolled her eyes at his sarcasm. Then her gaze dipped to the neck of his shirt that fell low to show off how defined his pecs were. Even worse, they were dusted with an inviting amount of dark hair. Not too thick, just enough to be masculine and sexy, but not so much as to be off-putting or gross. She'd always been a sucker for males with chests like that. Chaz's had been bare like all Andarions.

But Jullien's . . .

*Stop it!*

Forcing her thoughts away, she stepped back as he wrapped his scarf around his neck.

"The first restaurant district is this way." She led him toward the hangar and to the east. "You're in luck that it isn't very far from here, and one of my favorite restaurants is just on the corner."

He didn't speak as he trailed along after her. Yet she was well aware of his seductive lope. The way he kept his thumb hitched in his belt, near his blaster so that he could quickly draw it should he need to. He kept his head down, yet missed nothing around him.

A true predator.

It sent chills over her, especially given the massive size of him. Standing a bit over six feet herself, she was used to meeting most Andarion males at eye level whenever she wore her heeled boots. And she towered over the majority of human men. Jullien was a full head taller than her, and made her feel tiny in comparison.

She liked it a lot more than she should have.

When they reached the restaurant, he stepped around her to open the door so that she could enter first.

"Thank you."

He inclined his head to her.

Ushara greeted the cook and hostess as she grabbed two menus from the holder near the register and made her way to her usual table.

When she started to sit, Jullien hesitated. "Would you mind if we sat over there?"

She frowned until she realized why he wanted it. "Back to the wall where you have clear line-of-sight for the entire restaurant, but no one can see you sitting at the table. You've got eyes on both doors to know who's coming and going, and you're underneath the security camera?"

He nodded.

"Sure."

Without another word, he unlocked his holster before he sat down and made sure his coat didn't block his access to it. Likewise, he kept one leg out so that he could spring from the booth if he had to.

Sadness choked her over his hyper vigilance. "You ever relax your guard?"

"I'm still breathing." He didn't even look down at the menu, except in quick glances.

"Hi, Misha." Ushara smiled at the waiter as he joined them.

"Admiral . . . you got first shift again, I take it."

"Do, indeed. This is my friend, Dagger. He's new to our party, so I'm showing him around. I trust he'll be treated well here."

"Oh absolutely. Any friend of yours is family to us. I'll make sure and tell Petya. I know she'll want to meet him." He pulled out an e-tablet. "What can I get for you?"

"My usual. Dagger?"

"Unopened bottled water. Uncut canolay fruit."

Misha hesitated. "And?"

"That's it."

Ushara scowled at the paltry order. "Breakfast is my treat."

"Thank you. But that's all I want." He handed the menu to Misha.

Passing a wide-eyed stare at her, Misha gathered their electronic menus and left them.

Jullien stroked his whiskers before he caught the expression on her face that must have betrayed her shocked thoughts. "What?"

"You can't live on that. No wonder you're so thin. Why didn't you order anything else?"

"Have you *any* idea how many times I've had my food poisoned or tampered with? I'm lucky if they *just* spit in it."

"You're the tiziran."

"Yeah. The most hated tahrs in the history of Andaria and Triosa, combined. Remember? They took a poll. I won hands down. Ten years in a row on Andaria. If not for Justicale Cruel and my grandmother, I'd probably be the most hated royal in all Ichidian history. Which is weird given that my cousins committed far worse crimes than I ever did. I mostly assaulted inanimate objects. I never raped anyone or shot someone's dog, but what the hell? Why discriminate based on a belligerent drunk and disorderly criminal history?"

Misha brought their drinks, and, grimacing, set Jullien's unopened water down in front of him.

"Thank you." Jullien carefully checked the seal before he opened it. "Thank you, Misha."

He nodded, then left them alone again.

Even though Jullien had checked the seal, he still smelled the water and placed his finger inside to dip it in a bit of the water to taste for poison or pollution. Then, he pulled a small vial from his pocket and placed two drops in the water and swirled it.

"What's that?"

"It turns purple if there's any poison present. Blue if there's a paralytic. Yellow for hallucinogens."

Ushara gaped. "You do this every time you eat?"

"Only if I don't prepare it." He slid the vial back into his pocket and waited several minutes before he finally sipped the water.

"You didn't do this on board my ship."

"I was too hungry to care, then. Besides, I was already in your custody and at your mercy. Not like you couldn't have thrown me out an airlock had you wanted me dead."

He had a point, but still . . . "Were you always like this?"

Jullien shook his head as he continued to study his water. "No. I was suicidal at one time. Didn't care if they killed me or not. A part of me was hoping they'd succeed. The only reason I care now is I'm not about to let some asshole become a millionaire off my back because I laid down and let them cut my throat. They take me in, bastard's gonna earn it and I'm taking an equal amount of his ass to the grave with me." He gave her a lopsided grin. "I'm a contrary prick that way."

She leaned back as Misha brought out her food and put it in front of her. He grimaced as he placed the melon in front of Jullien. "Would you like me to bring you a knife for that?"

Jullien pulled his own out, and twirled it open. "No, thanks. I have it."

Misha beat a hasty retreat.

Ushara suppressed a laugh at Misha's reaction to Jullien's impressive knife skills. "Let me guess . . . fear of a poisoned blade?"

"That's what led me to you, is it not?"

Yet another very valid point. Ushara watched as he carefully examined the smooth shell of the melon. And by that, she meant *carefully*. "Is something wrong with it?"

"Looking for needle marks. Making sure nothing was injected into it."

Her heart sank at his matter-of-fact tone. It was a miracle he ever ate anything, given this amount of paranoia. He even smelled the shell, and rubbed his *solution* over it to test if something had been placed on it.

Finally satisfied, he cut up his melon. And as with the water, he still examined each piece before he cautiously ate it.

"You sure you don't want some of mine?"

Jullien hesitated. The hungry longing in his eyes was searing. "I would kill for it. But it's not worth the chance of getting sick."

Because he had no one to care for him, and no way to seek medical help. First thing any doctor or nurse would do was run his DNA and prints for medical records. And the moment they did that, it would pop up his warrant and notify them that he was a fugitive. They would be required by law to turn him in.

Aching for the way he was forced to live, she took a bite of her bread, then held it out toward him. "I'll be your food taster."

Jullien paused. Before he could stop himself, he opened his mouth and allowed her to feed him a bite.

She smiled warmly at him, then wiped at his chin. "See? It's delicious, isn't it?"

Honestly? He didn't taste a bit of it. All he could focus on was how beautiful she was and how warm her touch made him feel inside.

She held her fork up and fed him some of her breakfast scramble. "Thank you."

Inclining her head, she took a bite herself.

His cock jerked as he watched her eat and his thoughts went to a place he knew they shouldn't. But he couldn't help it. No one had ever been this kind to him. All his life, he'd wondered what it would be like to have someone who was nice to him for the hell of it. Not because they wanted something or a favor from his grandmother.

Nice because they *liked* him.

It was what had made him so mean to others, especially in school. In retrospect, he regretted how he'd treated a lot of his classmates, especially Dancer Hauk. But he still remembered that first day of school when Dancer had shown up and his mother had intentionally sat them together.

*"Remember Dancer, this is the tahrs. Be nice to him and he can do a lot of things for you and our family. I want you two to be best friends."*

Jullien would give Endine Hauk credit. At least she'd been open about it. Most weren't quite so blatant with their ass-kissing. But then, she was a distant cousin of his mother's. That kind of self-serving, backbiting bullshit ran thick in their genes.

And from that moment on, he'd been hard on Dancer. Suspicious and cold. Never trusting that Dancer was there for any reason other than the fact that Endine had made him tolerate Jullien's presence.

But no one had told Ushara to be nice to him. She had nothing to gain by sitting here. He had no more political ties to use. No strings to pull.

Nothing.

She cut up her ham and held it out for him. When he opened his lips, she playfully jerked it away and ate it instead. "Ha! Fooled you!"

Jullien laughed as her pale eyes sparkled with humor. Shaking his head, he held a piece of melon out to her. "Eat this with it. The juices will enhance the flavor."

Leaning forward she ate it from his hand. His breath faltered as her tongue skimmed the flesh of his fingers and sent another wave of desire through him unlike anything he'd ever felt before.

Holy gods . . .

"Mmmm," she breathed. "You're right. It's delicious. How did you know?"

He shrugged. "I spent a lot of time in the kitchen when I was a kid."

"Really? Not exactly the place I would imagine for an Andarion tiziran."

Snorting, he cut more melon. "Haven't you seen the pictures of me when I was Prince Ponderous?"

She choked on her food. "Excuse me?"

"Oh c'mon. You're not going to hurt my feelings. Not like I could miss it. The headlines were in every tabloid and newsfeed the universe over. Tahrs Tub-of-lard. Jiggly Jullien. Prince Jerkllien. Jolt-Head Jullien. And of course my personal fave, Tahrs Junkie eat-it-all Asshole. Whenever I was trying to stay sober, I sought refuge at the bottom of a barrel of cake batter. It was the only safe place I had in the entire palace where no one bothered me." He licked his fingers.

"Sorry."

"Don't be. Best memories of my life were sitting in the kitchen with our cook while she worked. I know she didn't really like me either, but at least she wasn't openly mean to me."

"Then how do you know she didn't like you?"

"Andarion hearing and I moved like a shadow for a fat kid. Heard a lot of things no one knew I did. But at least Karna quit complaining about me after awhile. Sometimes she almost even smiled when I came in. And at least she knew by the girth of my abundant ass that I appreciated her hard work."

Ushara offered him another piece of ham and this time, she didn't pull it away.

"So what about you?" he asked.

"What about me?"

"Who raised you?"

She tried not to react to something he really shouldn't have to ask. The fact that he was sincere with that inquiry said a lot about his world. "My parents. They're Tavali so I was raised here." She took a drink of her juice. "They're both still alive and my father continues to make some runs, but not too many. In fact, that's where Vasili is this morning. He spent last night with them after we got home. And he'll be with them all day. We're not letting him out of our sights for days to come."

"Really?" His voice was filled with disbelief. "He likes them?"

"Most beings like their grandparents, Jullien."

"Do they?"

She laughed at his genuinely shocked tone. "Yes. I promise."

But the expression on his face said that he couldn't quite wrap his mind around the concept of it. How tragic for him.

He wiped his hands. "Do you have siblings?"

"A large number of them. Three brothers and four sisters."

His eyes widened.

"And brace yourself . . . we love each other. Get along famously, most days. In fact, we live in a cluster together, within walking distance of each other's homes. Two of my brothers were even on board the ship that brought you here. The big giant who scowled at the door of the bar when I entered to get Vasili? That was my brother Dimitri."

"I have no ability whatsoever to relate to anything you've just said. I believe you spoke in Universal, but really, all I heard was bleh, blar, blurr, blah, bleakly, blar, blar."

She laughed at his gibberish. "It's true."

"I kind of, almost believe you. Of course I still believe in St. Daner who uses a pair of magical boots to bring presents to kids on Gal Day, too. So what the hell?" The laughter died in his eyes as he looked past her and his gaze sharpened and fastened on someone behind her.

She turned to see what had caught his attention. *Crap . . .* Speaking of her family. Her cousin Lev was headed toward them with his crew. They must have just come in from their latest run. And he didn't appear particularly happy.

With his thumbs in his holster, Lev paused beside her and eyed Jullien suspiciously. "*Kyzu,*" he said in greeting. "I wasn't expecting to see you here . . . with a new . . . servant."

Jullien leaned back in his seat. It appeared relaxed, but Ushara recognized it for what it was. He cleared the way for a clean shot at her cousin should he need it, under the table.

"Dagger," she said quickly, "May I introduce you to my *kyzi* Lev."

Jullien's eyes narrowed in disappointment before he returned his hand to rest on the table, letting her know that his finger was off the trigger. He passed her an irritated smirk. "Nice to meet you."

"You look familiar. Do you I know you?"

Jullien shrugged. "I have one of those faces."

"Lev . . ." Ushara drew his attention back to her. "Is there something you needed?"

Before he could answer, her link went off. She checked it and cursed. "Sorry. I have to take this." Scooting out of the booth, she headed toward the bathroom for privacy.

Jullien didn't move as the large, blond Fyreblood Andarion blocked him in. Because Jullien had yet to expose his fangs or stand up and he'd removed his sunglasses while talking to Ushara, Lev thought he was towering over a man and intimidating him. Dumbass.

"Do you know who she is, *schânkefrel?*"

"I know."

Two other Fyrebloods moved in to flank Lev, while he glared down at Jullien. "We don't like outsiders here. No one encroaches on our females. You don't touch an Andarion, *schânkefrel.* They're off limits to the likes of you. Understood?"

"I'm familiar with the culture."

The three of them stepped back as Ushara returned. Sighing, she grabbed a quick drink. "Sorry, they need me in my office. I have to go."

Jullien inclined his head to her. "It's fine. Thank you for the conversation this morning. And for the gifts."

Her features softened. "Good luck today. Try to make some friends." Then to his greatest shock, she leaned down and kissed his cheek. Turning around, she eyed her cousin and his crew. "Play nice."

But as soon as she was gone, they returned to glower at him.

Jullien let out a tired sigh. "Do I really have to kick your asses my first day here?"

"Lev," the female owner said in warning. "No fire in my restaurant."

"Don't worry, Petya. I don't need it to teach this piece of human waste a lesson."

"Ass-kicking it is." Jullien stood slowly. "Last chance to walk out of here on your own."

Lev hesitated as he realized that Jullien was taller than he'd assumed. And broader.

For some reason, no one seemed to appreciate his size. He'd never understood why that was. He towered over most beings and yet they didn't seem to comprehend that fact until it was too late.

Like now.

Refusing to back down and lose face with his crew, Lev reached for him.

In one fluid movement, Jullien caught him in the solar plexus, which would preclude him from making fire. Then he punched him in the throat. Catching him, he spun and set Lev into the booth before going after the next one.

Jullien punched and caught him fast, dropping him straight to the floor. When he went for the third, that one wisely stepped back and held his hands up.

"I've got no problem with you, brother."

Jullien cast his gaze around to make sure there were no other threats.

Misha and Petya stared at him, slack-jawed.

"You said you didn't want a mess in your place."

Petya inclined her head to him. "Appreciate it."

Jullien pulled out his wallet and left half his money, hoping the tip would cover the inconvenience. Keeping his back away from the third crewman, he made his way from the restaurant and hoped that he hadn't just signed his own death warrant with that outburst.

If he had . . .

His grandmother would be celebrating over his corpse tonight.

As he headed for his new job, he caught a glimpse of his reflection in the store windows and winced.

No wonder they'd attacked him. He looked like the worst sort of vagrant dog. Yeah, he was clean. But ragged as hell. Baggy clothes. Secondhand, stained coat that had been patched and repatched to the point he looked like he should be huddled over a flaming barrel with a bottle of hooch near some abandoned factory somewhere. Boots that were held together with electrical tape. He looked down at his bruised hands and torn claws.

*You're disgusting! A disgrace to the entire lineage of eton Anatole! No wonder your mother won't come out of her room. Who can blame her? I wouldn't sober up either if I had to face* you *as my son!*

It wouldn't have burned nearly as much had it not been the truth.

Pushing his aunt's harsh criticisms away, he turned the collar of his ragged coat up and headed toward the hangar for work.

When he went inside the office, he caught the clerk's sneer of revulsion, until she focused on his face. Then her look turned a bit more welcoming. "Can I help you?"

"Gunnar told me to report for work this morning."

"Oh . . . you must be Dagger. Hold a minute." She got up and went to another office.

When she returned, she was leading a blond male who slowed his walk as he focused on Jullien's form. He raked a calculating stare from the tips of Jullien's scuffed boots to the top of his head. "I was told to make sure and give you a thorough introduction of how we do things. Gunnar said that you knew about ships?"

"I do."

"How much you know about Tavali?"

"General information. Nothing specific."

"If you'll follow me . . . I'll show you where you can change into work overalls and store your gear."

Jullien headed into the back with him. As he started to remove his blaster, a bad feeling went through him. Honestly? He'd rather give up a testicle than his weaponry. Testicles he could live without.

Weapons . . .

*You're being paranoid.*

"You can't work in the bay armed. It's against all regulations."

Yeah, that was what he figured. Still . . .

Jullien placed his holster and weapons in the locker and followed his manager to the hangar. "Are you the OOD?"

"Yeah. And let me give you a quick tutorial on Tavalian culture and how things work around here. See this . . ." He pointed to his sleeve where The Tavali wore their national flags, individual Canting and ranks. "Designates the Nation we fly for. The solid black flag with the screaming skull is for the True Black Flag Nation, Gorturnum. That's us. We were the first of the Tavali Nations ever created. The patch under it is my personal Canting, then my rank. These three things mean that I'm a Tavali citizen with rights in this Nation. Notice you don't have any Canting, flag, or rank."

"Yeah. I know."

"No, I don't think you do. See, what that blank sleeve on *your* arm means is that you are a slag. Without rank or citizenship. You're not even a cock. So you don't speak to Tavali unless we speak to you. You don't count in our world, and you don't exist. You're a ghost here with *no* voice and *no* rights."

Jullien froze as he saw a group of Tavali moving in to form a circle around him.

"You damn sure don't dine with one of our admirals like you hold rank. You don't even look at our females."

"Yeah," another Tavali said behind him. "And you damn sure don't attack a commander, slag. Because you attack one of us. You attack us all. *That's* what being Tavali means."

"And *you* ain't Tavali, dog."

Jullien silently winced as he mentally did the math in his head. Not that he needed to. One to twenty . . .

This would hurt if they were planning to do it barehanded. The fact they were picking up tools for his beating . . .

Fuck it.

He swept his gaze around the group and smiled at them. "Well hell, boys. If I'd known you were throwing me a welcome party, I'd have brought some beer."

# CHAPTER 5

Ushara had promised herself that she wasn't going to act like some lovesick teenager with a crush on the latest crooning heartthrob. After all, she was the vice admiral of the oldest Nation of the Tavali fleet. The right hand of the most powerful commander they had. While she was young, she was as jaded as anyone ever born. Wise and strong.

Mature.

She was one of the best of Trajen's pilots. The commander he trusted above all others. She wasn't checking on Jullien over infatuation. Not even a little. It was merely gratitude for what he'd done with Vasili, and she wanted to make sure that he was settling in with his new job and quarters all right.

That was her duty as vice admiral—to ensure that any new member of their station merged well with their society. They had to mesh or be thrown out.

Of course, they didn't normally get such personal service from her, but Jullien had saved the life of her son . . . She owed him.

Yeah, she knew she was lying to herself and making excuses for why she was seeking him when she had no business doing so.

No matter how much she denied it, she was drawn to him even though she knew it was all kinds of stupid. There was just something about him that she couldn't get out of her mind. Something about him that touched her heart in a way no one ever had before.

Not even her husband.

Still, she was proud of herself. She'd gone almost two full days without bothering him or spying on his whereabouts. But after two days, she wanted to make sure that he didn't need anything.

Trying not to be obvious, she headed into the bay and acted like she was inspecting ships and cargo, which was technically within the parameters of her job.

Sort of.

She scanned the ground crews, seeking an exceptionally tall male, with black hair, broad shoulders, a lethal predator's lope, and a quirky sense of biting, self-deprecating humor.

Disappointment filled her when she didn't see him right away.

Where could he be? He was a hard one to miss, even in a large crowd. Face it, dark Andarion males tended to stand out among her Fyreblood breed. Especially ones with his noble, badass carriage.

"Hey, babe."

She paused as her brother Davel came up from beside her and placed a kiss on her cheek. She gave him a light hug. "Hey. You just getting in?"

Dressed black-on-black, her brother nodded. At six-two, he was a huge mass of overdeveloped muscles. Too big, in her opinion, with short, spiked white blond hair and silvery-white eyes that were identical to hers. As her older brother, he was forever overbearing and bossy—nosy to the extreme, and since the death of her husband, had tried to step in as Vasili's father with unwarranted advice and opinions on how her son should be raised. Something both she and her son weren't happy about. At the rate Davel was going, it was a race to see which of them took out a League contract for his life first—her, or Vas.

Still, she loved him and knew he meant well. She just wished he'd stick to sending his own family into therapy, and leave her son for her to screw up alone.

"Where's the rest of your crew?" she asked, looking around for them.

"They took off already for home. I saw you over here, nosing around, and wanted to make sure everything was okay. Paka told me what happened with Vas. How'd slavers get ahold of him, anyway?"

"I allowed him to go off with a small group of friends to Paraf Run." She glared at him as fury filled her over the near catastrophe. "Because of *your* wife."

He paled. "*My* wife?"

Hands on hips, she nodded as even more anger ripped through her. "Yes! Telling me that I was overprotective and ridiculous. That I needed to loosen my death grip on my child before I damaged his sense of independence and made him afraid to venture out on his own. So what happens the minute I relent? Sex slavers see his fair-hair and beautiful face, and grab him off the street. Thank you both for your expert opinions on parenting. You're both so awesome. 'Preciate it."

He cursed under his breath. "Am I a widower?"

"Not yet. You have your mother to thank for that, and the fact that your wife's pregnant and I didn't want the soul of your innocent unborn child on my conscience. But next time Fara interferes . . ."

"You know she would have never risked Vasili."

She held her hand up sharply to cut him off. "Don't care. She needs to stay out of my business. And so do you. How I raise my son is none of her concern, especially after this."

He must have realized how close to death he stood because, for once, he backed down. "All right. I will have this discussion with her. Though I'm sure you've already done so."

"Yes, I have. And yes, she's now terrified of me."

He nodded. "Point taken. Do I need to buy her a wig?"

Ushara snorted. "Don't push me, Davel. I'm still not over what could have happened to him. It was way too close and that boy is all I have in this realm. I've already buried my husband. I will *not* bury my son."

He sobered, "I know. We were all shaken by it and you know I would die before I allowed harm to come to my blood." Frowning, he scanned the bay with her. "What are you looking for, anyway?"

No sooner had he asked than her gaze fell to the very male she sought. Trying not to betray herself, she shrugged. "Nothing. Just passing through the area. Why don't you go on and say hi to your family? I know your kids have missed you. They need to know their paka's home."

"You're lying about what you're up to, but fine. I know when you don't want me around." He kissed her cheek again and wandered off.

Knowing her family wouldn't approve of her talking to an Ixurian, Ushara waited until he was out of sight before she headed straight to Jullien, who was working on the hydraulics system for a loader. Yet as she neared him, she noticed he wasn't moving with his usual fluid grace. Rather his movements were slow and laborious. Methodical.

It wasn't until he jerked around, ready for battle, at her approach that she saw why.

"Oh my God!" she gasped. One side of his face was swollen horribly from a beating. He could barely open his left eye and his lips were split and scabbed over. "What happened to you? Did you get run down by a freighter?" she breathed, moving forward to touch him so that she could examine his injuries.

Stepping out of her reach, he glanced around before he returned to working. "What can I say, *mu tara*? I make friends everywhere I go." As he bent over to retrieve a wrench, his shirt rode up his back to expose more bruises along his spine.

Horrified, she pulled it away from his skin to reveal the true nightmare of what had been done to him. Dear gods, she could see the entire outline of heel and toe prints. "What is this?"

He took his shirttail from her hands and tugged it down. "I believe the term is *boot party*."

"Jullien . . . did you report this to the HCs?"

"Why? It's the only time in my life anyone's ever thought enough of me to bother hosting any kind of party in my honor. I'm actually quite touched that they went to the trouble."

"You're not funny." She pulled her link out. "I want the names and descriptions of everyone you remember."

With stoic features, he pushed her link down. "I don't remember anything, Admiral. Now, if you'll please excuse me, I have work to do."

His curt tone wounded her. And come to think of it, he was acting very strange. Not his usual charming self. Rather, he was standoffish and cold. He wouldn't even meet her gaze.

"What's wrong with you?"

"Nothing, *mu tara*. I merely have a lot of work to do, and I really need to see to it."

Her heart lurched as she finally understood what had happened. "They beat you for eating with me, didn't they?"

He sighed, but still wouldn't meet her gaze. "I was merely educated on Tavali custom and code, and where I fit into your society."

"And you're okay with what they did to you? You're content to let them get away with this and not be punished for it?"

He shrugged. "Why not? Been known to employ such tactics myself to teach others a lesson. While I'm a lot of worthless things, Admiral, I'm not a hypocrite. And I'm a big believer in karma. Figured I deserved it. At any rate, it got their point across to me with resounding clarity. It's definitely something I won't forget any time soon."

"Hey!"

Ushara turned at the sharp, angry call to find one of her older cousins headed for them from the opposite side of the bay. From where she stood, he couldn't see her, but she had a clear line of sight to him.

Istaf stormed toward Jullien with his furious ass-kicking swagger. At six-six, he was a mountainous, muscled snow beast who intimated everyone around him, and always had. Most skittered from his path like mice fleeing a starving cat.

Jullien, however, held his ground courageously and didn't flinch at his approach. Rather, he calmly wiped his hands off and faced him with an irritated, challenging smirk that was as admirable as it was stupid.

"You the slag shit what beat my little brother down?"

While Jullien might have refrained from meeting her gaze, he leveled a killing stare at Istaf. "Depends. Your brother the pussy bastard who attacks an unarmed civ in a pack like a rabid dog?"

Growling in rage, Istaf started forward.

So did Jullien.

Ushara put herself between them. "Whoa! What is this? Istaf, explain yourself. Now!"

"He beat the hell out of Silig. Put him in the hospital. I'm here to make sure he pays for it."

Her jaw dropping, she faced Jullien. "Is Silig the one who attacked you?"

Jullien glanced away.

She faced Istaf. "Did Silig attack him?"

"You're not seriously defending a piece of crap slag over one of our own, are you?"

"When he's the one who single-handedly saved my son's life and returned Vas to me unharmed, I am. Are you telling me that my own blood dared harm the very male I brought here out of gratitude for saving my son? A male Trajen extended his own hospitality to?"

Istag paled. "What?"

"Yeah, you missed that part of it, did you?"

"What's going on here?" Davel asked as he must have seen the blood fury in Istaf's gait and doubled back to make sure everything was all right.

Ushara gestured toward her cousin. "This idiot was about to beat down on the male I offered sanctuary to, who saved Vasili." She spun on Jullien. "Look at what the imbeciles did to him already!"

Davel shoved at Istaf. "What the hell, man? What's wrong with you?"

"I didn't know. Besides, I was doing it to protect *your* sister. Silig said Lev caught some indigent comet slag snaking on her, and that he needed to be put in his place. How was I to know the indigent slag was the same slag that saved Vasili?"

Ushara curled her lip in disgust. "As if *I* need *you* to protect me. Really? Do I look like your wife? For your information, I happen to have two blasters, and a license to use them. Minsid hell, *kyz!*"

"Uh yeah," Davel agreed. "If you recall, the last male who tried to force a dance with my little sister is still undergoing surgeries to have both his testicles retrieved from his nostrils."

She rolled her eyes as her brother piled on. "I'm not *that* bad."

"No? I beg you to ask the guy whose testicles haven't redescended after three years. I promise you he would emphatically disagree. Testicle retrieval surgery is no laughing matter."

Ushara wasn't amused. "I still maintain that he racked his own balls."

"No male racks his own balls *that* hard. Trust me."

"You don't know," she snorted. "You weren't there."

"Yeah, but I've fought enough with you to know who racked what and how, and especially how hard. In fact, my balls still crawl back into my body out of survival instinct any time you come near me. And that's just from bad childhood flashbacks."

"Hey, where's he going?" Istaf jerked his chin toward Jullien who was slowly walking backward, toward the bay's offices.

Jullien froze as the three of them turned to face him. "This entire line of conversation was making me rather uncomfortable. Therefore, I thought it best I remove my testicles out of *everyone's* striking range."

Davel burst out laughing. "Smart male. I like him already." He sobered as he saw the damage done to Jullien's face. A tic started in his jaw as he returned to glare at his cousin. "You do that to him?"

"No. Silig and a group of his cronies did it. But——" Istaf held his hand up to cut off Davel's words when he started to interrupt. "You should see what this slag bastard did to *them*. He beat the utter hell out of every one of 'em. Honestly, I was expecting someone about twice his size."

Jullien tossed his wrench into the toolbox by his feet. "Yeah, me and Gondarion spiderweed. We don't go down easy."

"Then why'd you come after him alone," Davel asked Istaf defensively.

"Well I wasn't, at first, until I saw him. Then I just thought my brother was an idiot."

Jullien arched a brow at that. "In that case, you owe Admiral Altaan a debt of gratitude. She just saved you a universe of hurt and an operation for wrench retrieval from a place you don't want to know where I was planning to shove it."

Istaf stiffened. "You don't look like much of a threat, *boy*."

"Yeah, and I'm the one walking and working, while your brother's the one laid up in a hospital bed." Jullien twirled another wrench before he set it down.

Istaf took a step forward, but Davel caught him and forced him back. "Enough. You," he said to his cousin. "Go home."

Istaf passed a disgruntled sneer at Jullien before he complied.

Jullien returned to work.

Ushara placed her hand over Jullien's as he reached for a monitor and stopped him. "You need to see a doctor."

"I'm fine," he said without looking up.

She caught his chin gently in her palm and forced him to meet her gaze.

Jullien couldn't breathe as he stared down at the warm concern in her pale eyes. As he felt the heat of her hand on his skin.

"Please?"

He savored that single word before he spoke the truth. "I can't afford the down time. I have to make rent. Besides, I've had much worse beatings. Trust me. This isn't so bad."

She dropped her well-manicured hand down to his bruised one. The contrast between them was startling. Not just that hers was so pale compared to his, but the delicate bones and softness of her skin. "I'll go away if you do one thing."

"What?"

"Take your shirt off. If Davel agrees that he thinks you don't need a doctor, I'll leave you alone."

Her brother made a sound of supreme protest. "How did I get dragged into this?"

"You're an irritable ass who loves to fight, and you've broken and bruised enough ribs that I trust you to know whether or not Jullien should be working while injured. Plus I can judge by your facial expression how bad his injuries are 'cause I know you *that* well."

Jullien ground his teeth. "And if I refuse?"

"I'm going to suspend you from work and order you to the infirmary for a full eval."

Jullien growled at her before he dropped his tools and braced himself for the pain of pulling his shirt up. Not that he had to. He'd only lifted it to his armpits before her brother let out a foul curse.

"How the hell are you standing in that condition?"

Ushara grimaced. "It's bad, isn't it?"

Davel nodded. "Yeah, it's bad. *Shit!* If you've really had worse, I don't want to know how. Damn sure don't want to know why."

Lowering his shirt, Jullien winced as pain cut through him and he let out an agonized breath. For a minute, he feared he might actually pass out from it.

Ushara glared at him. "That's it. You're coming with me."

Jullien shook his head to clear his vision as he broke out into a sweat. *"Mu tara—"*

"Not a single word of protest. I'm not leaving you here to suffer. That's not how we do things."

"Take my advice, *drey*? Don't argue. She'll win by sheer stubbornness or meanness. Remember the earlier testicle discussion?"

Jullien snorted. "Fine." When he went to clean up his tools, her brother pushed him aside.

"I got this. You really should rest before you puncture a lung. Honestly? I don't know how you've missed doing it before now."

He was right. It was a miracle he hadn't done some serious internal damage. But then, as stated, it wasn't his first severe beating. He'd learned how to move with injuries and not worsen them a long, long time ago.

Grateful to Davel for his kindness, Jullien inclined his head to him. *"Pakti, drey."*

"No problem."

Ushara picked his coat up from the ground and to his complete and utter shock, took his hand into hers. For a full minute, he couldn't breathe as the warmth of her skin caressed his. "I can't believe you came to work in this condition. What were you thinking?"

"That if I didn't, I wouldn't get paid. Worse? I'd get fired. Somewhere between those two . . . killed."

"You're not funny."

When she started for the infirmary, he stopped her. "I can't go there."

"Why?"

Jullien was aghast at the question. "You've seen the bounty on my head. I'm not about to put my life in the hands of an unknown physician who's going to run my DNA and find my warrant. I'd sooner die of my wounds than feed a gutter rat who poisons me so that she desecrates my remains to make my bitch grandmother happy."

"You trust me, don't you?"

"Yes."

With his hand still in hers, she pulled him in the opposite direction.

Jullien had no idea where she was taking him until she came to another housing area. The condos here were much nicer than the ones where he was living. Larger. Lush. They reminded him of the politician district of Eris on Andaria where a lot of the upper aristocracy and older nobility made their homes.

Ushara stopped at one that was painted a sedate green and punched a code into the door before she entered. At first, he thought it was her home, until he looked around and saw older paintings of Ushara as a girl with her numerous siblings. There were all kinds of toys strewn about the carpeted floor, and something warm and sweet scented the air.

"Matarra?"

Eyes wide, he froze as she called for her mother. "What are we doing here?" he whispered between clenched teeth.

"Relax. She's a healer. She'll take good care of you."

Suddenly terrified at the very prospect of meeting Ushara's *Fyreblood* parents, he stepped back, intending to leave at the same time an older version of Ushara came through the door in front of them. Her mother took one look at him and curled her lip as the familiar glare of hatred filled her white Andarion eyes.

Jullien tried to flee, but Ushara refused to let go of his hand.

Suddenly, he felt a presence behind him. Turning, he saw an older Fyreblood male there who must be her father.

And he looked as happy to see him as her mother did. He was lucky her two parents weren't roasting him on the spot with their incendiary breath.

"What is *he* doing here?" her mother growled in a vicious tone that said she was about to launch her firespit at him any heartbeat now.

"*He* saved Vasili's life."

"I find that impossible to believe," her father snarled from behind him. "His kind doesn't do that. They save no one but themselves, and they have no use for us, except as target practice and morbid decoration as trophies for their walls."

"And I was there. I saw it."

Her father closed the distance between them. "Do you know who this is, Ushara?"

"I know, Paka."

"I don't think you do, *atalla*." He raked a cold, hate-filled glare over Jullien that reminded him of the ones his aunt Tylie would give him when he was a child and he'd try to see his mother. Just like then, it shrank his stomach and left him with that same sick, gutted sensation that made him wish he was low as they made him feel. At least then, he'd be invisible. "His grandfather murdered my father in front of me when I was a boy, and he laughed while he did so."

Jullien ground his teeth. Yeah, that sounded like something his family would do. "If it makes you feel better, Gủr Tana, my grandmother slit that same guilty grandfather's throat during breakfast over a rumor she heard."

That took the anger out of him. He actually gaped. "What?"

Jullien gave a subtle nod. "Ear to ear. Of course, it was a lie she'd been told. But she didn't bother to find out the truth until after the deed was done. *Oops* didn't quite cover it that day, and it was nothing compared to the rampage she went on against the one who'd lied to her. Just glad I wasn't *that* idiot."

His jaw dropping even more, her father gestured at Jullien while he grimaced at Ushara. "You see how they are! You can't trust any of them. And you dare bring *this* into my home? What are thinking?"

"He is not his grandmother. Jullien, tell him!"

Jullien glanced to her mother and then her father before he shook his head, and released her hand. "There's no need. I've already been judged and sentenced, and the one thing I learned most from my family is that once a verdict is rendered, there's no reprieve or mercy from it." He gave a curt, formal bow to her mother. "Forgive me, Ger Tarra, for bringing disharmony into your beautiful home and distressing you." He bowed to her father. "Mi Gủr Tana."

With that, he left.

Ushara glared at her father. "Really? After all the lectures you gave me as a girl about hospitality and repaying debts owed?"

"Don't you dare take that tone! If I taught you nothing else, it was to never, ever put faith in a darkheart. Your husband spins in his grave over this!"

"And my son lives because of that male and the sacrifice he made for

Vas. He has been cast out and spurned by everyone. I won't be like them. You taught me better. *The journey across the universe begins with a single step.* How many times have you said that to me?"

She turned toward her mother with a scowl. "His family taught him *nothing* but betrayal and cruelty at every point in his life. They threw him out with nothing and left him to die. I told him we were better than they were. Yet since he's come here, he's seen the same kind of brutality from us. Are we really any different from them? They attacked us because we weren't like them and what have we done to him? The same exact thing. Well, I won't be like that. I refuse to judge him by what his family has done."

Her father sputtered. "*He is wanted.* Have you not seen the bounty he carries?"

She nodded. "Yes, I have. He has a bounty, just as we do. Are we not every bit as wanted by The League? Is it not death to own Tavali Canting and flags? Is there not one of us here who would be imprisoned or hanged if caught by a League ship? Never mind what would happen to us should we ever venture into Andarion territory?"

Ushara gestured at the door where Jullien had gone. "Jullien is trying to turn his life around, and start over. Rather than become another mountainous obstacle he has to scale, I'd rather be a stepladder to help him."

Her mother snorted disdainfully. "More like a stepping stone to be cast aside after he uses you."

"That would be on him if he chooses to do so. But if I spurn him and treat him like shit for no other reason than the fact that he was born to the eton Anatole lineage, then that is on me. And I don't want that sin on my soul. I will not live as a darkheart. My parents taught me better."

Shaking and weak, Jullien sighed as he slid down the wall to crouch in the shadow of a dark alley. Honestly, he was too tired and in too much pain to walk anymore. Why did he even bother, anyway?

No one gave a single shit if he lived another day. No one would even know if he died. He had nothing left. Just a resolute will to carry on that he didn't understand. Probably because it was all he'd ever known.

His grandmother was right, he was a contrary bastard to the bitter end.

Closing his eyes, he tried to remember a time in his life when he'd had dreams. But honestly, he couldn't. As a child, the only goal had been to survive. To get through the day alive.

All he really remembered about being a boy was being scared all the time. Or angry.

Yeah. He remembered a whole lot of pissed off.

And how weird that the fear and anger had only left him after he'd looked into his brother's eyes and seen Nemesis staring at him. That soulless killer he knew wouldn't hesitate to gut him where he stood. In that sole moment of crystal clarity, of those human green eyes that burned him with ravenous fury, he'd seen his own reflection and had hated himself more than Nykyrian ever could.

Not that they'd ever really been brothers. Even before Nykryian had been sent away and "murdered," they'd never gotten along. Golden and fair, Nyk had been doted on by their mother and father. And Jullien had hated him for it. From the moment of birth, Jullien had done everything he could to try and compete. To make them see him as Nyk's equal.

They never had.

Second born. Second best.

Nyk was the heir. Jullien was their spare. And they'd never really wanted him. Nor had they tried to hide that fact, or save his feelings over it.

"Jullien?"

Tilting his head back, he saw his angel of torment descending on him. Weary and cold, he stared up at her. "Please leave me alone."

Ushara knelt by his side and frowned. There was something different about him. Something in his voice that wrung her heart. "Why?"

He didn't answer.

"Jullien . . . talk to me."

"It's just easier, okay? I know I'm an unwanted piece of shit and I accept that. But then you come around and you show me glimpses of a world I can't be a part of. You show me what it's like to be normal, and then when reality returns it's just that much harder for me to deal with." He met her gaze and the agony in those hazel eyes seared her. "I'd rather you beat and insult me like everyone else does, than do this anymore. It's far more cruel."

"I can't leave you here. In pain."

"Sure you can. Just turn your back and leave me in the dark like everyone else. It's easy."

"Jullien—"

He placed his finger on her lips to cut her words off. "Thank you for trying. It's more than anyone else ever did for me. Now go, *mu tara*. You have a family that loves you. You should never fight with them over something like me. Believe me, I'm not worth it."

A shadow fell over them.

She looked up to see her father glowering at them.

Growling irritably, he bent down to help Jullien to his feet. "C'mon, you worthless darkheart bastard."

Jullien hissed in pain.

"Careful!" she warned. "He's in bad shape, Paka."

Gentling his touch, her father draped Jullien's arm around his shoulders and helped him back to their home without speaking another word to him.

By the time they returned, her mother had the guest room ready and had set out a small medical kit. Her father helped Jullien sit on the bed before he stepped back.

"So what's wrong with him?" her father asked Ushara.

"Before or after he was knifed by an assassin?"

Her father sighed. "That would do it."

Jullien cracked a bitter, half-hearted grin. "What can I say? I bring out the best aim in everyone."

Her father grunted as her mother helped Jullien remove his work shirt. Only then did Ushara see real sympathy in her parents' eyes for him as they began to recognize what she was learning about the true horrors of Jullien's life.

Biting her lip, her mother pulled the bloody bandage back from the knife wound. "This is badly infected. Have you been to a doctor?"

"No. I was doing okay with it until I got jumped. It's been hard to keep it disinfected with busted ribs." He held his hand up and pulled the ragged, worn glove from it. "And a broken wrist."

Ushara gasped at something she hadn't even noticed.

Her father passed a shocked gape at her, before he stepped forward to glare at Jullien. "You've been working the bay like this?"

"Yes, Gůr Tana."

"How long?"

"Two days. It's actually not as bad today as it was yesterday."

"He needs to go to the infirmary." Her mother's tone was insistent.

Jullien shook his head. "I can't risk it."

"He's right," her father concurred. "There's not a Tavali here who wouldn't be tempted to turn him in if they figured out his identity. And since he's not one of us, he has no protection. Hell, he's lucky I haven't shot him for the bounty."

Her mother gave him a withering stare. "You're not funny, Petran."

"Nah, but I'm honest."

Tsking at him, her mother gently examined Jullien's bruised and swollen hand and tattooed forearm. Her features stiffened as she saw the jagged vertical scars on his wrist that betrayed an even deeper sadness about the tiziran's past.

Worse? He'd tried more than once to end his own life.

The moment he realized what her mother was looking at, he blushed and turned his wrist aside to hide them.

Her mother didn't comment on the scars. "Pet? Would you please fetch my oil chest for me? And Shara, I'll need an herbal tea. Lemon with honey and ornar."

Jullien braced himself as her mother moved to examine his eye and cheek. He had to give her credit, she had the gentlest touch of any he'd ever been near.

"Why do you keep flinching? Does my touch offend you that much?"

"No, Ger Tarra. Please forgive me. I'm not used to anyone touching me unless it's to strike a blow."

She cupped his unbruised cheek and forced him to meet her gaze. "When was the last time someone held you?"

Jullien looked away, unwilling to answer her.

"*Alteske?*"

"Jullien, if you please, Ger Tarra. There's no need for formality. I was disinherited four years ago."

Her gaze fell to the distinctive claw marks on his chest that proved his words. He was Outcast. No longer welcome in Andarion territory. To be caught in any of their lands would mean instant arrest at best, or death at worst.

Fitting really since it was what his cousin Merrell had done to Talyn

Batur while Talyn had been assigned to Jullien's personal guard. What they'd all had a hand in causing to be done to Talyn's father, Fain Hauk. Though to be honest, Jullien hadn't wanted Fain disowned.

That had been his grandmother's cruel dream because she personally hated the Hauk family so badly.

*What is cast out to the universe, returns with a vengeance.* Jullien could definitely attest to that.

Ushara's mother gently cleaned his eye. "You haven't answered my question."

"I should think it obvious, Ger Tarra."

"Four years?"

He laughed bitterly at her assumption. Then that old streak of venom reared up inside him and did what it always did. It lashed out from the vicious pain that he did his best to keep leashed in the darkest recesses of his soul.

"I've only been held by others long enough for punishment. If you're seeking some vestige of beneplacity within me, I assure you, I'm quite barren. Everyone, including my own mother, has told me since the hour of my birth that I am the least bene-merent of all Androkyn. Rather, I should have been suffocated upon arrival from her womb rather than suckled by my most unwilling wetnurse to live."

Her pale eyes filled with horror, she dropped her hand from his face. "What have you done to be so hated by your own mother?"

That was the question that had haunted him throughout his entire childhood. "The only answer I have is that I had the unfortunate luck of favoring my uncle Eadvard."

"I don't understand."

Jullien met her gaze and sighed. "They were barely a year apart in age. The favorite child of my grandmother, Eadvard killed two of my mother's siblings before he turned sixteen. He had my mother attacked and left for dead, and after she failed to die of her injuries, he attempted to murder her and my aunt Tylie himself. She, in turn, carved his heart from his chest while she was still a teenager. Apparently, he was a psychotic bastard from the moment he learned to walk. So you can imagine my mother's abject horror when they pulled a physical duplicate of the very creature she'd already killed for trying to murder her out of her womb and tried to hand it to her. I'm told she actually screamed and recoiled in terror the first time she looked at me."

"That's not your fault."

"And my mother and aunt are strict followers of Yllam Orthodoxy. They believe I have my uncle's soul and that the gods returned him to her to haunt her for her actions against him."

"What do you believe?"

"Perhaps I am Eadvard reborn. And my punishment is to return here and be cast into the care of those who hate me most. That at least gives me a reason for the hell that has been my life. And if that is why I'm here, then I can accept this fate and deal with it."

"So you're a believer, then?"

"Not really. It's just the lie I tell myself so that I can hold on to some semblance of sanity and explain the utter travesty that is my family. And why I'm forced to endure them."

Ushara returned with the tea and a large chest. "Paka had to leave to pick up Oxana. They blew a part of their engine and are stranded."

"Is she okay?"

"Yeah. Just a malfunction. I've got a tracer on him for you, and she's transmitting so that we can keep an eye on her to make sure everything's fine. We've already scrambled a fighter team to cover them until Paka gets there." Ushara handed the tea to her mother. "Oxana is one of my sisters," she explained to Jullien.

He didn't respond as he watched her mother mix the oils into his tea before she handed it to him.

"You should drink that while it's warm. It'll help with the pain. Once you finish, I'll clean and reseal the knife wound and set your wrist."

"What about his ribs, Mama?"

"We can wrap them after I tend the wound. The infirmary could fuse them and heal them a lot faster."

Jullien scoffed at the thought. "They could also sever my carotid and collect the bounty." He knocked back the tea in one gulp. It was actually really good. The warmth spread through him, but as it did so, it made his eyelids heavy.

The room started to spin.

What the hell?

He tried to focus. "What did you do to me?"

"You need rest. Just relax and breathe."

*Oh shit . . .*

"You drugged me?" He tried to get up, but couldn't. The next thing he knew, everything went black.

Ushara caught Jullien's head before he struck the headboard.

"Careful," her mother warned.

The care in that tone caught her off-guard. "You're concerned now?"

She helped Ushara position him on the bed, then nodded. "We had a moment while you were gone."

"What do you mean?"

"Meaning, I get it. I understand why you're drawn to his darkness." She picked up Jullien's arm where the tattoo was and turned it so that Ushara could see the scars underneath the ink where Jullien had cut his wrists. "But be careful, mu tina. When someone is in this kind of pain, it's not easy to come out of it. He's more likely to pull you down and drown you than you are to pull him up and save him."

"I agree. But he doesn't wallow in his sadness. And he doesn't blame others. He's trying. That is what I see, and it's what makes me want to help him. He's not like the other darkhearts we've met."

"No, but there is still a deep, unforgiving darkness inside him. From what I've read of him, he unleashed it against his own brother. Be careful that he never unleashes it on you."

Her mother was right and she knew it. Only a fool would ignore the danger of this male. While Jullien wasn't like his family, he was still a product of their cruelty. Still an eton Anatole. Which meant his idea of claiming her heart was more likely carving it out of her chest and putting in a box to be burned for entertainment.

"Don't worry. We're only friends. Something he seems to be very short on."

Her mother nodded while she worked on his knife wound. "Why was this not sealed?"

"It was. He must have torn it open again when Silig and his stupid friends attacked him."

She looked up, slack-jawed. "Silig is the one who did this to him?"

"Yes. Lev saw us eating together and they decided to teach him his place."

"Did they not know who he was?"

"Of course not. They're idiots. Thankfully, our side hogged all the brains."

Her mother laughed at that, then finished resealing his wound, and carefully bandaged his side.

Once they had his ribs wrapped, her mother hesitated. "He is extremely handsome, isn't he?"

Ushara felt heat rush over her face before she nodded in agreement.

Her mother gave her a speculative stare. "So you are attracted to him?"

"I won't lie and say no. He's tempting."

"Has he made any advances toward you?"

"No, he's been very respectful."

"Pity."

"Matarra!"

She laughed and wrinkled her nose. "Your father was an irritating beast, back in the day. I couldn't turn around without him shadowing me. I had my sights set on another, but your father wasn't having any of that. To this day, I'm extremely glad Petran was persistent. And that I came to my senses before it was too late. Otherwise, you would have had another paka . . . and another life."

Carefully, her mother applied her oils and rubs to the bruises and cuts on Jullien's body. All the while, she stared at Ushara from under her lashes. "Your Chaz has been dead for a long time, and I haven't known you to go near another male."

"True."

"So what's changed, my daughter?"

Ushara started not to answer, but she'd never kept secrets from her mother. There was really no reason to start now. "Vasili likes him. You've seen how Vas is now. He's talking again, and interacting, like he hasn't done in years. And the tiziran's been very kind to Vas. Amazingly so."

"Your paka will never accept a darkheart near us. You know that. I'm surprised he allowed him to return."

"I know. As I said, we're only friends. That's all." Yet even as she spoke those words, she knew them for a lie. Something was different in her whenever Jullien was around.

He broke her heart and made her feel for him in a way no male had made her feel for him since her husband. A part of her was more alive in his presence. More aware of him. More alert and giddy.

It wasn't just Vasili he touched.

She didn't even know why. Or how. But she recognized the danger signs. With Chaz, it'd been so easy. They had been similar creatures who'd gone to school together as children.

Their parents had been friends for as far back as either of them could remember.

Jullien was another matter entirely. His presence threatened them all. He was wanted. Hunted.

Hated.

Her gaze fell to the scars on his wrist that suggested he might even be psychotic like the rest of his family. The gods knew stability and dependability had never run in the veins of the Anatoles.

A sane female would walk away now before it was too late.

"Shara?"

She blinked at her mother's concerned tone. "Sorry, Mama. I was merely thinking that you're right. As soon as he's healed, I'll see to it that he's sent away from here. It's not worth the risk. We can't afford a darkheart among us. Too many of us have suffered at their hands. I won't dredge up that past or ask anyone else to suffer his presence because of my feelings. You didn't raise me to be so selfish. I will see to it that he's gone."

"Good girl. The Anatoles have never brought anything except heartbreak and turmoil to this universe. Rather than be content with their power and wealth, they have plotted and slaughtered their family and ours to extinction. Never forget that."

"I won't." Yet as she left the room to wash up, there was something that she couldn't get out of her mind.

Over the last two days, as she'd done more research into Jullien's past, she'd dug through thousands of media pictures that had been taken of him through the years.

As a royal prince and tiziran for two empires, he'd been dogged by photographers and reporters from the moment of his birth. They had literally documented almost every failure and shortcoming he possessed with ruthless acrimony. He hadn't been joking about the spoofing epitaphs they'd maliciously applied to his name in an effort to publicly ridicule him—something the Anatoles had never allowed done to one of their own royals before. But because he was half human and overweight, it'd been open season on him.

And what the Triosans had done to him didn't even bear thinking on. They'd made the Andarions seem benevolent saints in comparison.

Yet what had stuck out in her mind as she'd scanned articles and photos was that never once, not in all the tens of thousands of candids and official state pictures, was anyone from the royal family ever touching Jullien. There were photos of their mother cradling Nykyrian as an infant on her lap or in her arms while a nurse held Jullien in a cold, plastic carrier.

But none of him in his mother's arms. Or anyone else's.

Even the official Triosan state family photograph showed his father seated with Jullien standing behind him and his hand on his father's throne. Never on his father's body. And none where his father actually touched Jullien, or even looked at him. For that matter, Jullien was never looking at his father, either.

His gaze was always on the floor or on his hands. Or pointedly focused in the opposite direction of his family.

All the rest of the pictures showed Jullien with at least a foot of space between him and any member of his family. Most of the time, they had their backs to him. And in every one, the soul deep agony in his eyes was gut-wrenching.

How could no one see what was so painfully obvious and right in front of them?

Or did no one care? Were they really that heartless and unfeeling that they'd continue to insult and degrade him in spite of his unmistakable torment and rejection?

But then that was sadly the nature of the universe. Everyone was so wrapped up in their own concerns that it was hard sometimes to see that others had their own issues and pain. To remember that those who seemed to have it all, sometimes had nothing whatsoever.

And come tomorrow, she was going to have to find it in her to be as callous as everyone else and shove him back out into the universe that wanted him dead.

*How can I?*

She had no choice. While she felt bad for the prince, she couldn't risk her family. They would always take precedence over everything else.

Even her own bleeding heart.

# CHAPTER 6

Jullien lay in the dark bedroom, listening to soft voices of Ushara's family as they chatted in the living room about her sister's ship and how they planned to pay for its repairs.

"No, Paka. You can't take a loan for that. I'll figure something out. I have no idea what. But I'll come up something. I hear prostitution pays nicely these days."

"Ana! You have four little girls to feed. Your husband lost his last shipment and his ship. You're still paying off his medical bills."

"I know. But—"

"I can pick up more runs," Davel offered.

"Me, too," Dimitri said. Jullien had yet to meet that brother, but he knew his voice since he came by every night to check on his parents and sisters.

"Davel, your wife is about to have your next son any minute. You need to be *here*. Not off, who knows where. And Dimitri, you're already obligated for your son's and daughter's ship. You can't afford more debt." Oxana sighed. "I can manage something."

Still they argued about how to help her.

Jullien couldn't fathom it. His family had only argued about how to cut each other's throats. Who to screw over next.

And how hard.

The door to his room opened.

Ushara slid in quietly so as not to disturb him.

"I'm awake," he whispered.

"Did we wake you?"

"No. I can't hear you," he lied, knowing it would embarrass her if she knew he could hear her family's private matter. While most Andarions had heightened hearing, his was even more sensitive than theirs. His pediatricians had speculated that it must stem from some defect of being a hybrid. As a child, he'd been forced to wear special dampeners to keep his eardrums from shattering over any sharp sound.

On the run, it came in extra handy to be able to hear a fly squeaking from two clicks away.

She turned on the table lamp, then gently placed her hand against his brow to test for a fever and check his eye. How sick was it that he looked forward to this each day? This one fleeting encounter with her in the evenings where he could pretend that someone cared about him, and it saddened him that it couldn't last. All too soon, he'd go back to his hovel and she'd be out of his life.

Forever.

Not wanting to think about it, he forced himself to remain stoic. "How was work?"

She smiled kindly. "Fine. You feeling better?"

He nodded as she pulled back his bandage to look at the knife wound. Unfortunately, that wasn't what he wanted her to inspect. Before he could stop himself, he reached out and touched the incredibly soft strand of her pale hair that hung forward.

Startled, she looked up and caught his gaze.

Jullien swallowed hard before he brushed his thumb against her lips, wishing he had the courage to kiss her. But he knew better. Besides, he was Andarion. It would be wrong to dishonor her in the home of parents after they'd been so kind to him. What he was doing already by touching her hair without having spousal or betrothal rights to her was wrong.

She was a treasured daughter of their house and bloodline. An honorable widow with a half-grown son . . .

And so he dropped his hand and forced his gaze to the floor. "Forgive me, *mu tara.*"

"Ushara?" her mother called.

"Coming." She straightened up and left.

His body shaking from a need so strong it didn't bear thinking on, Jullien rolled over and clenched his eyes shut. But images of holding her tortured him. He might never have had a dream as a boy, but he had one now.

It was pure Tophetic madness the priests of Andaria would tell him would risk his eternal soul. Yet he didn't care. He'd be willing to pay that fee to have her.

Just once.

He'd never had a female in his bed who loved him. Only those who "serviced" his needs. Most of the time, they'd barely concealed their disinterest and disgust for having to tolerate his hybrid touch. Yet before he died, he wanted to know what it felt like to have a female ravenous for him. One who hungered for him as much he ached for her.

*Gah, you're a sentimental idiot. You sound like a woman.*

And he was. He admitted it. It was a stupid dream, anyway. That was why he'd chucked them all away as a kid. No need in having them. All they did was torture him worse than the guards who'd been assigned to him in prison.

*The only thing you need to focus on is getting back to work before you get tossed out of your box for lack of payment.*


"Did you know the darkheart fixed Oxana's ship?"

Ushara looked up from her reports as her father entered her office. "Pardon?"

"I just met with the tech rep to get an estimate on what the labor would cost now that her part finally came in. We opened it up and there was nothing wrong with the drive. *Ti. Dyti. Delidun.* In fact, it was upgraded and better than it's ever been. Looked brand spanking new."

That was stunning. Oxana's drive system had been burned completely out on her last run through the Solaras System. They'd all been worried sick about the cost of it. "How do you know it was Jullien who repaired it?"

"Who else has those skills and wouldn't bill us for them?"

He had a point, still . . . "Has he said anything about it to you?"

Her father shook his head. "He hasn't said a word to any of us after he thanked us for taking care of him and left three weeks ago. Has he spoken to you?"

"No. He's avoided me like a disease-carrying rodent."

"Well, I maintain that no one else would have had the skill-set to do it. Gunnar's been stalling us for the part, saying he couldn't get it in, and doubling the cost on it, like a rat bastard. I was told yesterday that it'd finally come in, after a League embargo and tax hike. He had it jacked so high that Oxana was about ready to sell her youngest on the open market. For that matter, I was scheduled to take out a loan with Frax to cover it, later today."

She cringed at the name of a notorious Tavali loaner who was best avoided at all costs. Most who took out loans with him ended up indentured for life, and it infuriated her that her family was being extorted like that. Especially from someone who was dependent on Trajen's good graces to stay in business. "Why didn't you come to me?"

"You don't have the creds for it, either."

"I'm still family."

"Which is why I didn't want to trouble you. My job is to take care of my children, not burden them."

She rolled her eyes at her father and his archaic principals. "Family helps each other."

"Anyway," he said, changing the subject, "we met for the labor estimate an hour ago. When we opened her ship up, there was nothing on it to be repaired. The ship runs better now than when she first bought it. Come see for yourself."

Ushara notified Zellen that she was taking her lunch break. Curious about the matter, she left her office and followed her father through the station, toward the north hangar where Oxana's freighter had been storage-docked since her father had hauled it in weeks ago.

While the station was governed by the laws of the Gorturnum Nation, each of the hangar maintenance and repair crews was an independent company that had an individual owner or boss. Gunnar was their direct overseer, or Chief Pit, who rented the hangar from Trajen and contracted with each company owner to keep the Tavali ships flying and cargo moving in and out of the station. He also helped fence "liberated" League merch, as well as moving legit cargo, and set up auctions for it. But his main job was to inspect the ships and hangar to ensure all ran smoothly and according to Tavali Code.

Last she'd heard, Jullien was working as one of Gunnar's base maintenance sweepers who ran and maintained their ground equipment and facility's systems. He was only cleared to clean and load ships if one of the other crews needed a hand.

But it was possible his position had changed.

Ushara had purposefully avoided talking to or about Jullien since he'd left her parents' home. It was a sensitive and sore topic for everyone, especially given the fact that she had yet to ask him to leave the base as she'd promised her family she would.

More than a dozen times, she'd started to, then chickened out. She just couldn't bring herself to hurt him. Not after the way he'd been treated by everyone else.

He had nowhere to go and she knew it. Not to mention, the small matter of a huge death sentence that hung over his head. It just didn't seem right to turn him out, knowing what waited for him on his own.

And why should she make him leave? He didn't bother anyone. He kept to himself, like a phantom ghost.

Case in point, as they went through the hangar in search of him, there was no sight or sound of his presence. While the other mechanics and engineers worked in boisterous teams or crews and chatted or obnoxiously played music, Jullien was forever solitary. A whisper of a breeze who clung to the shadows. He was only seen by others when he wanted to be found. Which was almost never.

After a few minutes of futility, she pulled out her link and called up his work file.

"Is he not on this shift rotation?" Her father stepped closer to look over her shoulder as she continued to read the schedule. "Is something wrong? Why are you frowning like that?"

"It's just . . ." She held her link out for him to see it. "He requested a transfer to Sheila's crew."

"Sheila?" His tone held shocked contempt. "Why would *anyone* want to work for *that* bitch?"

Ushara couldn't imagine. Everyone hated the old surly Tavali. Most quit after a day or two spent under her blistering insults.

No one had *ever* requested a turn on her crew. Most ran screaming out of the hangar whenever they were forced to work it.

"Are you looking for Dagger, Admiral?"

Ushara turned at the quiet, timid voice of a young woman who couldn't be more than twenty-two or twenty-three. Tiny and frail, she had short black hair and bright blue eyes. By her rank patch, she was a bait, a regular member of The Tavali. "We are. Do you know where he is?"

"He's not in trouble, is he?"

The concern in her voice sent a severe and unexpected wave of jealousy through Ushara. One that made her want to hurt the young woman.

She hadn't felt such an urge in a really long time and it took her a moment to get a handle on her emotions. "No, he's not in trouble. Are you his woman?" Well that came out before she could stop it. And it was a lot sharper tone than she'd intended.

Her father's eyes widened in shock.

The girl blushed profusely. "No, ma'am. Nothing like that. I just don't want to see him in trouble for doing something so kind. I was about to be fired and I really needed this job to feed my daughter . . . my husband owes a lot of money for his tithe. And everything I did made Sheila angry. She was always yelling at me and insulting me, giving me the worst assignments she had. Making me work late hours when I needed to be home. So Dagger switched crews with me to get her off my back. I don't know what I'd have done had he not taken it. It's so much better now. I can actually eat a meal and not throw it back up."

Ushara smiled at her. "I'm glad you're better. Do you know where I can find him?"

The girl glanced around before she leaned in to whisper. "Today's actually his day off. But he's been donating his after hours and off days to the Snitch Fund. You'll find him working on the *Jolly Harlot*, east quadrant. And speaking of, I better get back to work before Gunnar catches me slacking." She rushed away.

Completely shocked, Ushara met her father's equally stunned expression. The Snitches had been the married couple who had founded their Nation aeons ago after their daughter Tavali and her crew had been wrongfully arrested and slaughtered by a corrupt government. They, and a group of other independent freighters had joined together to form a coalition to protect each other from those out to exploit and prey upon honest independent pilots and freighters who didn't want to work for corporations or governments.

The Tavali had come a long way in the centuries since. But one thing remained the same.

They would fight and die for one another. You messed with one Tavali, you messed with all Tavali.

And the Snitch Fund was one of many programs they had to protect the families of their fallen, or those injured in battle. If someone had a ship they needed repaired and they couldn't afford the service or parts, they could apply for assistance and be added to a waiting list. Those with the skills and means then donated creds, labor, and parts as they saw fit to the fund. Or, in the case of punishment, they could be compelled to donate service or fees.

But it was exceedingly rare for non Tavali to participate in the program.

Ushara arched a brow at the expression on her father's face as they made their way through the hangar. "What's wrong, Paka? You look like you've swallowed your tongue."

"No. Just eating a large bite of humble pie. And it's sticking in my craw as it goes down."

She was tasting some of it herself as they finally found Jullien in a solitary corner, working on a really old freighter's cooling system.

His hand still bandaged from the beating, he was forced to hold an e-tablet at an awkward angle to accommodate his injury so that he could work. A faint bruise also continued to darken the skin of his eye and cheek, and he favored one leg over the other.

Even so, he was still incredibly sexy.

All of a sudden, he dropped the tablet and lunged at the ship. "Careful, *sprytan*. If you don't—" His words broke off as steam poured out and covered him, scalding his arm. Ignoring the heat, he grabbed a smaller body and yanked it up, out of harm's way.

It wasn't until that body was clear that she realized it was Vasili.

His breathing ragged, Jullien searched Vas's body for harm. "You okay?"

"I'm sorry! I'm sorry!"

"It's all right. It's fine. Are you hurt, *sprytan*?"

Terrified, Ushara ran forward. "Vas!"

Jullien immediately put himself between them. Literally. He cradled Vas behind him with one arm so that she couldn't reach or even see him, at all. "It's not his fault."

She tried to step around him.

He refused to let her near her child. "He didn't do anything wrong. It's all my fault. Not his. Don't hurt him."

Ushara paused as she saw the panic in Jullien's eyes and she realized that he actually thought she was going to harm her own son. "Jullien, it's all right. I just want to make sure he's okay."

Warily, he lifted his scalded arm and allowed Vasili to pass under it to reach her.

Vas approached her sheepishly. "Are you mad?"

She narrowed her gaze at him. "What are you doing here?"

Jullien moved to his toolbox and wrapped his forearm in a gel cloth. "He's been coming after school for help with math."

"And after I finish it, Jullien's been teaching me some things about engines and systems." Biting his lip, Vas frowned at Jullien. "Did I hurt you?"

"Nah, it's okay. It happens. I forgot to warn you about releasing the steam pressure on the valve before you loosened it. It didn't get on you, did it?"

"No. I'm fine."

Her father approached Jullian with a frown. "Let me see your arm."

"It's fine, Gŭr Tana. Just a steam burn. Not my first. Doubt it's my last. I'm just glad I got Vas out of the way in time. Sorry I was careless. I won't let him around the ships anymore."

Tears welled in Vas's eyes. "I can't come back?"

His gaze suddenly empty, Jullien appeared equally as upset by the thought, but didn't speak.

Ushara hesitated as she realized the two of them must have really bonded over the last couple of weeks. How strange. Her son was so incredibly standoffish. Vas rarely made friends with anyone. For that matter, he seldom spoke.

Even to her.

"Are you pestering Jullien, m'tana?" she teased.

He glanced at Vas. "He's no bother."

"Are you sure?"

Jullien nodded. "Positive. I've been getting my work done on time. Even with my hand busted."

"My grades have never been better. You can check with my teachers. Jullien's really smart, Mum. He's shown me all kinds of ways to understand math that I never knew."

Jullien scoffed. "I don't know about all that. I barely passed most years. All my teachers did was tell me how stupid I was when I was in school."

"Yeah, but you explain it a lot better than any of my teachers do. I actually get it when you show me. I have no idea what they're talking about when they do it during class." Vas picked up his tablet and handed it to her. "See. I've already done all my homework for the day."

She gaped at the sight. "So you have. I'd been wondering about that."

"And *I* did it. Jullien just shows me how so that I can understand what it means. He makes me figure it out for myself and double check the answers. He won't do it for me 'cause he says that only cheats me and my future."

She kissed his cheek. "Okay. Well, tell you what. Why don't you and Paka go grab something to drink and let me talk to Jullien for a minute, okay?"

Vas scowled. "You're not going to yell at him, are you? 'Cause it's not his fault that I've been coming to see him. He told me to tell you and make sure you were okay with it."

"I'm not mad at anyone, Vasi. I just want to talk to him for a second."

"Please don't yell at my friend, Ma. Not for something I did."

"Vas . . ."

"C'mon, *tana.* Let's give them a few minutes."

Reluctantly, he left with his grandfather.

Jullien sighed as he watched Vasili leave and waited for the raw ass-chewing he was sure Ushara had planned for him. "It's okay, Admiral. I'll be the bad guy and run him off from now on, so you don't have to. I understand. You're his mother. I'm the one he should be angry with. Not you."

"What?"

"That's what you wanted to say, right? Warn me to stay away from your kid before I ruin him with my darkheart ways. Sheila's already warned me that it doesn't look right, but since we're always in public and out in the open bay, in front of others, I didn't think it would hurt anything to help him with his homework during my breaks. I know what it's like to grow up without a father or a brother, or another male to talk to at that age, so I was just trying to be nice to him. But don't worry. I won't do it again. Unlike me at his age, he has uncles and a grandfather who loves him. I'll stay away from your kid. No problem."

Shaking her head, she closed the distance between them and took his arm in her hand so that she could check his injury. She grimaced at the raw, angry skin where he'd been scalded while saving her son, yet hadn't even raised his voice at Vasili. Instead, he'd been patient and kind.

Caring.

Protective.

Things he'd never been shown.

"That wasn't what I wanted to talk to you about."

"No?"

"No. I wanted to ask about my sister's ship. Do you know how it got repaired?"

A slow becoming red stain crept over his features.

She glanced up at him from beneath her lashes.

He looked away.

"Jullien?"

He tried to pull out of her grasp, but she held him fast.

"Why won't you answer?"

Refusing to meet her gaze, he let out a deep breath. "It was the least I could do after what your parents did for me while I recovered. I owed them for the food, medicine, and bed."

"You didn't owe my sister."

"I know. But I overheard your father talking about the loan while I was there so I knew it would keep him out of trouble."

She still couldn't get him to look at her. It was as annoying as it was sweet. "When did you work on it?"

"At night. After work. Days off."

She winced at the hours he must have spent on it alone. He would have been working on it until dawn to get it done so fast, especially with his injuries. "And the parts? Where did you get the creds for those?"

He tried to pull away again.

"Jullien?"

He finally met her gaze. His eyes were empty except for the anguish that seemed to be branded so deep in his soul that it held a permanent place there. "I traded my ring for them."

She was aghast at him. "What? Why?"

Shrugging, he blushed again. "Your sister has a family to support. I don't."

"But that ring—"

"It never did anyone any good. Trust me on that. Hell, I don't even know why I kept it."

"Admiral?"

Jullien finally managed to pull away from her grasp.

Ushara turned as Gunnar called for her again.

"You're needed at command."

"Coming."

Jullien had vanished so fast, she didn't even see where he went. There was no sign of him anywhere. How a male that size could vanish so completely and soundlessly, she'd never understand. He was more skillful than a League assassin.

Frustrated, she cursed under her breath. With no choice, she headed back to her office. But with every step she took, she kept wondering about him. Why would he help the very ones who despised him so?

Then again, it was sadly all he knew. Unlike her, he'd never had anywhere he really belonged. No group that accepted him. Neither human nor Andarion, he stood out among both races. Shunned, ridiculed, and hated by both.

The mean-spirited tabloids had taught her that he hadn't exaggerated in the least.

*Prince Potbelly. The Rotund Royal. Jumbo Jullien* . . .

They would all wet their pants to see him now. Lean and ripped. Even in ragged clothing, he was edible and irresistible. There wasn't a female anywhere who wouldn't slit her own mother's throat for a piece of that delectable ass, with or without a noble lineage attached to it.

And sadly, the tabloids had only given him peace from their viciousness after he'd been disinherited. With one last volley of cruelty, they'd run headline after headline extolling his brother's rise as heir and Jullien's fall from grace.

*Tahrs Jullien Banished to Obscurity! All Hail Tahrs Nykyrian! Huzzah!* Photos of Nykyrian's coronation had been run alongside those of Jullien's arrest mugshots where they'd overlaid the word *Exiled* or *Outcast* over his face. Or worse, they simply put an *X* over Jullien's image.

No wonder he'd traded his ring. In retrospect, why *had* he kept it?

If she lived to be a thousand years old, she'd never understand how his parents could have thrown him away, and not called to see if he was all right. Just once. Weren't they the least bit curious about what had become of their own son? If he was even alive?

It just didn't make sense to her that no one in his family cared for him. At all.

And that broke her heart completely.

Jullien let out a tired sigh as he finished working on the small freighter. He double-checked the coolant to make sure the tanks were filled to capacity and ran the last of the diagnostics. While the system tested the protocols, he wiped down the panels and polished them.

But his mind wasn't really on that. Rather, his thoughts were on things he knew better than to dream about. On a particular long-legged, curvaceous Fyreblood who warmed him when she shouldn't.

Angry at his wayward thoughts, he locked down the ship and took the command module back to the drop site. Unlike the other volunteers, he didn't personally hand it off to the owner. Honestly, he didn't want any kind of gratitude or acknowledgment for his services.

That wasn't why he did this. He did it for those in need, not for his own ego. He didn't deserve anything out of helping others. Rather he was trying to make amends for the ills he'd done in the past.

For all the wrongs his family had done to this universe.

So he quietly slid the module into the reclamation slot and vanished before anyone saw him. Then he grabbed another charity assignment from the listing wall and faded into the shadows.

*Your grandmother would shit to see you now.*

She'd disdained charity of any sort. To her, mercy was weakness. Compassion an even graver sin to be purged and punished.

Only power and discipline mattered. Unchallenged authority.

It was better to be feared than loved. And in that regard, she'd achieved her nirvana—for she was the most feared of any female ever born.

He definitely couldn't have hated her any more if he tried. It was why after she'd fled Andaria during the riots and taken refuge on the Porturnun Station that he'd gleefully hand-fed Parisa her location and had allowed his cousin to lead his grandmother's enemies straight to her there so that they could apprehend the lethal bitch and put his mother in power before his grandmother had killed her. It'd been the only way to guarantee his mother's safety.

Talyn Batur might hate him, but he and his mother, Galene, and the rest of WAR would have never succeeded in bringing Jullien's grandmother down and securing his cousins in jail had Jullien not covertly helped them to overthrow his grandmother's regime.

The Andarion rebel organization, WAR, had no idea that their key informant over the years—Dagger Ixur—was really Jullien eton Anatole, and that much of the sensitive information they'd relied upon to use against the aristocracy was gathered by his access codes. For that matter, he'd been instrumental in distracting his grandmother so that his mother and aunt could flee Andaria before the real coup had started, and his grandmother slaughtered them rather than see them on the throne in her stead. He was the sole reason his aunt and mother were still alive. The only reason his grandmother had kept his mother drugged instead of killing her outright as she'd done the rest of her family.

But Tylie would die before she gave him credit for anything. He'd risked his very life to cover their escape and allow them to reach his father's territory before all hell had broken loose on Andaria and the rioting started.

Instead of being grateful and realizing that he'd put his neck in a noose for them, what had they done?

They'd mocked him that day in the embassy after they'd met his brother for the first time.

In all the betrayals and beatings he'd suffered at the hands of his grandmother and cousins, nothing had cut deeper than his mother's own harsh words against him.

His mother hadn't slashed his heart.

She'd ripped it from his chest and fed it to him.

*"Did you see him, Tylie? My beautiful Nykyrian is the noblest of males!"*

*"Indeed. He's an honor to our blood. Unlike Jullien. I shall never understand how the two of them were born together."*

*"It's not Jullien's fault that he has the soul of the Koriłon. Oh, he gives me the shivers. I cannot bear to look at him for fear of what he might do next. I swear I see Eadvard staring at me through those cold eyes. It makes my flesh crawl every time he comes near me. I just . . . he's disgusting!"*

*"You, sister? I'm the one who's had to suffer his vile presence the most over the years. Every time he opens his mouth, I want to slap it shut. You've no idea how happy I'll be to sign his exile papers and have him finally disinherited. I vote we shove him on Onoria and let the convicts there have their way with his fat, sullen ass. Not that they would. We'd have to bribe them with pardons to touch him."*

His mother had actually laughed at his aunt's suggestion. *"Don't tempt me, little sister . . ."*

Jullien hadn't stayed to hear any more of their plans for his future. He'd been horrified and mocked enough.

Up until then, he'd been on the fence about helping Aksel take Kiara as a pawn to be used against his brother. But after their brutal words against him, he'd realized that if he didn't at least try, he would be cast out of both empires without any home at all, and no means to provide for himself—thanks to his parents, and his grandmother's heart-warming care.

While granted it was selfish, he'd felt as if they'd left him with absolutely no choice. They'd taken everything from him, and he'd had enough of it. He wasn't going to stand by and be left with nothing.

Not after all he'd been put through by them. The last thing he'd wanted was to see Nykyrian waltz in as the beloved son and replace him in his parents' callous, dead hearts and shove him aside like the garbage they proclaimed him.

And why not? They were already doing it.

His father's senate had moved earlier that year to have his distant human cousin named as the Triosan heir. And his father hadn't fought their decision.

*"It's for the best, Jullien. That way your loyalties won't be split between the two empires. And you won't feel the pressures of being divided, which is more than you can handle emotionally. Trust me. I'm deeply concerned about your immaturity and sullen disposition. The way you're prone to withdraw during any conflict, rather than engage. You're just not ready for the kinds of responsibility it takes to rule, or the pressures of maintaining your composure under pressure. Really, it's in your best interest, and that of the Triosans and Andarions. You'll see. Not to mention, you don't know enough about humans or the history of my empire to rule it effectively."*

Something completely untrue. Jullien held his doctorate in comparative political science with a primary focus on the history of Triosa and Trisa, and had done his doctoral thesis on the comparison of the fall of Justicale Cruel with the collapse of the Trisani Empire. Not that his father had ever bothered to spend five minutes alone with him to learn that.

And Jullien had never been withdrawn or distracted—nor did he lack composure under pressure. For six years, he'd been enrolled in the hardest university in the Nine Worlds and been focused on his research, and knee-deep in learning eight dialects of a dead language, plus Caronese, while dodging his grandmother's hysterics, his mother's insanity, and five separate attempts on his life—two of which had been nearly fatal.

Meanwhile his apathetic father who couldn't be bothered to take his son's calls, had no idea that Jullien had ever graduated with honors from North Eris University, first in his class, as that took place during the entire year his father's parents had maliciously banned Jullien from

Triosa because Jullien had refused to file down his Andarion fangs to please them—after they'd mocked him during one formal state dinner where his Andarion dental features had "embarrassed" *them*.

And his reward for surviving such glorious years of nut-wrenching endeavors?

Not the usual graduation ceremony and accolades most received for attaining such impressive goals.

No, not for Tahrs Jullien.

He'd been forbidden to attend his graduation—in fact, the entire event for that year had been cancelled by royal decree, as well as all degrees that were supposed to be handed out, and all students expelled on his behalf, for violating ethical code, thus guaranteeing that they would hate him forever.

Then Eriadne, in a fit of stellar rage, had destroyed all his school records once she realized his degree was in a human field of study. Worse? She'd executed his advisor and entire doctoral committee for daring to confer his degree on him.

So all his hard work and years of study were negated in the throes of one epic Eriadne bitch-sized tantrum. At the end of which, he'd been violently seized and imprisoned for a solid year, that included his twenty-second birthday, in her special hell-pit underground chambers that she reserved for those she hated most.

To say he'd emerged "a little sullen" from that precious experience was tantamount to likening a supernova to a pin light.

As for withdrawn . . . that stemmed from his respect of the fact that he was an Andarion and his father's people were human. The gravitational differences between Andaria and Triosa left him so much stronger that he was terrified of touching a Triosan lest he accidentally snap their delicate bones like a toothpick. With a hair-trigger temper, he didn't dare risk losing it around his father's race so he avoided any situation that could unintentionally ignite it.

Even as a boy, he'd stood as tall as most human men, and outweighed them by over a hundred pounds.

And once the Triosan senate decision had been made against Jullien's inheritance, his father had been in total agreement to let it stand in perpetuity. It was why Jullien had made so many trips there that last year. He'd been trying to make them reconsider, because he knew that Merrell and Chrisen were doing their best to overthrow him on

Andaria, and that it was just a matter of time before they either succeeded.

Or killed him.

He'd felt that noose tightening every day, until he could barely breathe
from it. Then to hear the mother he'd spent his entire childhood trying
to protect, plotting with his aunt against him to gleefully toss him to
the wolves to be slaughtered . . .

Or violated . . .

Jullien had wanted blood from all of them.

He was her son as much as Nykyrian.

Yet neither of his parents had ever once looked at him as anything
more than a tiresome burden. An unwanted obligation.

So yeah. He'd gone a bit bat-shit crazy on them all.

The unfortunate part was that Nykyrian had been caught up in the
crossfire of his fury as Jullien went against his parents and struck back
at them out of a lifetime of justified anger and hatred.

And that was what haunted him most about the entire ordeal. His
brother, alone, had been innocent. Nykyrian had never gone after Jullien.

Not until that night in the restaurant when Jullien had committed
an unprovoked, unforgivable act against Nyk's wife when he'd allowed
Aksel to take her.

Nyk had never deserved any of it. In that moment of desolate pain
and rage, Jullien had crossed the line he swore he never would and become his grandmother. He had used an innocent woman and his own
brother to strike at his parents.

To this day, Jullien hated himself for it.

He just wished he could tell his brother how sorry he was for what
he'd done. And let Nykyrian know that it was sincere. That he didn't
want or expect forgiveness for his actions against him, but that he did
owe him an apology.

*At least he's happy now.*

Nyk had the life he deserved. He was beloved by the Triosans and
Andarions alike. While they had never accepted Jullien as one of them
or respected anything about him, they were more than happy to welcome his brother as their future emperor. Nyk had a wife who adored
him. A beautiful daughter and two sons. Their parents respected and
listened to Nyk's opinions.

One day, Nyk would rule both empires.

Jullien wished him well. He wished him peace. Most of all, he wished his brother love, and a harmonious reign free of the treachery that had plagued their family since the moment their distant ancestor Anatole had first claimed the Andarion throne from the Hauk family thousands of years ago.

Legends said that the original Dancer Hauk's wife, out of a jealous rage for her husband handing the throne away to Anatole, had cursed Jullien's entire lineage to never have peace within their house until they abdicated their power back to the Hauks.

A part of him believed it.

But then, greed, treachery, jealousy, and lust didn't need a curse to propel them. While Andarions wanted to believe those were human traits, he knew better. Being born of both races, he was well aware of just how similar the two species were. And though they wanted to pretend they were nothing alike, humans and Andarions had a lot more in common than either wanted to admit to.

They both sucked and he hated being a part of either species.

Next life, he was coming back as an amoeba.

Maybe a shoelace.

Returning to the hangar, he paused to see his next project. *Stormbringer.*

Hmmm . . . interesting. There was no shortage of creativity for The Tavali when it came to naming their ships.

"Hey, Dagger! Over here! Now!"

He scowled at Sheila's sharp call.

Almost six feet tall and well built, she had short red hair and cold blue eyes. Gruff and brusk, she never asked for anything. She barked out orders like she was the headmistress of a kennel and everyone else was her obedient bitch. None of the others could stand her demanding ways, but having been raised by his overbearing grandmother who made Sheila look like a toothless kitten, he didn't mind. Not like she could have someone beheaded or gutted on a whim.

"You rang for me, *mu tara* and tormentor?"

She swept a bemused stare over him. "Um . . . yeah, could you lend me a hand for a second? I know you're off the clock. But this just came in and Dumbass went for lunch right before they landed."

"Well, since I don't know who Dumbass is, I shall be more than happy to stand in for him or her, provided a more suitable moniker is chosen for me. I'm rather fond of Shit-for-Brains, myself. Shithead for short."

She actually laughed. "Whatever. They need to get back into service. Can you program Caronese code and systems, and do you know anything about M-Class starships?"

"Yes and yes."

"Thank the gods! Get them flying and dinner's on me."

Jullien inclined his head to her then ducked inside the ship. He'd barely taken two steps on board before he recognized the ship for what it was and why it'd been damaged.

She wasn't a Tavali vessel. This was a Caronese battleship that had been taken in a fight. A brutal one by the looks of the blaster marks scarring the hallways.

And bloodstains on the floors and walls.

Jullien winced at the sight, hoping The Tavali had been merciful and killed the crew. If they survived to return to Caron and the loving embrace of Counselor Cruel's hands, Arturo would torture them as examples for the rest of his troops. He was one of the few modern leaders who made Eriadne appear benevolent.

Poor bastards.

Pushing the thought away, he went to the belly of the beast to override the security protocols and rewrite code so that The Tavali could fly her untraced.

Jullien had just started on the programming when he heard the sharp click of a blaster's settings being changed. He froze instantly.

"Well, well. Fuck me, if it isn't little Julie Anatole. And here I thought this ship was going to be our most valuable take today. Now, be a good little prince. Step back and kneel down so that I can kill you nice and slow, and get all the credits you're worth."

# CHAPTER 7

Holding his hands up, Jullien turned around slowly to face The Tavali behind him. From the way The Tavali had spoken, he'd expected to recognize the pirate.

He didn't. If their paths had ever crossed, Jullien had no recollection of it. From the size and smell of the male and the patches on his battle-suit, he was also a Chiller. One of the larger of that breed who'd been trained to hunt and kill Trisani. They were as lethal as League assassins. Lucky for Jullien, the Chiller, like everyone else, underestimated him.

But like the rest of Jullien's enemies, he was about to learn that the only beings who kicked Jullien's ass were the ones he allowed to kick it, those who came in a large enough group to overwhelm him by sheer force. . . .

Or the ones lucky enough to get a blind shot off first.

"*Titana tu, chiran.*" Jullien grabbed the blaster faster than the Chiller could react. It discharged, proving the Chiller had intended to kill him.

That effectively quelled his conscience.

All charity and reservation gone, Jullien wasted no time unbalancing the larger male, slamming him to the ground and snapping his neck.

Unfortunately, the Chiller screamed out before he died and brought his friends running. Jullien scrambled for the blaster and was on his feet before they came in, with Sheila behind them.

"Whoa!" she shouted as they held each other at an armed stand-off. "What the hell happened, Dagger?"

Jullien didn't take his eyes off the others as he toed the carcass at his feet. "He came at me."

"Bullshit!" the crew's captain snarled. "Larl wouldn't have done that." He started toward Jullien.

Jullien shot just over his shoulder. "Don't, slag. Next shot won't be a warning."

Sheila waved her hands at them. "Everyone, calm down. We'll get this squared."

The captain shook his head. "I want his life for my crewman. He's not even Tavali. You know the Code."

Jullien frowned. "What's the Code?"

Sheila sighed as she met Jullien's gaze. "The Tavali who brought you here is responsible for whatever you do. You can admit guilt and submit to the captain's justice, or if you don't, your sponsor has to surrender you or go to Calibrim for you."

"Calibrim?"

"Test of arms," Sheila explained. "The admiral will have to fight the captain. Similar to an Andarion Ring fight."

Jullien cursed under his breath. Oh hell no. It wasn't Ushara's fault he hadn't bothered to read the Tavali rule book before he'd defended himself.

Whatever. He wasn't about to allow her to risk her life or get hurt because of him. Not when she had a son to raise. He definitely wasn't worth it.

Jullien loosened his hold on the blaster and spun it in his hand so that he could offer the grip to the captain.

He grabbed it from Jullien's hand.

Relegated to his fate, Jullien put his hands behind his head and laced his fingers together, then surrendered to their custody. At least they didn't seem to know his identity. Maybe they'd kill him quickly.


"Admiral!"

Ushara let out an irritated groan at the sound of Sheila's voice through her door. She was so tired of dealing with crap today. As she was texting Zellen to tell him to brush Sheila away with an excuse, her door opened.

"Ma'am, it's Dagger. You have to come fast before they kill him. Please!"

The color drained from her face. "What?"

"He killed one of the *Razor's* crew. Said it was self-defense. When I told him you'd have to fight for him because of it, he surrendered to them and they took him on board their ship."

"Son of a bitch," she breathed. Grabbing her link, she rushed for the door. "Take me to them." She called Trajen to alert him of the situation as they ran for the bay as fast as they could.

By the time they reached the ship, they were locked out—which was illegal while docked in the bay. As part of Tavali Code, any ship that was granted landing privilege was required to remain open and accessible to any of that base's high command or Hadean Corpsmen.

Ushara hailed for entrance.

No one answered her call.

Panic and fury combined inside her to a dangerous level. And she wasn't the only one. Sheila pulled her blaster out and started to fire it at the hull. Ushara barely caught her arm before she pulled the trigger. "What are you doing?"

"Kicking their asses! This ain't right. He was doing me a favor by helping them degenerate ass-wipes in the first place. I know he didn't do nothing wrong. Dagger's a decent guy, Admiral. He's the only one what don't get mad or upset at me at the things I say. He understands me, you know what I mean? Everyone else is an effing asshole."

"Everyone?" Trajen arched his brow at her as he joined them.

Sheila shrank away without comment.

Ushara returned Sheila's blaster to her. "They've locked us out."

"Oh no, Mama, you didn't," Trajen said in the feigned accent of a teenaged girl. "Not on my base, bitches."

Using his powers, he blew the door completely off their ship. It went flying thirty feet into the air to land with a deafening clatter a full fifty yards away.

Trajen turned to Sheila who stood gaping. "Damn blast charge. Used too much."

She didn't say a word as she stepped back and put more distance between her and Trajen.

"You should probably wait out here for us, Sheila." And with that, he led Ushara on board while Sheila decided that it was best to stay put.

Wide-eyed as they entered the ship, Ushara was stunned that Trajen had used his powers like that. Trajen *never* exposed his Trisani origins to anyone, for *any* reason. But she was glad he'd made an exception as they wended their way through the dark, unfamiliar ship.

With Trajen's massive psionic tracking abilities, it didn't take long to find them. The crew was in the cargo area with Jullien, on the verge of gutting him. They even had him tied shirtless to a piece of damaged cargo like some kind of animal sacrifice for an angry god.

When Ushara started forward, they turned and drew weapons.

Placing his hand on her shoulder to hold her in place, Trajen burst out laughing.

She, however, wasn't so amused.

"Well, I'm glad I brought cheer to someone before I died," Jullien said churlishly.

Trajen continued to laugh. "Yeah, that you did, punkin'." He wiped at his eyes. "Boy, we have got to quit meeting like this. You get yourself into more shit. They have *no* idea who you are. What you're worth." He started laughing again. "Oh dear gods . . . this may be the dumbest group to ever live." He looked at Ushara. "It's tempting to kill them just on those grounds, alone."

"What the hell is this?" The captain stepped forward. "Get off my ship!"

That sobered Trajen instantly. He let go of Ushara and straightened as a look of feral death settled in his dark eyes. "You better find another tone, slag. Fast." He passed a pointed stare to the ones closest to Jullien. "Step away from my friend or your fondest body parts are going to start hitting the floor. And you will miss them. Trust me."

Jullien's ties came loose and his shirt returned to him. That instantly told them who and what Trajen was.

And it told Ushara a lot about Jullien's own persuasive powers and charisma over others. Trajen didn't lightly expose himself to anyone. Honestly, she hadn't expected him to help her rescue Jullien. She'd only alerted him to this situation as a matter of protocol.

The fact he was here . . .

That was impressive.

For him to call Jullien friend was unprecedented. In all the years she'd known Trajen, she'd never heard him laugh. Maybe a slight sarcastic chuckle.

*Never this.*

The captain stiffened. "Do you know who I am?"

"Yes and my buddy behind you iced a Chiller *you* brought on board *my* station. Do you really think I give a flying fuck who you are, who your father is or anything else?" Trajen stepped aside. "Ushara? Take Dagger and leave. Now."

She didn't hesitate to obey.

Jullien was another matter. He only went as far as Trajen's shoulder and stopped. "Don't do it."

Trajen scowled at him. "Excuse me? *Boy* . . . this is not your concern. Not the time or the place."

Jullien refused to back down or flinch. "And you heard *me*, *old man*. Let them go. Don't risk yourself."

Arching one feral brow, Trajen crossed his arms over his chest. "Rather difficult as their door is currently laying in the center of my bay."

"They have the Caronese battleship they hauled in. It's fully functional. Let them fly it out."

Something strange was passing between them. Ushara could feel it with every instinct she possessed. Yet she had no idea what it was.

After a few seconds, Trajen conceded. "Very well. There you have it, slags. Get off my station and be grateful for my mercy. I never want to see your faces again." He turned toward her. "Shara? Summon the HC to escort them to the edges of our territory and make sure they leave us without harm."

Jullien kept her shielded with his body until they were clear of the ship.

Once they were in the bay, she paused to call the Hadean Corpsmen, then turned toward Jullien who was working at a kiosk. "What did I just miss?"

"Hang on a sec, there's a few things I need to take care of, real quick."

Trajen didn't join them until after the crew was on board the Caronese ship, under heavy armed escort, and they were going through the launch clearance. "What *exactly* did you do to that ship?" he asked Jullien.

Jullien shrugged. "Deactivated their HD and LD. Reactivated the homing beacons. Sent out a hidden distress call on the Caronese EDB. By the time they hit the outer edge of Gorturnum space, the Caronese should have a full welcoming party for them. Since Senator Nylan's son was the ship's commander and they killed him while capturing it, he'll be hellbent on revenge. They won't make it back to Caron alive. And you won't have their blood on your hands, and will not have broken any Tavalian Code or law that you have to answer for with the UTC."

"You are one devious little bastard." Trajen shook his head. "Don't know if I should be impressed or afraid."

"Bit of both."

"Yeah . . ." Trajen glanced over to the door he'd ripped off their ship. "Guess we both have unresolved childhood anger issues."

"Yeah and I don't believe in burning bridges. Rather I bomb those mothers to the ground and toast marshmallows over their smouldering remains."

"I'm going to remember that."

They fell silent as the Caronese ship launched.

Sheila came out of her office completely distressed . . . until she saw Jullien standing at the kiosk. Then she ran at him, and to Ushara's complete shock, she threw herself into his arms. "Oh thank God! You're all right."

He looked as baffled as Ushara felt. "Um, yeah."

Sheila patted him on the back. "Well don't be so stupid next time, shithead."

"Honestly, I was trying not to be so stupid this time. You see how it turned out. Perhaps next time I should try for an all-out moron. That might actually work for me."

Laughing, she sighed. "No one else understands me like you do, boy. So stop being an idiot. If you're late for work tomorrow, I'm going to kick your ass."

He checked his watch. "Well, it's been a good fifteen minutes since my last ass-kicking. I should be due a new one by morning. I shall look forward to it, *mu tara*."

With one last growl at Jullien, Sheila chucked him on the arm and left.

Ushara grimaced at him as Sheila crossed the bay and returned to her office. "How can you stand the way she talks to you?"

"What *that*? I think she's hilarious."

"You're not serious?"

Yet he was. She could see the sincerity in his brownish-green eyes. "Trust me, I know the difference between someone who's churlish by nature because they're trying to protect themselves from being harmed by others, and someone whose barbs are meant to let blood. Sadly for her, others can't distinguish it. And so she does more harm to herself by trying to form a protective barrier from strangers than she would if she'd just be nice. But I understand the need to strike the first blow before they do. I certainly don't hold it against her, and I know she doesn't mean it. Besides my ego isn't that fragile. It would require that I actually possess one."

Trajen snorted. "Anyway . . ." He jerked his chin toward the abandoned ship. "It appears we have a spare vessel. Would you like it, Lord Jullien? Seems only fair since they were planning to gut you on it?"

"Don't need that piece of shit. Can't fly it after some thoughtless bastard ripped the door off its hinges." He passed an amused stare toward Trajen. "I'm thinking it should go to Sheila since she didn't get her payment for the work they'd commissioned from her. Besides, her daughter's treatments run high. I don't have any dependents. I drink rather cheap, as in free, tap water these days."

"Yeah, but you could replace those shitty boots." Trajen raked a sneer over them.

Jullien arched a brow. "Why? I like these boots. They're broken in. And they come with free air-conditioning. I hear they're even trying to patent this idea in the Oksana desert region, only there, they're called *sandals*. It's true. Look it up, if you don't believe me. It's the latest fashion craze."

Laughing again, Trajen shoved at him. "Shut the hell up." With an irritated growl, he started away from them, then stopped to look back with a fierce frown. "Why do I like you, again?"

"It's the fangs. It makes us look all cute and cuddly."

"Yeah. That must be it." And with that, Trajen wandered off.

Ushara cocked her head as she looked down at Jullien's ragged boots. "Why don't you replace those?"

He shrugged. "Don't know. Guess I'm too busy wasting creds on frivolous things like food, power, and rent."

"And my sister's ship?"

"Your sister has four daughters to feed."

"Then why don't you let me replace your boots?"

He wrinkled his nose at her. "Nah, see I know how this goes. It's called progressive entrapment. Come here, little boy. I got a piece of candy for you. Get in my shuttle . . . next thing I know, I'm drunk and naked in your bed. You're having your wicked way with me. My mama warned me all about females like you and taking candy from strangers."

She laughed at him. "I think I'd have a hard time getting away with that."

"Sadly, I doubt you would. Pretty sure I'd be an easy fool for you, which is why I have to pass on the boots. Besides, I hate shopping. If you took me, you'd see the beast that lives inside me and I'd rather you live with the myth of this noble hero for awhile longer."

Ushara tsked at him and that adorable grin on his handsome face. "You are so incredibly charming."

"Not really. I'm told I'm a giant asshole by most."

"Who?"

He screwed his face up. "Oh that is a frightfully long list. Terabytes of data, point of fact."

"They don't know you."

"They would all argue that they do."

"And what do you say?"

Sobering, he glanced away. "Maybe they know me better than I do, really. Are we not all a thousand characters in millions of plays throughout our lifetime? Is Ushara the mother the same character as Ushara the daughter? Or Ushara the admiral the same as Ushara the older sister? Or the younger sister? Did your husband not know a different side of you than anyone else in your life? What about the male who knows Ushara the testicle-launcher? I'm sure he would paint a very different image of you than I would. Who among us is not ever-changing? Ever evolving into someone new? Maybe someone better . . . or someone worse."

Dear gods, he was incredibly astute. "And who do you want to be, Dagger?"

"Honestly? I would sell whatever is left of my used up, blackened soul to be the hero Vasili sees whenever he looks at me and not the piece of worthless shit I know for a fact I truly am." And with those barely audible words, he turned and walked away with that sexy predator's lope that was uniquely his.

Tears choked her as she watched him go. He was exactly the male Vasili thought him to be. If only he could see it.

But sadly, his past was too brutal for that. And his conscience too riddled with guilt. Yet one day, she hoped he could find the ability to judge himself with the same compassion that he used when he looked at others. 'Cause the gods knew, while he wasn't perfect, he was as caring and kind as anyone she'd ever known. And if ever anyone deserved a second chance in their life, it was definitely him.

She just hoped he realized it before it was too late.

Sighing, she headed back for her office.

"Told you so, didn't I?"

Oxana blinked in total disbelief as she watched her older sister leaving the bay. "Wow . . . I've never seen her look like that before."

"I know, right?" Her twin sister, Jalyna, turned toward her, eyes wide. "I know what Paka said, but he's wrong. We have to do something."

"What?"

"What, what? You know what! *That's* what. Sheez, what? I can't believe you'd even ask me, what. Like you don't know." Her sister took off after the tiziran.

Oxana panicked. "Jay, stop!" she hissed. "What are you doing?"

"What we should have done while he was at Mum's. Now, are you coming? Or are you going to stand there, looking like Mary and being all scared of me? Are you a Fyreblood or a darkheart?"

Oxana hissed at her. "You shouldn't be using that term, you know? It's obnoxious and rude and insulting, especially for someone who's about to try and hook her sister up with one."

"Well it's not like he's a whole one. He's only partly darkheart."

"Oh 'cause he's human. Like that's *so* much better."

"Now who's being bad, huh?"

"Still you," Oxana said sullenly. "You're always the bad twin. Ask anyone who knows us."

"Bite-it!"

"What are you hens gaggling on about now?"

They froze as their little sister, Mariska, caught up to them. Almost identical in looks to Ushara, she was the smaller, more petite version of their older sister.

Jay glanced around with feigned innocence. "Nothing. Nothing at all."

"Oh yeah, right . . . um. . . . Never. What are you plotting and who's your victim, and can I help hide the body this time?"

Rolling her eyes, Oxana let out a long-suffering sigh. "Why don't you go find a cousin or brother to annoy? Davel's in. Better yet, go trash Axl's wife. We don't like her."

Mary shook her head. "I'd rather aggravate you two."

" 'Course you would."

"So leak the damage . . ." Mary poked each of them in turn.

They exchanged an annoyed frown. "Fine," Jay yielded first. "We're going to see the male who fixed Ana's ship."

"I thought you didn't know who repaired it."

Oxana shrugged. "Paka found out his name. I was going to thank him."

"See." Jay flipped her red hair over her shoulder, dismissively. "Now run along."

"Nuh-uh. There's more to this. He's hot, isn't he?" Mary gasped audibly. "Jay's going to cheat on her husband! Oh my God! That's it, isn't it?"

"No!" Jay snapped. "You're horrible! Why would you think that?"

"'Cause Ana can't cheat on hers. Then what's the deal?"

Oxana leaned in to whisper in her ear. "The tiziran is the one who did it. And Ushara is falling for him."

Mary gasped even louder. "No!"

"Yes!"

"No!"

"Yes!" the twins squealed in unison.

Mary's eyes widened. "Can I come?"

"Well you have to now or else you'll tell and we'll have to kill you." Jay grabbed her arm and they hauled her after them, toward Jullien's stark condo in the icky, awful section of the station where they tried to never venture.

Mary stuck her tongue out and shuddered as they approached his door. "Does he really live here?"

"Yes," Oxana said under her breath while Jay knocked. "Stop being rude."

"Is he not home? Knock harder. Place can't be *that* big." Mary pushed Jay aside. "Here. Let me help."


Jullien scowled at the insistent pounding on his door as he fastened his pants. He was still dripping from the shower. But the furious frenzy outside said whoever was there wasn't going to give him time to finish bathing and if he didn't answer soon, they might break through the door's meager hinges.

What the hell was so imminent?

Toweling his hair, he opened the door to find three very colorful, young females on his stoop. Three who gaped in an almost choreographed unison at his appearance. It would have been comical if he wasn't so damned irritated.

But at least it succeeded in taking the edge off his anger and allowed him to be cordial to them. "May I help you?"

The two with insanely bright fluorescent red hair were obviously identical twins. One was dressed in a yellow and red flightsuit and the other in a plain red one. Both were well-armed, but didn't appear threatening. The smaller of the three had stark white hair with pieces of it that she'd dyed bright pink and purple—the same colors that Ushara used as Tavali war paint on her face. And now that he looked at them, he realized that their features were extremely similar to hers, especially the youngest girl's.

She elbowed her way past the twins. "Hi." She extended her hand to him. "I'm Mariska, but you can call me Mary. Everyone does. These are my sisters and when they find their voices again, which will be any shrill moment, they're Oxana and Jay, or actually something unpronounceable my mother cursed her with because we're weird, as if Fyrebloods weren't strange enough already. Anyway, we came over because—"

"Oh shush, Mary!" the twin in the red suit said, pushing her sister back. "You weren't even a part of this. You hijacked our mission." Growling, she faced Jullien. "I'm Ana. Or Oxana and I'm the one you helped. I wanted to thank you, personally, for it."

Mary hadn't been kidding about the shrillness of their voices. Jullien had to resist the urge to cringe or cover his sensitive ears.

Instead, he forced himself to smile at her. "You didn't have to do that."

"Yes, I did. It was very kind of you and we wanted to do something for you to show how much I appreciate what you did when you didn't have to."

True, honest terror set in for the first time in his life. Jullien had no idea what they had in mind, but it couldn't be good for him.

All scenarios from sex to food ended with his bloody dismemberment, and pieces of his body being found all over the universe.

"Um . . . I don't think this is a good idea."

Jay laughed. "Look at that face! I think we scare him."

Mary grinned and elbowed Ana. "He should be afraid of us. We come with a herd of male relatives, but . . . we're harmless. We're actually here to set you up with our sister."

Jullien scowled, even more terrified now. "Excuse me?"

The twins took him by the arms. "Mary's right. We saw how Shara looked at you. She practically licked you all over."

Mary nodded. "She wants you and we're here to make you presentable to her."

"Pardon?" he repeated.

Jay tsked at her sister. "Listen to him talk. I could hear that accent all day. He's so proper! Just makes my motor hum. We should record that and play it at night. You think my husband would mind?"

Jullien choked. "Taras . . . please, I . . . um, have something burning in the kitchen."

"No, you don't. But that's a nice try." Mary grinned at him, exposing her fangs. "Just give in. It'll be a lot easier and less painful for you." She glanced to her sisters. "I'll grab a shirt for him and shoes."

Jullien let out a groan as he realized there was no way to protest this. They were not about to give up. "You're really not going to let me out of this, are you?"

"Not on your life." Jay grinned.

He kept trying to break free without harming them. "Don't you three have children and males of your own to torture?"

"Yeah," Jay said, "but you're new male steak. We have to break you in for our sister. Get you well seasoned."

"Besides, I have no male of my own. So I have to torture you." Mary scowled up at him. "Are you all right? You look rather green."

"You do realize that I've seldom been around females."

"Why? Are you gay?" Mary blinked innocently. "If you are, we have a cousin . . ."

"No. I come from a predominantly male family. On both sides. I've seldom interacted with the females, and whenever I did, it wasn't a positive experience."

"Oh. Poor you." Mary patted his arm. "You're in for an education. But we'll try and be gentle."

That might have carried more weight had Mary not punctuated it with a sinister laugh.

Little did Jullien know that they had no intention of showing him mercy. Of *any* kind.

Rather they spent the next couple of hours getting him groomed like some prized pet. They shoved and pushed and pulled and prodded until he was near insane from it all. He'd never been so groped or lovingly malehandled in his life. They gave him no choice in anything. Not even how they styled his hair or shaved his face.

Nor would they let him see what they were doing to him. He really felt like a show beast before a performance.

Every time he began protesting, Mary patted him on the arm. "It doesn't matter what you think, precious. We're doing this for Ushara. Just think about the benefits to come. I promise, she'll put a giant smile on your face."

He snorted.

Honestly, he found Ushara's sisters strangely amusing and quirky. They were a stark contrast to their much more serious-minded older sister, and he wondered why Ushara lacked their sense of whimsy.

Had she ever been like them?

And if so, what had stolen her smile?

It saddened him that she wasn't more like them. And the longer he was with them, the more he realized just how guarded and closed off she was in comparison.

No matter how hard he tried, he couldn't imagine her like them.

Bemused, Jullien watched as the twins fought over his clothes.

Oxana rolled her eyes at Mary and shoved a pair of pants back onto the rack. "If you put him in *those*, you'll sterilize him. No male needs pants that tight. Good gracious! That's not sexy. It's obscene!"

"I disagree. A body like that should be flaunted! Why hide it?"

"'Cause one day Shara might want to have another child. You don't want to lower his sperm count. Good grief! Besides, if he tries to sit in those, he'll rack himself and be out of commission for the night. Think about it!"

They turned to Jay to settle their disagreement.

"Well, Ana's *not* wrong. But Mary has a point, too. He does have an edible ass and arms. And his abs . . . if my Bar looked like *that*, I'd *never* leave my bed. I'm just saying, I'd have more kids than Ana by now."

The three of them turned to stare at him.

Yeah, okay, he felt naked, even though he was fully clothed.

Scowling, Ana handed him a jacket then snatched it back as she changed her mind for the tenth time.

Mary handed him another one.

Jullien hesitated before he took it and shrugged it on.

They screwed their faces up to study him like a lab experiment.

Yeah, he just couldn't envision Ushara part of their group, participating in this lunacy. "Was Ushara always so serious and stern?"

Oxana stepped forward to adjust his coat for him. "No. She was actually a lot of fun back when she ran her own crew. That's why they named her Star Skream."

"Star Skream?" What a peculiar call sign.

Chewing her lip, Mary handed him a different, longer jacket to put on. "She was so reckless and daring as a pilot, they say that you could hear the stars actually scream as she blazed past them in her ship. She would run against any Leaguer, anywhere, anytime. Fearless."

"Ridiculously so," Jay concurred. "She was a nut. Trajen kept her on report constantly for it. Then poof! After Chaz died . . . She, the best pilot in the Gort Nation, grounded herself so that Vasili wouldn't be an orphan."

"And she never really smiled again," Ana finished the sentence. "Not until you came along. She smiles a lot around you."

Jay nodded. "Gavin said that she even flew to rescue you. It's the only time she's been at the helm since Chaz died. Weird, isn't it? She took the helm to get you and Vas out of Steradore."

"That's why we're doing this." Mary wrinkled her nose. "Still not the right jacket."

She handed him another one.

Groaning, he changed.

Again.

They all three gasped, then clapped in joyous unison. Mary even did a little dance of happiness.

"What do you think?" Mary stepped back with an impish grin.

Relieved that it might be finally coming to an end, Jullien allowed them to turn him to face the mirror behind him. But the moment he focused on his reflection he was wholly unprepared for what he saw there.

It was no longer the bearded face of the ragged survivor Dagger Ixur.

That was the flawlessly groomed image of the bastard Tahrs Jullien eton Anatole.

In one heartbeat, his past slammed into him with a furious fist.

Bitter, horrid memories tore through him and unbalanced him. He didn't see the shopping parlor they were in. He saw the gilded and gaudy palace ballrooms. Heard the mocking laughter and the constant rapid-fire biting criticisms that came at him in thinly veiled barbed witticisms. The sneers and fetid backbiting that had gone on for years.

All that self-loathing and hatred came back with a vengeance.

And it shattered him.

"Dagger?"

The walls closed in on him as he staggered back and tore the jacket off, trying to catch his balance. But he couldn't. Everywhere he looked, he saw *that* hated face of a prince who disgusted him. Heard the voices that mocked and insulted everything he was and told him that he had no right to live.

Unable to stand it, he ran for the door.

Ushara left her office, intending to go home, make a nice quiet dinner for Vasili, and spend a night doing nothing.

But as she left the building, she almost collided with her youngest sister who met her in a screeching panic, that was followed by the twins running up behind her, and their equal ear-piercing tizzy as they piled on with Mary.

*Oh, this can't be good.*

"Dear God, what'd you do now?"

Jay bit her lip before Mary blurted out the answer. "We broke your boyfriend!"

Ushara scowled. "Excuse me?"

Breathless with her panic, Oxana nodded. "It's true. We were only trying to help. We took him out to thank him for what he did, and we got him a haircut and shave."

"Some clothes," Jay chimed in.

"And he ran like Coreła was about to ride up his ass with her thorny hammer."

Oxana nodded again. "We went to his condo and he's not there. We've no idea where else to look. But he was really, really upset."

"Really upset!" Jay repeated for emphasis.

"We're so sorry," Mary breathed. "We didn't mean to break him. It was going all good. Then . . . blam! He broke. No warning or nothing."

"We'll go watch Vasili for you." Jay pushed Ushara toward the street. "All night if we have to. I'll take him to my house and keep him. Just please . . . find Jullien. Fix whatever we did wrong. Jullien's a sweetheart."

Now Mary was nodding. "We had no idea. Please tell him that we're sorry."

Ushara hugged them. "Okay, I'll find him."

But the problem was, she had no idea where to look either. She hated to call Trajen again. Yet what choice did she have? It was a big station. Without Trajen, she didn't know where to begin a search.

*He's going to kill me.*

Both of them.

Pulling out her link, she cringed as she pressed the code for Trajen.

He answered immediately.

"Hey, boss. I hate to bug you. Jullien's gone MIA again, and I've no idea where to look. Can you point me in the right direction? My sisters accidentally upset him, and I just want to make sure he's okay."

He appeared at her side so fast that it startled her.

She hated whenever he teleported in. It creeped her out completely. "Little warning next time, please?"

A phantom hand tickled her neck.

"Really *not* funny, boss."

Trajen snorted, then went completely still. Until a strange expression came over his face. "What the hell did they do?"

Before she could answer, he grabbed her hand and ran with her through the station.

Ushara had no idea where they were headed until he took her to the oldest part of their base—up to the abandoned section where no one went anymore. This area had been closed off and abandoned for years. Probably since before she was born. Honestly, she'd never been here. She'd only passed by the area back when she'd first toured the station during her officer orientation. No one should have access here.

How Jullien had gotten in was beyond her.

Unless he hacked in and had bypassed the security . . .

While it still had a breathable atmosphere, it was thinly mixed. And it wasn't the safest place to be. Dust, debris, and cobwebs covered rusted out beams and deserted hallways. The entire section had been sealed off generations ago after an accident no one remembered or had even bothered to record had rendered it unsafe.

It was so eerie here. Silent and cold. Lonely.

Desolate.

Yet high up on the rickety scaffolding of an old building that had partially fallen down, silhouetted against the darkness of space sat an unwavering shadow in front of the shielded windows that looked out on the large uninhabitable gas planet the station hovered over. He was so still that at first glance, he appeared part of the scenery.

Until you looked closer and realized that was actually a ragged dark brown coat that trailed from the beam. And a pair of well-worn boots.

*No . . .*

"Jullien?" she called out.

He didn't move.

"Wait here." Trajen carefully began the dangerous, steep climb to where Jullien sat without moving.

Even though Trajen had told her to wait, she edged a bit closer. But there was only so far she could go without the risk of falling through something. It was a terrifying hazard that Jullien had traversed to get up there. And it made her wonder how many times he'd done such since she'd brought him here. From the looks of fresh tracks around her, this might have become a fairly common practice for her prince.

With a grace that was amazing for someone so tall, Trajen quickly maneuvered to Jullien's side on the narrow beam. "Hey, buddy. What'cha doing?"

Still Jullien didn't move. He sat quietly, staring out at the stars through the clear windows. "You know what I'm doing. You know what I'm thinking."

Sitting down beside him on the thin rail where Jullien was precariously perched, Trajen drew a ragged breath. "It's a long drop down to the station floor from here."

"I always wanted to fly."

Trajen hissed and placed the heel of his hand to his temple. "Damn, you have some fucked-up shit in your head."

"I know. You should live in my thoughts full time like I have to."

"No, thanks. I have my own fun house filled with twisted mirrors to deal with."

Snorting, Jullien handed him the bottle of Tondarion Fire he was drinking.

After taking a swig of the potent whisky, Trajen returned it to him. "I'll never mock your boots again."

Jullien sighed. "Yeah. I didn't realize just how screwed up I was. . . . I mean, I knew. I just had no idea."

"Don't beat yourself up, kid. Trust me. You got plenty of others willing to do it for you. No need in you doing it for them, for free."

"Can't help it." Jullien took a drink. "I was fine as I was. Then I looked and saw—" he scraped his claws against his cheek hard enough to leave a red mark on his skin. He grimaced in disgust. "Nothing ever changes, does it?"

Ignoring the question, Trajen hesitated before he spoke in a quiet tone. "I know your pain, little brother. You asked me about my eyes and what turned them dark, and you were right. I know the bitter cost of surviving what should have killed us. Of committing sins so wretched that you know there is no way back from them. They have seared scars on our souls so deep that they're craters in our hearts, and have left damage so severe we will never be the same. No apologies can be made for what we've done. Not to our adversaries or enemies, and definitely not to their innocent families who mourn for them, or to our loved ones we hurt. And no excuse we make to ourselves will ever quiet our screaming consciences. No redemption is possible for the likes of us. We are damned by our own hands and we know it. We consigned ourselves to hell and for what? This miserable existence of pain and suffering from which there is no end?"

Jullien closed his eyes as Trajen spoke aloud exactly what he felt. For the first time in his life, he didn't feel alone in his hell. He didn't know what Trajen had done, nor did he care. He was in no position to ever judge the actions of anyone else. Good or bad.

Trajen's dark eyes narrowed on him as he continued speaking in his lyrical Trisani accent that he no longer tried to hide or diminish. "And you look around at the world that walks by in total ignorant apathy while your soul screams in a bitter agony so loud that you think how is it possible that no one else hears it? How can they not see the abject pain and misery that you live in all the time? For you, there is no quarter or solace. No refuge from this madness. But the truth is . . . they don't see it because we're all lost in our own private torment."

Sadly, Jullien knew that for the truth it was. And he was as guilty of not seeing the pain of others as they were in ignoring his. Until now, he'd never been aware of it. It wasn't until Vasili had stumbled into his life that he'd ever seen another's pain for what it was.

And he wasn't sure why Vas had reached him and made him care. Something in that boy, that day, had opened his cold, dead heart and reached him. Since coming here, he'd been acutely aware of others in a way he'd never been before.

For the first time in his life, he really did care.

Still, Trajen gave voice to the exact emotions and truth inside Jullien as he continued to speak. "Life is nothing but a horror movie that we're all trying to survive as best we can while it does its best to leave us as bloody corpses lying hacked to pieces in shallow graves. Every single day is a new battle we face that leaves us weary soldiers, wondering what enemy lies beyond the next hill that might be a peaceful undertaking, or mined with unseen explosives waiting to rip us to shreds when we least expect it. And there comes a point where you find yourself standing on top of that hill after so many better beings than you have fallen, and you don't understand it. Why them and not you? They were pure, kind hearts and you are blackened and burned to the core of your rotten soul by your actions. So wasted and damaged. No wonder no one has ever loved you. And if no one could love you when you were shiny and new and unscarred and unsullied by the hell you've been through, how in the name of the gods could anyone possibly want you like *this*? Used up and ashamed, you're no longer even sure if you can love another when you can't even stand to look at your own reflection. You just want to crawl inside a hole and die because there's nothing left inside you now except that all-consuming pain and self-loathing. Yet you go on and on, and you don't know why you bother. Why you don't give up when it seems like every sign you pass says you should."

"I really hate *you* right now, Trajen."

He scoffed. "No, you don't. You hate yourself too much to have room inside your heart to hate anyone else and you know it."

*"Titana tu."*

"You're not my type, Andarion. . . . Besides, look around. You're still here. For whatever reason. Life isn't about finding answers. It doesn't make sense. Maybe it's not supposed to. It's just a random fucking universe determined to test us to our utmost abilities. And maybe that's its true purpose, after all. To help us see and find our real mettle. Because that's what it does. In those most dismal hours when we've been kicked in the throat and had our hearts ripped from our chests and our balls handed to us, when we're lying in the gutter with no more strength, we find out who and what we really are. Doesn't matter if you're born prince or pauper. Those trying times strip us to the core to show the universe, and us, what we're made of. You either get back up and into the Ring to fight another round, or you lie down and you let the buzzards have you."

"I was always too stupid to quit."

"No. You're not stupid. Maybe stubborn . . ."

Jullien snorted. "You make it sound so easy."

"It's never easy. Those blows are staggering. And the hardest ones are always the ones we give to ourselves. The flogging shrill sounds of our consciences that never lets us forget the cost of our survival or the voices of those who hurt us most. No matter how hard we try, we cannot drown them in alcohol or purge them with drugs. They return as demonic spirits to torture us long after we've buried them and moved on."

"Does it ever get easier?"

Trajen nodded. "But the relief you seek isn't at the bottom of that bottle in your hand or in the run of a drug line. And it damn sure isn't in the grave." He jerked his chin to where Ushara waited below for them. "It's in the comfort of making those small connections with others. For they, alone, are what guide us home when we're lost. And there is no home without them. They are the only shelter a weary soul can ever hope to have."

He sighed wearily before he took the bottle from Jullien's hand for another swig. "Let the past go, *merjani*. We have all hurt someone. Sometimes badly, by intent or by accident. With malice of forethought or neglect. You can't change the horrible things you did to survive. You can only change what you will do from this day forward."

Jullien knew that was true. Still, it was much easier said than done. Especially on nights like this when the past was so haunting and vivid. So biting and raw.

Trajen pinned him with a fierce glower. But unlike the others, those eyes never judged him. And yet he saw Jullien more clearly than anyone ever had.

"Tahrs Jullien eton Anatole died a lonely death on Andaria four years ago. The male by my side today rose out of the ashes of that betrayal, reborn a fierce warrior. Stronger, leaner, smarter——"

"I wouldn't go *that* far."

Trajen grinned. "You were never the male they thought you were and you know that. None of them ever saw the real you. You hid yourself from them to survive and stay sane. They underestimated you and that was their mistake. But now you have a chance to be the male you want to be. To be a male you can be proud of. To make the right choices and live the life you want to. And I've been watching you."

"You pervert."

Trajen smirked as he ignored the jab. "You haven't seen the consequences of your kindness."

"Because I know how much I hurt the ones I should have protected."

"You were a child then. And even so, you did save your mother's life. You're the only reason she lived. As for the other matter, you didn't know how to protect yourself, never mind how to protect your brother. You were right to be afraid, then. Had he been discovered, the results would have been disastrous for you both."

Jullien flinched as his memories surged. If only he'd understood the consequences better.

For all of them.

Nykyrian wasn't supposed to have been arrested over his ring. School policy had called for his brother to be expelled for theft. Nothing more. But everything had blown out of control so fast—Merrell and Aksel Bredeh had seen to that. And once his father had gotten involved with the situation, Jullien had been terrified of what Aros and his grandmother would do to him once the lie was uncovered. Where his father was concerned, lying was a worse crime than stealing.

His father hated him enough. To learn that Jullien had told a lie against Nykyrian would have had nuclear fallout.

And it had. The only good to come of it was that his father's lapse of control on his temper had been so severe that it had caused his father to never beat him again. But their relationship had never recovered from that fateful day.

Ashamed of the lie Jullien had told everyone, and his own overreaction that had only ended when the medics had been called to resuscitate Jullien's dead body, Aros had all but banished him from Triosa.

They'd barely spoken since that day.

Dancer had no idea what he'd cost Jullien when he'd come forward with the truth. And not just with Jullien's father. Merrell and Chrisen had used that event to their advantage to gain favor and rewards, and Jullien had been hung out to dry with his grandmother.

The one thing about Andarions, they definitely believed in severe and extreme corporal punishment, especially when his grandmother thought herself embarrassed by her half-human grandson. Nyk had gotten away with only forty-eight hours of punishment and imprisonment.

Jullien hadn't been so lucky.

Not that it mattered. Afraid his grandmother would see Nyk and recognize him, Jullien had panicked and tried to get his brother thrown out of school, and had almost exposed them both with that fearful act of stupidity.

Truth be told, in the end, they'd both gotten off easy, given the bloody executions that could have befallen them and their mother.

But what burned him to this day was the fact that Nykyrian had been innocent. Rather than try to play a duplicitous game he sucked at, Jullien should have just left his brother alone and ignored him.

Gods, if he could just take it all back . . .

"But we can't," Trajen whispered as he heard Jullien's thoughts. "Sometimes we are forced to build our futures over the rubble of our pasts. Yes, our foundations are shaky and cracked. But by weathering those storms, we've learned just how strong we are. And I don't see a shattered prince in front of me. I see a capable soldier I would be honored to have at my back in battle, and I don't say that lightly. Like you, my trust is hard won. And that boy you saved with what you thought was your dying breath? He was shattered, too. Vas was there when his father died. You want to know why Ushara defied my orders and risked her position here to shelter you? Why she has pissed off her entire family by not asking you to leave? Because you've somehow managed to reach her son when no one else has. For these last few years, Vasili has been a shadow of the boy you know him to be. No laughter. No curiosity. Just a wandering, lifeless ghost. Yet he seeks you out like a friend and a father. So tell me, Highness, how rotten a male can you really be if one so pure of heart sees only goodness inside you?"

"He's young."

"And jaded well beyond his years. Believe me. He sees more than others credit. He's extremely talented in that regard."

Jullien sat quietly as he considered Trajen's words. For some reason, they reminded him of an old passage he'd committed to memory during his studies. "Beware the soldier who seeks peace through war. The priest who finds comfort in tragedy, and those who can only love when the sun shines brightest."

Trajen drew back as if he'd slapped him. "A male who quotes the *Book of Harmony* in ancient Pralortorian? Damn, Andarion. It's a rare thing for anyone to impress me."

"Yeah, but I'm sure I screwed up the pronunciation."

"Actually, you did a remarkable job. We don't roll our Rs, that's an Andarion thing, but the rest . . . you had to have gone to serious effort to pick that up."

"Useless knowledge for cocktail parties."

Trajen shook his head. "Yeah well, it's good to hear it again. Been a long time for me. Now, do I need to call a cleaning crew to mop up your blood and guts from the floor or are you done feeling sorry for yourself?"

Jullien passed an ancient Trisani obscene gesture at him. "Great speech there, boss. Way to prop me back up."

"You're Andarion. I hear a kick in the crotch works better for your species than a pat on the back."

"Wouldn't know since kicks in the crotch are all I've ever had."

Trajen stood and held his hand out to Jullien.

Jullien hesitated before he accepted it and allowed Trajen to pull him to his feet. "Still not sure I shouldn't take the shortest route down."

"Would it make a difference if I said I'd miss you?"

Jullien let out a bitter, scoffing laugh. "I know that for the lie it is. Like you'd give a shit."

Trajen jerked his chin toward Ushara. "She would."

Jullien hesitated as he saw her in the pale dim emergency lights of the station. His breathing quickened against his will.

"Don't break her heart," Trajen whispered. "She's not as solid as she pretends to be. But she's loyal to a fault and when she loves, it's with everything she has."

He swallowed hard as he watched her shining in the darkness. She reminded him of the Trisani legends of its Darling—the guiding light ancient sailors used for navigation. There were a lot of legends and stories about it in their literature and religious texts. "Every soul is assigned its Darling upon its birth, and so we endeavor through our lives to find it. For it will always guide us home through the blackest storms. And when the final night comes and we take that last breath, it shall comfort us in eternity and remain forever by our side. Our one true Darling. The guiding light of my immortal soul."

Trajen scowled at him. "Just how much Trisani have you studied?"

Jullien let out a bitter laugh. "Obviously a lot."

"Yeah and I'm not the one you need to be quoting poetry to in the darkness. Unless you're trying to seduce *me*, and with enough Tondarion Fire, anything is possible."

Jullien laughed. "Well, I can't get down until you move your giant, hulking ass out of my way."

"Don't you get cheeky with me after I went to all this effort to save you or I might be tempted to toss you over."

"You know that's not really motivating since I'm okay either way. I still haven't decided if I want to be a stain on the floor or not."

"Then you'd be fine if I took some rec time with the admiral in your stead?"

A rush of fury cut through Jullien so fast and unexpectedly that he actually reached for Trajen and grabbed him. The only thing that kept them from falling was the Trisani's amazing ability to maintain his balance.

Ushara let out a sharp cry from below.

Trajen gave him a cocky grin. "I take it that you care?"

Jullien nodded weakly.

With an equally annoying playful slap to Jullien's cheek, Trajen steadied Jullien's balance before he let go. "Just so you know, Ushara's young enough to be my daughter. And that's how I view her. I only said that to wake you up to your feelings. There's never been anything between us."

"Good. I'd hate to have to gut you." Jullien followed him down the scaffolding.

By the time they reached the bottom, Ushara was waiting for them. She rushed forward.

Jullien felt like crap as he saw the worry in her eyes.

Trajen took the bottle from his hand. "I'm confiscating this as punishment for your bad behavior."

"Thank you, Trajen," Ushara said.

He inclined his head to her before he left them alone.

Jullien grimaced as he tried to think of what he should say to her. Honestly, he was embarrassed. "I'm—"

She cut his words off with a searing kiss.

Stunned, he growled at the unexpected taste of her as she filled his arms with warm, lush curves, and his head with the scent of sweet roses.

Ushara pulled back to stare up at him with a sheepish smile. "Sorry."

"Why? For *that* greeting, I'd light my ass on fire . . . Or *you* could."

She laughed, then sobered. "Are you all right?"

Cringing, he scratched at his ear in the most adorable fashion. "My ego will never be the same. I hope I didn't offend your sisters overmuch. It was kind what they attempted to do. I didn't mean to spoil it."

"So what happened?"

He tucked his chin to his chest. "I seem to have developed an aversion for soap. Took one look at a bar and it—"

She cut his words off with another kiss. "The truth."

"Why? I definitely prefer the rewards a lie brings me."

Snorting, she dropped her hands to his waist.

He sucked his breath in sharply as she lightly touched him.

"Because the truth will bring you much better ones."

His body turned molten as his throat went dry. "Don't, Shara." He tried to pull away, but she wouldn't let him.

She captured his coat and held him in front of her. "Not tonight. I know all the arguments why this is stupid and why I should jettison you out the nearest airlock. I hear everything as loudly as if I'm Trajen. But . . ." She placed her hand on his cheek and forced him to meet her gaze. "Then I look at you and I see those soulful eyes that burn me." She brushed her thumb against his lips. "This cute little smirk . . ." She pressed her lips together. "I've never felt like this about anyone else. And I don't understand it. I loved my husband. I did, but it was very different. It was comfortable and comforting. What I feel for you is scary and unnerving."

"Great. I terrorize you. Just the emotion I wanted to inspire." He tried again to get loose.

But she was ever relentless as she held him in place. "It is great in a terrifying way. It's like a part of me awakens whenever you come near me. And I know you don't feel the same, and that's okay."

She interrupted him when he started to speak. "I don't want to take anything from you, Jullien. You've had enough taken away. I just want to give you the one thing I don't think you've ever had."

"And that is?"

"Safe harbor. Come home with me. One night. And let me show you what it's like to lay your head down in peace . . . in a place where you're wanted."

Jullien couldn't breathe as his throat tightened. *Don't be stupid. It's a fucking trick.*

It had to be.

Suddenly suspicious, he stepped back and looked around. "Who's here?"

"What?"

"Is it The League? You're surrendering me, aren't you?"

She gaped at his assumption. "No one's here. Dear gods, Jullien. Really? You honestly think I'm lying about this? That I'm setting you up to hand you over to your enemies? What have they done to you that you can't trust anyone? For anything?"

Jullien let out a bitter laugh as her question triggered several memories he hated most. "You really don't want me to answer that."

She caught his arm as he started to leave. "Talk to me."

Where could he even begin? Seriously. There was so much pain. So much inside him that hurt and was broken. He'd been alone for so long, he didn't even know how to be with someone else.

But as he stared into her eyes, there was one memory that always stood out above the others. One nightmare that he could never banish no matter how hard he tried. And before he knew it, he told her the one thing he'd never told another soul.

"When we met you, you asked whose murder I was wanted for. Do you remember?"

Ushara nodded slowly as a bad feeling went over her. By his somber mood, she could tell this was going to be terrible. So she braced herself as best she could.

"It was the first life I took. You know how old I was?"

"Twenty?"

His laugh was even more bitter than the darkness in his eyes. "Seven."

Horrified, she choked at the last number she'd have ever expected to come out of his mouth.

Was he serious?

"What?" she gasped.

His gaze haunted and tormented, he nodded. "I killed him in cold blood. He *never* saw it coming."

A chill went down her spine as she struggled to understand what he was telling her, and the age he'd been when he'd done the most unspeakable crime. "Why would you do such a thing?"

Stepping away from her, he wiped his hand over his face as if he was trying to rid himself of the nightmare and couldn't. "I just wanted to make sure my mother was okay. She'd been crying all day for my brother—like she would often do. Then all of a sudden, she was quiet for no reason."

He turned to face her. "It made my blood run cold."

"Why?"

"I knew my grandmother was growing impatient with her. I'd been savagely beaten the year before for crying myself so I knew better than to shed another tear for Nykyrian. I wasn't about to risk my grandmother's wrath again. Ever. Trust me. One of Eriadne's beatings is more than enough to live long in anyone's memory. But my mother had been spared it, so far. Yet I knew it was only a matter of time until my grandmother turned her wrath on her, too. And something about the way she'd stopped crying that night told me it wasn't right. That this was the night my grandmother had had enough of it. It was a feeling deep in my gut. So I went to check on her. And when I pushed open the heavy door to her room, I saw my grandmother's personal guard smothering her in her bed."

Ushara gasped in horror.

Jullien swallowed, but still showed no emotion as he continued speaking in a whispered monotone. "I was so scared when I saw them, I didn't know what to do. He was huge and I was so small in comparison. One blow and he could have killed me. Just like they were always threatening to do. But I couldn't let him kill my mother. She was all I had left in the universe."

He raked his hand through his hair. "Terrified. Freaking out. In a total panic, I saw my mother's military Warsword on the wall, next to the door where I stood. Just a few inches from my hand. I was never to touch it because it was so sharp and dangerous. All my life, I'd been told that it could cut through flesh and bone like they were made of butter, and all I could think was that it would help me. So I grabbed it and cut his head off before I knew what I was doing. Before he even knew I was in the room. I had no idea anyone could bleed so much. And it was so hard to pull his body from my mother's. He was so heavy. I kept thinking his weight would crush her before I could get him off her and check to see if she still lived."

Ushara couldn't breathe at the tragic horror he described. "You didn't call for help?"

"Who, Ushara?" His voice finally held his anger, guilt, and turmoil. "It was my own grandmother, the tadara, who'd sent that male to murder her while she lay in a drugged stupor. The same insidious creature who'd just ordered the death of my twin brother. The very one who'd cut the throat of my own grandfather and everyone else in my family. Who was going to help me, I ask you? Who was I supposed to call that night for help? Who? My father wouldn't even take my calls. He was in mourning for my brother, and I was told that the sound of my voice was too mentally disturbing for him to deal with, at that time."

In that moment, the full horror of his childhood and situation hit her. He'd truly had no one in his life to turn to. Not for anything. "Your father really wouldn't take you in?"

"No. He refused to go to war for me. He told me as much. Repeatedly. His people mean more to him than a worthless, lying bastard son he can't trust. That's all I am to him. It's all I've ever been. He never once even thought of me as his heir. Not really. Nyk was the only one of us he ever loved. He *never* cared for me."

Ushara wanted to deny it, but he was right and she knew it. A contradiction would only sting him more. "So what did you do?"

"Once I made sure she was alive, I cleaned the blood from her as best I could and I sat there in shock for hours, holding the bloody towels in my lap, trying to think of what I should do. I ran so many scenarios through my mind, but I had no answers. All I knew was that my grandmother was as crazy as my mother. And that I was alone with them in that palace, with no one to help me. Worse, I knew my grandmother wouldn't stop. Sooner or later, she'd try again to kill her. So I did the only thing I knew to. I finally grabbed the guard's head and my mother's sword, and in the wee hours of the morning, I made my way to my grandmother's bedchamber."

Ushara could imagine the elder tadara waking to find the young prince in her room in such a grisly state. "And?"

"I placed his head at her feet and stared at her without flinching. Then with all the courage I could muster, I confronted her and said that tonight is the last night you will threaten my mother. Ever. Because there is one truth as tahrs that I know about you, *mu Tadara*. You are as vain as you are cruel. And while you hate me and are ashamed of me, you would die before you ever allowed a lesser Anatole lineage to occupy your beloved throne. Since you have killed my brother, I am the sole heir of your direct bloodline. The very last of it. Therefore you are forced to endure me. But I am not forced to tolerate you. With one cut of this sword, I could take your throne as easily as I took your guard's head. If you ever come at my mother again, I won't hesitate to take my place as the Andarion tadar. My mother is all that keeps you alive. Guard her well and know that your life is dependent upon hers."

Jullien sighed. "In retrospect, I should have speared her in that bed while I had the chance. That was my biggest mistake in life. . . . And my greatest regret."

"Does your mother know about this?"

He shook his head. "She was passed out from her drugs and remembers none of it. Only my grandmother and I know about that night. Eriadne had it all cleansed and erased. I didn't know any part of it had been kept as evidence until the warrants for my execution had been issued."

"How so?"

"Bitch kept the clothes I was wearing that night that had the guard's blood on them. Her version of the story omits his attack on my mother. With no corroborating witnesses . . ."

"You're a murderer."

"Wanted dead for it."

"But if you went to your family and told them—"

He laughed bitterly. "They don't care. My aunt Tylie's partner was the one who shot me when I escaped Andaria the last time four years ago . . . on Tylie's orders."

"But your mother—"

"Would stand beside Tylie against me. She believes I'm as guilty as they do. If she thought me innocent, she'd have rescinded the contract. But notice, it stands and so I'm hunted without quarter. I can't even get it reduced to a simple Bill-Kill. At least that would be a quick, painless death, instead of being tortured first."

Ushara felt sick to her stomach for him. She couldn't imagine how horrible he must have felt when his aunt ordered him shot.

How betrayed.

Jullien let out a tired breath. "Look, don't judge my mother. It's not her fault. I'm not going to lie and say I was this perfect, pristine angel. I wasn't. I cut the bastard's head off with a single stroke while he had his back to me. I spent my entire childhood in a fit of bitter rage. And you didn't want to be caught in my path when it exploded. Sometimes my actions were justified. Many times they weren't. Whether they were or not, I still have to live with them all. That's what's hard."

"And knowing all this about you, I still want to take you home." She held her hand out to him.

Jullien hesitated. "Why?"

"Is it that hard to believe that I might like you?"

"You'd be the first."

"Then let me be your first."

Still aghast, Jullien stared at her. But in the end, he couldn't deny what she made him feel. She was offering him the one thing he wanted most. The one thing he'd never had.

A kind touch. Someone who didn't look at him like he was utter shit.

Knowing this was probably as big a mistake as not taking his grandmother's head, he placed his hand in hers and let the warmth of her skin soothe him.

Without another word of protest, he followed her back through the station to a small grocery store. She glanced about nervously. "I need to get a few things before we go to my place."

"Okay." He trailed along behind her as she grabbed a small basket.

"Do you have a meat preference?"

He shrugged. "I've learned not to be picky these last few years." He took the basket from her so that he could carry it while she quickly filled it with dinner items.

"Wine?" she asked.

"Again, no preference."

Ushara hesitated in the aisle. "Suggestions, then? I don't usually drink it."

"I don't need it, if you don't want it."

She grinned up at him. "I normally eat with a certain young one who isn't old enough to imbibe. Since we're adults, I would *really* like some. My husband was a male of simple tastes who didn't care for it, but I have a feeling you are one who knows a really good vintage from a total waste of credits."

"Ah . . . that I do. However, do you want a robust bargain or something decadently obscene that will leave your panties on the floor, your head in the clouds, and your bank account screaming in agony?"

She laughed at his description. "Is there a happy compromise between those two options?"

Screwing his face up, he perused the shelves for a few minutes before he finally reached for a bottle. "This should meet your needs quite nicely with the flavors you've chosen for dinner." He added it to the basket. "Is there anything else you require?"

She bit her lip as she glanced about and tried not to be completely mortified. "Um . . . there is one thing. Wait right here." She tried to be subtle and fast.

Unfortunately and to her utter humiliation, Jullien followed after her. Damn it!

She really, really hated the amused cock of his brow as she placed the small box into the basket underneath the food.

When she started out of the aisle, toward the register, he didn't move. Rather he cleared his throat to get her attention.

"Those won't fit, you know."

"Excuse me?"

"They're sized for human males. They'll be too small and will probably break."

Heat erupted over her face. "Are you serious?"

He nodded. "I would tell you to look on the box. But given the degree of redness on your face already, I'm rather sure you'd die on the spot of embarrassment."

Grinding her teeth, she groaned under her breath. "I think you're too late. I already have."

He grinned at her. Then, in the most debonnaire manner befitting a prince, he kissed her hand. "Go back to your place and I'll finish this and meet you there."

"I have to pay for it."

"I'm not a whore, Ushara. I can buy your dinner for you."

"I wasn't implying that you were."

"Then go and I'll meet you there. Unless you really want to shop for condoms with me."

She let out an adorable squeak. "Fine, I'm out! I'll see you in a few minutes."

Jullien laughed at her hasty retreat. He found it precious and refreshing that a female so worldly and jaded could be embarrassed by something so ridiculously innocuous. It also told him a lot about her that she knew so very little about what she was buying, and how to pick them out.

Though why she'd waste time with him defied his imagination and humbled him.

In all his life, no matter how many times he'd tried, he'd never been able to convince a female to go with him on a date, of *any* kind. Not even a paid companion. They would accompany him to prearranged functions he'd contracted for, and he could visit the condos he provided for them for specified visitations hours or they would come to his palace rooms, but that was it.

Human women had always been terrified of his Andarion size, and fangs. So much so, that they'd cross the street at his approach or run from the room, even vacate an elevator. It'd given him a complex in his younger years.

Andarion females were far more cruel and unforgiving. His human eyes had caused them to view him as a deformed freak. That had been bad enough. Once he'd started gaining weight . . .

His Andarion social life had come to a screeching halt.

No female had ever looked at him the way Ushara did. They had never made him feel the things he felt whenever she met his gaze.

Like he was desirable.

He couldn't fathom it. Why would a female so beautiful and kind waste her time on him? It made no sense. But one thing was sure. Unlike other males, he wouldn't squander this chance. He knew how rare and precious these moments were.

How fleeting.

They might only have tonight. And all he had left to give her was his heart and respect.

His life.

But they were hers if she'd take them. And if she ultimately refused him and threw him aside like everyone else had, then he hoped she had the decency to kill him.


Ushara had just begun to worry that Jullien had lost his way to her condo when she heard the light knock on her door. She opened it to find him there with a huge bouquet of red and gold flowers in his arms.

And coiled in the center of them was a pair of thick purple socks. The exceptionally soft kind that she adored.

"What did you do?"

He dipped his head down sheepishly to peer at her from behind the bouquet. "I called your herd of giggling sisters for a consultation. They said these were your favorite. The socks more than the flowers."

Laughing, she pulled him inside to kiss his cheek. "They're correct, but right now, the male holding them outranks them all in my affections."

"I find that hard to believe. . . . The socks are much cuter."

She bit her lip as she took the flowers from him and carried them to the kitchen. He followed her with the groceries and set them on the counter for her.

As Ushara turned, she caught the hungry look in his eyes. It was absolutely searing and it riveted her to the spot. No one had ever looked at her like that. As if she was the air he needed to breathe.

And yet he stood away from her, rigid and aloof. With all the regal dignity of a prince.

"You know I give you permission to touch me, Jullien."

Still, he made no move to do so. It was so ingrained in Ixurian Andarion culture to respect each other's personal space that they never reached out to lightly touch one another. Only the closest of family would do such.

Even then, seldom in public.

Fyrebloods were different. They'd never been like his kind. It had been one of many reasons they'd been persecuted and hated throughout the centuries on Andaria. They were far more open and free. And, with no understanding of why they were like that, the darkhearts had been suspicious of them.

Stepping closer to him, she reached up to trace the chiseled line of his smooth cheek. He looked so different without his light beard and new haircut. Refined and elegant. Perfect, and even angelic. He was absolute masculine beauty. More akin to a Fyreblood's leaner, sculpted features than the rugged ones of the Ixurians.

Her sisters had said that this was what had sent him over the edge. When he'd seen himself clean-shaven and stylishly dressed. Which made a lot of sense to her. In all the photos of him before he'd been disinherited, he'd been immaculately groomed, in the latest fashions. No hair out of place. No trace of a single stray whisker. It was as if a valet and fashion consultant had traveled with him to keep every fiber of clothing and hair in line at all times. As if it'd been beaten into him that he must never appear in public unless he was perfectly coifed, and regally composed.

Rigid and imposing. Commanding and arrogant.

There were times when he still bore traces of that. But for the most part, he'd shed his aristocratic persona for that of a wary, watchful predator. One who was ever vigilant and on guard. Even now, when they were alone.

He'd still positioned himself so that his back was to the wall and he was facing the door. No one could see him from any window. And his holster was open, with his coat pulled back to clear it so that he could draw his weapon if he had to.

Yet he was more relaxed with her and Vas than anyone else. In their presence, he would cross his arms over his chest. Even put his hands in his pockets. Around others, he kept his left hand hovered near his blaster at all times. Either on the blaster's grip, or his thumb hitched in the belt near it.

It made her feel incredibly special to know that she and Vasili, alone, held his trust.

And as she moved closer to him, his breathing turned ragged. He dipped his gaze to glance down her shirt. Still, he didn't move to touch her in anyway.

But the sudden bulge in his pants gave away the line of his thoughts. More than that, it shoved away any desire she had for dinner.

She smoothed the scarf around his neck. "How long has it been since you've slept with a female?"

"I don't remember," he said hoarsely.

She gaped. "Seriously?"

His gaze didn't move from her breasts as he swallowed hard. "Four, six . . . thousand years."

"Jullien!" She splayed her hand on his chest.

Grimacing, he pressed his thumb against his brow as he thought it over. "Mmmm . . . last time I was under contract. Edrinius '60 . . . I think."

Aghast, she gaped at him. "That is literally five years ago."

"Yes," he said slowly. "*Well* aware of that fact. Hell, I probably don't even remember how to be with anyone else. For all I know, Androkyn aren't even doing it the same way anymore. They might even be using bells. Springs. I don't know. How would I know? At this point, I should cut things off and join the priesthood."

She laughed. "You poor baby. And here I thought I had it bad." She paused. "Wait . . . I do have it that bad. Ah, crap. I have it worse. Yeah, I haven't been near a male since I lost my husband."

"Ah good, I won't feel so bad, then, when I screw it up. You won't remember, either."

Laughing, she kissed him lightly on his lips. "Has it really been that long for you?"

He brushed his hand through her hair and lifted a lock of it so that he could twirl it between his fingers. "Trust me, you'll find out all too soon that I'm not lying. I'm sure my ineptitude will be stellar and embarrassing. I'm just putting it out here early to prepare you not to expect much. Please, try to refrain from laughing as it will devastate what tiny, little ego I possess."

"Hmmm . . ." Ushara pushed herself away from him. She rooted through the bag to find the small box of condoms and wine. Passing the wine to Jullien, she put the groceries in the fridge and grabbed a light snack and glasses.

Jullien wasn't sure what was going on until she hooked her finger in his belt loop and pulled him after her. His heart began to race as she led him down the beige hallway to the most *bizarrely* feminine bedroom he'd ever seen in his life.

Yeah, this was not what he would have expected from the tough, serious-minded tadara of the Tavali Gorturnum Nation. It was so incredibly frilly and *p-i-n-k*.

And *flowery*.

Painfully so.

Not just pink. *Bright,* dark pink. Like if pink could bleed pink, it would bleed *this* particular shade of pink. He had to suppress a shudder over it. The only good thing about the room was the size of the bed. It had four posters that were carved into the shapes of white columns wrapped with winding vines of ivy and even pinker flowers. A smaller white and pink settee was placed in front of the bed with more pink planters of flowers on the floor. The room reminded him of a garden that had thrown up all over the place.

Ushara let go of him to deposit the food, glasses, and wine on the white nightstand before she headed to the corner where a collection of large, scented candles were set on the floor in front of a rustic arched mirror so that she could light them to bathe the entire area in a cheerful, warm glow.

Jullien paused in the center of the room to look up at the ornate white chandelier that had been carved into spiraling vines and glass flowers that cast more shadows on the ceiling. It gave the room a fairytale appearance and went with the pink garden motif.

"You okay?"

He scratched uncomfortably at his whiskers. "Yeah, just feeling the sudden need to do something extremely masculine."

She laughed before she blew out the match and placed it in a tiny bucket of sand. "You sound like Vas."

Once she had all the candles lit, she came up behind him and pulled his coat from his shoulders. She tossed it over the settee.

Jullien cupped her face in his hands as she unbuckled his holster. Her features were so delicate and fragile. And as he stared into those clear pale eyes, he lost what little was left of his battered soul to her. Slowly, he lowered his head, waiting for her to turn away and deny his kiss.

She didn't.

Instead, she sank her hand into his hair and held him close. At least until she broke from the kiss long enough to pull his shirt over his head and toss it to rest on top of his weapons. He flinched as she bared his scarred body. But she didn't seem to notice as she ran her hands over his skin and pulled him into her arms.

Even more nervous, Jullien swallowed as he gently undid her shirt, and slid his hand inside to touch her supple skin for the very first time.

Honestly, he expected her to slap him for it. But as he gently cupped her, she sucked her breath in sharply and covered his hand with hers, urging him on. He growled at the satiny feel of her flesh.

His senses reeled as every part of him burned for her, especially when he felt her undoing his pants so that she could stroke him. As soon as her fingers brushed against his cock, he almost came.

The intensity was so fierce, he had to pull away. Fast.

"Jullien?"

Unable to catch his breath, he bent over and raked his hand through his hair. Cursing, he struggled for control. "Sorry. I warned you it's been awhile. I just need a second to quit seeing stars."

Instead of being angry, she smiled at him and then slowly stripped the rest of her clothes off before she turned on a low, soft tune and lowered the lights to a gentle glow. "It's fine, handsome. Take your time."

That put him right back in business.

With interest.

Jullien was pretty sure his tongue was on the floor as he watched her slide sensuously over the bed. Rising up on her knees, she sat back with her thighs spread while she gently gyrated to the music and rolled her arms and shoulders in time to the beat.

Ushara smiled as she saw how fast Jullien removed the rest of his clothes and launched himself into the bed beside her. He playfully tackled her and rolled so that she was sprawled on top of his muscular body.

"Hi gorgeous," she teased.

"Where did you learn that dance?"

"Oh . . . we need to talk. Fyrebloods have a very special kind of fertility dance we do. Didn't you know about that?"

"No. Damn . . ." He ran his hand slowly over her breasts before he lowered his head to tease them with is tongue and lips.

And speaking of . . . Ushara gasped as he tasted her with an unbelievable skill. Oh dear heavens! The things he could do with his tongue! He moved from one side to the other with a sensuous rhythm unlike anything she'd ever felt. It was so intense and incredible, so sensual and powerful that she actually came from it.

Unable to believe what he'd done, she stared in awe. "Jullien? What was *that*?"

Smiling as he laid her back on the bed, he slowly and methodically licked and teased his way down her stomach. "Did I forget to mention that I have a slight oral fixation? Hence my adolescent weight problem?"

She didn't know what he meant until he went a bit lower and lower still. Yeah . . . that was not a slight nothing.

That was a major set of skills and an incredible fixation her prince possessed.

Crying out in pleasure, she buried her hand in his thick dark hair as he licked and teased her without mercy. She lost count of how many times he brought her to climax before he finally took mercy and rolled away to reach for the condoms.

No one had ever been *that* thorough with her. Her entire body was shaking and weak. He'd left no part of her untasted.

But there was a strange somberness to him now that she didn't quite understand as he quickly, and quietly secured the condom without her help. He wouldn't even meet her gaze. Rather he reached out and gently brushed his hand through her hair with a great sadness that didn't make sense.

When she tried to roll to embrace him, he kept her back to him and entered her that way. Jullien nuzzled his face against her hair as he held himself rigidly over her, with as little weight against her body as possible. He very carefully and slowly thrust against her hips—as if he was terrified of crushing or hurting her.

He was so tense around her, that she wasn't even sure if he was enjoying himself. Honestly, she didn't see how he could be. For that matter, she was surprised he wasn't cramping from the effort of holding his weight off her. Rather, he seemed more focused on touching her as little as possible, and on keeping the condom secured.

Then the instant he came, he carefully pulled out of her—again so quickly she wasn't sure he'd climaxed completely. Making sure to keep everything in place, he was off the bed so fast that she was stunned by it.

What the hell?

And when he returned to her room a few minutes later, fully dressed to reach for his coat, she was pissed off totally. "What are you doing?"

With a baffled expression, he glanced at the bed and floor. "Did I spill some or hurt you? I tried to be as clean and gentle as possible."

She gaped at him. "You don't just get up and leave."

Now he looked even more confused. "You don't?"

And it was her turn to be shocked. "Do you?"

"Don't you?"

"No, Jullien. You don't. Ever." Scooting out of bed, she went to him and pulled the coat out of his hands. She returned it to the settee. "Have you always had sex like *that*?"

He nodded.

She scowled at him. "Are you telling me that *all* your girlfriends treated you this way?"

His frown deepened. "I never had a girlfriend. Only paid companions. Their contracts were always standard, and very rigid with how much physical contact was permitted between us during sex, and what positions I was allowed so that I didn't cause them harm from my size. And how long I was permitted to stay after I finished."

"Let me guess. Get out immediately?"

Again, he nodded.

She pulled his shirt off and ran her hand over his scarred ribs. "I'm not with an agency. And I'm not a paid booty call. Now get back in bed and let me show you what it's like to be with someone who actually likes you, and wants to be with you."

There was a strange hint of reservation in his eyes as he peeled his boots and pants off, and obeyed her.

Once back in her bed, she realized just how bad it truly was. He really had no idea how to cuddle or hold someone in his arms. It would be funny if it didn't break her heart.

"Jules? Relax and stop being so tense. I'm not going to bite you."

He turned even more stiff and rigid. "What did you call me?"

She froze. "Jules. Does it bother you?"

"No. No one's ever used that one before." He looked so awkward, leaning back on her pillows as he struggled to get comfortable.

Shaking her head, she handed him a glass of wine. "I'm thinking we should have bought something stronger to relax you. I would have thought a prince would have spent a great deal of time lounging about in bed."

All the humor went out of his eyes.

Her stomach tightened immediately as she realized she'd pissed him off. "What'd I say?"

"Nothing. You just a hit a sore topic for me. And no, though I was oft accused of it, I was never allowed to lie about in my bed. Or anyone else's."

"Obviously." She brushed her hand over his brow as she watched the haunted demons dance behind his hazel eyes. How she wished she could banish them from him. But as she skimmed her hand over the harsh, multitude of scars on his body, she knew it was impossible. They were a pittance compared to the ones that marred his bloodied soul.

How could they have been so cruel?

She paused at the mark by his heart where his grandmother had come so close to killing him. Wanting to soothe his pain, she dipped her head to gently lave the scar.

Jullien ground his teeth as he felt the heat of Ushara's tongue on his flesh, and he shivered. No female had ever touched him like this. His past companions had all been disgusted by his body. Revolted by his touch, they'd barely tolerated him in their bed. Seldom had they looked at him.

None had ever wanted to explore him the way she did. Never mind *cuddle* or hold him once it was over.

His breathing ragged, he cupped her pale head in his hand and marveled at the silken texture of her white, wavy hair. He'd never seen or felt anything like it. Or her skin either, for that matter. It was so pale and beautiful. Unblemished and perfect.

There wasn't a single mark on her.

It was as if the gods themselves profaned harming something so delicately pure and precious. He still couldn't believe she allowed him to touch her without conditions or restrictions. No female had ever granted him such an honor.

Smiling at him, she took the wine from his hand and set it aside, then slowly nibbled his scarred fingers. Chills spread over his body and sent a wave of searing heat straight to his groin, making him instantly hard again. And when she began to suck and tongue his thumb, he growled in pleasure.

Then cursed as he realized what else it was doing to him.

Ushara scowled as Jullien abruptly pulled away. "What's wrong?"

Cupping himself, he looked around her room and moved uncomfortably. "Do you have a towel?"

"For what?"

He gave her a strange look. "I assume you would know since you were married and have a child."

"You came again already?"

Offended, he shook his head. "No. But I am starting to leak."

"Yeah . . ." she dragged the word out, still confounded by his actions. "Males do that."

He gave her a confused stare. "Which is why I need a towel so as not to soil your bed sheets."

Ushara gaped as she finally understood. *"Keramon,* I don't expect you to be tidy in bed with me. It's okay." She pulled him back into bed and forced him to uncover himself so that she could stroke him and prove that she didn't care in the least whether or not he soiled her sheets. "I don't mind. They will wash."

Jullien couldn't fathom her tolerance for him. No female had ever treated him this way. The others he'd been with had been so repulsed by his body that they'd always acted as if every part of him was onerous and disgusting.

Biting his lip, he groaned as Ushara gently cupped and stroked him. And when she bent down to take him into her mouth, he found a whole new level of paradise he'd never known. His entire body shook from it.

Unable to believe this was real, he gently ran his hand through her hair and marveled at the miracle he'd been granted. He finally understood what Trajen had meant about finding peace in her arms. Right here. Right now, he was completely bare to her. And not just physically. Emotionally. He'd never been more honest with anyone else. She knew things about him that he'd never shared before.

And still she accepted him.

She *was* his Darling.

While he had no understanding or concept of love, he suspected that what he felt for her might be that. Or maybe it was cold-blooded terror.

He honestly had no way of distinguishing between the two. All he knew was that right now, she owned a part of him that no one ever had. For her, alone, he would kill or die.

Until this moment, he'd never once been touched by a kind hand. Never knew what it felt like to be wanted or desired.

And while he watched her tasting him, something inside him shattered wide open. Searing and hot, it flooded his blood with emotions he couldn't even begin to explain or sort through. With an audible gasp, he arched his back as she brought him to climax. He fully expected her to pull away and curse him for the lack of control.

Instead, she gently teased and wrung every last bit from his body until he was panting and weak. Only then did she slowly kiss her way up his abdomen and chest to lay herself over him like a soft, warm blanket.

Jullien held her against him as his head spun. He buried his hand in her soft hair and kissed her forehead while he savored this one moment of pure bliss. He wanted to say something profound, but words failed him. There was nothing that could convey the true depth of what he felt, and the last thing he wanted was to trivialize it.

Ushara looked up to catch the most open and unguarded expression on Jullien's face. His heart and soul were bared to her. Reaching up, she smiled as she brushed her fingers over his lips. "You are so handsome."

He shook his head. "I wish I still had something to give you."

"I don't need things, Jullien. Things have never mattered to me."

"I know." Rolling with her, he lay on his side so that he could reverently toy with her breasts.

Ushara bit back a smile as she watched him tentatively explore her body, as if terrified she was going to slap him or pull away at any second. "Don't worry. I'm not going to take it away from you."

He snorted. "You say that . . . but that's what always happened in the past. One wrong sound or move and my conjunctive rights were instantly revoked. Sometimes for a month or more as punitive actions for it."

"Conjunctive rights? Really? That's what they termed them?"

Nodding, he bent his head down so that he could blow a cool breath across her nipple.

She frowned as another awful thought went through her. "So how many different mistresses have you have over the years?"

He pulled back with a grimace. "Not that many. My grandmother had this uncanny ability to know whenever I was about to sign a new contract, and kept throwing my ass in prison right before I could make the meetings. Honestly, I think Merrell, Chrisen, or Nyran kept putting her up to it to make sure I stayed sexually frustrated."

Had she heard that correctly?

Ushara cupped his chin and forced him to meet her gaze. "Prison?"

He nodded. When he went to dip his head again, she stopped him.

"Jullien? What prison? When? I didn't see that in your records. Only a couple of arrests. But no real jail time. According to your files, you were always released."

He let out a bitter laugh. "There's a *lot* of shit that doesn't show up in my records. As for the prison, my grandmother has her own special hell that she keeps beneath the palace in Eris called the vörgäte. There are only two entrances. One in her bedroom and the other from the rooms of her personal bodyguard. It's reserved for the captives she can't afford to have in other prisons or dispose of through regular channels. It's where a large number of my family met their final fate and where one particularly mouthy tahrs spent a significant portion of his formative years."

Her heart lurching, she kissed his brow. "I'm so sorry."

He shrugged. "It's okay. At least down there, I didn't have to worry about one of my cousins knifing me while I slept. And you can always tell in photos whenever I'd just come up from a stint in her personal playground."

"How so?"

"I'm usually thinner. A lot paler and either squinting or wearing really dark sunglasses, even indoors."

Saint Sarn, she knew exactly the photos he was talking about. He also appeared very nervous or agitated in them.

No wonder.

"When were you in—"

"Shara," he breathed, cutting her off. "If you don't mind, I'd really rather not talk about it. I don't want to think about the past right now. I'd rather just be here with you, and savor every second of this."

Tears choked her. That was the sweetest thing anyone had ever said to her. "Okay."

He carefully positioned his body between her legs and kissed her before he slid himself inside her again.

Biting her lip, she cradled his hips with her legs as she ran her hands through his hair and watched him watching her. The feral light in his eyes scorched her while he nuzzled her neck and growled in her ear. This time, he made love to her ferociously.

And when he was spent, he lay in her arms and allowed her to cuddle and hold him until he finally fell into a fitful asleep. Ushara brushed her hand over his scarred body and winced at the pain it catalogued. No wonder he hadn't flinched at the beating Silig and them had given him. If she'd held any doubts about the veracity of his claims over the vörgäte, that alone would have told her that he hadn't exaggerated his past in the least. Only someone used to being beaten could have taken that and kept going.

*You are so different from Chaz.*

Her husband had been a pacifist. A very, very rare beast for an Andarion. Outgoing and extraverted to an irritating level, Chaz had kept himself forever surrounded by friends and family. To the point, she'd been forced to put her foot down and demand alone time with him.

She couldn't have found two males more different had she quested for polar opposites. Yet even though he was wanted and hunted, Jullien made her feel so safe.

How peculiar was that?

It made no sense whatsoever. He calmed her and excited her. Both at the same time. He was charming and unnerving. Belligerent and sweet.

Ever a surprise.

Ever unexpected. But they had no future together and she knew that. She couldn't bring a male into her life who was this hunted and hated. Not with a Thrill-Kill warrant. He was a danger to anyone near him. A danger to Vasili.

*I have to find the strength to let you go.*

*And break both our hearts.*

Ushara came out of the bathroom to the most delectable smell of her life. And the sweetest thing she'd ever seen.

Jullien had prepared a morning feast for her. Complete with fresh flowers, freshly squeezed juice, sliced fruit and the sexiest male who'd ever stood on two legs cooking in front of a stove she hadn't even known could make those mouthwatering aromas permeate her home.

As she entered her kitchen to find him humming a cheerful song, a jolt of horror went through her. "Dear gods, you're a morning Androkyn, aren't you?"

Laughing, he winked at her as he handed her fresh, hand-squeezed juice. "Sadly, yes. Especially after a night so sweet."

Then he amazed her even more by not just merely giving her the breakfast, he flipped the meat and eggs from the frying pans to the plate. Threw the plate up high enough to clear his shoulder, twirled, caught it and turned to present it to her with a mind-boggling flair and skill.

"I don't know what impresses me more. The fact you can do that at all, or the fact you can do it at this unholy hour of the morning. My eye-hand coordination doesn't kick in for another three hours."

Laughing again, he made a flourish of adding spices to her food and garnish before he set it down in front of her. And then, he sprinkled a bit of cheese over it all. He headed to the oven to pull out a tray of assorted pastries.

"You did all this while I was showering?"

"Told you I spent a lot of time in the palace kitchen."

"That you did." She took a bite and then moaned out loud at the savory goodness of it. "Oh dear gods, Jules! Forget working in the bay. We need to move you to the restaurant guilds. This is unbelievable!"

He pulled one of the rolls apart and smeared a creamy concoction over it. "You haven't tasted the best of it." He held it out toward her.

She opened her mouth and allowed him to place it on her tongue, then had to agree. "We could make a killing with this."

Smiling, he ate the other half.

As she reached for more pastries, the front door opened.

Jullien went pale. A wild look darkened his eyes. One that worsened as Vasili skipped into the kitchen with a wide smile.

"What is that deliciousness I smell?"

Jullien gulped audibly. "Um . . . um . . ."

Ushara laughed at his panic.

He glanced at her, then Vasili. "I was bringing some reports by this morning for the admiral, and I . . . um . . ."

She laughed even harder as Vasili sidled over to look at what was on her plate and she hugged her son. "Relax, Jullien. He knows you spent the night here. I don't keep secrets from my child." She kissed his cheek as Jullien finally calmed down.

Vasili cast a greedy eye at the pastries. "May I have some?"

"Sure." Jullien handed him the spread and knife, then a plate and napkin. "Want some eggs and ham?"

"Oh yeah!" Vasili took a seat while Jullien went to make them. "So, Mum. Why can't you cook like this?"

"Gee, thanks, Vas. Why can't you?"

"Probably because you never showed me."

"'Cause I don't know how."

Vas nodded as he licked at his fingers. "So, Jullien, how did you learn?"

"From a gourmet cook on Andaria who loved to experiment with different cuisines and spices. Not to mention, I like to eat. A lot." Jullien set the plate in front of Vasili.

Ushara checked the time. "You better hurry, babe. You don't have long before school."

"I know. I'm sorry I disturbed the two of you, but I left a book in my room yesterday. I swear I thought I'd grabbed them all. Somehow it leaped out of my backpack when I wasn't looking."

Ushara laughed. "It happens. And don't forget to pick up your recs from your teachers for temple. Tomorrow's the last day to turn those in."

"Okay."

"He's going through Confirmation?"

She nodded proudly. "He's growing up way too fast."

Vasili popped his head around the corner. "Would you like to go to temple with us tomorrow, Jullien?"

The request surprised him. He glanced to Ushara to see what she thought of the idea, but he couldn't gauge her reaction.

She merely arched an amused brow. "Vas . . . I'm sure Jullien's Yllam Orthodox. I doubt he'd want to attend our temple."

"Oh . . ."

Now it was Jullien's turn to arch his brow at her. "Are you Demurrists?"

She nodded. "Most Fyrebloods are."

Vas frowned as he rejoined them. "Is there much difference?"

"Enough that Jullien's great-grandfather systematically jailed and executed a large number of our practitioners for blasphemy against Asukar and the crown, and that to this day, there are no Demur temples allowed in any Andarion held territory or outpost. Any Androkyn found possessing a symbol of our faith in their empire is subject to arrest, imprisonment, or execution for it."

Vas gaped. "Really?"

"Those were my grandmother's Laws of Purification. My mother has been much more lenient about enforcing them." Jullien turned toward Vasili. "As for your offer, I would be honored to attend temple with you, provided your mother doesn't mind. I have no problem with the followers of Kadora. Goddess knows, they've been far kinder to me than the Asukarians."

Ushara cocked her head. "Yeah, but——"

"I was never confirmed in the faith," he said, knowing the protest she was about to make. "While I was forced to go to temple as tahrs, the priests refused me communion and all holy rites, including exordiom and Confirmation."

Ushara gasped at something that would have been a public embarrassment every week for him to endure. And without exordiom, he wouldn't have been allowed some of the most basic Andarion customs such as burial rites when he died. And if one believed their priests, he wouldn't be allowed into the blessed lands of Eweyne without it, either, but rather would be condemned to eternal suffering in Tophet. "Why?"

"Half-human. I'm unfit for benediction and redemption."

"Wait . . . your brother was given exordiom. I saw photos of the ceremony when he was an infant."

"My brother was eldest born and heir. As such, my mother forced them to honor him. I wasn't allowed in for his services. And after he was supposedly killed, she was too indisposed to be concerned with my immortal soul. So to answer your concerns, I won't be violating either temple doctrine to attend with you. . . . Don't worry. I won't embarrass you. I'm well aware that I can't take your communion, or the sacred-affirmations."

"That never occurred to me and we would be honored to have you join us."

Vasili cheered before he ran back to his room.

Ushara's link went off while Jullien cleaned up Vas's plate.

At her sound of irritation, he turned. "Something wrong?"

"I have to run." Then louder, she called. "Vas? I need you to hurry. I have to go."

"I can get him to school for you, if you need to go on."

She looked up with a gape. "Really?"

"Sure. I'll finish cleaning this and head right out. We can lock up without a problem and get him to school on time."

The smile on her face warmed him. "You are wonderful." But nothing was as wonderful as the kiss she gave him.

Closing his eyes, Jullien savored the taste of her.

She nipped his lips before she pulled away. "I'll see you later, handsome."

He could barely think straight as she left, and he quickly set the kitchen to rights. He gathered his things and Vas, then walked him to school while the boy chattered incessantly. Even so, he liked the kid a lot. That being said though, he had no idea why the boy liked hanging out with him. Yet he did.

When they reached the school, Vas hesitated.

"Did you forget something?"

Vas tugged at his ear, then shook his head. With an adorable bashful move, he stepped into Jullien's arms and gave him a quick hug. Then he dashed off like battle-lorinas were after him.

Jullien grinned, warmed by the gesture. He waited until he was sure Vas was safely inside before he went to work.

But the strange normality of the day wasn't lost on him. How weird that here in this Tavali base with some of the most dangerous creatures in the universe he felt safe for the first time in his life.

Yeah, it was off.

And it was payday, he realized as he saw the bright orange slip in his locker. Grateful, he took it to the accounting office to trade it in first. But when they handed him the cred envelope, he knew it was a mistake.

He headed straight to Sheila's office where she was already in full rage mode with someone on the other end of her link. Yeah, he didn't really want to be on the receiving of *that*. Waiting patiently until she'd fully vented spleen and insulted every member of their gene pool, Jullien went inside to speak with her.

After slamming a few things around on her desk, she glared at him. "What's your damage?"

"Head injury at birth. Lack of parental love and support. Oppositional defiant disorder. And a blatant disregard for authority figures, particularly those in uniform and with badges. But that's not why I'm here."

That succeeded in making her laugh. "All right, Dagger. What do you need?"

He handed her the extra creds from his pay. "There was a mistake with my voucher. I wanted to make sure it got back to you."

Her gaze softened before she returned it to him. "There was no mistake. It's yours."

"I don't understand."

"It's a bonus, and a raise. You work harder than anyone else on my crew. Most days you do the work of three, and don't think I haven't noticed. You don't take all your breaks. You don't laze around or socialize. You come in, go straight to, and don't stop until you clock out. Plus I heard what you did yesterday. Admiral Trajen offered you that ship and you passed on it. It ain't right for you to take nothing when you could have had it all to yourself."

"Sheila—"

"Don't go getting soft on me, shithead. You know how I feel about that."

He grinned. "Okay."

"You earned that, boy. And you got a ship out there that needs to be stripped and cleansed for resale."

"Yes, ma'am." He started to leave.

"And Dagger?"

He paused to look back at her.

"You're a good male. Thank you for understanding why I'm such a bitch all the time. Ain't many what do. And for thinking about my daughter. I really appreciate it. You ever need anything, you let me know."

Inclining his head to her, he headed off to work.

"That was unproductive."

Ushara snorted at her council as they finished their video conference with the Tavali Qillaq ambassador. "Yeah well, I'm not interested in helping the Qill start a war. Officially. Trajen would kill us all. What the pilots do independently is on them. As a Nation, we are not getting involved in that mess. Now, if you'll excuse me?" She left the briefing room and headed for her office.

It had been a miserably long day. Dreadful to extremes. Nothing could make her smile at this point.

"Are you all right, Admiral?"

She growled at her receptionist. "I need a jug of painkillers."

Tyra laughed. "There's some in your top desk drawer. Should I get you a fresh bottle of water?"

"I would love you for it."

"Yes, ma'am." She got up to fetch some.

Ushara fell into her chair and opened the drawer. But instead of seeing the painkillers, her gaze fell to a single rose wrapped in a gold ribbon. A small card and beautiful bracelet was tied to the end of it. Her heart quickening, she pulled them free and opened the card to see a bold, masculine script.

Mu Kira,
I hope this brings the same smile to your heart that you have brought to mine.

                                        Faithfully yours.

Even though it was unsigned, she knew it was from Jullien. Pressing her lips together, she swallowed hard at the winged heart bracelet. On Andaria, these were never lightly given. And as she turned the heart over and saw that he had engraved her initial in front on the right wing and his was hidden on the back, beneath the left, she knew that he'd understood the gift and had done it with full knowledge of its significance.

These were reserved for Andarions who dared fall in love with those considered out of their caste. Star-crossed lovers who were forbidden by law to have a relationship.

It was a symbol of unrequited love or that which was unattainable.

And it was always given by the one who held the lower caste standing, and offered humbly to the one they deemed themselves unworthy of having—which was why her initial was on the front right and his hidden in the back, on the left.

Tears choked her as she cradled it in her hand.

"Admiral?"

Ushara cleared her throat. "Sorry. Did you see who brought this?"

"Brought what? No one's been in your office."

Leave it to Jullien. Her phantom prince. "Nothing." She held her hand out for the water and took it.

Ushara fastened the bracelet to her wrist and watched the way the light played in the red crystal. Her gaze fell from it to the picture on her desk of Vasili and Chaz that had been taken just days before Chaz's death. They were laughing and waving at her. It was the last time she'd seen that untainted happiness in her son's eyes.

Until today.

Why did he respond to Jullien the way he did? It made no logical sense.

"Admiral?"

She looked up at Zellen's voice to find him standing in her doorway. "Yes?"

He came forward with his link and handed it to her. "Your brother Dimitri just sent this over and he wanted me to make sure you saw it immediately. I told him I'd put it in your hand myself."

His ominous tone was terrifying. She clicked the news report and waited for the file to load.

A reporter stood outside the Overseer's Trigon Court on Gondara. "While details are currently sketchy, the reports are confirmed that it was the Outcast Andarion prince Jullien eton Anatole who raped and robbed the victim last night. In response to this latest heinous move, The League has increased the warrant on his life and updated the charges. We've been trying to get a statement from Anatole's parents, but neither the Andarion tadara nor Triosan emperor will comment publicly. The most we have is a statement from the Triosan ambassador who assures everyone that they will not harbor any fugitive from League justice and that Anatole has no landing privileges or haven within their empire. Likewise, the Andarion ambassador has confirmed that Anatole was officially Outcast from their society and holds no rank or protection under Andarion law."

Disgusted, Ushara turned it off and returned it to Zellen. "Jullien didn't do that."

"Doesn't matter. Someone is out there, using his name and upping the bounty on his life. They're trying to flush him out."

Yes, they were.

Meanwhile, his parents most likely believed that bullshit. "Send out two sifters and see what they can learn about this. I want to know as much as they can dig up."

"Why?"

"Because I don't like to see anyone framed for something they didn't do. And if it was this easy to pin this on him, doesn't it make you wonder about the rest of what he's charged with?"

Zellen shrugged. "He's an aristo. Who cares?"

"I care and I'm your CO. You're under orders. I suggest you follow them."

"Yes, ma'am."

As soon as he was gone, Ushara pulled up the updated warrant on Jullien. *Twenty-five million creds.*

Her head spun at the exorbitant amount. She'd never seen a bounty *that* high. What had they done? Taken up a collection?

Worse? Her well-meaning sisters had shaved off his beard. Now, there was no mistaking his features. Anyone who saw him would know instantly he was the Andarion prince.

They might as well have painted a neon target on his forehead and marked it "hey, shoot here!"

Her heart racing, she left to tell Jullien the wonderful news before he learned it in the most fatal way possible.

# CHAPTER 8

Jullien knocked on the door, then grimaced as he tugged nervously at his jacket. He'd forgotten how much nice clothes itched. Then he shrugged his shoulders, trying to alleviate the sudden irritant there. It literally felt like his skin was crawling.

Even more annoying, his chin was burning and itching like a mother as he tried to let some of his beard grow back. *Gah, I think I'm allergic to bathing.*

Honestly, it was a psychosomatic overreaction to anything that reminded him of his royal duties. He knew it. But understanding the cause and living with the consequences were two entirely different things.

And why was it taking Ushara so long to answer the door?

Had they left him? He checked the time. He was a little early . . .

Jullien knocked again.

Vasili opened the door, wearing an ornate red jacket that was trimmed in black and gold. His face had been painted and his white hair pulled back into a tight ponytail. He gave Jullien a wide grin that exposed his fangs. "Sorry it took me so long. I was trying to get the lines straight."

"No problem. I was afraid I'd gotten the time wrong."

Closing the door, Vasili frowned at the items in Jullien's hand. "What's that?"

"I didn't know if you used them or not. It's what we're required to have for temple entrance in Eris. But since you're looking at them like foreign objects, I assume they're unnecessary here."

He cocked his head to study them. "But what are they?"

"Prayer beads and a prayer wheel. Asukarian cap."

Vasili bit his lip. "May I touch them?"

"Sure." He handed them to the boy.

"What do you do with the beads?"

Jullien showed him. "You lace the chain through your fingers like this, and use the beads to count your prayers while you go through them. The wheel helps keep track of the prayer order and reminds you of where you are in the annual cycle so that you're honoring the proper god for the season."

"And why do you wear a hat?

Jullien smiled. "Warriors pride themselves on their braids. To cover them is an act of humility. You're showing the god Asukar that you are humble before him and his pantheon by covering them in his temple, and that you are a willing subject to the dictates of the gods."

"Ah. That makes sense."

"But you don't do that in your temple?"

Vasili shook his head. "Do you paint your faces on Andaria?"

"We do. However, given the history of the Fyrebloods and Andaria, I didn't think it prudent to walk into your temple bearing the marks of an Anatole or Nykyrian lineage on my face. While I have definite suicidal tendencies, I can think of far less painful and quicker ways to end my life. Like funneling liquid drain cleaner."

Ushara paused as she came out of her room and heard the tail end of Jullien's words to her son. Her breath caught in her throat at the sight of the two of them.

*Holy gods . . .*

This was the first time she'd seen Jullien truly dressed in finery. And he was absolutely stunning. He must have returned to the store her sisters had taken him to for clothes and purchased his new outfit for temple. While she'd seen suits like that worn by other males, they'd never done the justice to them that Jullien did. The black shirt and slacks hugged his ripped body as if they'd been tailor-made and cut exclusively for him. Likewise the dark red jacket he'd chosen was well-cut and understated. Nowhere near as fancy as most males wore for temple and yet it didn't need to be. Something about how he wore it made it debonair and highly fashionable. Especially with the plain black knit scarf that was wrapped and twisted around his neck with a shabby chic, casual style.

Wearing a pair of dark red-tinted, black-framed glasses, he didn't even look like the same individual. His features seemed more rigid and chiseled. More elegant and noble. High fashion and urbane. He held himself straighter, as if by putting on those clothes his royal training had

kicked into gear and it was as innate to him as breathing. While his regal mannerisms were evident at times normally, they were currently on
high display right now.

Yeah, she could easily see the royal, arrogant prick in him and yet
because she knew his other side so intimately, and because of the kindness
he was showing Vasili, she still found him utterly charming and adorable.

And when he glanced her way, and stumbled over his words, then
lost his composure entirely, he become totally lovable again.

*That* was definitely her Jules.

Smiling, she headed to him and kissed his whiskered cheek. "Hi,
handsome."

Jullien couldn't breathe as he felt her lips on his skin. Her breath
against his ear. Chills tore through him and left his brain malfunctioning. Worse, it left him so hard and aching for her that he couldn't think
straight.

And what she was wearing *really* didn't help his situation in the least.
"Is that normal temple fashion?"

The smile on her face only worsened his condition. "Is it not what
they wear on Andaria?"

"No. If it were, I assure you, I'd be the most faithful follower of all
time. And would have *never* missed temple a day in my life."

Vasili snorted at him. "Do you mind? That is my matarra, you know?
And I'm standing right here."

"Sorry, Vas." Still, Jullien couldn't take his eyes off her skimpy outfit.

While the skirt was long, it was made of a light silk that hung in
brown, green, and maroon panels from a leather and feather low-riding
belt. One that left glimpses of her upper thigh and hip exposed. Her top
was nothing more than an elaborate bra embellished with jewels that
fell down in waves over her stomach. Around her neck was a feather and
beaded neckpiece in the shape of a bird that had a trailing sheer white
cape in the back that attached at her wrists by beaded cuffs. Her hair had
been braided and coiled into an elaborate fall from the crown of her
head that was embellished with an ornate white beaded and feathered
headpiece that covered her ears. Beadwork framed her painted face
with chains and beads that crested over her forehead.

He toyed with the beads that hung to the side of her face. "You are
beautiful."

She smiled warmly. "Thank you." Then she held her arm up to show him that she was wearing the bracelet he'd left for her. "And thank you for my gift."

Now it was his turn to turn bashful again.

Wrinkling her nose, she jerked her chin toward the stool behind him. "Now take a seat, and I'll paint your face for you. And don't look so worried, Gŭr Tana. Sadly, it'll mean a cut in your caste, but as you said, we can't have an Anatole marching into temple without bloodshed. So today you'll have to go in as a lowly Altaan."

His hazel gaze burned into her with fury and snapped vivid brownish-green fire. "There is nothing lowly about the Fyreblood Clan Altaan or Davers. It is you who honors me by allowing my putrid skin to sully the reputations of your noble clans."

Tears choked her at his indignant tone. He meant every bit of that. It was truly heartfelt. And she hadn't even known that he'd learned the clan name of her husband. She'd never told him that Chaz had been a Davers.

Before she could stop herself, she kissed him.

"Oh, I'm out." Vas headed for the back of the condo.

Laughing, Ushara pulled away from Jullien. "Sorry, *mi courani!* Come back! I promise we'll behave."

Vasili returned, but he gave them both a stink eye as he did so. "You better."

Removing his glasses, Jullien closed his eyes, and held himself perfectly still while Ushara began painting her clan symbols across his face to match the ones on hers and Vasili's.

"The glasses are new," she said as she worked. "They're darker than the ones you were wearing when we met."

"These are prescription. I'd forgotten how much I missed seeing straight."

She blew across his forehead to help the paint dry. "Really?"

He opened his eyes to look at her. "Yeah. Up close it's hard. And because I'm hybrid, I have spectral problems with color distortion. Gives me massive headaches at times."

"Is that why they're tinted red?" She returned to painting.

He nodded. "It helps a lot. I'm also sensitive to UV, especially with artificial light."

"Can they not fix it with surgery?"

"They don't know how. 'Cause they're not sure what it is. Benefits of being a hybrid life form—there aren't enough others like me to understand it. As soon as the word *hybrid* ever left a doctor's lips my grandmother stopped listening and walked away. Her philosophy was always that I could suffer with it as punishment for not dying at birth."

"I'm sorry."

He shrugged. "Wasn't that big a deal until the last few years when I couldn't get replacements for broken lenses. Luckily, when assassins attack up close, they're large enough I don't need clear vision to find them."

She rolled her eyes at his humor. "So you're fine at a distance, then?"

"Yes. I only have trouble close up and with small print."

"How have you been programming?"

"I know how to blow the screens up. Have you see the size of my giant font, baby?"

She staggered back, laughing at the way he said that. "You're such a mess."

Someone knocked on their door.

"I'll get it." Vasili jumped from his stool.

"You ready to meet the whole Altaan clan?"

He actually blanched. "What?"

"You didn't realize that part of this when you agreed to it, did you?"

"*All* of them?" he choked.

She gave a solemn nod. "But don't panic. Don't get overwhelmed. Stick to me and Vas. We'll protect you."

"So how many Altaans are we talking?"

She shrugged as she added more paint to his face. "With in-laws . . . seventy-two."

"Holy *shkyte*!" He gaped. "Seventy-two? Please tell me you're screwing with me."

Ushara shook her head. "But it's okay. They may not all be in port. I'm just preparing you, in case. The only one really to avoid is Dimitri. He's got the biggest problem with Ixurians."

"And the ones who beat the hell out of me?"

"And them. They go without saying."

"Great." Sighing, he put his glasses back on. "Thinking right now when my brother gave me the option of answering his question or having my brains blown out, I chose poorly."

"Stop whining." She pulled him to his feet.

Jullien followed her to the door and braced himself for the *warm* reception he knew they were about to receive. Her parents, who were talking to Vas, fell silent as soon as they saw him.

Her father's eyes bulged as his cheeks darkened with anger. "What's *he* doing here, dressed like *that*?"

Ushara pulled Jullien out the door and locked it. "He's going with us to temple."

Petran turned toward her mother. "Katira? Have words with your daughter. Now!"

"Shara—"

With her head held high, Ushara pulled Jullien by the arm and kept going. "I've no wish to be late, Matarra."

Jullien looked back at her parents with an apologetic grimace.

Petran glared at her mother. "I blame your side of the family for this."

Rolling her eyes, she said nothing as she followed after them.

Ushara rushed to catch up to her sisters who were walking together as a group with their husbands and children. Dressed identically to Ushara, Oxana screamed the instant she saw them together and drew her sister into a hug.

Then she hugged Jullien and kissed his cheek. "Love the face! Altaan looks good on you." She took his hand and led him to the male who was carrying a small toddler girl dressed in a more modest version of her outfit. "Sparn . . . this is Dagger. He's the one who repaired my ship for us."

Sparn paused and shifted his daughter in his arms to shake Jullien's hand. "All blessings to you." He glanced around to the other three girls who were running between them. "As you can see, your help was deeply appreciated. Thank you so much."

"My pleasure."

Oxana brushed her hand through the hair of the infant girl in Sparn's arms. "This is our youngest, Olya." She pointed to the eldest. "Nadya, named for our yaya. Then the twins Iryna and Fena. Girls, say hi to Dagger."

Nadya, who was probably four or five, pursed her lips at him. "Why do you have dark hair?"

"Nadya!" Oxana snapped. "Don't be rude! Dagger isn't a Fyreblood."

"But he gots fangs? Why he got dark hair and fangs?" She gasped and ran to her father.

Jullien knelt down on one knee and held his hand out toward her. "I won't hurt you, Nadya. I promise."

Eyes wide, she looked up at her mother for confirmation.

"It's true, *couriana*. He's the one who saved your cousin Vasili."

"Really?"

Jullien nodded.

She approached him slowly. He held his hand up for her inspection. "See. I'm harmless."

After a few seconds, she laced her fingers with his and smiled. "Okay. I'll believe you if you carry me."

Jullien laughed as Oxana groaned.

"She's my con artist in training."

Gathering her in his arms, Jullien stood. "It's my honor to carry her."

"You say that now," Sparn grumbled. "But she's heavier than she appears."

Nadya stuck her tongue out as she settled herself into Jullien's arms and grinned happily. "Look Yaya! Naddi gots a ride to temple!"

"So you did, Naddicakes. So you did."

Ushara smiled at the sight of Jullien carrying her niece while walking with Vasili. It did the strangest things to her breathing. And gave her a strange, weepy feeling inside.

Mary snuck up behind her to grab her into a hug. "He's gorgeous, isn't he?" she whispered in her ear. "And tell me . . . how sexy is a male who carries a baby without complaint? Couldn't you just gobble that up with honey and biscuits?"

"Would you stop?"

"Can't stop. Not when it's something that fine." She made a purring noise.

"We're heading to temple and you're being awful."

"I need something to confess. And given that you had unlimited access to that hard, nice *crowpyn* I'm amazed you're walking straight."

Grimacing at her sister's vulgarity, Ushara prayed that Jullien couldn't hear them. But the devilish grin he cast her a few minutes later over his shoulder said that Mary's voice carried plainly to his exceptional hearing.

Great. That was all she needed.

As they reached the doors to the temple arena, Ushara sobered. Especially when she caught the expression on her older sister's face as Daryna waited for them inside.

It was chilling.

And by that cold, sinister glower, she knew Ryna would have an

earful for her as soon as she reached her. Though honestly, she had
no idea what she'd done to upset her older sister. Was it because of
Jullien?

Ushara glanced around at all the Fyrebloods coming to temple and
flinched at the large number. Before she faced her sister's wrath, they
had to get through the temple gate and the high priestess who was waiting to greet them and bless them on their way in. Maybe this wasn't the
best idea after all.

Suddenly, she felt sick.

Her heart pounding, she returned her gaze to Jullien. If he had any
fear or reservation about this, he didn't show a bit of it. Instead, he kept
his spine straight, his head held high and acted as if this was where he
should be. As if he had as much right to be here as anyone else.

But boy, did he stand out with his darker coloring. There was no missing the fact that he was a darkheart in the midst of those who'd been
brutally persecuted by generations of his predecessors.

*They're going to sacrifice him on the altar of my blatant stupidity . . .*

As they neared the priestess, Jullien set Nadya down so that Oxana
could take her hand and have her blessed. Then Jullien went up to the
high priestess.

"Greetings, blessed High Mother." He held his hands out, palms up-
ward, as if he'd done this a thousand times and was a practicing Demurrist.

She brushed them with her touch and marked them with her sacred
oil, then looked up and froze as she saw his face and took in his Ixurian
features.

Ushara heard her father curse under his breath as she held hers, fearing that Jullien was about to be rudely thrown out or asked to leave.

Or worse, set afire on the steps of their temple.

Instead, the elder priestess smiled warmly at him as she cupped his
hands in hers. "Welcome, *drey*. The gods truly smile upon you this day.
I often speak of a warrior's courage, but seldom do I see such in reality.
And I know it took a true Kadurr to walk unarmed and in peace to these
temple doors, knowing the hatred you'd face here." Kissing his hand,
she bowed before him. "I am humbled by your warrior's heart."

Jullien returned the gesture and kissed each of her hands in turn. "I'm
the one who's humbled by your gracious welcome, High Mother. And
perhaps not so much courage as simple contentious stupidity."

She laughed out loud. "And modest to boot." Clearing her throat,

she shook her head and struggled for composure. "Be welcome and blessings to you."

"And to you, High Mother."

As Ushara stepped up, the priestess narrowed her gaze on her. "Are
you the one who brought him here?"

"I am, High Mother."

She smiled. "The goddess is most pleased with you, *mu tina*. Rare is
the soul that sees the heart beneath its worldly trappings. Rarer still
is the one who isn't afraid to walk her own path through the brambles
that strive to prick her heels and cause her pain. For some thorny paths
are well worth the agony, for the rewards they bring are beyond measure."

"Thank you."

Once she was blessed, Ushara joined Jullien on the other side of the
entrance and waited for Vasili.

Ryna continued to glare a hole through her.

Irritated, she walked over to her older sister who had gone back to
having white-blonde hair again. Normally, Ryna dyed it a dark brown
or rich caramel to help blend with other Andarions since she tended to
fly into their territory more than the rest of them.

"What?" Ushara asked in agitation.

"I'm not talking to you." She turned her back on Ushara and spoke
to Vasili instead. "Did you know your matarra, my irritating little sister,
introduced this male to your aunts and not me? Did you? The gaggling
gander of geese, they get to meet him. What? Is she ashamed of the only
sister she has with a brain?"

Vasili stood there, wide-eyed and terrified as if afraid to even attempt
an answer or comment for her.

Then she turned to Jullien. "I'm Daryna or Ryna, by the way. You
can't miss me as the only female sibling she has who doesn't make you
wish you were headless or on another planet when I'm in a room with
you."

Jullien glanced about nervously. "Um . . . hi?"

"It's a pleasure." She turned back to Ushara and glared at her. "You're
such a thoughtless creature. Call me later."

Ushara let out an irritated sigh as Ryna flounced off. "Have I mentioned that all my sisters are crazy?"

"No, but I'm beginning to wonder."

Smiling, she took his hand and kissed it. "I have to go sit with the chorus. You two behave."

Vasili led him to an empty bench on the left, near the back of the open temple that had a dark burgundy canvas spread across ornate, arched columns. They sat down toward the middle, and almost instantly a group of males swarmed them. One he knew. Two more he recognized from his "welcoming" party in the bay. The rest . . . .

Well, judging by their similarity in features, he assumed they must be some of Ushara's seventy-two relatives. Strangely amused by them, Jullien leaned over toward Vas. "Let me guess . . . your uncles?"

"And cousins." He glanced over his shoulder. "My gre paran and gras-paran are on the pew behind us."

"Nice. . . . Glaring at me?"

Vasili nodded vigorously. "With a lot of hatred."

"Awesome. I'm not as paranoid as I thought." Jullien straightened and flashed his link on the icon for the liturgy so that he could review their schedule.

Vasili tugged at his sleeve. "Yet you appear amazingly calm."

"Well, they'll either gut me or they won't. No use worrying about it until happens. Although . . ." He scowled at the huge bastard on his left. "I do wish this lovely beast would either buy me dinner or put a bit more space between us before he publicly fondles me."

Muffled laughter erupted from the bench behind them. "You heard the boy, Kirill. Move over a bit and let him breathe."

Smoke literally came out of Kirill's nostrils before he complied.

Jullien turned around to see the elder Fyreblood seated next to Ushara's father. "Thank you for protecting my innocence, *Gûr Tana*."

"By the gods, you are a cheeky little bastard, darkheart."

"Vidarri! Mind your tongue in temple!" Scowling at him, she softened her expression as she leaned forward, toward Jullien and extended her hand. "I'm Ushara's yaya. Nadya. It's a pleasure to meet you. Dagger, was it?"

Pressing her hand between his, he bowed over it. "Yes, Ger Tarra. And the honor is all mine. I assure you. Until this moment, I thought Ushara took all her beauty from her mother. Now, I can't tell who she favors after more. Never has any family been blessed with more amazing females than yours."

She tsked at him. "You are a handsome charmer."

"I only speak the truth."

Kirril curled his lip. "Now can I hit him, Graspa?"

Vidarri actually considered it. "I'm quickly getting there."

Vasili snickered.

"Traitor," Jullien said under his breath.

He looked up with a stricken expression.

"I was only joking." Jullien put his arm around him and hugged him. "Relax, *mi tana*. I'd never be upset at you. Just don't get upset at me if I have to trip you to be an obstacle for them should I be forced to make a hasty run for the door."

He laughed again.

"Shh!" Nadya snapped at them all from her seat. "Service is starting."

Sobering, they rose as the chorus procession started and began leading the priestesses toward the dais and altar. It was only then that Jullien could truly appreciate how many of his enemies surrounded him.

And how much of an odd Androkyn out he was in this massive crowd. Yeah, this might not have been best idea.

Sadly, it wasn't his worst, either. Although, it was starting to rank up there rather high on his list of, "oh shit, I shouldn't have done that."

*It's not the first time you've stuck out like feces in a punch bowl.* And at least none of the individuals around him were pissed-off inmates who'd been imprisoned and tortured by his grandmother without due process.

Nor was he an unarmed, untrained child.

He flinched as a bad flashback tore through him. It took him a second to control his breathing and keep his composure. To maintain himself and remember where he was.

That he was safe. In control.

He placed his hand on Vasili's shoulder to remind himself that this was real. *This* wasn't a dream or hallucination. The other was just a bad memory. He wasn't there anymore.

*Breathe, Jullien. Breathe.*

But there had been a time when he couldn't control the panic attacks. When they had rendered him useless and left him a cowering wreck of volatile emotions.

And he wasn't the only one who'd suffered because of them in the past. Talyn Batur had been taken and brutalized because he'd been too far gone with one to stop his cousins. Had he been able to think straight and to control his panic attacks then, he would have never allowed

Merrell or Chrisen to arrest and exile the boy. Their stupidity wouldn't have sounded so rational to him that day. But when Talyn had violently attacked him, Jullien hadn't seen a boy coming for him, he'd gone to the darkest places of his past and had lashed out from there like a cornered dog. Talyn had paid dearly for the wrongs others had done him.

It was why Jullien didn't complain about being judged or punished for the ills of his family. Why he accepted it as his due.

He'd committed his own sins and wrongs while trying to protect himself.

And he hated himself for it.

Squeezing his eyes shut, he forced his thoughts away from the past. Away from the pain. He might have been a prince, but the whole time he'd lived in that palace, he'd lived like a feral animal, in constant survival mode. Striking out at everyone who ventured near him.

*Let it go and breathe.*

Jullien listened as they began to play a soft harp, electric piano, and drum, and watched as Ushara and the chorus danced and led them in song. Unlike the somber, depressing hymns he'd been taught, theirs were uplifting. They were about coming together and uniting. Standing together and defending each other. Being a family. And as they sang, Vasili hooked his arm through Jullien's.

A foreign warmth filled him, and before he could stop it, a forgotten dream sprang out the mental dungeon where he'd kept it locked down deep. It was the one where he was actually part of a real family.

He placed his hand over Vasili's and wished that he'd been lucky enough to have been the boy's father. It pissed him off that Vas's childhood had been tainted by such a tragic loss. The kid didn't deserve it, anymore than Ushara did. Jullien would never understand why hearts as gentle and kind as theirs had to be hurt. It just didn't seem right. He'd give anything if he could protect them and keep them safe from the universe.

A weird surge of protective possessiveness rose up inside him so fiercely that for a moment, he couldn't breathe. It was primal and raw. Overwhelming. He hadn't felt anything like this since the night he'd seen the guard strangling his mother. A furious need to make sure that no one and nothing came near what he loved.

*Loved . . .*

Jullien went cold as that random thought rattled around his three existing brain cells and iced every part of his being. As much as he wanted to deny it, the truth slapped him right in the face.

*I love them.*

Both Vasili and Ushara. The thought humbled him and he wasn't really sure what to do with it. Honestly, it scared him and made him want to run screaming for the nearest door. He'd never really loved anyone before. No one had allowed him to.

As the song finished and Jullien grappled with his rising panic, Vas grinned at him and sat down.

Knowing it would be bad form to run out on the service at this time like a screaming lunatic on an acid high, Jullien sat down, too, and forced himself to calm down.

He'd just begun to level out his panicked breathing when Kirill hissed and jumped beside him for an annoyed little bit of fluff who pounded on the male's beefy leg with her tiny fist until Kirill moved it aside to make room so that she could squeeze past him. With angry eyes, baby Nadya glared up at Kirill as she wiggled to the other side of his legs and then she smiled at Jullien and held her arms up toward him.

It took him a second to realize that the younger Nadya wanted him to pick her up again. "You want to sit with me?" he whispered.

She nodded eagerly.

Since her mother was in the very front chorus with Ushara, he glanced over his shoulder to make sure it was all right with her grandparents. When neither moved to murder him, he slowly scooped the little girl up and awkwardly perched her on the edge of his knee beside Vasili. She put one booted foot on Vasili's thigh, then leaned back against Jullien's chest and began sucking her thumb. Within a few minutes, she was sound asleep in his arms.

Completely at a loss, Jullien had no idea what to do. He'd never had a child fall asleep on him before. For that matter, he'd never really been around children. In a family that tended to eat its young before they grew into adults, they weren't in abundant supply.

So when it came time for the sacraments, he stayed in his seat with her and allowed the others to line up for the altar.

Instead of returning to her own seat in the chorus after she'd taken hers, Oxana came and sat beside him. "Sparn said that she'd escaped him by climbing under the pews. He thought she'd gone to my parents, but

I panicked when I didn't see her with them for sacraments, and then Vas told me she was with you. Are you okay?"

"Fine. She's been asleep the whole time."

"I can wake her."

"You don't have to. I can carry her home, if you want. She's really not heavy."

Nadya blinked and yawned. "Mama?"

"Right here, Naddicakes."

Rubbing her eyes, she fell forward, into Oxana's arms. "Is temple over?"

"Almost."

She frowned as she looked at Jullien. "Is Dagger my new basha?"

Laughing, she kissed her daughter's cheek. "No, honey, he's just Ushara's friend."

"Okay, but I like him. He smells nice. Can we make him my basha anysways?"

Oxana was still laughing as they stood for the final prayer and dismissal.

As the males of Ushara's family attempted to swarm him again, the females took flank positions around him as a layer of protection. That stunned him completely. The fact that it included her mother and grandmother shocked him most of all.

"Go on with all of you," her grandmother said, gently pushing the males back. "You can punch at him later. But let the boy alone for now. You've all growled at him enough for one morning."

As the males stepped away and left, Nadya the elder turned around with a pointed stare that reminded Jullien of a royal interrogator about to begin a torture session. "And what is your lineage, Ixurian?"

Jullien refused to flinch or let her know how much that question stung. Since Andarions were matriarchal, her opinion mattered and she was asking him for his own mother's opinion where he was concerned.

His shoulder itched, reminding him all too well how little his family valued him. "I'm Outcast, Ger Tarra."

"You weren't born without caste. What was it before you angered your mother and she slashed you from her lineage?"

"Does it matter?"

Her stare turned harsh and biting. "Depends on your intentions with my Ushara. What are they?"

"Yaya," Ushara chided. "What are you doing?"

"You bring him to temple, with your son. I'm doing what is my right." She faced Jullien with a ball-shriveling glare.

Ushara wanted to kill her family as she recognized the hurt in Jullien's eyes. It was subtle and unless you knew him as well as she did, you wouldn't recognize it.

To his credit, Jullien held his ground and didn't waver or show any weakness whatsoever, which was a good thing when dealing with her grandmother. If there was one thing Nadya Altaan hated, it was any kind of enervation in any creature. If she sniffed out vulnerability, she went for the throat of it.

It was what Chaz had despised most about her and it had kept them at odds the entire time Ushara had been married to him. The only reason he'd been allowed into the family at all was because they'd been pledged as small children. Years before her grandmother had discovered Chaz's dislike for fighting and weaponry.

Two things the prince had never shirked from.

When Jullien spoke, his voice was smooth and steady with its rich, noble accent. "My intentions toward her are extremely honorable, Ger Tarra. But I can give her nothing material as I have nothing left to give. That being said, I would gladly lay my life down to protect hers. And Vasili's. I would never allow anyone to do harm to either of them."

"Are you Tavali?"

"I am not."

"Then you need to go and find another female to shame. My *grastiya* is the vice admiral of this Nation and the well respected widow of a former admiral. I will not have her reputation tarnished by being linked to an Outcast comet slag such as you. Do you understand?"

He didn't so much as blink under the cruelty of those harsh words. But then, he'd heard worse from his own parents. "I understand, Ger Tarra. Forgive me for my dishonor to your family."

Ushara gaped as he started away. "Jullien, you stay right here." She gently took his hand in hers to keep him by her side. It was only then that she felt how rigid and tense he was. That she felt the slightest trembling in his touch.

Her grandmother glared at her.

Yet for the first time in her life, she defied their matriarch. "There are a few things he left out. He has nothing material to give because he traded his extremely valuable royal signet ring to pay for the repairs on Oxana's ship, and refused to take any repayment for the parts or labor. And in case you missed that first part, Yaya. His *royal* signet ring."

Her grandmother curled her lip in disgust. "You dare to bring one of *them* before *me*."

Ushara lifted her chin. "Depends. Are you going to slash my lineage, too?"

Jullien released her hand. "Shara, please. Don't fight with your family. Not over me. Stop before it's too late and you say something you can't take back." He urged her toward her grandmother. "I can't stand being the wedge that divides you from them. Take it from someone whose entire family ate itself whole. It's not worth the trauma. Don't let my blood poison yours. I'll go."

"But—"

"No," he said, sharply, cutting her off. "Mend this with them before it's too late. You've no idea how rare and valuable your family ties are. You take for granted what the rest of us would sell our souls for and I won't let you sever something that no amount of money can replace."

And with that, he was gone.

Tears welled in her eyes as she turned back toward her mother and grandmother who appeared far too satisfied with themselves.

"It's for the best."

"For whose best, Mom?" she asked.

"Everyone's."

But as Ushara saw the stricken expression on Vasili's face she knew better. It wasn't best for him. He wanted a father of his own so badly that it'd burned in her heart for years that she'd been unable to find a male tolerable before this.

And if she was honest, it definitely wasn't in her best interest.

Her grandmother frowned. "Would you really choose a darkheart over your family, Shara?"

She swallowed hard against the tears that choked her before she answered that with a question of her own. "Before you force me to that decision, Yaya, you might want to stop and think if you want to lose me and Vasili over your hatred of the Ixurians."

# CHAPTER 9

Heartsick and weary, Jullien ran his hand along the outside panel of the *Stormbringer*. Though she was an older ship, she was a thing of absolute beauty and grace. Antique with fine, subtle lines. Unlike modern ships, she'd been custom designed by a master engineer. Not stamped out in a factory by cold mechas and drones. This one had a human touch to her. Someone had taken personal care with her construction, and left no detail overlooked.

"Should I leave you two alone?"

He scowled at the familiar voice. Turning his head, he was surprised to find the high priestess there in regular Tavali gear. Strange, the High Mother seemed much tinier now than she had in her temple garb. Her white blond hair was pulled back into a severe bun. With her entire face painted stark white over her already extremely pale skin, she still had the black Samari clan wings drawn around her white eyes, with streaks of gem blue bisecting the wings and her lips. Even as an elder female, she was strikingly beautiful and must have been incredibly breathtaking in her younger years. Yet the loveliest part of her was her compassion and kindness. The way she had of looking at others as if she actually cared about them—like a mother should look at the children she loved and cherished. Not that he had personal experience with that. He'd only seen that expression when other maternal beings had gazed at their young, or when his own mother glanced at his brother and Nykyrian's children.

He lowered his hand and approached her. "Can I help you, High Mother?"

Shifting the basket in her hands, she smiled warmly. "A *xetetic* would call this a coincidence."

He snorted at the Demurrist term for a nonbeliever, or anyone not of their faith. "And what do you call it?"

"I'm more interested in what you think the odds are that you'd be working on my ship with such caring devotion?"

Jullien froze. "You own the *Stormbringer*?"

She ran her hand over the filigree design that wrapped around the underpanels. "I do and here I've been praying and praying for someone to get her back into service for me. Then lo and behold, I make my weekly check to see if my prayers are answered, and I find that someone has, indeed, finally accepted my repair request. I come to bring my generous benefactor a care basket, and thank them for their kindness, and it turns out to be . . . well, *you*. Again, what are the odds?"

As much as he'd like to believe in a higher power working magic behind the scenes to do good things for them, the delusion of a benevolent creature who gave a minsid damn about them belonged to small children and morons. His trust in such had died in childhood the day his grandmother had viciously told him she'd murdered his twin brother. "It's a random universe, High Mother. Weird shit happens without rhyme or reason every day."

"So you say. I choose not to believe it. The gods work their will in their own good time, to benefit us all." She held her basket out toward him. "I still wish for you to have this."

"Thank you, but I can't accept it. I don't do this work for payment, but rather my own penance." He sifted through the toolbox to find the right wrench for the access panel. "If anyone can understand that, I'm sure it's you."

"Are your sins that great, *m'tana*?"

He didn't comment as he opened the panel to look inside the drive and check the wiring there. At least now he knew what the priestess's given name was. According to the ship's manifest, she was Unira Samari.

"So what did you do to the old girl, anyway?"

She moved to stand behind him so that she could peek over his shoulder and watch while he rooted through the guts of her ship. "I primarily make relief runs through League blockades . . . which is why I haven't had the money to repair her. There's not a lot of profit in charity, as I'm sure you know. Things got a little hot on my last run and the Garvons took out a big piece of her drive and shield systems. We limped back into port. But she hasn't been the same since. She's been very testy with me over it. I can barely start her engines. Because she's so old, it's hard to find anyone willing to work on her, or anyone who has any knowledge of how to repair her. Many don't even know how to access her core or can read her old code. Every year it gets harder to find parts for her since they stopped manufacturing them decades ago."

"Why don't you replace her?"

She cast a weepy look at her ship. "We go way back, she and I. As I'm sure you can appreciate. You don't get rid of your best friend simply because she gets a little age on her, and isn't to most folks' tastes. I like to think that we're both getting better with experience. Not washed up. Besides, no one would value her. They'd simply buy her for the metal and circuits, then crush her for scraps, and I can't bear the thought of seeing something so precious needlessly destroyed because others can't take a minute to see the truth of what's right in front of their eyes."

Smiling at the inner beauty of the priestess's soul, Jullien linked and reviewed the diagnostic on his handheld. "Well, it doesn't look too bad. I think I can have her back in service for you in a couple of weeks."

Her entire face lit up. "Really?"

He nodded. "A little horse-trading with Sheila and some custom work, but it should be manageable." He paused as he studied the schematics. "And if you want, I should be able to boost the auxiliary firepower. It's a little dated as you said . . . still, it'll take a higher round than what you've been using for defense. That should keep the Garvons and others off you a bit. I can update the system, do a patch and make it carry more, too. If you're interested?"

"Really?" Unira repeated, excitedly. "That would be wonderful!"

"I can also tap the intake, boost your speed and slow the fuel lines, which will save you a lot on your annual running costs. She'll be a little slow on the initial takeoff, but you won't notice it in flight, or when you hit HD. So as long as you're not rabbiting out from a base, you'll be fine. Do you do that a lot?"

"No. It's usually mid flight when I encounter authorities."

"Well, I can rig a booster switch should you need more speed on takeoff. That would bypass the fuel savings and settings in an emergency."

She gaped at him. "You can really do all that?"

"Sure, it's extremely easy on these older-model ships. It's not that hard on the newer ones. You just have more code to bully and bypass. More coders and mechas you want to hunt down and slap."

Laughing, she stepped back and held up her gift in a teasing manner. "You'd really do all that for me and take nothing from my basket for yourself?"

Jullien shook his head. "I'm sure you can find someone far worthier and in greater need . . . such as the widows and orphans fund."

She lowered it to stare up at him. "Very well, then can I ask another question?"

"Sure."

"When can I look forward to seeing you at temple again?"

His stomach tightened at the reminder of the last time he'd seen Ushara and her family. It was what he'd been doing his best to not dwell on or think about.

Four days. It still hurt and felt like he'd been gutted. But then he should have known better than to let his guard down. To let himself think for one moment that he could have something for himself.

*"What's it like to know your own mother can't stand to look at you, Julie? That she screamed the first time she saw your hideous, hybrid form?"* He grimaced as he heard Merrell's hateful words being snarled in his ear with spiteful glee.

Sighing, he forced himself to face the cold, harsh reality that while he might have entered the world with a twin brother, he was going to remain forever alone in it. "I don't know."

The high priestess pulled a small wrapped, gilded book from the basket and held it out to him. "Here, m'tana. I insist you take this for yourself, if nothing else. It's a prayer book and cloth. Ushara told me that you were never given exordium on Andaria. It would be my honor to exord and confirm you in our faith. The classes are easy. If you're interested in joining them and converting, my number is in the back of the book. You can scan it into your link and contact me, whenever you're ready, should you ever choose to be."

Jullien took the book and stared at the bright purple cloth that was embroidered with their symbols of faith and the gold flower charm that dangled from the embroidery. "You'd exord me even though I'm Ixurian?"

She smiled kindly. "I see no Ixur before me. Only a rare Kadurr. If you're going to invent an alias for yourself, child. Pick one that actually fits your true nature." And with that, she walked off and left him.

Not sure what to think about her words, Jullien tucked the book into his pocket while he went to order the parts he'd need to begin repairs on her ship.

As he walked through the main landing bay, three other ships and their raucous crews were in the process of being unloaded and inspected for code and inventory, and logged for possible repairs by other crews. He didn't pay them much attention.

Not until an unknown object came flying at his head. Reacting on pure instinct, he caught it without hesitation.

The fact that it was a Caronese war-star and he hadn't cut his hand on it brought out an impressed noise from the reckless lunatics who'd thrown it at him. But it pissed him off to no end. Had he missed the catch or not seen it coming, he would have needed stitches, and it could have killed him or caused serious injury. Only a careless moron with no regard for the life of another would throw *that* at someone.

It was something his cousins or grandmother would have done for entertainment, and *that* definitely didn't help his soured mood—which was also why he was so good at catching such things. He'd been struck so many times as a young child that he'd developed heightened peripheral vigilance and assassin reflexes that allowed him to catch or deflect any object that came flying at him without warning.

Even in pitch blackness.

Jullien held the war-star in his hand, testing its heft, and debating the sanity of returning it to the sender.

With interest.

*Don't. Hold your temper.*

But it was a hard, hard thing to do when he was desperate to punch the Caronese bastard who was approaching him with a smug, dismissive smirk. Especially when old memories and flashbacks burned through him and added a need to strike out.

Damn the consequences.

"Sorry, slag. It slipped." He yanked it from Jullien's hand.

Jullien continued to hold himself perfectly still. *Ushara will have to answer for any action you take against him.* That alone allowed him to stay the course.

Even though his soul screamed for blood.

Something definitely not helped when another piece of scum from the bastard's crew stepped up to Jullien and slapped him, then laughed about it as he and his cronies danced off. The pain and metallic taste of blood in his mouth really set his fury into overdrive.

They had barely vanished before Davel Altaan was in his face, too.

Jullien ground his teeth. It was the first time a member of Ushara's family had come near him since their grandmother had publicly reamed him at temple. He curled his throbbing lip. "What is this? Tavali Ass-hole Day?"

Davel ignored his sarcasm. "Why didn't you hit them?"

With the pad of his thumb, Jullien wiped at the blood on his lips. "The last time I bitch-slapped one of your brethren who attacked me, I was told the blowback for it went to your sister. Contrary to what you think, I do care about her and I wouldn't hurt her for anything. So if losing my dignity and some blood saves her from a Calibrum, I'll take their shit and do nothing even though it galls the Tophet out of me."

"Is that the real reason?"

He gave Davel a droll stare. "You saw what I did to your cousins. You really think that group of *human cocúpün* scares me?"

"Oh well, in that case. Let's go teach them some manners, shall we?"

Jullien cocked his brow. "Don't tease me, Davel. It's cruel."

"I never tease about fighting, drinking, or sex. And don't worry. This blowback is on me, *drey* . . . and so's bail."

For the first time in days, Jullien smiled as he finally had something to look forward to. "Then lead on *mi dryht* Tavali." He pulled his glasses off and put them in their protective case that he left in the bay, along with his weapons—no need to tempt himself for a murder charge.

By the time they reached the bar where the others had gone, Jullien had his gloves on and was ready for payback. "I want the Caronese *chiron* who started this shit."

Davel gave him a sinister grin. "And I claim his slap-happy friend."


"Admiral? You're needed in lockup immediately."

Ushara scowled at Zellen, who wore a strangely amused expression on his face as he stood in the doorway of her office. "Pardon?"

"Anders said it was imperative for you to come, in person, ASAP."

Irritated that the commander of their Hadean Corps would dare summon her like that, she got up and headed for their quarters. She had no idea why the HC would be bothering her. Normally Anders was more than capable of policing the station without any interference from either her or Trajen. That was the entire point of having their division. Normally, HC only bothered her or Trajen whenever a verdict or sentence needed to be rendered for Calibrim—or a trial, or banishment.

But as she arrived in the HC offices, and saw her brother and Jullien handcuffed together on a prisoner bench like two guilty teens who'd boosted their parents' favorite skimmer for a joyride, she began to suspect why he'd demanded her presence this day. Their clothes were torn and bloodied, and both were sporting the kind of injuries that said they'd been in a violent and prolonged altercation of some sort.

*Please tell me they weren't fighting each other.*

Though, to be honest, had they gone at one another, she'd have expected them to be in far worse shape, given their skills and size. Plus she doubted they would have been able to handcuff them near each other after such a fight.

Once two Andarion males engaged in violence over a matter, they seldom quit pummeling each other until one of them was carried away on a stretcher. Unless they were blood brothers or held off at blaster point, they never stopped until an ambulance and enforcers were called.

"What did they do?" she asked the intake officer at the front desk.

She looked at Ushara and shook her head. "You want the whole grocery list or just the fun highlights?"

Ushara covered her eyes and sighed as horror filled her. Embarrassed and ticked off, she lowered her hand to her mouth so that she could glare at her brother, then Jullien. "Really? Really? How old are the two of you?"

"It's not Davel's fault."

"It's not Dagger's fault."

They spoke in unison.

"So now you're bonded. You're what? Fight bros? Browlers?"

"Could be Bringers," Davel said, which caused Jullien to laugh until he saw the fury in her eyes.

He sobered instantly.

Davel leaned against Jullien's shoulder. "Look on the bright side, *drey*. Your girl can't make you sleep at your mother's tonight. You don't have to go to bed to the wonderful sound of your parents bitching at you over what a disappointment you turned out to be."

"*Zēriti.*"

"Ah, don't be. It was so worth it. I just hate they took that ear from us so they could reattach it. I wanted to frame it for my wall."

"Oh dear God!" Ushara gasped. "You ripped off someone's ear?"

"I didn't." Davel pointed to Jullien. "He's a vicious bastard in a fight."

Jullien was unrepentant. "He came at me first. I was unarmed. He's the one who introduced cutlery into it. Besides, it was the lesser evil of what I was tempted to snatch off his body."

Ushara turned back toward the intake officer. "What do I have to do to get them out of here?"

"They've been bonded out. But after the damage they did, the HCXO marked them IRIS."

"IRIS?"

"I Require Intense Supervision. Anders didn't want to release them without direct supervision so he had me call you to take custody of them."

Davel let out a tired sigh as another HC unlocked their cuffs. "Yeah, the tattletale puss wanted to make sure Mom knew so she could spank our asses." Rubbing his freed wrists, he looked over at Jullien. "You might like that after dinner. But remember, she is my little sister. So, no gru-gru without pledging. Or else I'm going to have to bleed on you." He stood up and held his hand out to Jullien.

After helping him to his feet, Davel gave him a brotherly hug. "Later, *kiran*."

"Later, *mi drey*."

Walking sheepishly to her, Davel kissed Ushara's cheek. "Go easy on him, *kisa*. He's had a bad day. And you should know I've offered to sponsor him on my crew. We need to get him off the docks before someone kills him. It's open season for anyone out there without a patch, especially someone like *Dagger*. He's had a couple of really close calls today. If you have any feelings for him at all, don't send him out there again."

Stunned, she watched her brother leave, then turned back toward Jullien. "What did you do to him?"

He paused by her side as the IO handed him his things. "Nothing. But he did get bashed in the head pretty hard. *That,* I tried to prevent."

She led him from the office, back toward the landing bay so that he could pick up his coat, weapons, and glasses. "So what happened, anyway?"

He shrugged nonchalantly. "Assholes came in. Davel saw them in all their *charming* glory. We decided to teach them some manners."

"There are easier and much cheaper ways to teach manners."

Jullien snorted. "Not if you're Andarion."

Ushara paused as she realized what Davel had said to her. And what it meant. "Did you tell my brother who you really are?"

"Your father did."

While she trusted her brother, she wasn't sure she liked so many people knowing about Jullien's outstanding warrant. Davel wouldn't hurt him, but he wasn't always the most judicious when it came to keeping secrets, either. He ranked right up there with her gaggle of sisters.

"You know, if Davel sponsors you . . . you'll be gone from base most of the time. I'd rarely see you."

Tucking his hands into his back pockets, Jullien gave her an adorable, boyish sideways glance as they headed out of the bay, toward the living quarters. "Will you miss me?"

"I think I will." She couldn't tell how he felt about that. He had an irritating ability to hide his emotions.

"Well, I'm not leaving right away. He won't go until after the baby's born."

"That's any day now."

"Yes, but he said he won't leave until after the Day of Division."

That wasn't *that* far away. And the thought of Jullien leaving with Davel's crew made her ache deep inside. Much more than it should. It was actually excruciating. "Then I expect to see more of you between then and now."

"Really?"

"Yes."

"Okay." He rubbed his chin. "I'll gain more weight."

She laughed at his teasing tone. "Jullien!"

"Oh . . ." he said, drawing the word out. "You meant *come over.* Like play at your house . . . 'cause I'm just a *juvenile* delinquent. Right?"

She bit back a smile at his light, teasing tone and the playful light in his eyes. "Well, if you insist on behaving like one. . . ."

He brushed his thumb speculatively over his bottom lip while they walked. Then he gave her the most adorably charming grin she'd ever seen on any male's face, and it made her incredibly warm and tender inside. "Do I still get my spanking later?"

How she could find him so desirable, she had no idea and yet, she'd never been this attracted to anyone. "Do you want one?"

"Not really." He paused for a second to consider something. "Unless you're wearing that outfit you had on at temple. Then I could be per-suaded to take it like an Androkyn . . . and relish it."

She snorted. "Now you're being sacrilegious."

"Yeah well, if I'm bound for Tophet, let it be for something good, I say."

Shaking her head at him, she laughed. "You're incorrigible."

"Can't help it. My mind runs on inappropriate thoughts. Besides, you bring out the worst in me."

"Really?" she dragged the word out, slightly offended by that thought. "The *worst*?"

Jullien nodded playfully as he stared at the most beautiful female he'd ever seen in his life. Before he could stop himself, he brushed the pale hair back from her soft cheek. The light in her eyes scorched him.

More than that, it made his mouth water for a taste of her. God, how he'd missed her these last few days. She was all he could think about. Whether she was with him or not, she stayed with him like his own private demon.

Damn her for that . . .

And damn him.

"No, Shara," he breathed honestly. "It's not true. You make me a much better Androkyn. I actually walked away from the fight at first, *because of you*. And I've never done that before in my life. Believe me. If there's trouble to be had, I'm always there with both hands out."

"Then how did you get pulled back into it?"

Cringing as he realized he'd accidentally screwed her brother, he brushed his fingers along her jaw. "I'm going into stealth mode now. I just walked into a bad place with no clear, safe exit."

Regretfully, he stepped away from her.

She narrowed her gaze on him as she invaded his personal space to confront him. "So Davel dragged you into it, I take it?"

"I didn't say that. I was definitely a willing participant for the entire event. Walked there on my own two feet, and everything."

Ushara let out an agitated breath as she pressed her forehead against his cheek, and sank her hand into his soft hair to hold him close. One of the best things about him was also the most aggravating. He accepted all blame as his due.

With full responsibility.

The true mark of a leader. Whether it was hardwired because of his birthright or beaten into him from his parents and grandmother, he never tried to weasel out of blame. He might hide the truth a bit, but he didn't hide his part in it.

She'd also discovered these last few days as she'd done more research into his warrant and past exactly how much his grandmother hated him. There were no records left of him on Andaria.

At all.

Nothing other than the hostile, mocking articles of reporters roasting him and holding him up for public ridicule. No birth registration. No caste listing. Every trace of Jullien eton Anatole had been erased from their systems. It was if he'd never been born. He wasn't even listed in the royal family histories.

They'd purged him entirely.

For all intents and purposes, he was persona non grata.

And it wasn't much better on Triosa. There were no birth or school records. While they hadn't gone so far as to remove him from their royal family tree, he'd been relegated to not much more than a footnote and listed simply as the younger half-Andarion bastard son of Aros Jullien Triosan. Disinherited from royal succession on the seventeenth day of Elembiuos, 8561.

No first or last name given for him. He had been erased from their lives as if he didn't matter at all. As if he had no significance to his family whatsoever.

But that wasn't true where she was concerned. In spite of what they thought and how they treated him, she saw his noble heart beneath his bluster. The insecurity that undermined his arrogance. And the adorable, playful bit that peeked out from under the rough countenance of a fierce, weary warrior.

"Come home with me, Jules. Vas is spending the night with a friend. I can make you dinner and listen to you complain about my cooking instead of my son."

He chuckled lightly. "Remember, I'm easy to please. No matter how bad you think your cooking is, it'll never be the worst thing I've tasted, and I would never complain. As long as you don't poison me, spit or piss in it, I'm ecstatic and grateful."

Those words made her stomach ache. "I really wish that were a joke."

"Not as much as I do, I assure you." He took her hand and placed a searing kiss on her palm. "Lead me home, *mu tara*. As always, I am helpless against your will."

It didn't take long to swing by the grocery store and pick out a light dinner, then head back to her condo.

Jullien started washing and cutting the vegetables while she changed out of her uniform and into more casual clothing. Then she took over so that he could open and pour their wine.

"You sure you don't want me to cook?" he asked as he handed her a glass.

She fed him a piece of bread. "No. I've got this. While I may not be as accomplished as you are, I can do basic comfort foods. Now let me dazzle you with my ineptitude."

He snorted as he drifted away from the counter to look around her living room at the pictures on her walls and shelves of Vas and her family. When he came to the old keyboard console she had near the sofa, he frowned. "Is this what I think it is?"

"Electric keyboard?"

He glanced at her. "You play?"

She shook her head. "Not a single note. Vasili wanted lessons a few years ago. It lasted about six days before he got bored and gave up. I keep it around in case he gets interested again. It's one of those things I know the day after I sell it, he'll want to do it again." She caught the reverent way he was looking at the abandoned instrument. The way he caressed the dusty case. Like a lost, forgotten friend. "You play?"

"Used to. But it's been a long time."

"Go ahead and amuse yourself. I promise I won't laugh. There's no way you can torture it more than Vas did. It sounded like a dying yaksen the whole time he attempted to play it."

Snorting, Jullien sat down, opened it up, and tapped a few keys, then winced. "It's way out of tune. That might have been part of it." He hummed and toyed with the sliders on it for several minutes until he brought it back into harmony.

Ushara was impressed that he could tune it so easily by ear. She knew from watching Vasili and his instructor that it wasn't that easy to do even with a tuner. Because it was old and had been well used at the time she'd purchased it, they'd struggled to keep it in tune and had complained about it incessantly. However, Jullien didn't seem to have any problem finding the right pitch.

Once he was satisfied, he began to play an extremely complicated piece. Her jaw dropped at the unimaginable skill he possessed.

*Holy gods . . .*

It was like listening to a recording of a master virtuoso. His touch was so light and delicate. Precise and elegant. He didn't miss a single note. She'd never heard anyone actually play like that live before. Not with *that* kind of accomplishment. He made the instrument come alive as if it were a breathing creature. Her chest tightened with the emotions he wrung from her as he played as if he were divinely inspired.

She wouldn't have thought anything could sound more incredible.

Until he closed his eyes and started singing in a deep, rich bass. It was only a low rumble as if he was too timid or embarrassed to sing out loud. But it was beautiful, and his pitch was as tone perfect as his playing.

Tears blinded her as she struggled to listen to every note. He sang like an angel.

Breathless, she crossed the room to stand by his side.

He stopped instantly and cleared his throat. *"Zēritui."*

"Sorry? Oh my God, Jullien! That was incredible. Where did you learn to play and sing like that?"

Reaching for his wine, he gave a humble shrug. "Lessons were required as part of my education, six times a week. But I was never good enough for a recital."

Never good enough? Was that a joke? "Said who?"

"Everyone. My grandmother and instructors. My aunt. Father. Cousins . . . guards who groaned whenever I sat down to practice. Even the guard dogs and trained battle-lorinas would howl and whine at me, then run and hide under furniture."

Anger poured through her at their vicious, jealous cruelty. At what they'd stolen from him for no reason whatsoever. "Jullien, they lied to you. You have to know that. Surely you can hear how well you play and sing. Can't you?"

Yet the sincere light in his eyes said that he honestly thought himself incompetent. "I was okay, maybe when I was younger. But that was a long time ago. As I said, it's been years since I touched one. I'm way out of practice."

She let out a scoffing laugh. "If this is you out of practice, I can't imagine what you must have sounded like then. I want to hear more. *You* keep playing." She put his hands on the keyboard. "I mean it."

"Gah, you're bossy."

"That's why I'm the vice admiral."

Snorting, he ran through a scale. "I really don't remember too much more."

By the time she finished dinner, he'd started playing and singing a ballad she'd never heard before. "That's beautiful. Who wrote it?"

Getting up, he gave her a bashful grin. "I did, just now."

"Seriously?"

He nodded, then in the sweetest of gestures he wrapped himself around her and held her with her back to his chest and his face buried in her hair. She could feel his fierce heartbeat against her shoulder and his erection against her hip, as he surrounded her with his strength and warmth. His muscles flexed while he gently rocked her.

She leaned back in his arms, surrendering her weight to him. "Are you all right?"

Jullien couldn't speak as he let her gentle presence soothe him. He'd felt safe so rarely in his life that he knew to cherish it while he could. This wouldn't last.

It never did. There had never been a time in his life when he'd had even a glimpse of heaven without there being massive hell to pay for it.

He was terrified of letting her go. Terrified of this night ending and being banished back to the cold where he was forced to live. All he wanted was to stay here. To have the right to share his broken life with her.

Forever.

"Jullien?"

Closing his eyes, he kissed her cheek. "I just wanted to thank you for dinner. I know how hard you worked all day. The last thing you needed to do was come home and feed me, especially after having to get me out of jail."

Ushara growled at him as she suppressed her anger over that little bit that dampened her tender feelings. "Don't remind me."

Impishly, he nibbled her fingers. "It smells good." He gave one sexy nuzzle that left her breathless before he moved to hold a chair for her. "You sit and I'll serve you."

"Really?"

"Only fair. You did the hard part."

She slid into the chair and watched as he quickly made plates for them and refilled their glasses. He could be so incredibly thoughtful and sweet. She'd never met a male like him before. He appreciated every little kindness he was given in a way no one else did.

Yet even so, she couldn't help teasing him. "Hmmm, I think you just wanted to make sure I didn't contaminate your food."

Laughing, he pushed his glasses up on his nose before he sat down next to her. "Notice, I've given you my complete trust. I've barely examined anything." He playfully pulled his own cutlery out of his coat pocket.

She let out a high-pitched laugh. "No! You really carry your own set?"

He folded them and returned the cutlery to his pocket. "I do, indeed." Then, he reached for his napkin and placed it in his lap and took her fork. "See." He wiggled it between his fingers. "Total trust."

He playfully sniffed at it.

Shaking her head at him and laughing, she took his hand in hers and caressed his fingers. "You break my heart."

He gave her a stricken look. "I don't mean to. You're the last one I'd ever hurt."

"I don't mean it that way. What they've done to you. . . . It's so wrong."

"Not really." Clearing his throat, he wiped his mouth and took a deep drink of his wine. "I promise you, I have an equal share in the fate that's befallen me over the years. I've spent a great deal of my life playing hard to get along with. Most of what happened in my past stems from my utter lack of cooperation with others. In case it's escaped your notice, I'm quite the contentious asshole."

She laughed so hard at his dry, serious tone that she choked. After clearing her throat, she smirked at him. "Name me one thing you could have changed." She held up her index finger. "One."

He sat back and crossed his arms over his chest. "I did not have to piss in the courtyard pool of the Triosan palace during my grandfather's sixtieth birthday party."

Shocked and horrified, she burst out laughing again. "No! What? Why?"

Sighing, he rubbed adorably at his forehead before he sat up and returned to eating. "I was seven and it was the first time I'd been allowed back to my father's for a visit after my brother's death. So it was awkward to say the least—they were all virtual strangers to me and I was rather angry that my father had abandoned me for two years after Nyk's death without so much as a single *hey surviving son, are you still breathing?* Plus

I wasn't used to being around humans anymore. They kept staring at me and whispering and gossiping bad things about me."

"Like what? What could they possibly say about a seven-year-old child?"

"How fat and revolting and animalistic I was. Speculating on how many humans I'd eaten to be my freakish size at my young age. I'd been rudely inspected, pinched, grabbed, and prodded in some rather private places by far too many, and I was done with it. For the two days I'd been there, I'd kept trying to talk to my father and he'd kept brushing me off with sorry excuses. Pawning me off on a viciously rude nanny who sneered at me whenever she glanced my way, and pinched me every time I said or did something she didn't like. Which was every time I opened my mouth."

"Is this where your Amazonian cousin comes in?"

He paused while buttering his roll. "You remember that?"

She nodded.

Jullien set his butter knife aside. "Well, Lil's not to blame for this one. Rather, it'd been a particularly grueling day without her. I'd felt like shit. My mother was in a mental institution at home, which was why I'd been sent to my father. After an all-day session of being told how repugnant I was, what a crazy whore had birthed me, and how unwelcome I was on Triosa, I just wanted to be left alone and was trying to be as invisible as possible. At some point as I hugged the shadows and silently went for more cake, I overheard my grandfather sneering to his friends about how my very presence there embarrassed him on his birthday. He said I was being obnoxious and going out of my way to take attention away from him. And here I thought I was being good, staying out of everyone's hair, and being inconspicuous by hovering alone in my dark corner all night. I really had been doing my best to stay out of everyone's sight, with my head down, and hadn't spoken to a soul in hours. But as he continued to rail about what a sorry excuse for a grandson I was, and how he hated that the grandson who looked human was the one who died and I was the one he was stuck with, the Koriłon sank his bloody talons in me and I thought, fine, old man . . . you want embarrassment? It's on, bitch. I set my cake down—and you know I mean business when I lay uneaten cake aside—put my shoulders back, waddled my little fat ass over to the fountain, unzipped my pants, whipped it out and colored their fountain water right there in front of them all while yelling, Happy Birthday, you old bastard. Hope you choke on your fucking happiness. You want to see what an Andarion penis looks like, bitches? Here it is."

She burst out laughing. "Oh dear Saint Saren. No, you didn't!"

"Yes, I did. I still have my father's hand prints on my ass from the beating I got afterward to prove it. And at least I finally got the old bastard to talk to me. Granted, all he did was shout, but it was words and they were directed at me, in the same room."

Covering her mouth, she stared bug-eyed at him. "I can just imagine the humans screaming in horror."

"Yeah well . . . As I said, I am guilty of a lot of instigation when my Fuck-it List kicks in. My temper and mouth are not my friends. I have a bad tendency to walk around half-cocked on my best day. And that was one of my particularly stellar evenings. If there is a right or wrong thing to do in any given situation, my innate tendency is always for whatever is going to get me into the most trouble."

She watched as he ate his food. "You are definitely not a peacemaker."

"Most Andarions aren't. And I, in particular, am not."

She reached for more wine. "My husband was."

He arched a brow at that. "Seriously?"

Nodding, she took a bite of bread. "Chaz flew on a human Tavali crew. He was actually a pacifist."

"And you agreed with his philosophy?"

"I didn't disagree with it. It was soothing to be around him, especially after being raised in the middle of my lunatic brothers who would run at each other's throats over every little insult. In comparison, Chaz was very tender and quiet."

She paused at the stricken expression on Jullien's face. "What's that look for?"

"What look?"

Ushara gestured at him. "That one. Right there. . . ." She brushed her hand against his brow to smooth his frown away. "It's not an indictment against you, Jules. I like the fact that you're different from him. I don't want you to be the same as Chaz. Ever. Besides, it was his convictions that got him killed."

"*Zēritui.*"

"Me, too," she said sadly as her throat tightened. "I miss him a lot." She brushed at the tear on her cheek that fell past her control.

Before she realized he'd even moved, Jullien was by her side, pulling her into his arms. He held her against his chest and cupped her face in his warm hand.

Biting her lip, she swallowed hard at the tenderness she felt for him. He'd never been held when he'd been hurt and yet he didn't hesitate to comfort her. She leaned her head back to stare up at him.

"I can't believe you allow me the honor of touching you," he whispered as he lightly brushed the backs of his fingers over her cheek.

"It's because I love you, Jullien." The words were out so fast and effortlessly that she couldn't even stop them.

And he didn't take them the way she would have expected. He released her and staggered back as if she'd slapped him.

"Jules?"

With a panicked frown, he blinked slowly.

"Did you hear what I said?"

"I heard. But I don't understand."

She rose to her feet. "What part?"

"All. Any . . ." He scowled at her. "Why?"

"Why do I love you?"

He nodded. "Um, yeah. Let's start there."

"Really?" she asked with a bitter laugh. " 'Cause this is not how these discussions usually go and you're beginning to piss me off. Which for the record, doesn't usually go well for the male."

Stepping back from her, he brushed at his brow with his knuckles—a gesture she was beginning to recognize as one he did anytime he felt extremely uncomfortable in a situation. "Discussions of any sort don't usually go well for me, so that's nothing new. But this—" He waved his hand between the two of them. "This is an entirely foreign landscape. I have no ability to comprehend what you're even talking about."

A horrible realization went through her suddenly. "No one's ever said that to you before, have they?"

"No." He shook his head. "No, they have not."

"Never?" she tried again.

There was a strange, panicked look in his eyes as if he might bolt. "Only that they'd love for me to die. That they'd love for me to contract a venereal disease and rot. But *no*. The *I love you,* period. Only been said around me to others. Closest *I've* ever personally come to it was a priest telling me once that he hoped the gods loved me because no one else ever could. So you'll have to forgive me if I'm a bit skeptical that you alone possess this incredible supernatural ability to love that which is unlovable. By *anyone* else."

She was completely aghast at what was obviously the truth and yet so far beyond belief that it floored her. But it made sense as she remembered seeing the pictures of him with his family.

No one had ever held Jullien. Not even as a child.

They always stood apart from him, giving him their backs. No, none of them would have ever told their son that they loved him.

"I can't imagine anyone knowing you and not seeing how wonderful you are. Or maybe, I'm defective, too. I'll go with that. Because all I see is a warm, hilarious male I love spending time with." She walked slowly forward and reached up to lay her hand against his cheek.

He cupped her face in his hands and gave her the hottest, hungriest kiss of her life.

Ushara shook from the force of his passion. Reaching up, she pulled his glasses off and set them aside. His breathing ragged, he scooped her up in his arms and carried her to the bedroom where he wasted no time stripping her clothes from her, and then removing his own. He didn't slow until he got to her panties. Those he removed at an excruciatingly snailish pace as he teased and stroked her skin with his hands.

"Are you trying to torture me?"

"No." He looked around uncomfortably.

Determined to show him how much he meant to her, she rose up on the bed and forced him to lie back.

Jullien couldn't breathe as she gently stroked and teased his cock. Whenever she touched him like this, she owned him, mind, body, and soul. He had no will where she was concerned. She had no idea how much control she had over him.

Since the day he'd drawn his first breath, he'd been a defiant bastard. Contentious. Smart-mouthed. Belligerent. Surly and nasty.

But his admiral had declawed him completely. Effortlessly. No one else had ever made him heel. Not the guards of his prison. His grandmother. His father.

Well, Nykyrian had quelled him in Camry's. But only because Merrell and Parisa had overdosed him on Bliss with the intent to kill him that night. Had he been sober, that scene in the restaurant would have played out differently, too.

Nyk had no idea how lucky he was that Jullien had been too high to fully react and counter his assault that night.

And that was the last thing he wanted to think about right now.

His heart pounding, he watched as Ushara gently rolled a condom over him. Then, she kissed her way up his abdomen until she reached his lips. Taking his hands into hers, she lifted her hips and impaled herself on him.

He growled deep in his throat as she led his hands to her lush breasts and started the sweetest swaying dance against his hips.

She leaned forward over him, allowing her white hair to sweep against his chest while her pale gaze held his captive. The warmth of her hands sent chills all over his flesh.

"I love you, Jullien eton Anatole. And I intend to keep saying it to you until the day you actually believe it." She gave him the hottest kiss of his life.

He tried to catch his breath as she made love to him. But honestly, he couldn't think straight. Not while he felt like this. There was something feral and primal in him that wanted to wrap around her and protect her. To make sure nothing ever harmed her again.

It was fierce and demanding and undeniable. Taking her hands in his, he pressed one against his racing heart and the other to his lips. The scent of her skin and the sensation of her thrusting against him sent him over the edge. With a primal growl, he came so forcefully that he shook against her.

Ushara smiled in satisfaction, but as Jullien opened his eyes, she gasped.

They were blood-red in the darkness of her room.

He froze instantly. "Ushara?"

She swallowed hard before she responded. "You're stralen?"

"What? No."

Eyes wide, she nodded before she reached to touch his cheek. "Baby, you're stralen." As gently as she could, she slid from him to pull the mirror from her nightstand drawer and showed it to him.

Gaping, he poked at his eyes. "How's this possible?"

"You must have the gene."

"Anatoles don't have it. They've *never* had it. And neither do the Nykyrians. No family on either side of mine has ever possessed the gene."

She wiggled the mirror in his face. "Jullien. You can't argue *this*. You know the rules of genetics. Same as me. There are only three carrier families in all of Andarion history known to be stralen. Two warrior clans. One Fyreblood. You have to be related to one of them."

He let out a nervous laugh as he sat up and took the mirror from her hand to study his eyes more closely. "Well ain't this a bitch? Nyk and I are freaks, but not just because of our father. What do you want to bet that the real truth behind the insane Purging on Andaria is that Eriadne screwed a Fyreblood?"

"What?"

"Think about it . . . Nyk's blond. *White*-blond. I'm stralen. I'd bet a million creds if there were any surviving records . . . but we'd never find them now—Eriadne's not that stupid or careless, that my mother's father would be a Fyreblood Samari—the carrier family. It makes sense, right? Originally, Eriadne didn't go after the Fyrebloods at all. Only the Winged clans and that was a personal grudge against the Baturs who'd threatened her power. Once they were chased out, she'd calmed down and stopped the slaughter, until about the time she became pregnant with my mother. Then it came back with a vengeance against the Fyrebloods, and in particular the Samari clan. I'd always wondered why she went after them so vehemently. *This* would definitely give her a reason."

"But you said you looked like your uncle?"

Jullien let out a bitter laugh as he considered it. "Yeah. That makes even more sense. Eadvard was only about ten months older than my mother and he was always my grandmother's favored child—above all of them. They both could have been illegitimate. Would explain why they were born so close together when the rest of them weren't. And why my grandmother really cut my grandfather's throat. He might have found out the truth and threatened to say something, or he could have confronted her over it. With Eriadne, who knows? Hell, I could actually be a War Hauk. Wouldn't that be some shit?"

"But whatever you are, Jullien, you're stralen for me." She smiled at him.

That sobered him instantly as reality sank in. "You are in so much trouble . . . Damn *Ger Tarra*. What have you gotten yourself into? You don't want to be involved with my sorry ass. I'm just not worth this kind of trouble."

"I emphatically disagree."

Reaching up, he pulled her down across his naked body so that he could hold her.

There in the faint light, Ushara saw the anguish in his red eyes. She felt the tenseness in his arms as he pressed his lips to her forehead.

"No, Ushara, you don't want to be with me. Ever. Everything I love is violently ripped from my life," he whispered, his voice filled with the same misery she'd seen in his eyes. "Therefore I dare not love anything." He brushed his hand through her hair. "Yet I cannot live without you. What am I going to do?"

"Trust in me, Jules. I'm not going to abandon you."

"It's not abandonment I fear, Shara. I can take solitude. I actually prefer it." He swallowed hard as he stared at her. "It's betrayal I can't handle. Don't ever choose another over me. I've always taken second place in everyone's affections. That's what I can't forgive. Just once, I want to come in first."

"That you do."

He kissed her again, then rubbed his nose against hers. "With one exception."

"And that is?"

"I will understand that Vasili is always first in your heart. As your son, he should be there. He's the only one I will cede your affections to."

Tears filled her eyes and choked her. "That's one of many reasons why I love you."

"I love you, too, *mu tarra*. And it terrifies me. But I swear by every god you believe in that I will never break your heart."

"You keep that vow, and I swear that you'll never again be left out in the cold."

Jullien wished it were that simple, but he knew better. Her gods had no use for him.

And neither did this universe.

Cupping her cheek, he nibbled her lips. "I meant what I said, Shara. I won't divide you from your family."

"Then we will make them accept you."

The way she said that, he could almost believe in miracles. But he wasn't a dreamer. He knew the futility of reaching for things he couldn't have.

Still . . .

She made him want to believe again. To hope. To dream. She, alone, mended the broken pieces of his life and made him feel whole again. It was stupid, but he couldn't deny what he felt.

He wanted to believe in the impossible.

But did he dare? How many times could one being be kicked down in his life and still find the strength to stand up again? It was one thing to take shit for himself—to have his nose rubbed in it, but another to watch that flak fly at someone he cared about. He had a hard enough time navigating the barbed missiles aimed at his own head. He didn't know how he'd deal with those that would come for Ushara.

*You're an unstable, psychotic bastard.*

Nyk had been right about that. Not even Jullien knew how he'd react to things.

Until it was too late.

Yet Ushara calmed him in a way no one ever had. If he ever had a hope of being normal—of fitting in—she was it. *Maybe there is a future for me here . . .*

Jullien was just starting to relax when her link went off with Vasili's ring. He reached for it and handed it to her.

She kept her head on his bare chest as she answered it. "Hey, Vas, what's . . ."

He heard the tears in Vasili's unintelligible voice as he struggled to speak. Concerned, he rolled out from under Ushara and got up to turn on the lights while Ushara scrambled from the bed.

"I'm coming, baby. Don't worry. I'm on my way." She hung up and searched for her clothes.

"What happened?" Jullien handed her what she'd been wearing earlier.

"I don't know. He was too upset to say really. I haven't heard him like that in a long time." She took the clothes from his hand, then paused as she realized he was dressing, too. "What are you doing?"

"I'm coming with you." Whoever had upset Vas was about to meet the worst side of him. "They hurt your son, they hurt you. And *no one* hurts you, *mu* tarra."

Ushara would normally argue, but right now, she was grateful to have someone else with her. She didn't know what she was walking into or what she'd find. Over and over, she kept seeing Vasili as he'd been the night Chaz had died.

Her baby had been so traumatized, he'd been a walking ghost, refusing to speak, eat, or sleep. He'd been inconsolable. They'd all been terrified that Vasili would follow his father to the grave.

Then when he'd finally spoken again, he'd sounded just like he did tonight.

"Shara?" Jullien paused as he caught the panicked hurt that was deep in her eyes. It concerned him to see her like this.

She balled her fist in Jullien's coat. "You don't know what it's like to have a vital part of you out there where you can't protect it. To know it's vulnerable to the cruelty of others. I can't breathe, Jules. I can't stand for my baby to be hurt."

He cupped her face in his hands and locked gazes with her. "No one will harm your son. My blood honor."

Ushara felt the power of him as he released her, and she saw the feral determination as he walked away. In that moment, she realized just how deadly Jullien really was. The stories of his family's cruelty went through her.

The Anatoles had finished second only to the War Hauks in that first Plenum. They were one of the most violent and capable blood lineages in Andarion history. And they had protected their heritage by marrying and breeding with only those families who produced the strongest and best warriors of every generation. If not the sanest, always the strongest.

Her stomach tightened. *What have I done?*

Had she just set loose the true Dagger Ixur?

Just how much blood-fury would he unleash this time?

And who would he kill?

# CHAPTER 10

Nervous and desperate to find Vasili as soon as possible, Ushara waited with Jullien by her side outside a small home near the shopping district, for someone to answer the door.

"He's in a back room. You want me to kick the door in and get him?"

Horrified at the suggestion, she glanced over her shoulder and frowned at Jullien as he read something on his link. How strange that with the red glasses on, it hid the fact he was stralen. Rather, it created an odd optical illusion that made them appear like normal Andarion eyes now instead of his human ones. "What are looking at?"

"I have him tagged." Completely unabashed over his illegal and immoral action, he showed her his link. "I chipped him as soon as he started hanging out with me in the bay, weeks ago, to ensure you didn't lose track of him again. Unlike the external biolink you were using, this chip is embedded in his body, and won't run out of juice. It charges off his electrolytes."

She wasn't sure if she should be grateful.

Or mortified.

"You did that without my permission or Vas's?"

"Figured you wouldn't care if you lost him again. It's a good, noninvasive program. He doesn't even know I did it. Neither did you."

"Jullien!"

"What?" he asked innocently.

She wasn't going to argue privacy issues with him right now. That fight would come later.

The door finally opened to show a larger Fyreblood male. He grimaced at them. "Yeah?"

Jullien barely held his temper at that tone. It brought out the royal beast in him that wanted to put the male through a steel wall.

Ushara went into her commander's role. "I'm here to get Vasili."

"Why?"

Jullien's nostrils flared at the disrespect. He glanced to Ushara, waiting for any cue that she wanted him to go on an attack. Unfortunately, she was in a cruel mood and gave him nothing.

Damn it! She wanted to handle this.

Oh, the Andarion frustration!

"I'm his mother. I don't need a reason. Would you please get him?"

Dismissively, he turned his back on her. And that seriously pissed off Jullien. But he managed to keep his temper leashed. Barely. And only because he'd promised Ushara on the way over that he would let her deal with this matter.

Until he heard the bastard speaking to someone in another room, under his breath. "No wonder the boy's a *cocúpün*. You should see what just walked over to claim him. He must have cried to his mama that he couldn't be away from her tit for five minutes."

Locking his jaw, Jullien forced himself to keep his feet planted. To take no violent action.

*You made a promise to Ushara.* He chanted that silently.

It held solid until he heard the sharp sound in the back of the house of someone being hit and Vasili crying out in pain . . .

*Fuck it.*

Ushara saw a peculiar expression darken Jullien's features a split second before he pulled his glasses off and went storming through the doorway with murderous intent.

*Well, this can't be good . . .*

She rushed after him, knowing by the set of his jaw and bloodlust in his stralen eyes, he was about to start something, and most likely wind up back in the brig.

How he knew where to go in the house, she had no idea—he must be using his program. He made his way down the hall as if he were intimate with the layout, straight to the backyard. There, a group of boys had Vasili surrounded, taking turns shoving and hitting him.

Before she could run to protect him, Jullien descended on them like the Dagger Ixur he called himself. And the moment he did, the elder Andarion males of the house joined the fight.

Faster than she could blink, Jullien literally lifted Vasili from the group and shielded him with his body until he had her son tucked safely in her arms. Then Jullien returned to the fray with an unimaginable fury.

No, not unimaginable . . .

The fury of the famed Kadurr. Ancient warriors, they were said to be the children of Kadora and the Koriłon. The Andarion war goddess and the trickster god of the damned. Fearless and bloodthirsty, they were invincible and unstoppable. Skilled beyond mortal means.

Long ago, before Andaria was civilized, those warriors would drink the sacred Adiem, a blessed drink that was supposed to summon their spirits before battle so that the Kadurr could hopefully possess Andarion warriors for the fighting to come. But only the best and bravest could commune with the gods and would be selected as hosts for the Kadurr.

That was what Jullien reminded her of. Now she understood exactly what the high priestess and her brother had meant. He caught the largest of the males a blow that lifted him clear off his feet and knocked him straight to the floor. Turning, he kicked the next one into the wall so hard that he busted through the paneling. Jullien didn't falter or flinch. Not even when they hit him. He took the blows as if he barely felt them. She'd never seen anything like it. He was equal to the best of any Andarion Ring fighter she'd ever witnessed.

In a matter of minutes, he had every male lying on the floor, screaming and crying in agony.

And as he went in for a fatal strike, Ushara panicked and caught his arm. "Jullien!"

He turned on her with a growling snarl and moved to hit her. But before his fist made contact, he caught the blow and froze. Horror replaced the dark rage in his eyes. "Shara?"

She nodded.

His breathing labored, he blinked and swallowed, then pulled her into a fierce hug. He held her so tightly that she could barely draw air into her lungs.

Reaching out, he grabbed Vas toward him, too.

Only then did he move them toward the exit.

Ushara wasn't sure which of them was more rattled by his martial skills. And as the females began to scream and demand heads, she knew there would be an inquest and arrest over this. "We have to get you out of here."

Jullien hesitated.

"Now!" She forced him to leave the grounds before the HCs arrived to take him into custody. He'd been extremely lucky that they hadn't run his prints or DNA for the earlier fight. No doubt her brother had kept them from it since Davel was known and well liked at the station, and the crew they'd attacked had been outsiders. But this was different. Jullien was the outsider now and the Zarens were a long established Tavali family on this base.

She might be able to pull strings, but the best thing would be to get him away from here and out of the line of fire as fast as possible.

As they headed home, Vasili was completely subdued and quiet. Jullien didn't speak either. He kept his arm around Vas as if to assure them both that her son was safe and that no one could harm him again.

Ushara kept glancing behind them, waiting for the HCs to show up and arrest him. "What happened back there?"

Vasili rubbed at his eyes. "They called me a coward. Said Paka died because I ran like a scared mouse, and that I'm an embarrassment to you and both my lineages. That I shouldn't even be here. I should have died."

Jullien stopped and started back toward the house.

"Hey!" Ushara grabbed him. "What do you think you're doing?"

"I'm already going to jail. We know that. Probably my execution. So if I'm going to die, I'm going to make it count and take those bastards with me."

"Really?"

"Told you I was a contentious bastard."

She arched a censoring brow at him.

Jullien shook his head. "No one hurts you or Vas. They have no right to insult him like that. I won't stand for it. Ever," he snarled.

For the first time, she saw tears in his eyes. "Jullien?"

His breathing ragged, he pressed the heel of his hand against his forehead and doubled over.

"Mum?" Vasili passed a fearful look to her.

"It's a panic attack, Vas." She moved to cup Jullien's face in her hands and forced him to focus on her. "Jules? Can you hear me? Where are you?"

Anguish furrowed his brow before he covered her hands with his. A single tear fell down his cheek as he finally met her gaze. "I just want to keep you safe. I don't want you insulted or hurt. Neither of you."

She placed Vas's hand in Jullien's and cradled them together. "We're safe and we're here with you. See? No one's hurting us."

He nodded, then growled as his gaze went past her shoulder to focus on something behind her.

She turned to see a group of HCs heading for them. Crap at their timing.

Jullien went into what she now recognized as his assassin stance. With his legs apart, he had one hand on his blaster and the other at the center of his back where she knew he kept additional weapons. God help them if they came at him when he was in this mood. They had no idea what they were stepping into. No doubt, this was when he'd ripped that poor guy's ear off in the bar fight.

Honestly, she was only just learning exactly what her tiziran was capable of, and it terrified her.

Bracing herself for the confrontation, she faced them. "Can we help you?"

Their captain jerked his chin toward Jullien. "We're here to arrest him. We have a complaint against him for assault."

"No, you don't," she said calmly, trying to diffuse the situation before it exploded. "I was there for the entire event. Dagger was extracting my son, who was being brutalized in their home. If they wish to pursue charges against Dagger, then I will be forced to do the same with their entire family for what they were doing to my child."

She gestured toward Vasili's battered face and torn clothes. "You can see for yourself what they did. Dagger acted in defense of a minor. He was well within his rights to do what he did on my behalf. I fully sanctioned his actions. If they have issue with him, then they need to take it up with me in my office tomorrow."

The captain hesitated before he inclined his head. "Very good, Admiral. I'll tell them." He turned around and left.

Finally relaxing his stance, Jullien raked his hand through his hair. "You can't keep doing this."

"Doing what?"

"Putting your neck out for me." He glanced at Vas and shook his head. "I screw things up, Shara. Ruin lives. It's what I do. It's *all* I do. Everything I touch goes to Tophet. Your grandmother was right. You hang with me and you'll be hanged beside me. And I can't let you do that to yourself. You deserve better."

He turned to leave, but Ushara grabbed his coat and held him by her side.

"You're a fighter, Jules. One of the fiercest ones I've ever seen in my life. So why are you so willing to run now when you have something worth battling for?"

"Because I don't care what happens to me. I never have. But you and Vasili . . ." He looked from her to her son, and growled. "I can't stay and risk you." Grinding his teeth, he tore himself from her grip. "I can't do it, Shara. I won't."

Vas began crying as he walked away from them. "Don't go . . . Paka. Please!"

Jullien froze at Vasili's whispered words. Barely audible even to him, they struck him like a fist in his gut.

*Don't you dare turn around and look at him. You keep going, you stupid half-wit, hybrid bastard, and you leave. Now! For once in your sorry life, do the right thing!*

But no matter how much he told himself to go—that this was the best for them all, he couldn't do it. He turned to look at Vasili and saw the tears streaming down the boy's face. Saw the agony in those white eyes that he'd learned to love.

Worse, he saw the tears glistening in Ushara's pale eyes and the pain that was etched on her face.

Against all odds, they wanted him as worthless and broken as he was.

And he was done for.

How could he leave the only two beings who'd ever given a single shit about him? How? In all the universe, they were all he loved.

Before he could stop himself, he opened his arms and Vasili ran to him. Jullien caught the boy against his waist and held him while the boy wept against his chest and broke his worthless heart. His own throat tightened to the point he barely kept his own tumultuous emotions reined in.

With a ragged breath, he watched as Ushara closed the distance between them and placed her hand on her son's head. Jullien sank his hand in her hair and laid his head on her shoulder.

"I will stay," he whispered.

She kissed his cheek and smiled up at him. "And we will teach you what it means to be part of a family that doesn't seek to harm you."

Nodding, he gave Vas one last squeeze before he let him go and screwed his face up at her. "Just be patient with me. You know going into this that I'm one fucked-up animal. If I go too far, promise me you won't hesitate to put me down before I damage your life or reputation in any way."

"Jules . . ."

"I mean it, *kira mia*. I would rather die by your hand than live knowing I'd caused you to shed one single tear in my name."

She choked on a sob as she realized that she had the most coveted type of Andarion male in existence. A *straleneur . . . a stralen heart*. And Jullien's was completely virgin. Never touched or claimed by anyone before her. To be so worldly and jaded, so hardened, he knew nothing of relationships. Nothing of being loved or of loving.

He was hers, alone.

Taking his hand, she led him and Vasili home.

Once they were settled inside and safe, she put a pot of tea on while Jullien tended Vasili's injuries at the counter with her first-aid kit. Though they were minor, it infuriated her to the point, she was glad Jullien had torn through the Zarens.

Unlike Chaz, she'd never been a pacifist, especially when it came to her son. Had Jullien not been there, she would have beaten them herself. Granted, not to the extent or success he had, but she would have put forth her best effort and most likely shot a few of them.

But what surprised her was how well Vas tolerated Jullien's care. He normally whined and complained whenever she tried to wash or bandage his cuts. He didn't even hiss when Jullien brushed alcohol over the deepest injury on his brow.

"This one needs a stitch." Jullien scowled as he examined it more closely. "I can do it, but it might be better fused by a medtech."

"You can do it," Vas said bravely.

Jullien passed an adorable grimace to her. "I leave it up to your *matarra*."

Skeptical, she glanced at them. "Do you have any experience stitching wounds?"

"Four years on myself. At least with Vasili I won't be doing it one-handed or in a mirror." He winked at Vas. "Besides, scars are sexy. *Qeres* like them."

"Jules! Don't teach him that!" *Qeres* was the Ixurian term for low caste females of easy virtue who often traded sexual favors to the nobility for a night out in expensive clubs and restaurants.

"What?" he asked innocently. "Don't act so offended after I spent an entire afternoon being mauled by your sisters, and hearing how they view males and talk about *us*."

Vasili snickered as the teapot sounded.

Unamused, Ushara went to pull the kettle from the stove and pour the tea. "That's beside the point. And you forget that we're Andarion. *We* don't like scars on our males. They're hideous and gross." As she turned back, she caught the hurt and stricken expression on Jullien's face. Too late, she remembered how many scars lined his body. "Jules . . ."

Completely somber, he moved away from her. "I should be going. I have an early shift."

"Jullien?" But it was too late. He was out of her home before she could apologize.

"Mum? What happened?"

Furious at herself for being so thoughtless, she cupped her son's chin and sighed. "I accidentally hurt his feelings. I forgot that Jullien has a lot of scars that bother him."

"How could you forget?"

"'Cause I don't see them, Vas. They don't matter to me." She brushed the hair back to look at his brow and was about to take him to the doctor to have it stitched when she realized that Jullien had already done it. "He stitched you?"

Vas nodded. "He did it so fast, I barely felt it."

She should have known that Jullien wouldn't have left with it unfinished. Sighing, she kissed Vas's bandage and hated that she'd hurt Jullien's feelings. "Come on, honey. Let's get you cleaned up and ready for bed."

"Don't you ever sleep?"

Jullien cursed as Trajen startled him while he worked. "Don't you make any noise when you move?"

"No. I like that sound of horror people make when I sneak up on them."

"Not people."

"You're half people."

Jullien snorted. "Is your sole purpose here to insult me?"

"Not my *sole* purpose. Just a nice bonus."

"Awesome. Well since you are here, can you be useful and toss me that wrench over there?"

Trajen used his powers to teleport it to Jullien's hand.

Jullien didn't comment as he continued working on the *Stormbringer* while trying to ignore Trajen's presence.

"So what happened tonight?"

Jullien growled in frustration. "You're a Tris. Don't think I have to relive it. Pretty sure you've already plucked all pertinent details from my mind. Among other things that I probably didn't want you to know about."

Trajen laughed. "I don't intimidate or bother you at all, do I?"

Jullien crawled out of the panel and sat up on the ship's stabilizer so that he could meet Trajen's dark gaze. "Not really. I lived my whole life with everyone spying on my most intimate moments, every second of the day, right down to how often I jerked off. They all thought they knew what I was thinking. It's actually refreshing to have someone who truly does. Besides, I'm not that complicated a creature. When pushed, I shove. When confronted, I attack. I rabidly protect what few things I care about. And I strive to be left alone. . . . Simple."

"Yet if there's trouble to be found, you sniff it out like pigs on truffles. And hump it like a dog on a fresh leg."

Jullien let out a tired sigh at something that was all too true. "That I do."

"Two *massive* fights in one day. You know that's a record, even for this station."

Jullien rooted through his toolbox and grabbed his water. "Can't help it. Everywhere I go, there's always an asshole."

"Well you know the old saying?"

"If everyone's an asshole, maybe the real asshole's you?"

Trajen laughed again. "Paraphrased, but yeah, that's the gist of what I was going for."

Not really wanting to think about the truth of that statement, Jullien wiped his hands off and took a drink. "Yeah well, I resemble that remark, so I'm not even going to defend myself. Are you here to arrest me or ask me to leave?"

"Neither. Just wanted to give you a heads up."

"On?"

"The fact that the family you attacked tonight is rather highly connected. They're old Tavali and they don't think much of Ushara as my vice admiral. In fact, a lot of the Gorturnum weren't real happy with her as my choice of adjutant. They've always thought she was too young for that much responsibility, especially after the way her husband died."

Jullien frowned at the odd note in Trajen's voice. "How did he die?"

Trajen materialized to sit by Jullien's side on the ship, and held his hand up, fingers spread.

Jullien hesitated. He wasn't sure if he wanted to be *that* personal with Trajen. It was one thing for the Trisani to rifle through his thoughts without his consent or knowledge. It was another for him to lock in with Trajen's and to share them and his emotions.

But he did want to understand what had happened with Ushara and Vasili, and he'd refrained from asking either of them since it would have forced them to remember the death of someone they loved. Having lost his brother, he knew how brutal those memories were. The guilt. The anguish. He'd always hated whenever someone asked him probing questions that brought up a bitter memory.

So he set his tools aside and placed his palm to Trajen's. The instant their skin touched, he felt an electrical jolt as the Trisani's mind merged with his. For a second, he thought he might vomit as everything spun around. It was extremely disorienting—like the worst sort of carnival ride.

He saw flashes of images he couldn't place. Though some he was sure belonged to Trajen's distant memories.

"Breathe steady, and focus." Trajen's voice soothed the churning in his gut. "Don't fight me. Just follow my lead."

Jullien took a deep breath. Suddenly, he was inside a Tavali freighter that was docked on a Starken outpost, alongside a large group of other Tavali ships. Most of them were Gorturnum by their Canting and flags, but a few were Wasternum. He had no idea which one was Chaz until he saw Vasili. Even though Vas was only five in this memory, he knew the boy instantly.

He was the perfect five-year-old-male version of his mother, with bright, curious eyes and the happiest disposition Jullien had ever seen on any child. Vas was running mad circles around the adults, laughing while he did so.

How adorable.

"Vasili!" his father snarled. "Stop it, this instant!"

Freezing in place, he opened his mouth like a fish. "Like this, Paka?"

Jullien laughed at the boy's game. But his father didn't find it amusing. Instead, Chaz picked him up and spanked him for it. Then set him down hard in a seat to cry.

"Don't move again. I mean it! And stop that noise, or else I'll give you a real reason to weep!"

Fury shortened Jullien's breath at those harsh words.

Ignoring his son, Chaz went back to the group that was meeting on the ship. He returned to the starchart. "Are you sure we can take him by surprise? Trajen's a slippery bastard. No one's been able to get near him since the night he murdered my father."

"You're his FA. When you make your report, you'll have to take the shot. You're the only one who can get close enough to him for it. He won't let anyone else into his offices."

Chaz nodded, then glanced over to one of the Wasternum pilots. "What about Dane?"

"I've got my agents in. I can move on Hermione and her bastard immediately. After they're gone, and you're in place, we'll let the Septurnum take the fall for it—then we can put in one of our own to lead them. At that point, the Council is ours. Venik's already said he won't interfere so long as we keep his name out of the takedown and stay out of his business. We'll rule the other three Nations and they'll tithe to us. You'll have vengeance for your father, and I won't have to take anymore shit from another Dane ever again."

Chaz shook his arm. "Sounds good." He glanced to the others. "Are we all in accord?"

One by one, they nodded. Until he came to a Wasturnum who was off to the side. Tall and athletically built, he still wore the face paint and mask that they used whenever they were hauling illegal cargo that kept their identities hidden from enemies and authorities. He stood with a slightly taller member of his Nation. The two of them exchanged a frown.

"What do you think?" the taller one asked.

The shorter one let out a heavy sigh. "I don't know . . . I got a little problem with the plan."

Chaz glared at them. "What?"

The shorter one lowered his mask to reveal his chiseled, patrician features, dark olive skin, and long, wavy dark red hair. "For starters, that you're planning to murder my mother, you fucking bastard. Secondly, Trajen's a friend of mine. You go for my brother, you go for me.

Oh, and yeah, that's the third thing. You're coming for me, too." Ryn Dane drew his blaster at the same time the others opened fire on him.

Vasili started screaming in terror as total chaos erupted. Shots flew thick. Two struck Ryn's armor as he ran to save the boy Chaz had abandoned to the fight while Ryn's friend covered him.

Somehow, Ryn managed to get off the ship with Vasili in his arms. He handed the boy off to a blue-skinned woman before he locked the ramp with the others trapped inside the ship.

"Blow that bitch in six!" he snarled into his link. "I don't want a single one of them left alive. Make sure we're clear and that no one gets off it. Then we'll call Trajen and let him know he was right to be suspicious."

"Hey, Dane?" the woman whined. "What do I do with this? Not maternal and it's leaking and loud! Did you break it?"

He cursed under his breath. "It's a child, Yra, not a poisonous reptile."

Softening his features, he took Vasili from her and walked quickly with him away from the ship as he tried to soothe the boy. "It's all right, little guy. I'm Uncle Ryn. I'm going to get you home to your mama, okay? Shh . . . it's all good. It's . . ." His voice trailed off as he froze mid step.

Chaz came out of the shadows with a blaster aimed at them. "Call off your orders. Now!" He clicked the blaster's setting from stun to kill.

Ryn scowled at him. "Davers, I'm holding your son. Let me set him down and we'll discuss this."

"You think I care about that brat? I didn't even want him. Now don't fucking move! Do what I told you. Call off your orders or I'm shooting you!"

"Paka?" Vasili cried.

"Shut up!" he snarled. He tightened his grip on his weapon. "I'm not playing, Dane. Don't try anything. I know how your family works. You brought us here 'cause we can't breathe fire in this atmosphere. You're sneaky bastards. And I'm not going to die on my knees like my father did. Nor am I spending another day serving a piece of shit Vaqim whore and her family. Now release my friends!"

Vasili cried even harder.

Tightening his grip on the boy, Ryn's gaze went past Chaz's shoulder. He covered Vas's eyes with his hand and kept the child's face buried against his shoulder.

An instant later, Chaz hit the ground, dead. Splintered into pieces as if a bomb had detonated inside him.

Repulsed by the vision, Jullien pulled his hand away from Trajen's as he let the reality of what he'd just seen go through him. That wasn't a memory tainted by emotion and perception. It was the harsh, unvarnished truth.

"Damn, Tray. You're a cold-blooded bastard."

*"Era suera."*

Jullien snorted at the idiomatic Trisani expression that was literally translated to *like eats like*, but meant *it takes one to know one.*

Maybe he was right.

"You didn't murder his father."

Trajen shook his head. "No. I fought him for my position, per Tavali law and custom. While I'm Trisani, he was a Fyreblood. And I didn't use all my powers in our Calibrum. I could have killed him as easily as I did Chaz. But rather, I battled him relatively fairly."

He particularly liked Trajen's use of the word *relatively*. "And you never told Ushara the truth about her husband?"

"No, I let her think that our enemies attacked him and his envoy, and did that to them. It would destroy her to know that Chaz had been involved in that kind of treachery and had pointed a weapon at his own child."

Yes, it would. She honestly thought Chaz had loved her and her son. But the truth was far from her delusions. "He was using her for her family's position and ties?"

Trajen nodded. "Back then, I kept myself cloistered and left the running of the station and Nation primarily up to Ushara's father and family. Chaz was my field admiral and his brother was the VA under my predecessor. Since I was an outsider, I thought it best to let things stay as normal as possible . . . my mistake."

"Ushara told me that Chaz was a pacifist."

"A lie he lived. He battled his way to become my field admiral, then kept his head low while moving into position so that he and his brother could assassinate me. I believe you're familiar with such tactics."

"Little bit." Jullien rubbed his hand over his face. "And Vas? Does he remember any of that?"

"No. I made sure of it, but . . . my interference had unforseen consequences."

"Mindwipes usually do."

A tic started in Trajen's jaw. "I didn't know what else to do. I couldn't leave the boy with that memory. Could you?"

"No. Trust me. You did right by him. Having been on the receiving end of many similar father-son exchanges, I'm a walking advertisement of what happens to sons whose fathers are in bitter need of parenting classes. We come out all kinds of effed up and arselings back." Jullien narrowed his gaze on Trajen. "So if you weren't interested in leading the Gorts, why did you battle to become their HAP?"

"I had my reasons."

"So you did and they're all yours and none of my concern. Gotcha, boss."

Trajen snorted. "I can't believe how much I strangely like you." He pulled a flask out from his pocket and handed it to Jullien. "You're the only one, other than those who were there, who know the truth of what happened that night."

Jullien was impressed by his compassion. "You left all of them with their memories?"

"You and Ryn Cruel are the only ones who know what happened that night."

With a scoffing laugh, Jullien took a swig, then choked on the potent drink. "What the hell is in this thing? Ship fuel?"

Grinning, Trajen took it and knocked back a large gulp. "Trisani Starfyre. Forget that watered-down shit the Tondarions make. We brewed the malt whisky that put hair not just on your chest, but on your knuckles and tongue."

Jullien laughed as he continued to wheeze. "Is that legal?"

"Of course not. Outlawed by every known government. Melted the brains of lesser species." He held the flask out toward him.

"Well then . . . gods know I never needed my brain activity. Pretty sure I was brain dead on arrival at birth." More prepared this time, he drank it and let it burn its way through his system. It was toxic going down, but had a smooth aftertaste that mellowed into something very pleasant after a few minutes.

Trajen clapped him on the back. "I'll make a Tris out of you yet, Andarion."

Snorting, Jullien ran his thumb down his right fang. "So you've confided in me. Poisoned me . . . dare I ask why? 'Cause I got be honest, these little chats of ours scare the Tophet of out me."

"You don't believe in Tophet."

"Not true. I currently live in it."

Trajen confiscated his whisky for another swig. "Truthfully? I don't know. I think it's because I can't hide from you. I still haven't figured out how you saw me so clearly when no one else ever has. You see everyone."

He locked gazes with Jullien. "And I see you, little brother. You're as fucked up as I am. It's why I wanted you to know the truth. I didn't want you to keep comparing yourself to a ghost that never existed. You held Chaz up as this shining beacon of perfection in fatherhood and husbandry, when the truth is he didn't give a shit. He took his wife for granted and ignored his son. I think it's why Vas glommed on to you the way he did in that bar. You protected him when you didn't have to. And I know you're stralen. It's faded for now, but I can still see the traces of it in your eyes. The more you're around Ushara and Vas, the stronger it'll become."

"That's what I'm afraid of."

"It's what we're all afraid of. Love makes us weak. 'Cause you know you're no longer in control of anything. *She* is."

Jullien let out a tired breath at that single truth. *"Swáhytsý,* brother."

Trajen capped his flask. "Congratulations, by the way."

"On what?"

"Your marriage."

Jullien blinked as those words hung in the air between them. "Pardon? My *what?"*

"Ah. . . . Didn't know, did you?"

Confused, Jullien stared at him. "Am I drunk?"

"I don't know. Are you?"

Jullien scowled as he held his hands up to test their stability. No. He appeared sober. Everything was relatively right, except . . .

"What makes you think I'm married?"

"I don't think anything." Trajen pulled out his link and handed it over to Jullien. "Know it for a fact. It's how my favorite admiral kept your ass out of jail and off the bounty sheets after a certain family went to file formal charges on you behind her back. She done went and changed your name, lineage, bio, and your address, and everything else in your files."

Jullien's jaw dropped as he read through his personnel files. Trajen wasn't kidding and he wasn't drunk. According to this, he did indeed have a wife, and a new last name.

Furious, he handed the link back to Trajen and jumped down from the ship.

"Hey! Where are you going?"

Jullien glared up at him. "To make myself a widower."

# CHAPTER 11

Ushara came awake to a giant, hulking shadow standing over her bed. She started to shoot it until she recognized the muscular outline. "Jullien? What are you doing here?"

"According to my files, I live here now."

"Wha . . . oh." She cringed. "I was going to tell you about that in the morning."

"In the morning? *Really?*"

She bit her lip and cringed. "I had to do something. After you stormed off, there was more fallout over the fight. And . . ." She paused at the low feral growl he let out over her words. If he'd been a Fyreblood, she'd have expected smoke to come out of his throat to punctuate that guttural sound. "Why are you so mad, anyway?"

"Why?" He stepped back from the bed and gestured angrily toward the door. "Oh, I don't know. You married me without my consent, or even notifying me of the event. How would you feel if I did that to *you?*"

While he had a valid point, she wasn't going to let him know it. "You're stralen."

"So?"

"So . . . you're stralen," she repeated. It wasn't like he could just run off and find another female now. Unfortunately for his rare breed, it didn't work that way. Once that gene kicked in, the male became pair-bonded to a frightening level to the one who'd caused it. While they could be with another female, their loyalty and *heart* would always remain with the one who first awoke the chemical change in their bodies. It biologically altered the male for the rest of his life, and there was nothing he could do about it.

Given that fact . . .

"I thought this would make you happy."

He was aghast. "That you legally filed us as married without asking me?"

"Well, kind of, yeah."

Jullien laughed bitterly as he neared the bed again. "I'm not some stray dog you found on the street and took in, Shara. I'm a sentient being and still do have some semblance of pride. Believe it or not."

"I know that." She sat up and pulled her legs under her. "And before you come in here all pissy with me and yelling about this, you need to stop and remember that you're not the only one who goes a little nuts when it comes to the safety of the ones he loves. I've already buried one husband. I'm not about to stand aside and bury you because you're a fucking idiot, too. You ran off. I didn't know where you were. The HCs showed up demanding your head, and I panicked, knowing what would happen should they run your prints or DNA—which I didn't know if they had on file or not, given your earlier stupidity of ripping off someone's ear. And like you, I did what I had to to make sure you stayed safe and that they couldn't touch you. And at least I didn't put anyone in the hospital while protecting you, unlike someone I could name!"

Jullien backed up as he saw the pain in her eyes and heard the tremor in her voice. In his own fury and hurt, he hadn't thought about that.

Now he felt like a total prick for attacking her.

"I'm sorry, Shara. I'm not used to anyone protecting me. Only stabbing me in the leg so that I fall while they get away." He brushed the pale hair back from her face as he sat down beside her on the bed. "I told you that I didn't want to separate you from your family and I'm afraid of how they'll react to this. What they'll do to you because of me. I mean, shit . . . is there anyone worse you could take home to them?"

"I know. But my family will get over it. They're not Anatoles. They will scream and yell about it, and pout. They might even shun me a bit. But after a few . . . decades they'll learn to love you as much as I do."

He laughed at that as he fingered her delicate cheek and marveled at the screwed-up miracle that had brought them together. He couldn't decide if he was the luckiest bastard ever.

Or the most cursed to love her this much. Because in the back of his mind lived the terror that somehow his presence in her life would end it.

And knowing it was his fault would ruin him. He couldn't live with the guilt of knowing he'd caused her harm. It would be the one thing that would utterly destroy him.

"This is not how marriages are contracted."

"I know," she whispered. "But you don't have a matarra for mine to negotiate with."

He brushed his thumb over her lips. "And your matriarch has already denounced me as unwanted rubbish."

"True, but I'm a widow and a mother myself. So I claim autonomy to forge my own marriage."

"With an Outcast."

"You're a cock now. With prospects." She smiled up at him and it knotted his gut. But more than that, it made him feel like he was finally worth something. "Both my brother and Trajen have offered to sponsor you. Honorary Tavali today. Full citizen in two years. I know you, Jules. You'll be a captain in no time. I have my own ship in storage that you can run. She's not much, but with your abilities, you can breathe new life into her and get her running again."

He laughed bitterly. "You make it sound so easy."

"What else do you have to do with your life?"

Closing his eyes, he ground his teeth.

Ushara scowled. That reaction terrified her. "Jules?"

He met her gaze, then took her hand and placed it over his heart. "An Ixurian and a Pavakahira. This is a recipe for absolute destruction."

"I know. But you're a contentious asshole. Remember?"

He laughed. "I am that and I'm still angry at you."

"Good," she said, pulling her nightgown off, over her head. "I'm still mad at you, too."

"Then why are you getting naked?"

She slowly began undoing his pants. "Because we can't consummate the marriage with our clothes on."

Jullien's breath caught as she reached down to cup him. "Shara . . ."

"Hmmm?" She nipped at his chin with her fangs.

He struggled to remember his reasons against a marriage with her.

Or any thought at all.

But it was useless when she was in his arms. He had absolutely no will where she was concerned, especially when she licked and teased him like this. God . . . every part of his body felt like it was on fire. Sucking his breath in, he buried his hand in her hair and struggled with the intensity of emotions he could barely understand. The feral need to hold her and protect her.

He cupped her cheek and kissed her.

Ushara moaned at the passion of his kiss. She didn't know if it came from his stralen or something else, but no one had ever been like this with her. It was as if he lived solely to touch her skin.

Toeing his boots off, he pulled his shirt over his head while she pulled his pants down.

She laughed at his eagerness as he tripped on the pants and cursed. "You all right?"

He grunted in response. Then he was on the bed with her again, back in her arms.

The warmth of his skin sent chills through her that were heightened as he scraped his whiskers against her breasts. With a fierce growl, he pulled back. "Where are the condoms?"

"Consummation won't count if you use them."

He froze to stare down at her. In fact, he was still for so long that she began to worry he'd gone catatonic.

"Jules?"

Finally, he blinked slowly. "I-I've never done that."

"Why do you look so scared?"

His breathing ragged, he rolled over onto his back and stared up at the ceiling. "It's been beaten into me my whole life that I'm a hybrid. That . . ."

She waited for him to speak. When he didn't, she sat up and draped herself over his muscular chest. "What?"

Jullien swallowed hard before he spoke again. "I was pledged twice, Ushara."

"You were tahrs. That would have been expected. So why didn't you marry them?"

He took a deep breath. "They killed themselves the day after the pledging ceremonies."

"What?" she gasped. "Why?"

Pain darkened his eyes. "They said they'd rather be dead than bear my defective lineage."

Bile rose in her throat over their cruelty. That would be harsh to say to any male. To say it to one who was of royal birth, who should have one day been the ruler of their empire, was unheard of. "Oh Jules . . . I'm so sorry."

He swallowed hard. "And even though the companions were all on birth control, they were so afraid of accidentally conceiving a hybrid child from me that I had to agree to only sleep with them during the infertile days of their cycles and to make sure I was covered at all times and to spill nothing near them."

No wonder he was so paranoid when they had sex.

"*Mi keramon*——"

He placed his fingers gently over her lips to stop her protest. "It's okay, Shara. Having been unwanted by my own mother, I was glad for it. The last thing I want is to father a child on a female who can't bear to look upon its face. I don't want the first sound my child hears to be its own mother screaming in horror that she birthed it. A child should never hear its mother say the things I've heard my mother say about me." He drew a ragged breath. "I don't think I can do this."

Straddling his hips, she cupped his face in her hands and forced him to meet her gaze so that he could see the sincerity in her eyes. "Do you know what I see when I look at you, Jullien eton Anatole?"

"The discarded bastard of the family that murdered yours to extinction."

She wrinkled her nose. "In the beginning, but I don't see that anymore. All I see now is the handsome face of my stralen husband. In my life, I've only allowed two males in my bed. The father of my son and *you*. No one else. I would never trust my son's safety to anyone not of my blood save you and Trajen. And I can think of no greater happiness than holding your son or daughter in my arms and watching it grow into an exact copy of *you*. And if the gods were to ever grant me such a blessing again, I promise you that the first sound your child would hear would be the cries of his or her mother's joy as I gladly welcomed our baby into this world."

Jullien couldn't breathe as those words choked him. "I don't deserve your heart, Ushara. I damn sure don't deserve your love. But I swear to you that I will never betray you and I will spend the rest of my life doing everything I can to bring no shame or harm to you or what you love."

"I love you, too." She gently nibbled his lips as her taut nipples brushed against his chest.

Closing his eyes, Jullien couldn't imagine anything feeling better until she slowly impaled herself on him. The pleasure of being inside her uncovered was so intense that he shook from it and growled deep in his throat.

Ushara hesitated at the ferocious, primal sound as Jullien gently grabbed her hips and thrust against her. His eyes turned a deeper, darker red. He rose up in the bed to hold her close before he flipped and took control of their passion.

With the gentlest of caresses, he scraped his fangs along her throat as he quickened his strokes. Taking her hand into his, he kissed her palm, then held it to his heart as his breathing turned into an all-out seductive purr.

If she didn't know better . . .

"Jullien?"

He didn't speak as he came and when he did, he threw his head back and let out a burst of flames that lit up her entire bedroom.

Shocked, Jullien started to pull away, but Ushara held him close and refused to let him go. "Shh . . . finish. It's okay. I'm right here."

Then she began a soft, old Andarion lullaby while she ran her hands over his back and through his hair until his body was completely drained and sated.

His breathing ragged, he lay on top of her trying to come to terms with what had just happened to him. And with the fact that he was something he'd never known. That his whole life and heritage had been a complete lie.

He *was* a Fyreblood Andarion.

So was Nykyrian.

"You okay?" Ushara asked.

Even though he knew the truth, he still had to double-check that he wasn't hallucinating. "Did I . . ?"

"Yes."

"Is it always like that?"

"No. That was your second set of lungs opening up to allow you to make fire. Is your throat burning?"

"Very much so. It's also really dry."

She kissed his cheek. "Let me up. I can get you something for that."

As he moved, he started coughing. Then he panicked, afraid he might belch fire again.

Ushara rubbed his back comfortingly. "It's okay. You won't spew fire accidentally, trust me. You'll always know by the way your breathing sounds. You can't make fire unless your second set of lungs is engaged."

He laughed bitterly. "Andarion doctors said the extra lung chambers were a birth defect from being part human. No wonder I always had so much trouble breathing, especially whenever I ran. Human doctors tried to treat me for asthma and bronchial disorders. I used to get so dizzy at times, I could hardly walk."

"It's why we preferred to live in higher elevations on Andaria. It was easier to breathe there." She kissed his shoulder. "I'll be right back." She got up and pulled on her bathrobe.

Jullien coughed again and struggled to catch his breath as he came to terms with all the lies he'd lived with for so long. About everything. He'd never had anyone he could trust or believe in.

Not even himself.

Until Ushara.

For the first time in his life, he had a home where he was wanted. A hand that touched him without scorning him, or hurting him. He now had something to lose.

Something they could take . . .

"Are you okay?"

He glanced up as she returned. "What?"

"You look terrified."

"Panic attack." He got up and started pacing the room as it hit him full force. Damn it.

He'd always hated when they struck. They'd started the day his grandmother had told him she'd killed his brother. Since then, they'd come and gone, always without warning. Sometimes he could go for long stretches between them, and then at others . . . it seemed like they'd strike back to back.

Suddenly, Ushara was in front of him. "Shh, breathe, baby. Just breathe. I've got you." She pulled him into her arms and rocked him. Her breath fell against his neck while she teased his hair with her fingers and soothed him with her humming. "You're not on Andaria. You're not running. And you're not alone."

"That's what scares me most. I need to make sure Vasili's okay."

"I just checked on him. He's asleep in his room."

"Are the doors locked?"

"Yes. It's all good, Jules. We're surrounded by my family. They all live within shouting distance." She handed him the cup in her hand. "Now drink this. It's not poisoned or tampered with. There are no drugs in it. It's a honey tonic that will soothe your throat." She took a sip of it first to show him.

Jullien drank it and let it soothe the rawness. "Thank you."

"You're welcome. Tomorrow, I'll show you how to use and control the fire."

"Okay, but can we keep this between us?"

"If you want."

He nodded. "Thank you. I'm a big enough freak. Last thing I need is for anyone else to discover that my grandmother was an even more indiscriminate whore than my mother."

Gasping, she arched a brow at his choice of words. "Should I be offended by that?"

"No." He scowled at her, not understanding why she would take that personally. "Not at all. You're not the one who violated your marriage vows."

"Neither did your mother."

"True. What she did was worse. She crawled into the bed of a human who was too big a cocúpün to marry her because he lacked the backbone to stand up to his father."

"Is that really what happened?"

Nodding, Jullien took another drink. "He loved her. But he cowed to his father in every way while the old bastard lived. It was sickening." He opened his mouth to show her his fangs. "Notice one's shorter than the other?"

"Yes."

"My grandfather tried to have them filed off and my father stood there, saying nothing."

"What did you do?"

"Before or after I bit the dentist and assaulted the guards holding me down, and was exiled from Triosa for it? Those are part of my arrest records you saw, by the way. The destruction of property and vandalism on Triosa? It's a large part of why I was disinherited by my father." He laughed bitterly. "Aside from the fact that I actually am part Andarion and my dental features don't bother me, can you imagine the shit-storm had I gone home without my fangs?"

"They'd have killed you."

"Yeah. Especially since Eriadne had me imprisoned again shortly thereafter. They'd have eaten me alive if I'd appeared fully human in that hellhole of hers. It was bad enough how fucked I was with human eyes."

Ushara grimaced at the images in her mind that she hoped were only her imagination and not his reality. "How old were you?"

"Barely twenty." Jullien picked his pants up and pulled his link out. He turned it on and handed her the photo of his parents. "I'll never understand how any male could refuse to fight for a female who looked at him with that much love. I've never understood it. For *that*, I would have gone to war. I would have fought until there was no more life left in me."

"And that's what makes you Andarion." She kissed his cheek. "Now come to bed, husband. We have a lot to do tomorrow."

Jullien swallowed as she dropped her robe and went back to bed completely naked. The sight of her like that made him hard all over again.

This was not the way he'd seen this day ending.

He was now married. With a family—a wife and son.

And still hunted with a foul death sentence hanging over his head.

"Jules? Are you panicking again?"

"Lot-a-bit. There's a reason I used to do drugs and eat my feelings."

"And where did that get you?"

She had a point.

"Tossed out on my ass." Sighing, he set the mug and link on the nightstand and slid in to bed beside her, then gathered her in his arms. "Yeah, okay. This is much better." He buried his face against her hair and let the sweet vanilla scent of her shampoo soothe his ravaged nerves. She gently traced his tattoo in the darkness before she moved her hand to play with the hairs on his chest.

As he listened to the silence, he remembered what Trajen had shown him. But one thing still didn't make sense. "How did you become Trajen's vice admiral at such a young age?"

She stiffened in his arms, then sighed. "You want the truth?"

"That's why I asked."

"I was a little upset when my husband died."

"I would expect so."

She let out a sad sigh. "Let me backtrack. I was extremely upset when my husband died."

"Okay."

She glanced up at him from beneath her lashes while her hand continued to stroke him. "The former vice admiral was his older brother and he knew that Chaz was . . . not the best fighter. Or pilot."

"Yeah."

"He shouldn't have been making runs through Trimutian territory."

"Are you talking about the Golden Lightyear?"

"Yeah. A lot of The Tavali were making runs back then from Starken to Altaria. The League had just started really cracking down on that area. We all knew it. But it was still highly profitable and Chaz wanted to make one last run through it to make a big score on a Trimala freighter he'd heard was shipping a lot of rare minerals the Probekeins were paying top creds for. So his brother helped him lie to me about it, and sent him on his way with Vasili on board the ship. By the time I found out where he'd really gone, it was too late to stop him or get to him and Vas."

"*Zēritui.*"

She swallowed hard. "Thank you. So three days after Chaz's funeral, I sat in our home, trying to get Vasili to eat and he wouldn't move. He wouldn't speak. He was comatose and traumatized. And I heard Chaz's brother laughing as he walked by outside our door."

She rose up on her arms to look down at Jullien in the darkness. "Something in me snapped. I actually heard it. And I picked Vas up, handed him to my mother, then went outside and challenged Pietr to a Calibrim. Thirty minutes later, he was dead at my feet and Trajen named me vice admiral of the Gorturnum. And while many aren't happy about my meteoric rise from captain to VA, there was nothing they could do about it. It's his right to choose whomever he pleases, and he didn't trust any of them. Not sure why he trusts me, either." She sighed idly. "Anyway, they make shitty comments about it behind our backs. The most common, of course, is that we were sleeping together and he murdered my husband. Pietr found out and I killed him over it—which is the other thing Vasili was fighting about tonight that he didn't want to tell you. It's ridiculous, but it doesn't stop some from gossiping."

"I've not heard it, if it makes you feel better."

"Good."

He reached up to brush her hair back from her cheek. "And now you've given them a whole new topic to gossip over."

She smiled. "I don't care. Just remember, I'm Andarion, too. I protect what I love, and I don't play well with others. The only thing more frightening than an Andarion male protecting his *meiran*—"

"Is an Andarion female protecting her blood lineage."

"Exactly. And that now includes you, Dagger Altaan."

But even as Jullien settled down to sleep in her arms, he couldn't shake the feeling that this was only temporary. That something was coming for him. It was as if the real Dagger Ixur was standing in the room, staring at him, just waiting for the moment to strike them all down.

Why else would the gods have given him so much unless they wanted to watch him suffer when they snatched it all away?

It was something he'd almost convinced himself was ludicrous until a few hours later when he got up to check the doors and Vasili. Even though Ushara had told him everything was locked, he just wanted to make sure.

He picked his link up to charge it and noticed that for once he had a message.

Weird . . .

No one had his number, except for Ushara. He turned it on to check it and his heart stopped.

*Where are you hiding, little rabbit? We haven't forgotten you. We will find you, Julie. And we will feast on your entrails. The hounds of Coreła will not rest until they see the betrayer punished for what he did, and the rightful tadara back on her throne. We will have your head as a trophy.*

While that was ominous, he really didn't give a shit. What bothered him about the text wasn't the threat, it was the next bit of code attached after it. The encrypted cipher he'd used and sent when he'd worked with WAR before his grandmother had been deposed.

*Eriadne is with Braxen Venik on his Port StarStation. They've been working together for years, preying on Andarion ships and anyone she views as a threat to her reign. She's been releasing information and skimming profits from The Tavali for it. She scales back Andarion forces, allowing The Tavali to travel through lesser patrolled areas so that they can eliminate her enemies and knock out her competition.*

*XX Dagger Ixur*

Shit. Did they know he was still using that alias? If that were to surface, it could still get him killed. Not just with the Andarions, but now with The Tavali. Venik was the High Admiral for the Portnurmum

Nation—a rival clan to the Gorturnums. No matter how much Trajen might like him, he'd be honor bound to hand him over to Venik.
And given the bad blood between the two Nations, Venik wouldn't
hesitate to cut Jullien's throat.

Now that he was married to Ushara, Venik could also demand her
head, too.

His heart pounding, Jullien yanked the chip from his link and destroyed it. He didn't want to take a chance on anyone using it to backtrace him here. If they were able to transmit to it, then they could locate
him with it. There must have been something embedded in the photo
of his parents that he accidentally activated earlier when he'd shown it
to Ushara. It was the only way they could have found him.

*I have to be more careful.* Another mistake like this and he'd be finished
for good.

If he wasn't already.

# CHAPTER 12

"What the hell's he doing here?"

Jullien arched a brow at Zellen's *warm* greeting the instant he walked into Ushara's office. He cracked a devilish grin at her adjutant. "It's official Take A Psycho To Work Day. Didn't you get the memo?"

Ushara burst out laughing. "Would you stop taunting my crew?"

"He started it," Jullien said in a tone to let her know he was still teasing her. "Besides, I *was* behaving. It's not like I shot him or anything . . . which was what I started to do."

Zellen paled at those words.

"He's joking." She headed for her office.

Jullien paused at Zellen's desk to give him a deadly scowl. "No, I wasn't," he said in an ominous whisper. "But let's keep that between us, shall we?"

"Get your cute little ass in here. Now."

Jullien gave one last glower to Zellen before he obeyed. Then he cast an arrogant smirk to her on his way into her office. "Does this constitute sexual harassment under Tavali law?"

"Only if I spank you."

That caused him to raise his other brow with sudden hopeful interest. "Really? And how bad do I have to be for *that* kind of reward?"

Trying not to laugh again, she grabbed his jacket and hauled him into her office to slam the door before any other curious onlookers started gossiping about them. "What gets into you and makes you do things like that?"

Lifting his red glasses, he rubbed at his eyes. "I don't know. Maybe my aunt was right. I am the Koriłon incarnate."

Ushara frowned as she realized his irises were still vibrantly red. She pulled his glasses down over them again and now they appeared as normal Andarion silvery-white. "Why do these make them appear to be white when they're on?"

He stared at her. "Optical illusion from the lenses. Since they have a spectrum filter, I assume it has something to do with that."

She pulled his glasses off again. "Is the stralen permanent now?"

"No idea. Given that no male in my family has ever had it before, I know nothing about the condition. But I would assume so since they haven't faded."

She brushed her fingers along his brow. "Is it painful?"

"No. I can't tell a difference . . . other than *this* happens every time you come near me." He pressed her hand against his swollen groin. "That is *quite* annoying and highly distracting." His breathing ragged, he bit his lip as he stared down at her with the hottest, needful look she'd ever seen on any male's face. "All I can think about is being inside you." He rubbed himself against her open palm and kissed her before he stepped back and grimaced. "Yeah, that condition definitely qualifies as uncomfortable and makes me glad my pants are baggy."

Someone knocked on the door.

"Come in."

Zellen entered with a furious glower. "You married . . . *him*?" By the way he spat the pronoun, it was obvious he was substituting it for what he really wanted to say.

"I take it the paperwork came in."

Zellen made a pain-filled noise. "It did."

"I need you to file it and make sure Dagger has access to everything. He's now assigned as a cock to Davel's crew so he'll need ID and badges."

"Under what name?"

"Altaan."

"Have you cleared this with your parents?"

She gave Zellen a withering stare. "I'm a matriarch in my own right and your CO. I don't need to clear it with anyone."

"I'll keep Ixur."

"Ju—"

"Shara," he said quickly, cutting her off before she used the wrong name. "It'll keep your family off your back. Zellen's right. They're going to balk enough. No need to salt an open wound."

She hated the fact that he was right. They would pitch a fit and that might help a bit until they came around. "Very well."

"And do we really have to put this on record?" Jullien asked her.

"What do you mean?"

"Just that I've got a lot of enemies and I don't want them to find you or Vas. Less paper trail, the safer you both are. I'd rather they continue to hunt me solo."

Zellen nodded. "He's right about that."

Ushara balked at what he suggested. "That will leave *you* with no protection under Tavali Code."

"I'd rather be exposed than you. And I think we'd both rather hang me than Vas."

She narrowed her gaze at Jullien. "Now you're playing dirty."

"I know. But I won with that hand, didn't I?"

"I hate you."

Jullien winked at her. "Yeah, me too."

Zellen crossed his arms over his chest. "So what am I doing with his paperwork?"

"Put him in as single with Davel's crew."

"You're sure this time?" Zellen asked.

Tears glistened in her eyes. "No. I don't want to lose another husband."

"I won't break your heart, Shara. My word of honor to you."

"You better not. My word of honor to *you*. I'm descending into Tophet, roping the Koriłon myself and riding him straight to you to beat your ass for it if you do."

"Yes, mu tarra."

Zellen inclined his head to her. "All right. I'll get his orders in and have him added to our rolls as a candidate. I assume Davel knows about this?"

"He does. Both Trajen and I second his candidacy for citizenship. Back date it to yesterday. I don't want him on the docks another minute without some Tavali protection."

Zellen nodded. "Okay. I've got a few cock badges in my desk I can give him now that he can take with him."

"Thank you."

"Anything for you, Admiral. I'll get his paperwork pushed through by this afternoon. We'll have him badged and coded by dinner."

"I appreciate it."

Zellen saluted her, then turned a discriminate eye to Jullien. "You do know you're going to have to finally give up your hobo style, right?"

"What is it with you people and how I dress? Damn, you're worse than the snobs at court." Pulling his glasses down to the bridge of his nose so that he could peer over them, he cocked his hip and hand in the perfect gesture of a snotty fop. "What is *that*? Last season's Yetur and Babineaux? Have you fallen into penury or are trying to start a new trend of plebeian workaday wannabe haute couture?"

Ushara laughed while Zellen rolled his eyes. "You're way too convincing in that role, love."

"Yeah." Jullien scowled and pushed the glasses back into place. "Having bad psychotic flashbacks. Don't ever let me do that again."

"And her brother isn't going to let you on his ship looking like some hobo they rolled or conscripted. We have a rep to maintain. And vagrants aren't frightening."

Jullien scoffed. "I beg to differ. I think I carry psycho off quite nicely in my own clothes. I'll have you know I've caused some pretty tough characters to cross the street at my approach."

"I'll bet you have, but more from a fear of your stench than anything else."

"Perhaps, but they still blinked first and ran."

"All right, boys." Ushara broke them apart before their verbal sparring could take on a more sinister bend. "We do have work to get to. And Zellen's correct—to fly as Tavali, battlesuits are necessary. You'll be required to purchase and maintain at least five soft and two hardsuits that are up to Code."

"Really?" Jullien asked.

They both nodded.

"And you have to submit them and the rest of your equipment to inspection every six months to make sure that they're of the right quality, colors, and standards as determined by the UTC."

Jullien groaned.

"I'll get him a manual, Admiral."

"Thanks, Z."

Curling his lip, Jullien scratched at his brow. "Damn, y'all tough."

She shrugged. "Tavali is an honor that comes with obligation. No one is entitled to anything. You earn the right to bear our ranks and badges.

The whole purpose of the next two years is to see if you have what it takes to be a fully vested citizen of our Nation."

"But if you make the cut," Zellen said earnestly. "You'll never be without family again. A Tavali who commits a crime against another of our own is hunted with extreme prejudice and brutally executed. You don't ever want to be on the wrong end of our justice."

Jullien had to bite his tongue at the blind optimism Zellen was too old to believe in. Surely, he had to know that it wasn't that simple. And that no one could be trusted so completely. Ushara's husband had been only one example of how easily someone could allow their hatred and jealousy to corrupt them.

And he'd grown up in a court filled with such yapping dogs who'd been eager to tear each other apart over every little scrap piece of meat or shoelace.

Petty creatures. Petty issues. He'd seen females poison one another because one wore a similar gown to a ball, or another had a younger spouse, or fewer facial wrinkles. Males who'd knifed each other to get Eriadne's favor, only to have her slit their throat a few weeks later because she didn't like the scent of his cologne.

How he wished he were making that up. And from what he'd seen, The Taveli were just as capable of corruption and brutal acts as anyone else. However one thing would always be true where Jullien was concerned . . . "I don't betray anyone who doesn't slash my throat first. But if you come for me, all bets are off. No one kills me and lives."

Zellen snorted before he turned back toward Ushara. "Do you need anything else from me, Admiral?"

"No, thank you."

After he left, she faced Jullien and straightened his jacket for him. "You ready for this?"

"For what?"

"When you walk out that door, you're TNT. Tavali-in-Training. They will test you and haze you. Every member of Davel's crew will do their absolute best to try and break you over the next two years to see if you have what it takes to be Tavali. They'll be looking for any reason to deny you citizenship. You will have to prove absolute loyalty to captain and crew, no matter what. Above all, you'll have to prove loyalty to Nation. When you're Fetchyn or Tavalian, they mitigate some of the hazing."

"When you're what?"

"Related to someone who's already a citizen, which is why I wanted you listed as my husband. Without them knowing, I'm terrified of what they might do to you. You've no idea what I've seen them to do some of the cocks on crews."

While he appreciated her concern, he wasn't worried about it. "I was thrown into prison as the tahrs and grandson of the tadara who put the inmates there. I seriously doubt there's anything they could do to me worse than what I've already been through."

Ushara winced at those emotionless words that she knew masked unbelievable horrors in his past.

He brushed the hair back from her cheek. "Believe me, *Ger Tarra*, there's a reason I chewed through my wrists with my own fangs in an effort to kill myself."

She choked on a sob.

He tilted her chin up with his fingers and offered her a tender smile. "I will be fine so long as I'm away from you and Vasili, and none of my enemies know to look for you here. I'd rather they be chasing me while I'm on the move, anyway."

Nodding, she held him as she tried to imagine all the nightmares he refused to share with her. The ones that caused him to pace the floors at night when he thought she was still asleep. "I wish I could wrap you in a padded room where nothing bad could ever touch you again and keep you safe forever."

"Only if you join me there." He kissed her cheek as her link buzzed. "You have work to attend. As do I. I'll see you later."

Reluctantly, she released him.

He paused at the door to turn back toward her. "Don't forget Vasili has a practice test after school today. Do you want me to pick him up for you?"

"I'd totally forgotten. Yes, that would be incredibly helpful. Thank you."

Inclining his head, he slid out the door and pulled it closed. Ushara stood there for a moment, feeling his absence like a physical ache. How he'd come to be so important to her so quickly, she had no idea. Honestly, she should hate everything he stood for.

But she couldn't. Instead, all she wanted to do was protect and keep him safe from harm. It made no sense and yet she couldn't deny the need she had inside her.

Now she was going to have to tell her family and they were going to absolutely flip. While she'd shown a brave face to Jullien, the truth of how they were going to react terrified her.

She only hoped that they could find it in their hearts to understand and forgive. If not . . .

This might have been the worst mistake of her life.

"Hey!"

Jullien paused at Zellen's sharp call.

"You forget your badges and manual access code."

"Sorry. Focused on other things." Jullien headed to his desk.

Zellen didn't hand them over. Rather he kept them in his lap and pinned a hard stare on him. "Why are your eyes white now? They weren't before."

Jullien pulled the glasses down to show him their real color.

"*Titana ræl.*"

He smirked. "Yeah, exactly, and I am."

Scowling, Zellen glanced to Ushara's door, then back to Jullien. "Well that settles my mind at least."

"How so?"

"I know you're not being a total self-serving bastard. My first thought when I saw the orders this morning. Then I had some doubts that you might be okay when you didn't want to use her name or let anyone know about the marriage. I guess she warned you what to expect by not letting her list you as her husband?"

"She did."

Still, he hesitated. "I almost feel bad doing this to you, darkheart. Davel runs an almost exclusive Fyreblood crew. They all got an axe to grind against your kind. Two of them have their eyes on the admiral. They find out that she's yours and they will gut you for her."

"Anything else I need to know?"

He sat up and scribbled something on a piece of paper, then tore it and handed it to Jullien. "Take this to the local optometrist. She makes a contact lens that can mask stralen eyes. As long as she knows I sent you, she'll work with you off record and ask no questions. Keep that shit under wraps."

"Thanks."

Zellen nodded and handed him another slip that was already on the desk, filled out. "This is a line of credit at the TBX. They'll get you what you need to fly and won't jerk you around or add on anything that isn't absolutely necessary. It's in my name so you'll owe tithe to me for it. But don't worry, I won't charge you interest. I'll dock a straight five percent of your take until you pay off the balance."

"Why would you do that?"

"Sheila's my sister, and I know all the things you've done for her and my niece. She's going to be really sad to see you go, and I figure you can't be too bad if she got that attached to you."

Jullien smiled wistfully at the thought of having to turn in his notice. "Yeah, I'll miss her, too. She's a lot of fun to work with."

"Believe me when I say you are the *only* one who thinks that."

"Then they ought to get to know her. And don't worry. I won't leave her in a lurch. I'll get all my projects finished for her before we leave."

Zellen narrowed his one good eye at Jullien. "She said you already had her working almost eight weeks ahead of schedule."

He shrugged nonchalantly. "I don't sleep much."

"And you don't log all your hours, either. According to her, you only charge her for one in three hours you actually work. You didn't know she knew about that, did you?"

Jullien fell silent.

Zellen let out a slow breath. "You are not what I thought you were when Ushara dragged your sorry ass onto our ship. . . ." He handed the patches to Jullien. "Don't forget that you can't patch up unless you're in full Tavali sanctioned gear. If a Tavali asks if you're a cit, you can answer that you're a cock, candidate, CC, candy-ass, or TNT—those are the terms we use for those going through initiation. Don't call yourself Tavali yet or someone will cut your throat for it. And whatever you do, don't let any League or local LEO catch you with *any* Tavali paraphernalia on your body or in your possession as they are felonies and carry a death penalty in most systems."

"Trust me, that's the *least* of my concerns should I get caught by any LEO anywhere."

Zellen laughed. "I guess that's true." He held his hand out to Jullien. "Welcome aboard . . . Dagger."

"Thanks."

"I'll call Sheila and let her know that you'll be a little late in to work.

You should take care of your eyes and get some Tavali gear on before you head in. After yesterday, you don't need anymore drama on your record."

Jullien bowed to him. "Yes, Gûr Tana. I'll see right to it." And with that, he headed out. But honestly, he hated the thoughts of changing his clothes. He'd just gotten comfortable with his new persona.

Now he was stepping into someone else. Another uncertain role.

Jullien reached for his link, then remembered he didn't have one. Crap. He couldn't access the manual without it. Maybe the TBX would have them there and he could pick a new one up without a scan that would alert bounty hunters and The League where he was.

But as he entered the optometrist's office, he had a weird feeling.

Like he was being watched.

Turning, he scanned the street.

No one was there. Yet the feeling persisted, and he'd been followed enough in his lifetime to know he wasn't paranoid. This was real.

*Where are you, you bastard?*

More to the point, *who* was it? How much of a threat were they to Ushara and Vasili?

Memories flashed through him like a strobe light and threatened to send him to his knees.

From the moment of his birth, he'd felt like he'd been standing in the middle of a killing field—with enemies rushing him from every side, trying to stab him through his heart. Many times they'd succeeded and he'd stumbled to the ground, but through it all, he'd forced himself to climb back to his feet.

No matter how hard the blow, no matter how much he'd wanted to lie down and die, he'd stubbornly refused to fall.

*Indurari.*

"You want me, bitch . . . you better be prepared for war." Because the one truth that had remained constant, he would not go quietly to his grave. And the one thing he knew how to do was fight past his pain—to bite the hand that both fed him and bled him to the bone.

This time, he wasn't just protecting his own ass. He was protecting something far more precious to him.

And that made him deadlier than ever.

# CHAPTER 13

"This is bullshit! I demand to see the Gorturnum HAP! Now!"

Standing in the main landing bay where Ushara had been summoned twenty minutes ago to deal with this *lovely* situation, she shook her head at Malys Venik. As the wife of Brax Venik, the High Admiral of the Porturnum Tavali and a Qillaq warrior, this creature was a handful. She'd come in with a few of her husband's ships that had been damaged in a League ambush. As such, Malys was demanding that Ushara turn over a dozen of the Gorturnum's fastest ships to her crews to get them home.

Yeah, like that would happen.

When the hottest pits of Tophet froze over.

While they were all Tavali, they were not that close a family and it didn't entitle Malys to Gorturnum ships that were personally owned by their crews or Trajen.

Not to mention, this blatant disregard for Ushara's rank and position was really beginning to piss her off, and it was taking everything she had not to resort to punching out the female for it. She was, after all, Pavakahira Andarion, and the urge to light this Qill on fire was hard to suppress. "I'm the VA in charge here, Commander Venik, and you will deal with *me*."

Tall and insanely gorgeous in her skintight red battlesuit, Malys raked a withering sneer down Ushara's body. "I don't deal with the second string, sweetie. Yerek? Move this little fluff out of my way."

When the giant mountain stepped forward at Malys's command, a deep, resonant voice rang out.

"Yerek, that would be a *profoundly* bad idea for you, that would have devastating consequences on your future health and mobility. Seriously, I suggest you retreat and take a coffee break."

Ushara had to bite back a smile at Jullien's cold, deadly tone that carried the full weight of his regal birth. That was the voice of a male used to commanding armies and being obeyed without fail. She glanced at him over her shoulder and then had to do a double-take as she caught sight not of the vagabond male she was used to seeing, but of a stunning stranger.

This wasn't the immaculate, haughty fop she'd seen in old media photos who'd been the tahrs of Andaria, or the adorable ragamuffin who'd won her heart. The male approaching them was barely recognizable.

Dressed black-on-black in a Tavali armstitch battlesuit with a long leather and suede coat, he was all lethal predator. And the flared colonial style looked good on him. Each side of the coat was tied back to show the presence of his custom silver-handled blasters. Not that he needed them to look tough with the deadly aura that surrounded him. It was enough to terrify anyone with an ounce of self-preservation.

His silver-trimmed holster matched the garrotte chain he wore around his left wrist and his new buckled boots. He now sported a pair of black leather fingerless gloves and a custom holster, as well as dark sunglasses that hid his eyes from them so that no one could tell where he was looking. An unnerving tactical advantage that was employed by League assassins.

The only thing left of the old Jullien was the long black scarf that he still wore around his neck, and his sexy, well-trimmed whiskers that he somehow managed to keep from ever becoming a full beard.

He was gorgeous and seductive, and she wasn't the only one who noticed.

In fact, the amount of attention that was on him now was beginning to anger her more than this current situation. Even Malys's features softened as a slow, appreciative smile spread across her face.

"Well, what have we here?" The smile faded as she saw Jullien's arm patches and she realized he held no real rank. "You dare threaten your superior with violence?"

Jullien snorted derisively. "He's not my superior in *any* way, and it's not a threat, *mu tara*. Rather an absolute promise of extreme and gory violence on his body. He approached my admiral with hostile intent. He's lucky I haven't gutted him." Then he passed a charming grin to Ushara. "I got around to reading the manual."

"God help us now," she teased him.

"Or at the very least, your brother since it's his ass in the hot seat for my actions. . . . He's so going to seriously regret being *my* CO." Jullien turned back toward Malys. "Means I have free rein to make you unhappy. I sincerely like that thought."

"Have you any idea who I am?"

"No, and I honestly don't care when you threaten the VA of this Nation."

"I will have you whipped."

Jullien gave her a chilling smile. "Last one who tried that died in agonizing pain, while calling my paternity into question."

Malys's nostrils flared as she realized that Jullien wasn't about to heel. She faced Ushara. "Are you going to let him talk to me like this? With impunity?"

Ushara ground her teeth. Andarion males didn't back down, especially not stralen ones. Jullien was protecting her. But Malys was a Qill and they didn't retreat either. This was a bad situation and she had no idea how to diffuse it.

A tic started in Jullien's jaw. "I believe what we have here is what the Overseer of Justice and her council would call a failure of competing goals. You broke your ships. And that's a damn shame. You should learn to pilot them better. Now you expect us to hand over ours without compensation. Were we to march into your territory and do that, Venik would tell us to kiss his large Andarion ass. Given what I know about the history between Venik and Thaumarturgus, I really don't think you want to take that meeting you're insisting on. So instead of trying to manhandle my VA, I suggest you thank her for saving your lives."

Malys closed the distance between them. "You're Andarion?"

"Yes, I am."

"Caste?"

"Given my bearing and syntax, I should think it obvious."

"Then you should know my husband will do as I request of him. As the mother of his children, I hold Brax's full loyalty. Therefore, you should fear him and me."

"And my wife holds mine. Therefore, you better damn well fear me, and you should be quaking before her."

"Your wife?"

Jullien stepped back to bow toward Ushara. "I believe you are more than acquainted with her."

Malys paled instantly as she finally understood the full dynamic of what was happening.

Ushara closed the distance between them while Malys leaned in to whisper near Jullien's ear.

"Are you wearing those glasses for the reason I suspect?"

"Yes."

She paled even more. "It appears I've overstepped my bounds, Admiral Altaan. However, it's imperative that I get our ships and cargo out of here as soon as possible. What accommodations can you make?"

"I'll get our CP right on it, and let you know. Please feel free to partake of our hospitality until then." Ushara stepped back. "Zellen? Would you provide an escort for our Porturnum guests and make sure they're cared for until we can see them on their way?"

"Yes, ma'am."

Jullien didn't speak until they were gone. "Nice code for *watch them*."

She snorted, then grimaced at him. "I thought you wanted to keep our marriage a secret."

Screwing his face up into an adorable expression, he scratched at his whiskered cheeks. Now that was the less-than-cocksure Jules she knew so well. "Yeah, I screwed up. And we're all lucky I didn't deck her. If she'd taken one more step at you . . . it wouldn't have been pretty for any of us. What's the penalty for assaulting a HAP's wife?"

"You don't want to know."

"Didn't think so."

Her heart quickened as she tried to see him through those dark glasses. She reached up and removed them. Instead of red, his irises were green, but not their usual hazel color. "What's wrong with your eyes?"

"They're colored contacts to hide the stralen."

"Is that safe?"

He blinked a few times as if they annoyed him. "It limits my peripheral a little, but not too badly. I've got this set and a pair of solid white ones so that I can look full-blooded. I thought I'd let you pick the ones you preferred since you're the one who has to see them."

She folded his glasses and handed them to him. "I like your real eyes, whatever color they are. It makes no never mind to me so long as you're happy with them. . . . But," she paused to smile up at him. "I have to admit to having a preference for the stralen. Only because when I see them, I know it means you're still mine."

"That I will always be."

Ushara bit her lip as she ran her hand along his scarf. "Tavali looks good on you."

"Good enough to eat?" he teased lightly.

She laughed. "Someone might overhear you."

"It's not the overhearing that concerns me." He cast a pointed stare downward.

Ushara followed the line of his gaze to see the large bulge that was quite evident in his tight pants. Her husband had been rather gifted by the gods in that department. Heat exploded over her face.

Clearing his throat, Jullien reached behind his back to untie his coat. "Don't move away for second," he said under his breath.

"I should."

"Only if you want to embarrass us both." He quickly buttoned his coat all the way down and folded his arms over his chest. "I'm heading to work now. You?"

"Work."

He gave a charming nod before he took a step back. "Oh, I forgot to mention that I have a new link." He pulled it out. "I need your digits again."

"What happened to your other one?"

"Got compromised."

"How so?"

When he didn't answer, she became worried. "Jules?"

"A threat came through. No idea how they traced me."

"Viable?"

"Enough that I destroyed it."

Her heart sank at the thought of what he'd lost. "Did you salvage anything?"

He shook his head. "Wasn't worth the risk."

"You have *nothing* left from it?"

"I don't need anything from my past."

No! Tears filled her eyes as she thought about the picture of his parents. It was all he'd been able to keep from his former life.

Now he had nothing whatsoever.

Not a single memory at all.

"*Keramon*—"

"Don't, Shara," he said sharply. "I'm not like you. I don't have those happy memories of a warm childhood that I want to hang on to. Really, I'm okay with letting go. There's absolutely nothing I want from my past except to forget it ever happened. As far as I'm concerned, my life began when I opened my eyes on Gavin's ship and saw you standing over me."

Choking on a sob, she hugged him. "I love you so much."

"Not the way to keep our marriage a secret, love."

"I know." She kissed his cheek, then linked their lines. "Go to work. Try not to go to jail."

He snorted irritably. "Make no promises."

Shaking her head, she watched as he headed toward Sheila's office.

Dayam. That loping swagger . . .

She wanted to follow him, rip those clothes off, pin him to the nearest wall and ride that long hard body until he begged her for mercy. How strange that she'd never felt this degree of desire for Chaz.

But then Chaz have *never* looked like *that*.

"You are drooling, *kisa*."

Ushara growled at the sound of Ryna's voice in her ear. "What are you doing here?"

"I came to give you a heads-up that Paka knows about your marriage."

She went cold with dread at those unexpected words. Crap . . . "What? How?"

"You know how it goes. Zellen told his wife who called her sister who called her sister who called her friend who called our mother who ran to Paka who is now furious at *you*." Ryna hugged her. "For what it's worth, I'm on your side. So are the twins and Mary."

"Thank you."

Pressing her cheek to Ushara's, Ryna purred in her ear. "He has a fine little ass, doesn't he?"

"You're not supposed to be ogling my husband's ass, sister."

She stuttered. "I can't help the fact he's bending over in that office. You think Sheila dropped her stylus on purpose?"

"Are you trying to piss me off?"

Ryna laughed. "Sorry. I'll stop admiring his ass now."

"So how mad is Paka?"

"On a scale of one to ten . . . about thirty."

Ushara cringed. "Great. Let me deal with Venik, then I'll deal with this."

How much worse was this day going to get?

And when she'd asked that question, she'd meant for it to be rhetorical, not a personal challenge to the gods. Yet everything went wrong for the rest of the day.

*Everything.*

By the time she'd found transport for Malys and crew, and had a workable solution for them, she'd been ready to pull her hair out from dealing with the older shrew.

She was already two hours late heading home and her nerves were raw and ravaged, ready to break in half.

Exhausted and irritable, she opened her door and was greeted by the foreign sound of raucous laughter. And clashing metal. Sounds of battle and cursing.

What the . . . ?

Curious and a little worried, Ushara went to the back courtyard where the door was ajar to find Jullien and Vasili outside, playing with toy battle drones. They were attacking each other's "beast" and insulting their abilities, and running around like two small kids. She'd never seen anything like this as they went in circles around each other with total careless abandon, jumping over furniture, shrubs, and each other.

"I thought you said you were good at this, *chizzi*?" Jullien ducked as Vas's drone fired at his head and narrowly missed it.

"Ha! You're old, *žumi*!"

"Old? Ha! I'm the one winning."

Vasili blew him a raspberry as Jullien stumbled and almost tripped over a potted plant. "You're not winning. Falling on top of it 'cause you're fat doesn't mean you won."

"I'm not fat," he said indignantly as he continued to fight. "I'm fluffy."

Vasili turned his entire body as he attempted to control his drone to tackle Jullien's. "You're hairy and gross. Not fluffy!"

Laughing at them and the fact that they didn't stop for anything—not even when Jullien stepped in a bowl of plant water and Vas ran into her wind chimes and became tangled with them, she pushed the door open to watch a few more minutes of their adorable play. "What are you two lunatics doing?"

They froze and the drones instantly crashed to the ground.

"We didn't have them in the house." Jullien said that so fast and defensively it made her wonder how many times he'd gotten into trouble as a child for playing with drones in the palace.

"I figured as much. Where did they come from?"

Vasili picked his up and ran it to her. "We built them! Aren't they neat?"

She was in awe of the intricate devices. "Yes, they are."

Vas turned it over to show her the propulsion gears and tanks they'd used. "Jullien was teaching me about engineering. This was part of my project."

Ushara smiled at Vas's exuberance. She'd never seen him happier. Jullien still looked as if he were afraid he'd done something wrong and was waiting for her to start yelling at him for it.

While Vas explained the drone to her, Jullien went inside.

Subdued and unusually quiet, he came back a few minutes later with a small serving tray of food for her.

Stunned at the unexpected bounty, she gaped at him. "What's this?"

"Dinner. We already ate. We would have waited, but we didn't know how long you'd be and Vas was starving. So we kept yours warm for you."

Touching her heart, she smiled up at him, grateful beyond measure for his kindness. "This is why I love you."

He gave her a bashful smile before he pulled away.

Vas grabbed his drone from her hands. "Rematch!"

The smile finally returned to Jullien's face as he ran after him. "You're on, *bryth*! Arm up!"

Smiling at them, she watched their war while she ate. Jullien had just conceded defeat when her door rang.

"I'll get it," she said, rising with her plate to carry it back inside. She set everything in the kitchen and noted how clean Jullien had left it all before she went to see who was visiting.

It was her father and grandfather. How strange for them to ring, though. They never did such, which told her exactly how furious her father was over her marriage that he would be so formal. He must have assumed she'd still be at work. Or he was doing this to be a pain in her ass.

She released an exhausted sigh as she let them in. "Paka, I'm too tired tonight. Can we discuss this tomorrow?"

"We're not here for you."

Those cold words froze her to the spot. "What's that supposed to mean?"

He handed her the papers in his hand. "Dagger's been reassigned to the crew of the *Night Rain*. We're here to help him gear up since they're launching within the hour."

Her stomach hit the floor. "What?"

"Kirill lost one of his men. He's agreed to take Dagger on to train him."

She shoved the papers back at him. "This is bullshit. I'm not letting you to do this."

"Do what? He's a candidate. It's his duty to go where he's assigned."

"Davel—"

"Won't be traveling for awhile. Dagger has to have two full years in as a cock to be admitted to the Nation. You know the Code. He has to be active on a crew immediately for his status to stand. No one is above our laws."

She glared at her father and what he was doing.

And why.

"Kirill's a savage. And he hates Jules. You know that."

"Careful, daughter. That's your blood you're talking about."

"And this is my husband you're sending out with a vicious crew you know will treat him like shit. You do this, Paka, and I won't forgive you for it."

"It's already done."

Tears blinded her over their cruelty. She couldn't believe that this was the same male who'd preached benevolence and kindness to her, her entire life. *Never judge until you've seen their circumstances.*

What happened to *that* father?

"Where is he?" her grandfather asked.

She curled her lip at him, unable to believe he was in on this. "Follow the laughter," she said, her voice breaking on those words.

And that laughter died a few seconds later when they went outside and told Jullien to pack his gear.

"No!" Vasili screamed. "No!" His shrill cries broke her heart and made her want to claw out her father's eyes.

Jullien swallowed hard as he knelt on the ground by Vasili's side and handed him his controller. "It's okay, *luden*. I'll be back before you know it. Just remember to keep your grades up, and watch after your *matarra* for me, okay?"

Tears flowed down Vasili's face. "Will you be here for my Confirmation?"

"I'll do my best. And I'll call every chance I get."

Nodding, he hugged Jullien, who in turn held onto him. "I'll miss you, too, *tana*. Be a good boy for me."

"Love you, Paka."

"Love you, too." Jullien balled his fist in Vas's hair and kissed his cheek, then released him. Rising to his feet, he refused to look at her father or grandfather. Instead, he held his hand out for her. "You okay?"

"No. I'm furious."

"Don't be. And now when the seat gets left up in the bathroom you'll definitely know who to yell at."

"You're not funny."

He took her hands into his and held them to his lips to kiss them. Then he cupped her face and kissed her lips. "I was going to give this to you later tonight. But I guess I can't wait." He reached down into his pocket to pull out something he wouldn't let her see. "I know it's not much . . . one day I promise I'll get you a bigger one."

Tears choked her as he slid a pitch-dark wedding ring onto her finger. The black center stone came up like a rose that was nested in dark leaves formed by the black rhodium band and white melee diamonds. The side band was a delicate, intricately carved filigree. Tiny and extremely feminine, the ring was a very unorthodox choice. "Black?"

Jullien nodded. "I don't want you to ever forget that you alone hold my dark heart. You're the only one I've ever trusted with it. And I'm leaving it here with you for safekeeping . . . in your hands." He brushed his thumb over her lips. "After all, an Androkyn is never where he lives. But where he loves. And true love will always find its way through paths where even feral lorinas fear to prey. You are my Darling star, and no matter how dark the night or how perilous my journey, your divine light alone will always guide me home."

Those words shattered her heart. Sobbing, she pulled him against her and wept. In that moment, she hated her father for doing this to her.

How could he take Jullien away?

Even worse, she had nothing to give to him. He was so much more thoughtful than she was. "You better come back to me, Jullien eton Ana-tole."

He pulled the ring from her finger and showed her the engraving inside the band. "My oath to you, *mu Ger Tarra*. Any time you need me, glance at this and know that I will never fail to keep it."

*Urtui æbre gevyly frag. I will never break your heart.*

Jullien kissed the ring and replaced it on her finger, then kissed her softly. "I am and will ever be yours."

And with those words spoken, her father and grandfather took him to join her cousin's crew. A crew she knew would hate him for every-thing he'd never done.

This was wrong and she knew it. Somehow she was going to get him back. She didn't know how, but she would. Even if it meant alienating her family to do so.

Jullien didn't speak to Ushara's father or grandfather as they made their way to Kirill's ship. A part of him kept waiting for them to shoot him in the head so that they could collect the multimillion cred bounty on his life.

Honestly, even though they weren't licensed for it, it was what he expected.

So it was almost a relief to see that they really meant for him to board as part of Kirill's crew.

Her father roughly shoved his bag of gear into his hands. That was as close to a goodbye as they came. At least it was far kinder than the send-off his own parents had given him.

But the look in Petran's eyes was the same. He stared at him as if Jullien disgusted him. As if he were the lowest form of life to ever belly crawl from the cesspit of genetic mutations.

Kirill came down the ramp to add his glare to the group. "I've got him from here."

"Thanks," Vidarri said. "We owe you."

"No problem, *Graspa*. Happy to help out, anytime." Inclining his head to them, Kirill led Jullien on board, and stopped him as soon as they were inside the ship. He held his hand out. "I need your link."

Jullien started to ask why, then remembered that as a cock, he wasn't allowed to question his captain. Grinding his teeth, he dug it out of his pocket and handed it over.

Kirill dropped it to the floor and stomped it to pieces. "So you can't be a cry-baby bitch and tattle to Ushara about your treatment."

Jullien held his temper in check and said nothing. *You can do this. You survived your stints in the vörgäte. You can handle this bunch of pussies, too.* They weren't nearly as tough as the guards and definitely not as frightening as the Ixurian inmates who'd taken their hatred of his grandmother and royal status out on him.

Kirill stood right in his face. "Are you pissed?"

Jullien blinked slowly and ignored him. One thing he'd learned from his "lovely" experiences was that non responses infuriated his tormentors much more than his smart-ass retorts.

"You think you're a badass, don't you?"

He smirked at Kirill before he quoted another passage from the *Book of Harmony*. "Only those who aren't, think it. Those who are, know, and don't have to prove."

Kirill curled his lip. "You think you're cute?"

"Adorably precious."

Snarling, he shoved Jullien forward, toward the cargo bay. As he headed for the crew quarters with his gear, Kirill stopped him.

"You haven't earned the right for a bed, slag. What do you think? You're a tiziran?"

That made him want to slug the bastard and Kirill was lucky he caught the urge before he had Kirill searching the floor for his fangs.

"You'll bunk in the engine room and when you prove yourself worthy, we might allow you a blanket."

Jullien felt his nostrils flaring as he followed Kirill to his new "quarters."

Over and over, he reminded himself that he'd survived a lot worse than this. Crueler tormentors with a much bigger axe to grind, who'd shoved it up his ass with a vengeance.

*This too shall pass.*

This would be a child's play, with a group of infants who thought they knew cruelty. They were amateurs.

Jullien stored his gear in a closet in the engine room and made his way up to the cargo bay to help secure their load for takeoff. What he quickly learned was that Kirill's attitude was contagious, and he was as welcome to their crew as a lethal STD in a whorehouse.

Still, he held his tongue and his temper. For Ushara. She was the goal in this. In the long run, they were inconsequential. His days here would drag by, just as his months in prison had. If his grandmother's cruelty had taught him anything, it was to bide his time and focus on what mattered most.

Survival.

He grimaced as the stryper shoved him from behind. "Watch where you're going, slag!"

Jullien clenched his fist to keep from hitting the bastard. He hadn't been the one moving. Whatever.

The tone sounded to alert them to secure themselves for launch. When Jullien headed for a seat, the stryper stopped him in the doorway and pushed him back through it. "Slags to the bay. You're just cargo."

"Excuse me?"

"You heard me, slag." He slammed the door in Jullien's face and locked it.

Stunned, Jullien watched as they headed down the hallway away from him and laughed at what they'd just done. Turning around, he stared at the cargo bay. Was it even pressurized? Or sealed for an atmosphere? Some of these older ships weren't.

And there was no place for him to secure himself for the launch.

Shit. So this was how they were planning to kill him.

# CHAPTER 14

U shara waited in nervous excitement with Vasili as the *Night Rain* docked in the bay. This was what they'd been counting down to for weeks on end now, and ever since she'd gotten word that they were returning, she'd been breathless with anticipation.

Oxana had even brought little Nadya out to join them to welcome Jullien home.

Strange, she'd never been like this before. Not since she'd been a small child and had waited eagerly with her mother and siblings for her father to return home from his missions. She was absolutely dancing with her eager enthusiasm.

Nadya squealed as the ramp lowered. "Basha Dagger!"

Oxana laughed. "He probably won't be the first one off, Naddicakes. Cocks have duties that take them a few minutes to attend before they can leave their ships."

"Oh, okay." She looked up at Vas. "You gots to hold the sign up higher for him to see it, though."

Ever patient with his younger cousin, Vas smiled down at her. "He'll see it."

Ushara chewed her nail as the crew finally started leaving. She felt as giddy as Nadya. And even though she knew her sister was right, she still scanned every member who came off, looking for any trace of Jullien's swagger.

And each one disappointed her.

After half an hour, and when they'd virtually stopped departing, she scowled. "This is weird. Where is he?"

While he wouldn't have been among the first to disembark, he should have been eager enough to not be among the last either.

Kirill and his stryper were laughing as they came down the ramp.

At the sight of *them*, Ushara felt the blood drain from her face as dread welled up inside her. She met Oxana's gaping stare. That could mean only one thing.

Jullien wasn't with them. The captain was always last crew off. No one else would be left on that ship.

What the hell?

"Stay here with the kids." Scared and angry, she closed the distance between them. "Kirill?"

He sobered at the sound of her voice. They both did. "Hey, *kyzu*. What can I do you for?"

Ushara glared at him, resisting the urge to pull her blaster and beat him with it. "You know what I want. Where's my husband?"

Kirill shrugged. "Don't know. I assumed you saw the transfer orders."

"What orders?"

"Two months ago. I traded him out with one of my brother's crewmen. No offense, he was a mouthy, worthless piece of shit. I needed someone I could rely on. Check with Lev for his whereabouts."

She felt as if she'd been slapped.

Without another word, they brushed past her.

Oxana brought the kids to stand by her side. "Hey? You all right? What happened?"

"They traded him with one of Lev's crew." She could barely choke out those words past the stabbing pain of disappointment she felt.

Oxana scowled. "Why didn't someone tell you?"

Ushara shook her head as a new fear began to manifest. He was lying. She knew it. "I don't know."

"He's not here?" The hurt in Vas's voice mirrored her own.

"No, baby. Sorry." She hugged him as she met her sister's gaze and saw in Oxana's eyes the same doubts and fears that she had. No transfer had been put in for Jullien. She'd have seen the order go through. In fact, she'd been monitoring his orders since she hadn't been allowed to speak to him as part of Kirill's dictates and hazing for him.

Given that crew transfers for cocks were a normal practice and not something that her cousin would have to hide with nonexistent paperwork, it begged a single question . . .

What had they really done with Jullien?

*You better not have collected his bounty, you son of a bitch.*

Determined to find out the truth, she headed across the bay.

"What are you doing?" Oxana called.

"Getting Davel." Kirill might brush *her* off, but he wouldn't be able to do that to her brother. Davel would get to the bottom of this, and if it was what she suspected, he'd help her kill her cousin, too.


At noon the next day, Ushara knocked on Trajen's door. She very seldom disturbed him at his personal residence, but she really needed some peace of mind.

And either backup or an alibi.

The door opened on its own. She walked in slowly. There was no telling where Trajen was. His home was massively large and always eerily silent.

She waited for the lights to turn themselves on to lead her toward wherever he was keeping himself. After a few seconds, they began to flicker and guide her.

Yeah, her boss was a freaky creature of habit.

The phantom lights slowly led her down to his training room where he was working out with more weights than he should be able to lift. She didn't know if he was actually that strong, or if it was a mental, Trisani thing. Either way, it was impressive and terrifying.

As soon as she entered the room, he placed the weights on their stand and picked up a towel from the floor. He draped it around his muscular shoulders so that he could wipe the sweat from his face. While she knew that as a Trisani, Trajen was a lot older than he appeared to be, his body didn't show it. He didn't look a day over thirty.

And like this . . .

His physique would rival Jullien's.

She had to catch herself fast before he picked up on any thoughts of desire from her. From experience, she knew he didn't react well to anyone who lusted after him. Trajen claimed he was celibate to preserve his "wizard powers" from being drained.

However, she suspected it came from the fact that he was even more paranoid and suspicious of others than Jullien. Trajen very seldom touched anyone and he allowed no one to touch him.

For any reason.

In fact, he maintained a four-foot minimum distance of space be-tween himself and everyone else, at all times. He didn't just keep walls around himself, he had it mined with explosives, barbed wire, and a flaming moat that teemed with crocodiles. She'd actually seen folks drop dead for stepping too close to him, too fast. Or rebound off an invisible force field.

He wouldn't even take items from the hands of others. Rather he waited until they set it down before he reached for it.

For whatever reason, Jullien was the only exception to that rule. He was the only one Trajen had ever allowed inside his personal perimeter.

Trajen met her gaze. His muscles rippling, he reached for his water. "Are you sure Davel was lying?"

His powers were so incredibly frightening at times . . .

"No. But he sounded really weird and he wouldn't answer my ques-tions about Jullien. And I hate how easily you read my mind."

"Sorry. It saves time." He opened his water and drank it while she explained what was going on.

"It's been six months and no word from Jullien. I'm scared, boss. Davel wouldn't even look me in the eye. Rather, he bypassed me, beat the crap out of Kirill and has refused to speak to my father since. Given that, and the lies I know Kirill was spewing yesterday, I know some-thing's seriously wrong. What is it they're not telling me?"

He scowled as he got up and moved a little closer to her. "Where's your father now?"

"He was on the dock with Axl and my grandfather. Axl's crew just came in and they're unloading cargo."

Using his mental powers, Trajen changed clothes instantly as he walked, leading her upstairs. It was so unnerving how he did that. And she envied him that ability. Oh to be able to save time by dressing with-out touching anything. She could only imagine what it must have been like to live in a world where everyone could do such things.

Silent and brooding, he walked with her back to the bay where her grandfather was still standing with her brothers while they chatted about nothing in particular.

Even so, they stopped talking immediately when they saw her and Trajen.

"Vidarri." Trajen narrowed his gaze on her grandfather. "Don't you think you should tell your granddaughter what you've done?"

Her grandfather shrugged nonchalantly. "No idea what you're talking about."

"Oh, don't play this game with me. I can bypass you. But really, I think it best if she hears it from you, than if I tell her."

Ushara felt sick to her stomach. This had to be bad for Trajen to go this route. He didn't do things like this.

"Tell me what?" she prompted.

Her grandfather hesitated before he finally spoke. "It was for the best."

Oh yeah, this was going to be *real* bad. "What?" She all but shouted the word.

Her brother Axl sighed. "They'd found him, Shara."

"By him, I assume you mean Jullien. He does have a name, you know? So who had found him?"

"Bounty hunters." Her grandfather snarled. "They saw him and attacked him on one of their stops, and almost shot Kirill. It was just a matter of time till they showed up here and came for you or Vasili."

Ushara felt sick to her stomach as dread consumed her. "What did you do?"

None of them would look at her.

"Answer me!"

"They sold him."

She turned to face Davel, who'd come up behind her to join their group. "You knew?"

"No. Not until you sent me to rendezvous with Kirill last night. Kirill lied at first, then told me the truth after I beat it out of him."

She choked on her tears, but forced them down. This wasn't the time for hysterics. She had to remain calm if she was to help Jullien. "How long ago?"

"Four months."

Those words ran into her with the force of a starship in hyperdrive. Was he serious?

Four *months*? They'd sold Jullien *four* months ago? Blind fury exploded inside her as she gaped at the group of betrayers. How could they?

"He was Tavali!" she growled at them.

"In Training," her grandfather said defensively. "A candidate. They needed the money for repairs. It was for the good of the ship and crew."

"You bastards!" Never had she felt so betrayed. And to think it was her own family who'd done this to her!

To Jullien!

"He's a darkheart!" her grandfather snarled.

She sneered at him. "He's a Fyreblood!"

The color faded from her grandfather's face. "What?"

Ushara wiped at the tears on her cheeks as she confronted them all. "Yeah, you heard me. You sold out one of our own, *Graspa*. Jules didn't want me to tell anyone. But his lineage isn't just eton Anatole. It's also Pavakahiri Samari. More than that, he's stralen for me. *That's* what you've betrayed with your actions. Not just my husband, but one of the most sacred and rare of the Fyreblood lineages. The last of it, no less."

Crossing his arms over his chest, Trajen gave a slow nod. "She's not lying. He's the grandson of Edon Samari. One of the last two surviving heirs of the original and direct ruling Samari bloodline, and the only one who carries that incredibly rare stralen gene. Not even his twin has it. Jullien dies, your race loses their connection to your beloved goddess and her Kadurr warriors *forever*." Trajen emphasized the last word in a sinister whisper.

Axl cursed. "Are you telling us that Edon Samari really did have a child—that it wasn't just some bullshit legend handed down to amuse kids? And that darkheart bastard is the one we've been waiting for to restore our original monarchy?"

"Ironic as Tophet, ain't it?" Trajen laughed bitterly. "Edon Samari seduced Eriadne eton Anatole so that he could overthrow her and take the Andarion throne, and instead she went on a vengeful killing spree to wipe out all Fyrebloods over his betrayal. Ultimately, it would be his very spawn that dethroned her and took her place. In the end, Samari succeeded. But lost."

Her grandfather shook his head as he realized what he'd done. "We've got to find him! We can't let his bloodline die out."

Ushara glared at her grandfather. "You're not doing *anything* else. You've done enough already. *All* of you are grounded until Jullien returns." Furious, she began hailing her sisters—the only ones she dared trust at this point.

And Davel. Right now, he was an honorary sister. He might not approve of the designation, but she was so mad at the males of her family that it was the only way she could allow herself to be in a room with him and not do him harm.

Armed and ready for battle in full Tavali gear and war paint, Ushara and her sisters walked slowly through the dense, smelly crowded Ladorian pleasure club, looking for any sign that they were in the right place while they waited for Davel and Trajen to join them. The stench in here was nauseating. Sweat, blood, and other things she didn't want to think about.

Jay curled her lips in distaste as she pressed her hand to her nose in a useless attempt to blot out the odors. "Please tell me he's not really here."

Ushara barely stifled her gag reflex as she stumbled past two humans who really needed to find a private room. "I hope not."

But Trajen was never wrong and this was where he'd brought them. She shuddered at the thought of Jullien being trapped in this godforsaken hell where they sold others for sex, fights, and any kind of imaginable perversion. The depravity sickened her.

"Well, well, ladies. What I can I do for you?"

Ushara turned a jaundiced eye to the well-dressed human male who approached them. He appeared to be one of the ringleaders of this wretched establishment, which didn't endear him to her. Rather it made her want to take a note from Jullien and punch the man in the throat for no other reason than just condoning the existence of such a horrid place that peddled sentient misery in the name of profit. "We're looking for an Andarion fighter."

"For carnal pleasure, recreational hunting, or blood sport?"

Her stomach lurched at the question and the joy in his tone. Oh yeah, she seriously wanted to punch him, especially given the option that Davel had told her they'd sold Jullien to. "Blood sport."

He grinned at them with a sick satisfaction that gleamed in his eyes. "Ladies after my own heart. And you're just in time. We open the next round of betting in fifteen minutes. If you want to see tonight's menu . . ." He handed them a card with a scancode. "Minimum bet is listed under each fighter. And we have some fierce animals in the cage for tonight's fun. Good luck. Once you bet, you'll receive instructions on where to go for the viewing. And what seats you're entitled to for the amount wagered. We also have refreshments, as well as companions listed under other menu options. Whatever thrill you seek, we have something that'll make you peak."

As he walked off, she was tempted to shoot him in the head.

Maybe later.

Desperate to find Jullien, Ushara quickly scanned the fighters. Her heart sank as none of them looked familiar.

At all.

This was useless.

"Wait!" Ryna flipped it back two. "Look." She pointed down. "His arm."

Ushara wanted to vomit as she saw the familiar bleeding winged heart that was pierced by a sword. *Indurari*. She didn't even recognize the hooded male in that picture. They'd beefed Jullien's size up, most likely from steroids or some other dangerous drug, and his lower face was misshapen by bruises and cuts. His eye color was hidden by the dark hood that fell over them.

But for the tattoo and the scar near his heart, she'd have never known it was him.

*The Annihilator.*

Fury tore through her as she saw the other photos they'd posted of him in brutal, gory fights. They'd shaved his head and beard. And kept him caged like an animal.

Her hands shaking, she met her sister's gaze. "I might yet kill your father when we return home."

Ryna didn't flinch. "I might help you."

By the time they were able to place the bet to locate him, Trajen and Davel had finally joined them. Ushara waited impatiently for the coordinates that would guide them to Jullien.

And she was terrified of what she'd find when she got there. As bad as Andarion Ring matches were, this was so much worse. These weren't just fighting matches meant to show off skill and stamina, these were all-out savage bloodbaths that were meant to be as ruthless and raw as possible. The kind of primitive gore-fests that were banned by any civilized government. Which was why they were held on stations where no government held any jurisdiction.

The crowd was so thick, they could barely move through it. And she had no idea where they kept the fighters or how she and her sisters and Trajen and Davel would go about getting Jullien out of this mess.

She looked up at Trajen. "What do we do?"

Trajen let out a deep growl as they neared the stark, fenced arena where Jullien would be fighting. "The cage is highly electrified."

Which meant even he would have trouble with it. While Trajen could manipulate and play with low electrical currents, higher ones tended to go awry and have unforeseen reactions. His powers could detonate that cage like a bomb if he tried to use them to access it.

"Can we blow the circuits?" Davel asked.

Oxana gave him a droll stare as she pointed out the fact that those circuits would be kept outside the station, in space, and they had no way to access them. "Sure. You get right on that, *drey.*"

He rolled his eyes at her sarcasm, then scowled as he glanced around for more viable options. "Do they not clean the cages out between fights?"

Ushara frowned at Davel's question. Before she could think better of it, she glanced to see what he was talking about, then wished she hadn't as a wave of extreme nausea hit her.

No, they didn't clean the cages out between fights and what remained of the losers was barely identifiable in the dirt and sawdust that covered the floors.

Bile rose in her throat. She shook her head to clear it before she gave in and undignified herself in public. "We've got to get him out of here before the next fight."

A deafening roar went through the crowd.

Davel cursed. "I think we're too late."

Ushara watched in horror as a buzzer sounded and two fighters were literally slung into the cage from opposite doors. They rebounded off the electrified bars that sent green and blue sparks arcing out into the cheering crowd. And the instant she recognized the Andarion with red eyes, it ignited a fury within her that she'd only tasted one other time in her life.

The day she'd gone after Chaz's brother.

In that heartbeat, everything went dark and her sight dimmed. . . .

Davel stepped back in fear at the same time Trajen caught the expression on Ushara's face.

"What do we do?" Davel asked him.

Trajen had no idea. This was what he'd hoped to avoid and it was why he'd chosen Ushara as his VA. While Jullien's Samari lineage was the first among the Fyrebloods, Ushara's Altaan was the second. Unlike the other massive warrior tribes of Andaria, the Fyrebloods had always been extremely reclusive. They'd taken to the highest mountains to cluster in small family clans. Their numbers had intentionally been kept tiny in comparison to their darker counterparts on the ground. Mostly in an effort to keep the Ixurianir from noticing them and attacking them.

Though they were as war-loving as the rest of their Andarion brethren, they were also every bit as honorable when it came to the rules of battle and conflict. The Fyrebloods knew they had a distinct advantage with their pyrokinetics, and so they'd avoided conflict with the Ixurianir, seeing it as dishonorable to battle those who couldn't defend against them. They turned to philosophy and became the teachers and priests of Andaria.

Until technology arose that leveled the playing field and forced the different species to merge together again. As Andaria became civilized and their castes were set, the Fyrebloods, unlike the winged and Ixurianir Andarion clans, were barred from the noble and warrior ranks, and given to a caste below both groups. They weren't even allowed to fight in the First Plenum for a place in their ruling government or military.

Something that hadn't set well with a group that believed themselves to be descended and birthed from the original gods of Andaria. So the Fyrebloods had become even more reclusive and withdrawn. Resentful. And that had led to more suspicion from the others who feared what the Fyrebloods might be plotting against them in seclusion.

Until the inevitable happened and war broke out between the groups. Overwhelmed by sheer numbers and no match for the growing technology that could launch a targeted missile from a farther distance than their incendiary breath, the Fyrebloods were pushed into an even lower caste and their numbers reduced to near extinction levels.

Those who possessed the stralen genes were the first to sacrifice themselves for the protection of their families. And they were the ones systematically targeted by the Ixurianir for execution.

Then just as it seemed the Fyrebloods were done for, a miracle happened. A single Altaan warrior rose through the ranks to lead her people in rebellion against the Ixurianir. And she was the one who had been entrusted with the last Samari son—her own nephew. An infant whose mother, Zira, had died moments after his birth of the wounds she'd sustained in battle, fighting beside her sister warriors. Yvera Altaan was the one who'd taken that infant into hiding and raised him.

It would be his son, Edon Samari who would be sent years later as an envoy to negotiate peace with their tadara, Eriadne eton Anatole. Renowned for his charm and wit, Edon won more than Eriadne's support.

He, alone, had won her frigid heart.

Even though she was already married, with children, Edon had set out to seduce her and had plotted against her husband. In true, ruthless fashion, he manipulated and vied for power, hoping to save the last of his race. His goal was to bring down the tadara and her consort who'd already purged the winged clans from Andaria.

Wanting to save the Fyrebloods from another "Cleansing," he intended to murder Faran and replace him as tadar, then kill Eriadne and see his own children as the reigning monarchs of Andaria.

That had been his plan.

Until the unthinkable occurred. Somehow during his seduction of his queen, he became the one enchanted and lost his heart in the process. By the time she conceived his son, he was thoroughly in love with his enemy. So much so, that he could no longer bear the thought of causing her any harm.

Edon knew then that his days were numbered.

And so they were. As soon as her husband uncovered her scandal and learned that two of Eriadne's children had been fathered by another, he ended their affair in the most brutal of ways.

It was a courtesy she returned to him tenfold, delivered to her husband by her own hand while he ate breakfast at her table.

Only to learn that he hadn't been the one who'd uncovered the lie or the one who'd killed her lover. Rather, it'd been her own sister who'd murdered Edon.

And so she'd handled that betrayal in true Anatole fashion.

She'd gutted her sister by dinner.

It was that kind of cold-blooded ruthlessness that had ended Trajen's family, too. While he despised bloodshed with every part of his being, he understood that there were times when it was a necessary part of life. A time when to preserve life you had to brutally take it.

Some sacrifices had to be made for the greater good. To save the body, the cancer had to be cut out.

Trick was to know how to prune and how to surgically remove only the part that was bad. And to not damage the rest.

That was where Ushara came in now.

His powers were worthless here.

Hers . . .

"Heads down!" Trajen shouted to her brother and sisters as Ushara's eyes turned as red as Jullien's. Fire shot from her hands up her arms and danced all over her body.

No one could summon or control fire like a female Altaan Fyredancer. They were as dangerous as any stralen male.

Patrons screamed and ran, as fire exploded all around them from Ushara's well-placed firebombs.

With her head bent low, Ushara stalked toward the cage like the fiercest of predators. Trajen pulled out his blasters and took up point for her to cover her advance. Guards came running. Ushara blasted them with her fireshots before they could shoot her. Not even the electricity of the cage could slow her down when she reached the door.

She wrenched it from the hinges with her bare hands and sent it flying with the same ease he'd used when he'd gone after the morons on his base. This was that mysterious "god-gene" that inhabited the Pavakahir females. It was as rare and unpredictable as stralen for the Ixurian male. Maybe one in five billion would be born with it.

Probably fewer.

To marry these two genes . . .

No one would ever attack his base and win, especially not with a Trisani at the helm.

The Gorturnum were now as solid as any Tavali Nation ever created.

Provided they got out of here alive tonight.

Trajen fell in behind her and opened fire on the slags coming up from the hallway.

Ushara ignored Trajen as she focused on the fighter in the cage who was still trying to kill Jullien. She blasted him away from her husband.

"Jules!" She grabbed his arm.

He spun on her with a growl so feral that she fully expected him to hit her. But he stayed his hand as his gaze focused on her features. Agony drew his brows into a stern frown as he stared down at her as if he wasn't sure she was real.

"*Keramon?*" She recalled the fire from her hand before she reached up to cup his face.

Jullien didn't seem to understand her.

Suddenly, he snarled and fell to his knees, then started clawing at the collar on his neck. The other fighter moved in to attack again.

Too late, she realized they had a neuroinhibitor around Jullien's throat they were using to control him and lock down his ability to protect himself. Ushara blasted the fighter away from them, then tried to rip the hinged collar from Jullien.

It wouldn't budge.

Shrieking in frustration, she let go of the collar and released as much fire into her hands as she could. She let it arc up, into the ceiling until it set off the fire extinguishers, which in turn released every alarm in the building and short-circuited their electrical systems.

All of their electronics shorted out and went down, then everything went dark.

"Trajen?"

Finally, he was able to use his powers to release the collar from Jullien.

It sprang free instantly.

Coughing and wheezing, Jullien fell forward while she fireblasted more guards. They continued to shoot at them. Dodging the blasts, Ushara fried any and every one of the bastards dumb enough to get in her way and to try and stop them from leaving. She'd had enough of this. Anyone between them and the door was a crispy fritter.

Davel helped Jullien up and put his arm around his shoulders so that they could quickly get him to their ship. But they had to blast their way back, every step.

Not that she cared. She was more than willing for the payback, given the condition Jullien was in. Even Trajen seemed to be enjoying it.

"I thought your race profaned violence," she reminded her boss.

"Some days. Sadly for them, today isn't one of them. Today, I'm rolling around in it like an Andarion on holiday."

Yes, he was.

With her sisters covering their retreat, they made their way through the ensuing chaos left in their wake back to Oxana's ship.

By the time they launched with Trajen at the helm, most of the Ladorian base had gone up in flames.

Davel let out a low whistle as he helped her put Jullien down on an infirmary bed. "Well, we can all add arson to our League warrants. Thanks, sis."

Rolling her eyes, she ignored him. "Get a blanket." She cupped Jullien's bruised and bloodied cheek while he lay on his side, facing the wall. He still hadn't spoken a single word to anyone. "*Mituri?* Can you hear me?"

Jullien didn't respond at all. Rather, he continued to stare straight ahead, his breathing ragged and pain-filled.

Davel covered him with the blanket. "I think he's in shock."

She couldn't blame him for that. She'd be in shock to have survived that hellhole, too. "Can you take the helm from Trajen and send him back here?"

"Sure." He left her alone with Jullien.

Ushara knelt down until she was eye level with him. Stroking his cheek, she wanted to cry over what they'd done. He was like Vasili had been. Completely traumatized and comatose. Unresponsive.

She glanced over her shoulder as the door opened.

Trajen hesitated as he saw Jullien's condition.

"Can you hear his thoughts?"

"Yes."

"Where is he?"

Trajen let out a weary sigh. "Some place you don't want to know."

Tears gathered in her eyes. "What can I do?"

"You're doing it. He hears you, Shara. He's just not quite ready to face it all yet."

She choked in a sympathetic sob as fury and pain racked her. Never had she wanted to hurt her family so much as she did right then. "Just so you know, I'm busting their Canting for this. I mean it. *All of them.* Even my father."

"I won't argue," he said in a flat, even tone. "Whatever punishment you decree, I will back completely. Jullien was entrusted to them as a Tavali cock, and they betrayed him. You're not wrong. And he wasn't just crew. He was *your* blood family. Back in the day, the Snitches would be the first to demand their lives for this. This is exactly the kind of bullshit our Nation was created to protect us from. When we don our gear and board as crew, we are Tavali. We're supposed to be able to rely on each other, regardless of where we're born. Above all things. That's the sacred oath we all take. We don't betray our own. Not for *any* reason. Tavali stands together. No matter what. Blood for one. Blood for all."

Tears blurred her vision. "Why do they hate him so much?"

"You know why."

"*He* didn't do anything. He wasn't even born when it happened!"

"Doesn't matter. Hatred is a blind and deaf, unreasoning beast that doesn't stop to ask why it attacks. It simply slaughters everything in its path without mercy until there's nothing left to salvage. It rots us from the inside out and leaves nothing of the host but an empty hollow shell incapable of compassion. It's why you can't let it take root. Once it starts to grow, it's the hardest weed to prune. And just when you think you have it under control, it explodes and consumes you entirely. All it needs is one target, perfectly placed, and your soul is the price you pay for having courted that beast you thought you could keep caged. It's the one beast we should never dare feed."

"Is this what happened to your family?"

He shook his head. "Fear and ignorance, and lack of understanding more than hatred are what destroyed the Tris. They are an even deadlier beast, at times."

Her heart aching, she stroked Jullien's cheek. "Can you heal him?"

"Physically. Yes. Those wounds are always easy to repair. What they did to his soul, only the two of you can heal, and that will take time, patience, and a lot of understanding on your part."

She winced. "He was just learning to trust."

"I know."

Tears blinded her. "Is there any hope for us, Trajen? Tell me the truth."

He was silent for so long that she began to fear he'd left. But as she turned to find him still in the room, she saw his eyes glowing a faint orange in the dim light. "You and the Danes are the only beings in this entire universe I consider family, Shara. You know this. There are none I give a damn about or that I'd cross the street to avoid running over. If I didn't absolutely believe you could be happy with him, if I thought for one moment that he would harm you in any way, I'd cut his throat myself and bleed him out at my feet. But happiness is never a guarantee and the path to it isn't always an easy one. And the gods know you two are stubborn, and you both have the worst tendency to undermine yourselves. So who the hell knows what future, if any, any of us have?"

With those words spoken, Trajen turned and left.

Ushara choked on a sob, especially when the wounds and bruises on Jullien's body began to heal. "You hear that, Jules? You're going to be fine. You swore to me that you wouldn't break my heart. I'm holding you to that vow. And I swear to you that I will not leave you alone, ever again. No matter where you go or what happens, I will come for you and I will find you. Even if I have to traverse the bitterest flames of Tophet and battle the Koriłon to steal Coreła's thorny hammer to do it. You will not live another day alone in the darkness. I will be your Darling. And I will guide you home."

But if he heard her, he gave no indication. In spite of what Trajen had said, he was still lifeless and cold. Vacant. A living corpse. It was as if their betrayal had killed something inside him and she didn't know if they'd ever be able to reach him again. He was in the same exact state Vas had been in when Chaz had died.

It'd taken her years to get her son back.

She'd been so lost trying to find her child. And Vas she'd known his whole life. She had no idea where to begin to find Jullien. All she knew was that her family and his captors had put him through absolute misery. While Trajen had healed his injuries from her sight, they were still implanted in her memory. Those animals had torn him apart in that cage. They'd fought him like the worst sort of mindless beast in death matches.

For that, she'd never forgive her family. How could she?

But right now, the most important thing was her husband.

Leaning forward, she kissed his bruised cheek and whispered in his ear. "Come back to me, Jules. I need my smart-ass Ixurian to keep me grounded and make me laugh. I don't like who I am when you're not around."

Still, he didn't move or speak. The only clue she had that he might have heard her was that his grip tightened on her hand, ever so slightly. "Follow me home, Jullien," she whispered. "If for no other reason, so that you can see me gut my entire family for you on our return. I promise, you don't want to miss the fireworks that will come when I bust my father's rank in your name."

# CHAPTER 15

O nce they were back at base, Davel and Mary helped Ushara walk Jullien off the ship while her other sisters locked everything down. His movements were so slow and stiff that it broke her heart. She hadn't seen him move like this since Silig and crew had attacked him on his arrival and it made her crave even more blood from her family.

This was twice now they'd gone after him for no reason whatsoever. Enough was enough.

On the dock, Sheila was waiting for them, along with Unira. Neither said a word of greeting, but Sheila threw herself against Jullien and held him close for several seconds as he returned her hug without comment. Patting him on the back, she gruffly cleared her throat and inclined her head to Ushara. "Good job, Admiral." Then she was gone.

With a gentle hand, Unira cupped his bruised cheek and gave him a sad smile. "I'm glad to have you home, *m'tana*. We've all prayed for your safe return."

A tic started in his jaw. His breathing turned ragged as if those words angered him. But he still didn't speak.

Dropping her hand, the high priestess stepped aside, then she placed a comforting touch on Ushara's shoulder. "I have a gift for you later, sweetling. I'll stop by tomorrow with it."

"Thank you, High Mother."

As they started toward her condo, Jullien's eyes flared and he let out a low, fierce growl. Before Ushara realized what he was doing, he broke from them and headed across the bay with a determined, murderous stride. If anyone else had been around, she'd have feared for their life. But no one was here. So she had no idea what he had in mind until she saw what was in front of him.

"Ah crap," she breathed.

He was going for Kirill's ship.

She started after him, but Davel stopped her. "Let him go."

Was he serious? If Jullien harmed that ship, there would be Tophet to pay for it. "Are you out of your mind?"

Davel shrugged. "Let him burn the motherfucker to the ground. They deserve it. Don't you agree?"

She looked past Davel to Trajen, hoping one of them might have some degree of common sense. "Boss?"

"If you don't want the Koriłon to fly, don't flutter his wings."

Nope. No sense here, whatsoever.

Granted, Jullien's wrath was justified, but the fall-out on this would be the equivalent of a nuclear level holocaust.

Cringing over the war that would come once word of this spread, she screwed her face up in sympathetic pain as Jullien ripped open a side panel, reached into it and, with his bare hands, yanked out a fuel line to let it spew its highly flammable contents all over the main engine bay. An impressive feat of strength in and of itself.

If not one of all-out idiocy.

"Um, guys? Should I make mention that if he lights that, he's about to blow a quarter of this station straight to Tophet?"

Davel went pale. "She has a point."

Trajen didn't move. "Give him a minute."

Covering her lips with her hand, Ushara cringed in expectation of the massive explosion that would also probably kill them all.

But it didn't come. Rather, Jullien walked calmly over and used the bay's hydraulics to send the ship out the main doors, and didn't ignite it until after it was clear of the station.

Then it went up in a massive boom of glory so powerful that it rocked the building around them.

Thankfully the vacuum of space protected the station from being damaged and the ship quickly settled down into nothing but a burned-out skeletal husk of what it had been just minutes before.

Without a word, Jullien turned and headed out of the bay.

Trajen expelled an elongated sigh. "Well, I certainly think he made his point about how he feels where Kirill is concerned. Comments?"

Davel shook his head. "All I'm thinking about is how pissed off Kirill will be when he finds out."

With a deep sigh, Ushara shrugged at something that couldn't be un-
done now. "You can tell him to address the bill in care of I don't give a
shit, and shove it up his ass. With interest."

Laughing, Davel saluted her. "Will do, little sister."

"Now, if you'll excuse me . . ." She left them to go after Jullien to
make sure he returned to her home safely.

But as she rounded the corner, she realized that he was heading back
to his old quarters.

She ran to catch him. "Jules? You don't live there anymore. Vas and
I moved your things to our place and returned the card to Gunnar."

Still, he didn't speak. He just continued to stare blankly at her.

And that broke her heart even more. "Come on, *mi keramon.*" She took
his arm and led him home where everything was calm and quiet.

Since it was late, Vasili was still at her mother's, asleep. They had
her condo all to themselves.

Ushara took Jullien to the bathroom and stripped his clothes off so
that she could bathe the stench of the cage, ship fuel, and fire from him.
The new scars on his body tore her apart. There were so many more . . .

"Jullien?" She tried to get him to look at her and he emphatically refused.

No matter what she tried, he kept his gaze averted as if he was too
ashamed to look her in the eyes.

"I wish you'd tell me what's going on inside you. I just want to help.
I see the pain you're in and it's killing me that I can't make it better.
Please, baby, tell me what I can do."

Jullien heard those words and they shredded him. But the truth was,
he didn't know how to answer her. How to reach out to someone.
Because he'd been alone all his life, he didn't know any other way to
cope other than to withdraw into himself. This was what he did when
his world collapsed. It was how he survived it.

In all the worst times, he'd been left alone to face them. The death
of his brother. His mother's violent tantrums. His father's verbal or physical assaults. The deaths of his fiancées. His stints in prison. His exile
from Andaria and Triosa. Any time he screwed up, he was isolated and
locked away.

No one had ever checked on him or reached out to see if they could
soothe him. Not a single conversation or even a simple, *hey, you. You
okay?*

So he didn't know how to let her help. All he knew was that it hurt deep down inside and he didn't know why this burned so much worse than all the others. Maybe because he'd wanted them to accept him this time, and in the past he hadn't cared.

Not that it mattered. He'd been a fool to think for even a nanosecond that he could ever be a part of a family of any kind.

And yet when she was with him like this . . . he wanted to believe it was possible. He wanted to believe in her.

If only he could.

Closing his eyes, he trembled as her hands glided over his body and washed away the dirt and filth that clung to his skin. The agony that stained his soul.

She was the only one who'd ever touched him without giving him pain.

Why couldn't he be whole for her?

She deserved a normal male. One who could bring honor to her home and not the shame and turmoil that came with him.

*You're a disgrace! And I will never allow you to bear my Triosan surname. Your mother and grandmother can do what they will with theirs, but I will die before I see something as worthless as you on our throne!*

He could still feel his father's hands on his throat as he choked him and shouted in his face. See the hatred in his father's eyes that were so similar to his own as they condemned him even more than those words had.

It'd been a promise his father had kept to this day. Unlike Nykyrian, Jullien had never once been allowed to use his father's surname on any public record. For any reason.

Stupidly, Jullien had thought no one could ever make him feel worse or lower than his father had that day when Dancer Hauk had told Aros that Jullien had misplaced his signet ring in his gym bag and that Nykyrian hadn't stolen it, after all.

Jullien had thought nothing could hurt more than his own father choking him to death and walking out to leave him in the hands of medtechs without so much as an apology for his brutal assault.

Not until Kirill and his crew had torn the Tavali patches from his sleeves and thrown him to the Ladorian slavers.

"Isn't he one of your crew?"

"Nah, he ain't shit to us. We're just hoping to get some free entertainment out of him before we go. It's all he's worth."

"Jullien?" Ushara's voice cut through his memories. But all that did was hurt even more. . . .

Ushara tried again to pull Jullien away from wherever his thoughts were taking him.

A single tear fell down his cheek.

"Oh baby." Her heart lurching, she kissed it away and wished she knew what to do.

Finishing his bath, she dried him off and took him to bed. There she snuggled beside him and held him as best she could.

"I'm right here, Jules. Whenever you're ready to talk or not talk, or whatever you need." She wrapped her body around his, and listened to his ragged breathing. For the longest time, she thought she was wasting her efforts.

Until she felt him wrap his arms around her body. A few minutes later, he finally fell asleep while holding onto her like she was his lifeline.


"How's he doing?"

Ushara shook her head as she opened the front door and allowed Oxana to enter with Vas and Nadya. "He still hasn't spoken."

"I'm sorry."

"Is Basha Dagger sick, Mama?" Nadya frowned up at them.

"He is, *mia*."

She pursed her lips. "We made him a card." She tugged at Vasili's sleeve. "Show your mama what we did for your paka so . . . so that he'd feel better."

Vas handed Ushara a piece of paper. "It's what her and her sisters did yesterday while we waited for you to come back."

Ushara smiled at the pictures of Jullien with them at temple. "Why don't you two go give it to him while I finish making breakfast?"

"Okay." Vasili took Nadya to the bedroom.

Ushara led Oxana to the kitchen where she'd left everything cooking. "Thank you for picking up Vas. I don't know what I would have done to Paka had I seen him this morning."

"Yeah, it was bad. Basha Klavdii was there and he was furious about what Jullien did to Kirill's ship. He was demanding Paka do something."

Ushara curled her lip. "Like what?"

"No idea. But it's nuclear."

"Bring it with both hands. As much as he might want a piece of my Jules, I want a piece of Kirill's jewels. And I assure you, I will get my way first."

"I know you will, sister. I know you will."

Jullien opened his eyes to find a small, happy face surrounded by white blond curls, peering at him over the mattress.

"Nadya, stop!" Vas whispered loudly. "He's still sleeping. Just leave it by the bed and let's go before you wake him."

Giggling as she pulled the mattress down with her little hand, she smiled even wider. "He's not sleeping. His eyes are open. You're awake, aren't you, Basha Dagger?"

Jullien wasn't sure what to say as he stared into a pair of innocent white eyes that studied him curiously.

Cocking her head, she gave him an adorable scowl. "Why you so sad, Basha Dagger? You're home! We missed you so much! We were sad while you were gone and then Mama said you were back and we've been so happy that you were home again." She shoved a piece of paper in his face. "We made this for you to say how much we love you. Well . . . me and my sissies drew the pictures and Vasi wroted the words 'cause we can't writed yet. But we did the pictures. See the pictures?" She climbed up on the bed to sit on her knees next to him.

His eyes teared up as he saw the images of her with him in temple, sitting beside Vasili and the rest of her family. Pushing himself up in the bed, he forced himself to smile at her. "It's beautiful, Tara Nadya. Thank you."

Smiling, she threw herself against his chest and hugged him. "Love you, Basha Dagger!"

He looked up and met Vasili's gaze.

Tears were flowing down his cheeks, too. "When Davel came back and wouldn't say anything . . . I-I thought you were dead. That I'd never see you again."

Jullien held his hand out to Vasili. "I wouldn't do that to you, *mi tana*."

Vasili tackled him with a hug. "Don't ever die."

Closing his eyes, Jullien held them.

Ushara froze in the doorway as she saw Jullien and the children locked in a tight embrace.

He opened his eyes as if sensing her presence. If she lived a thousand years, she'd never forget the haunted pain in their red depths.

She moved to set her tray on the nightstand before she neared them. "Are they bothering you?"

He shook his head. "Not at all." He kissed Nadya's head, then Vasili's. Clearing his throat, he picked up the picture. "Where should we put this beautiful work of art, Naddimaer?"

She giggled at his nickname for her. "Where can we put it, Lyr Shara?"

"How about on the mirror so that Basha Dagger can see it every day?"

"Okay!" Excitedly, she scooted off the bed and ran to hang it at a crooked angle from the mirror with Vasili's help.

"I have sweetcakes ready in the kitchen for both of you, if you're hungry."

Balling her fists with her excitement, Nadya squealed and ran for the door, then double backed to hug and kiss Jullien. "I'll bring you some, Basha!"

Vasili hesitated at the foot of the bed with a troubled frown.

"What's wrong, baby?" Ushara asked.

"Jex said last night that even if you succeeded in bringing Jullien home that our graspa and yaya weren't going to allow him to stay. That his paka and the rest of the clan would block his citizenship. He said they were going to force you to make Jullien leave."

She gave him a chiding stare. "No one makes me do anything I don't want to do. Haven't you learned that yet?"

"But if they won't vote him in . . ."

"Jullien is my husband and your father. They can't do anything about that. It's already done. As for blocking, they wish. I'm about to bust their Canting and suspend *their* citizenship. None of them will have a vote, one way or another. That's what they need to be worried about, instead of his."

Vas's eyes widened. "Do they know that?"

She shook her head. "And don't tell them. The trial will be tomorrow. I'll render my verdict to them then."

He turned back to Jullien. "So then you're staying? Right? You're not leaving us?"

Jullien looked at Ushara. "Your mother and the gods are the only ones who have the ability to keep me from you. . . . And I'm not so sure about the gods."

Vasili sniffed back his tears before he followed after Nadya. "You better save some for me, Naddi!"

Alone with Jullien, Ushara approached him slowly, unsure of his mood. She smoothed his furrowed brow and sat beside him on the mattress. "How are you feeling?"

"Lost."

She took his hand and cradled it between hers. "You're not lost. You're home where you belong."

Jullien trembled as those words sank in and warmed the coldest part of his soul.

Ushara reached to the table and picked up a mug of the hot cider he liked. He didn't know how she remembered that. But she did.

"Thank you." He sipped it and noted the time. "Aren't you late for work?"

"I took the day off."

"Why?"

Smiling gently, she traced circles around his chest. "I wanted to be with you."

"I don't understand."

She looked at him with that same stunned expression she wore any time he said something that was ludicrous in her world and yet normal for his. God, to have grown up in her environment.

"The last thing you need right now is to be alone. I stayed home to take care of you. Hasn't anyone ever done that for you before?"

He shook his head.

"Not even when you were sick as a boy?"

Again, he wished he'd been able to live the life she took for granted. But such things had never been known to him. "No, Shara. I was always quarantined to keep from making anyone else ill."

Ushara arched a brow at his choice of words. Surely, he didn't mean . . . "Quarantined?"

"I'm a hybrid species. They were terrified I'd contract something harmless, mutate it into a deadly form, and cause it to become unresponsive to treatment for others, both human and Andarion. So whenever I was ill, I was moved into a sterile environment until the doctors determined I was no longer a biological hazard or intergalactic health crisis waiting to happen."

Yes, he had meant that. She couldn't believe it. "And no one sat with you while you were sick?"

"No. It was always too risky. Trust me. One sneeze, and I can clear a room faster than a bomb threat."

She sat in stunned disbelief of their blatant disregard for him. Of all the things he'd told her, she didn't know why this one seemed so much more horrible than the others, but it did. She couldn't imagine being ill as a small child and not having her mother tend her. Having someone bring her soup and . . . well, *care*.

"For the record, Jules? I hate your parents."

"I don't."

"How can you not?"

"I don't know." He rubbed at his forehead. "I guess I just feel sorry for them."

"Why?"

"They could have chosen to be happy together. All they had to do was stand up for each other and their sons. And they didn't. Instead, they chose rank and position over family. My mother refused to give up her job as prime commander to marry my father when she found out she was pregnant with us, and my father refused to give up his empire to marry her. They wanted everything, and they ended up with nothing."

"It doesn't excuse what they've done to you."

"Maybe, but had they not done it, I wouldn't be here with you now. I'd be in their empires, married to someone else. And I wouldn't cherish you as much as I do. So honestly? You should be grateful to them for making me able to appreciate you the way I do."

She gave him a suspicious glare. "You don't really believe that. Do you?"

He swallowed hard as he took her hand in his and caressed her fingers. "When I was younger, I hated them viciously. I did. I stayed angry all the time. At everyone . . . even myself. It wasn't until the night my brother confronted me that I was able to finally let that anger go. But the one thing I learned from being with your bastard cousin and his crew . . . it doesn't matter when you try to make them like you. If they're determined to hate, they hate, these last five years, I kept thinking that if I'd just been a better son. . . . If I'd done what my parents had wanted me to, and kept my mouth shut, and not fought them like I did. If I'd followed the rules and played along, that things would have been different. That they'd have accepted and loved me."

His gazed burned into hers. "It didn't matter. I did everything Kirill asked of me, Shara. *Everything*. I kept my mouth shut and sucked it all up. And they still gave me away like I was garbage."

"Oh honey . . ."

He finally looked away. "So no, I don't hate or blame my parents. Apparently, the flaw's with me. Whether I try or not, I'm the one who never fits in. It's the old saying, right? If everyone's an asshole, maybe the asshole's you. I guess I'm the real asshole, after all."

She tugged at his hand. "You know better."

He laughed bitterly. "You have twin sisters, right?"

"Yes."

"You know how they talk about the unbreakable bound between twins? How close they are from the moment of birth and how they have their own language with each other?"

"Of course."

"I never had that with my brother. Not once." His voice was scarcely more than a whisper—that tone told her just how much this confession bothered him. How long he'd kept it his own secret without telling it to anyone else. "My earliest memories are of watching him and Galene Batur playing together in our nursery."

Meeting her gaze, he laughed bitterly. "I had the biggest crush on her. I thought she was the most beautiful girl on Andaria. Like some angel that had fallen from the gods to grace us. Whenever she'd visit with her father, I wanted to make her smile at me the way she'd smile and laugh at my brother. But she never did. She could barely stand to look at me and was always so impatient and annoyed with everything I did. I'd get so frustrated over it that I'd end up fighting with both of them, and they'd shove me out of the room to leave them in peace so that they could play without my interfering. And all I wanted was to be part of their group. Then when Nyk was gone, I had so much guilt over it all. Like I'd wished it on him because I wanted to play with her on those afternoons. And it always made me think that I must have been defective from birth and that Nyk somehow knew it. Why else would my own twin have rejected me?"

"Jules—"

"Don't, Shara. I know the arguments you're going to make. But when you strip them all away, you do have to wonder at the truth. Really. There has to be something defective within me at my core soul. My parents aren't bad people. My father is extremely well-respected by everyone who knows him. His parents adored the ground he walked on. My brother and his family think the universe of him. My mother has always been in love with my father since the day they met. My mother and aunt are completely devoted to each other. They love and respect Nykyrian, who in turn loves and respects them. They have the devotion of the entire population of Andaria and the media. I, alone, am the one they all hated and ridiculed from the moment I was born."

"They never gave you a chance."

"Honestly, I don't think it would have mattered. It's like when a dog or lorina attacks a predator or a damaged pup or cub. They instinctively know there's something wrong with the newcomer and that it's harmful to their group so they attack and kill it before it has a chance to damage the rest. Maybe I'm that defective, harmful cub that needs to be culled or killed."

"I don't believe that."

"Surely they can't *all* be wrong. There has to be something defective with me."

"Is that really what you want to put your faith in?"

He swallowed hard. "I don't know. But if the same thing keeps happening everywhere I go . . . the problem has to be with me. It's the only rational conclusion to be drawn."

"And maybe it's simply that you're different. Not defective. A lorina will attack any species that isn't its own. Any scent it doesn't recognize to protect its cubs. They will eat their own offspring if you spray the scent of another creature on it. People and Andarions can be the same. You know this. Look at what the Ixurianir have done throughout history to the Pavakahir and Murakhir—the darkhearts persecuted the winged races before they came after the Fyrebloods. They even went after the stralanuer at one time in our history, before they understood the science that caused male eyes to turn red. Humans are even worse. Trajen's entire race was put down because they feared them so. Was your brother always treated better than you?"

Jullien flinched. "No. And to my eternal shame, I'm to blame for some of that."

"What do you mean?"

He pressed his hands to his ears and doubled over in the bed as if the agony of the memory was more than he could bear. His breathing ragged, he curled into a ball and shook.

Terrified, she rubbed at his back to comfort him. "Jullien? What is it?"

He didn't speak as silent tears shook him. In all the times she'd seen him upset, she'd never seen him like this.

Aching for him, she held him until his misery and grief were spent.

Oxana almost came in during it, but caught a glimpse and quickly reversed course. Before she went, her sister pulled the bedroom door closed and left them alone.

After awhile, Jullien finally calmed. He moved to lay on his side, facing the wall. His breathing ragged, he swallowed hard and toyed with her fingers.

Ushara remained snuggled against his back, holding him close. With her arm under his head, she nuzzled his neck. "Are you all right?"

He nodded, but when he spoke, he contradicted the gesture. "Not really." She felt his hot tears on her skin as he swallowed again. "I've wronged my brother in so many ways that it shames me to the depth of my immortal soul. In my all my life, it's the only thing I truly regret. The only thing I wish I could change. I'm so sorry for what I've done to him and I can't even apologize for it. There's no way I can ever make it right."

"If you don't want to tell me, you don't have to."

He fell silent for several minutes before he finally spoke again. "I thought him dead for so long. He was an axe that hung over my head. A threat my grandmother used against me that I used against her."

"What do you mean?"

"With him dead, I was heir. She kept threatening to kill me as easily as she'd killed him if I displeased her. And I had a degree of arrogance that she wouldn't actually kill me. I knew Tylie was a lesbian and wouldn't have children. Not just because of Kelsei, but because she can't abide them. She hates kids passionately. And her partner isn't any better. Their idea of watching a child is, *here, little boy. Stick this metal hair clip in the wall socket.*"

Ushara laughed in spite of the seriousness. "Sorry."

"Yeah, so was I when I did it."

"Are you joking?"

"No. Would you like to see the scar? It turned my entire hand black. Learned more about electrical currents at age three than any toddler needs to know."

Well that quelled her humor. She grimaced. How he could find such gallows humor in his past, she had no idea.

"Anyway, given that, in spite of my grandmother's constant assertions that she'd put my cousins on the throne in my place, I was relatively sure she was arrogant enough to keep her own blood there, even though it was half human and tainted. So we bickered and I bled for it until the day I was in school and a new student arrived. At first, I didn't recognize him. I thought it was just another human they'd let in. It was a weird program they'd started a couple of years earlier to integrate us. As a result, we'd been having a huge surge in human enrollment. I thought nothing of it until they said he was the adopted brother of Aksel and Arast Quiakides—a hybrid human-Andarion they'd found in an orphanage."

Jullien fell silent as he saw himself again in class and felt the fear of that afternoon so clearly. Merrell had sat beside him as a pall had fallen over both of them.

At first, Jullien had thought that maybe, just maybe there might be another hybrid in existence. It was possible another Andarion had slept with a human.

Until Nyk had looked at him. The moment he saw the gut-knotting hatred for him in those human eyes that were so similar to his, in the face of his father . . .

There had been no doubt. Though Nyk's features were younger, he was the very image of their father. And he carried himself with the same arrogant bearing and mannerisms that Jullien despised with every part of his being. Gave him that same condescending look of disgust and disdain that said he was struggling with every breath to barely tolerate Jullien's presence.

Just a child, Jullien had panicked as he sat there, terrified someone would realize this was his long-dead brother. His cousin Chrisen knew instantly. The expression on his face had confirmed it as he swung around in the desk in front of Jullien to glare at him.

Jullien had hastily glanced around to see if anyone else caught on. Thankfully, no one else was bright enough.

Only the five of them knew. Him. Nyran. Merrell. Chrisen. Nykyrian.

And he'd been torn between wanting to run to his brother and throw his arms around him in gratitude that Nyk was alive, and terrified of what it would mean to have him returned to their lineage. Eriadne had "killed" Nyk for a reason she'd never fully explained.

End of the day, the bitch was bat-shit crazy. She was tadara with unlimited power over everyone's lives. He was barely able to keep his mother alive as it was. Barely able to keep himself alive and out of the hole beneath her palace.

He knew from experience that his father wouldn't step in. He'd already asked his father to help him and his answer?

*It's not worth a war with the Andarion empire. I will not fight your grandmother over you. Don't bother me again with your ridiculous requests. You're Andarion. Act like it. Strap up, and stop whining like a bitch.*

His human grandfather was even less likely to step in, especially after he'd pissed in his pool. Literally.

So Jullien had done the only thing he knew to do. He'd ignored his brother and pretended he didn't know him.

Nykyrian had done the same. He'd walked right past him and sat down in the desk three feet away. No words. Not even a nod of acknowledgment.

Nothing.

That had cut, too. When class had ended, Jullien had fully intended to talk to Nykyrian, but as he headed for him, Merrell, Nyran, and Chrisen had cut him off. Merrell had sent Dancer on to his next class and Jullien's three cousins had dragged him off to the gym where they'd cornered him.

Merrell had grabbed him by the neck. "It's *him*, isn't it?"

Jullien had said nothing. He'd known better.

"What are we going to do?" Chrisen was already sweating.

Panting, Nyran was in an all-out panic. "Mom pretended to be Cairistiona. She's the one who gave the orders to have him killed as his mother. That bastard speaks and they'll kill her. They'll kill us all!"

Merrell had slapped his younger brother. "Jullien didn't know any of that, you idiot!"

"Julie won't tell. Will you?"

Jullien's mind had whirled as he stared at the three of them. He knew from experience that while he could take Nyran and Chrisen individually in a fight, he was no match for Merrell. And the three of them together could kick his ass without effort. "I'm not saying anything."

Merrell slapped his brother. "Stop panicking. He can't tell anyone, anyway. Eriadne did it. She's the one who had our mother impersonate Cairie. She'd be the first to cut his throat if he spoke."

Jullien had winced as he finally had the details of what had really happened to his brother. While his grandmother had confessed to killing Nykyrian, she'd never told him how she'd done it.

Now he knew.

And he'd hated her even more.

"Jullien?"

Blinking, he let the sound of Ushara's voice return him to the present and away from that horrid moment. "I was such a bastard, Shara. I was so afraid and angry. The four years we were in school together, I kept waiting for someone to realize he was my brother. I knew if they did, that I'd be killed. If he was alive, they wouldn't need me. My grandmother was so unstable. My cousins even more so. Worse, their mother was the one who'd played the largest part in his supposed death. Hell, she'd impersonated my mother—which was a crime in and of itself. And her sons were at me the whole time to do something to get rid of him. I was under constant attack from all of them. I didn't know what to do. And my father kept screaming at me for being sullen and withdrawn. Mostly because Parisa and Merrell were pumping me full of drugs to keep me sedated so that they could control me. They overdosed me eight times, which my father thought I did. Of course, that made him attack me more because he thought I was a raging drug addict. Tylie and my grandmother, too. I still don't know why they didn't outright kill me, then. Although I suspect a couple of the overdoses were meant to end my life, and I was just too stubborn to die."

Biting his lip, he turned to face her. "I antagonized Nyk in school. Part of me wanted him to tell others I was his brother. I figured if he outed us, then I couldn't be accused of it. Another part of me wanted to hurt him for leaving me to deal with all of them on my own, and I was just lashing out. I didn't understand then how bad *he* had it at home and honestly, I was so wrapped up in my own hell, that I didn't care."

He closed his eyes and winced. "I just wanted him to bleed as much as I did. It seemed like he'd come back for no other reason than to show everyone else what a second-rate piece of shit I was and rub my nose in it. All those feelings of inadequacy from my early childhood returned with a vengeance. He was always smarter. More handsome and lean. The better athlete and student. Better son. It's why they loved him more. I was jealous. I admit it. Still, he didn't deserve what I did to him. Maybe if I'd just told my father who Nyk was when he'd first shown up . . ."

"Why didn't you?"

"Honestly? I didn't think my father would do anything to help him. Or even believe me—which he never did. He wasn't emperor then. His father was still alive and anytime I'd ever asked him to help, he'd refused, saying he didn't want to start a war with my grandmother. And I had no doubt that telling him about Nyk would start shit with her. So I swear to the gods, truthfully I feared that if I told him it was Nykyrian, he'd tell my grandmother and hand us both over to her and she'd kill us in a fit of rage."

"Really?"

He gave a bitter laugh. "Shara, you can't imagine the things I've seen her do. The things she's done to me out of sheer spite. She's psychotic. When I was eight years old, she gutted my uncle in front of me, during dinner, because she'd seen him speaking to someone she suspected of plotting against her."

"Oh my God, Jules."

"Yeah . . . then she cleaned her knife off on his shirt, sat down and started eating again with his corpse right there, between us. Her own child. And made me eat, too, and had me beaten every time I gagged. Believe me, anytime we had an unexpected dinner guest, I was terrified why."

"How could your father leave you there?"

"I don't think he realized how bad she was. To be fair to him, he probably couldn't conceive of the level of evil she exists on. Whenever I tried to explain it, he would call me a liar. Let's face it, it really is something you have to witness firsthand to fully appreciate. So I understand why your father and family hates mine so vehemently. They're a special level of Tophet all to themselves."

"But it's not fair to put you on par with them when you don't deserve it."

He scoffed at her. "As I said, I'm not innocent. You don't grow up in that palace, surrounded by her level of evil without being damaged, inside, out. I promise you, Kirill is lighting a special missive to Kadora right now with my name all over it."

She laughed as she remembered his fit last night. "I'm sure he is. Did you have to blow up the whole ship?"

"It was the lesser evil since what I really wanted to set on fire was Kirill. So it was a good thing I came across the ship first, as restraint is not one of the virtues generally associated with my name. Hence the pool incident on my grandfather's birthday and the statue of my grandmother I blew up with ship fuel."

"In that case, you made a good call."

Expelling a heavy breath, he fingered the wedding ring he'd given her. "You need to see about annulling our marriage and extricating yourself from me before I drag you down."

She closed her hand over his. "No. I made my commitment to you and I meant it. I love you, Jules. And I will fight for you."

"Why?" he asked with a sincerity that made her heart ache. He truly couldn't fathom that anyone could care for him.

She couldn't imagine having so little self-worth.

Wanting to tease him, she cupped his cheek. "I've no idea. You make me crazy. You worry the snot out of me, but I can't stand the thought of not having you in my life. When Davel came back and told me what they'd done to you . . . Kirill's lucky *I* didn't set him on fire."

Bowing his head, he pressed his forehead against hers and held her. "Can I tell you a secret?"

"Of course."

"When I was a boy and it would get unbearable, I used to run and hide in the old archives or cellars of the palace. There I would imagine that I really was the long-lost son of Samari, and that she was in the shadows, looking for me. She would take my hand and turn me into one of the Dagger Ixurir so that I wouldn't have to go back to my room and deal with my aunt or grandmother. But no matter how hard I looked for her, she never came for me."

"Is that why you chose your alias?"

He nodded. "I would also pray that my mother or father would come for me. That they'd remember they had a son." He twisted her ring around on her finger. "But they never did."

Then he locked gazes with her. "The whole time I was on that Ladorian base, I wanted them to kill me. I was so tired and hungry and hurt. Yet in the back of my mind, I saw your face, and all I could think about was how sad you look whenever you talk about losing your husband, and I didn't want to be your sadness. So I fought on and hoped that you'd come for me. But I didn't really think you would."

A tear slid from the corner of his eye. "I will never doubt you again." He dipped his head to give her the sweetest, tenderest kiss of her life. Never had she tasted anything like it.

His breathing changed as he rolled with her and he lifted the hem of her gown. "In all my life, you are the only one who has never disappointed me."

"*Kimi ti,* Jules," she whispered in his ear as he slid himself inside her.

He tightened his arms around her and held her close against him and cupped her cheek in his hand as he stared down into her eyes. "Just promise you'll never let me go."

"Never."

For the first time in his life, Jullien trusted and it terrified him. He was so vulnerable right now. In a way he'd never been before. Ushara alone had the means to utterly destroy him. No one had ever held this much power over his life and heart.

No one.

She possessed a part of his soul he hadn't even known existed. Closing his eyes, he lost himself to the warmth of her body wrapped around his. To the pleasure of her limbs sliding against his as she caressed his body and held his dark heart. She was so tiny and frail compared to him. Yet she was the most powerful creature he'd ever met. One frown on her face could cut him to the bone.

One cruel word from her lips could kill him.

And when she came a few minutes later in his arms, calling his name, he finally felt like he was home.

Most of all, he felt wanted. Growling low, he buried his head in her head and joined her in her release.

Ushara smiled as she felt Jullien tremble in her arms and surrender his weight to her. It was the first he'd done that. Normally, he was so careful to move away and not crush her. But she loved the sensation of his massive size pressing her down in the bed.

"Am I killing you?" he asked with a light laugh.

"No."

He stayed there a moment longer before he rolled with her and settled on his back with her draped over his chest. "Will you stay in bed with me all day?"

"If that's what you want, yes."

His gaze burned into her. "I do."

She lifted his hand and kissed his scarred knuckle. "Then let me check to make sure my sister got Vas off to school and that she'll pick him up, then I shall be right back to stay right here until tomorrow morning."

"She doesn't have to get him from school. I'd like to have dinner with him. I missed him, too."

"Okay, then. Half the day in bed." She kissed his cheek before she got up.

Jullien listened as she walked down the hallway. He glanced around the garishly pink and horrendously feminine room that had been hideous to him before he'd left. Now he found it the most beautiful place he'd ever seen. There was nowhere else he'd rather be.

After a few minutes, she came back with more food and drink. "They're all gone." She followed his line of sight up to the rose and vine chandelier that cast rainbow prisms on the ceiling. "We should probably redecorate some, shouldn't we? Make it a bit more appealing for you?"

He dropped his gaze to her as she set the tray next to him. "No. There's nothing about you or your home I want to change."

"Really? It's *very* pink in here."

"And the best memories of my life have taken place in this very pink room. It doesn't bother me at all." He reached for a piece of toast.

She gave him a suspicious tilt of her chin. "I thought the room made you want to do something masculine?"

He gave her a devilish grin. "I did do something very masculine with you. And I plan to do again very shortly, and much longer, and more thoroughly this time."

Laughing, she handed him a glass of juice. "You're incorrigible."

"I've been called worse." He took a sip and reached for the fruit. "But there is something I'd like to do to your house later, if you don't mind."

"As long as you don't launch it into space and set fire to it, it's your home, too. You can make any change you want."

"Really?"

Nodding, she got up and went to the closet. "Really." She opened the door.

Jullien gaped as he saw that she'd bought him an entire wardrobe and placed it there. "When did you do that?"

"After you left. It was meant to be a welcome home surprise. Vas helped me pick them all out. I also paid off your tithe with Zellen."

"Why?"

"You're my husband, Jules. I wasn't about to have anyone else own a piece of you. Call me selfish, but I plan to keep you all to myself. The only ones I don't mind sharing you with are Vas and Nadya . . . maybe Trajen when he wants a drinking buddy. But only on occasion."

Suddenly, her link started buzzing.

He frowned at a tone he wasn't familiar with. "What's that?"

"Not a good sound." She went to the nightstand and answered it.

Jullien could tell by her expression and silence that it was extremely serious. After a few minutes of listening, she let out a tired sigh.

"Tell them that I'll be in shortly." She hung up.

"What is it?"

"My father and uncle are demanding I resign as vice admiral."

# CHAPTER 16

Jullien stared at Ushara in disbelief. "They want you to resign? Because of me?"

"No. They want me to resign because I'm about to bust their Canting and they know it. This is over *their* actions. Not yours."

"Because of me," he repeated insistently.

But she was being just as stubborn with her position as he was. "They broke the Code. They're the ones who did wrong in this. Not you."

"I have a hard time faulting them for what they did when they were only trying to protect *you*."

"Be that as it may, I'm not that forgiving for what was done to *you*. I want blood over this, too."

He snorted. "Oh, don't let *this*," he gestured at his calm, relaxed pose, "fool you. I'm not a saint or a martyr. I'm not about to forgive them. I'm going to exact my revenge. On my own. But that's between us. After all, I am a contentious bastard—the son of all bastards, for that matter, and an eton Anatole. We don't let shit go. Ever. That ship was just the first round. But they're your family. I don't want them angry at *you*."

Laughing, she pressed her hand to her forehead as she finally understood why he was protesting her interference. He wasn't telling her to let it go because, like Chaz, he was trying to make peace. Rather, he wanted a piece of them himself. "That's so . . . messed up. But sweet. In a psychologically damaged way."

"You knew I was broken when you took me in. This is on you, *mu tara*. I came into this marriage with a massive warning label. *And* a kill warrant. You knew, baby. You knew."

"Yes. Yes, I did." Sighing, she got up. "Let me go deal with this and I'll—"

"Oh, I'm coming with you."

"Jules—"

"I'm fine, Shara. I had my nervous breakdown. Licked my wounds. Now I'm back. The one thing you can thank my psychotic grandmother and aunt for—I learned to snap back fast from the brink of insanity. I had to. I take the hard hit. Withdraw inward, catch my breath, get fucking pissed and come back fighting twice as hard, with renewed vigor and determination. That's what I do. It's why I'm still here and alive while the rest of my family is in their graves. Bitches rang my bell—their mistake. They let me up off the ground. Now, I'm answering the door. They want a piece of me? They're going to earn it. I'm not about to send you in there to fight without me. You go. I go. I'm your husband. My place is standing at your back, supporting you, every step of the way to Tophet and back. And defending you with my dying breath. You will never stand alone, so long as I'm here."

He was so different from her first husband. So different from anyone she'd ever known. While she was used to strong males who would rise to fight and defend, they were much more overbearing with it. They were all too quick to shove her aside and take charge. Jullien knew when to lead and when to pull guard point. Unlike them, he wasn't threatened by the latter. He would defer to her as leader and remain in the background so long as she was given the respect he felt they owed her and only rise up to strike them down when they didn't.

Honestly? She adored that about him. He was like having a tamed battle-lorina on hand. Only he was much more charming and sweet.

Although, *not* better behaved when confronted, and a lot less predictable.

Definitely a lot more terrifying.

"All right," she relented. "Arm up. This isn't going to be pleasant."

"Did you miss the hole you just dragged me out of?"

She flinched at the memory. "I'm going to kill them."

"Oh baby, please . . ." He bit his lip seductively. "I want the full honor, and first shot." With an eagerness that actually terrified her, he scooted off the bed and went to shower.

Ushara let out a bitter laugh. He was a fighter. The high priestess hadn't been wrong about that. A true a son of Kadurr. She could definitely see the blood of the Samari in him. It made total sense. That unflagging spirit was what had saved her race and kept them going against

overwhelming odds. In the face of it all, they had chosen to be dangerous.

Even so, this was going to get bad. Her father was very well respected
and she was a young commander. Many here had never agreed with her
appointment under Trajen's leadership.

Many had never appreciated the way Trajen had taken over, especially
since he'd come in from a competing Nation.

That included certain members of her own family, such as Kirill's
father who had never liked Trajen, or appreciated the fact that they were
being led by a non-Andarion. They thought Trajen a normal human,
and in their eyes that made him weak.

If they only knew . . .

By the time they were dressed and headed for the meeting, Ushara
was sick to her stomach with worry and dread. If Jullien was nervous
or apprehensive, he did a remarkable job of hiding it. He appeared completely calm and confident. Smooth even.

"How do you do that?"

"Do what?" he asked.

"Remain perfectly calm and composed when you're walking into the
den of your enemies. Vas asked me that when you went to temple with
us the first time, and he's right. Nothing seems to rattle you. Is it an
innate aristocratic trait or something else? How do you manage such raw
confidence and regal grace at all times?"

"Simple. You and Vas walk in with the fear that you're going to say
or do something wrong and they won't like you anymore. Or that you'll
screw up and lose their respect. I know going in they hate my guts.
There's absolutely nothing I could say or do, including set fire to a baby
or kick a puppy, to make them hate me any worse. So I have no ground
to lose where they're concerned. It's actually quite liberating to know
there's no way to make them like me. An act of the gods themselves
could not swing them to my favor. So I have no pressure or fear of any
kind. There is *nothing* I can do to fuck up. Anything I say or do will be
socially unacceptable, talked about in the worst way imaginable, and misinterpreted by all. Might as well have fun with it and embrace the whole
King of All Bastards they're going to accuse me of, anyway."

She laughed and shook her head. "That is sad and yet terribly true,
isn't it?"

He shrugged nonchalantly. "It's a blessing, really."

Before they entered her office, she took a moment to straighten his coat. It was adorable to her how he always managed to have it slightly askew. He'd gone back to wearing his red glasses instead of the contacts, and in spite of his harsh, brave words, she saw the pain that haunted his stralen eyes. While he didn't comment on what had been done to him, she knew it hadn't just left new physical scars on his body. He had fresh ones on his soul, as well.

For that, she could murder her family. She saw the traces of it whenever he touched his bald head and winced in shame. The way he hunched his shoulders, then caught himself and straightened his spine as if determined to not show it to anyone.

Even himself.

He had an inner quiet strength and dignity that awed her.

With his full swagger in place, he opened the door and held it for her so that she could lead the way into her office.

And when they saw that he was with her, it set every pair of eyes on them, and a number of whispers began. Ushara didn't say a word to them as she swept into the room and headed for Zellen's desk.

"So much for my day off, eh?"

Zellen nodded. "Conference room?"

"Why not? Seems like a good place for a kangaroo court, doesn't it?"

Her father rose to his feet as she headed for the hallway that led to it. "Do you think it's a good idea to bring *him* here?"

"Better than provoking him to violence." She leaned forward as if imparting a secret. "Let me tell you the one thing I've learned about dealing with my husband. Think of him like the giant lorina in the wild, sleeping happily in his cave. He might stick his head up to watch you walk by, but so long as you don't get his full attention, he won't attack. Whatever you do, for the sake of the gods, don't throw a rock at him. Because once you do come under his full attention, he's going straight for your jugular. Just ask Kirill."

That got her uncle on his feet.

Which caused Jullien to turn and face him.

Kirill's father Klavdii took one step forward until he took in the exact size of Jullien's height and width, and saw the color of his eyes.

Then he retreated.

Ushara swept her gaze over the males gathered in the waiting area. "Shall we move this to the conference room, eh?"

"Who's overseeing it?" her father asked.

"I am." Trajen, who appeared from the shadows, swept past him.

Her father actually jumped in startled alarm.

Trajen paused at the conference room door to look back at them. "Unless one of you wants to challenge me for *my* position?"

One by one, they looked away.

Trajen passed an arch stare to Jullien.

"Tempting, but I'm too tired to bother with it."

With a snort, Trajen gave him a playful, brotherly slap. "Ironic. You're the only one who'd stand a chance of taking the seat from me and you're probably the last one who'd ever make the try for it."

"'Cause I'm not a fucking idiot. . . . I'm only partially brain-damaged."

Laughing, Trajen led the way into the conference room to take the seat at the head of the table. His smile died instantly as the rest filed in and took chairs.

Ushara sat to his right while Jullien stood behind her. She glanced up at him. "Aren't you sitting?"

He shook his head and stood with his legs braced. Arms crossed.

That certainly wasn't intimidating or scary at all. She passed an amused glance to Trajen who was smirking at Jullien's stance.

Trajen cleared his throat. "I'm thinking before we start. . . . Should we disarm your bodyguard, VA Altaan?"

"I already took the blasters from him. Thought it would be a bad idea to have them on his body for this."

"Good call. Knives?"

She glanced around again. "Just one. It's his security blankie. I hate to take it from him. He gets a little edgy without it."

"Well, we don't want that. Any other weaponry I should know about?"

"Just hands and fangs, but we can't really detach those."

Trajen stroked his chin speculatively for a second. "Yeah, guess not. Very well, then. Let's keep in mind that we should all be on our best behavior, shall we?"

Ushara had no idea why Trajen was trying to provoke her family, but she didn't say anything as her cousins, uncle, father, and brothers crowded in. Davel was one of the last to show. With a grimace, he elbowed his way past them to shove his way to stand next to Jullien.

"Morning. Sorry I was late." He kissed her cheek to let everyone in the room know whose side he was decidedly on. Then he moved to stand next to Jullien. He attempted the same stance, but for some reason it wasn't as badass when Davel did it. It was, however, adorable.

Trajen sat back in his chair. "All right. First bitch up."

Kirill rose. "He blew up my ship. The whole damn thing. There's nothing left!"

"I know," Trajen drawled. "Was there. Saw it. Laughed my ass off."

"And you let him?"

"*Let* is a strong word. Not sure I could have stopped him, given his state of mind at the time. At least not without losing a vital piece of my anatomy. Decided it wasn't worth it. Especially not for your sorry ass."

"I can corroborate that as I stood back myself and watched it go up." Davel laughed. "It was quite . . . impressive."

"And I expect restitution!"

Ushara arched a brow at Kirill's indignant tone. "I suggest you take it from the money you made selling my husband into slavery. Or perhaps from the creds someone on your crew made from his gear that was taken and never returned to him, and I know the full value of it first-hand. I have the billing tithe on it. Would you like me to forward that to you?"

Kirill glared at her. "I didn't make any creds on him, for your information. I had to pay *them* to take him."

Too late, he realized what he'd said.

Ushara couldn't breathe as those words slapped her hard. Jullien didn't move.

Her gaze went to her father, then her uncle in turn. "Were the two of you in on this conspiracy?"

"Your father wanted him out of your life. We took care of it."

She cocked a brow at that.

Her father blustered. "You've not been the same since he came here. You're distracted and your loyalties fractured."

"My loyalties are *exactly* where they should be. Where they've always been. With my high admiral, this Nation and with my family. I've not broken an oath or wavered on *any* duty."

"You have risked us all by bringing a *hunted* darkheart into this Nation knowing we hate him. That he's not welcome here. That he'll *never* be welcomed here."

"Man, that's harsh." Davel winced. Then he spoke to Jullien in a low tone. "I, for one, welcome you, *drey*. Love you, too, in a purely platonic, brotherly way."

" 'Preciate it."

"No problem. Just don't set my ship on fire, especially if I'm in it."

Jullien snorted.

Their father glared at Davel.

Trajen let out an irritable sigh. "Look, you're all wasting my time. I'm not picking another VA. Ushara has done nothing to shake my confidence. I'm only holding this little soiree to placate you. End of the day, get over it."

Klavdii shot to his feet. "This is an outrage!"

Ushara shook her head. "No. The outrage is yet to come. Check your standing. Every member of the *Night Rain* has lost rank, effective immediately. Those with Canting have lost it as well. And that includes you, Klavdii, *and* my father."

*"What!"*

She looked at her father without flinching. "Anyone who had a hand in what happened to my husband is busted. We do not betray Tavali. Even a cock. For *any* reason. I placed my husband in your hands. When you betrayed him, you betrayed me *and* this Nation. You all violated your most sacred oaths. In the eyes of Tavali, you have committed treason and I will not allow that to happen."

Her father glared at Trajen. "You're allowing this to stand?"

"Her husband. Her call. Unless by some miracle, you can find someone to speak up on your behalf?"

"I will."

They turned in shock as Jullien spoke.

Ushara gaped at him. "Excuse me?"

"Just thinking that sadly these bastards have all spawned. While I couldn't give a shit about any of them, some of the spawn who aren't in this room are rather cute. The younger ones are still innocent. It's really not fair to punish them because these assholes couldn't wear a condom or behave like sentient beings with a conscience. I don't want to see their young on the street or starving."

Davel was seized with a sudden coughing fit that he finally gave up on and allowed to turn into hysterical laughter.

Ushara managed to hold her composure, but it wasn't easy, especially with her brother and his hyena fit. "Fine. You're all on probation for a year, and your voting rights regarding my husband's standing in the Nation are permanently suspended. Any other infraction and your Canting is gone, forever. You so much as frown in my husband's direction and I'll bust you to his personal slag. Furthermore, ten percent of your take for the next year will go to pay for Jullien's lost wages and tithe."

When they started to protest, she held her hand up. "Keep bitching and it'll be twenty percent. And Kirill, you're down two ranks, Captain Altaan."

"That's bullshit!"

"No, it's not. You're lucky, you're still even a bait at this point, given how mad I am at you. So don't even whine about it. Now you're all dismissed. Get out before I let my husband have at you!"

They left slowly, and very grudgingly.

Davel sighed. "It's going to be fun at our house during family holidays for the next few years."

"Ah, you love it." Ushara smirked.

Davel snickered. "Yeah, you're right. I do."

Her father glared at them as the room emptied.

She waited for him to speak. That expression on his face always meant a caustic lecture was brewing. Honestly, she wasn't in the mood for it. She was too old for his speeches, especially when she wasn't the one who'd done something so morally reprehensible.

But before he could start on her, the door opened.

Ushara frowned as her grandparents came in with the high priestess. She had no idea what this was about, but it terrified her, especially given the glower on her grandfather's face as he neared them.

"Vidarri," Trajen greeted. "What can we do for you?"

"I wanted to verify my granddaughter's news that she gave me before she left." He approached Jullien with Unira Samari flanking him.

Jullien immediately stiffened and went into that warrior's stance that never boded well for the ones facing him.

"Easy, *m'tana*," the high priestess said, touching him lightly on the arm. "It's all good."

He cast an uncertain glance to Ushara.

*"Graspa?"*

Without responding to her, he gently pulled the glasses off Jullien's eyes to look at them. He sucked his breath in sharply at their red color. "Dear gods . . . it *is* true. You weren't lying."

"Paka?" Her father rose to his feet. "What's going on?"

Tears welled in her grandfather's eyes. Reverently, he and her grand-mother went down on their knees in front of Jullien and bowed rever-ently.

Which infuriated her father. "What are you doing! We do not kneel before—"

Her grandfather cut him off with a sharp hiss. "You show respect be-fore the last Samari son!"

Her father scowled. "What?"

Jullien grimaced in pain. "Yeah. My grandmother got around a bit."

Her father shook his head in denial. "Bullshit! It's not possible. Only males carry the gene. He couldn't have inherited the stralen from his mother. His father's human."

Trajen shrugged. "The human DNA must have mutated the Fyreblood genes and somehow activated the stralen within him. It's the only thing that makes sense. But you can't deny the fact that he's stralen, *and* a Fyre-blood."

Ushara nodded. "I've seen him breathe fire. And he was tested against Unira's DNA. He's definitely Edon Samari's grandson."

"How long have you known?" her father asked.

She glanced at Jullien. "I found out not long before he left."

"Why didn't you tell me?"

"I asked her not to."

Her father looked ill at Jullien's words. "You really *are* one of us?"

Unira nodded. "I suspected as much the first time I saw him when he came to temple—he looks a great deal like some of my family. In particular, my father. It was why I did such a double take that day. And then once the admiral told me he'd gone stralen, I knew he was the one the old prophecies spoke of. Through him, the rarest bloodlines of Andaria are united. And if he fathers a son with your daughter, every bloodline could finally be merged—winged, Fyreblood, darkheart, and stralen. For the first time in centuries, there could be a full-blooded An-darion child born of all lines."

Her father's eyes teared as he realized the magnitude of that. "My grandson could be the *onakenedd*?

"Yes." Unira smiled at Jullien. "And as the very last of the Samaris, I would be humbled if you'd allow me to adopt you back into my lineage so that your children could carry our name, if they, and you and your wife, so choose to honor us."

Jullien couldn't breathe as those unexpected words hit him. He was too used to being disparaged and rejected by everyone.

Accepted?

He turned to look behind him to make sure she was actually speaking to him and not someone else. But there really wasn't anyone there.

Unira smiled kindly. "You all right?"

"Sorry . . . yes, I would be thrilled to be part of your lineage. I was only making sure you meant me and not someone else."

Unira laughed at him, then gave him the envelope in her hand. "And this was the gift I wanted you to have that I mentioned yesterday."

Frowning, he opened it and gasped as he realized it was the title for her ship. "I don't understand."

"I'm old and I don't need to be running blockades anymore. The gods were trying to tell me something when they grounded me. And I've been thinking a lot since I saw you working on my old girl with such loving care . . . I want you to have her."

"But I'm not Tavali."

"Not yet. You will be and you'll need a ship. She needs to go to someone who understands her and who will love her as I have. You not only love her, but you can repair her and keep her flying in a way no one else can. I can think of no better captain for her than you."

"High Mother—"

"Matarra," she said with a twinkle in her eye, cutting him off.

Jullien gifted her with a rare smile. "I—"

"Don't say you can't accept her. She was meant for you. I know it with every part of my heart. The gods wanted you to have her and so do I."

Jullien took her hand. "I will accept her only on one condition."

"That is?"

"You remain as part of her crew."

Unira tsked at him. "You'll have to convert. I won't fly with a heathen captain and risk the wrath of the gods."

He laughed at her less-than-subtle manipulation. "It's a deal. Besides, I was going to convert anyway for Ushara and Vasili."

Rising on her tiptoes, she kissed each of his cheeks. "I've always wanted a child of my own. The gods could not have given me a better or a more honorable or handsome son than you."

Jullien swallowed hard as those words sobered him. He wasn't sure how to take them. No one had ever wanted him before.

Ushara placed her hand on his shoulder. "You've stunned him speechless, High Mother. That's quite a feat."

Her father approached him sheepishly. "And I've done you grievously wrong. I should have welcomed you into my family as my daughter urged me to do, and instead, I conspired against you. Can you ever forgive me for what I've done?"

"For the sakes of your daughter and Vasili, I can ignore the past."

Her father inclined his head and shook his hand. "I promise you that I will never again give you cause to doubt me or my honor."

"Thank you."

Davel draped his arm around Jullien's neck and kissed him on the cheek. "Aw! I think this means you're all mine now, *drey*. I get to torture you on my crew."

"Beautiful," Jullien said in the driest of tones. "Eighteen months?"

"Yeah."

Jullien sighed wearily. But there was a gleam in his eye that said he didn't really mind it.

Her grandmother finally approached Jullien. Her expression was a cross between pain and disbelief. "I still don't know what to feel about you. And I will never understand why the gods would place the last surviving son of our greatest family in the body of our mortal enemy. Surely they must have their reasons, although I'll never understand them. That being said, you are stralen for my blood. I could ask for no greater gift or honor for my granddaughter. She's been harmed enough in this lifetime. It's time for her to have a male worthy of her heart, even if his heart is a dark one. I welcome you to our family, *m'tana*. Whichever name you choose to go by, I will gladly stitch it to your uniform, and pray for your safe return every time you leave us."

"Thank you, *Ger Tarra*."

She kissed his cheeks and bowed to him.

Davel clapped him on the back. "Welcome to the Altaan clan, *drey*. I'll start getting it changed on your papers."

Jullien ruffled Davel's hair. "While I appreciate the thought, I think I'll continue using Ixur."

"Why?"

He jerked his chin toward their father's disgruntled expression. "So as not to provoke your paka any worse and to keep your uncle from entirely losing his shit. I think it best to maintain some semblance of family harmony for the time being. Plus it keeps a layer of protection between me and Ushara and Vasili. I don't want any of my enemies to use them to come after me."

Unira placed a motherly hand on his shoulder. "You are a good male, and a devoted husband. I would suggest at least switching to Samari to protect yourself from those who are looking for your current alias. We can easily fabricate all new paperwork for you, to protect you as well as them."

Jullien swallowed hard as his throat tightened in gratitude. "I'm honored, *Ger Tarra*." It was the first time anyone had sought to protect him from his enemies. Honestly, it kind of scared him to have someone consider his well-being now. "Thank you. I swear I will do nothing to bring shame to your lineage or name."

"I have full faith in you, *m'tana*. From the moment I first saw you, I knew you were an Andarion of high integrity and utmost nobility."

"I wouldn't go quite that far. But I strive to do right . . . sometimes."

She smiled. "The Kadurr occasionally were forced to commit a few sins in order to set things right. Yet the gods forgave them. It is the intentions behind the actions that the gods take into account more than the actions themselves."

"I'm not sure that puts me on any better ground, as my intentions are not often any better than my actions."

"At least you're honest." Laughing, the priestess shook her head. "And with that, I have much to do. I shall take my leave now."

Her grandmother took Ushara's hand and Jullien's. "Once your Dagger converts, we'll expect a real wedding from the two of you. Not the hackneyed civil travesty you did without your family present. I shall get with your mother and sisters, and start the planning. We want the full obnoxious fare."

Ushara laughed. "My poor love has no idea what he's in for."

Davel tsked at him. "Brother, take my word. Run."

Her father nodded. "You're going to wish I'd shot you in the head."

Jullien turned toward Trajen. "Joke?"

"You wish." Trajen let out an evil laugh. "So glad I'm celibate. It saves me so much drama." He headed for the door, then stopped to look back at them. "For the record, had I replaced Ushara as my VA today . . .

my second choice would have been Dagger. I'd have expedited his Canting based on his exceptional military and political knowledge, diplomacy skills when he chooses to use them, and proven battle skills. So you wouldn't have gained any ground. Just FYI to chew on. Once he has citizenship, he will be moved to Canting and through the ranks as quickly as I can make it happen. There's no one else I'd put at Ushara's back or mine." He cut a stern glower to Davel. "Let it be known when you take him to crew that I consider him *my* family. Anyone else harms him, they deal with *me* personally. To me, he's my little brother. And I will fuck up any Tavali who touches him." With that, Trajen left them.

Zellen let out a slow breath. "I shall let everyone know. And get started on the new paperwork."

Davel tapped fists with Jullien. "*Estra, mi drey.*"

Jullien inclined his head to him. "*Estra.*"

Petran pulled Ushara into his arms and held her before he kissed the top of her head. "Now I know how your mother's paka felt when she dragged me home to meet him."

"Paka!"

"It's true. He threw me out. Took your mother a solid month of convincing her yaya that I was worthy of courting her. I still had to undergo a full purification with her father and brothers before he'd let me near her. Hate that bastard to this day."

Jullien arched his brow. "Purification?"

"Survival training," Petran explained. "And just so you know, they weren't supposed to sell you off. They did that without my knowledge or consent. They were only supposed to return you to where they found you and leave you there. That was what we'd agreed to."

She frowned. "Then why were you fighting with Davel?"

Her father scratched sheepishly at his ear. "I didn't believe him when he told me what they'd done. I accused him of lying about it."

"Paka!"

"I know. But it's hard to hear something like that and believe it. I didn't want to hurt someone I loved over . . ." A red stain spread over his face.

Jullien's expression turned to stone. "Someone like me?"

"I won't ever do it again, boy. I promise you." Her father held his hand out to Jullien.

After a brief hesitation, Jullien took it.

Her father pulled him in and hugged him. "From this day forward, I consider you mine, and I will defend you as such."

"Thank you, Gůr Tana."

Clearing his throat, he pulled back to look at the two of them. "And I'll be expecting that grandson from the two of you. Along with some granddaughters."

Ushara laughed. "We will get started on that right away."

"Good! I'm not getting any younger. Days like today are aging me quick."

Her link began buzzing with Vasili's tone. She answered it, then went pale. "Honey? What is it?" She paused. "Vas? Breathe, baby."

Jullien scowled at her worried tone.

"Are you still at school?" Her voice trembled. "All right. Stay right there. I'm on my way. Don't move." She hung up.

Jullien rubbed her back. "What is it?"

"I'm not sure. He was too upset to speak clearly. I couldn't really understand what he was saying. But I've got to get to him." She headed for the door.

All three of them went with her to Vas's school, which ended up being a good thing since Vasili wasn't in his classroom. Rather, he was hiding in the boys' bathroom, refusing to come out.

"Vas?" Jullien called as he went inside with Petran and Davel to find him. "Are you in here?"

Sobbing, Vas ran from the last stall and threw himself into Jullien's arms.

Jullien held him while he met Petran and Davel's shocked stares. "What's wrong, *mi tana*? What has you so upset?"

Vasili pulled out a small box and handed it to Jullien. He spoke in broken words through his sobs. "Was . . . in . . . my . . . b-b-b-backpack."

Scowling, Jullien opened the box, then cursed out loud as he saw a bloody, severed finger wearing the signet ring he'd traded to buy parts for Oxana's ship. He slammed the lid over it and handed it off to Davel before he pulled Vasili against him again and held him tight. "Did you see who put it there?"

He shook his head and cried even harder.

Davel's curse matched Jullien's as he saw it and passed it to his father.

"Where's the backpack?" Jullien asked.

"R-r-room."

Jullien kept his arms wrapped tightly around Vasili as he walked him out of the bathroom and to Ushara. He looked around, trying to find someone who didn't belong here. So help him, when he laid claws to the one responsible, he was going to rip their throat out with his bare hands.

No one would upset Vas like this and live. No one threatened his family. Ever.

Petran and Davel came out behind him. "Who do you think did this?" Davel asked Jullien.

"Nyran," Jullien growled. "Has to be. No one else is this sick." Not even his grandmother would have done that to Vasili. She'd have sent a head to Jullien with a threatening note.

As a rule, she didn't terrorize children unless she knew them personally. To her, there was no fun in scaring a stranger unless she was there to witness it.

"What happened?" Ushara asked.

Davel actually started to give the box to Ushara.

Tempted to punch him, Jullien snatched it from his hand. "You don't give that to your sister, you moron!" He slid it into his pocket before he explained it to her. "It's the signet ring I traded for your sister's ship."

"That's not all that's in there," Davel said under his breath.

"It's all she needs to know." Jullien glared at him. "Don't make me beat you with a chair. Since I can't lay hands on the one who did this, I will make you a worthy substitute for my wrath."

"Brother, you got some serious anger management problems."

"Yes, I do." Jullien ground his teeth. He wanted blood for this. Anyone who would traumatize a child so needlessly . . . "We need to search his backpack."

He and Davel went to get it while Ushara and her father took Vasili toward the office to check him out for the rest of the day.

As they headed for the classroom, Davel sighed. "You need to relax. They can't hurt him on this base."

"Excuse me if I disagree. They got close enough to plant a disembodied finger on him. They can get close enough to hurt him."

"Someone had to have seen them."

"Then point them out so I can end their life."

As they entered the room, the teacher started to protest.

"It's all right," Davel said, placating him. "This is Vasili's father. His mother is with him in the office and we're checking him out."

The teacher raked a curious stare over Jullien's body. "Are you Tavali?"

Davel answered for him. "He's TNT. Is there a problem?"

"Fyreblood?"

Davel nodded. "Samari."

Jullien arched a brow as Davel continued to answer for him.

The teacher appeared impressed. "Does he ever speak?"

Jullien smirked. "Those who don't know me think I'm quiet. Those who do, wish I was."

"Beg pardon?"

He slung Vasili's backpack over his shoulder and cracked a shit-eating grin at the teacher. "I typically practice excessive sarcasm since random throat punches tend to get me arrested in most systems."

"And that's why we don't let him talk much. Have a nice day." Davel pulled him out of the room. "Gah . . . I can't believe Shara lets you out in public without supervision."

"What? Nobody bled, died, or was bashed in the head during that meeting. My social skills are vastly improving, especially given the mood I'm in."

"Now there's a terrifying thought. Explains so much about Andarion politics."

"Yes, exactly. That's why the Anatole standard of diplomacy has always been . . . sure we'll negotiate if any survivors happen to remain." Jullien started searching through the backpack as they headed for the office.

He paused outside the door as he found the note that had been shoved inside with the box. Opening it, he read the words and his fury mounted with every one.

*Just when you think you're safe . . .*

*Sooner or later, we all pay the Korilon's fee. Your bill is coming, Julie. Look out for it.*

His vision turned dark. *Bitch, please. You're the one who better watch the shadows at your back. I'm coming for you, Nyran. And you're about to bleed. Hard and profusely.*

# CHAPTER 17

Y ou have to go out on Davel's crew. We've been over this a thousand times. You can't gain citizenship without training time on an
active ship."

"Then screw it. I'd rather not have it than risk you or Vas."

Standing in her bedroom while she finished painting his face, Ushara held Jullien close as she savored those stubborn words and fought
the urge to choke him for them. "I know, *mi kiri*. But we're fine. Trajen
has told you as much. It was just a threat to rattle you."

"It succeeded. I'm rattled. More than rattled, I'm pissed."

She rolled her eyes at his obsessive paranoia. "It's been two months
and nothing else has happened. We're fine."

He growled at her.

She growled back and bared her fangs at him.

That succeeded in making him smile, especially as she straightened
his jacket. "How do you always manage to put your jacket on crooked?"

Jullien shrugged adorably. "I don't know. It's part of the CAS I developed in school."

"CAS?"

"Contentious Asshole Syndrome. It made my grandmother and instructors insane, which delighted me to no uncertain end."

Laughing, she kissed him. "Well, I find it charming and it gives me
a reason to malehandle you."

He sucked his breath in sharply as she brushed her hand against his
abdomen. "Then I'm glad I developed it so early that it's now an ingrained
habit."

"Mum? Paka? Are you ready?"

"We're ready, Veelee," Ushara called, stepping past Jullien to open the bedroom door. "Are you?"

Vasili was on the other side in full face paint for his Confirmation—something the two of them had requested Unira delay to the next cycle of candidates when Jullien had gone missing, since Vasili had wanted Jullien here for the ceremony.

Jullien's breath caught as he saw that it wasn't Altaan and Davers painted on Vasili's face.

It was Altaan and Samari.

Vas hesitated as he saw Jullien's stunned expression. "Is it all right that I did this, Paka?"

Recovering from the initial shock, Jullien pulled him in for a hug. "Absolutely. I'm more honored than you'll ever know. It just caught me off-guard. You are more than welcome to everything I have. Especially my name."

Ushara swallowed back her tears at the sight of them. She was grateful how much the two of them loved one another. Her greatest regret had always been not having a father for Vasili.

What amazed her was that Jullien had never tried to replace Chaz in either of their lives. Yet he couldn't love Vas any more had he been his real father. He doted on him constantly, in ways that continually floored her. She'd never seen any male love a child who wasn't his so thoroughly.

Her gaze went to Vas's door where Jullien had even painted the Gorturnum screaming skull logo against a solid black background with the words *Vasili the Brave and Terrible* circling it—that had been the one change to the house he'd wanted to make that he'd asked about on his return.

Jullien had done the same thing inside his ship and hers for Vas to counteract the "overwhelming" feminine influences that she'd unwittingly subjected her poor son to—something she hadn't even been aware of until Jullien had moved in and she'd seen them together. Even though she'd grown up sandwiched between her unruly brothers, she'd never been so keenly aware of the male code of conduct until now, and it amused her how they playfully teamed up against her to tease her until she smiled and laughed about it.

A knock sounded on their door.

Vasili went to answer it while Ushara turned toward Jullien. "We'll resume our fight later. And I will win it. So prepare yourself mentally for your eventual defeat."

With an irritable mumbling under his breath, he followed her to the front where her family was fussing about running late. Little Nadya ran straight to Jullien for her ritual ride to temple in his arms.

While they walked on ahead, Mary grabbed her. "Have you told him?"

"Not yet. Shh! He'll hear you."

Her sister scoffed at her. "You have to tell him." She mouthed the words at her.

"No!" she mouthed back. If she told Jullien she was pregnant, he'd never leave to finish his citizenship training. He was too afraid of his cousin harming them. Since the school incident, he hadn't slept through a single night.

He'd hardwired their house with the most frightening security system she'd ever seen in her life. Both she and Vasili wore rings that transmitted their vital signs to his link at all times.

And he checked it constantly anytime they were out of his sight.

She could barely go to the bathroom alone now. In fact, Jullien walked only slightly ahead and continually stepped back to check where both she and Vasili were peripherally to ensure they were with the group. She was amazed he didn't insist on a tether line for them.

He really was *that* ridiculous.

But at least most of her family was slowly acclimating to him as her husband.

Kirill, Gavin, and Klavdii, and their branch, notwithstanding. In fact, they wouldn't even walk with them to temple anymore. And they sat away from them during service. Which was probably for the best, given Jullien's hostile, unforgiving temperament where they were concerned.

And hers.

Unira greeted them as they approached the temple. "There's my beautiful boy." She winked at Jullien. "Has he behaved this week, *m'tina*?"

"Not too much bloodshed, High Mother. No arrests. He's getting better."

The priestess touched Jullien's cheek where Ushara had painted the Samari symbols on his face. "Are you still heading out in the morning with Davel's crew?"

He glanced to Ushara. "Depends on who wins our fight tonight."

Unira laughed. "In that case, after the ceremony, I should like to exord him before we send him out."

Ushara smiled at them. "I think that's a great idea."

"You say that now," Jullien said churlishly. "Until the holy water touches my flesh, starts to boil, and we burn down the temple. For that matter, we're all lucky I don't burst into flames whenever I walk beneath the arches."

With a gentle push, Ushara urged him forward. "We're holding up the line. Go, you silly *žumi*."

He obeyed without another comment.

When Jullien started to sit off with her parents, Vasili stopped him. "I wanted both my parents with me. If that's all right, Paka?"

Jullien brushed his hand through Vasili's hair and nodded. "Absolutely." He offered his arm to Ushara and allowed them to lead him to the candidate section.

It was still strange to him that Vasili accepted him as his father without hesitation. More used to being rebuked, Jullien continued to have a hard time being part of their family. Every time, he automatically expected Ushara or Vasili to hurt him.

They never did.

He wondered if his stomach would ever stop habitually shrinking in expectation of being rejected. If he'd ever grow accustomed to this new existence where they didn't kick or hurt him. He was trying, but it was so difficult when he'd lived defensively for his whole life.

His gaze went to Ushara's family.

No. *His* family now. Why did he have such a hard time accepting that? Over the last few weeks, they'd gone out of their way to prove to him that he really was a member of their *nyth*.

And yet . . .

He kept waiting for the betrayal to come. For them to throw him into a hole or sell him off again.

Davel inclined his head at him and smiled as he held his infant son in his arms. Maksim. Their other son was named after the cousin who currently wasn't speaking to him because of Jullien. Davel's daughter, Yasha, lay curled against her mother. Fara was a beautiful blonde, but she paled in comparison to Ushara.

Jullien had mixed emotions about Fara since she was essentially the reason he was here. For that, he owed her his entire life and existence. But for Fara and her insistence that Ushara loosen her hold on Vasili, he'd be dead now.

Yet that insistence had put the boy in danger, and like his wife, that angered him at the female. So Jullien treated Fara with polite deference.

And she was utterly terrified of him. Anytime he neared her, she ran like the Koriłon himself was after her.

He had yet to formally meet Ushara's brother Dimitri who had been with her at Steradore. The one they'd all warned him would hate him most.

Perhaps it was a blessing they'd been kept apart.

Ushara reached over and took his hand. Jullien's heart sped up at the contact. Glancing over, he smiled at her.

"You all right?" she whispered.

He nodded. But it was a lie. He wasn't used to this sense of normal. Like wearing a pair of oversized shoes that had been stretched to someone else's feet. It wasn't uncomfortable, per se.

Just didn't feel quite right.

Not to mention, he still had that feeling he was being watched. That someone had eyes on him. No matter what he did or where he went, he couldn't shake it. He never could find them. But the sensation wouldn't let up, either. It was so unnerving.

There were times, when he swore he could feel Nyran or his grandmother standing over him.

Even now.

By the time the solemn religious ceremony was done and the young candidates who'd been confirmed were free to mingle with friends and family, he was having a hard time breathing and focusing as Ushara led him toward the open area that was decorated for the public temple party and celebration. The crowd was thick with extended family and celebrants.

And still his paranoia persisted. Even though he knew there couldn't be any other Ixurianir here. In this sea of pale blond Fyrebloods, they'd stand out as much as he did.

Ushara called out to him. "Jules?"

He drew a deep breath and mentally shook himself as he tried to keep her from knowing his state of unrest and shoved his panic attack down. "Yes, *mu taru*?" he answered, using the Andarion term that meant *lady of my heart*.

"Do you dance?"

A slow smile spread across his face. "Of course I do."

With an impish grin that made him so hard it was extremely uncomfortable, she crooked her finger for him. Worse? She started dancing in a small crowd with her sisters before he reached her. In a circle, they joined hands and swayed their hips in perfect synchronization. Then broke apart to move their hands and shoulders in a provocative swaying beat that thrummed through every fiber of his being.

Damn . . . she was the most seductive female to ever breathe. No tara should be that limber or sensual. Then again, he was glad that if one had to exist, that she belonged to him and that he had the privilege of tasting those moves all night long when she wasn't in her clothes.

And when she took his hand and began to dance with him, he was grateful for every long, frustrating, and tedious afternoon his grandmother had insisted he endure lessons in spite of his endless whining against them.

Ushara's laughter filled his ears as she danced with him. "You've been holding out on me, *mi tiri*."

He wrapped his arms around her as they swayed toward the ground. "You never asked me about *this*."

"True, but now that I know what you *can* do . . . you're going to be doing a lot more of it."

He grinned down at her. "*Trevisa, Ger Tarra. Bauertui hæfre.*" *Yes, my lady. I am forever your servant.*

But as the song finished, Jullien realized that they had attracted a *lot* of attention from the Fyrebloods who didn't normally attend temple with them. Or if they did, they hadn't noticed him among their congregation as he usually sat in the back and stayed seated throughout the liturgy.

Instinctively, he put himself in front of Ushara and kept one hand on her waist as whispers echoed, and malevolent stares focused on them.

To his shock, it was her grandfather who came forward to stand with them against the gathering angry crowd that was starting to demand Jullien's scalp be mounted on the wall.

"What's going on?" Vidarri asked.

One of the more hostile members Jullien didn't know neared them. "What is this darkheart doing here, desecrating our holy place?"

Vidarri lifted his chin. "He's a Samari."

The male curled his lip in repugnance. "You dishonor their nobility and memory by painting him as one. But it doesn't make it so."

"He's a Samari by blood and DNA." Still dressed in her full high priestess's robes, Unira came to stand beside Jullien. "He's also my son— fully Vested and acknowledged as such by me. He's a Fyreblood with as much right to be here as anyone."

"Prove it." That cry was taken up by the entire crowd.

"He doesn't need to prove himself."

Jullien gaped at Vidarri. That stunned him. But when Petran, Katira, and the elder Nadya took positions beside him and agreed, he was absolutely floored. Never before had *any* family stood at his side to defend him.

Ever.

Nadya glared at the crowd around them. "Dagger is a member of the great house of Altaan. If you take issue with him, you have issue with us. *All* of us."

Ushara took his arm and placed it around her waist so that she could splay his hand over her stomach and hold it there. In Andarion culture, it was a matriarchal declaration of family and a powerful statement for a female to make since they didn't normally touch each other in public, especially so intimately. It was the same as saying she would kill or die to protect him. That he, alone, was hers.

Likewise, her grandmother and mother each placed their hands on his shoulders.

Jullien's eyes watered, forcing him to blink quickly as unshed tears choked him. This was the first time in his life he'd truly felt like part of a family. He couldn't even begin to describe what it meant to him that they were willing to make this stand on his behalf.

And when her sisters moved in to stand at his back and touch him . . .

An unfamiliar warmth spread through his entire body. With it came the rage and hatred he knew all too well—that furious need to shove back whenever he was pushed.

"You dare question the honor of my family and especially the word of *mu Ger Tarra* Samari?" Jullien challenged the group.

His gaze never leaving the bastard who'd first spoken, Jullien gently lifted Ushara's hand from his stomach to place a kiss in her palm. Then he removed his glasses and handed them to her.

As soon as they saw the color, those around him gasped and shrank back.

*Yeah, bitches, you better run . . .*

With his fury mounting, Jullien stepped away from the Altaans so as not to hurt them, and let the powers he'd been working on with Unira for the last two months rip through him. Fire shot down his arms and to his hands. Something as a male Fyreblood he shouldn't be able to do, but apparently stralen wasn't the only mutation his father's screwed-up genetic donation had caused.

He let the fireballs fly out straight to the one who'd spoken.

Opening his mouth, he spewed his fiery venom at them. One thing about the Samaris, they didn't just breathe fire, they controlled it better than any of the other bloodlines. It was what had always made them the deadliest of the Fyrebloods and why they were the first among the Pavakahir lineages.

Several members of the crowd screamed and ran. Others stood completely still as they realized who and what he really was.

Dampening his fire, Jullien cornered the one who'd been rudest and dragged him toward Ushara. He forced the prick to kneel on the ground in front of her. "Apologize to *mu Ger Tarra* Samari and her family."

"M-m-my apologies."

"And mu matarra."

"Forgive me, High Mother."

Jullien finally released him. "Any other questions you have about the veracity of my lineage?"

"N-n-no, Gůr Tana."

"Good. By the way, you should never, *ever* overestimate my affection for Androkyn in general or any particular desire I have to preserve your individual lives."

Petran let out a long, weary sigh as he shook his head.

Ushara laughed. "Well, Paka, he is a work in progress. And we've come a long way. He didn't shoot or kill anyone, this time."

"Only because you made him leave the blasters at home," Davel said under his breath.

Her grandfather snorted. "Don't be so hard on the boy. They wanted to see him make fire. He gave them what they asked for. I got no problem with it."

Her maternal grandfather, Carak, clapped a hand on Jullien's shoulder. "Proud of you, *tana*. It does my old heart good to see such spirit. Reminds me of my own *Koriłon-be-damned* fire-in-the-gut I had at your age. I was a bastard soul on its way to Tophet myself until the day Katira's mother tamed me. You think we were hard on *you*? You should have seen the way her father and brothers reacted when she brought me home the first time."

Katira gasped. "You *never* told me any of this."

"Not something a father tells his daughter. I didn't want you to take up the challenge. And it worked. You picked a male with a quiet, peaceful disposition for your husband."

Petran stiffened. "Why do I feel suddenly insulted?"

Laughing, Carak popped him so hard on the back, he stumbled forward. "You've been the perfect balm for my Katira. There's no other son I'd want for her." He jerked his chin at Jullien. "But I'm glad to see a Kadurr back in our bloodline. Keeps things interesting, eh, Vidarri?"

Jullien scowled as Vidarri and Carak walked off together, commiserating about the good old days. He glanced down at Ushara. "Did your grandfathers just admit to actually liking me?"

"I think they did."

"This has got to be a sign of the Ormadum. I can't leave tomorrow. You're going to need me for the End Times."

"Oh my God . . . Jules! Really? We're back to this fight already?" Ushara rolled her eyes at him. "Am I going to have to bash you on the head, knock you unconscious, and carry you on board?"

"Probably. You'll need a lot of help, though. I weigh a shit-ton. I also suggest Trajen. He's the only one here large enough to beat my ass with impunity."

Laughing, she kissed his surly lips until he smiled again. As the crowd dispersed and the music returned, he slowly began to relax and enjoy the rest of the night.

By the end of it, the young males and females who'd been confirmed came together for a final dance and to show off their fire skills.

Jullien wrapped his arms around Ushara's shoulders and held her as they watched Vasili.

In two parallel lines, the group stood, facing each other. Vasili slid an eager glance toward them as he pulled his Þinsan-boll—a sacred, elaborately embroidered thick ribbon that held a large ball at each end—from his neck. As they'd been confirmed earlier, each of the balls had been dipped in blessed oils for the ceremony, then Unira had placed the ribbon around their necks.

Starting at opposite ends, each of them used their incendiary breath to light the balls so that they could begin swinging them by their ribbons in a beautiful, choreographed dance.

Ushara tilted her head back so that she could watch Jullien's face. "You don't have anything like this for your confirmations, do you?"

"No. Ours are much more somber events. With candles that we light through more conventional means."

She caressed his forearms while they watched their son. "Are you ready to join our world completely and leave behind everything you grew up with?"

He glanced down at her. "I told you, Shara, I had no life before I met you. Nyk should have gutted me the night I betrayed his wife into the hands of his enemy. It would have been the kindest thing he could have done for me back then. But I'm grateful that he showed restraint and mercy when he had no reason to do so. And for what I have now, I owe him a debt that I can never repay."

Jullien buried his face in her hair and took a deep breath to savor the sweetest scent he'd ever known. "This life you've given me . . . my greatest fear is waking up and finding it all a dream. As far as I'm concerned, I am Dagger Samari, Gůr Tana to Ushara of the Pavakahira Nyth Altaan, paran of her incredible and honorable son, Vasili Davers. This is the only life I want, and I will fight the Koriłon himself and all his *kybyks* to keep it. So there's nothing for me to leave behind."

Ushara bit her lip to keep from crying as her love for him overwhelmed her. She started to tell him about the baby, then caught herself. He would never leave with Davel if he found out. She knew that with every part of her being.

*He's going to be furious if you don't.*

She laid her hand against his whiskered cheek and savored the rough texture of it. "I love you, Jules."

"Love you more."

Smiling, she watched as Vasili finished his dance and extinguished his Þinsan-boll in the fyreboll near the altar, then hung it up with the others. Unira blessed them each and passed them to their families.

Ushara sent Vasili on ahead with her parents so that she and Jullien could remain behind.

Once everyone was gone and the temple closed, Unira turned to Jullien. "You didn't want anyone else here to witness your exordium?"

He shook his head. "No one else knows I haven't received it. Not exactly something I brag about since it shows a genuine lack of regard for me on the part of my birth family."

"That is an indictment against them, *tana*. Not you."

He leaned down to whisper to Unira. "Doesn't feel that way, High Mother."

Shaking her head, she gently pinched his ear. "Come, we can do this quickly in my office, and then you can go home to finish celebrating Vasili's Confirmation."

Unira led them toward the small alcove that was one of the few enclosed areas in the temple compound. Her office was small and opened into a larger dressing room and antechamber. The antechamber held the door to the confessional area and a larger, extremely ornate room for private infant exordioms.

This had always been one of Ushara's favorite places in the Gorturnum station. The paneling had gold inlaid over the carvings and filigree, and it highlighted the historical paintings that chronicled the birth of the Fyrebloods as the descendants of the gods. She'd been here many times for the exordioms of her family, and soon she'd be here again to present their child for his or her first blessing.

Biting her lip, she couldn't resist caressing her stomach as she watched Jullien glance around the unfamiliar space.

In the shape of an elongated octagon, the room held a basin in the center and curtain recess at the far end where the priestess's small altar was placed between two columns that held up an ornate arch.

"Remove your jacket and shirt while I prepare the sacrament."

Jullien obeyed quietly and handed his clothes and his scarf and glasses to Ushara to hold. She was grateful that his back was to Unira. Because when the priestess turned around and saw the multitude of scars on his body, the horrified expression on her face would have cut him deeply.

It took the priestess a moment to regain her composure before she rejoined them.

With an uneasy smile, she placed a small stool in front of the basin for him to kneel on.

His stare empty, Jullien hesitated. "We don't have to do this."

Unira frowned. "Are you having second thoughts?"

"No, but I can tell you are after seeing . . ." His gaze went to his scarred chest and arms. And especially his wrists that bore out the harsh tragedies of his past.

Sheepishly, he reached for his shirt in Ushara's hands. "It's okay. I accepted the fact that your gods abandoned me a long time ago." When he started to pull his shirt over his head, Unira stopped him.

"I don't have reservations about this, Jullien. I only weep at the trials the gods have put you through, and can't help wondering why."

"Obviously, I chafe their asses."

Unira tsked at him. "You shouldn't blaspheme here."

"Is it blasphemy to speak an obvious truth?" he asked honestly.

She took his shirt and handed it back to Ushara. "Kneel, child. Benediction has been wrongfully withheld from you for far too long."

Jullien let out a long sigh. "Here's hoping I don't burst into flames."

Unira laughed so hard, she had to step back for a moment to catch her breath.

After a few minutes, she returned to brush her hand through his cropped hair that was only just starting to grow back as she began the prayers of invocation, benediction, and blessing. She tilted his head forward, across the basin, and poured the water and oils over his head.

Once finished, she wiped and dried his hair with her sacred cloth and kissed each cheek and his forehead. "There, child. You didn't burst into flames, and since you are definitely past the age of consent, if you wish to sign the registry, I can go ahead and confirm you."

"Sure."

Unira handed him a regular towel before she folded and tucked away the sacred cloth and pulled out the registry that Vasili had signed earlier.

Jullien paused. "Shara?"

"Is something wrong?"

"Did you see how Vas signed this?"

He stepped back for her to look at it.

Ushara let out a small gasp in surprise, then smiled. "I think it's sweet."

"It doesn't bother you?"

She rubbed his arm before she kissed his cheek. "Not at all. Are you okay with it?"

"Of course." He towel dried his hair. "I just didn't want it to upset you."

"I'm actually happy that he thinks of you as his father. He was so young when Chaz died that he doesn't really recall him. It's time that he had a paka to claim."

Smiling, Jullien signed just below Vasili, then put his shirt and jacket on while Ushara took a picture of the registry. "What are you doing?"

"I want a photo of it to show my parents. They'll think it's sweet, too."

Jullien wasn't so sure about that. Seeing their grandson using his new Samari surname might incite them to riot against him again. It definitely would make Chaz's parents want his head on a pike if they ever saw it.

Unira handed him his own copy of their holy book, the *Gæst Hælend* that she'd already had imprinted with his name on the cover. "I thought you'd prefer J.D. Samari on it since I've noticed that's what you've been using on official documents."

"Yes. Thank you."

She patted his hand and gave him a small box. "The gods' blessings to you both. I won't keep you any longer. I know you have a party to attend. *Cald mitta*."

"*Mitta, Matarra*. Thank you, again." Jullien kissed her cheek.

"Thank you," Ushara repeated before she gave her a hug. "For everything."

Unira patted her back kindly. "Good luck," she whispered before she released her.

Ushara reached up to clean some of the smeared paint from beneath Jullien's eye. The exordiom had removed almost all of it from his face so that practically none of the Samari crest was left. She tweaked his nose playfully. "Now that you're a sanctified Demurrist, you have to marry me at temple. Full ceremony."

He draped his arm over her shoulders as they headed for her parents' home where everyone was gathered for Vas's party. "You know you'll be stuck with me after that. Demurrists don't believe in divorces from sanctified temple marriages."

"True." She sobered as she saw the expression on his face. "What's wrong, *mi'ki*?"

"Are you sure that it doesn't bother you for Vas to use Samari as his surname? I know that you loved Chaz and—"

"Jullien, I was a child when I married Chaz. We were children when we were pledged. It was an arranged marriage between our parents. Yes, I *loved* him, but it was a girl's love. Naive and innocent. What I feel for you makes a mockery of what I thought I felt for him. I honestly don't know what I'd feel for Chaz if he were still alive. We were very different creatures. As you so often say, that was my past and I don't want to live there. You are my present and my future. You *are* my life."

He scowled at her. "I just don't understand how you can love my irritable, contentious ass."

She laughed at the angst in his tone. "You are warm and sweet. Intelligent and protective . . . a little psychotically so," she teased. "You give without asking. No male has ever made me feel as loved or needed as you do. What is there not to adore?"

"I'm belligerent. Crass. Ill-tempered. Quick-tempered. And half of your family, and the entirety of mine want to kill me. That's just for starters. And as you noted, I'm psychotic."

"Well, no marriage is without its problems."

Snorting and rolling his eyes, he opened the door to her parents' house to let her enter first.

The party was already in full swing and every corner of their home was packed with a family member or friend.

Trajen met them a few steps inside the door and handed Jullien a bottled ale. He smirked at Jullien's damp hair. "Congratulations. I see you're finally sanctified."

Jullien wiped at the oil that was still clinging to his forehead. "Indeed. You can kill me now."

"Later. I'm in a peaceful mood at present. Though I'm sure you'll ruin *that* in no time." He inclined his head toward Vasili. "You've no idea how much it meant to him to have you here tonight."

"He's a good kid."

"That he is." Trajen took a swig of his own ale before he pinned a hard stare on Jullien.

"You know you shrivel my nuts when you do that. Get your Tris ass out of my head."

Trajen laughed. "Ah, see, you've already slaughtered my happy place." He sighed irritably. "And if it makes you feel better, nothing's going to happen to them here. I will keep watch over them both while you're gone."

"Yeah, but you didn't keep the finger out of his backpack. No offense, Tray. Hard to trust your Tris sense, after that."

"They didn't come in here with the intent to harm."

Jullien cocked his brow. "That *was* harmful. Trust me. I was there. I saw what it did to Vas's mental state. Kid still has nightmares from it."

Trajen shook his head. "Sadly, I can't detect those kinds of attacks. But I can tell if they were here to harm them physically. And I can stop those. You have my word to you, little brother. No one will touch them in your absence. I'd shut them down and send you their hearts in a box if they were to dare such."

A bad feeling went through Jullien at Trajen's nagging insistence. "Why do you want me gone so badly?"

"Honestly? I don't. I'd much rather have you here. I sleep better knowing you're at my back. But I want you with citizenship and Canting. As much as I like you, I can't break protocol. I can only bend it so far. The sooner you make full Tavali, the happier we'll all be. So get it done. Sooner rather than later."

That didn't help his mood. If anything, it made his hackles rise more. "What aren't you telling me?"

"You know what I'm not saying."

"There's a storm coming."

Trajen nodded. "You know what sucks the most about seeing the future?"

"Not being able to stop it."

"Yeah. And knowing that more than one outcome exists is the worst of it all. I can see multiple truths at the same time. So I know what happens if you listen and if you don't. While I can advise you, I can't make your choices. Only you can."

"I'm listening, but I have one question . . ."

"Yes, I have been," Trajen said coldly. "But it's been a long time since I was wrong."

Jullien sighed at something he really didn't want to hear. "What made you wrong, then?"

"There are certain people who can lie to me. Certain minds I can't read. Things that will drain my powers. It's why I stay secluded. It's harder to be weakened this way. I don't ever want to be weak again."

Jullien glanced over to where Ushara was laughing with her sisters, then to Vas who was gaming with his cousins. "I know what you mean." He now had his heart on the outside of his body where he could no longer protect it at all times, and he *hated* it.

Trajen snorted at him. "She's not your weakness."

"What do you mean?"

"Haven't you realized it yet, brother? That little girl is the heart that beats inside your chest. She's the air inside your lungs. While she is the very tool that can bring you to your knees, she's the only reason you're still standing today. And she's the only reason you'll be standing tomorrow. . . . *For on the darkest night when the storms come and batter at the helm, even the best-made ship and crew will be forever lost at sea—*"

"*Without their Darling to guide them home.*"

Trajen tapped his bottle against Jullien's. "You seriously read way too much our literature, little man."

Jullien laughed. "That I did. Forever ruined my sorry ass."

"Basha Dagger!"

Jullien handed his ale to Trajen as little Nadya came running toward him and launched herself into his arms for a massive hug and kiss. "Umph! You've been eating a lot of cake, little Naddimaer. I think you've gained thirty pounds since this afternoon. Or I'm getting really old."

Laughing, she offered him a piece of candy. "I saved some for you!"

"That looks good, but I'll let you eat it for me."

Davel came up to them and ruffled Nadya's hair before he spoke to Jullien. "Remember, we've got an early start in the morning. Don't stay up too late."

"You taking Basha Dagger from me, Basha Davel?"

"I am, Nadya. Sorry."

She stuck her tongue out at him. "Who's going to carry me to temple?"

"I'll carry you till my paka gets back."

Nadya screwed her face up at Vasili's offer, then sighed heavily. "All right. You'll do, I guess." Still, she poked her lip out into an adorable pout. "He's not as comfortable to sleep on though. And he don't smell near as good. I will miss you, Basha Dagger. Don't be gone long."

"I'll be back as soon as I can."

"Okay." She hugged his neck, then started crying.

Jullien panicked at the sound. "Did I break her?"

Trajen laughed. "No. She wants you to stay."

Oxana came rushing over to check on her daughter. She glared at her brother. "What did you do?"

"Nothing!"

"H-h-he's taking Basha Dagger away, Mama. Tell him no!"

"Oh, baby. It's okay." She pulled her daughter from Jullien's grasp. "He'll come back."

She cried even harder.

Stunned, Jullien felt terrible and had no idea what to do. All of sudden, a pair of arms wrapped around his waist. He jumped until he realized it was Ushara.

"I know exactly how she feels," she said against his shoulder.

He covered her arms with his own. "Please tell me you're not going to do that to me tomorrow."

"I might."

"And if you do, I definitely won't leave."

Davel snorted. "Yeah and I'd be a member short for my crew. I'll shoot him and carry him onboard before I allowed him to stay behind."

Ushara glared at him. "And that's when I started hating my brother."

Jullien laughed.

Ushara kissed his shoulder, then reached for Vasili. "You ready to go home?"

"If it's okay, I'll stay with Yaya and Graspa tonight. They said they'd walk me to the bay in the morning to say goodbye, but we figured the two of you would want tonight to yourselves."

"Vas," they said in unison.

He hugged them both. "It's okay, parental units. I know I'm loved. My ego will survive this. But I'm old enough to know that the two of you need some time alone without Vasili in the house. It's all good. I already packed a bag and stashed it upstairs earlier. I will brush my teeth and everything. Now go."

Ushara kissed his cheek. "Love you."

"You, too."

She waited while Jullien hugged him. Her throat tightened as he buried his fist in Vas's hair and held him close. Vas fisted both of his hands in Jullien's jacket. When Jullien finally released him, Vas patted him on the back and inclined his head. Neither spoke, but the expression on their faces said more than words ever could and it almost reduced her to tears.

Jullien clapped him on the shoulder, then they and Trajen left.

Trajen paused outside their condo. "I will not be getting up in the morning as that is a side of me no one needs to see. However, safe journeys, my friend. May you never need to carry more than you can hold. And let the gods' conscience keep you clean and hoist you back before you reek."

Jullien laughed at the nonsensical words. "Just puckle your breath, brother. We'll be jock'n the devil's mickle ladly in the dale, come the pitch dingle on the dreich moon's back."

Ushara's eyes widened as Trajen held his hand out. When Jullien took it, he pulled Jullien in for a brotherly hug.

Jullien had no idea how rare it was for Trajen to allow anyone to touch him.

"*Valé*," Trajen said before he literally vanished.

Ushara arched a brow. "What was that gibberish?"

"Old Trisani sayings. Just means we'll raise some hell when I get back."

"No wonder he loves you."

"Love is a strong word. Tolerate, I think, would be more apropos." He opened the door for her and let her in.

Ushara hesitated as she saw his bags and gear by the couch, and the reality crashed down on her. He would really be gone in a few hours. Even though she knew he had to do this, it hurt to think of his not being here. She choked on a sob.

"Shara?"

"Sorry," she breathed, trying to blink back her tears. "I warned you."

"Shh." Cupping her face, he kissed her. "Don't. You cry, I cry, and I'm really not attractive when I cry."

She laughed at the very thought of her tough male crying. "I doubt anything could break you."

"Not true. But . . . I made something for you." He reached down and pulled her link out.

"What'd you do?"

He turned it on and downloaded something to it. "Hold on a second." He pulled his out and synced them. After a few seconds, he pressed his watch.

Her scowl deepened as she watched him.

Until she felt her wedding band begin to vibrate. "Is that . . ."

"My heartbeat." He returned her link to her. "You can check my vitals and location at any time through my watchband. You'll always know where I am, and that I'm all right. Likewise, I can check yours. And Vasili's."

"Does Vas know?"

He grinned. "I told him. He's the one who helped me wire your band without your knowing. I wanted to surprise you. This way, we'll never lose each other again."

"Have I told you how much I love you?"

"Not as much as I love you. I can't stand the thought of not being here should you need me." Worry creased his brow as he stared down at her. "I know you're keeping something from me."

"What?" she gasped.

"You've been whispering and cutting off your family for days whenever I come near. I'm not stupid, Shara. But I trust you. Whatever it is, I'm sure you have your reasons. I won't pry, even though it's killing me."

"Jules—"

"It's okay. Really. I don't want to fight my last night here. I just want to savor these precious few hours."

"I hate the way you say that. It's like you're not coming back."

"I fully intend to. But you never know what the gods are planning and I have a lot of enemies who want me dead. In case they decide another fate, I don't want your last memory of me to be a bad one."

In that moment, she almost told him about the baby. But she couldn't. Instead, she pulled him to the bedroom and stripped him bare. Then spent the rest of the night making sure that he would definitely want to come home to her as soon as possible.


Jullien woke up almost an hour late to the sound of Vasili knocking on their bedroom door.

"Mama? Paka?"

Yawning, he gently shook Ushara awake. "We overslept, Vas. We'll be out in a minute."

"Okay. I'll start breakfast."

"Oh good grief!" Ushara shot out of bed as she saw the time.

"Guess you're showering first," Jullien called after her.

She mumbled something unintelligible from the bathroom. Reaching for his link, he quickly texted Davel to let him know he was running late.

Ushara came running out a few minutes later. "You're up."

He went to the shower while she frantically pulled her uniform out of the closet and set about dressing. Suppressing a smile, he quickly bathed and dressed. Then went to join them in the kitchen.

Ushara handed him his juice. "Davel came and grabbed your bags. He said to put it in gear and get to the bay."

Vas swallowed his toast. "She's politely paraphrasing his words for my delicate sensibilities."

"Yeah. Knowing Davel's vocabulary, I don't doubt that." Jullien grabbed a piece of toast from Vas's stack and hugged him. "I better go."

Ushara winced. "I'm not sure I can do this, after all."

"I'm one heartbeat away. You can feel me anytime you need to." He touched his band and sent it to her finger, then kissed her.

"Stay safe. I will kill Davel if any harm befalls you."

"I'm more worried about the two of you. No wild parties while I'm gone."

When she started for the door, he stopped her. "Stay with Vas. It'll be easier. Just pretend I'm heading for the bay to work with Sheila, and that I'll be home tonight."

She swallowed against the tears that choked her. "Okay."

As he started to leave, she pulled him to a stop. He arched a curious brow as she unwrapped his scarf from around his neck.

"I need something with your scent on it. I won't be able to sleep otherwise."

Smiling at her, he brushed his thumb along her jaw. "Anything else?"

She wrapped his scarf around her neck. "I'm good."

Jullien tied his coat back so that he could access his blasters and headed out. In spite of his brave talk, he was sick to his stomach at the thought of leaving. This was the hardest thing he'd ever had to do. Every step he took felt like it was gutting him.

It was effing brutal.

By the time he reached the bay, he wanted to stab Davel. In the throat. With something dull and rusted.

But as he passed Sheila's office, he slowed down. There was a group of Septurnum Tavali there. Outsiders, and they were as pissed as he was.

"Can I help you?"

They turned to glower at him.

"You work here?"

"I know the owner. What do you need?"

"Where is she?"

Jullien wasn't about to give them any information about her. "What do you need?" he repeated in an icy, demanding tone.

"My brother was the captain of the *Razor's Edge*. He was brutally killed by the Caronese and this was his last stop before they got him. I'm here to get answers and kill whatever bastard cost my brother his life."

# CHAPTER 18

*W*<sub></sub>*ell, since the bastard who caused your brother to be killed by his enemies was me, I probably shouldn't comment on that.* Jullien stared at the Septurnum crew and decided that feigned ignorance would be the best course of action. "Not sure what exactly you want with us. . . . If the Caronese killed your brother, why are you here?"

"This was his last stop."

"You said that."

"He left his ship here and took out on a Caronese battleship with his crew and I want to know why. My brother didn't do things like that. I'm thinking someone here forced him to it, knowing they'd kill him for it. That's the bastard I want."

Again, t*hat would be* me. *But since your brother had planned to gut me for no other reason than he was an asshole . . .*

*Fuck him,* and *you.*

Jullien smiled coldly at him. "Their ship had been damaged in battle. They flew out and were supposed to come back for it and didn't. The Caronese got them, you said? Damn shame, that."

The Tavali pirate came up and raked a glare over Jullien. "You seem to know a lot about this." His gaze narrowed on Jullien's sleeve. "Cock? Aren't you a little old for such a low rank?"

"Hey? What's taking you so long, *now?*" Davel paused as he saw the other crew in front of Jullien. "What's going on?"

"I was taking out some trash before I left."

The Septurnum stepped forward to intrude on Jullien's personal space . . . something highly unwise when dealing with an Andarion. "Who you calling trash, candy-ass?"

Davel inserted himself between them as he noted the flaring of

Jullien's nostrils. "My brother isn't a morning creature. Could I be of service to you?"

Jullien stepped back. "He wants information about the *Razor's* crew. Apparently, the Caronese ate them after they left here and he's raw about it."

"What's that got to do with us?"

"That's what I said." Jullien crossed his arms over his chest. "They put in here for repairs. Sheila did the intake, they departed in another ship they'd captured with their cargo, and when they didn't return to pay for the repairs and pick up the *Razor*, she salvaged it."

Davel turned back to the Septurnum. "So what's your problem?"

"My brother wouldn't abandon his ship, which was paid for. I think he was set up."

"You got any proof?" Davel challenged him.

"No."

"Then take it to the UTC or Hinto. You don't come into our station and start making accusations at folks. Bad form."

"Look, Commander . . ." he dropped his gaze to Davel's name patch, "Altaan, I want to speak to whoever is in charge here. And I want to speak to them now."

Davel lifted his chin. "That would be my sister and *his*," he cocked his head toward Jullien, "wife. I can assure you that VA Samari will tell you the same thing I just did. And if you upset her, I'll feed you to her husband who is an extremely vicious bastard when his wife is stirred. The Caronese will be the least of your worries then. Now, if you really do think there was foul play, then go to your own command. Gadgehe Hinto will contact our admiral, and he and Trajen can work things out. That's how we do things peacefully."

"I want to talk to the one who salvaged the ship."

"You're talking to him," Jullien said drily. "I cut the bitch up myself. Personally."

"Under whose authority?"

"I told you. SOP. We were owed creds. Had no name or way of contacting the owner. No one returned to claim it. We can't have that kind of debt tied-up on a ship that's not running. After two months of storage-dock, she was divested of our work. Three months, I started stripping for stray parts. The original crew took their personals with them. Left nothing behind. Which also made me think they had no intention of returning. I assumed the ship was stolen since the numbers they used for docking were washed. Another reason we didn't want it here. No idea who might come looking for it and be pissed to find it hiding under our banners."

Davel shrugged. "There you have it. He speaks the truth. That is the standard by which all Tavali bases work. You know the protocol."

"Still don't seem right." He narrowed his gaze on Jullien. "We're going, but if I find out there's more to this, I will be back."

Jullien didn't move as he watched them walk away.

Davel didn't speak until the Seps were on board their ship and getting ready to leave. He turned his back to them and faced Jullien. "There was more to it than that bullshit you were spewing, wasn't there?"

He gave a subtle nod.

"Do we need to warn Shara?"

"Trajen's the one his brother crossed. I don't think they want to talk to him about it. But if they do . . ."

"I want to be the spider in the room for that." Davel clapped him on the back, then led him toward his ship. "All right. I got your gear stored. Because you are family and I know how little you tolerate others, I pulled you out of gen-pop to give you your own room. It's not much, but it is private space. My Fyreblood crew is warned to be gentle with you. This is not Kirill's ship. You have a problem with anyone, tell me before you put them through a wall. My stryper's named Gallatin, and she's in charge of most of the cocks and baits. Since she's also a commander, refer to her as XO, strype, firstmate, or SIX. She's fair, but a hot-tempered human . . . who is currently glaring at us. . . . What? I bathed this time."

Lithe and athletic, Gallatin had jet-black hair and eyes with grayish skin that was strangely attractive. She had a commanding presence in spite of the fact that she barely reached the center of Jullien's chest.

And she didn't flinch at all over the irritation in her CO's tone of voice. "Supposed to leave half an hour ago, Commander."

"Well, we're leaving now. Let's not dally."

She pressed her forefinger to the center of her forehead before she narrowed her gaze on Jullien. "Dagger?"

"XO?"

She nodded. "You're my shadow till you get used to the crew, who, with the exception of me, is all Fyreblood. Have you any flying experience?"

"A lot."

"Pilot?"

"Yes."

"Licensed?"

"Yes."

"With practical hours?"

"Only with combat experience and leisure. Not commercial."

She arched a happy brow at that. "Ever crash?"

"Not intentionally."

Laughing, she clapped him on the arm. "I love this male. All right, Captain Krunch, are you taking us out?" she asked Davel.

"For that, I am. You can give him the tour."

She groaned as Davel headed for what must be the flight deck.

Jullien arched a brow at Gallatin. "Captain Krunch?"

"So named for his wonderful landing capabilities."

"Oh, goodie."

She laughed even harder. "Someone who gets my sarcasm. You will fit in well here, my child. Welcome to the family. I only have one more question . . . outstanding warrants? Who do I need to hide you from?"

Ushara went by her parents' house to pick up Vasili. Like her, he'd avoided going home today. Neither wanted to be there without Jullien. Strange how it didn't seem like home anymore without him there.

The thought of being in the condo now . . .

It hurt so much she could barely breathe.

She pushed opened open the door to find her mother at the table with a huge meal laid out across the top of it. "What in the name of Saint Sarn is this?"

Her mother sat back with an amused twist to her lips. "You tell me."

"Tell you what?"

Vas looked up with a huge grin. "Paka sent it for us."

"What?"

Her mother nodded. "It was actually scheduled for your house, but when they called Vasili's link for the delivery, we had them bring it here." She picked up a pair of very pink fluffy socks that were in a small basket with a note. "I accidentally opened this and read the note before I realized it was meant exclusively for you. Sorry."

Ushara bit her lip as tears gathered in her eyes at the sight of something only Jullien would think to give her. Her hand trembled as she picked up the note to read it.

*Shara,*

*I know how tired you've been lately in the evenings, and I wanted to make sure you're still able to nap when you get home. Don't worry about dinner. I've taken care of it for you in my absence. I just wish I were there to hold you right now. I miss our naked cuddle time. Will be home as soon as I can.*

*Ever your darkheart*

She sniffed back tears as she held the note to her chest and looked at the steak and vegetables. He'd made sure to send over her favorite foods from the diner they'd first gone to.

"They said that Paka had arranged for dinner to be brought over every night for us so that you wouldn't have to cook when you got home."

Her mother nodded. "And he left a dated note and gift to be brought with it for every day he's supposed to be away, too. Misha said it was the sweetest thing he'd ever seen. He also paid for their sister to come by and straighten up once a week and help do laundry, and any shopping you need. If you leave a list or e-mail it, she'll take care of it while you're at work. Jullien also has a tutor who'll be working with Vasili so that you don't have to stress with his homework."

Ushara gaped. "Are you serious?"

She nodded. "He arranged it all. Said he didn't want you to have to worry about anything while he was away."

Ushara wiped at her eyes as his kindness overwhelmed her. "I can't believe he did all this."

Her mother paused as she sorted through the food. "Did you tell him about the baby?"

"No. He doesn't know yet."

Her mother let out an elongated breath. "Then I take back every ill thought I ever had about him. Go call your husband, precious. Give him my very best."

"Thank you, Mama." Ushara made a quick plate and took it home before she called and hoped that it went through.

Jullien was just coming off his maintenance shift when he felt his arm vibrate. His heartbeat sped up as he thought about Ushara and he reached for his link to see if everything was all right.

It rang with her tone.

Worried, he answered it as he entered his room and then went to lie down on his narrow bunk. "Hey. Are you okay?"

"Your presents arrived. So tell me, honestly . . . were you afraid I'd poison your son with my cooking?"

He smiled at her question. "Well . . . he is a bit underweight for his height."

She sent over a request for video.

Jullien switched it on and was greeted by her beautiful face. "Are you mad at me for it?"

"Why would I be mad?"

"I don't know. I debated whether or not I should do it. I didn't want to insult you, but I know cooking and homework aren't your favorite things to do either. I just wanted to make sure you were cared for since I wasn't there to help you with it and I know how busy and stressful everything's been lately."

"It was so sweet and thoughtful. Thank you." She made a kissing face at him. "So how's my brother treating you? You need me to beat him up?"

He laughed. "Nah. I think I can take him. Just don't want you to hold it against me if I do have to beat his ass." He traced the lines of her face on his screen, wishing he were there with her so that he could feel the softness of her skin beneath his fingers. "Hey now, don't look so sad."

"Can't help it. I miss you so much. It's like a vital part of me is gone, and it hurts."

"Yeah, but remember, it's not the part that's good for you, anyway. I'm the part that hogs all the covers and steals your sweets."

She laughed. "And who lets me bury my cold feet under him at night and never complains about them." She burst into tears.

Jullien froze at the sound of her utter misery. It was the first time anyone had ever cried like this for him. He'd only seen his mother weep for his brother in this manner. "Shara? *Mu taru?*"

"I'm sorry. I just really miss you. I forgot what it was like to need someone else this much and to have to live without them. You kind of snuck up on me."

"I'm not sure what to say to that."

"That you love me and you'll be home safe and sound as soon as you can."

"You know I do and that I will. I've never loved anyone but you."

That made her cry even harder.

Jullien sat up, feeling all kinds of worthless. "Honey? What did I do now?"

"It's not you . . . well, it is you, but it's not."

He felt completely helpless and lost. "Shara, you're killing me. I can't stand for you to be in pain and not be there to help."

"I know. I'm sorry. It's just a hormonal thing. I've been really emotional lately. It'll pass. I promise." And still she sobbed.

"Is there anything I can do?"

"Just stay safe."

Suddenly, the ship's alarm rang out.

Her eyes widened. "You're under *attack*?"

"I'm sure it's nothing."

With a droll, irritated glare, she cocked her head at him. "That's an alarm for battle stations, Jules. It's not *nothing*."

"I know. I've got to go. I'll call when it's over. Love you."

"Love you, too. Be careful." She hung up.

Jullien tucked his link into his pocket as he rolled from the bunk to head for the bridge so that he could see what was going on. They weren't supposed to be anywhere near a League-controlled zone. Nor any kind of enemy territory. Since he was wanted so severely and Davel was a new father, this was supposed to be a low-risk training run. Simple in and out. Legal supplies, with legit paperwork. No complications.

They both should have known better.

As he entered the bridge, Jullien drew up short. A few feet away, Davel was engaged in a heated discourse with a League patrol and the last thing Jullien wanted was to be seen by anyone in a League uniform. While he'd been out of the limelight for years now, he still didn't want to chance anyone recognizing him from any of the media blitzes that had once run constantly against him.

Davel let out a tired breath as he reiterated his point. "We're an independent contractor on our way to pick up a shipment. I don't understand why you need to inspect us. You've got the live-feed on our cargo bay and can see it's currently empty."

"We have it on good authority that you're hauling contraband. Now prepare to be boarded and inspected, or we will be forced to attack."

Davel passed a suspicious glower toward Jullien as he muted the channel. "Anyone have a confession before I let them on board?"

Gallatin shook her head. "I inspected every piece of cargo and personal item. We're clear. Nothing illegal came on board."

"Except for me." Jullien jerked his chin toward the League officer's image. "I'm the only thing they can be looking for."

"That's what I was thinking, given how vague they're being." Davel met Gallatin's gaze. "We've got to hide him."

"I'm on it. Buy us time."

Davel opened the channel. "All right. Cargo airlock. Prepare for boarding."

Gallatin led Jullien toward the head of the ship, away from the cargo bay. "I've got a bad feeling."

So did he, but he didn't want to make her even more nervous. "How many others have warrants?"

"All of us. But only yours is a kill warrant. Our IDs and codes should pass muster without any problems. Yours . . ."

His face was too well known, even with his beard, different eye color, and hairstyle. Hard to hide when you were the former heir of not one, but *two* major empires, and had once been the most photographed spoiled bastard of all time. Not to mention the small fact that he was a rare hybrid of two species not known for screwing each other and breeding children together.

*Thanks, Mom and Dad, for sheltering me.*

Suddenly, blaster fire rang out.

Gallatin cursed. Jullien grabbed his blaster and started for the flight deck. Before he took more than a few steps, his link went off.

It was Davel.

"Yeah?"

"We were right. They're here for you. Take one of the fighters and launch out. We'll cover it."

Was Davel out of his mind? "They'll mark you for harboring a fugitive if I do."

Davel fired at someone. "They'll capture you if you don't."

"I'll surrender, then. It's not worth the risk to you and your ship or crew. You have an infant and children to consider."

"Yeah, so do you."

"Vas will—"

"Ushara's pregnant, Jules. She didn't want you to find out until after we got back, because she knew you wouldn't leave her. It's why she's been so tired and emotional the last few weeks. Now go and let us cover you. Don't make her raise another baby without its father. I can't do that to her."

Jullien stared at Gallatin as those words sank in.

Gallatin patted him on the arm. "Come on, let's get you out of here."

Even though it wasn't in Jullien to run from a fight, he went this time. For Ushara.

Gallatin led him to the small rear bay where her own fighter was docked. She gave him her passcodes and main blaster, along with her patches and the ship Canting, and all the creds she had on her. "Find another Tavali crew to shelter you. We'll scout as soon as we can."

He gave her a quick hug. "Good luck."

"Same to you, Dagger. Godspeed you."

He holstered his blaster and climbed into her ship. She manually uncoupled the anchors and let him drift out to space for the launch so that they didn't alert any of the League soldiers that he was launching.

Jullien stayed dark until he was far enough back to see that there were three League ships and a battlecruiser. Damn. They'd seriously wanted a piece of his ass.

*Don't do it.*

*Think of Shara.*

She was pregnant. That news still hit him like a sledgehammer to his stones. The dream of having a child of his own was something he'd given up on so long ago, that honestly he couldn't even remember having it. Hell, Merrell had even fabricated a medical report that said he was sterile and given it to Eriadne in an attempt to have him disinherited.

Jullien had never bothered to denounce the report, even though he'd known at the time it was a lie. Since he'd never found a female who could stand his hybrid presence, never mind abide his touch to breed with him, it'd been a moot issue to argue.

To have a baby with a female who actually loved him . . .

Inconceivable.

All common sense said to tuck his sorry ass in, keep his head down and crawl back to her as fast as he could. Take no chances and live a long, uneventful life in eternal gratitude that he'd found the only female in existence who was able to overlook his shortcomings and worthlessness to spawn with him.

That's what he needed to do.

But that was her brother under heavy fire, putting everything he loved on the line to get him home.

Jullien couldn't buy his happiness for the price of Davel's. He damn sure couldn't do it if it meant her brother's life.

*In the end, we all face the Rekkynynge.* All souls had to account for every action taken during their lifetime. Good and bad. Eri would judge them and determine if they were worthy of eternal peace spent in Eweyne.

Or damnation in Tophet.

And while Jullien was pretty sure his past guaranteed him a straight shot through the fiery gates of Tophet, and no amount of good at this point would ever bail his rotten soul out of that sentence, he wasn't about to stand by and watch a good male go down to save his sorry hide today.

"*Titana ræl.*" He fired the engine and headed straight for the League ships, full throttle. "You want a piece of me, bitches? Come get some."

# CHAPTER 19

"What do you mean you lost my husband? Davel, so help me, this better be a really bad joke." Ushara could barely breathe as she struggled not to scream at her brother over the video link.

"I'm so sorry. Somehow The League knew he was on board my ship. I have no idea how. They attacked and we were badly hit. He did escape during it, so we're hoping for the best. We're searching for him right now, but we really need his locator from you to find him."

"You're lying to me. What aren't you saying? I know you. Tell me!"

Davel glanced away.

Ushara rose to her feet. "Gal . . . Answer me now, or so help me I'll sic both my mother and Tray on the lot of you! And if that doesn't scare you like it should, I'll call the twins after you and send them to your location, *with Mary!*"

That threat broke Gallatin immediately. The truth rushed out of her, like Nadya running from Oxana at bedtime. "Dagger attacked The League to help us get away, and was hit really hard by them. He made a hot landing. We found what was left of my fighter . . . It looks like he got out though, but there was no sign of him anywhere."

" 'Cause the little bastard's good at covering his tracks," Davel muttered. "He detonated everything to keep the League assassins off him. In the process, we lost him, too."

Ushara covered her face as she fought against the wave of hysteria that threatened to overwhelm her. This couldn't be happening.

Not again. She couldn't lose another husband. Not while she carried his baby. It was bad enough to have to raise a baby who knew their father and could barely recall him, she couldn't stand the thought of her child not knowing his or her father *at all.*

And even worse was how much Jullien meant to her. While she'd loved Chaz, she'd never depended on him the way she did Jullien. He'd never allowed her to.

Jullien *was* her partner. In every way.

"Shara?"

"Give me a minute." She breathed and fought against the tears that threatened to send her into hysteria. This wasn't the time for them.

Clearing her throat, she took a deep breath to hold herself together. "I'm sending his frequency, but he'll have changed it by now." She racked her brains to think like her husband would, and to remember the survival lessons he'd given Vasili. "I'd try odd numbers, then back it four digits. He's into random sequences like that. He won't be in a huge population center. You have to think really smart. Look for an outpost with just enough tech to be relatively current, but not one that's overly monitored. He's more likely to be in an unpopulated zone or near a smaller spaceport that would be Tavali friendly. He won't be near anything Sentella or Andarion." Ushara paused as a thought occurred to her. "Hold on a second."

Her hand shaking, she reached for her wedding band and prayed for a miracle as she activated the heartbeat function. *Please work. Please work. Please work.* The words became a frantic chant in her head until that miracle happened.

She felt his heartbeat on her finger.

"He's alive." She burst into tears as her hands shook in relief. "Oh, thank the gods!"

Davel and Gallatin looked at her as if she were crazy.

Ushara wiped at her face as she calmed herself. "It's something he did for me so that I'd know he was okay while he was gone. He put a tracker on his vital signs for me."

"Can we use it to locate him?"

"That's what I just sent you. I hope so. Find him, Davel."

"You know I will, *kisa*. Let us know if you hear from him."

"Okay. Love you."

"You, too." He cut the transmission.

Ushara closed her eyes and held her black flower wedding ring to her trembling lips. "You better come home to me, my darkheart. I will *not* forgive you if you don't."

.   .   .

"Stall it now, slag, or we'll be terminating you right where you be standing."

Jullien froze at the sound of the thick, lilting accent unlike anything he'd ever heard before. He held his hands up so that no one would misunderstand his intent. "It's all good, brother. No harm intended. I'm just an orphan, trying to find my way home, hoping to find some family to aid with my journey." He used the Tavali code words that would signal to a fellow member that he'd been separated from his crew and was invoking Safe Harbor law. Under Tavali Code, once those words were spoken, no fellow Tavalian could hurt or betray him without risking the loss of their rank, Canting or life.

"Family, eh? Then turn about slow-like, and you be telling me all about how we be kinfolk. Who's your da, *cade*?"

Jullien turned to find a tall, muscular male who was much younger than he'd have thought given the authoritative, cocksure tone. Human by the looks of him, he had short blond hair and sharp, chiseled features with intelligent eyes that missed absolutely nothing. While he held a jovial air about him, there was a lethal undercurrent that said it was a lie meant to mislead. Something this man did to give others a false sense of security that they were safe in his youthful presence, but Jullien had met enough creatures like this one to know he was a deadly predator who was well-trained and capable of striking down any enemy who crossed him without mercy or hesitation.

One wrong move would be his last.

"*Tevi Era Essa Seakea' alah. Fashe Tah.*" Jullien started the explanation with the official Tavalian motto and oath—*Tavali is an honor that comes with obligation. Hem me never.* "My tithe is to the northern True Black Flag Nation. My father's Trajen Thaumarturgus."

He laughed. Then, as Jullien had predicted, the humor died and his blaster came up like lightning and with unerring aim. The targeting dot hovered without wavering between his eyes. "Ach, you lie, man. Now tell me the truth or I'll be scraping your brains off me ship."

"No lie. Hard as it is to believe, as I admit I am a totally unlovable bastard, Trajen sponsored me himself. You blow out my brains, he's going to be seriously pissed, and I would not want to be you." Jullien held his hand up, palm out with his fingers spread. "Check it before you pull."

Narrowing his blue eyes, he approached Jullien slowly. He hesitated before he holstered his blaster and pulled out his link to scan Jullien's thumb. After a few seconds, it accessed his Tavali records.

One blond brow shot north. "Be damned and blessed. Dagger, eh? You don't look like a typical northern son. But I won't be judging you for that." He cracked a charming grin. "Jupiter Hinto, at your service, *cade*."

"Hinto?"

"Yeah . . . and yeah, I be the son of the man you be thinking of. I'm also captain of that fair lady behind you, *Ship of Fools*. It'd be me honor to see you home to your family, in particular your cranky da."

Jullien let out a relieved breath. When he'd first stumbled upon the small remote outpost after hours of hiking through godforsaken barren landscape, he'd been hoping there was Tavali docked here in the small town.

Given how remote the port and how well-maintained the ships, it'd been a good gamble that this was a trading port of some kind they used. He'd learned about these over the last few years while running for his life, and had become dependent on them for short-term work, and quick, no-questions-asked transport between other remote locations.

"I can't thank you enough."

"Ah, no problem. Always glad to do a favor for me family, even me distant northern cousins."

Suddenly, a huge body dropped down on top of Jupiter from above and grabbed him into a fierce hold while the newcomer growled and moaned.

Jullien started forward to help until he realized they weren't actually fighting. Rather Jupiter was playfully slapping at the dark-haired male who was laughing and dodging like an irritating kid brother.

"Hey, Ju-Ju Bear, you getting slack, old man. I could have had you." He wrapped his muscular arms around Jupiter's shoulders and kissed his cheek.

Jupiter ruffled the newcomer's wavy dark hair until it stood straight up on top of his head as if he'd had a bad electrical shock. "Suck it, Psycho Bunny. You're lucky I didn't slit you to appetite just then. What you thinking, slipping up on me like that?"

"I was thinking you were all cute and cuddly, and I had to get me some of this adorable ass of yours." He tossed his head, then frowned as he saw Jullien. "Who's your new boy-toy?"

"Dagger. And he don't know you're joking about that, and that you're me brother, you dolt, so stop it, will you now, before he takes you seriously?"

Psycho Bunny sobered to study Jullien with a jaundiced eye that said he was every bit the warrior Jupiter was. "Crew member?"

"No . . . he swings from the True Black Flag Nation."

He gaped. "No, minsid way. He don't look like a Fyreblood."

"Yeah, I checked it meself. He definitely tithes to the north." Jupiter gestured toward Jullien. "Chayden Aniwaya, meet Dagger Samari. Dagger, this is Chayden, who used to be Septurnum with me, till he turned into a little mercenary Rogue bastard."

"Still am Sep, really. I only wear Rogue 'cause I don't like tithing to one Nation, but my daddy continues to spank my ass regularly when I misbehave." He released Jupiter to hold his hand out to Jullien. "Pleasure to meet you, brother."

"You, too, Captain."

Jupiter crossed his arms over his chest. "So what brings your lady dancing into me space these days, Chay?"

A devilish dimple flashed in Chayden's cheek. "Was passing through, heard you were here and . . . I've got a take to share with you, my precious brother." He winked at Jupiter. "Yeah, I'm so screwed on this one. Tattoo my ass and slap it hard. . . . Yet it was so worth it. Will split the cargo later. But . . ." He pulled a bottle from underneath his long brown coat and handed it to Jupiter. "Who's your best friend *ever*?" He said the last word in a tone that sounded like a possessed being that made Jullien wonder if perhaps that was why they called him Psycho Bunny.

Jupiter kissed his cheek. "Ahhh. . . . You keep this up, *cade*. You might be changing me religion yet."

"Yes, but can I change your sister's?"

"Hey, for a crate of this," Jupiter held up the bottle and kissed it—"I might be persuaded to give her to you with me blessings."

"Don't tease me about Mack. You know she's the one woman I'd sell my soul for."

Jullien stepped back at that and hoped Chayden wasn't a full-blooded brother to Mack as this line of conversation was a bit strange if he was. . . .

Jupiter screwed his face up into a painful expression as he pulled at the cork. "Funny, I've been hearing that a lot lately, from way too many men." He opened the bottle and took a swig. Then, he made a sound of deep appreciation. "Ach now, that's some sweetness, there. What Leaguer did you make cry for this?"

Chayden let out a deep, sinister laugh. "Didn't. Was a Sentella supply ship. That special brew was actually earmarked for Darling Cruel from Caillen Dagan, which is why I had to pilfer it. Moral imperative for what that dodgy bastard owes me. So enjoy it in good health. May Dagan's head explode when he finds out it's gone."

Jupiter gaped at him. "Are you out of your ever-loving mind, *cade*? What are you thinking? And you admit it in front of a *crawler*, no less."

Jullien held his hands up. "I heard nothing about it. Besides, I've got no love for The Sentella and they have a lot less for me. Especially Dagan. That is one hot-headed little troll who jumps to bizarre conclusions only the gods understand."

Chayden snorted. "What? He accuse you of raping one of his sisters, too?"

"Yes," Jullien said between clenched fangs. "Kasen. You?"

"Kasen," Jupiter and Chayden said in unison.

"He got me last year," Jupiter said as he passed the bottle to Jullien. "I swear. Me hands were nowhere near the *shenandoah*. Word to the gods on that. But he thought he saw what he didn't and that was all she wrote."

"What is his problem?" Chayden shook his head. "If I was going to snake one, it wouldn't be Kase. While she's attractive physically, her personality shrivels all interest—*if* you know what I mean, and I know you do."

"Truth." Jullien handed him the bottle. "My cuff got caught on her jacket, and I was trying to run for my life as fast as I could. I was ready to cut off my own arm to get away from her. Next thing I know, Caillen's all over me, screaming rape, trying to have me arrested. He was so insane, I filed charges on *him* for it."

Jupiter laughed. "You know he did that to his brother-in-law, too, right?"

"What?" Chay asked in gaping disbelief.

"Aye, he did. Cried rape with Syn on Shahara."

Chayden snorted, then laughed. "Bullshit! He's not that stupid. . . . Oh wait, it's Caillen. Of course he is. Did Syn shoot him?"

Jupiter took the bottle. "Sadly, no."

"Well, that's disappointing. I shall have to lecture Syn on his behavior next time I see him."

Jullien laughed. He really liked these Tavali.

Chayden took another drink of the Tondarion Fire and passed it to Jupiter. "All right, new friend, so you have issues with The Sentella. Anything else we need to know?"

"Let's just say that if we can avoid meeting up with any of them or The League, I will be grateful. Because whatever they do to you for lifting that," he indicated the bottle, "pales in comparison to what they'd do to me. We have assured mutual destruction there."

After his own swig, Jupiter passed the bottle to Jullien. "Here's to brotherhood, then. Mores to the merry, and to drowning on dry land. Hem me never, me *cades*."

Jullien took it and drank to the toast. "Can I ask a favor?"

"Bathroom's on board."

He snorted at Chayden's assumption. "Actually, I need a secure transmitter."

"Blood?"

"Yeah. Someone I need to let know I'm still breathing."

"We've all been there." Chayden jerked his head toward Jupiter's ship. "I'll take you up and hook you in." He glanced to Jupiter. "Am I still in the system?"

"Depending on how mad you've made me Mack lately."

Chayden clapped Jullien on the back before he hit the release to the ramp. He led him up and into the immaculate ship. It was high tech and well-maintained. And unlike anything Jullien had seen before.

This was . . .

He paused at one of the panels to look over the impressive schematics. "Who designed this?"

Chayden put his hand over it to block Jullien's view. "You don't want to get too nosy about that. Jupiter is really protective when it comes to his lady. Let's leave it at that, okay?"

"Sure."

He led him to a small XO office. Jullien tried to put the call through, but there was too much interference.

Damn it. He couldn't even transmit his vitals right now.

"Is everything all right?" Chayden asked as he left the room.

"Couldn't get through."

"Nervous mother?"

"Pregnant wife."

Chayden sucked his breath in sharply. "Oooh. Sorry."

As Jullien started to close the door, a distress transmission came through. Chayden brushed past him to answer it.

"Yo, POW, this is Psycho Bunny. I have your coords. Hang dry. Passing to big bad will round a posse and head out ASAP. Repeat, we are on our way. ETA one hour or less. Hang dry. Help is on its way." Chayden switched it over and signaled a recall for Hinto's crew.

"POW?" Jullien asked.

"Piece of Work. He's Jupiter's cousin. Dumbass can't fly for shit. They're always going down from League run-ins, hence the call sign. Never knows when to shut his mouth."

Jullien followed him back toward the ramp.

Jupiter met them at the top of it. "Teex again?"

"Oh, how did you know?" Sarcasm dripped from Chayden's tone. "I'll run point. I locked his location in already. He's on Oksana."

"Great. Me favorite place to land. Never." Jupiter growled irritably. He passed a sympathetic grimace to Jullien. "Sorry to be making you wait for seeing home again. Let me save me cousin's sorry hide, so as not to listen to me aunt and moora crying at me, then I'll see you back to yours."

"No problem. Anything I can do to help?"

Chayden took off as more of Jupiter's crew ran in to take their stations. And as the crew came on board, Jullien noticed something unusual about Jupiter's staff.

With the exception of Jupiter, there wasn't a male among them.

Jupiter caught Jullien's quirked brow, but didn't comment on it. "We got this. You be wanting a ringside view for the fun, or to rest a bit?"

"I'd like to keep trying to get word home to my wife. Wherever that makes you most comfortable."

Jupiter shivered as he led the way through the ship's corridor. "Marriage. Half your rights and double your duties. I do not understand this madness that has sunk her claws into so many lately. Saints preserve me." He made a holy gesture as they entered his command bridge.

Half his crew passed him an angry glare at his comments on marriage.

He passed the look right back at them. "Ach, don't be giving me your stink eyes, me *shenandoahs*. Not like that whole lot of you don't know how I feel about it. You've heard me rant enough on the topic when I'm flagged." Jupiter paused to smirk at Jullien. "And I know what you're thinking. . . . A thread will tie an honest man better than a chain a rogue."

"Got to say that was not in my thoughts. At all. Especially since I have *no* idea what that even means. Or even how that's applicable."

Jupiter laughed. "I'm not the lecherous piece of dog you be thinking." He pulled out his link and turned it on to show Jullien a picture of an extremely attractive red-headed female in a t-i-g-h-t Tavali battlesuit that hugged an impressive body. "Meet me own special piece of hell that comes wrapped as me sister Mack." He nodded at Jullien. "Yeah, exactly. Learned early in me life to keep me crew away from her or to take on crew she didn't want to torture me with. Me life's much happier this way as I don't have to gut a crew member I rely on nowadays."

Laughing at Jupiter's solution, Jullien headed for an observation seat while Jupiter took the captain's chair and locked in.

Jullien kept trying to get through to either Davel or Ushara with his link while they launched. But for some reason, he was still dark.

"Why's there so much League traffic here, all of a sudden?"

Jullien looked up at the question from Jupiter's stryper.

Jupiter was studying the maps around them. "Yeah. It's a lot more intense than normal. Something stirred them up." He opened a channel. "Psycho Bunny? What'd you do?"

"I swear this isn't me . . . this time."

Jupiter turned to look at Jullien. "Do I want to know?"

"While I have an outstanding warrant, I should be a low priority to The League. Seriously. Way down on their hit list. Not like I'm Idirian Wade or Justicale Cruel. Nowhere near the level of Emperor Abenbi or even Counselor Cruel. I'm only a personal hemorrhoid, not an intergalactic threat."

"Well, someone's been a pissing in Kyr's whisky. And I know *I* didn't do it."

Jullien admired the way Jupiter cut and banked away from the patrols to miss engaging them. For a young pilot, he was extremely talented. But there was something really odd about all of this.

If he didn't know better, Jullien would swear he had a tracing chip in him that they were using. But he'd burned his out years ago. It'd been the first thing he'd done when he and his grandmother had parted company on bad terms. Last thing anyone wanted was a way for a vindictive bitch to hunt him down.

The crew remained completely silent while Jupiter did amazing stunts with the ship. Jullien would love to get his hands on the engine of this thing and see what was in it. It ran unlike anything he'd ever seen before.

And though it took some serious maneuvering, they managed to finally elude the League ships and land in the Oksanan desert by a broken-down Septurnum freighter without any further confrontations or problems.

However, as the new crew came onboard and drew up short the instant they saw him, Jullien realized his old luck had returned with a vengeance.

Teex wasn't just Jupiter's cousin. He was the captain who'd come inquiring about the *Razor*'s crew that Jullien had thrown out of Sheila's office, and off their base.

And the rotten bastard remembered the encounter.

"Well, well . . . if it isn't the Gorturnum trash done washed up on our shores. Looks like I am going to find out, after all, what happened to my brother and his ship, or skin every bit of flesh from your bones, Andarion. And there's no one here to stop me from it this time."

# CHAPTER 20

When Teex stepped toward Jullien, Jupiter stopped him. "Whoa, now. Calm yourself before you be doing something we're all regretting."

"The only regret is the one you're going to have if you don't get out of my way, cousin."

Jupiter stepped between them. "He's Tavali and he's declared Safe Harbor."

"I'm sure my brother did, too."

Actually, he hadn't. But Jullien withheld that technicality.

Not that he needed to as Jupiter continued to stand between them. "Need I be reminding you, *cade*, what happened the last time a Septurnum broke Safe Harbor? Think about it, man. Almost four *hundred* years later and our name continues to be tarnished for it. The Dane family *and* the Wasturnums *still* be wanting all our asses. The last thing we be needing now is another clan war from another Nation, and me da would take it harsh for it to be his own blood what done it."

"They killed my brother, Jory!"

"The Caronese killed your brother, man. You know this. Your brother picked a fight with them. He brutally slaughtered their crew. Mercilessly, while they were down on their knees before him. They might have shown him some mercy had he not done what he done, but the way he treated them when he took their ship . . . I hate to say he got what he earned 'cause what they did was brutal, but damn it, Teex, use your gourd. You know what I'm telling you's harsh true."

Teex glared at Jullien. "I know there's more to this. I'm going to prove it."

And with that he brushed roughly past him.

Jullien didn't move.

Jupiter sighed heavily. "Sorry about that. Didn't know there's bad blood between you."

"Didn't realize the asshole was your cousin."

"What can I say? Every family has its asshole."

Jullien nodded. "Yeah. . . . I'm the one in mine."

Jupiter laughed. "On with you, now. You don't seem so bad as all that."

"Believe me, my entire family would argue."

"Now that you mention, me family would probably say the same of me. Guess we assholes should hang together, then."

"Maybe so." Jullien returned to the bridge where Teex continued to glare a hole through him. It was like being in royal court all over again. So he did just as he'd done as a kid. Held his head high, locked his jaw, and ignored the bastard while he continued to try and reach Ushara.

Teex and crew put on the news while Jupiter and his crew were hooking up their ship to tow it with a tractor beam.

Jullien paused to listen to the reports he normally avoided like they were the patient zero for an incurable plague, since most of the news was about his birth family and old friends who'd abandoned him the instant his parents had cut him off.

He didn't want to care about any of them, but it was hard not to, especially when they flashed a picture of Nykyrian with his parents and he saw how happy they were. A pregnant Kiara held one of their sons while Nyk stood with their father, who had his arm on Nyk's shoulder in a proud embrace.

Yeah, that stung like a vicious kick to the stones. Jullien swallowed hard at the familial scene. He was glad to see them thriving. But it hurt to know that his father had never once welcomed him like that, not even when he'd been a child. And that his father never would.

Back in the day, his father had always sighed heavily whenever Jullien approached him, or ground his teeth as if struggling not to strike him in exasperation.

There had been a time once when Jullien would have sold his soul to have his father look at him with that kind of love, pride, and respect.

Instead, his last words with his father had been harsh and biting.

*"You've made your bed, boy, and since you enjoy wallowing around in your sheets so much, I hope you enjoy the ones you've chosen. From this day forward,*

*you're dead to me. As far as I'm concerned, I only have one son and you're not him."*

Jullien had glared at his father's back as he'd walked away and shouted his own parting shot. *"If you felt that way, you old bastard, you should have done us both a favor and left me dead when you choked the life out of me, instead of calling to have me resuscitated. Oh wait, it wasn't my life you were saving that day, was it? It was yours 'cause you were afraid you'd be put to death for my murder."*

His father had spun on him then and swept him with a ruthless glare of hatred. *"You're absolutely right. I wasn't about to throw my life away for a lazy, drugged-out, piece of shit like you. I begrudge every single second of my life I wasted on you, trying to make you passably human and decent. You've never been anything but a disappointment to me."*

Jullien winced at the harsh memory. Damn, it still hurt when he thought about that night.

But then, it didn't matter. At least that was what he tried to tell himself. He had a new family now, and while they didn't love him either, they weren't cruel to him. At least, not like that.

Plus, Ushara and Vasili loved him. They made it all worthwhile.

He turned his link on again and flipped through his photos. It was the first time in his life that he actually had some worth glancing through. A collection where no one had been captured glaring or sneering at him behind his back. Where the memories were all happy and worth reliving.

An image of Vasili and Ushara came up on the lock screen, which was also new now that he had information to protect. Their picture had been taken during Ushara's birthday party at her parents' house about a month before Vas had been confirmed. The two of them had looked at him with so much love that he'd snapped the picture, wanting to preserve and keep that expression forever. The rest were candid photos taken of Shara and Vas at different times, and a few of little Nadya and her sisters, as well as Shara's sisters during their many visits to their home. They were over so often, he was surprised they didn't keep a change of clothes in the closets.

Then again, they ranged freely and borrowed whatever they wanted whenever they felt the urge. He'd never seen anything like it. Their husbands were literally the only things the sisters didn't share.

Everything else was fair game for them.

"Hey, Ju Ju?" the stryper called from her seat. "We got something strange here. You might want to take a look at this." She put it up on the main screen. "That's a lot of ships. But they don't appear to be a League fleet or military."

"Convoy?"

"Maybe. They just dropped in on us from hyper. Picking up some cruisers and fighters. Definitely capable of doing a lot of damage."

Jupiter scowled. "Have you hailed them?"

"Working on it."

Jullien frowned as he kept an eye on the small fleet in front of them.

"It's a Porturnum group." His stryper arched her brow curiously. "They're requesting a conference with you, Jupiter."

"Pull them up."

Jullien folded his arms over his chest as an image of an obvious human-Andarion hybrid came on the screen. Since there weren't many of them, it got his interest immediately.

"Venik," Jupiter said in a chiding tone that told Jullien he was fairly well acquainted with the male. "What's the meaning of this shite? Are you trying to piss me off, *cade*?"

And that caught his curiosity even more as Jullien remembered Malys mentioning that her husband was Andarion. Given the age of the male on the screen, this must be one of Brax's and Malys's sons.

"I just need a few minutes of your time, Jory. We mean you no harm, whatsoever. We're just passing through Sep space. So tell your little Bunny to simmer down and back off the targeting of my ships before I feel compelled to do something about it."

Jupiter flipped open the comm channel for Chayden. "Chay, behave."

"Ah, do I have to?" Chayden's disappointed tone was comical. "I want to be Payne's pain as I don't feel he gets his due daily chafings."

"Not today, *drey*. Let's see what they need before we rub up their grains, shall we?"

Chayden said something in a language Jullien didn't speak, but it was obvious by his answering laughter that Jupiter was fluent with it.

"Does this mean I can send over an ambassador you won't shoot?" Venik asked.

"Aye. Send your ambassador over." Jupiter hesitated. "Airlock or bay?"

"Airlock. So drop your shields to let us in. . . . And Jory?"

"Yeah?"

"My ambassador wants a private word with your Gorturnum guest."

To his credit, Jupiter didn't flinch or blink. "What guest be that?"

"Don't play stupid with me. Teex already told us all about your Gorturnum friend who was exceedingly rude to my mother when she pulled into their port and asked for assistance from them."

Jupiter's face turned to stone. "And I be hauling him under Safe Harbor. So if any of you be thinking of doing ill to me guest on behalf of your moora's sake, I'll be taking it quite personally. On me honor that."

"Relax, Grandma. Now drop your shields, open the airlock, and let us in."

Jupiter cut the transmission. "I don't trust those bastards." Getting up, he headed for his cousin and slapped him on the back of his head.

"Hey! What the hell?"

"You called them? To what purpose? Where's your head, man? Up your arse?"

"Where's yours, Jory? Since when are you up the ass of the Gorts?"

"You get us crossed with Trajen Thaumarturgus and that'll get us crossed with the Danes, and the whole of the Wassy Nation. You do that, you stupid dropping, and me da will eat your head arselins back. You best trust me on that. Your parents and blood be damned." He drew back to hit him again, and then growled and refrained.

With a disgusted sneer, he turned toward Jullien. "Me deepest apologies about this."

"It's fine. I'm the one who was rude to her. I'll go see what they want."

"You know her boys'll be wanting a piece of your hide for retaliation." Jupiter turned back to his cousin. "Why are you even talking to them, T? You've no reason to be speaking to the Ports."

"I ran into them while asking Tavali about my brother and his last take. They're the ones who told me that he was at the Gort station and that he'd been put in harm's way by the hybrid bastard who worked there."

Jullien went cold. "They said what?"

"Yeah, but I didn't see a hybrid at the Gort station. Do you know who they were talking about?"

Jullien ground his teeth as it all fell into place. The Gorturnums had sent Teex after him, but because he was now stralen, Teex didn't realize he was the "hybrid" they'd meant.

He'd forgotten about that. With his eyes a different color, his complexion, while paler than the average Andarion, was still dark enough to pass as a lighter skin-toned lineage, especially among the Fyrebloods. Unless someone knew Jullien had been born with green eyes, they'd never be able to tell now that he wasn't a full-blooded Andarion.

But why would the Veniks think him hybrid? Malys had asked if he was a stralen Andarion, and he'd told her that he was. For all she knew, he was full-blooded. There was no reason for her sons to think him anything else.

Unless . . .

Jullien cursed. "It's a trap." Just as he stood, a bright light flashed.

Venik and six others appeared on the bridge with them, blasters aimed at their heads.

An eighth member caught Jullien from behind with an Andarion wire-collar. The three cords cut deep into his throat and lifted him from his feet, instantly incapacitating him.

While Venik and friends held the others at blaster point, Jullien was dragged, choking and coughing, from the bridge and down the hallway into a small rec room. He fought against the collar, but they were designed to cut off the victim's air supply and tighten with every attempt made for freedom. It was a tool mostly used in their prisons to control inmates. Or by special forces who targeted sentries or guards. There was nothing he could do. Once a collar was in position around the victim's neck, it was a most effective weapon that could only be removed by the one wielding it.

He couldn't even breathe or make fire with it in place.

By the time his attacker wrenched it from his swollen throat, he was barely conscious. He threw Jullien to the ground where he wheezed in an attempt to breathe again.

Before Jullien could catch his breath, his attacker delivered a staggering kick to his ribs that knocked him flat on his back. His vision blurred and head throbbing, Jullien tried to focus as his assailant stomped him hard in the crotch.

Cupping himself, Jullien cursed while excruciating pain crippled him and he tasted bile.

An angry fist wrapped itself in his hair and wrenched his head back so that he could finally see the face of his attacker. For a full minute, he thought he was hallucinating.

But it didn't dissolve.

The vision only grew clearer into the snarling, twisted image of his cousin, Nyran. Tall, dark and insidiously handsome, he'd always been a psychotic bastard.

"Well look at you, little Julie . . . stralen. Appears my mother isn't the only Anatole whore after all, eh? No wonder you were always wanting to cuddle up to the Hauks and kept trying to get us to leave them alone. Guess you could smell their putrid blood in your veins." He kicked him again, then slammed his head down to keep him dazed, and unable to fight back.

Or so he thought.

Unwilling to bend to the bastard, Jullien growled and moved to catch him to counter his assaults.

Just as he would have flipped Nyran and beaten the hell out of him, he felt the sharp, bitter sting of a needle in his neck. An instant later, everything began to swim as his empty stomach violently heaved.

"Yeah, you remember that, don't you, little Julie?" Nyran held him down in a practiced lock-hold until the drug took his will away from him completely. Since he hadn't eaten in the last two days as he'd walked through the desert after his crash, its effects were almost immediate, and left him even queasier than normal.

In spite of his best attempts, there was nothing Jullien could do. Everything swam and twisted.

Laughing, Nyran stroked Jullien's whiskered cheek. "I told you I'd be back for you, didn't I?"

Unable to fight at all now, Jullien waited to die from an overdose. But after several seconds, he realized that wasn't what Nyran had planned for him.

Instead, Nyran lifted Jullien's shirt and began marking his back, making a thousand stings across it. The pain was unbearable, but he couldn't move or make a sound due to the drug.

"In case you're wondering, I'm implanting you, but you'll have no idea where it is. So this time, you can't dig it out to escape again. See, I have plans for you, Julie. You owe me, you little shit." He straightened and kicked him again. "Because of you, my mother's dead. I lost my holdings. My titles. My lineage. My Andarion fortune. Everything! My brothers are dead!"

Nyran kicked him over, onto his back so that Jullien could look up at him. "Or at least some of them, I should say." He knelt on the floor by Jullien's side. "Did you ever stop and wonder why Eriadne and my mother had such tight ties to Venik and The Tavali? Eriadne wasn't the only one who fucked him, you know? My mother did, too. In fact, she's the one who introduced Eriadne to Venik and arranged for him to use Andarion space to ply his trade. And she gave him a son to cement the deal. I actually spent a great deal of time on my father's base as a kid. Bet you never knew that, did you?"

He smiled coldly. "Had you gone anywhere other than The Tavali to hide, I would have never found your stupid ass. But the minute you attacked my stepmother, and she came home screaming about you . . . then pointed your file out to my father. I had you by the testicles."

Jullien started to pass out.

But Nyran slapped him back to consciousness. "Stay with me, *kyzi*. See, I was going to kill you when I heard you were with the Gorts. Gut you like the bastard mongrel you are. Until it dawned on me that you owe me a throne." He slammed Jullien's head against the floor. "Are you listening, Julie?"

"I hear you," he whispered as his voice slowly began to work again.

"Good. Because you're going to help me and my surviving brothers take over the UTC and get rid of Thaumarturgus. You will do *everything* we tell you to do or I will take everything from you, the same way you stole everything from me. Starting with that pretty little wife of yours. Do you understand?"

Jullien shook his head.

Nyran backhanded him. "Do you understand?"

"I'll kill you!"

"You can try. But remember, I am a son of the Porturnum Nation. A Venik and an Anatole. More than that, as the last of our family, I'm still talking to Eriadne. And she would give me *anything* I wanted if I told her where to find *you*. I breathe one word of your current location . . . you don't want to know what she'd do to you and that little family of yours in retaliation for losing her throne."

Nyran screwed his face up as he considered those words. "Actually, you do know, probably better than anyone, what fate awaits you in her hands." He rubbed at Jullien's chin. "For that matter, Tylie would reward me for a chance to carve out your heart. She always hated your guts. So I have many options where you're concerned. And if I go missing or anything happens to me, my brothers will make sure that your yaya gets your full address, as well as that of your wife and her entire Fyreblood family. You really want to roll that dice, Julie?"

He lifted up the front of Jullien's shirt and traced the scar that his brother Merrell had given him when he'd almost sliced Jullien's throat. "Pity he didn't kill you that day. But my mother always said the gods had their reasons for everything. Perhaps this is the plan. They're finally going to give me my due while I give you what you've earned. And I will enjoy every minute of this. Now go home, little Julie. And remember, if you cross me . . . say one word about this to your whore or to that bastard you serve, I will call down The League and Eriadne on you so fast, you won't even have time to run again. I'm through playing with you. You've seen how easy I can track you down. You're my little bitch and you're going to heel at my command, or I will crush you. For as Tavali as you want to pretend you are, I was born into their world and have their blood flowing for generations in my veins. Me, they respect and will follow for all time. You're nothing but a pathetic pretender. An imposter everyone sees through. No one wants you. They never have. Not even your own mother could love you. She won't even let us say your name in her presence."

And with that, Nyran got up and left him on the floor.

Ashamed and aching, Jullien lay there, wishing himself dead. He hadn't felt like this since he'd lived in the palace. Powerless and hurt. Unable to protect himself or anyone else.

This was the exact kind of head game that Eriadne, Tylie, Parisa, Merrell, Nyran, and Chrisen had specialized in and tormented him with his entire childhood. Between them, the courtiers and the rest of his family, he'd never known a moment's peace or any kind of security or happiness.

Now . . .

He couldn't even run. If he tried, they'd kill Ushara and Vasili just to punish him. It was how they operated.

*I have to kill Nyran.*

There was no other way. But he'd have to do it carefully so as not to draw Ushara and her Nation into a war with the Porturnum.

*Titana ræl.*

He heard the door open again. Still unable to move more than his head, he swallowed as he saw Payne and two other males who were similar enough in their features that they must be his brothers.

Jullien laughed.

"What? You think this is funny?" Payne Venik snarled.

"Hysterical. Really. I'm supposed to be worthless and yet you three badass Tavali pirates had to drug me to kick my ass. Guess that makes you the three biggest *cocúpüni* in the universe to fear me this much."

Payne seized him. "You know what your problem is?"

"Yeah. The fact that I like the way that vein throbs in your temple when my mouth sets your fury off."

He backhanded him.

Tasting blood, Jullien laughed again. "Now you're just trying to turn me on, *giakon*. Is that the best you can do?"

Payne's nostrils flared. "Hold him, Trygg. Time we taught this bastard respect."


"Holy gods . . ."

Jullien jerked as he felt someone touch his face. Pain burned through him, but at least he no longer felt the effects of the drug Nyran had injected in him. His breathing ragged, he rolled over to see Jupiter kneeling by his side.

"I'll kill those scabbing Porty bastards for this! I told them they weren't to touch you."

Jullien sighed and winced as he wiped at the blood on his lips. "They were avenging their mother's honor. It's fine. The day will come when I won't be on the ground and I will return the favor. I promise you."

Jupiter growled as he tapped his link. "Terris? They've left our guest in quite a mess of a shape. I'm taking him down to your clinic now. Can you meet us there?" He paused. "See you shortly."

As gently as he could, he helped Jullien to his feet, then slung his arm over his shoulders and walked him down to the ship's infirmary.

"So what's the deal with you and the Porties?"

Jullien considered the best way to answer. "I apparently chafe everyone's ass."

"Don't be treating me like a fool, *cade*. They came in here with blasters and violated me lady. Then they broke Safe Harbor. That weren't done lightly. It's an act of war should I choose to make it so. I want to know why they'd take such a chance for you. Just who are you, really?"

"I'm nobody. Really."

With a snort of disbelief, Jupiter didn't speak another word as he led him into the infirmary and helped him onto the bed.

Once Jullien was settled, he pinned him with a fierce grimace.

"I know you're lying. But I assume you've got your reasons for it and I'll be leaving you to them. We're still planning to take you home. As I promised." And with that, he turned and left him alone with the crew's medtech.

Jullien fell silent as she came forward to treat him.

"You're Andarion?"

He nodded.

The sympathetic expression on her face told him just how awful he must appear. "I'm Doctor Exten. Is it all right if I touch you to treat your injuries?"

"You must have dealt with a few of us to know our protocols."

"We're well warned about Andarions in med school. And it's reiterated when we take Tavali med certs since there can be a fairly large number of Andarion Tavali in some of our Nations."

"Ah . . . and yes. I grant you permission to treat me."

Jullien remained quiet while she went over his injuries. It wasn't until she got to his back that she let out an audible curse.

"What did they do?"

He didn't respond since he knew it wouldn't matter. Nyran's implant would be so small, it would take a subatomic scope to find it, and surgery to remove it.

If they could. Knowing his cousin, it was most likely embedded in his spine which would make its removal impossible without paralyzing him. At least that had always been Nyran's SOP, and there was no reason to think Nyran would have changed his practice.

But in coming after him, Nyran had made one strategic mistake.

He'd told Jullien where *he* was hiding.

Like Ushara had said—don't get his full attention. Until now, Jullien's focus had been scattered. He'd had no idea where to look for his cousin.

Now he did.

Yet getting to Nyran while the coward was holed up on the Porturnum base wouldn't be easy.

Closing his eyes, he held his breath as the doctor worked and tried not to feel the pain, either inside or out. In all honesty, he was so tired of these games. He just wanted it to end.

Why couldn't his family ever let him live in peace?

He should have never tried to have a life with Ushara. He should have known better. Now he was the biggest threat to not only her, but Vas and Trajen.

To their entire Nation.

Nyran wouldn't stop. He knew that from experience. And Jullien had no idea what Nyran's brothers would do. What all they might be capable of. Not that it mattered.

*I will fix this.*

He had no idea how. Or even where to begin. But it didn't matter.

*Wrong is never right . . . And you can never be strong while you're standing upon weak legs.* The old Trisani words went through his mind. When he'd been a boy, the *Book of Harmony* had been his only source of comfort. It alone had given him some semblance of conscience and guidance in the middle of the insanity that had made up his grandmother's court.

Now he had that same lost, drifting feeling again. Like he was in the middle of an ocean without a raft or life jacket, surrounded by sharks determined to eat him alive.

Yet as his panic surged and threatened to take him under, he thought of Ushara and pictured her beautiful face. He made himself focus on the sound of her voice saying his name whenever she whispered in his ear.

*Kimi tu, Jules . . . kimi asyado.*

No one else in his entire life had ever told him that they loved him. Not until Ushara, Vasili, and little Nadya.

They had found him in the darkness. Brought him home and made him feel warm and accepted.

He would not lead them into war. And he would not allow Nyran to threaten them.

"Can you take Meracin?" The doctor held a bottle near his face.

Jullien glanced longingly at the painkiller. Had Nyran not injected him, he could have. But it wasn't worth the risk of a lethal interaction that could kill him. "No. I have to suffer with it."

"Is there anything I can give you?"

He shook his head. "Don't worry. I have a high tolerance for pain."

"Yeah, you must. Anyone else would be crying like a baby, given the extent of your injuries. And I wouldn't think any less of you if you did. You took some hard hits."

Jullien sat up slowly and pulled his shirt from her hand. "Sadly, I've taken worse."

She glanced at the scars on his body as she put the medicine away. "Yeah, I guess you have."

He settled his shirt over his chest without comment.

After she cleaned up, she returned with a small cold pack for him. "Twenty on, twenty off."

"*Paktu.*"

"Pardon?"

"Thanks," Jullien said as he realized he'd responded habitually in Andarion and not Universal.

"You're welcome." She hesitated. "How would you say that in your language?"

"To you, I'd say *lützul.* To me, you'd say *lützil.*"

"*Lützil?*"

Jullien smiled at her attempt to roll her ls and pronounce the Andarion monothongs and umlaut. It wasn't an easy language for any non-Androkyn speaker to pick up, especially his Erisian aristocratic dialect and accent, and he gave her credit for even attempting it. Most humans didn't bother. "Very good."

"Yeah, right. Thanks for not mocking me."

"Hey, it's better than my first attempts at Universal. I promise you. Took me forever before I could make a human understand anything I said to them. For the longest time, all I got were peculiar frowns and a lot of pointing to the bathroom when what I'd said to them was *good day* or *hello.*"

She laughed. "I don't know about that. I love Andarion accents. It's very sexy, the smooth way the words roll off your tongue . . . like music. I could listen to yours all day long." She took the ice pack from his hand and activated it, then placed it against the bruise on his cheek. "You really need to keep this on your eye so the swelling won't be so bad."

When Jullien put his hand on the bag, he expected her to step away.

She didn't. Instead, she dropped her hand to finger the bruises on his throat below the collar of his shirt. "This has to be killing you. Are you sure there's not something I can do for your pain?"

Before he could answer, she dipped her head to nuzzle his neck.

He shot off the bed and collided with the tray. "I'm married."

She arched a brow at him. "Why aren't you wearing a wedding ring, then?"

Mainly because he was Andarion and they had a different custom with rings since it was a given most any legitimate or free-born male would be spoken for as soon as he entered puberty.

Unlike humans, they didn't exchange rings automatically, or see them as a universal sign of matrimony. Since marriages were arranged between matriarchs, a familial matriarchal pledge ring was given to the female at the time a contract for a future unification was negotiated as collateral to guarantee that the male would fulfill his promise to marry her. Females only gave rings to their husbands on anniversaries or at the birth of their first child, and then strictly as a show of extreme affection.

Because it was rarely done, it was a mark of high honor for an Andarion male to own a wedding ring. But it was not a given, nor customary. Males were naturally deemed either the property of their parents or their spouses and therefore they didn't need a ring to prove ownership. It was simply assumed by all.

Plus he had a natural feature that told the universe he was taken.

Jullien pointed to his red eyes. "I'm stralen."

She gave him a blank stare.

"Means I'm married and rabidly in love with my wife. It's an Andarion condition that's unmistakable. Don't need a ring when you have stralen, as it's far more obvious."

She swept a wistful pout over his body. "For the record, cutie-pie, you might want to rethink the ring since the rest of us have never heard of your stralen. And update your Tavali personnel files to list the wife, so we know."

Stunned and still gaping, Jullien watched as she left him.

Yeah, okay . . .

What a screwed-up day this had been from beginning to end. He felt as if he'd fallen into an alternate dimension.

What the hell? Women didn't do things like this to him. He'd never had a female of any species come on to him before.

Except Ushara.

*This is just . . .*

*Effing weird.*

If not for the pain, he'd think himself dead. It just didn't seem real or even plausible. He was an anathema to sentient creatures. At least that was how he'd always been treated. The concept that anyone would want him . . .

Totally screwed with his head.

Unable to cope, he sat down on the floor as he tried to make sense of everything. Maybe he had a severe concussion. That seemed highly plausible given the number of times Nyran and Payne had slammed his head against the floor and the force they'd used to do it.

Definite possibility. He only had three working brain cells on his best day, anyway.

As he sat there, thinking it all over, a plan began to take form. The rust and cobwebs were coming off. While he hated court politics, those old skills were still there in the darkest recesses of his mind.

And they were coming back now, sharper than ever as he considered what he wanted to do with Nyran and Eriadne. How to get the upper hand against them.

*Fine, you little bitch. You want to play with me . . .*

*Set the board.*

Nyran thought he had him in check. He was about to learn what Jullien had taught Chrisen and Merrell the hard way. While they had spent their youths conspiring against him and trying to ruin his life, the little fat kid hadn't just eaten his way through the kitchen. Jullien had devoured every political and military handbook ever written about strategy and philosophy. Not just in Andarion, but for all the Nine Worlds.

Silently reciting those passages and verses had been the only thing that had kept him sane in prison and during his months of forced seclusion and isolation whenever those pricks had betrayed him. In the end, it was the very survival skills Merrell, Parisa, and Chrisen had forced him to learn from his cradle that had led to their deaths.

Come Tophet or Koriłon, he was going to win this. And plant both Nyran's and Eriadne's heads on his wall.

Entering the bridge, Jullien rubbed his eyes and winced as he accidentally brushed his hand against the bruises on his brow.

"Morning to you," Jupiter greeted. "Did you sleep well?"

"Not really. You?"

"No." He handed Jullien a mug of coffee. "Happy Universal Theian Day."

Jullien scowled as he swallowed a sip of the bitter brew. "Is it the third already?"

Sitting in his chair, Jupiter nodded and turned on the news so that

Jullien could see some of the celebrations that were already in full swing on the various planets, especially since it was well after dark on some of them.

The newscaster had tears in her eyes as she watched the elaborate memorial wreaths being placed on the walls of the League's main headquarters on Gondara at midday by the highest League officers under the watchful gazes of The League Prime Commander, Kyr Zemin, and the Trigon Court's Overseer, Alia Mureaux. "As you can see, it's a beautiful tradition that marks the five hundred and eighty-sixth anniversary of the worst genocide in Ichidian history when Justicale Cruel destroyed an entire planet and forever extinguished the entire Theian race."

She sniffed daintily. "Ten billion souls were lost in less than one week to his madness. Such a horrid, horrid tragedy. . . . And now, we'll cut to the Caronese royal family as they leave League headquarters to provide their annual donation to the League fund before they lead the Overseer and her court of advisors into their local embassy to renew their treaty and loyalty oath that the Caronese Governor was forced to sign after the tyrant Cruel was defeated and executed. Then they'll perform their annual act of contrition."

Jullien let out a low whistle. "You know that has to suck and burn."

Jupiter nodded. "Don't it though? And I know how they feel, given that me own blood has to hang low on St. Hestia's Day every year, for much the same reason. It chafes to be reminded of your family's ills in such a public forum. As you so eloquently said, me friend, every family has its asshole. And some have more than one. Really shafles when that asshole is so egregious he screws the lot of you for generations to come."

"Not talking about that." He jerked his chin toward Darling Cruel and Kyr Zemin. "I mean the prince and prime commander. They're bitter, longtime enemies who can't stand each other. Kyr's even made an attempt on Darling's life."

"Really? When?"

"During Kyr's brother's wedding, when his brother Maris decided to come out of the closet with Darling's help and leave his bride at the altar— it was a huge scandal for all of them. Maris and Darling have been best friends since grade school. They're still inseparable, which makes Darling Zyr's mortal enemy, especially since he's still sheltering Maris from the Phrixian royal family after they've cut him off and declared him dead. It has to burn Kyr's soul to be that close to Darling and not kill him."

Jupiter cocked his head as he studied Jullien. "You know them?"

"What makes you think that?"

"Way you speak about them. It's personal, as if you've been up close with them all, many times."

Jullien steeled his expression so that he gave nothing away. He'd actually been in attendance at that wedding when Kyr had tried to geld Darling over Maris's unexpected disclosure that he had no intention of marrying a woman. Ever. It'd been one hell of an entertaining free-for-all.

Luckily, he was spared from having to lie about it when Jupiter's stryper spoke up. "Hey, Ju Ju? We got an alert coming in." She replaced the newsfeed with a huge number of ships that were headed straight for them.

Armed and targeted for Tavali.

Jupiter sat up straight in his chair and set his mug aside. "What the hell, man?" He flipped to the channel on his con. "Chayden? You awake?"

"I see them. They're not League. I think they're us. But they're not answering my calls."

"Ours, either."

Suddenly, Jullien's link buzzed. He answered it to find Ushara on the other end. "Hey, I've been trying to call you."

"I've been in hyperspace. Are you safe?"

Jullien watched as the crew around him scrambled for battle stations. "Not exactly sure." He glanced back to the screen as an amused thought went through him. "Where exactly are you, baby?"

"Ninth quadrant. Solaras System."

"I had a feeling . . . brought a lot of friends, did you?"

"Why do you ask?"

"Thinking you might want to back them down a bit as we're about to have a riot here if someone gets twitchy." He pulled the link away from his head. "Uh, Jupiter. It's okay. That would be my ride out there."

Gaping, he turned toward Jullien. "Seriously?"

"Precious? Could you answer their hail? You're making them a wee bit nervous."

Ushara, in full Tavali war paint, appeared on their main screen. "Identify yourselves."

"*Ship of Fools,* 8C-RUN–QIL1-CO-NCOB-Z, with Commander Hinto at the helm. To whom am I speaking?"

"Vice Admiral Ushara Samari of the Gorturnum Nation. I'm told you have something priceless that belongs to me."

Grinning, Jupiter held his hands up in surrender before he gestured toward Jullien off on his side. "So it would seem, Admiral. It was ever our intent to return him home to your loving arms."

"Jules?" she gasped as she saw him.

"Really. They've been quite gentle with me. Extremely hospitable."

"Why are you bruised then?"

"It wasn't the Seps who did this. I swear. I ran afoul of another group of assholes."

"Beg pardon, Andarion?" Jupiter asked with a laugh. "*Another* group of assholes? I share me best whisky with you, and *this* is how you insult me . . . bloody figures."

Jullien winked at him.

Shaking her head, Ushara turned her attention back to Jupiter. "In that case, I'm in your debt, Jory. You ever need anything from us, let me know, and it's yours."

"Think nothing of it, Admiral. Always me pleasure to help out a beautiful lady. Glad to have been of service to the both of you, and to have met your husband. He's a good *cade*. Congratulations on your marriage, by the way."

"Thank you."

Jupiter stood up to walk Jullien to their airlock while Ushara sent over a small shuttle for him. "Well it's a good thing I didn't let me idiot cousin have you, eh?"

"Probably so. And I am thankful for everything."

Jupiter nodded. "I'm just sorry about Venik and his *chirani*. I will pay them back for what they did to you. That I promise."

"You don't have to worry about that tab. It's one I plan to collect on myself."

As soon as the shuttle docked, Jullien opened the door while Jupiter left to return to the bridge. He expected it to be Davel.

It wasn't.

Ushara grabbed him by the jacket and pulled him fiercely against her for the hottest kiss of his life. "I'm so mad at you I could skin you alive."

His breathing ragged, he arched a brow. "Only if you let me spank you first."

"Pardon?"

"Pregnant? It seems you told everyone *but* your husband."

She blushed. "Only a few others."

"Define *few*."

"Dozen . . . roughly." Biting her lip, she straightened his jacket before she gently examined the bruises on his face and neck. "Maybe I was a little naughty. I didn't want to worry you while you were gone."

Too grateful to see her again to really fight about it, Jullien brushed his hand against her stomach that was only just beginning to bulge ever so slightly. "I should be angry at you, but I'm not. I'm just glad to see you. I still can't believe that we're going to have a baby."

"Brace yourself, *mi keramon*. Not one baby . . . two. It's twins in there."

For a full heartbeat, he couldn't breathe as those words slapped him hard. "What?"

Nodding, she picked up her link and turned it on. "I haven't been feeling well and my mother made me go to the doctor. She did the ultrasound and this was what she found."

Jullien's breath rushed out of him as he saw the images of two very small fetuses. He grinned as he watched them. "We're having jumping beans."

She laughed. "Yes, this fall, we will have your jumping beans. They're due at the end of Cantlos. But I'm told that twins usually come early, so we shouldn't waste any time preparing the nursery."

Tears filled his eyes as love and fear overwhelmed him. He was going to be a father.

*Him.*

What were the gods thinking? Were they insane?

Unable to sort through everything he felt, he sank to his knees and placed his head against her precious stomach that held the most incredible miracle he'd never dared to imagine for himself. How could any male be so happy and terrified at the same time? So proud of what would come and yet humbled by the gift of the female in his arms?

Closing his eyes, he did the one thing he hadn't done in so long, he hadn't even known he could still do it.

He prayed.

The gods could have his worthless life and soul, and do with it what they would. All he asked was that they kept Ushara and her children safe.

Ushara bit her lip as she brushed her hand through Jullien's soft hair while he kept her locked in a tight grip for so long that she began to worry about him. "*Mi'ki?*"

He placed a gentle kiss to her stomach before he spread his hand flat against it, and looked up at her. "I will not let anyone threaten you or your children. On my honor. With my last drop of blood. I will keep you safe."

"I know, *mi tiuri*." But she sensed that there was something else bothering him. Something deeper than his normal concerns and paranoia. "Are you sure you're all right?"

Nodding, he took her hand and placed it to his cheek. An Ixurian sign of extreme affection.

She stroked his bruised cheek gently. "Are you ready to go home?"

He rose slowly and led her to the shuttle. Yet even so, there was a profound change in him and she could feel it.

"Jules?"

He met her gaze with an arched brow.

"Who hurt you?"

"It doesn't matter. They're not important."

She stared aghast at him. "How do you figure?"

He nudged her down into the pilot's chair and fastened her into her seat. "Do you trust me, Shara?"

"Of course."

"Then let me handle this." He moved to sit next to her as he began the prelaunch sequence for her.

Her breath caught as she had a sudden bad feeling. There was only one thing it could be. One thing he would refuse to discuss with her like this.

His family.

Somehow they'd found him. Nothing else would make him act this strangely. Or have him this upset and secretive. And as she scanned the bruises on his body while he prepared the launch, it all made sense.

Those marks were from someone who'd wanted to seriously hurt him. They were personal injuries that came with a vendetta. Injuries that made her want to hurt his family all the more.

*Haven't you done him enough harm?* Why couldn't they leave him alone?

But it wasn't until they'd landed at home, late the next morning, and she had him back in her house that she saw the full extent of his injuries. And then, not until he came out of the shower and she caught sight of him dressing in their bedroom.

"Oh dear saints, Jules!" She gasped at the welts, cuts, and bruises along his spine. The footprints on his ribs, chest, and stomach. "Can I not leave you alone for five minutes?"

"Probably not." He smirked at her. "I'm a contentious asshole with severe dysfunctional relationship issues that lead me to extreme forms of antagonism and aggression against my peers in most social situations. Even I'm surprised by what comes out of my mouth most days."

Ushara rolled her eyes at his playful sarcasm. "Get in bed. Right now." She reached for her link to call her mother.

But Jullien didn't make it to the bed. He collapsed at her feet.

"Jules?" Ushara knelt down by his side, then panicked. He hadn't passed out.

He'd stopped breathing completely.

# CHAPTER 21

Jullien came awake with a violent, painful jolt to find Trajen leaning over him. His head pounded as he scowled up at the dark, dangerous Trisani. "What the hell, man?"

Scowling furiously, Trajen let out a relieved breath before he slapped him hard. "You ever die on me again, Andarion, and I'll rip your throat out. I mean every word of that."

"Okay, then. I see those employee motivational courses Ushara insisted you take have really been paying off. You haven't wasted your creds on them, at all," he said drily.

Trajen snorted. "You're such a smart-ass." He helped Jullien sit up. "How you feeling?"

"Extremely confused." He rubbed at the pain in the center of his chest as he looked around the room. "Why am I half naked in my bedroom with you fondling me? Is there some confession you need to make?"

Trajen shoved at him. "You're not that cute. Even with the fangs. And I'm too sober to be tempted to lose my wizard powers for your sorry ass. . . . Do you remember what happened?"

Jullien rose slowly to his feet. "I was coming out of the shower."

"Yeah?"

"Then you were rubbing and slobbering on me."

Trajen made an obscene gesture at him. "The main detail you're missing is the part where you fell dead on the floor at Ushara's feet."

Jullien froze. "What?"

He nodded slowly. "You want to talk about it?"

"Talk about what? I have no memory of it. . . . I really died?"

"Yeah, you did. I just ran enough electricity through you to power half this station. It's why you're so sore. Honestly, you didn't seem to want to come back." Trajen caught him as he stumbled. "Careful. You might want to sit." He helped Jullien toward the bed.

His lungs felt thick suddenly as the room tilted and spun around him. Jullien struggled to breathe. He stretched out on the bed and coughed, then choked and gurgled.

Trajen caught his arm and stretched it over his head. "You using again?"

He shook his head. Truly, it felt as if his lungs were solidifying. No air could get past his throat.

"Don't lie to me."

Unable to speak, Jullien started wheezing. He had no idea what was happening. Pain tore through him. The harder he tried to use his lungs, the less they wanted to work. Tears blinded him. He shook all over.

Trajen rolled him to his side. "Breathe, little brother. Slow and easy."

He was trying, but there wasn't anything easy about it. It hadn't been this difficult since he'd been a kid and his stupid cousins' uncle had made him run maneuvers on Kirovar.

*Damn you, Barnabas Cabarro.*

Climbing onto the bed with him, Trajen wrapped his arms around him and squeezed his chest so hard that for a moment, Jullien feared he'd break a rib. But after a minute, the pressure started helping to loosen whatever was seizing his lungs. "Deep breaths. Don't fight me."

After a few minutes more, Jullien's breathing returned to normal and the wheezing finally stopped.

Trajen slowly backed the pressure off and laid him down on the bed. "Just stay there and take it easy." He covered him with a blanket before he slid off the mattress.

"Does this mean we're dating?"

Trajen let out a sound of supreme aggravation. "A simple *thank you, Tray, for not letting me die* would be nice."

"Thank you, Tray. But next time, you could buy me dinner before you fondle me in my marital bed."

He hit him with a pillow. "Gah. You're such an obnoxious ass." He conjured a small vial and handed it to him. "You need to drink this."

"What are you poisoning me with now?"

"You don't want to know. But it'll clear the remnants of Bliss out of your second set of lungs so that they don't keep seizing on you."

Jullien went ramrod stiff.

Trajen let out a tired sigh. "Tell me I'm wrong and I'll believe you. But I've been around enough Fyrebloods to know the symptoms when I hear them rattling in your chest. Once you start breathing fire, there are some things you have to avoid. And Bliss is poison to your species."

"I didn't take it voluntarily." Grabbing the vial, Jullien opened it and drank the bitter liquid. With a fierce grimace, he cursed, then handed the vial back to Trajen. "So no, I'm not using again. But yes, it is in my body."

"Okay."

Jullien glared at him. "Why are you playing this shit with me, anyway? I don't like it, Trajen. I've been head-fucked my whole life. By everyone. I know you can pull the truth out of me quicker than I can tell it. So why this mind game?"

"Because I *can* pick and choose what I pull out of you. And I've *chosen* to trust you, which is an exceedingly rare thing for me to do. You've earned the right to keep your privacy. I won't go digging inside your head without your permission. No games, Jullien. I would never do that to you."

"Appreciate it."

Trajen inclined his head to him. "We good?"

"Are we?" he asked belligerently.

He scowled at Jullien. "Well, I was till you got that tone with me. Is there something else you need to confess?"

Jullien shook his head. "I'm just out of sorts. Sorry. I had a bad day. And falling down dead for no reason hasn't really helped my mental state any."

Trajen clapped him on the shoulder. "No problem, *drey*. I'm here if you need me." He hesitated. "I do feel that I should warn you about one thing before I let Ushara back in."

"And that is?"

"End of next week, the UTC has its annual meeting. This year we're hosting it here at the station."

"Yeah, okay. . . ?" He let his voice trail off, unsure as to why this concerned him or why Trajen was bringing the matter up at this particular inconvenient time.

Like he gave a shit, right now.

"You familiar with Ryn Cruel?"

Since Ryn was Darling Cruel's older half brother, and had lived in the royal palace at Caron while their father had been alive, Jullien had attended a large number of functions with him. But given that Jullien was Andarion and a few years older, they'd never been friendly with each other. Ryn had his crew of humans he ran with, and their only interest in Jullien had been as a punchline.

"We've crossed paths a few times over the years."

"Enough that he would know you on sight?"

Jullien grimaced. That was hard to say. Ryn's royal cronies had picked on him enough when he'd been overweight that they might, yet Ryn had never really participated in their cruelty. A time or two, he'd even tried to get them to stop. But that being said, Ryn had mostly avoided all contact with Jullien and the Andarion royal family.

Ryn's little brother, Darling, however, was another story. Jullien and Darling were well acquainted and had run up against each other several times over the years.

So . . .

"Maybe."

"Then you need to be wary. As his mother's VA and virulent protector, he always runs scout for her. More than that, they sometimes have Darling with them. Although it's been a few years since Darling's attended with him—he and Ryn had a bit of a falling out a few years back, but it's not unheard of for Darling to come, especially if he's had a fight with his uncle."

"Noted."

"And . . ." Trajen paused for effect. "The one you have to be on guard against most is Venik."

"Because of Malys."

Trajen shook his head, then dropped the last name Jullien had ever expected to hear. "Because of Hauk."

"Hauk?"

"Yeah. Fain Hauk is his right-hand pilot. Even though Hauk flies under a Rogue's Canting, Braxen Venik is his Tavali father, and he's fiercely loyal to Ven. Hauk functions as his field admiral and he's always with him for these. I know you two have bad blood between you. So I wanted you to know to keep a low profile while they're here. And take special note that because Hauk, as a Rogue, isn't supposed to be aligned to any one Nation, he hangs back away from Ven, and in particular the Danes and Hintos to keep them from getting suspicious about his loyalties. So he'll be ghosting the area and not officially with us. You'll find him in the bays or the bars, trying to be inconspicuous."

"But not in the meetings."

"Exactly. Same for Ryn. They have no idea that I know anything about them. Especially since they're not allowed to attend the closed sessions. Ryn usually hangs around or in his ship. Same for Fain. In fact, the Danes don't even know he exists. Not sure the Hintos do either. That's how low a profile Hauk keeps. But if he sees *you*—"

"He'll know me instantly and bust my ass . . . as will Darling." And while Jullien could take Darling without much effort, Fain could go either way. He was a former titled Andarion Ring champion.

Because Jullien was a hybrid, he'd been banned from Ring matches—even in the Open league—but he'd seen Fain fight enough to know he would be a handful in battle. Jullien wasn't afraid of him. Just respectful of the fact that if it came down to it, Fain wouldn't be an easy victory, and could possibly be the end of one former Andarion tiziran.

Fain would definitely be motivated to tear his throat out.

"They'll be here two days. Watch your back." With that, Trajen quit the room.

A frown drew Jullien's brows together as he considered an interesting tidbit Nyran had left out during their "meeting." Fain was *also* a member of the Porturnum Nation . . .

*With Nyran.*

How the hell did that work? That had to be fun at family get-togethers.

Hauk served as the right hand of Nyran's father? And while Fain would kill to have Jullien's testicles on a platter, it was nothing compared to what he'd do for Nyran's.

Especially if . . .

The door opened, breaking his thoughts off as Ushara ran into the room with a worried scowl. "Jules?"

He caught her against him as she literally threw herself onto the bed by his side. "Hey, baby." He kissed her while she sobbed. "Shh, what's this?"

She popped him on the stomach. "Don't you *ever* die on me again! You scared me to death."

"Ow!"

She was instantly contrite. "Did I hurt you?"

"It didn't feel good." He rubbed his offended area.

"I'm sorry."

Instantly, the room filled with her sisters, mother, Vasili, Davel, and Axl as they came in to assure themselves that he was alive and breathing.

Jullien could barely follow all their rapid-fire questions.

"Please," Ushara said, holding her hands up. "You're giving the poor baby a headache. He's fine."

Mary scooted to sit next to him on the bed. "You love all the attention, *big drey*. Admit it."

He laughed at Mary as she forced Ushara off the bed so that she could check his forehead for a fever. "How is Ushara doing? Really?"

She grimaced in her sister's direction. "She's supposed to be off her feet most of the day. Doctor's orders. *Watch her.*"

"Mary!" Ushara gasped.

"Well, you are," Oxana chimed in. "He needs to know."

Jay pushed her toward the bed while Ryna pulled Mary off. "Ushara's the one who should be sitting. Not you."

Axl groaned at his sisters. "Gah, I'm so glad they don't barge into my house all the time. How do you stand it, m'drey?"

That comment sparked a playful slapping match between him and Mary that their mother had to break apart. Jullien bit back a smile. As the youngest of the Altaan brood, Axl seldom spoke a word. He claimed it wasn't worth the effort and that he had nothing all that important to say that it was worth the fight, anyway.

Putting more distance between his brother and sister, Davel scratched at his forehead. "All right, I'll wrangle everyone out for the sake of peace. Jules, rest up. I'm not taking all the heat on this. I plan to share it with you as soon as you're back on your feet."

"Thanks, Dav. You got a serial for that knife you just planted in between my shoulder blades?"

"Nah, but . . . I do have another legal run to make in three weeks. And I need my best cock back on my crew for it."

Ushara pulled her blaster out and aimed it at her brother. "Don't even."

Axl disarmed her. "Hey, when did this escalate to violence?"

"Look at my husband. I'd say a few days ago when your brother dragged him out of here against my protests. And it will instantly return if your brother tries to take him out of here again."

"Yeah, right. As I recall, Dagger was the one protesting and you were making him go." Axl handed the blaster to Jullien. "*Drey*, I do not envy you her temper."

"It's okay. I don't envy her mine."

"He ain't kidding on that." Davel herded the group out.

Snickering, Vas came over and offered Jullien one of his cookies. "I'm glad you're home, Paka. I missed you."

"Missed you, too." He hugged him.

"All right, Veevee. We've got homework. Let's give them a rest for a little bit and we'll check on them after we get done." Kitari led him out of the room and shut the door.

Ushara frowned. "Is that your link I hear?"

"Yeah." He pulled it off the nightstand and turned it on to see a photo of Nyran with Eriadne at a restaurant. His vision darkened at the implied threat that came in a disguised news article.

"What is it?"

Refusing to react to it, Jullien deleted it immediately. "Just a news report. Nothing important." He pulled her into his arms and held her close, savoring the warmth of having her safe.

*You better lay off me, you little prick. You're playing with a Fyreblood now.* And Jullien was about to unleash a wealth of Samari vengeance on him. Nyran had no idea how much Jullien had changed these last few years, but he was about to learn.

Up until now, Jullien had left them alone and been on the run. He'd given them plenty of time to let bygones be bygones.

*Vengeance is a cruel mother who inevitably eats her spawn.* The Trisani were right about that, especially when you didn't know when to let it go.

Closing his eyes, he sucked his breath in sharply as Ushara gently raked her fingernails through the hairs on his chest and abdomen. For some reason, that hair fascinated her and she would always spend untold hours toying with it until he was hard and insane from her caresses. Especially whenever she nibbled and teased it with her lips and tongue.

He bit his lip as she drew circles around his navel. "You keep doing that and your mother and Vas are going to get an earful."

She nipped his chin playfully. "Sorry. I've missed you so much."

"I was only gone four days."

"Five. And it seemed like an eternity."

Smiling, he kissed her. "One minute away from you seems like forever."

Ushara returned his smile, but even so, she knew he was keeping something from her. There was a shadow behind his eyes that hadn't been there before. Jullien had come back to her with a ghost haunting him. Something horrible had happened while he was gone.

And it wasn't just his beating.

She didn't know what. But she was going to find it. One way or another, she was going to make him feel safe again.

And if his family was trying to harm him as she suspected, she would finish off every last one of them.

In the bloodiest way imaginable.


Jullien frowned as the Porturnum ships landed in their bay. Malys was nowhere to be seen. And neither was Nyran. But Fain was there—just as Trajen had predicted. He'd landed in a fighter first, as a scout for Venik.

Careful to stay hidden, Jullien watched him from the shelter of Sheila's office. Fain looked a lot different from the boy he'd gone to school with. He still wore the Andarion warrior braids, only now half of them had been bleached white. Instead of the Hauk war paint on his face, he had Tavali markings.

But the most curious mark was the Batur tattoo that ran the entire length of Fain Hauk's left arm. Strange because Merrell and Chrisen had forced Fain to break his pledge with Galene Batur before Fain had been disinherited from his Hauk family. Why Fain would have her Batur family lineage put on his arm to pay eternal homage to her was beyond Jullien's best comprehension.

Then again, Fain had always loved Galene. And given her beauty and grace, Jullien could well understand his devotion. While Galene had never been particularly kind to him, she'd been very caring toward Nyk, Dancer, and Fain.

It must have killed Hauk to give her up to save his brother's life. And if Fain ever found out that Galene had given birth to his son after Merrell had forced Fain to leave home . . .

There would be Tophet to pay for all of them.

Of course, *his* head would be the first Fain would mount on a pike over that event. Still . . .

Jullien went to Sheila's desk and began to do some research as he considered the best way to use this new information to his advantage. Yes, he was in a precarious position where Fain was concerned.

But Nyran's wasn't any better.

*Beware the sword of vengeance, for its blade is just as sharp on the back as it is the front. Lacking all sight, it doesn't see what it hits, nor feel the pain that it causes. It tastes every bit of the blood it draws, and it cries more, more, more. For once started, its appetite becomes insatiable. So think you twice before you grasp that hilt, and find your hand locked to a fate that is as likely to strike the one who wields it as the one it's meant to lay low.*

He shook his head as the Trisani warning went through his head.

Fuck it. End of the day, he was an Andarion and they didn't carry a sword of peace.

They carried insatiable Warswords.

And he planned to shove his straight down Nyran's throat. As the old Andarion saying went, *blood vengeance spilled hot burns to the bone, but blood vengeance served cold soothes even the most battered of souls.*

There was a reason why the Trisani national flag was a blue peaceful bird rising in flight against a field of solid white with a single "Darling" star over its head, and the Andarion flag was a black-and-white Warsword standing on a field of bloodred as a promise of strength and unity should their empire ever be attacked. While it did have two black stripes and one red that represented the three original races—winged, darkheart, and fyreblood—they were united against the vertical red stripe that signified their warring blood-ties.

Of course, in theory, Andaria did have a "peace" flag that was white and black. But it was only used by their ambassadors, royal family, and diplomats on specific missions, and seldom seen on actual Andarion soil. The first time Jullien had seen one, he'd thought it was a joke—something his father's people had done to mock his mother's race. He'd been stunned silent when he realized that it was authentic.

Which brought him back to his original question . . .

How was Nyran living among the Porturnum with Fain and keeping his presence there a secret? If Fain ever laid eyes on an Anatole in his domain, he'd kill him without hesitation or care of consequences.

*Sometimes the most obvious things hide in plain sight.*

*Think, dumbass.*

Why would Parisa have crawled into bed with a Tavali? He knew his cousin. What could she have been hoping to gain? Parisa didn't do anything without a game plan.

He was missing something . . .

Frustrated, Jullien got up as more ships were landing. One was the *Cruel Victory*, which would be Ryn's.

"Are you reconsidering working for me now?" Sheila asked as she returned to her office and eyed his battered face.

Jullien laughed as he lightly touched his bruised lips. "I don't know. I got knocked around pretty good working for you, too, as I recall."

"Yes, but I bring you pastries." She handed him the sack in her hand. "And coffee."

Grinning roguishly, he took the cup from her. "That you do, *mia müra*. Thanks."

She squeezed his arm as she moved past him, toward her desk. "We get anything interesting in yet?"

"Nah. Same old shit." He pulled out a pastry to eat while he watched Ryn's crew come down the ramp. They were a peculiar bunch. The Wasturnum crew reminded him more of a group of the princes he went to school with than Tavali pirates.

"Are all the Wasturnums snotty bitches?"

Sheila laughed. "Noticed that, did you? Yeah, they are. And that's just the males. In fact, you won't even see His High Highness Precious Cargo while they're in port. He'll be holed up on his ship the whole time they're here 'cause he's too good to mingle with us commoners."

"High Highness Precious Cargo?"

"Ryn Dane? That's his code name."

Jullien laughed. "Seriously?"

"Well, not the High Highness. I added that. But yeah. Precious Cargo."

"Should I ask why?"

"The way his mother treats him. In fact, I think he's still breast-fed. I know I've seen her burp the little shit after his meals."

Still laughing, Jullien drank his coffee. "I think I shall reserve judgment on that."

"Feel free. I judge him an ass enough for both of us."

"And while you do that, I'm going to work on my ship. If you need me for anything, you know where to find me lurking."

"Fine. Abandon me to those assholes."

Jullien didn't comment as he slipped outside and made sure to keep an eye out for both Fain and Ryn. Ushara had told him that they would arrive an hour or two before their leaders to make sure everything was ready for the high admirals. Once they were satisfied with accommodations and security, they would signal the HAPs for a landing. But interestingly enough, the VAs never interacted with each other or with the HAPs of other Nations. They avoided each other so as not to raise suspicions or to cause anyone to gossip about them.

There was never any cross-pollinization.

Ushara and Jupiter were a rare exception, and only because Jupiter had been forced to land here once for repairs and had intentionally made friends with as many as he could. Because . . . well, he was Jupiter. And apparently, friendliness was the way he rolled and flew.

And since Trajen could read minds, he wasn't worried about it.

As Jullien headed for his ship, he caught sight of a slight hooded figure on his left. Immediately suspicious, he moved his hand to his blaster, expecting it to be an assassin after him.

But the figure made no moves in his direction and didn't seem the least bit interested in what he was doing.

She or he was oblivious to everything except what lay before them.

Keeping to the shadows, it skimmed the wall until it came to the small cargo door for the *Cruel Victory*. There, it pulled out a link and typed something.

An instant later, the hatch opened to show a nervous Ryn Cruel, who glanced about to make sure no one was watching them.

With a happy shriek, the figure jumped into his arms. Her hood fell back to expose a wealth of bright red hair as she gave him a kiss so hot it left Jullien gaping.

Laughing, Ryn pulled her into his ship and quickly sealed his hatch shut, locked it down tightly, and armed it.

Well then . . .

Jullien now knew why Ryn wouldn't be coming up for air while they were here. Unless he missed his guess, that little red head was Mack Hinto.

Jupiter's sister.

*Well, I won't have to worry about running into him for the next two days.*

Ryn was going to be too busy dodging Jupiter and Gadgehe who would have his balls for *that* trespass.

Suddenly, a shadow fell over him.

Jullien turned and pulled his blaster only to meet the shit-eating grin of Jupiter as he held his hands up.

"Didn't mean to startle you, me large Andarion friend. Fasten your heart down, *cade*. Sorry I interrupted your daydreaming."

Holstering his blaster, Jullien laughed. "Yeah, right. I was just plotting devastating revenge on my enemies. You know . . . the usual." He pulled Jupiter in for a hug. "I didn't realize you'd be here already."

"Came in a few ago, and I saw your brother-in-law in the bay. He told me where to find you. Thought I'd stop in and say hi to you. See what trouble we could get into here in your backyard."

"Are you here with just your crew?"

"Me sister and her crew came in with me. She lit out, but she's around."

"Yeah. I'm sure she had some *Precious Cargo* to see about."

Jupiter groaned out loud. "Ah, dear gods . . . you know?"

Jullien hesitated as he saw the agonized expression on Jupiter's face. "*You* know?"

Grimacing, Jupiter motioned him in. "Can I trust you?"

"Of course."

"This be a big a secret, *cade*. And I'll know if you tell it. But since you know, I don't want you to be thinking bad things about me Mack. She and Ryn are married. But no one's to know, especially not our father. He'd flip it if he ever learned it."

"Seriously?"

He nodded. "They've been together since she was eighteen. It was about time he made an honest woman of her, if you ask me. Took the bastard long enough to put a ring on her finger. He's lucky I haven't killed him before now."

"Why the secrecy?"

"You know why we have St. Hestia's Day, right?"

"Yeah, she reunited the Tavali Nations into the single UTC after The League demanded The Tavali split into four separate companies and not call ourselves a single nation anymore."

"Right, but you know why St. Hestia did that?"

Jullien shook his head. "No. Not really."

Jupiter sighed. "Back in the day, Hestia Waring was the HAP of your Gorturnum Nation, and they were at constant war with the Wassies for territory. Some say she went after Isiah *Dane* who was the VA and heir of the Wasturnum Nation to seduce him so that she could use him against his father. Others say she loved him from the moment they met. However it began, they fell in love and united the two nations. Everything was going well until Dane and their son and crew took refuge from The League with one of me ancestors in the Septurnum Nation under Safe Harbor. Moglidice Hinto slaughtered them and Hestia Waring-Dane slaughtered him brutally for it. For two hundred and fifty years, the name Hinto was banned from all Tavali rolls and our Nation punished horribly for the deed. It's why we're still not really trusted by the other three Nations. So . . . The UTC don't like for the sons and daughters of two high-ranking officials to hook up to begin with. To have a Hinto and Dane be married . . ." He screwed his face up. "Is a bit of scandal. See? And me da would be horrified. Ain't no telling how our Lady Tavali, Hermione Dane, would react to finding out her precious, only son done gone and married a Hinto. None of us want to be around for that explosion."

"Got it, and I'll take it to my grave."

"Good male. Now lead me into temptation, brother. For it is the one thing I cannot resist."

But as Jullien headed with him out of the bay, they ran into Jay and Ryna who were standing with two attractive Porturnum females. Something about them seemed very familiar.

And when Ryna called him over to introduce him, Jullien understood why.

"There he is. Jules, come meet Venik's daughters. Vyra and Lyssa. We were just talking about you."

"Really?"

Laughing, Ryna nodded. "They said that you're old friends with one of their brothers, and that he's told them a lot of fond stories about you. Apparently, you went to school together?"

Ryna's polite words made his blood run cold. Yet not half as much as the speculative glimmer in the pale eyes of the two Veniks as they studied him way too intently.

"Pleasure to finally meet you . . . Dagger," Lyssa said.

Jullien slid a furious glare toward Jupiter who caught on fast that this wasn't a friendly exchange. Nyran was tempting the Koriłon badly and involving innocents who should know better than to come between two Andarion males at war.

But if they were that stupid . . .

"You're the crew of the *Black Widow*?" Jullien smiled.

"We are." Vyra glanced to her sister. "Why do you ask?"

"Making sure I have the correct crews matched to the right ships in my head, especially with those newer models. Their circuitry's so pissy these days. You never know when it's going to get a worm in it. Jam up and freeze at the damnedest time. It's why I don't fly them. They're terribly unreliable. Like some family members I know. Bastards turn on you when you least expect it. Leave you hanging out to dry, while they save their own asses. Got to be careful what you put your faith in. And whose battle you pick up to fight."

Lyssa lifted her chin as she caught Jullien's *other* meaning. "Porturnum doesn't work that way. Family backs family. Always."

"Do they?" He arched a sardonic brow. "You seriously might want to rethink the veracity of *that* statement. As I have much evidence to the contrary."

She glanced to Ryna and Jay. "Yet *you* expect loyalty from *your* family? What kind of hypocrite would hold others to such a higher standard given all the ones you've betrayed? Is there anyone you *haven't* knifed?"

"Hey now!" Jay snapped. "You don't insult our brother."

"Why not? He just threatened us."

Ryna started for Vyra, but Jullien caught her and forced her back.

"Don't. Just let it go."

"Listen to him, Fyreblood," Vrya spat. "And mark our words. To save his ass, he threw his own twin brother into jail. He cut the throat of his own cousin with his bare hands and shoved his pregnant sister-in-law into the hands of a rabid psychopath. You think he's changed? He hasn't. He can't. A lorina is incapable of changing its spots."

This time, Jullien went for them.

And Jory stopped him.

But not before Jullien saw the shadow in Jory's eyes that doubted him and believed what those bitches said. Worse? He saw it in Jay's eyes, too, and on Ryna's face.

No matter how hard he tried, he was still a worthless piece of shit. No one was ever going to allow him to forget the mistakes he'd made in his past. Not so long as Nyran and his grandmother lived.

There would never be peace for him. And they were never going to allow him to have a home he belonged in. Sooner or later, they would steal this from him, just as they'd taken everything else.

It was already beginning.

*So help me, gods, I'm going to kill you both.* One way or another, he was going to end this.

And them.

# CHAPTER 22

Ushara glared at Jullien and her brother. "I can't believe you're even contemplating this. Every time he goes out, it ends badly."

Jullien cracked his most charming grin at her. "This time I'm instigating it. It's a small run, with Unira, to test the *Pet Hate.*"

"The *what?*"

Unira laughed. "My former *Stormbringer.* Once Dagger finished the repairs, *m'tana* renamed my lady-ship *Pet Hate.*"

Ushara scowled. "Why?"

"Seemed a fitting name for something I'll one day run, provided I ever make citizen."

Mary came up behind her and gave her a sisterly hug. "Let him go, bossy pants. We're all going out with him to cover his cute little bottom for you. He's got more guards than a Vistan virgin on her way to her wedding night."

Ushara laughed. "Thanks, Nightmare."

"No prob." She grinned at the priestess. "I'll be needing to confess this weekend, won't I?"

"I'll hold an appointment for you."

"Damn."

"An extra long one."

Mary let out a painful whimper.

"He has to get some hours in," Davel reminded her. "You know that."

"I know. Fine." Sighing, Ushara kissed Jullien. "Please be careful."

"I will."

"Okay." She kissed him again. "How long will you be gone?"

"Three days."

She cringed as dread filled her. In three days, there was no telling how much trouble her husband could fall into. He had a frightening ability to seek it out in the safest places. "Stay in touch."

"I will. Promise."

Sick to her stomach, she watched as they boarded their ships.

*I should have never taken a base position.* Had she stayed as a ship commander, she could have flown out with them. But she'd accepted the VA assignment so that she would be grounded to raise Vasili. As his only parent, she'd wanted to make sure that she wouldn't be required to leave him for any reason.

Now it sucked.

Her heart heavy, she didn't move until they were gone. Then she returned to her office and turned on the news to make sure there was nothing going on anywhere, on any planet or outpost, that might threaten their safety.

And she meant *no-thing.*

But as she flipped to the Andarion news, there was definitely something important happening. It was a day later in the Andarion empire, and festivities were in full swing for a massive birthday celebration. Citizens lined the decorated streets where music played and a parade was in motion. The way they carried on, she assumed it was for Cairistiona.

Until she saw the banners that were posted all over.

For Tahrs Nykryrian.

Her jaw went slack as that hit her like a slap across her face.

"Wait a minute . . ."

If was it Nykyrian's birthday, it would have to be Jullien's, too. They were twins, after all. Born only minutes apart, according to Jullien.

Why wouldn't he have mentioned it before he left?

Then again, Jullien had never said a word about his birthday, really. Other than the most generic things about his birth, he'd never really mentioned a specific date, or even a time of year for it.

Her stomach shrank as guilt shredded her over the fact that she'd never even thought to ask him about the date. *Please tell me I haven't been this thoughtless . . .*

She went to her desk and pulled up his files.

No birth date was listed. So she went for his Andarion records, only to remember they'd been erased completely. He had no registration files left of any kind. Not even a library card.

She traced Nykyrian's and sure enough, the sixteenth of Ogronios, *today*, was his birthday. Tears filled her eyes as she realized that they'd met just a handful of days after his birthday, almost a year ago.

In her mind, she saw an image of how Jullien had looked that day.

Starved. Bedraggled. Half-dead and bleeding.

Lethal and desperate.

She couldn't believe how much had changed in so little time. Although Jullien still had trouble sleeping through the night and he didn't eat food unless he prepared it. Nor did he sit with his back to open doorways or cameras.

His hyper-vigilance continued. As did his paranoia.

Yeah, okay, in some ways, he hadn't changed at all.

But he had learned to cuddle. And he seemed to trust her. He sought out her company and Vas's, which for him was monumental.

Sometimes he even talked about things when they bothered him instead of withdrawing into himself and closing down.

Yet not a word about his birthday.

A part of her wanted to throw him a huge birthday party for his return. The kind her family was known for. But as she thought more about it, she remembered the way he was at any large family gathering. He always stood in a corner for the duration. While he'd interact with Nadya and her sisters whenever they'd tease at him, and Vasili and Davel's son and daughter, he didn't really look comfortable at any such event. More like he was visiting the dentist and they'd just run out of the last batch of painkiller and novocaine.

No, her introverted Jules wouldn't want a crushing celebration. He'd want something much more intimate and meaningful. Something that was a long time overdue.

"You're going to get us murdered. And that's just from my little sister should she find out I let you do this."

Jullien ignored Davel's dire tone as he grabbed a crash helmet from the closet. "Just be on standby in case I have to come in hot. This is something I have to do for my own peace of mind."

"Fine. *Cald cadaire.*"

Jullien appreciated the Andarion sentiment since he would need all the luck he could get.

Without another word, he climbed into the fighter and launched. Honestly, he was a lot more nervous about this than he was letting on. He had no idea how this would go.

What he would find.

But he had to try.

Hoping for the best, Jullien headed the fighter into the oldest port on Eris. Time to put his new eyes to the test and see just how well stralen worked for him with a regular Ixurian Andarion population.

As soon as he landed in Eris, he popped the cockpit and climbed down. The landing bay's CP came over to grill him, but luckily bribes still worked on Andaria.

And so did his forged credentials.

Jullien pulled his collar up and took a deep breath as he headed for the street. He hadn't been home in five years. Not since the night Tylie had thrown him out and Kelsei had shot him and almost severed his spine.

He'd sworn he'd never come back here.

*Damn you, Nyran.*

Things had definitely changed. Not just because of the activity on the streets for Nyk's birthday celebration. Fashions were a lot less restrictive. Their soldiers weren't as heavily armed and the citizens seemed a lot happier.

He was also attracting a lot more attention than he wanted.

Irritated by it, Jullien pulled his sunglasses out and put them on as he did his best to blend in with the crowd. He drifted out, toward the river where the old drainage pipes had once allowed his grandmother's guards to float bodies out of the basement and dispose of them without being seen.

Now, those same pipes would hopefully allow him private access into the palace, provided Nyk and his mother didn't know about it and hadn't destroyed them.

Hoping and praying, he held his breath until he located the old, rusted-out pipes. Unbelievably enough, they were fully intact. It appeared his mother and brother had no idea the vörgäte existed. Lucky them. His mother must not have *ever* pissed her mother off as a girl.

Jullien crawled inside the smelly, filthy pipes and slowly made his way to his grandmother's private dungeon. Curling his lip in disgust, he turned his torch on and suppressed a shiver as old memories returned with a bloody vengeance. He hated being back here. But thank the gods his paranoia had been such that he'd known one day he'd need evidence.

Experience had taught him not to keep it anywhere his family could get to it. Any place someone might stumble on it and out him.

Choking on bile and bitterness, and a potent rage that he hadn't tasted in a long time, he finally entered the vörgäte and headed to the cell that had been reserved exclusively for his numerous stays here.

As he walked through the doorway of the tiny cell that was still decorated with his blood, a wave of painful memories hit him so forcefully that for a moment, he thought he might go down with it. His breathing became labored and for a moment, he was that child again. All the years of hopelessness. Of fear and horror.

Those feelings of being unwanted. Unloved. Undeserving of anything, even compassion or mercy.

Damn, how many years would have to go by before he could let this shit go?

Disgusted, he refused to think about it. Or them. They didn't matter anymore. None of them did. It was all in the past.

*Think of Ushara. Vas.*

*The babies . . .*

That was the present. Not this shit-hole. But it was harder than even he had thought it would be. Damn.

Breathing slow and easy, he knelt on the floor next to the commode and removed the bricks from behind the bottom of it where he'd burrowed a small hiding spot. He'd once risked life and limb to secret the chips he'd stored down here.

And for a moment, he could see himself as a boy again, feel the pain of their cruelty ringing in his heart and ears. Tears stung his throat as he glanced around the walls where he'd carved the words *JULLIEN IN-DURARI* with his claws, over and over again to help himself stay sane.

It hadn't helped. Not really.

All he'd wanted was one day of peace. One family member to reach out to him and show him kindness. A modicum of compassion or care.

They never had.

Brushing at his eyes and refusing to let them have another minute of his life, he cleared his throat and tucked the chips in his pocket. As fast as he could, he got out of the hole he'd hated with every fiber of his being.

Without thinking and because he was so upset, he made a wrong turn in the tunnels and came out inside the palace, instead of near the river where he was supposed to.

*Shit!*

He'd instinctively headed toward his old bedroom. *That* wouldn't have been so bad, except the door locked behind him and there was no way to access tunnels from this side without it being really obvious, since he was right outside the door for the head of the royal guard. And the only other access point was inside the tadara's bedchamber.

Yeah . . .

His mother or one of her staff would definitely notice if he were to walk into her bedroom and access the doorway there.

With no choice except to brazen this out, he held his head high and put on his best royal swagger, then headed for the front of the palace.

"Excuse me?"

*Titana ræl . . .*

Grinding his teeth, Jullien inwardly cringed at the sound of Kelsei's deep, hostile voice. He turned ever so slightly toward her and prayed she didn't recognize him. "Yes?"

"Who are you, and what are you doing here?"

"I was separated from my tour group. Just trying to locate them."

She narrowed her gaze on him. "What's your name and caste?"

*Shit.* Time to get really brazen.

And extremely stupid.

He pulled his glasses down to show her his stralen eyes and let his sleeve fall back to discreetly reveal the tattoo on his arm that would add veracity to his lie. "I'm a War Hauk, obviously. Another reason I just want to get out of here. *Mu* Ger Tarra thought this would be amusing, and I just find it uncomfortable and in poor taste. So if you could point me to the nearest exit, I won't bother you anymore."

Kelsei relaxed and actually turned kind. Wow. He'd never witnessed a non-bitch expression on her face before. She was actually quite beautiful. No wonder Tylie was so devoted to her. He saw the attraction now. "I should have known, given your size and build, and carriage. What made you leave the military?"

"Merrell Anatole," he said, throwing his cousin under a shuttle since Merrell had single-handedly chased most of the Hauks out of the armada. And every Anatole and Hauk knew it.

"Oh. My apologies, Gűr Tana, if I dredged up any bad memories."

Jullien didn't speak as they literally came face-to-face with Tylie who entered the hallway in front of them.

*Son of a bitch, can't I catch one break today?*

"Where have you been, Kels? I need—" Tylie's sentence stopped as she saw Jullien. She scowled. "Do I know you?"

Kelsei smiled pleasantly. "He's a War Hauk. Came in with a tour group and got lost. I'm showing him out."

Tylie said something else, but Jullien wasn't paying attention to her. He was staring up at Nyk, who was holding one of his sons as he and an obviously pregnant Kiara walked by on the landing above them. With her arm wrapped through Nyk's, their mother laughed and joked with his brother and Kiara. Now, there was a kick to the stones Jullien could have seriously done without.

*What? Were the gods fucking bored today?*

In that moment, he felt every single rejection and slap his family had ever given him. All at once. They hit him with a massive hurricane force that left him breathless and dizzy.

Weak and reeling.

*Damn you all to Tophet!*

*And damn me.*

Needing to withdraw, he started to turn away when his gaze fell to a servant.

No, not a servant. He was too attentive to everything around him. Too ripped. And he was wearing boots with sliding heels that were custom-made to conceal blades. The kind of boots used by assassins, seaxes, and Tavali. Having been on the run for the last five years, Jullien had learned well to spot bastards like him in a crowd.

And while he wasn't the target today, he knew the assassin was most likely going for Nykyrian, who was distracted by his family.

Without a second thought, Jullien ran for the beast and tackled him. The assassin came up with a blaster. And when he did, he revealed three of his friends in the room, who moved to cover him.

Nykyrian rushed his mother and wife across the landing to safety while Jullien disarmed the first one. He twisted the blaster out of his hand, then knocked him unconscious. Guards fired on the other two while Jullien shot the last one.

Then he quickly dropped his weapon and held his hands up so that no one misunderstood his intentions.

"It's okay!" Kelsei shouted to the guards. "He's the one who saw the attack coming. Don't shoot him!"

Jullien heard footsteps rushing down the stairs. His stomach shrank at the sound. Glancing up, he saw Nyk headed straight for his position.

Unlike Tylie, his brother wasn't an idiot. Nyk would definitely ID him.

Jullien bolted for the nearest door and didn't stop running for blocks. Not until his sides ached so much, he couldn't breathe, and he was sure no one was following him. Only then did he slow down and wheeze in an effort to catch his breath again.

Grateful he'd made it out, he headed back for the fighter.


It was almost midnight before Jullien made it home. He opened the door, trying to be as quiet as possible so as not to wake Ushara or Vas.

But once he shut and locked the door and turned around, he froze. Ushara was asleep on the couch underneath a huge HAPPY BIRTHDAY banner that Vasili and Nadya and her sisters must have made for him. And speaking of, Vas and Nadya were curled up on the floor near an uneven cake that had *Happy Birthday* scribbled on it in writing that must have been Nadya's attempt with someone else's help. It also had a Nadya-sized bite taken out of it.

His throat tight, he took a quick picture of them before he slowly crossed the room to brush the hair back from Ushara's face.

She came awake with a start. "Hey, baby."

He kissed her cheek. "Looks like someone was busy."

Her face pinkened. "We wanted to surprise you. I can't believe we fell asleep."

"Definitely surprised. It's beautiful."

Rubbing at her eyes, she sat up. "Why didn't you tell me it was your birthday?"

He shrugged nonchalantly. "They've never meant much to me. Since my mother was ill while I was growing up, no one ever celebrated mine. They came and went without comment."

She scowled at him. "You've never had a party?"

He shook his head. "Just this one." He smiled at her. "It's my favorite by far."

Her expression turned weepy as she cupped his face in her hands.

She scratched playfully at his whiskers. "At least you came home un-scathed this time."

"I did. See, you *can* let me out of your sight."

"I don't know if I'd go *that* far."

As Jullien started to pick her up to carry her to the bedroom, some-thing fell to the floor. He scooped it up and frowned. "What's this?"

"Your present."

He opened the tiny box to find a black wedding ring with the Sa-mari family symbols engraved over it. Tears choked him at the sight. "It's incredible."

"I tracked it down through an auction house. It actually belonged to your gre paran, Adron Samari. Look inside it."

Jullien tilted it so that he could see the engraving. As he read the words, his throat tightened with a fierce rush of overwhelming love and gratitude for the female before him.

KITRÍEWE GEVYLHYT YVONA HÆFRE STRADA ROWGH
FAUR LORINAS SĂLBATIC GEVAAR PRAEGU.

It was an old Andarion saying—*True love will always find its way through paths where even feral lorinas fear to prey.*

"I don't know what to say."

She tugged gently at his hair. "Well . . . you can always start by ex-plaining to me why you were at the Andarion palace yesterday."

His jaw went slack in shock. "What?"

"I'm not an idiot, Jules. I saw the newsfeed about the mysterious Hauk hero who helped stop an assassination attempt. While the footage is blurry, I know my husband when I see him. Now, you can tell me the truth or I can pull the logs on everyone's ships. If that doesn't work, I'll interrogate my sister and she'll crack like an egg. Mary fears me."

He sat back on his haunches. "Shara—"

"I know something happened with your family while you were miss-ing. Whatever it is, I can help. But you have to trust me. You're not alone, Jules. Not anymore. I am here for you."

He looked away as fear and anger tore through him. "It's not that easy, Shara. You don't know what they're capable of."

"And you've no idea what I'll do to protect my family, and that includes you." She took his hand and led it to her stomach. "I want you here to see your children born. More than that, I want you to help me raise them. But I can't help you or protect myself or Vas if I don't know what's coming for us. If you really love or respect me, then you have to trust me enough to be honest about what's going on."

She was right, and he knew it. But it was so hard.

Taking her hands into his, he held them and choked on the words. "I can't lose you, Shara. You are all I have in this life."

A tear slid down her cheek as she took his ring and slid it on his finger. "And you are my heart."

Nodding, he lifted her hand to his lips and kissed it, then forced himself to do the one thing he'd never done before.

He trusted her with the whole truth. "Nyran is the bastard son of Braxen Venik."

Her jaw went slack. "What?"

Jullien let out a tired sigh. "I had no idea they were related. He's the one who had the finger planted in Vasili's backpack. He has spies everywhere. Apparently, he went to hide with his father after his mother died, and Merrell and Chrisen were killed in the Ring by Talyn Batur. When I left Andaria, he was in jail with his two brothers Talyn later killed. His father or Tavali brothers must have helped him escape. Once I came here, he found me through them."

"What does he want?"

"Me to help him and his Tavali brothers unseat Trajen."

Her jaw dropped again.

"Relax. I have no intention of hurting Trajen for that piece of shit. I know better than to ever trust Nyran. But . . . as Tavali, he is able to come and go here. As are any of his Porturnum brethren. We can't ban them from the station."

"No. So why did you go to Andaria?"

"I grabbed some files I had hidden as self-preservation. Recorded conversations. Some of them, I'd already turned over to WAR years ago to help overthrow my grandmother and save Talyn. But I didn't have copies until now. Others only I knew about. They're of Nyran and his brothers scheming against the Hauk family. I was thinking of leveraging them against him."

"How so?"

"I found out Fain Hauk is also Porturnum Tavali. I'm thinking that if he finds out Nyran helped to hide his son from him, he'll kill him for me."

"And where does that leave you in Hauk's affections?"

"Probably in the grave next to Nyran."

"Unacceptable."

Jullien sighed as he rubbed her hands against his chin. He had to make her understand what they were dealing with. "Baby, listen. I know my cousin. If I don't do this, he will come after everything we love. He's insane on a level you can't even begin to comprehend."

Ushara saw true fear for the first time in his eyes. There was something more to all of this than just the backpack. Something deep and dark in Jullien's past. "What did he do to you?"

Tears filled his eyes, but he quickly blinked them away. "I won't go there. They won't own another minute of my soul. I couldn't stop them in the past. There's no way I'm going to let them have your future. Or mine."

"And before you go off half-cocked, let me give you info you don't have. Venik owns Fain Hauk. Even though he's a Rogue, Fain won't cross Venik. I don't know why or what for. But I'm telling you right now that there's something really weird about their relationship. If Nyran is Venik's son, Ven will protect him with everything he has, and Hauk will do whatever Ven says."

"Then what do I do?"

"We pull your cousin in. Set him up, and we cut his throat. Here. Away from his father. But we do it together."

Laughing, Jullien rose up on his knees to cup her face in his hand. "I can't believe how lucky I am to have my bloodthirsty Pavakahira."

She nipped his chin as she lifted his shirt to brush her hands over his stomach. "Blood's not the only thing I thirst for."

He sucked his breath in sharply.

"Basha Dagger?"

Jullien spun away from Ushara as he heard Nadya's sleepy voice. "Hey, *mia*."

She stumbled across the floor to fall against his chest. "Happy birthday."

"Thank you." But she was already asleep again.

Ushara laughed in his ear as she leaned over his shoulder to peek at the sleeping girl. "She loves you so much. She's already told the entire family that when she's old enough, she wants you to be her captain and train her for citizenship."

"It would be my honor, provided I have *mine* by then. Though at the rate I'm going, I might still be training under her."

Ushara laughed.

Rising with Nadya in his arms, he carried her to the guest room and put her to bed while Ushara woke Vasili. Jullien came out just in time to take over putting Vas to bed.

Like Nadya, Vas was still groggy. "You want me to carry you, *luden*?"

Vas shook his head as he stumbled into his room and fell across his bed.

Jullien tucked him under his covers and was about to turn the lights out when he noticed the troubled expression on Vasili's face. "What's wrong?"

Rubbing at his eyes in a manner freakishly similar to Ushara whenever she was tired, he frowned at Jullien. "Mum and Oxana started ordering things for the nursery today."

"Yeah?"

"It just got me thinking."

"About?"

Vas dropped his gaze to his hand, which he wound in the blanket. "They were arguing if they should make it ready for boys or girls. I hadn't really thought about it before now, but then I did, and I . . ." He pursed his lips as tears swam in his eyes. "I know that when the babies get here that you won't love me the same way anymore."

"Whoa!" Jullien snapped as he stepped back into the room. "What? Where did *this* come from?"

Tears fell from his eyes. "It's what everyone says about stepkids. I know I'm not your blood son. And—"

"Stop right there." Jullien braced his arms on each side of Vasili and stared down at him. "*Mi tana,* how could you *ever* think for even a nanosecond that I wouldn't love you as much? Boy, girl, mutant rabbit, I don't care. I will love whatever your mother gifts me with, but you will *always* be my firstborn child that she allowed me to love."

Vas started to roll his eyes, but Jullien caught his chin and forced him to meet his gaze.

"Listen to me, *akam*. Fathers normally give their sons life. You, Vasili, gave me mine. Do you understand that? Do you think a single day goes by that I don't look at you and feel an overwhelming love and gratitude for everything you've given me?"

Tenderly, he brushed away Vas's tears. "I was dying in that bar, that day. I wouldn't have lived another hour. Now, because of *you,* I have a home and an unbelievable family." He chucked him on the chin. "And the most incredible son, who fills me with absolute fatherly pride every time I look at him. I love you, Vasili. I do."

Jullien pulled his knife from his boot. "And if it's the blood that bothers you . . ." He laid the blade against his palm and cut it, then took Vasili's hand and made a smaller slice on his. Placing them together, he allowed their blood to mingle. "There now. You are blood of my blood. My true son."

Vas sat up with a sob and hugged him. "I love you, Paka."

"Love you, too. No matter how many other sons and daughters we have. I will always love *you.* And you will always be my firstborn." He kissed him on the head.

When Vas pulled back, Jullien saw the dark shadow in his eyes.

"What else is on your mind?"

He glanced at the door before he lowered his voice to a whisper. "Can I tell you a secret?"

"Of course."

Vas swallowed hard before he spoke again. "On the night my father died, he almost killed me."

Jullien went cold. "What?"

He nodded. "I've never told anyone that. Please don't tell Matarra. It's why I didn't speak for the longest time. Why I've been withdrawn for so long. My paran held a blaster pointed at me and threatened to kill me. Those are my last memories of my own father. That's why I saved you in the bar. 'Cause you had no reason to stand up for me. But you did. You did what my own father refused to do."

Jullien silently cursed that Vas still had the memory Trajen had meant to erase from the child. "I'll never let anyone hurt you, Vas."

"I know. And I'm glad you're my paka."

Jullien hugged him again before he tucked him back into bed and turned out the light.

Honestly, he didn't know what disturbed him most. The fact that Vas remembered that night when he shouldn't, or that Trajen's powers weren't as well-honed as Trajen and everyone else thought they were.

It meant that their fearless leader could be defeated. Not that he had any ambitions in that area. Far from it.

And speaking of . . .

Trajen was waiting for him in the hallway.

Jullien pulled up short as he caught sight of him. "Should I ask what brings *you* here?"

"Sure. Heard you were planning to unseat me. So I'm here to kill you."

# CHAPTER 23

Jullien stepped back, ready to fight.

Trajen burst out laughing. "Wow . . . you took me seriously. Damn, boy, you really do have some severe trust issues."

"*Titana tu, tu cocúpün caxam—*"

"Hey now, simmer down. I cannot believe you kiss my vice admiral with that mouth. Why so hostile over a joke?"

Jullien glared at him. "You're lucky I didn't shoot you just then."

"Yeah. Glad the wife makes you disarm when you come in the door. Otherwise, she'd be cleaning stains off the wall and I'd be friendless again. Though I'm not sure what we have qualifies as friendship . . . since it's been too long since I had one, and you have no experience whatsoever in that department to draw on."

"Yeah, and I'm beginning to understand why I'm a solitary beast. Friends like you? I don't need them."

"Ah now, that's just hurtful. Careful or your wife'll force us to kiss and make up."

"What is going on out here?" Ushara arched a brow as she joined them. "You sound like two toddlers fighting. Do I need to separate you?"

Trajen tucked his hands into his pockets. "I was trying to tease your mate, but he's in a foul little mood. You should have warned me to bring a rabies shot and muzzle."

Jullien snorted irritably. "I'm always in a foul *minsid* mood. Haven't you noticed that the crews I deal with all leave sweets on my desk like frightened villagers making an offering to a vengeful god?"

"You know, they make meds for Irritable Bitch Syndrome. Maybe you should consider seeing a doctor about that?" Trajen said with a hint of laughter in his tone, which caused Jullien to roll his eyes. "And now that you say that, Sheila has mentioned it to me. And the fact that she pays tribute to you with pastries and coffee herself, which given her charming personality says a lot about *yours.* Anyway——" Trajen cleared his throat as he glanced to Ushara. "——you summoned me from the bowels of my pit, mistress?"

She gestured toward the living room. "Is what I suggested to you doable at all?"

Trajen led the way. "No."

"Why not?"

"He's hybrid. There's not a doctor in the universe who would touch him. We've no idea how his genetics would react to it. Or what to do for him if there were any complications."

Jullien glanced between them, curious about this new line of discussion about his body and well-being, that neither one had seen fit to include him in on. "What are you talking about?"

"Ushara wanted to make you a Rogue. Which we can't do anyway unless you're a Canted citizen. Besides——" Trajen returned his attention to Ushara. "——you know the stats for survival on mentally stable, well-adjusted Rogues are slim. You really want to chance that with Captain Happy over there?"

Jullien made an obscene gesture at him.

"And thus my earlier point over the IBS was duly illustrated with juvenile glee."

Ushara ignored the two of them as she struggled to keep them on point. Some days, her job as Trajen's VA was more like herding squirrels with ADD through busy intersections. And Trajen could be the king of squirrelly squirrels. "So what do we do?"

"I have a suggestion, but you——" Trajen gave her a pointed stare. "——are not going to like it. Not sure our Jules will be any happier with it."

"What?" they asked in unison.

"Teterrimous."

She scowled. "Bless you."

Trajen snorted at her.

But Jullien knew exactly what he meant. "I thought that was a myth."

He shook his head. "No. *We* had the tech. Remember, the Tris are the ones who invented space travel, Verkehrs, AI, intergalactic communications, modern robotics, *and* time travel. We didn't just have the tech. We made the tech that made the tech possible."

Ushara felt completely lost in their conversation. "What specific tech are you talking about, though? I've never heard of this."

Jullien sat with his elbows braced on his knees and stroked his whiskers with his thumb while he considered it. "To merge consciousness with machines."

Now she was even more confused. "You mean AI?"

Trajen shook his head. "And by the look on Jullien's face, I think he's seen what I'm talking about. Although I have no idea how, since we keep a vicious guard on who gets our tech these days. And there's less than a dozen of us left alive who know how to do it, or even that it exists."

Jullien dropped his hand from his face. "Jupiter Hinto. His ship runs on it, doesn't it? It's how he flies the way he does."

Trajen nodded.

"I knew there was something weird about the *Ship of Fools* . . . so what all does it entail? How do you do it?"

"With our powers, and *I* can't do it. But I know who can."

Ushara bit her lip as fear cramped her stomach. "Is it safe?"

"If Jullien goes through the training and does what he's told, yes. But if he fights it and doesn't listen, there's always a chance it could fry his brain and leave him a vegetable."

She scoffed at his words. "Well, then, that's not an option."

"What *exactly* do they do?"

Ushara turned an angry glare toward the maniac. "No, Jules, I don't like the way this sounds."

"Shara . . ."

She growled at him. "Have you met yourself? There's no way you're going to obey anyone and not fight whatever they say. Just because they said it, you won't do it. You're hardwired for rebellion. You can't help yourself."

Trajen didn't respond to her comment as he answered Jullien's question. "There's a small implant they'll have to make. Similar to being chipped, but it won't interact with your body. It's a booster for your brain's electrical impulses that will allow you to communicate with certain devices, and you'll have to wire your ship. Think of it like a networking signal."

Biting her lip, Ushara shook her head. "I don't want him put in harm's way, especially if it's harm he could bring upon himself with his disposition and mouth."

Jullien gave her a droll stare. "Gee, thanks, love. Appreciate your support."

She returned his stare tit for tat. "Oh, like you don't know. You're the first to admit it."

Trajen laughed. "So what exactly is Nyran asking you to do, anyway?"

Jullien handed over his link. "He wants meetings and the things he's asking me for require that I go alone. I don't want anyone else with me that he could use for leverage. Plus, he claims to have eyes on me here. So I don't know who to trust."

Trajen spent a few minutes reading through Nyran's messages before he handed the link to Ushara. "He's right. While I agree with you that Jullien needs to learn a bit more about teamwork, there's still a time and place for solo. This would be it. But what I'm suggesting will allow us to be with him from a distance. We can still run point. It's the only solution, really."

He gave Ushara a moment to read through the threats Nyran had made against them before he spoke again. "And let me explain something. . . . This isn't easy for me, either. I'm trusting you both with a part of my past and with someone I swore I'd never open up to anyone else. I'm not taking this step lightly. I only trust Jullien because he knows the cost of betrayal. And you both know how I'll react to it."

"And I've got no place else to go."

Trajen snorted. "There is that."

Ushara turned the link off. "I still don't like it."

"I know." Trajen sighed heavily. "But you know I wouldn't suggest this if I didn't feel it necessary. There is absolutely no one else I'd ever offer this to. And I do mean no one."

Ushara choked on her tears as she considered every negative scenario that could go wrong. Not to mention the fact that her life was a case study in disasters that defied the odds and should have never occurred. "How long will it take?"

"About two hours. But the training will take a few months. He'll have to be away for it."

And that stung even more.

Jullien took her hand. "I will be here for you when the babies are born. Come Tophet or Koriłon, nothing will keep me from your side."

She laced her fingers with his and met Trajen's gaze with determination. "I want to be there when it's done to him."

"Shara—"

She held her hand up at Jullien. "I won't give on this. If you're going to be stupid, I want to be there to support it and beat you should it go wrong."

Jullien lifted her hand and kissed it. "There's the sane, rational female I fell in love with. Glad to hear her voice of reason."

Trajen laughed again. "You two get some rest. I have to make contact with someone who's going to be less receptive to the idea than Ushara, and arm-wrestle him to the ground for it. So it'll be a couple of days before we have to leave."

"What about Nyran?" Jullien asked. "I need to tell him something to keep him from getting suspicious."

"I've got information you can give him to string him along. I'll send it over to your link."

"Thanks."

He inclined his head. "Oh—and, Shar? Ignore your sisters' earlier words of wisdom. Go with your gut. This one'll be fine for the nursery. The babies will love it." He pushed one of the paint cards on the coffee table toward her, and with that, he literally vanished.

Tears filled her eyes as she looked down and saw which card Trajen had chosen.

"We're having daughters." She held up the light pink paint swatch she'd desperately wanted, but her sisters had all thrown a fit about it being too early to choose colors yet. "I hope you didn't have your heart set on a son."

Jullien shook his head. "I already have a great son, thanks to you. All I ask is that our beans are healthy. Nothing else matters to me."

Ushara got up and tugged at Jullien's hand until he stood and allowed her to take him back to their bedroom. "You're not mad at me for calling Trajen, are you?"

He drew his brows together into a stern expression. "I would never be angry at you for loving me enough to try and protect me. I've waited a lifetime for someone to care."

Those words broke her heart. And it made her realize something about his trip. . . . "Are you all right? It had to be hard to go home again."

"That was never my home. It was only the place I was once forced to live."

Wincing silently at those words, she knew the pain his dry tone concealed. She couldn't imagine feeling that way about her childhood home. While it wasn't large, and no longer held much of her personal items, it still made her warm inside to be there. Like walking into an all-body hug. The sights. The smells. Everything about it soothed her and brought back the happiest memories from her past.

But then, Jules never felt like a part of his own family. They had never given him those gifts of warmth and security. The gifts of love and acceptance.

And they'd never treated him like a member of their family. He'd been shut out his entire life. An unwanted stranger.

"Did any of them see you?"

He laughed bitterly. "Actually, I had a conversation with my aunt and her partner. They had no idea who I was."

Her jaw dropped in shocked disbelief. "Seriously?"

"Yeah. Tylie would have arrested me immediately had she known. Kelsei would have shot me again."

How could they not recognize him? He hadn't changed *that* much. But then, they'd never cared or even looked at him. The fact they could stand that close to him and not know him said it all.

Their indifference disgusted her. Try as hard as she could, she just couldn't imagine a family that didn't love or protect its own.

Especially an Andarion one, where blood, heritage, tradition, and lineage were everything.

When she started for the bed, Jullien caught her. With the gentlest of touches, he pulled her against him and pressed his cheek to hers. He didn't say a word. He merely held her against him in a tight embrace.

Ushara felt more tears gather in her eyes. This was how he coped now whenever he was deeply and emotionally hurt. Without words.

Because he'd never had anyone care for him, there had been a time when he hadn't reached out for her, but he'd finally gotten past that. Finally learned to trust her enough to seek comfort in her arms whenever something bothered him.

Closing her eyes, she savored the warmth of his body against hers. The scent of his skin. He was so incredibly strong and independent that it made her weepy to know she was the only comfort he craved whenever he was hurt. She, alone, was his security blanket that he needed to have by his side. She suspected it was why he never complained whenever she burrowed her icy feet against his warm skin. So long as her feet were there, he knew she was with him.

But the moment she no longer touched him, he awakened instantly. And wouldn't settle down again until she returned to bed.

Jullien nuzzled his face against her neck. "Thank you for my birthday," he whispered against her ear. "And thank you for my life."

Pulling back, she smiled up at him. "You don't have to thank me. I'm so grateful to have you. It's why I'm afraid that something's going to tear you away from me like it did Chaz."

"I'm not going anywhere. I have nowhere else to go. Besides, I'm hard to kill."

She narrowed her gaze at him. "You're not funny." She pulled his shirt over his head and hesitated as she saw the scars on his body that bore out the truth of his words. Her Jules was a fighter.

Fierce. Determined. Lethal and skilled.

And though he was definitely hard to kill, he wasn't invincible. She knew that, and it terrified her. It was, after all, how they'd met. He'd been on the verge of death that day.

While she had no doubt he'd fight to the bitter end, it didn't change the fact that the unthinkable could happen. And Nyran's threats against him were harsh and horrid.

His grandmother's even more so.

She ground her teeth. "We will find Nyran and we will end him."

"It's not just him we have to worry about. It's his Tavali brothers. You saw the e-mails. They will come after me if I kill him. I can't ask the Gorturnum to go to war with the Porturnum for me. And I doubt they would. I'm still not accepted by the majority here. I don't have my citizenship. And half your family still refuses to talk to you or even look at us."

"It's not the good half."

"Shara . . ."

Sighing, she hated the fact that he was right. Even her brother Dimitri was siding with Kirill. Because of Jules, he refused to come home so long as they harbored him. His wife was so mad at her right now, she was lucky Madina hadn't poisoned her food on temple days.

Jullien cupped her face in his hands and pressed his forehead against hers. "I'm so sorry that I brought disharmony to your family."

Those words choked her, as did the anguish in his voice. On Andaria, the role of a male was to keep peace in his home, at all costs. To protect his family and guard them against all threats. It was impressed upon them from the moment of birth. For females, it was to protect the sanctity of their bloodlines and lineage, and to keep it sacred.

While Ixurian males were expected and encouraged to fight and rage against others, they were never to bring that fury home to their families.

*Ypasunga bafthrex. Crossing the threshold.* That was the term they had for it. Once a male entered his home or that of any family member, he was to immediately check his emotions and restrain himself. Failure to do so was considered an act of flagrant dishonor against his lineage and was considered highly shameful. Such behavior was corrected swiftly and harshly by his family—male and female. It could even cause a male to be disinherited.

And for a male to allow others to disrupt the harmony of his home was an even greater shame to his honor and name. Failure to maintain peace within the family and home was the leading cause of suicide in their society among their males—second only to debilitating injuries that the males felt made them a burden to their families. Harsh customs and beliefs she'd never personally agreed with, but it was all Jullien knew. All he'd been shown.

Rigid rules in a harsh, unforgiving, martial society.

Pulling back again, she stared up at him so that he could see the sincerity in her eyes. "You have brought nothing but happiness to my home and heart. What they have chosen to bring here is on them. You are never to take responsibility for their hatefulness."

She took his hand and led it to her stomach, where their unborn children slept in safety. "I never thought to find another male I could love at all, and what I found was one who showed me a whole new depth to that emotion that I didn't even know existed. One I cannot live without. I need you, Jules. I cannot imagine my life without you, and I don't want to ever go back to *that* existence."

Jullien sucked his breath in sharply as those words made his heart speed up and she dropped her hand to cup him through his pants. He dipped his head to kiss her while she slowly opened his fly to stroke him. She had no idea what she did to him whenever she loved him like this. What the warmth of her hand on his body meant. The fact that she would face him, and explore his scarred body while they made love, and accept him . . .

Grinding his teeth, he toed his boots off while he kissed her, and she peeled his pants down his body. He lifted her gown over her head before he picked her up and set her on the bed.

He slowly took his time sampling her breasts, savoring each one until he was drunk from the scent of her skin and taste of her.

When he started to move lower, she tugged playfully at his cheek and wrinkled her nose. "Your whiskers are getting so thick."

"What?"

She nodded with a serious scowl. "You're becoming quite woolly."

After kissing her rounded stomach, he crawled up her body to flash his fangs at her. "I thought you liked me woolly."

She brushed her hands through his chest hair. "I do, but there's a fine line between sexy and stalker." She returned her hand to tug at his chin. "Two more days, you'll be scaring small children."

Laughing, he nipped playfully at her fingers. "Fine. I'll shave in the morning. Unless you want me to stop now and take care of it." He started to roll away, but she caught him between her legs to keep him right where he was.

"I can live with it for the night." She rolled him to his back so that she straddled him.

Jullien's breath left him in a rush as he felt her wetness against his stomach. Even now, he couldn't believe that she allowed him so much freedom in her bed. That she accepted him as he was, and that his hideous body didn't bother her in the least. After a lifetime of females who saw him as deformed and revolting, he still had the urge to hide at times and rush to be done as quickly as possible so as not to bother her with his biological needs.

But Shara wouldn't let him do that. She forced him into the light so that he could see he wasn't the freakish monster they'd made him out to be. For whatever bizarre reason, she enjoyed his company.

And she loved him, even with his flaws and scars.

Her eyes hooded, she smiled down at him as she slid herself onto him.

He growled at how good she felt. She rode him so slowly that it was sheer, exquisite torture. Closing his eyes, he lifted his hips, driving himself as deep into her as he could. *"Kimu tu, mu kitríewan."*

She took his hand into hers and kissed his palm. "I love you, too." Sadness darkened her eyes as she ran her fingers over his tattoo and the scars it covered. Scars she pressed to her lips while she made love to him.

Jullien trembled at the sight of her kissing his wrist. Her faithful heart humbled him to the core of his rotten soul. He'd felt so hopeless and alone the night he tried to kill himself. In that hour of absolute misery, where he'd been slammed down so hard that he thought he'd never rise up again, he'd been unable to conceive of a moment like this. Of having a female like Ushara to share his life with.

And he wasn't about to let his family take it from him. Not without a brutal blood-match.

As gently as he could, he rolled with her and pinned her beneath him so that he could bury his face in her neck and inhale her warm sweet scent while she wrapped her body around his. This was what he loved best. The feeling of being cocooned by her while he was inside her.

Ushara wrapped her legs around Jullien's hips as she felt the change in his mood. She laid her hand against his cheek while he kissed her and intensified his thrusts.

Like this, she could feel every muscle in his body rippling. It'd taken her forever to convince him that he could lay his weight on her and not hurt her. That she welcomed it. Yet even so, he was still very careful with her, as if afraid he'd inadvertently crush her with his weight. While it was true that Andarion males were massive beasts with dense bones and muscle mass, she wasn't exactly frail.

And honestly, there was nothing she loved more than their handful of private moments when she saw a side of Jullien that no one else did. A side that he kept for her alone. Here, he was vulnerable. Gone was any hint of arrogance or bluster. That protective layer of barbed sarcasm he used to push everyone away vanished entirely. He was so incredibly sweet and loving. Thoughtful. Even timid and bashful.

If anyone else came near, his defenses came up immediately and shattered this version of him that he kept solely for her. Not even Vasili was given the privilege of this Jullien. The father he saw was very loving and respectful of him, but also stern when he had to be. Jullien never let Vas forget that he was the elder male or see that he had any vulnerabilities. Rather, he remained steadfast and strong in all matters.

*"Just because I changed my opinion about him doesn't change the fact that I'm still right, and you can't go."* She laughed as she remembered a mini argument Jullien and Vas had had over a friend of Vas's.

Jullien lifted his head to frown at her. "Do I want to know why you're laughing at me while we're having sex?"

Smiling, she kissed him. "Love you, my sweet. Only thinking of how precious you are."

"And that made you laugh?"

"Would you rather I cry?"

"No, that would definitely be worse for my ego."

Laughing again, she nipped his throat and then his chin and ear. "Is this helping to show that I'm not laughing at you or your awesome skills, baby?"

Jullien sucked his breath in sharply as she did the most wicked things with her tongue while she cupped and squeezed him. He wasn't sure if he'd ever get used to her lighthearted ways in bed. She liked to tease and have fun, but his knee-jerk reaction was to assume she was mocking him and to take offense at it. Though he was slowly getting better about it, it was still sometimes hard for him to hear laughter and not think it was meant to ridicule.

Yet all he had to do was look into her eyes, and he saw the truth. There was no ridicule there. No hatred or disdain.

Only love and acceptance.

And only Ushara looked at him that way. No one else. Ever.

"You are so beautiful," he breathed an instant before he watched her scream out in release. He moved even faster, heightening her pleasure and waiting until she was completely finished to join her.

And when he came, he buried his face in her hair and let the softness of it and her body welcome him to the first real home he'd ever known.

In the quiet peacefulness, he held her. Until his link went off with an irritating sound that made him want to splinter the damn thing against the wall.

"Davel?" she asked as he reached for it.

It was normally who disturbed them. Her brother had an unerring ability to know when they were in bed together.

Reluctantly, he slid out of her and reached for his link on the nightstand. He flipped it on and froze. "No. It's my grandmother."

"What?" She sat up with a gasp to look at it over his shoulder.

He held the link so that she could see it. His breathing ragged, he tried to contain his rage, but it was impossible. Every word made him even more furious until all he could do was crave eton Anatole blood.

So help him, if he ever laid hands to his family again, he'd rip them apart. . . .

*Since you've proven yourself worthless to me, time and again, I had originally in-*
*tended for you to rot in your impoverished misery. But you couldn't let well*
*enough alone. Therefore, I shall have to punish you for your treacherous interfer-*
*ence. Know that you've brought this on yourself. And that you have a choice to*
*make—stay out of my way and live with your little whore, or continue to protect*
*your brother. Every time you stop me, I will take a pound of your flesh for it.*

"What does she mean, *a pound of your flesh?*"

"I have no idea. As a boy, it would have meant some quality time spent in the *vörgäte.*"

"Her private prison?"

He nodded. "I have no idea where she is now. The picture Nylan sent was of the two of them inside a restaurant that could have been on any planet, in any city. All I know is that she was banned from Andaria. The Triosans wouldn't touch her. But we have extended family all over. And allies who would harbor her, including the Porturnum. She's a devious bitch, capable of anything."

Ushara watched as he began trying to backtrace the transmission. After a few minutes, his anger and frustration built to the point he lifted the link to slam it down.

She caught his hand. "If you destroy it, you'll never be able to use it against her."

Tears gathered in his eyes. "If she harms you . . . Shara . . ."

"She can't harm me, Jules. Don't even go there. I'm not your mother. I'm a warrior in my prime, and I won't underestimate her. But don't sell me short, either."

"My brain hears you. My heart, however, has no ears."

Her own tears choked her as she realized what this meant. "They're not going to leave us in peace, are they?"

"No. It's not in them to do so."

"What are we going to do?"

Jullien cupped her face in his hand. "Do you trust me?"

"With my life and everything I hold sacred."

"Then you're going to have to let me go and finish this."

Her heart sank at the lethal tone of his voice. "For how long?"

"As long as it takes to bury them."

Even though it killed her, she nodded.

# CHAPTER 24

Lararium?" Jullien turned his chair toward Trajen as they landed on what had to be the most remote outpost in the Nine Worlds.

It was so cold here, he didn't even know how it could sustain life. "Now, there's a name you don't see advertised in tourist brochures. Even *I* never made it out this far during my death-defying jaunts, running from League assassins."

Trajen gave him a caustic stare. "Good thing, too. As you would have been gutted on landing."

"By what? The imaginary ice cap people who can live without the all-crucial, life-sustaining atmosphere?"

Trajen didn't elaborate. "I know I'm asking a lot, but rein down your tongue. Stop playing hard to get along with. And remember that the individual you're about to meet can melt your brain, and has about as much prick tolerance as you do."

"Duly noted. May I ask how many live here have that special talent?"

"Since it only takes one having a bad hair day to kill you, do you need a precise head count?"

Not really, but Jullien was in a particularly spiteful mood at the moment and couldn't resist poking the irritable beast in front of him. "More than a handful, then?"

Ushara laughed. "Admit it, Tray. You have to love him. It's like having a giant toddler around with an autoresponder set to Annoy."

"Really don't." Trajen let out a low growl. "This might have been a mistake." Rising, he headed for the ramp. "Shall we get this slaughter over with?"

Jullien wasn't sure what he'd expected, but it damn sure wasn't *this*.

His jaw went slack as they stepped out into one of the most elaborate and advanced landing bays he'd ever seen.

And it did, in fact, have an atmosphere, contrary to what the schematics had read.

While the bay was small, it had tech the likes of which he'd never seen or heard of before. He'd kill for a tour of it.

*Stay focused.*

He arched a brow at Trajen's voice in his head. And as they walked through the area, he noticed they were attracting a lot of attention in spite of the jackets and hoods they wore.

Trajen ignored the people around them and forged ahead with long, deadly strides. Jullien matched him, but made sure that Ushara was keeping up with them, as he didn't want her to fall behind and get attacked by one of the humans here. There was something about them that didn't seem quite right.

Something that set him on edge and gave him an urge to slap them as they passed by to see if they'd react like people.

Or mechas.

Trajen didn't stop or slow until they were on the street, where three low, domed buildings were made of the strangest material Jullien had ever seen.

"What is *that*?"

Trajen glanced at the buildings and shrugged. "Keeps anyone from knowing there's life here. It also makes them think that this part of the planet is uninhabitable."

Ah, that explained the fictional readings. Damn. . . . If the surly HAP had access to all *this* insane technology, it begged one question— "So tell me, Tray . . . why are you Tavali again?"

Trajen drew up short with a harsh stare. "Don't ask questions you don't want to know the answer to." That tone said the subject was closed, and for once, Jullien backed off the topic.

His mood more severe and guarded than normal, Trajen took them into a small warehouse where a group was working on mechas. Only these were unlike anything on the market. Some were close enough to pass for human. As in, they were completely indistinguishable from humanity.

They were even perspiring.

Damn . . .

Jullien glanced to Ushara, and now he really wanted to go back outside and see if he'd been right. Had all those "people" on the street really been mechas instead?

"Hey! Badges!" A guard rushed to challenge them.

Trajen lowered his hood and gave the man a withering glare.

The guard immediately backed down and actually bowed. "Blessed Born, forgive me. I didn't know it was you I was addressing. How may I be of service?"

"Is Thrāix around?"

*I'm always around, but I'm not kneeling to your sorry ass. Bugger off.*

Jullien glanced about for the source of that deep, raspy voice. But he didn't see anything.

Trajen inclined his head to the guard. "Seems we found him. Thank you."

As soon as they'd walked away from the guard, Jullien cocked a brow at Trajen. "Oooh, aren't we the haughty bitch when we get back amongst our own?"

"Do I need a rolled-up newspaper to slap you with?"

"Good luck finding one around here. Besides, you smack my nose, it'll just compel me to piss on your leg for spite."

Sighing, Trajen met Ushara's amused gaze. "Can you please muzzle him?"

"I'm the one who tried to keep him at home. You brought him here, against my wishes. I told you not to have him in public. You know as well as I do that he completely flunked home-training. What were you thinking?"

"Trajen doesn't think. It's always been his shortcoming."

Ushara jumped at the deeply accented, disembodied voice that spoke beside her.

Jullien watched as a male manifested there who stood a good two inches taller than him—which was impressive, given his height. He also had the build and carriage of a well-trained soldier.

But not just an average soldier . . .

Special Forces.

It bled from his pores, as if he'd been carved from generations of military servicemen. Coming from a heavy martial society, Jullien could spot the breed from a mile away. Which was strange, given that the Trisani had always been a culture of peace.

But not this one.

The man locked gazes with him as if he knew exactly what Jullien was thinking—which, being Trisani, he most likely did. "Peace never fights, but I do."

"Never heard the latter part of that verse in the *Book of Harmony*."

"Fine, then. *Insecure peace is even worse than war. And peace maintained through fear and intimidation is the most malignant form of tyranny.*"

"As an Andarion, I couldn't agree more. War is our happy go-to place—*If there's a battle to be fought, let it be in my lifetime, that my children may sleep safely in peace, and dream of better days.* However, I always thought the Trisani national motto was—*In peace sons bury their fathers. In war, fathers bury their sons. Therefore, make me a weapon of peace, and where there is hatred, let me sow love.*"

"Sadly, it was. By the time our people realized we needed more soldiers than idiot politicians and philosophers with no real-world experience or understanding of their opposition's mind-set, it was too late to save us. They learned the hard way that it takes two to make peace, and only one bomb to destroy our world. That it's a complete waste of time and total insanity for cooing doves to try and negotiate peace with unreasoning jackals when they are hell-bent to feast on your bones."

Jullien nodded. "*Why did you bite me,* the fox asked the snake, *knowing we'll both drown and die now? . . .* And the snake answered, *Because it is ever my nature to do so.*"

Approving Jullien's Trisani quote, Thrāix saluted him with two fingers. "And speaking of jackals and snakes . . ." He turned to glare at Trajen. "I can't believe I let you talk me into this. Your father would be proud of your evil powers of persuasion. And you didn't even try to use your real powers on me. I'm just that fucking gullible."

"What evil power was this?" Ushara asked.

Trajen winked at her. "Guilt."

Thrāix snorted. "I didn't even know I could still feel that emotion. So double kudos." He met Jullien's gaze. "Are you completely sure you want to do this? Once we do it, there's no going back. Ever."

"What exactly are you doing to him? Trajen was a bit vague."

"Of course he was." Thrāix cut a peeved, gimlet stare toward Trajen before he softened his expression for Ushara. "We're rerouting and remapping part of your husband's brain. Opening up a trench, as it were."

She paled noticeably. "Trajen said there wouldn't be any surgery."

He inclined his head to her. "I don't need surgery. But it's not without risk. It takes total supplication to me. He fights me, it could cost him some brain cells."

"Jules," she said with a warning tone, "I don't think you're capable of doing that."

"I can do it."

Aghast, she gaped at him. "You're the most argumentative Androkyn ever born. Your first words to me on the day we met were that you're a contentious asshole."

"I can control it for this."

She shook her head in total disbelief before she turned back toward Thrāix. "Fine, but please make a note that I am *not* Trisani. Anything happens to my Jules, and your jewels are the first set I'm coming after."

Thrāix actually grinned at that. And then, shockingly, his eyes filled with tears. He swallowed hard as his smile faded.

Trajen stepped forward. "You all right?"

In truth, he looked as if he'd just been cold-cocked with a sledgehammer. His breathing ragged, he all but doubled over. "You're weren't kidding. I see now why you chose her. If she were a little taller . . . She looks just like her."

"Her?" Jullien asked.

"My wife." Thrāix cleared his throat and shook his head. He pulled out a small locket and opened it to show the photo to Jullien. Inside was the image of a female who bore a shocking resemblance to Ushara. Except her hair was darker and her eyes were a silvery-blue, and she didn't have fangs. Yet their features . . .

Damn.

"That's eerie."

Closing the locket, Thrāix returned it to his pocket. "Yeah, it is."

"Where is she?" Ushara asked.

Thrāix's eyes flashed red. "She was murdered."

Ushara touched his arm in sympathy. "I'm so sorry. My first husband was murdered. I know how hard it is to carry on after such tragedy."

He patted her hand. "I will make sure that you don't lose this one. Contentious asshole or not."

She laughed even as Jullien let out an irritated growl. "Can I go in with him when you do it? Since it's not surgery?"

Thrāix hesitated, then nodded. "It'll do him good to have you there, I think. You can help keep him calm for it."

"He's going to be awake?"

"Again, not surgery. He has to be awake while I do it." Thrāix passed a troubled look to Trajen that said they were speaking privately while Thrāix led them to a set of doors and into the rear of the building.

There, he showed them to a large sterile room with a hospital bed.

"Lie down and get as comfortable as you can."

Jullien reluctantly obeyed.

Ushara fluffed the pillow and ruffled his hair. "Don't bite the doctor."

Thrāix arched a brow at that. "The doctor bites back."

A blanket appeared on top of Jullien, reminding them of just how powerful Thrāix was with his powers.

Trajen stayed back, in a corner of the room. "What do you need me to do?"

"Nothing. You're here for his moral support and to help keep Jullien comfortable, since he doesn't know me. This is more about trust than anything else. He has to stay calm."

"It's really not *so* bad."

Jullien shot up at the familiar voice. "Jupiter?"

He came through another door to grin at them. "Hey, Jules." He inclined his head to Ushara as he approached the bed and shook Jullien's arm. "VA." Then he looked to Trajen. "HAP."

"What are you doing here?" Ushara asked.

Thrāix moved a tray closer to the bed. "I asked him to come, since Jullien knows him, and Jory went through this himself."

Ushara gaped. "How did *you* know about this procedure?"

"Me mother's part Trisani. Mack was actually born with the skills I had to be given. Chafes me arse quarters that I had to have this done, but in the end, me powers ended being stronger as a result of it."

Ushara chewed her lip. "Is it painful?"

"Stings a bit. Nothing too bad. Just a fierce headache for a few days. I doubt your male'll feel it at all. You've just got to stay in a happy place and don't be letting the darkness swallow you."

Thrāix pulled a chair up. "Ushara, if you'll take his hand? Jory . . . standby to help Trajen hold him should we need it."

They moved into position while Thrāix leaned over Jullien's head. "I'm going to touch you now, if you're ready?"

Jullien nodded.

Thrāix gently placed his hand on Jullien's forehead. "Just breathe deeply and close your eyes. Let me guide your thoughts and don't fight me. Ignore what you see. And follow me through, okay?"

"Okay." Jullien moved Ushara's hand to his heart while strange images and patterns floated through his mind. At first, nothing made sense. But that didn't last. He saw his past playing out in vivid, biting details.

*Shh,* Thrāix whispered in his head. *I'm with you,* kiran. *I'm not judging. Just move with me past it. We have to open this shit up to get where we need to go. Sorry about that.*

Jullien tensed as he saw himself in prison and felt the pain of it all anew. *Why am I here?*

Thrāix tightened his grip on him. *Part of the process. It's normal. We have to go through the temporal lobe before we move to the frontal. Unfortunately, it'll release kickback emotions and visions as we tunnel into it . . . from both of us.*

No sooner had Thrāix said that than Jullien saw what he meant. At first, Jullien thought it was Ushara, but as noted, Julia was taller and thinner, with blue, human eyes and dark hair.

And she was in a jail cell with both Thrāix and Trajen when they were all a lot younger. Thrāix and Trajen were trying to fight off guards who were dragging her away, but they were no match for the Chillers and the tech that had been specifically designed to negate their Trisani powers.

"Don't you touch my sister!" Trajen shouted, rushing them.

The guard nearest him caught him a blow that broke his jaw.

Thrāix attempted to blast him with his powers and ended up screaming out in pain as it damaged a part of his own brain.

Jullien flinched.

Thrāix tensed and released a shaky breath. *Calm down. It's my pain, not yours, brother.*

*I'm sorry, Thrāix.*

He felt Thrāix's jaw flexing next to his. *It's all right. We all got shit to deal with.*

And as their memories merged, Jullien realized just how much they did have in common. But not even that was enough to save him from the resurgence of his past as he was thrown back to the horrors of reliving his childhood.

Ushara panicked as Jullien jerked on the bed and Thrāix, Trajen, and Jory struggled to hold him down.

Thrāix cursed out loud as both their noses started bleeding. "Hold him or we'll lose him!"

Chilled to the bone, she tightened her grip on Jullien's hand and pressed hers to his cheek. "*Mi turi?* Can you hear me? I'm here with you."

"Shara?" With that single whisper, he calmed.

"I'm not going anywhere." She moved to lie down beside him and cuddle against his ribs like she did at night when they slept. She even placed her leg over his and draped her arm across his waist.

Jullien settled down instantly. His breathing remained heavy and ragged, his body tense, but with her pressed against him, he didn't move.

By the time Thrāix finally pulled back and let go, he was pale and shaking. Weak. He stumbled and almost fell. When Trajen went to help him, he curled his lip at him. "I'm fine."

Trajen held his hands up and backed off.

Jullien was unconscious.

Terrified, Ushara rose up and started to wake him, but Trajen stopped her. "He needs to rest. His brain's healing right now. Don't disturb him."

"Are you sure?"

He nodded.

She glanced to Thrāix for confirmation.

"He's being honest. Jullien's fine from this." But there was an odd note to his tone.

"What does that mean?"

Thrāix shook his head. "Has Jullien ever talked to you about his family?"

"Some."

Wiping the blood from his nose, Thrāix let out a bitter laugh. "No. He hasn't." He met Trajen's gaze. "You haven't really gone into his past, have you?"

"Hell no. The unintentional bits I've caught scarred me enough that I keep my shields up around him at all times."

When Thrāix glanced to Jory, he shook his head. "I don't really have those powers."

"Be glad." He turned his attention back to Trajen and drew a shaky breath. "How the hell does he manage to trust anyone? With anything?"

"I don't think he does."

Sniffing against the blood, Thrāix cleared his throat. "Ushara? Walk with me."

"What about Jullien?"

"He's not going anywhere. Besides, Jory and Trajen are here with him."

Reluctantly, she followed him from the room. He didn't take her far. Just outside the door. There, he turned and narrowed his gaze on her. "There's something I think you need to see."

"What do you mean?"

He held his hand out to her. "It's about Jullien. If you want to really understand him . . ."

She took his hand, then gasped as she instantly saw images of Jullien as a young male in the Andarion palace. He was dressing alone, preparing for his graduation ceremony from primary school. But what burned her was the turmoil inside him. Instead of the joy she'd felt when she was his age and getting ready for her ceremony with her sisters surrounding her, he was utterly despondent.

He winced as he caught a glimpse of himself in the mirror. His eyes were hollow from the drugs Merrell had been feeding him. And he was so pale, his skin rivaled the whiteness of his shirt. He felt ill and dizzy. Nauseated and weak. But he'd worked hard for this, and he was determined to stand strong and be there tonight in spite of them all.

Determined to hold his head high, he pulled his jacket on and buttoned it, then wiped at the clammy sweat on his forehead. He checked the time. His valet should have been back by now with his water.

Whatever.

His link rang. Picking it up, he saw that it was his father. Joy brought a rare smile to his face that his father had arrived early to pick him up and take him to school. "Paka! I was just—"

"Your Highness? This is His Majesty's secretary. Unfortunately, the emperor has a pressing issue that has come up, and he must cancel his appointment with you today. He regrets that he can't be there. But this is an urgent matter of national importance and can't wait. Thank you for your understanding." He cut the transmission.

Jullien stood there in stunned disbelief as his joy withered under a staggering wave of disappointment.

A pressing issue?

Seriously? Tears gathered to choke him, but he held them back.

Of course his father had something else to do. He always did. Why should today be any different than normal? And there wasn't anything pressing about Triosan security that needed his father's attention. Did his father forget that he watched the news, too?

Screw it.

Trying not to think about it or the fact that his father had probably forgotten to add it to his calendar, he finished buttoning his coat and put himself together as best he could. Once he had himself impeccably groomed, he left his room and tried not to let his father's callousness hurt him. He should have known better than to expect anything else.

With a deep sigh, he hesitated as he passed by his mother's suite of rooms. They were eerily quiet.

Hurt and wanting comfort, Jullien went toward the doors. His breathing ragged, he put his hand on the knob, then stopped short of turning it.

*Don't. She'll just yell at you.*

If she even knew it was him. Most of the time nowadays, she thought he was his uncle, come to kill her. Ever since he'd hit puberty, she couldn't tell them apart. One look at his face and she would scream and threw something at him.

Aching to the core of his soul over something he couldn't change, he pressed his head to the door and splayed his hand against it, wanting her love and approval with everything inside him.

Suddenly, the door opened.

Jullien stumbled into the room to meet the startled gasp of his mother's favorite guard, Lieutenant Galene Batur. Tall and gorgeous, she hated every one of his guts and didn't hesitate to let him know it.

"Why are you skulking outside the door?"

His hurt turned to anger. "I wasn't skulking. I wanted to see my matarra."

The unusual sound of his mother's laughter stunned him.

"She's awake and alert?"

Galene didn't speak as he stepped around her and into the room. He followed the sound of his mother singing to find her in a rocking chair with a young boy in her lap. Talyn Batur. The sight struck him like a kick in the groin, especially since the child held one of Nykyrian's prized toys that his mother didn't allow anyone to so much as breathe on without a shrieking fit.

"What's this, Yaya Tizirah?"

His mother smiled down at the boy and smoothed his long hair back from his face before she kissed him. "It's a lorina, like you!" She tickled him until he squealed in laughter.

"Matarra?"

Sobering, she met Jullien's gaze. "What are you doing here?"

The sharpness of her tone cut through him like a knife. "It's my graduation night. Do you not remember?"

She tightened her grip on Galene's son. "You're not supposed to be in here." She stood up with Talyn and cuddled him in her arms. Something she'd never done with Jullien. "Get out! Guards!"

"Matarra? I'm not Eadvard. It's me . . . Jullien. Don't you remember?"

"My son's dead. *You* killed him."

Galene took his arm. "You should leave, *Alteske*. You're upsetting her."

He felt the childish urge to shout that she was his mother, not Talyn's. But he knew it wouldn't do any good. Instead, he allowed Galene to push him out and shut the door in his face.

Jullien turned to find Tylie rushing toward him while his mother continued to shriek from inside the room.

"What did you do now?"

"Nothing."

Shoving at him, she pinched him on the arm. "You know better than to disturb Cairie. Why can't you leave her alone and let her be happy?"

"I happen to be her son."

"Then act like it and do something for her, you selfish little bastard."

His breathing intensified under the hatred in her gaze. "And whose fault is it that I'm bastard-born? I'm not the whore who screwed a human dog."

Tylie slapped him. "You filthy mongrel! That's your mother you're insulting! Why don't you go sober up for once? You reek of alcohol!"

Wiping the blood from his lips, he watched as she entered his mother's room and left him alone.

His link went off, warning him it was time to leave for his graduation.

Jullien pulled it out and turned the alarm off, then slammed it against the floor and stomped it. There was no need to go. He'd been to enough ceremonies where his family abandoned him and left him to stand alone. He had no desire to attend another one. It was too embarrassing to be the only one there with no family present. To have to make excuses and to see the mockery or pity in the eyes of others.

Screw it.

Disgusted, he headed for the study, intending to grab a bottle of the strongest Tondarion whisky his grandmother had in her cabinet and have his own celebration in his room. But as he reached the foyer, he met Merrell coming through the main palace door.

"What are you doing?" Merrell had demanded.

Disgusted, Jullien held his hands out. Was he totally stupid? Couldn't he tell he was headed for alcohol? "What does it look like?"

Merrell's eyes had flared as he shoved Jullien toward the study that had been his destination. He literally threw him into the room and shoved the doors closed behind them. "Are you out of your mind? You can't go to graduation!"

Jullien's contentious spirit kicked in. If Merrell was so thick he couldn't figure out he'd already abandoned that idea, far be it from him to correct the moron. "You don't order me, asshole!"

Merrell grabbed his collar in an angry fist. "Have you given thought to what would happen if someone were to see you and that hybrid bastard together and realize he was your twin? You can't risk this!"

Rolling his eyes, Jullien shoved Merrell away. "You don't tell me what to do! I'm the tahrs! Not you!"

Merrell caught him in a headlock and twisted him, pinning him to the ground.

Jullien tried to speak, but the way he was held, he couldn't say another word. All he could do was wheeze and choke.

"I'll see you dead before I let you jeopardize our lives!" Merrell injected him.

A few heartbeats later, everything went black.

Ushara came out of the memory, gasping. "His cousin overdosed him on his graduation night?"

Thrāix nodded. "What I didn't show you was his grandmother's reaction to it all. Because he wasn't in the top one percent of his class, she refused to acknowledge it. To quote the bitch, *I don't celebrate mediocre accomplishments.* And the whole reason he wasn't in the top one percent had nothing to do with his abilities, intelligence, or study habits as much as it did with the fact that he was a hybrid prince attending a predominately Andarion school, and overweight, and neither of his parents gave a shit when his teachers attacked him and lowered his grades out of jealousy and spite. He had one teacher who took off an entire grade because he handed the paper to her upside down. He never had anyone champion him, for anything."

She swallowed hard against the swell of pain inside her. "I knew it was bad. But I had no idea just how isolated he was."

Thrāix took her hand. "I want to show you one more thing."

"I'm not sure I can take it."

"Yeah, you can. You need to see this."

She doubted it until she took his hand and saw herself through Jullien's eyes.

It was the day she'd brought him clothes and taken him for breakfast. There was no way to describe the feelings inside him when he'd opened the door and seen her. An act of random kindness that she hadn't thought very much about—she'd have done it for most anyone. But one that had changed his life and given him his first taste of compassion.

That single morning had changed his entire perspective and outlook— had given him hope.

And made him hopelessly hers, forever.

That succeeded in breaking her completely. Sobbing, she let go and staggered back.

Thrāix didn't take pity on her. "I wanted you to understand what he'll *never* be able to say to you. The depth of emotion mere words won't ever convey. I thought you should know. I didn't have the chance to tell the woman I loved like that what she meant to me, and I've had to live out my life wondering what it would have been like had Julia fully understood what she was to me."

He swallowed hard. "I know you've been hurt, Ushara. That you're afraid of losing him. Life is never the fairy tale they sold us on when we were kids. More often, it's the nightmare we can never wake from. What they don't tell us when we're little is that the trick is to find the one who will be there in the middle of the night to hold us when we're screaming and tell us that it'll be all right. The one who doesn't shirk or run from our nightmares, but who holds us through them and makes sure we never face them alone. I promise that I will do everything in my power to make sure you don't lose him."

"Thank you."

Nodding, he stepped away from her. "When he wakes, he'll be extremely ill. Don't be too concerned. It's normal. He'll have a high fever. Chills. Severe headache. Dizziness. Disoriented. Confusion. Even vomiting. Some motor control might be compromised. Things to watch for are slurred speech and memory loss. Vision problems. Nose bleeds. Numbness in his extremities. If he has any of those, let me know immediately."

"Okay." Wiping at her tears, she returned to the room where Jullien had yet to move.

Jory and Trajen scowled at her, but didn't say a word. Rather, they withdrew to give her privacy.

Alone with Jullien, she sat on the bed and pulled the collar back from his neck so that she could gently finger the scars where Merrell and Parisa had injected their venom into him for years. And not carefully. The scars showed their savagery where they'd purposefully stabbed the injectors to cause him as much pain as possible and to make it obvious to everyone that Jullien was using.

A true junkie would have hidden his use and chosen a concealed spot on his body to access his veins. Like everything else in his life, this was done to scar and humiliate him. To hold him up for public ridicule.

Worse? Once his guards had discovered him overdosed on the floor, his grandmother had punished him for it.

As had his father.

She winced as the images Thrāix had shown her played through her mind, along with all the articles she'd read about Jullien. Those that had shown him alone in harsh rehab clinics where they'd sent him to recover and recuperate. Not the cozy, cushy ones most aristocrats were sent to, like the one they'd chosen for his mother.

No, his grandmother and father had sent him to the ones that were barely a step up from prison, where he'd been resented and hated. A target because of his noble birth by both the staff and other patients. Hospitals where he'd sat alone on visitation days in a solitary corner while everyone else spent time with their family and friends.

A weary soul.

"I will never leave you alone again," she whispered in his ear.

Jullien came awake with a start.

Ushara sat up instantly to let him know that she was still with him. "I'm right here, baby," she breathed, cupping his face.

Hissing, he placed the heel of his hand to his eye.

"I know. Thrāix said your head would be hurting." She reached for the water on the table next to the bed. "Sip this slowly. It'll help."

To her astonishment, he obeyed. "How long have I been out?"

"A few hours."

"Shouldn't you be headed back for Vas?"

"He'll be fine with my parents and family for a couple of days. He knows we love him and that he can call us if he needs something. Right now, you need me more, and I don't want you here alone."

Jullien placed her hand on his cheek. The tender expression on his face seared her.

Until he opened his eyes. There was a strange light behind them. Dazed and haunted.

"Jullien?"

He started to get up, then cursed and stumbled. "Trajen!" His shout rumbled through the room. "Jory!"

"Baby, you need to get back in bed."

He wasn't listening. Instead, he was trying to get to the door.

Luckily, Thrāix, Jory, and Trajen didn't dawdle in their rush to join them.

They stared at him in flabbergasted awe.

Trajen gaped. "What are you doing, Andarion?"

"Eriadne's going after Shara's brother. We have to get to Axl. Now!"

Ushara felt her stomach hit the floor. "What?"

Jullien tightened his grip on her hand. "That's what the bitch meant. She's got The League coming down on your brother. We have to warn him, or they're going to kill him."

# CHAPTER 25

"What the hell did you create?"

Ushara drew up short as she entered the room with Trajen, Jory, and Thrāix.

Thrāix glared at Trajen for that accusation. "I did *nothing* you didn't ask me to do. You know what I know. Everyone responds differently to it. He's a hybrid being. His brain isn't wired like anyone else's."

Terror and panic mixed inside her over their fury. "What happened? Is Jullien in danger?"

"No," Jory said quickly. "Definitely not in danger. At least we don't think so."

Trajen let out a tired sigh as he turned to face her with pinched features. "Sit down, Ushara."

"Why?"

Thrāix helped her to a chair. "Because we've accidentally made your husband Trisani."

Yeah, okay, she needed to sit. "W-w-what?"

Trajen nodded. "Somehow he's got more powers than just the ability to communicate with machines."

"We're not sure what all he can do yet." Thrāix rubbed at his chin. "I've never heard of this happening. With anyone . . . ever."

Jory made a sound of supreme disgust. "Man, why couldn't it have been me? I never catch the great breaks like this."

"Not sure this is that great a break." Thrāix exchanged a brutal grimace with Trajen. "These powers are their own form of hell at times."

"Especially if you're not born with them." Trajen kept trying to signal her brother. "I can't get through to Axl. I've sent word to every ship we have near him . . . but there's no way we can reach him in less than a week."

Tears filled her eyes. "I already called Dimitri and told him. But he's too far away to get to him, or Kirill, either, for that matter. No one can reach him in time to warn him. Eriadne picked her target well."

"She always did."

Ushara wanted to scream in frustration. "What are we going to do?"

Jory sighed. "I've got the word out to me sister and me Sep brothers and Ryn Cruel. He said he'd contact The Sentella and Wassies. With luck, one of them can get to Axl before The League does."

Thrāix scowled. "What's that sound?"

"It's a ship starting. Dear gods, tell me he isn't . . ." Trajen ran for the bay.

Ushara ran after him, along with the others. She had the same bad feeling about Jullien that they did. And as she got to the bay, she cursed at the visual confirmation of Jullien's stubborn stupidity. "What's he thinking? He can't make it any faster than we can."

Trajen cursed. "I don't know."

Jory ran for his ship.

Trajen turned to Thrāix. "Got a ship I can borrow?"

"Follow me."

Ushara ran after them. But as soon as she got on board, she realized the same thing Jory did.

Jullien had them locked out. Nothing could launch.

"I'm going to kill him." Ushara grabbed her link and immediately hailed her husband.

Instead of answering, she got a prerecorded message.

*"I know you'll be mad. I would annihilate me in your place. But I'm to blame for this, and I can't sit by and let them kill your brother to get back at me when he's innocent in this. You won't grieve any less for Axl than you would for me. And this way, no one else in your family will be hurt, except for Vasili. For that alone, I am eternally sorry. You know I wouldn't hurt the two of you for anything if I could find any other solution. But this is the best one I can think of. Tell Vas that I love him. That I'll always love him. That I'm depending on him to take care of you and the girls for me. There's no one else I would trust with your safety. I love you, Shara. Please understand and forgive me. This really is the only way to make things right."*

Thrāix let out an explosive curse as he blasted the ship's control panel with fire. His eyes turned a bright orange as he faced Trajen. "You feel that?"

Trajen's curse matched Thrāix's. "I don't have a single League contact. Not one. Do you?"

"Ryn does. We can have Jory call—"

"We can't use *him*. Are you out of your mind?"

"Why?"

Trajen passed a sick look to Ushara. "Jullien's brother. The minute Ryn Cruel sees Jullien's face or name, he's not going to lift a finger to help. He'd kill Jullien himself, for the bounty, and laugh while he did it."

Ushara scowled. "What are you two talking about?"

Trajen sighed. "Jullien isn't trying to reach your brother, Shara. He's got The League coming after *him*. He's already contacted them and offered to give himself up if they agree to leave off their pursuit of Axl."

No . . . Horrified that he'd dare do such, she immediately tried to hail Jullien again.

When he didn't answer, she left a message. "Jullien . . . Listen to me and listen well. I will not forgive you for this . . . Do you hear me? You are not to surrender to them. Not for any reason. You better get your lumbering Andarion ass home to me, or so help me, gods, I'm going to find my way down to Tophet and kick your ass every step of the way home. I mean it!"

Her voice broke on tears. "Don't do this to me," she repeated. "Please. For the love of the gods. I love you, too. And I need you home with me. Don't make me have to raise our daughters alone. They need their paka. Please don't make me break Vasili's heart. And don't break mine. You promised."

But as minutes went by and the line stayed silent, she knew it was too late.

He was gone, and he wasn't coming back.


"Honey, you have to stop crying. It's not good for the babies."

But Ushara couldn't stop. It'd been six weeks since Jullien vanished. Six weeks without a single word of his fate.

And now . . .

She looked down at the image of her babies that the doctor had just handed her during her checkup and today's date, and cried harder.

Her mother sighed as they left the doctor's office. "C'mon, *mia*. Let's get Vas, and you two can spend the night at my house."

Ushara was so distraught, she could barely walk. By the time they reached her home, she was hiccupping and incapable of speech. Thankfully, her mother had her own access to the door—otherwise, Ushara would have never been able to open it.

But as they walked inside, the scent of something warm and delicious hit her. The shock of the aroma interrupted her crying jag.

As did the sound of deep laughter coming from Vas's bedroom. What the hell?

Confused and concerned, she rushed down the hall to see what was going on with her son, who'd been moping around even worse than she since Jullien had gone AWOL.

She drew up short at the nursery door where someone had painted the Gorturnum screaming skull logo in pink to match the one Jullien had drawn on Vasili's room. Only where Vas's had VASILI THE BRAVE AND TERRIBLE, this one had VLADMIRA AND VIVEKA THE COURAGEOUS AND BOLD.

Only one person knew what she wanted to name her daughters. . . .

And he was supposed to be dead.

Her heart pounding, she went to Vas's room and pushed open the door. Tears filled her eyes again as she saw Jullien standing beside Vas while the two of them played one of Vas's games.

"Go right! Right!"

Jullien was trying to obey Vasili's orders when he was blindsided and tackled to the ground.

He gasped, only to have his lips claimed in a kiss so hot, it left his head reeling. Tossing the controller over his shoulder, he laughed and wrapped his arms around Ushara, then lifted her up over him to hold her against his chest. He growled at how good she felt in his arms. "I think someone missed me."

Her pale eyes sparkled as she cupped his face and stared down at him. "How are you alive?"

Shrugging, he got up and helped her to her feet. "Hard to kill. You had to know I wouldn't really surrender to them. I just had to get them off your brother's back."

Color rushed into her cheeks an instant before she balled her fists into his coat lapels and jerked him forward. "And you couldn't take five minutes to let me know? You bastard!" She kneed him in the groin.

Doubling over, Jullien hissed in pain as he saw stars from it.

Vas let out a high-pitched squeak in sympathy. "Ma! I can't believe you did that!"

Jullien stumbled back as he struggled to breathe. "It's okay," he choked out. "I deserved it." Biting his lip, he struggled with the agony. Damn, Davel hadn't been kidding about the power of her kicks. Holy shit . . . "Really glad we're having twins, 'cause I'm pretty sure that just capped any chance of me fathering kids ever again."

Her mother laughed from the doorway. "What did I just walk in on?"

Ushara gestured at Jullien. "The wretched beast lives!"

"So I see. I would have thought that would have made you happy."

"One e-mail," Ushara growled between clenched teeth as she gestured angrily toward him. "One! Is that too much to ask?"

Jullien slowly straightened. "I assumed the food and items I sent to you would clue you in that I was alive."

Ushara froze. "I thought all that had been arranged before you left."

"How would I know to send the maternity clothes?"

Pausing, she eyed him suspiciously. "Yeah? How *did* you know about that?"

He rubbed at his crotch, trying to offset some of the damage. "I've been spying on you and Vas. Hello? You know I do that. Why you think I have the house wired?"

"Oh! I could beat you!"

*So long as you do it naked, knock yourself out.*

Ushara gasped as she heard his voice in her head.

And the devilish grin on his face said he was more than willing to submit to her abuse. Rolling her eyes, she sighed. "You're incorrigible."

"I know. I'm sorry. Really, I didn't mean to upset you." He gave her a contrite smile. "Happy anniversary, by the way."

Her mother let out her own gasp. "Is that why you've been so torn up all day?"

Ushara nodded.

Jullien pulled her against his chest and held her. "Even though it's dangerous, I had to see you. I couldn't stay away on our anniversary."

Katira came forward with a sweet smile. "Have I told you how much I love you as my son?"

Jullien panicked at her actually being nice to him. "Not really."

"I do." She kissed his cheek. "Vas? Turn everything off and come spend the night with us. Your paka and mom need some time to themselves."

"Yes, *mur tarra.*"

Jullien released Ushara. "I need to check on dinner before it burns." He went to the kitchen.

Ushara took a minute to help Vas pack an overnight bag and collect his homework. "How long has your paka been here?"

"He picked me up from school and helped me do homework. Then we made dinner for you and started playing games." Vas threw his pack over his shoulder. "You really naming the babies Vladmira and Viveka?"

"Yes, why?"

He screwed his face up and stuck his tongue out with a noise of supreme displeasure. "I'm sure it'll grow on me. Eventually." He hugged her. Then he went to the kitchen. "Love you, Paka."

Jullien growled as he gave him a tight hug. "You, too, *luden.* See you in the morning." He inclined his head respectfully to her mother. "Thank you, Ger Tarra."

"Matarra."

He actually blushed. "Matarra."

And with that, she took Vas and left them alone.

Jullien scowled as he looked at her. "Did you perform an exorcism on your mother while I was gone?"

"No. You did when you took care of me so sweetly. And when you committed suicide to protect my brother from The League. She's been lighting candles and saying prayers for your soul at every service. She's now convinced you're a saint."

"Really?" He choked on the word.

She nodded. "Have you seen Unira?"

"Yeah. I saw her first thing when I landed, right before I talked to Trajen."

"Did they know you weren't dead?"

"Only Thrāix knew."

"Good. I don't have to kill them." Grinding her teeth, she continued to glare furiously at him. "I can't believe you didn't tell *me.*"

He set his spoon aside and tried to kiss her, but she pushed him back. "What can I say that you don't already know? I'm an inconsiderate asshole."

"Yes, you are." She took his hand and placed it on her stomach. "Feel that?"

Jullien froze when the tiniest movement brushed against his palm. "Is that one of the babies?"

She nodded.

Stunned and humbled by the feathery flutter, he fell to his knees in front of her as his breath left him in a rush. Tears blinding him, he lifted her top up so that he could brush his lips against her stomach where he'd felt them. "Hey, *mia kikatalli*," he said gently, rubbing the area where they frolicked. "Don't be too eager to join this world. You're much better off where you are. Trust me. But I promise, whether in there or out here, your mother and I will make sure no one hurts you."

Ushara brushed her hand against his whiskers as she smiled down at him. "You're such a goof."

He wrapped his arms around her waist and held her gently. "I've missed you so much. You've no idea the hell it's been not talking to you. But I had to get them off you and your family. It was easier to let them think me captured and dead than to risk anything happening to you."

She tugged playfully at his hair, which made him harder than hell. "You're still not forgiven."

Jullien rubbed his whiskers against her skin, teasing it playfully before he gave her a sensuous nip. "Not even a little?"

"No." Unrelenting where he was concerned, she held her ground without the least bit mercy for him. "How much Trisani power do you have, anyway?"

He held his hand out, and the spatula flew from the counter into his palm.

"Oh my God, Jules!"

"Yeah." He set it down before he rose to his feet and adjusted himself so that his pants weren't biting into his erection. "It's been interesting, trying to harness my new wicked friends. Honestly, I'm glad I haven't been around you and Vas for some of it, as it's been dangerous at times. I've exploded a few things. Knocked over a lot more. Embarrassed myself to no uncertain end. Really, *really* glad you missed out on that."

She laughed as he fed her a piece of oil-soaked bread. "And the quest for your grandmother?"

"Frustrating. The one thing both of them excel at is hiding. But I haven't given up."

The lights dimmed.

She arched her brow. "You?"

He nodded as he used his powers to find one of her favorite love songs to play over her system. While he didn't normally like them, he would suffer it for her. "I wanted to take you out dancing tonight, but the risk of someone seeing me . . . Thrāix made me promise that I wouldn't leave the condo until tomorrow night. If I violate his dictates for my release, he won't let me out of his custody again."

"He sounds like a warden."

"Basically. He's a tough bastard. But I respect him. He's so paranoid, he makes me feel normal. . . . I like that in a person."

She laughed as she began that seductive swaying that never failed to set him on fire.

Yeah, for that, he'd suffer the worst music in the universe. Watching her practice for the temple chorus and exercise were two things he'd missed most these past weeks. While he had several of her sessions recorded, it wasn't the same as being able to reach out and touch her. Or having her dance around him and touch his face and smile at him as she was prone to do.

Just thinking about it was almost enough to make him come.

His breathing ragged, he had to force himself to focus on what he was doing.

Twirling around, she took a bite of bread, then held the last bit of it out for him to finish off.

He swallowed it and then tried to distract himself from where his thoughts were going. "Did you know Thrāix's father was Vashaw Flavian Sparda?"

She almost choked on the bread at something that was extremely shocking. "Thrāix is a Sparda?"

Jullien nodded. "Yeah. I was stunned when I found out, too. His father went down protecting him and the last of the royal Trisani family."

Ushara let out a low whistle. That was an impressive lineage. The Spardas had been instrumental in ending the Scythian Age of the Warlords and overthrowing Justicale Cruel.

"Had Trisa not fallen, Thrāix would have most likely gone on to be the next *vicegerent* and *vashaw*, like his father."

No wonder Jullien liked him. They had a lot in common. Both displaced by war and misfortune.

And as he reached around her, the scent of his skin hit her. Closing her eyes, she savored it and the warmth of having him with her again. She'd forgotten just how much space he took up in a room and how much she enjoyed standing next to his massiveness. He made her feel so petite and tiny. And she loved that sensation. Loved his massive size.

Especially his muscular shoulders and those biceps . . .

She only had *one* complaint with him.

He glanced down at her and frowned. "What's with that look?"

Wrinkling her nose in distaste, she reached up to tug at his whiskered chin. "Why is it whenever I let you out of my sight, you regress to your woolliest state?"

He flashed a devilish grin at her that exposed his fangs. "It's to keep all the other *qeres* at bay. You don't want them chasing after me, do you?"

"You better not be chasing after no *qeres*. I don't share my male."

Laughing, he took her hand and pressed it against his swollen groin. "Believe me, I haven't been near anyone else. That requires a level of trust that I only give *you*." He dipped his head down to kiss her, but his words had already broken her heart and lodged a sob in her throat.

He pulled back with a frown. "What's wrong?"

Before she could answer, her link went off. She started to ignore it, but it was Zellen. "Hold on a sec. That's a command call." She pulled it out and answered it.

"Admiral? We have a situation in the bay. Not sure how to handle this one."

Weird. He didn't normally have such problems. "What's going on?"

"I have six Porturnum ships seeking Safe Harbor."

"Okay. . . . Why is that a problem?"

He lowered his voice. "Two of them are Andarion, and they're wearing warrior braids. I swear one looks a lot like your husband's cousin who was executed during their coup. Does he happen to have a relative named Varan Enole?"

She glanced over at Jullien, and by the fury in his stralen eyes . . . "I'm going to say yes."

"That's what I was afraid of. They're asking a lot of probing questions that are above my rank and pay. How do you want me to handle this?"

"Call the HCs. . . ." That was the most she could get out before Jullien was heading for the door with an intent that said he was on his way to confront them and blow this situation into a fatal outcome.

# CHAPTER 26

J ules! I order you to stop! Now!"

He paused outside the door and turned to face Ushara with a look that actually frightened her. *"Order?"*

"A little harsh, but you can't go down there and confront them when they're here under Safe Harbor. You know better."

And still that expression made her blood run cold. She'd never really been afraid of him before, but right then . . .

This was a side of him she really didn't want to be on.

"I'm currently under Jory's banner. He won't care if I rattle their cage or snatch the door straight off it. He'd be the first one to do it, especially after what they did to me while he harbored me under it and they broke Code. Today, I intend to be payback's two-fisted bitch."

He turned toward the bay, and as he started for it, he almost slammed into Trajen as he manifested in front of him to block his path.

"What the fuck?"

"Tone," Trajen said in a voice that was deceptively calm. "Don't be thinking you're all that with those powers, boy. Remember, some of us have had ours a lot longer and mastered them long before your daddy got busy with your mama. You jerk that chin at me and take that tone, and I'll slam your ass down, bare it, and spank it."

A tic started in Jullien's jaw. "So I'm just supposed to let them encroach with impunity? Need I remind you that I'm Andarion, and that's not how we do things."

"Yes, and they know you're Andarion, which is why they're doing it. They're trying to flush you out after your last attack on them. Tit for tat. And if you'd stop being an idiot for three seconds, you'd know that."

Jullien flung his hands out and manifested fire into both of his fists. "Then let me roast the bitches."

"Ushara? Leash him."

"I'm trying. But he's not really broken in. As you say, he flunked home-training. There's not a lot I can do when he's like this."

Trajen let out a tired sigh. "This is going to be bad, then." He snapped his fingers and Jullien vanished.

Ushara gasped. "What'd you do?"

"Gave him a time-out." Growling low in his throat, he rubbed at his eye. "He's going to be so pissed off. But you and I know what will happen if he storms into that bay and starts his shit with that crew."

Sadly, she did.

War. All-out, and nasty.

With another heavy sigh, Trajen dropped his hand. "C'mon. Let's go deal with this drama, then we'll deal with Jullien's trauma. And you have my permission to bust their asses for wrecking your anniversary."

"Thank you." Not looking forward to it, Ushara headed for the main bay, where Zellen was waiting with a group of Ports she'd never seen before.

Since Trajen was in regular clothes, they had no idea he was the HAP of their Nation. Not that it seemed to matter—they didn't show her much respect, and she was in full Tavali gear with her Canting and rank clearly displayed on her sleeves.

Zellen saluted her. "Admiral, our guests would like access to some of our personnel files."

"To what purpose?"

The Andarion, who did indeed look a lot like Jullien's cousin Merrell, eyed her suspiciously and didn't identify himself past his Canting and the name on his uniform. "We have a runaway slag we're tracking. We have reason to believe he might be seeking refuge here."

"Give me his name, and I'll look and see."

"He might be using an alias."

"I can search for that, as well."

The Andarion didn't back off in the least. "We need to do facial cog."

*Nice try* . . . But the unstoppable wind had just met the immovable object. She wasn't about to hand over her husband to anyone.

Ushara arched her brow with the same haughty disdain. "I can scan for photos."

"We don't want to trouble you."

She crossed her arms over her chest. "But you already have interrupted my dinner. So why not hand over what you need, and let me get started on your trace?"

An angry tic started in his jaw as he narrowed his white gaze on her name. "Altaan? You're a winged military caste, are you not?"

She didn't dignify that with a response. Mostly because it was a sore, sticking point with her family that they alone held that distinction. Of all the lineages on Andaria, her father's sole branch was the only one that was both Pavakahir and Murakhiran—Fyreblood and winged—two of the strongest and rarest bloodlines. And they had been chased from the military and "cleansed" from Andarion soil by the tadara herself.

Anole rudely picked up a strand of her blond hair from her shoulder and curled his lip at it. "You're hybrid?"

In that moment, she was *so* grateful Jullien wasn't here. For that insult alone, he would have gutted his cousin.

There were only a handful of crimes an Andarion male viewed as worse than having another male touch his spouse. In their society, it was viewed as a felony, and Jullien would be within all legal rights to kill his cousin for such an offense.

Glaring at him, she snatched her hair out of his grasp. "Anole? You're a branch of the royal family, aren't you? Second cousin of the tadara?"

"Yes, he is. How clever of you to know that . . . Or perhaps someone told you?"

Ushara's blood went cold at the sound of Eriadne's voice. Holy gods . . . It tested every shred of sanity she had not to react to the female's presence in her hangar. No wonder Trajen had sent Jullien out of here.

It would have been an absolute bloodbath.

With a deep breath for strength and patience, she turned to face the one creature she wanted to kill most in this universe. And it took every single piece of restraint she'd been born with not to shoot the bitch on sight.

Complete and utter shock riveted her, and that alone kept her from reacting—and probably saved her life. While she knew Andarions aged *much* slower than humans, she also knew the tadara was at least a hundred years old, if not over. But the female in front of her didn't look a day older than fifty, if that. In fact, her caramel skin was virtually flawless and smooth. There was barely a wrinkle or pore on it.

She was stunningly beautiful still. High cheekbones were set against a regal, patrician face with perfectly arched black brows that contrasted sharply with her white Andarion eyes. Her long black hair had been braided with a gold band and fell over one shoulder to her tiny waist. With a cool aloofness, she commanded attention and respect.

Eriadne arched a brow at Ushara. "You don't bow to your tadara?"

Ushara lifted her chin defiantly. "If I were in the presence of her, I would. But I'm not an Andarion citizen nor do I see any tadara here."

That had the desired effect. It pissed her off. Her nostrils flaring, bloodlust darkened her eyes. "You're playing with fire, *kikatalla.*"

*Little girl? Really?*

Refusing to be intimidated or belittled by such a ridiculous ploy, she offered Eriadne a cool smile. "I'm told I do that well."

Eriadne wasn't amused. "You remind me of someone, but I can't remember who . . ." Her gaze fell to Ushara's stomach. "You're with child?"

"I am."

"Your husband must be proud."

"He was very much so."

*"Was?"*

Ushara allowed her eyes to tear up. "We're Tavali. He was taken by The League two months ago. They executed him."

Eriadne narrowed her eyes speculatively. "You're sure about that?"

"Given the warrant for his life . . . quite positive. After all, they're not known for hesitation or mercy. I'm sure that's something you can appreciate."

Eriadne snapped her head back as if she'd been slapped. "You're rather cheeky, aren't you?"

Ushara shrugged. "Since I hold the second-highest-ranking position in my Nation, it's a bene that comes with my seat."

Eriadne grimaced in distaste before she glanced to Anole. "Would it be amiss of me if I inquire about the name of your husband, Admiral? I should like to add him to my prayers."

"We're Demurrists here. But if you still feel the need, by all means. It was Dagger . . . Samari."

Eriadne paled. "Samari? I thought them all extinct."

"You were misinformed."

"You lie!" Varan stepped forward. "Jullien's your husband! Admit it. We know he's here. That you're harboring the slimy little bastard!"

Eriadne held her hand up to silence him.

Ushara passed a smug sneer to Varan. "Feel free to check my marriage records, as well as the records of my children. They're all public. My husband's name is clearly registered. He was the captain of the *Stormbringer*." She pulled out her link and accessed the documents for them. "As you can see, his paternal lineage and name are filed. As is his mother's. My husband's paternal bloodline was confirmed at the time of our marriage through DNA as Samari Pavakahiri, and his maternal is registered as Altaan Pavakakiri, not the Nykyrian-Anatole Ixurian bloodlines, which I believe Tiziran Jullien's would be, is that not right?"

Fury darkened Eriadne's eyes as she reviewed the documentation that had to be her worst nightmare, as it publicly called her a liar.

And a faithless whore.

"Yes, that is correct. My grandsons are of the Nykyrian-Anatole lineages, and they are Ixurian. We have no Fyreblood within our noble house."

"Then my husband obviously never had anything in common with your family. My Dagger was born a proud Fyreblood."

Varan gaped while Eriadne continued to glare a murderous line through Ushara. "You're playing a dangerous game. Be warned."

"I'm not playing a game at all. Games are for amusement, and there's nothing amusing when someone's life is at stake. But then, perhaps that's your problem. You never understood the difference between games and reality."

Hissing, Eriadne took a step toward her before she caught her composure and stopped. "You don't want to push me."

"And I'm Tavali Pavakihira," Ushara said, holding her ground and refusing to back down. "You don't want to threaten or challenge me. More than that, I'm a mother who loves her young, and unlike you, I will kill anyone and any*thing* who dares to threaten what I love."

Eriadne laughed coldly. "That's the trick . . . though, isn't it? I hope what you love always returns it to you, and doesn't betray you as mine did me. There is no more bitter a pill than to birth your own destruction."

She started for her ship, then paused to look back at Ushara. "Oh, and if perchance you do happen upon my grandson one day while he slithers about in hiding, tell Jullien that Ives sends his best to him and can't wait to spend more time alone with him. I, for one, can't wait to reunite them."

And with that, she gathered her men and left.

As soon as she was out of sight, Ushara scowled at Trajen. "What in the Nine Worlds was *that* about?"

"Cold-blooded viciousness."

"Meaning?"

Trajen appeared sick to his stomach before he answered in a low tone that was barely audible. "Jullien told you about her private *vörgäte*?"

"That she'd lock him into for various things. Yes."

He gave her a hard stare. "You're not naïve, Ushara. You know what happens to boys in prison, especially to a prince whose family is as hated as his. . . . Ives was one of his more malicious abusers."

Her stomach heaved. She ran as fast as she could for the nearest bathroom and barely made it before her stomach emptied itself.

Shaking and weak, Ushara couldn't breathe as her anger and horror wrapped themselves around her heart and made her sick to her stomach. Tears for Jullien filled her eyes as she tried to calm down. But it was hard, given the imagined nightmares that played through her mind.

Her poor Jules . . .

What she imagined, he had to live with.

Trajen followed her and handed her a cool cloth when she finally stopped retching. "Sorry. I shouldn't have sprung that on you so callously. I'm as upset as you are. That was wrong of me."

She held the cloth to the back of her neck and flushed the commode. "He never talks about it."

"I know. There's a lot he doesn't mention. To anyone."

She looked up at Trajen. "How could she be so cold?"

"I've no idea. Anymore than I understand how Jullien was able to remain even remotely sane in that palace with them clawing at him constantly. But you did great. They came here specifically to flush him out and kill him. You caught them completely off-guard. Now she doesn't know what to think. She's not sure if he's alive. Captured. Dead. Where he is. And the bit about his being a Samari . . . brilliant. She has no idea if you're trying to blackmail her or just set her down. If anyone else knows that Dagger is Jullien or that she fucked his grandfather . . . It was beautifully done. You put her in retreat, and that's not an easy thing to do."

"She'll be back, though, won't she?"

"Yeah, and we have to go release the rampaging beast I caged. Something I'm not looking forward to." He sighed heavily. "Maybe I should give you the key and take a vacation."

She snorted at his fearful tone. "You're not a coward."

"Normally. But I'm sure Jullien's a special kind of pissed off right now. I really don't want to face it, and I'm not completely sure just how much power that little bastard currently wields. Especially as pissed as he's going to be over what I did to him. Honestly, and between you and me? He scares me."

She thought he was kidding until he took her to the room in his basement where Jullien had torn the whole thing asunder. It looked as if a hurricane had exploded inside it. The whole room was scorched and destroyed.

Literally.

Yet that wasn't the terrifying part.

What truly made her want to wet her pants and had Trajen turning the palest shade she'd ever seen on his face was the fact that Jullien had calmed down to a stoic level. In fact, she'd never seen him calmer as he greeted them with his arms crossed over his chest.

Yeah, *that* was horrifying.

She exchanged a panicked look with Trajen before she spoke to Jullien. "Are you all right?"

"Only because you are. That was an extremely reckless thing you did."

"You're not angry?"

"Beyond furious." Jullien wiped one regal finger against his bottom lip before he straightened his red-tinted glasses in what had to be the most aristocratic gesture she'd ever seen anyone make. "Am I free to go?" he asked Trajen.

"Depends. What are you planning?"

"After I give my wife her anniversary present, I'm going to deliver Varan's head and testicles to my grandmother, along with my best wishes for her most grueling and laborious death."

"The minute you do that, they'll know you're alive. Right now, they're not sure. It gives you a tactical advantage. Why not make use of it?"

"What do you mean?"

"Think about it. She's Yllam Orthodox. Just like your mother and lyra. What's more, she doesn't know you're stralen or that it's physically possible for you to carry that gene."

Jullien scowled at Trajen. "I still don't follow your logic."

"Bleach your hair, Jullien. You don't just look like your basha Ead-vard. But for his darker coloring, your uncle was a dead ringer for *his* father—it's why Eriadne favored him above all her other children. Crazy as she is, she did actually love your grandfather. And with *your* lighter skin color and blond hair and those red eyes, you would be a clone of Edon Samari . . . haunt the bitch."

Jullien fell silent as he considered that. It made sense. He didn't favor anyone else in his family, on either side—including his own twin brother. As a boy, he'd been bothered by that fact to distraction. The Anatole genes were unbelievably strong. Most of their family bore an uncanny similarity to one another. It was what had allowed Parisa to pass as a twin to his mother, even though they were first cousins.

Trajen gave him an evil, chilling smile. "They tortured you with the lie that you were your uncle's spirit come back to punish them for their crimes. Fine, then. Be Edon Samari's ghost and wreak your retribution. Go for Eriadne's throat. With the powers you have now . . . think about what you could do."

Jullien laughed. "I don't know if I should be impressed or scared."

A slow smile spread over Trajen's face. "Bit of both."

"If you were a little cuter and less hairy, I'd actually kiss you for this."

"And if I weren't stone sober, I might let you."

Jullien held his hand out to him.

Trajen took it and pulled him in for a brotherly hug before he pounded him hard on the back. *"Te amo, fratrem meum." Love you, my brother.*

Jullien knew to savor words that came from Tray's heart. Words the man didn't say lightly and had rarely spoken to anyone in his lifetime. They were as foreign to the Trisani's tongue as they were to his. He tightened his grip in Trajen's hand and inclined his head to him. *"Et tu. Unus ex meis intimis. Animae plusquam dimidium meae." And you. My friend, whom I dearly love. My second self.* In Trisani, that was the deepest avowal of friendship—their code of brotherhood that their warriors swore to in the rare times they went into battle for each other. It meant that they would kill or die for one another's safety. Which in a society that didn't believe in war or violence, meant a lot more than it did in his.

Ushara choked as she saw the tears in Trajen's eyes. "I'm going to make a Tris out of you yet, boy."

"Not if I make you an Andarion first."

Laughing, Trajen clapped him on the shoulder. Then the humor died on his face as he glanced around the room. "*Et per ego te Deum oro!* Clean this *minsid* hell up! I'm not the maid, and I'm not picking up after your brat-ass tantrum. What is wrong with you?"

Jullien snorted. "That is a long and mighty list of psychological problems that would keep us here all night. However, the short answer is you locked me in. You fucking knew better. You're lucky I didn't burn the entire station down. But for the fact my son sleeps here, and baby Nadya, and my wife and her family, I *was* tempted."

Trajen growled at him. "Why do I like you, again?"

"I speak your language . . . raw anger and fluent sarcasm."

His nose twitched. "Call the cleaning crew. Good thing I have one . . . or two dozen. Don't tell them you're an idiot. And don't forget to commit a couple of felonies with your League files. And suicide."

"Already done. It's why I didn't take down the access panel or monitor in the midst of my earlier tantrum. And what stopped it. Once I realized what Ushara was doing with my family, I offed myself quite beautifully in Kyr's League database. Made it a particularly gory report that was filed with high command and is backlogged in League bureaucracy. Gave my kill to a lower-ranked assassin who died a few days later, fighting against a Sentella–Caronese Resistance joint Task Force so they can't do a verbal confirmation with him on my demise, and there won't be any video evidence for the kill, other than a single photo of unidentifiable remains and his fabricated sworn testimony that I wrote, since The League forbids *their* key assets from taping themselves when taking out political targets. Burns my ass that the bitch doesn't have to pay for it, though. I'd like to see her choke on a bounty that high. But what can you do?"

Trajen ruffled his hair. "Bleach your hair blond. Become her throbbing hemorrhoid."

"There is that to look forward to." He flashed his fangs at Trajen. "And on that note, I have something else I've been looking forward to for weeks now." He took Ushara's hand. "If you'll excuse us?"

"Yeah, go on. She needs something to smile about. She's been flooding the station for weeks now. You've been setting fire to my rooms. I'm getting too old for this shit." Grumbling, he vanished.

Ushara screwed her face up at Trajen's departure. "I have no idea what to make of your relationship with him. He is so different around you. I wish you could see him interact with others so that you could truly appreciate how much he really does like you. He's a strange combination of doting father and watchful big brother. He doesn't tolerate or speak to anyone else the way he does you."

"Tray's always nice to you."

"I'm his VA."

"Maybe that's why he's nice to me."

She shook her head. "He liked you from the moment he met you in the bar, and offered to adopt you as a Gort cock. And again, he doesn't do that. I've never known him to be so open with anyone. Ever. We have some members who have been here since before I was born he won't even speak to."

Jullien shrugged. "I guess he has a fondness for assholes." He traced the line of her brow before he kissed her. "I'm sorry our night was ruined."

"I'm sorry I upset you."

"*You* didn't. And neither did Trajen. Not really. My grandmother did. I meant what I said to you. I will never be angry at you for loving me and trying to protect me. Truly, I'm not used to anyone trying to save me from my stupidity, so it takes a few to realize that's what's going on. My thoughts don't automatically go there, as I'm too used to being thrown to the Ring, weaponless and naked."

She flinched at a truth that made her ache for him. "But things are different now."

"Yeah," he breathed, cupping her cheek. "You've got to be patient with me as I acclimate to that." And as he spoke, his eyes changed from red to green to white.

Ushara gasped. "Jullien?"

He grinned. "I have control of them now. Not the stralen itself. It remains intact. But I can camouflage the color, and do basic Trisani abilities. A limited amount of teleportation."

"Seriously?"

He nodded. "Not much, and it drains me horribly. I'm not able to fight after I do it."

"Jules, that's amazing!"

He wrinkled his nose at her. "I owe it all to you."

"How do you figure?"

He swallowed as he fingered her cheek and stared at her with an adoration that left her breathless. "I was done that day I met you, Shara. I'd completely relegated my soul to the gods. Made my peace with this world. I was just waiting for the Koriłon to come claim my rotten soul." He brushed his hand through her hair as he let out a breathless laugh.

"While I sat dying, this boy came in so full of piss and life. Fire and venom. I could only imagine the glorious mother who had birthed a son so strong and willing to stand against them. I knew you had to be incredible to give him that kind of confidence while surrounded by his enemies, especially at his age. He didn't wear that mantle of hopeless, betrayed fatigue that cloaked me at his age. Vas was indomitable. And then there you were like Kadora herself, ready to slay me for threatening your child. You were the most beautiful creature I'd ever seen. And as I fell, I was so grateful that my last sight in a life that had been filled with nothing but brutal ugliness and violence was one of perfect beauty and grace—that just once before I died, I finally got to see an act of unrestrained and pure, untainted love."

"Jullien—"

He placed his finger over her lips to keep her from speaking. "You will always be my Darling star, Shara. Now that I have found you, not even death will keep me from you." He put his hand into his pocket. "Close your eyes, *munatara*."

She obeyed without question.

Chills rose along her skin as he placed a chain around her neck and his breath fell against her cheek. His fingers lingered there while he positioned the necklace to rest between her breasts. Then he placed the sweetest kiss to her lips. "Okay."

Love for him warmed her as she opened her eyes and looked down to see a beautiful round filigree gold locket that held an ornate white flower in the center.

It was the Kadora's rose. Legends said that it bloomed in the center of her garden in the heart of Eweyne. And that on the day when the gods Kadora and Asukar had created the Andarion race to be the absolute embodiment of war to fight for them and to worship them, that the goddess of balance, Eri gazed upon their beauty and wept, and said that they were perfection except for one thing.

*They lacked heart. Warriors cannot fight if they cannot love. For battles are not won through the strength of a soldier's hand. They are won by the determination of a warrior's devotion to those he values more than himself.*

*We fight not for ourselves. We fight for our families and we cannot fight for our gods if we do not know how to love them.*

And so determined Eri went to the garden of her sister and plucked the leaves of her sister's favorite flower, knowing that within its sweet petals was a serum so potent, it would open the warriors' eyes to the beauty of Andaria, and that once they saw the beauty, it would open their hearts and fill them with its sweet nectar and allow them to love their homeworld.

One by one, they were given drink distilled from that perfect, pristine rose. And as they tasted its sacred, oil-infused water, their eyes were opened and transformed into the pure Andarion white that was unique to their race. Through those eyes, they saw the beauty that surrounded them and wept, and through those tears, they learned to love and to value their gods and each other above all else.

To this day, that rose was the Andarion symbol for justice and balance. Most of all, it stood for eternal love and was a promise from one partner to the other that they would lay down their life for them.

Ushara stared up at Jullien through teary eyes. "You are ever determined to reduce me to a blubbering basket case, aren't you?"

He winced as if she'd wounded him. "Never my intent, *mia.* I only want to make you as happy as you make me."

"Oh, Jules . . . that you do." She nipped his lips, then took his hand.

"Where are you taking me?"

"Home so that I can strip you bare and beat you."

"Gah, how sick am I that you made me harder than hell with just those words?" He pressed himself against her to prove it.

She squeaked. "Oh, good grief. That is frightening!"

"Well, it has been two months. . . . Have you *any* idea how miserable that is for an Andarion male?"

"At *your* age, your urges should be slowing down."

"Ach!" he groaned. "You wound me! A dig at my age—and on our anniversary, no less. That's *so* harsh. Besides, I'm still in my prime, and I'm not supposed to go more than eighty hours without sex, ninety-six, tops."

She was still tsking at him a few minutes later as she opened the door to their house. "Good thing you're stralen, then. I'd hate to be murdering another female *and* you."

He shut and locked the door behind them. "No worries there. Even if I wasn't stralen, I would never betray my vows. I'm an asshole and a bastard, not a faithless dog." He pulled her into his arms. "I would never take your heart for granted. Not after having lived for so long without it. I don't ever want to be banished to that lonely hell again."

Ushara was completely unprepared for the intensity of his kiss.

His breathing ragged, he pulled back to stare down at her with a raw, desperate hunger. "I need you, Shara. I swear I'll make it up to you all night long, but right now I have to have release."

Playfully biting at his lip, she whimpered in sympathetic pain for him as she reached for his fly. "My poor baby. It's fine. I know you will. You always do."

The relief on his face was comical as she lowered his pants for him. His breathing intensified as he pinned her gently to the wall with another scorching kiss and quickly peeled her uniform from her. Dipping his head down to suckle her breast, he entered her and made love with a frenzied need. Ushara cried out in pleasure as he filled her completely.

Normally, she would have been upset at him over the harried pace, but his desperation only proved to her that he'd kept faith with her, especially given how quickly he finished and the bashful expression on his face.

It was so sweetly endearing.

He groaned out loud in aggravation, then banged his head against the door.

Laughing, she kissed his cheek and tugged playfully at his whiskers. "Are you okay?"

"No. I'm as irritated by that as you were. It was way too quick for both of us." He brushed his fangs along her collarbone. "But I'm far from finished for the night." He pulled his pants up, then carried her to the bedroom, where he spent the rest of the night making good on his promise, and reminding her of how much of an oral fixation her Ixurian had been cursed with.

By the time she fell asleep in his arms, she was completely sated and worn out.

Ushara wrinkled her nose at Jullien's new blond hair and smooth cheeks. She was so used to his dark bewhiskered looks that it was like meeting a stranger whenever he shaved all traces of his beard-shadow away. "You look so strange like this."

"I would have thought you'd prefer it."

She shook her head. "I love my darkheart. I have no desire to change you."

"Glad to hear it." He stared at himself in the mirror as if trying to get used to it as well. "It is weird."

" 'Cause it looks so natural for you. Like this, you can easily pass as a Fyreblood. Trajen's right." She handed him her link, where she had a picture of Edon Samari she'd found from old archive files. "You *are* his clone. It's chilling, really."

Jullien shuddered as he compared it to his reflection. "It's so spooky to look so much like someone you've never met. Who died so long before I was even born."

"Yeah. You're definitely going to screw with her head."

And that made him smile like a cat locked in a creamery. "This will get her off my mother's and brother's backs. And your family's. She won't have time to screw with your lives, and plot a takeover while I have her on the run."

"That is true. But what about your Tavali training?"

"I've talked it over with Trajen. Kirill and your uncle are still gunning for me. And the Ports. For now, I'm abandoning all Canting and flying without any colors. Unira will fly independent with me and continue the training so that I can qualify for membership, but I'm keeping off everyone's radar in the Nation, and staying clear of your family to protect them while I do this."

Pain choked her. What he was doing was *so* dangerous. Without Canting, he'd have no quarter anywhere. No Safe Harbor. While not all Tavali obeyed the Code they'd sworn to uphold, they were subject to it. But only so long as you wore the badges.

To fly without Nation, colors, or Canting . . .

"It infuriates me that you have to do this."

He shrugged. "It is what it is."

That didn't make it right. The whole point of being Tavali was to fly as family and to have a brotherhood that stood at your back. It wasn't to have to guard against this kind of treachery from your own kind, as well as everyone else. He couldn't even rely on Tavali allies such as The Sentella, Kimmerians, Dread Reckoning, or Mavericks.

He was truly alone. Still hunted and subject to be killed by anyone who found him, with no place to hide.

"I wish I could go with you."

"You're my ears and eyes here. We're still a team. I can't do what I do without you."

But this wasn't how she wanted it. Even though they were married, they still couldn't be together. Damn his family!

And hers.

"Hey," he said, cupping her chin in his hand as he saw the tears swimming in her eyes. "I'm one call away. I'll be back whenever you need me. I reactivated your rings. And I will be here when our girls are born. I swear that to you. Nothing will keep me away. If Vas needs anything, he knows I'll come running. You can screen me, anytime. Day. Night. I'm yours whenever you need to be horrified by my ugly face."

"You are not ugly." She reached down to cup his hard, shapely rear. "What you are is all kinds of sexy."

He nuzzled his face against her neck. "Yeah, you keep doing that, and I will not be leaving . . . ever."

Nipping his chin and running her tongue down his throat, she grinned and slid her hand around to cup him.

He sucked his breath in sharply. "Definitely *not* going anywhere, you do that." His voice dropped a solid octave as his breathing turned ragged.

Her link rang.

Jullien cursed and whimpered as she stepped back. If that was her brother, he would beat holy Tophet out of him. "I'm going to stomp that thing."

She gave him one last squeeze before she answered it. That only made it worse for him.

When she returned a few minutes later, her face was pale. "Something wrong?"

She nodded. "It was Davel wanting to make sure that I warned you the Garvons are stepping up their efforts against all Tavali, and anyone they think is committing any illegal activity in their territory. Caillen Dagan was arrested last night and is going to be executed for smuggling."

That effectively killed his amorous thoughts. "You're shitting me?"

She shook her head. "Davel said you knew the Dagans?"

"Yeah. Never was particularly fond of Caillen. He's an overreactionary bastard who jumps to ridiculous conclusions, but I hate to see him die like that."

Grimacing in sympathy, Jullien rubbed at his neck. He felt awful for them, especially Caillen's older sister Shahara. "This is where I wish I still had some political pull. If I could get my father to take a call from me, the Triosans should have some diplomatic ability to negotiate an exchange for him."

"Can't your brother do that?"

"I would assume so, but I don't know how well they get along. For all I know, especially given Caillen's mouth, Nyk might be rooting for the Garvons." Jullien sighed as his stomach cramped for the poor smuggler. "I still feel like I should put a call in to Evzen, and at least get him to look at the kid and consider a pardon or prison term. Run the specs and make sure it's not a case of the territorial governor being a douche and trying to further his own career at the expense of Caillen's life. While I've no doubt Caillen's guilty of something, he wouldn't have been carrying anything so bad, it would warrant a death sentence. He's not *that* big an idiot. . . ." He hesitated as if he reconsidered that statement. "Well, he is, but he's not a capital felon. Just terminally stupid."

Ushara laughed at his uncharacteristic rant over Caillen's personality. Jullien normally only reacted to his own family like this. Seldom did anyone else motivate him to this degree of rancor. "You really don't like him? What did he do to you?"

He gave her a dry, withering glare. "He once accused me of raping his sister."

That instantly sobered her at something she didn't find the least bit amusing. "What?"

"Swear to the gods." He held his hand up to testify to it. "Yeah. And no, I didn't do anything. He's just *that* stupid."

Well, that certainly explained the rant and why he didn't care for the man. "Then why do you want to help him?"

"I don't. But I feel for his sisters, and I don't want this to tear their family apart. They were orphaned as kids. And while I don't think much of Caillen and even less of his mental capacity, I do respect Shahara Dagan. She's one of the few truly decent people I've run across in my life and I hate to see her done wrong now. For whatever reason, she adores her little brother, moron that he is."

Ushara arched a brow at his passion, and honestly, a part of her was a bit jealous of his obvious respect and defense of another woman.

And that, too, was extremely unusual for him. Especially since he, as a prince, shouldn't have had any knowledge of someone in their line of work. "So how do you know her?"

"Trigon Court." He cleared his throat as a strange and becoming blush crept over his face. He was suddenly, adorably bashful. "She was always professional and courteous whenever I escaped my cousins and she arrested me."

Well, that definitely explained how he'd come across someone in her profession. And it was the last thing she'd expected him to say. "Excuse me?"

He nodded. "You saw my records. Not like you don't know how often I rotated through various legal systems. Unlike the others who hauled me in, she didn't gloat, degrade me, or put my head through a wall or window while I was in her custody. She actually treated me with compassion and acted like I was a sentient being. She'd even try to protect me from the media and wouldn't call and tell them where to line up to photograph my delivery to jail. Says a lot about her integrity . . . and it's how I met Caillen and her sister Kasen, too."

"So just how much time did you spend in the Trigon Court system?"

He snorted bitterly. "Remember, you married a contentious asshole who has extreme anti-social tendancies and major problems with anyone in a position of authority. Let's just say I held the upper tier of their frequent flyer program for deliquents."

She arched her brow. "I don't understand. Didn't your family post bond immediately?"

"Not really. My father's position was always that if I got myself into trouble, I should get myself out. So he left me there, hoping they'd *scare me straight*."

Ushara scowled. "Scare you straight from what?"

"The drugs my cousins kept shooting into me against my will."

Every time she thought about that, she wanted to do them harm. "Didn't you ever tell your father what they were doing to you?"

"Tried, but he never believed me. First rule of being a junkie is lying about it, and blaming your addiction on others. All the experts will tell you that. They won't let you leave rehab until you admit that it's all your

fault and you accept total responsibility for your addiction and actions."
He sighed. "Anyway, it doesn't matter. It was a long time ago."

Yet it did matter. It made her sick what his family had done to him.
And he'd just let something slip that he'd never told her before. "Wait.
Back up a second. . . . What do you mean by *escape* your cousins?"

An angry tic started in his jaw before he rubbed uncomfortably at
the scars on his neck. "I wasn't given any real freedom. Everything I did
was watched and monitored. Because I knew what Parisa had done to
my brother, Merrell, Chrisen, and Nyran were my wardens for her to
make sure I didn't let it slip that she'd had anything to do with Nyk's fate.
If I said or did something they didn't like or that they misinterpreted,
they immediately injected me with some toxin that would either overdose me or induce a reaction that ended with me in jail, rehab, or a
psychiatric ward. They had my behavior so erratic, I could barely think
straight most days. It was why I was so angry when Nyk returned out of
the blue, for the throne. I kept thinking how unfair it was that he'd just
show up and get it all, and I'd be thrown out with nothing after everything they'd put me through for it."

Sighing, he shook his head. "Gah, I was so pissed and stupid. So many
wasted years, waiting for a destiny that was never going to be mine. How
strange that it seemed so important to me then, and I couldn't care less
about any of that now."

"Because you had nothing else."

"True." Jullien swallowed hard as he laid his hand against her rounded
stomach and felt the slight fluttering of their daughters at play. "Now I
have so much more than I ever deserved. More to lose than I can bear
the thoughts of."

Kneeling down, he placed a kiss where they frolicked. "I hate the
thought of leaving my girls."

She brushed her hand against his cheek. "We hate the thought of you
going."

He pressed her palm to his cheek before he rose to kiss her lips. "I
will be back as soon as I can."

"I know." This was a new chapter in both their lives. But as he led
her from their home, toward the landing bay, she couldn't get the image of his new files out of her head.

Jullien eton Anatole was dead.

It was in the official League records now. In the back of her mind, she couldn't help fearing that they might have turned that into a self-fulfilling prophecy. Especially given how many enemies he had.

He was going out today as a true ghost.

The more she thought about it, the worse it seemed.

*What have we done?*

She was sending him out there without Nation. Colors. Harbor.

And if anyone ever learned he was still alive, he would be instantly killed. Yes, he'd been alone before. But she didn't know him then. This time, he traveled with her heart.

This time, he was chasing after the devil for vengeance. Terror filled her. As he said, never before had either of them had so much to lose.

# CHAPTER 27

Jullien cursed in frustration.

Thrāix turned in his chair to look at him as they flew dark through League-controlled space. "Problem?"

"No . . . yes. Not *our* problem. Someone else's. But something I can't seem to let go of."

By the expression on Thrāix's face, he could tell the Trisani was using his powers to read his thoughts. Irritating, but he was getting used to it. He just wished Thrāix was more like Trajen and would respect his privacy and leave his mind alone.

"Don't take it personally, Andarion. They didn't listen to your brother, either. Nykyrian couldn't get a stay of execution, any more than you could. So it's not just you the Garvons are being assholes with."

"Doesn't make me feel better. Damn shame, no matter how you look at it." Jullien rubbed at his chin. "At least tell me Dagan deserves to die."

"Not really. Definitely not for this. He didn't even do it. Caillen's taking the death sentence for his sister. But you knew that without anyone saying it. It's why this has been eating at you."

Jullien looked away as Thrāix said a truth he didn't want to hear spoken out loud. Yeah, he'd known it. Caillen was always taking the rap for his sister Kasen. He always had. "No good deed goes unpunished. Damn."

"Do you really want to help him?"

"Bad blood between us aside? Yeah, I do." For whatever reason, he hated to see anyone unjustly punished.

It was his worst genetic defect.

"Then make sure the DNA for Caillen is run through the Exeter database *before* his execution. Don't let them backlog it, like they normally do capital cases."

Jullien scowled. "Why?"

"Trust me. Use your newfangled powers, and run it through their system today . . . *if* you want to save his life."

Jullien had no idea what difference that would make, since they only ran the samples to see if the convicted felon's DNA matched any other unsolved crimes on file. It was one of the reasons why they weren't in any hurry to run them before execution. Since the felon was about to be out of circulation, what difference did it make if he or she had committed other crimes? They wouldn't be committing any future ones. At least that was *their* philosophy.

But . . . who was he to argue with Thrāix?

Screw it, he'd do it. At least this way, if Caillen was guilty of something else, he'd die for a crime he'd actually committed and not one his sister had dragged him into.

Small consolation, that. Still, better than nothing, he supposed.

His link went off. Jullien pulled it out to see Ushara's image smiling at him. His heart and mood instantly lightened. How weird that it took so little to brighten his day. Worse? Just the thought of hearing the sound of her voice made him hard and aching, especially since it brought to mind an image of her wearing that lacy confection she'd surprised him with on their anniversary.

Smiling at the cruel dichotomy while hoping Thrāix was completely out of his head right now, he answered it. "Hey, beautiful."

"Where are you?"

He checked his coordinates. "Still in the Solaras System for a few more. Why? You need me to head back?"

"No. The League is locking down the Garvon Sector hard. I wanted to make sure you weren't near it."

"We're headed to Oksana to rendezvous with Jupiter."

"Good. Opposite direction works very well for me. Although, knowing you, you could still find utter disaster, with both hands tied behind your back and blindfolded."

He laughed. "So what's going on over there that I need to avoid?"

"Oh, you know. You're the Tadar of Politics, and usually understand these nuances better than the rest of us. Anyway, the Summit's about to meet, so the Caronese Resistance is revving into high gear for their attacks while their Grand Counsel's away. The Sentella's backing them, as they always do. The Qills are trying to start a war with the Trimutians, and for some reason I can't learn, they've got Septurnum help—see if you can find out from Jory who that idiot is. If that's not enough to make the hair on the back of your neck stand up, your grandmother's running loose in the streets, doing who knows what. I have a hangnail, and Vas drank the last of my juice this morning and didn't tell me. He stayed late at school and forgot to remind me, so I thought he'd been kidnapped again. Then he left his backpack in his locker without thinking, so we had to find his teacher to let us back into school after hours to get it. World is coming to an end. I'm telling you. See what you miss when you leave? Oh, and the toilet seat was left up again, and I fell in, in the middle of the night! And you're right, you didn't do it. I raised a thoughtless beast of a son."

He laughed. "Well, I'll kill Vas as soon as I get home, and hide his body. For now, I'll give him a stern lecturing when I hang up from you. In the meantime, I can do absolutely nothing about anything else. I'm feeling grotesquely worthless as a husband and Androkyn."

Laughing at him, she shook her head. "I miss you so much."

"Miss you, too. But I am willing to take the bathroom heat for Vas if it'll spare him your wrath until I get back."

She gave him an adorable grin. "I have to say, you do endure my wrath with much more grace than he does."

"Only because I'm used to being yelled at."

Gasping, she touched her heart. "Now, that hurts."

"I didn't mean for it to," he said quickly. "Just stating a fact, and I wasn't implicating you. You're not the one who insults or beats me. You merely speak about certain subjects with great passion. That doesn't bother me at all."

Ushara winced at his teasing. She knew he was making light of something that, while it didn't bother him, made her ache in sympathetic pain. She'd often wondered how he managed to stay so calm whenever others began shouting at him.

Now she knew.

Trajen had shown it to her. But she hadn't really made *that* connection before. This time, she did. Shouting and insults were all he'd known for communication growing up. All his family and teachers had ever given him. They yelled and he mostly stayed silent while they did so. Because to speak only escalated their tempers and made it worse.

In that moment, she would give anything to hold him.

Jullien frowned at her over the link. "What's that noise?"

She smiled at the discordant sound. "Your legacy."

"Pardon?"

"After hearing you play so well so often, it seems your son has rede-veloped his interest in music. He's out there practicing . . . thanks," she said sarcastically.

He screwed his handsome face up into one of sympathetic pain. "God, I am *so* sorry."

"You should be." She winked at him, then laughed. "Actually, it warms my heart to have him diligently practice every night. I'm glad to see the old keyboard put to use again, and that he sees you as a role model."

Jullien groaned. "Fine, go on and be cruel. Just pile the guilt on. Make it worse."

"Worse?"

"Um, yeah. I'd much rather our child pick a role model I'd like for him to emulate. God help us both if he ever behaves like me. I can think of no worse curse."

She rolled her eyes again. "I can think of no greater blessing. I would love to have a son who acts just like his paka."

Making a noise of protest, he appeared horrified by her suggestion. "Don't say shit like that, Shara! The gods might take you up on it."

"Jules?"

He paused at Unira's soft voice. "Yes, Matarra?"

"We need to go dark. Immediately."

Ushara's face paled. "Stay safe. Love you."

*Itu, munatara.*

Ushara cut the transmission so fast, Jullien wasn't sure she heard him. But then that was what he adored most about her. He didn't have to say it.

She knew.

His safety was more important to her than words. Still, the sight of that blank screen made him ache. He hated to be apart from her.

Another thing he despised his family for as he shut down everything on the ship with his thoughts.

Thrāix gave him an approving nod. "You're getting scary with that."

"Yeah, I don't even feel it anymore. It's like breathing to me now."

"That's good. It's what you want. The ship to become part of you. Indistinguishable."

It was becoming that way. Fast. As were a lot of other objects around him. He wasn't sure at times how Thrāix and Trajen remained sane with their powers. The universe held a whole new scary level when viewed through Trisani eyes.

Such as now . . .

Jullien frowned as he heard the approach on their port side. "Three League ships are moving in."

Unira started to reach for the sensors, then stopped as she remembered that Jullien had cut all power except basic life support. "Can they sense us?"

Jullien shook his head. "They're not probing." He listened to their communications and engines. "They're not slowing." Closing his eyes, he leaned back in his chair and did what they'd come here to do.

Used his powers to scan through their secured onboard systems for classified information that not even his best abilities could access from outside their lines. As good as he was at filching League info, there were some items not even Syn Wade could access.

No one was *that* good by conventional means.

But with these new psychic powers, there was nothing Jullien couldn't access, because he no longer had to do it through an I/O method. His thoughts connected seamlessly to the binary so that it couldn't detect that he was an outside party. The computer thought he was merely another onboard component, and it accepted him as such.

No questions asked.

By the time the ships moved out of range, Jullien had a headache from it.

"Well?" Thrāix asked.

Jullien rubbed at his temple. "Nothing on Eriadne. Bitch is more ghost than I am. Varan, however, is shacked up with one of his other cousins. Since he's a Morlatte assassin, he's registered with The League. Go, moron. I have his address." He started the engines for the ship and set their course. "That being said, it got me thinking."

Thrāix snorted. "Glad something did, Captain."

Jullien chose to ignore his sarcasm. "Nyk's adoptive brother had a base on Oksana, and back when all that shit broke with WAR's rebellion on Andaria, Aksel had a full dossier on all of us."

Unira scowled. "Why?"

"Aksel hated Nyk from the moment his father adopted him. To him, it was the worst insult Huwin could give him and his brother. You're not good enough sons to be my legacy for The League and to carry on my Quiakides name. I had to go adopt a male of another species and make him an assassin instead of my two natural sons."

"Ouch," Thrāix whispered.

"Exactly. Anyway, because of that hatred, Aksel took the contract on Nyk's life the minute President Zamir made it live. And with that madness, Aksel dredged up everything on my brother's past. More than that, Aksel had approached me about helping him to set up Nyk before anyone else knew Nyk was my brother. No one had figured that out yet. *No one.* Yet somehow, Aksel had put it together. He knew all kinds of dirt on my family that no one else had."

Jullien pointed to the nav screen, where he'd laid their course in for Oksana. "I'm thinking we should get to that base and see if anything remains of it. . . . If we can find any of those old files intact."

"That's a long shot."

"True," Unira agreed. "But one definitely worth taking."

Jullien landed them not far from where Aksel's old Morlatte base was now nothing more than a shambled, hollowed-out wreck of the high-tech assassin's lair it'd once been. Five years of neglect, plus the bombing run his brother had laid down on it, had left its scars on the place. The harsh desert landscape had virtually reclaimed it.

Thrāix manifested his fake, holographic people to watch over their ship while they disembarked to check things out.

Jullien had learned that those mental projections, combined with his lifelike mechas, were what had populated the outpost where Thrāix lived. The surly Sparda Trisani was the only actual sentient creature on that rock. The rest had been his fabrications. Either androids he created in his lab, or those holograms he projected with his powers.

Impressive and terrifying.

Just like Thrāix himself.

As they approached the run-down remains, Unira let out a slow whistle at the annihilation that spoke of extreme violence and fury. "What happened? The League?"

"No. My brother. The mother of his daughter, Driana, was murdered here, and his wife was held as hostage. Aksel wanted Nyk to come for a visit." Jullien shook his head at the burned-out walls that had been obviously bombed. "Needless to say, Nyk was a bit perturbed when he arrived. This is a prime example of *be careful what you wish for.*"

Thrāix snorted as they picked their way through the debris to enter the rusted-out remains. Cast against the harsh desert landscape, the building looked like some giant skeletal beast.

As Jullien started for the rickety stairs, he froze the instant he picked up the subtle sound of someone else near them.

Before he could warn the others, he heard the click of a blaster being switched from kill to stun.

"Don't."

He held his hands up slowly. "We mean you no harm."

"Then why are you here?"

Jullien hesitated at the odd question. Before he could answer, Thrāix used his powers to disarm his attacker and pin him to the rusted wall. As his friend went to snap the man's neck, Jullien stopped him. "Wait!"

"For what? A fucking invitation?"

No, there was a strange prickling he didn't understand until he faced the man.

Jullien's breath caught as he instantly recognized the ragged dreg there. Though he was in bad need of food, a bath, shave, and clothes that fit and weren't worn out, this was his once-proud cousin.

Bastien Cabarro.

*Son of a bitch.*

*I thought you were dead.* Those words were almost out of his mouth before he could stop them. Luckily, he bit them back before he betrayed himself.

Sympathy for Bastien poured over him. What the *minsid* hell? How sorry was their family that they could cut their children loose to suffer and die so easily?

"Set him down."

Growling low in his throat, Thrāix obeyed. "A living enemy makes for a dead you."

Jullien gave him an amused stare. "I see you've been reading the *Book of Harmony* again."

"Fuck you, Andarion," he snarled under his breath.

"And another lovely quote from your peaceful scripture."

Bastien scowled at them before he glanced to Unira. "Who are you people?"

"We're just passing through." Jullien shrugged his survival pack off his back. It contained medical supplies, water, and dehydrated emergency food rations. He held it out to Bastien. "Let us look for what we came after—has nothing to do with you—then you can grab a shower on our ship. I'll leave you with some clothes, food, and water."

Bastien raked him with a suspicious glare. "Why?"

"Because you look like you could use it."

Bastien, who bore enough of a resemblance to Jullien's father that it made him want to punch him, took the pack with a grimace. "Do I know you?"

"No," Jullien answered honestly. Six years younger than him, Bastien had never really hung around much the few times their families had forced them together. Bas would head to a corner with his handheld in an attempt to avoid his obnoxious siblings while Jullien would do the same.

For the same reasons.

Bas's human family had been its own special kind of hell, as evidenced by the man's current shitty condition.

Thrāix glanced to Jullien before he spoke to him in his head. *Who is this asshole, and what's he to you? Don't waste my time by saying "nothing" or I'll smack you. I know better.*

Jullien let out a tired sigh. *He's my cousin, Bastien Cabarro.*

Thrāix arched a disdainful brow at the name. "You're that Kirovarian prince who slaughtered his whole family?"

Fury darkened Bastien's eyes. Slamming the pack down, he started for Thrāix only to have Thrāix throw him against the wall again with his powers.

Aghast, Thrāix glared at Jullien. "You would really spare a snake this treacherous?"

"I didn't do it!"

Thrāix scoffed. "That's what they all say."

Jullien exchanged a glance with Unira, who was remaining oddly stoic and silent. "I believe him. They never had any evidence against him, other than the word of his own uncle, who now sits on the throne he inherited after he testified against Bastien."

Thrāix laughed bitterly. "Oh, okay, 'cause the younger son *never* murders the older one for a throne."

That bitter accusation, which had been leveled against him more times than he could count, ignited Jullien's own rage, and if anyone else had said it, they'd be searching the ground for their teeth. "Yeah, and sometimes the second son just makes a ready-made patsy for others to pin their own crimes on. Because everyone *but* that second son is smart enough to figure out that when the entire family dies, he's going to be blamed for it. Funny, he's creative and ambitious enough to remove the direct obstacles to his succession, yet doesn't ever consider that in the obvious chain of suspicion, he's suspect number one and that either jail or death is a much more permanent hurdle against his ruling. Yeah, right. . . . That thought *never* occurs to him, until it's too late. Now, put him down."

Bastien hit the ground with a solid thud and a loud groan.

"Really?" Jullien said in the same tone an irate parent would use with a petulant toddler.

Thrāix smirked. "You didn't specify *gentle* as a condition of his release."

Sighing irritably, Jullien growled in the back of his throat while Bastien pushed himself to his feet. He struggled for patience, knowing it wasn't worth a fight against one of his few friends.

Irritated, he tried to ignore Thrāix's pissy mood. "Aksel's office was on the second floor. What we need, if it's still intact, should be up there." He led them away from Bastien.

As they left the room, Bastien called out to Jullien. *"Paktu, mi kyzi."*

*"Estra, mi pleti."* Jullien silently cursed himself as soon as that automatic response was out of his mouth, and he realized what he'd done.

How slick Bastien had been.

Dammit. He was the one who'd taught Andarion to him when they were boys. Not much of it. Just a few key phrases.

*Thank you, cousin* and *anytime, my blood* being among them.

Holding the pack to his chest, Bastien approached him as Jullien turned slowly around to face him again.

His breathing ragged, Bastien swallowed hard. "Tell me I'm wrong. But it's you, Julie, isn't it?"

The sane part of himself said to tell Bas he was mistaken. To deny it, and his cousin, with everything he had.

He couldn't. Not after everyone else in their family had turned their back on Bas. He knew exactly how bad it hurt to be cast out and denied. Be damned if he'd do it to someone else. "Yeah."

Bastien stared at him as if he were a ghost. Then he laughed and reached out to pull him in for a hug. "Damn, if you don't look good, cousin. Running looks much better on you than it does on me. You wear banishment well."

Jullien held him close even though he had to ignore the stench of him and breathe through his mouth. "You wouldn't have said that two years ago. Trust me."

Clapping him on the back, Bastien released him. "Thanks for not cringing when I touched you. Believe me, I know I'm disgusting and it's more than I deserve."

"It's all good, *m'drey*."

"No, it's not. And for what's worth, which isn't much, I tried to get my father to harbor you. It sickened me how they did you after your parents threw you out. I'm really sorry."

Jullien gestured at him. "I'm sorry for *this*. What happened to you?"

"League. I'm a Ravin. Been running since Barnabas murdered my family and stole our throne."

He cringed in sympathetic pain. "I figured you were dead by now."

"Same here. Thank the gods for my Gyron Force training. How the hell have you survived?"

Jullien smirked. "Thank the gods for Gyron Force training. Had your uncle and father not been such bastards those times I visited, I wouldn't have lasted a week on my own."

Bastien snorted. "Ain't it a bitch? Barnabas had no idea he was doing us a favor. One I pray I get to return to him by planting my Gyron axe in the center of his skull."

"*Gealrewe!*" Jullien clapped him on the back. "Well, since you know who I am, you want me to drop you somewhere? Get you off this rock?"

He let out a long, tired sigh. "Yes—but no. Not unless you know how to pull a League chip out of me."

"No." Jullien looked to Unira and Thrāix.

"Sorry," Unira said. "Not a clue."

Thrāix shook his head. "Beyond my abilities. I could try to do it with my powers, but it's as likely to explode the chip, which could cause internal damage, and depending on where it's located, that could paralyze or kill him."

The only thing that had saved Jullien from being tracked by Nyran's toy was that he'd discovered how to jam the one in his spine—something

Nyran hadn't figured on him learning to do with his new Trisani powers. The beautiful bonus about his being a hybrid, he didn't have the same limitations that Thrāix and Trajen had. But when it came to surgically removing Bastien's or jamming League tech . . .

That he didn't want to risk. As Thrāix said, he might hurt or kill his cousin.

Eyes wide, Bas held his hand up and backed away. "Rather not chance death. My life sucks enough without a maiming or fatality."

Thrāix nodded. "Figured you'd feel that way."

Bastien narrowed his gaze on Thrāix. "Were you really going to kill me?"

"Had you not been his cousin? Yeah. And I still might. If you give me any reason to." Thrāix headed for the stairs with Unira.

"Duly noted." Bastien ripped into one of the meal packs as he followed them through the base. "So what brings you here. Really?"

Jullien decided there was no reason to hide the truth. Besides, if Bastien lived here, he might be a resource who could help them with the search. "Looking for the files Bredeh ran on my family back when he was trying to kill Nyk. I'm hoping I can find something to lead me to my grandmother and the rest of my cousins who've sided with her."

"To what end?"

"Theirs, I hope."

Bastien swallowed a bite of his bar. "I thought you and Grandma were always tight?"

Jullien froze and gave him a bone-chilling glare that caused him to take two steps back.

"Sorry," Bastien said quickly. "That's what your father always said whenever he came around. He thought it showed an utter lack of judgment on your part."

"What in the Nine Worlds could *ever* make him think that? I never could stand the old bitch."

Bastien shrugged nonchalantly. "No idea. But he was fully convinced of it."

Jullien snorted. "Anyway, I love my grandmother as much as you do your uncle, for about the same reasons. Had my father ever bothered to have a conversation with me, he'd have known that. And if I don't stop her, she will find some way to kill my mother and brother, and retake her throne. I didn't wipe out an entire portion of my family to put my mother in power to watch that happen."

Bastien scowled. "No. Wait . . . what?"

"You heard me."

"WAR and your aunt put your mother in power."

"Yes," Jullien said slowly, "with the information *I* gave them over the years. And particularly at the end. Trust me. No one else could have brought down Eriadne. It's why I'm the only one she put a hit on."

Bastien's jaw went slack. "Do *they* know that?"

"They never bothered to ask. But one would think with their brilliant intellects, they'd have discerned it by now. Again, doesn't take much to figure it out, since I'm the only one my grandmother has come after with a vengeance. Everyone else was spared her wrath. Kind of makes you wonder why, huh?"

"Damn, brother. You got screwed."

"Don't we all?"

Bastien nodded. "So why you want to help them?"

Jullien shrugged with a nonchalance he really didn't feel. "She's still my mother. Nyk's still my brother. My grandmother's done them enough harm in their lives. I'm not about to let that bitch do any more. Be damned if I'm going to let her win after everything else she's done. I'm a bastard that way."

"And here all this time, I thought you were nothing but a vindictive asshole."

"Oh, you were *not* wrong about that. I am vindictive asshole. This is all about payback to the whore. Just the whore, in this case, isn't my mother."

Bastien sucked his breath in sharply. "That's harsh."

"I am the callous bastard they raised me to be." Jullien scowled at Aksel's system, which Thrāix hadn't bothered to touch. Rather, he stared at it with a bemused grimace that matched the one on Unira's face.

One quick glance over it, and Jullien understood their reservation. "It's booby-trapped?"

Bastien stepped around him to enter in his password. "Yeah . . . sorry about that. I did it. First thing when I found this place and moved in was secure everything so that if one of the League bastards happened upon it, they couldn't use anything to figure out if it belonged to me or not." He opened the files. "There you go."

While continuing to eat his way through the supplies Jullien had given him, Bastien drifted back to watch.

Jullien took over and began searching through Aksel Bredeh's database with an expertise Bastien had never realized his cousin possessed. This was not the useless piece-of-shit prince the Triosans had railed against. Bastien couldn't count the hours he'd listened to his father and Uncle Aros as they discussed what they needed to do to block Jullien's inheritance. *"I don't know what to do with his sorry ass, Newell. It's not like I have another heir to choose from. But you've seen what I'm talking about. He sneers at me as if he could rip out my throat, and he's large enough to do it. Plus he's Andarion. And he's high most of the time. I'm so terrified of being alone with him. I never know when he's going to decide he's had enough, and go for my crown. The way he looks at me scares the shit out of me. I know he's plotting with his grandmother to invade my empire. Why they've waited this long, I have no idea. Why else would he keep begging to come live here when it's obvious he's more Andarion than human? Hell, he can barely speak Triosan or Universal coherently. I only understand every third word out of his mouth. Can you imagine him as the emperor of my people? My father would roll in his grave. I know he's only after my crown."*

Instead, Jullien had willingly given up his Andarion inheritance when he put his mother in power. It would have been easy during the Andarion coup and riots to kill off his entire eton Anatole family, and to have emerged as the sole survivor of that mess. No one would have suspected anything, given the way the Andarions had gone after the royal family.

Had he wanted to, he could have seized the Andarion throne and then taken his father's empire in the blink of an eye. Hell, with the turmoil that rapidly followed on Kirovar, Jullien could have even made a play for theirs, too. Since Bastien's mother, their queen, was the younger sister of Jullien's father, Jullien had as much blood rights to it as Barnabas did.

More so, really.

But that wasn't the cousin Bastien remembered from his childhood. While they hadn't been close, the Jullien he recalled had always tried to stay low and in the shadows. Off everyone's radar. True to Aros's words, his studious and portly Andarion cousin had been sullen and quiet. Extremely reserved, and at times rude. Bastien had assumed it came mostly from the language barrier and Jullien's frustration with their strange, "foreign" customs, which were seldom explained to him until after he'd unknowingly violated them and he was mortified and ridiculed when his father or another relative made a grand show of publicly correcting him for it.

Because Jullien was seldom allowed to visit his father, his Universal had been extremely difficult to understand through his thick Andarion accent, and he'd spoken even less Triosan and no Kirovarian—which everyone kept insisting he answer them in. Uncle Aros had refused to allow Jullien a translator, since as a prince of the empire, he "needed" to know and speak the people's language. Then they would laugh and mock him when he spoke with a childish vocabulary and syntax, which understandably had made Jullien even more churlish and silent. Withdrawn and belligerent. It got so bad at one point that Jullien refused to speak even when their grandfather tried to beat answers out of him.

Bastien flinched as he recalled that afternoon of them striking Jullien, and Jullien standing there, unflinching with every blow, but willfully silent through every bit of it. He'd never seen anyone stand so strong, especially at such a young age.

It was why Bastien had attempted to learn Andarion. That had given him a whole new appreciation for Jullien's intellect. God knew, Andarion was one screwed-up language. Hard to pronounce and harder still to comprehend if you weren't born to it.

Honestly, he'd always felt sorry for Jullien. He'd seemed horribly lonely and sad. Wounded even. He seldom smiled. Always looked at the world around him through those dark glasses with a suspicious frown, as if waiting to get slapped or kicked.

While Bastien's father had been doting and kind, Aros wasn't. At least not to Jullien. Aros might bring presents and praise for Bastien and his siblings, but he'd always complained about Jullien's obesity, Andarion traits, and mannerisms. His red-tinted glasses that he had to wear. The way he rolled his *r*s and *l*s. His father had accused him of lisping like a toddler when he spoke, but it wasn't a lisp. More like a deep brogue or growling sound.

Basically everything Julie did got on his father's nerves. In fact, all Bastien remembered from family get-togethers was Aros relentlessly dogging his son. *Sit up. Stand straight. Sit down. Your coat's crooked.*

*You mispronounced that. Why can't you learn how to greet a human? Stop slouching. Are you paying attention? Where's your head? Did you hear what I said? Or are you too stupid to understand it?*

Their grandfather had been even more critical and cold. Mostly because he couldn't stand the Andarions, and he'd been infuriated that his grandson and future heir was one of their dreaded breed. Furious at Aros, he'd taken his rage out on Jullien as if it were all his fault that his father had slept with his mother.

Every time Jullien came to visit, Quinlan had gone to war on both Aros and Jullien, making both their lives hell until Jullien was returned to Andaria.

Now Bastien sighed as he watched his cousin searching through files.

Yeah, Julie knew an entirely different Triosan grandfather than the doting old man who'd bounced Bastien and his siblings on his knee. And that made him saddest of all. He had a hard time reconciling how his grandfather could be so kind to him and so hard on Jullien, who'd never deserved such harsh treatment. It'd really screwed with him as a kid to see those different sides of his family.

Made him extremely suspicious of people in general.

Sadly, not suspicious enough. If he'd been a bit more, he might have seen Barnabas's treachery coming before it was too late.

Jullien scooted the chair back from the desk for Thrāix to lean in. "This is it. But it's not really helpful. Venik has a secured base that's unknown to The Tavali outside of his Nation. He had it built for my cousin as a precaution should something happen to him, so that Malys wouldn't be able to kill Nyran or Parisa in a jealous rage. I will lay odds that's where my grandmother is."

Thrāix studied the schematic. "That's so deep in their territory . . . and the Phrixians. We go near that, they'll know."

Jullien raked a frustrated hand through his hair. "We've got to do something. I can't let them kill my family. She's not going to stop trying for my mother's throat."

The woman with him rubbed his shoulder. "At least your immediate family is safe from them."

"That's not good enough."

"You know . . ." Bastien moved forward to access another database of old smuggler routes. "There are some ancient trading wormholes that aren't in use anymore in that sector. They don't really appear on most maps." He showed it to Jullien. "I stumbled across this one back when I went through a teenage phase we won't talk about."

Jullien snorted. "I remember that phase."

"And we're not talking about it." Bastien pointed to one of the routes that paralleled the station's orbit. "That would drop you in, clear of their surveillance."

Jullien nodded as he studied the map. "Mind if I take a copy?"

"It's all yours."

He quickly downloaded it. *"Thöky."*

Bastien's eyes widened at his use of the Kirovarian term for *thanks.* "Glad I could help."

Jullien jerked his head toward the door. "Want to see about that shower?"

"You know I do."

"We can also drop you somewhere else. Really, I don't mind."

Bastien shook his head. "As much as I would, I better stay put. This place plays havoc with League tracking equipment and most electronics. Not sure why Aksel's shit works. But this is the safest place I've found to bed down. While it's not much, it gives me peace of mind at night. I know I don't have to tell *you* what that's worth."

No, he didn't. Sad to say, Jullien would have killed for a run-down safe shit-hole like this to call home before Ushara took him in. But even so, he hated to leave Bastien like this.

Desperately, he wanted to offer him Safe Harbor, but since he wasn't a Canted member of the Nation, he didn't have the right to make that invitation. And while Unira had her Canting, she was terrified of Trajen and would never dare bring someone wanted by The League near their base.

Thrāix wasn't Tavali and, like Jullien, couldn't extend it on Trajen's behalf. That being said, the Trisani glanced around. "You want me to make the place a little more hospitable?"

Bastien frowned. "What do you mean?"

"I have some skills that can clean this place up and make it more solid and habitable . . . if you want."

A slow smile broke across Bastien's face. "A solid roof that doesn't leak during the rare rains we have would be incredible. But don't make it too inviting. I don't want it to attract any undue attention. Only things I want crawling in here are the spiders and insects."

"Got it."

Jullien led Bastien and Unira toward their ship.

Bastien frowned at the ship's name on the side that was written in Andarion. "*Pet Hate*?"

Jullien grinned as he lowered the ramp. "Seemed fitting for me."

Shaking his head, Bastien laughed. "Damn, Julie, you look *so* different from the last time I saw you."

"Yeah, I'm surprised you recognized me."

"I would always know my favorite cousin."

He arched a brow at that. "Not how I remember our relationship."

Bastien grinned. "I will admit that you intimidated me."

That admission stunned him. "What?"

"Honor to the gods. Yeah. You were massively tall and huge. Twice my size, and you always wore a frowning expression that said you were contemplating the death and dismemberment of the next person who made the mistake of speaking to you."

Unira passed a curious look at Jullien. "Did you?"

"No. Honestly, the frown came from my confusion as I tried to understand what they were saying to me. Triosans speak fast, and their accents are incredibly thick and unlike the language files we were given in school. The court dialect was completely different from what I'd been taught."

Bastien nodded. "He's right. It took me a few minutes to reacclimate every time I visited. But man, Julie, that's not what it looked like on your face. Your expression was one of perpetual pissed off. Not that I blame you for it. . . . Yet even so, I always looked forward to seeing you."

"Why? You mostly ignored me."

"I always sat by you, if you remember."

Jullien scowled as he thought back to their childhood and vaguely recalled that fact. Bastien *had* done that.

Bastien grinned at him. "I just always thought you had some kind of secret knowledge the rest of us lacked. And I wanted to know more about Andarions and if they were as different from us as everyone claimed. Because honestly, you didn't seem like you were all that strange to me."

"Thanks . . . I think."

Bastien winked as Unira laughed before she headed down the hallway that led toward the bridge. Sobering, Bastien narrowed his gaze on Jullien. "In all seriousness, though, you look really good now, and not just more fit and trim. You look happy. Like there's a weight missing from your shoulders. I don't know what happened to you, but I hope it's as good as it seems. You deserve to have some peace from the hell they gave you."

Jullien pulled the glasses down past his eyes so that Bastien could see their true red shade.

Bastien gaped. "What's the Andarion term for that?"

"Stralen."

"Means you're married, right?"

Jullien nodded as he replaced his glasses. "To an amazing female. Like your Alura."

Tears filled his eyes as anger curled his lip. "For your sake, I pray she's nothing like Alura. That faithless bitch is one of the reasons I'm here."

"I'm sorry, Bas. I didn't know."

"Yeah. Neither did I. Until it was too late."

Feeling bad for the man, Jullien took him to his room and showed him where the shower was. He pulled out some of his own clothes for him. "Take whatever you need."

Inclining his head, Bastien stepped into the bathroom and closed the door.

While Bastien showered, Jullien went to the galley to make him something hot and nourishing to eat, and to pack him some better supplies.

Unira joined him. "It's really decent what you're doing for your cousin."

"He was always a good kid."

"Still, it has to be hard for you."

Jullien pulled down their canned supplies. "Not as hard as I would have thought."

"Meaning?"

He paused to look at her. "I think I've finally listened to you, Matarra, and learned to let the hatred in my past go, and find peace with it, and with my birth family."

She arched a quizzical brow.

He laughed at her shocked expression. "I know. I didn't think I'd ever be able to forgive any of them, either. Now . . . I just don't want to see him suffer."

Unira pulled his head down so that she could place a kiss on his forehead. "*M'tana* . . . today you have become *il Pryne Kadurr*. You no longer fight with fury in your heart. You have transcended to the next level and have found the *Træxeri*. The rarest of rare. I envy you that. It is said that only one in every ten generations will ascend to such a state, and here you have."

With a wry grin, he hugged her. "Don't give me too much credit, Matarra. I'm still a surly war-beast."

Laughing, she pulled away. "You will have a new mastery of your powers when you fight now. Especially your fire. Mark my words."

Jullien didn't believe it for a second, but he didn't want to contradict her either. He felt no differently. Not really. Other than he'd been in Bas's worn-out shoes and he knew how hard it was to be alone in the universe, without friend, ally, or even a pet to call your own. It was a fate he wished on no one other than his grandmother.

His heart heavy, he finished preparing the meal and packing supplies, then returned with them to his room to find Bastien coming out of the head. He had the towel wrapped around his face and was inhaling the fresh scent of it as if it were a bouquet of flowers. Sadly, Jullien had been there, too.

"You can have some of the towels, if you want."

Bastien actually blushed. "Pathetic, right?"

"Not about to judge. You don't want to know how sorry my state was when my wife found me." He handed the tray to Bastien, who attacked it with much the same fervor he'd frightened Ushara with on the day they met.

And like him, Bastien cringed the moment he realized that he'd become more animal than sentient being. "Sorry."

"Again, no apologies. Ever. I get it."

Bastien wiped at his mouth, and for the first time they were truly bonded kin. "Who would have ever thought this would be our lives, huh? I thought by now I'd be ruling by Alura's side, in complete bliss."

"I never thought I'd live long enough to rule. Gods' truth to that. Every day I woke up alive in that palace, I counted it a miracle."

Bastien set the tray aside. "Seriously?"

He nodded. "Once Nykyrian was gone, I figured it was just a matter of time until one of my cousins grew brazen enough to take the fatal shot."

"That's why you wanted to live with your father?"

"Why else?"

Bastien let out a bitter laugh. "Your father thought it was a ruse of your grandmother's so that you could take his throne."

Jullien rolled his eyes at the stupidity. "Of course he did. All he had to do was marry and screw another whore for a son. I wouldn't have cared. I just wanted away from Andaria."

Scowling, Bastien gaped at him. "You know why he never did, right?"

"No idea whatsoever."

"Jullien . . . he loves your mother. I mean, *loves* her. They were supposed to marry. Everything had been arranged, in spite of our grandfather. Uncle Aros was willing to give up his throne for her, then Nykyrian was killed and she went into an institution. After that, his father and the Triosan senate absolutely forbade it."

He gaped at something he'd never heard or known before. "What? When was this?"

"Before I was born. But I heard my mother and your father, and our grandfather fight about this most of my life. Aros categorically refused to ever take another bride—that was his FU to his father and his people over what they did to him by banning his marriage to Cairistiona. He has been loyal to your mother all these years. Your mother is his heart and soul."

That made no sense whatsoever. "Then why did he allow them to banish me and then replace me as heir?"

"Truthfully? Aros thinks you hate him. He says that the first time he picked you up when you were an infant, you screamed like you were being murdered and didn't stop until he put you down. That anytime he tried to touch you, you cringed and recoiled, or ran away to hide. So he learned to leave you alone and focused on Nyk. After Nyk was gone, he didn't know what to do with you."

Jullien ground his teeth as those words reopened old wounds deep inside his soul. While he had no knowledge of being an infant, he knew well that when he was a child, the only time anyone touched him was for punishment. Given the rough and callous treatment of his nurses, he imagined they must have been the same in his infancy and that he would have had an automatic flinch factor to being handled by anyone, even his own parents. So of course he'd have screamed if anyone touched him.

He still involuntarily flinched if anyone other than a small handful of well-trusted family came near his personal space.

And he did remember hiding from his father when he'd been young. But only because his father rarely came to visit and had been a virtual stranger to him. As an Andarion boy, he'd been taught to fear humans, who hated their species.

Even his own father.

Bastien sighed. "Every time you visited, you and Aros always ended up in a bitter fight. So he thought it would be best if you stayed on Andaria. It's why he didn't fight them when they removed you. He thought you'd be happier there. That it would be best for everyone."

Jullien scoffed bitterly. "My father never bothered to get to know me at all."

"I'm sorry, Julie."

"It doesn't matter. My parents orphaned me the day I was born. I never expected much from them, and sadly, they never failed to meet my low expectations." Jullien jerked his chin toward his closet. "Take whatever you need, brother. I'll make sure and bring supplies here whenever I pass through."

Bastien drew his brows together in consternation. "Why are you being so kind to me?"

"Because I know what it's like to be left out in the cold. I don't want to do that to you. If I can find a surgeon who can remove your tag, I'll come back with him, too."

Tears welled in Bas's eyes before he pulled Jullien against him and hugged him. "Even if you leave and never think of me again, the fact that you offered . . . I love you, my cousin."

Jullien pounded him on the back and released him. "I won't forget. I put my hailing numbers in while I ran my searches. If you come under attack, get sick, or need anything, you call me. I mean that. I'll return immediately. Anytime. Don't hesitate."

With that, Jullien showed him the way back to the ramp and to where Thrāix waited with extra ammunition and weapons.

Bastien gasped at the sight of it. "I wasn't expecting all this."

Thrāix grimaced. "Yeah, well, I wasn't expecting to let it go either. But after what I saw in that building . . . reevaluated my opinion of you. It's not often I'm wrong. But I'm man enough to admit when I make a mistake. I made sure to conceal you, so you should be left alone."

He inclined his head to them. "Thank you."

Unira joined them and handed Bastien one of her prayer books. "I know you probably don't read Andarion, but I want you to have this anyway, for the gods to watch over you and keep you safe."

"I will treasure it, High Mother." He paused to meet Jullien's gaze. "Peace be with you, cousin."

"And you."

Suddenly, an alarm sounded.

Jullien scowled as he heard it. "It's Jup. He's under fire."

Bastien inclined his head to them. "Go. Help whoever it is. Thanks again, all of you." And with that, he sprinted down the ramp and vanished.

Thrāix cupped Jullien's face and turned it toward him. He gave him a poignant, sincere stare. "He'll be fine."

"Reassurance or truth?"

"Both. Plant your emotions and you can see it yourself. You did a good thing and kept me from a stupid one. My thanks on that."

"*Y'blent'i.*"

Thrāix sucked his breath in sharply. "Oooh, I love it when you speak Andarion to me. No idea what it means, but it's sexy as Tophet."

Snorting, Jullien shoved him away as he rushed to take his seat for launch. "Means *no problem.*"

"Sounds better in Andarion."

"Everything does," Unira said as she locked down the ship and took up her own chair for take-off.

Jullien fired their engines and launched while he scanned for Jory's position and situation.

Thrāix let out a low whistle when he found it by more conventional means. "Damn, they're taking heavy fire. This is where I'm supposed to remind you that Ushara wants you to stay safe and away from battle."

"Your warning is noted."

He passed a disgruntled smirk to Unira. "I know what those words mean in Universal, but when did they become Andarion for *I'm ignoring you, and doing it anyway?*"

She laughed. "The day we allowed my son to take command of this ship."

"Ah, our stupidity. Gotcha."

Jullien leaned back to smirk at his copilot. "You planning to keep bitching? Or are you ready to help me implement Operation *Strûghênyi Pamutir.*"

"Bless you. When we finish with battle, you should see someone about that head cold." Thrāix secured himself to his chair. "But if that wasn't a sneeze and you meant Operation Mind Fuck . . . I'm locked and loaded, Captain. Let's do this."

# CHAPTER 28

Working as a team, Jullien and Thrāix flew in completely unde-
tected and appeared like a phantom wraith behind The League
cruiser that was hammering Jupiter's ship.

Unira opened fire.

The cruiser sounded the alarm to launch fighters for a counterstrike,
but it was too late. With his powers, Jullien already had access to their
systems and was shutting down every part of their ability to defend themselves.

One by one, the fighters went dark and drifted harmlessly away. He
left them only enough power to sustain life support.

But as he crawled through their databases and files for the information he wanted, he heard a strange buzz. An instant later, a fierce ache
began in his head. All of a sudden, he felt weak and peculiar.

"Jules?"

He barely heard Thrāix's voice through the shrieking in his ears.

"Unira! Grab him!"

Jullien didn't understand those words. His eyes began jerking as
everything went dark. . . .

Thrāix cursed when he saw Jullien fall and couldn't get to him in
time.

Unira paled as she cradled Jullien's body in her arms. "What's wrong
with him?"

"It's an old Chiller attack. I-I didn't recognize it in time." Thrāix
grabbed a manual headset. "Jupiter? If you're locked in, disengage. Repeat. Disengage. They have a Pulsator on board."

Jupiter's curse matched his as he pulled back. "What do we do?"

Thrāix checked the monitors visually, but hesitated to use any of his powers, lest he get hit, too. "I think Jullien's hacks are holding. We should retreat while we're able."

"Hintos don't retreat."

"Fine. We're advancing in a new direction."

Silence rang out for several interminably long seconds before Jupiter responded. "And that direction would be?"

"South." Thrāix plugged in their new coordinates and prayed nothing had been burned out with Jullien's brain. Since his friend was Andarion, he had no idea how this attack would work on him as opposed to a Tris.

Hopefully, nowhere near as severely.

And he didn't breathe again until their engines came online without Jullien's assistance and fired up to full throttle. "SOF? How you doing over there?"

"Keeping pace. Our friendlies are not. Appears the good captain knocked them down permanently before they took him out of commission. How's he doing?"

Thrāix glanced over to Unira, who shook her head that she had no idea. "We're not sure."

Jupiter sighed. "All right. I'm moving to hyper. Want to rendezvous at our usual?"

"Yeah. I'll see you there shortly." Thrāix let Jory take the lead. Once he had them in hyperdrive, he moved to check on Jullien himself.

Blood was slowly leaking from his left ear and nose.

Unira wiped it away with a tissue that was soaked. Even though she appeared composed, her hand shook, letting him know exactly how concerned and upset she was by Jullien's injuries.

Thrāix covered her hand with his. "I'm not going to let anything happen to him."

Tears welled in her eyes. "I know it sounds crazy, but I really do think of him as my own child." She laughed with a bit of hysteria in her tone. "I always thought I was so content with my life as a charity worker and high priestess. Taking care of my congregation and helping others. That was always enough for me." She brushed the bleached blond hair back from Jullien's face with a mother's caress. "I looked at everyone as my child and thought that was what love meant. It was all there was to it."

Wiping at her eyes with the back of her hand, she choked on a sob. "I was such a fool. I had *no* idea how much more I could love someone until the day this surly little beast stood so bravely in his defiance before me at my temple door . . . with that irritating grin of his that dared me to throw him out. And then when I watched him on those quiet after-noons where he patiently tutored Nadya and Vasili in the bay when he had no idea anyone else was around. . . . Where other males would have been shouting angrily in impatience at the children over their careless-ness and rambunctiousness, he never once raised his voice above a gentle whisper with them while they interfered with his work. Rather, whenever Vasili would yell at his cousin that she was going to break something, Jullien would pick her up and tickle her, then kindly remind the boy that objects can be fixed or replaced. But the feelings of loved ones are not so easily mended."

Thrāix ground his teeth at the paraphrased quote. "That's from the Trisani *Book of Harmony*."

She let out a half laugh. "An Andarion tiziran who quotes peace, and a Trisani warrior who craves vengeance entrusted by the gods into the hands of a priestess who had all but given up on this world and her place in it. What a strange family we are."

"Family?" Her word choice startled Thrāix. It'd been a long, long time since anyone had included him in such a grouping.

"Surely you know that's how I view you as well? You're as much a son to me as Jullien is."

Stunned, Thrāix stared at her. His own mother had died so long ago that he couldn't even recall her face or form. Not even the sound of her voice or color of her hair. Honestly, he had no memory of her as any-thing more than the vaguest of shadows. While he remembered more of his father, he'd lost him the night Trisa fell. He'd died fighting beside Thrāix's older brother.

As for Julia . . . he tried never to think of their brief time together. The pain was too much for him to bear.

Like Jullien, he'd lived alone for so long that it was all he knew now. He'd been forced to teach himself to live in a state of perpetual empti-ness and denial—otherwise, the loss of family, culture, and home burned so deep that he couldn't function at all. The rage of injustice wouldn't let him.

For this one broken Andarion and a vice admiral Trajen had taken under his wing out of guilt, Trajen had called in his long-standing debt and forced Thrāix back into the land of the living. It was something he'd sworn he'd never do.

Not for anyone or anything.

Yet for reasons he still didn't comprehend, he'd allowed Trajen to pull him back. And Jullien and Ushara had kept him here.

But a family . . . ?

Unira cupped his cheek. "Are you all right?"

A tear slid past his control as his emotions overwhelmed him and he realized that somehow all of them had slipped past his numbness and burrowed far deeper into his heart than he'd ever wanted them to.

Damn his soul for it. The last thing he wanted was to care again. The price was just too fucking high.

Now it was too late.

They were there and there was nothing he could do for it.

Embarrassed, he wiped it away. "I need to see about Jullien."

"Thrāix—"

"I'm fine, High Mother."

"You're not fine, *m'tana.* I don't have to be Trisani to know that. You've been alone for a long time, and I understand that. But Jullien and I do consider you our family. He may not say it, but you know it's true. And I feel the same. I just wanted you to know how much my boys mean to me."

He swallowed hard. "I have no real memory of my mother. But I should like to think that she would have been as kind and beautiful as you."

As if sensing her words and their mood, Jullien came awake with a curse, ready to battle.

Thrāix caught him before he accidentally punched one of them. "Easy, *m'drey.* You've no enemies here."

Jullien blinked past the pain that was slicing through his skull. "What the hell happened? Did you hit me?"

"No, but I'm tempted," he scoffed. "Old Chiller weapon. No one was expecting *that* to be on board."

Jullien panicked as he realized that they must have detected his presence. "Are they after us?"

"No. We appear safe."

*"Appear?* That's a bullshit word."

And his body wasn't listening to anything comforting as his breathing turned ragged and he rushed for the con to double-check their settings and make sure of it.

After a few nerve-wrecking minutes, he realized Thrāix was right. He didn't see any sign of the cruiser.

Still . . .

*They had detected him.* Booted him out of their system. He ran more analysis to see if they were after them.

Thrāix exchanged a worried frown with Unira. "Jules, what are you doing?"

"Making sure they're not tailing us."

"They're not."

"You don't know that."

Thrāix put his hands on his hips. "Pretty damn sure."

"Yeah, but—"

Moving to stand by him, Thrāix gently cupped Jullien's face in his hands and forced him to meet his gaze. "Look at me, buddy. Focus. You're safe. It's just a panic attack. Breathe through it."

Dizzy and belligerent, he had to curb the impulse to strike out at Thrāix. In the past, it was what he'd have done to anyone else. But the well-trained Trisani warrior wouldn't react well to such an attack. Not that the fear of bleeding stopped him—it never had before. He just didn't want to rupture their friendship with his stupidity.

Thrāix kept his gaze locked on his. "Come on, Jules. In and out. Slow and easy . . . First time you get knocked down with a Pulsator, it's a beast. Trust me, I know. It's what caused our army to fail. We thought we were indestructible. No human could touch us with our psychic powers. We got blindsided, just like you. And when you find out that you're not the baddest ass on the block, it takes you a few to recover."

He tightened his hand in Jullien's hair. "You still with me?"

Jullien finally began to calm a degree. "Yeah. Think so."

Thrāix patted him on the shoulder and let go. "Just remember that warning sensation, *drey*. Next time, pull back the instant you feel it. It's that weird-ass hum and buzz. Treat it like a live electrical wire. And remember that unlike us, you're Andarion. You got all that strength and the ability to breathe fire. It won't leave you in a coma for a week. Most of all, you're not alone. You have reinforcements."

Unira placed her hand on Jullien's back.

He would never get used to this feeling of having a family. Of unity.

"*Sanguine inter fratres devoto,*" Jullien breathed.

Thrāix smiled as Jullien spoke the words that had been the official motto of the Trisani royal armed forces. "That's right. *For my brothers, I will bleed.*"

Jullien pressed the heel of his hand to the ache in his forehead. "Did Jory make it out?"

"He did. Otherwise, I'd be all over them. Probably have my brains scrambled as a result. I laid the course in for Haven II, where we're meeting him."

Jullien nodded as he checked everything one more time . . . just in case. "Uh. . . . I feel like I've gone a round with Talyn Batur in a Ring match."

Thrāix laughed. "I don't think you'd be standing upright if you'd done that."

"Yeah, trust me, I know. I'm still dizzy from the last punch he gave me."

Thrāix arched a brow at his comment. "Seriously?"

Nodding, he pointed to the scar on his forehead. "Oh yeah. They don't call him the Iron Hammer for nothing. He took down my entire guard while they were firing point-blank at him." He laughed at the memory. "Never saw anything like it in my life. Still don't know how he took that many stun blasts without going down. That giant shit's a beast."

"Adrenaline. If you want, I can teach you both how to do it."

Unira screwed her face up at his offer. "I'd rather go down if I get blasted. After I shoot them back, of course." She winked at them. "While I'm a priestess, I am an Andarion one."

Thrāix laughed as he replaced Jullien at the helm. "You rest and I'll take the ship. Call your lady. Rest your nerves. It won't take long to reach Jory."

"All right. Thanks." Jullien headed for his cabin while he tried not to let his paranoia overtake him again. He didn't like being overpowered by anything. It brought back too many bad memories of his childhood, and always sent him into a vicious panic attack. Things he wasn't ready to deal with. While he tried to joke about it, it really wasn't funny.

PTSD never was.

He tended to go rabid in those situations, even catatonic. His reason fled so fast that he couldn't think straight. Or rationally. He lost all sense of himself and the world around him. Even time. Worse, he never knew how he'd react. Sometimes he could fight back and protect himself, and at other times . . .

It was like being as helpless as an infant. His body locked up and paralyzed him, until he couldn't move or breathe. He just sat there, shaking uncontrollably as memories flashed through his mind on a strobe-like playback that made him want to rip out his eyes.

Gah, why couldn't he get a handle on this? He'd tried everything in the Nine Worlds to move past it. Still, it lingered and kept on until he felt as if he were going mad from it all.

Needing peace, he went to his bunk to rest, and there, he pulled up the videos on his link of Ushara and Vas. Of Nadya and her sisters, and his Tavali family.

He watched them as they did nothing remarkable. . . . They were baking cookies. Coloring pictures they'd drawn. Working on, or rather screwing up the ships he'd been assigned to repair. Doing Vas's homework and teaching Nadya her letters and basic colors. And yet everything they did amazed him. Biting his lip, he traced the lines of Ushara's smiling face, wishing he were with her. Wishing even more that he was inside her, because truthfully, she was so deep down inside him that he felt as if he were drowning.

And at the same time she was the only thing that kept him afloat. If something were to happen to her, he would lose his mind for real. In all his life, he'd never had anything. Not until she'd made him hers.

She, alone, gave him purpose and sanity. And he wasn't about to allow the Anatoles to take her from him. Not without a brutal fight.

He clutched the link to his chest as anger consumed him. One way or another, he was going to finish this and make sure no one ever threatened her again.



Jullien froze as they entered the Tavali café where they were to meet Jory and his crew. The instant he stepped inside the quaint Ritadarion-themed decor that made him feel as if he were outside on the dual-sunned planet, he had an instant déjà vu that he'd been here before. He glanced around at the blue walls, gold, scuffed tables, and hand-carved, rustic furniture and chandeliers.

Yeah, even though he'd never stepped foot in this place, he knew it intimately.

Thrāix duplicated his scowl. "What's wrong?"

"I've seen this restaurant."

Unira arched her brow. "When you were on the run?"

Before he could answer, his gaze went to the back corner, and he saw the exact table from the picture he'd been sent. . . .

More than that, he saw the ones who'd sent it.

Nyran *and* his grandmother. This must be their usual haunt.

*Shkyte!* Cursing under his breath, he backed out of the door hurriedly so that neither caught sight of him and blew *his* surprise that he'd been working so hard to give them.

*It's Eriadne.* He sent the warning silently to both Thrāix and Unira so that they could duck and cover, too. Which they quickly did as they followed him outside. Since they didn't know for sure who they were ducking, the way they dodged would be comical if he wasn't so pissed off about it.

Once safely on the street, he quickly vanished into the shadows of a nearby alley so as not to be seen by any of the Andarion bodyguards or entourage.

Silently spewing profanity, he met Thrāix's gaze. "What are the odds they'd be here? Having fucking tea?"

"For you? Good. 'Cause, let's face it, your luck sucks."

Jullien snorted. "Ain't it the truth?" He raked his hands over his face as he tried to get a handle on this.

And on his temper, which really wanted to go back into that restaurant and choke the life out of both of them until they were dead at his feet.

Or at least cut into bloody chunks.

"So what do we do?" Unira asked.

"Don't, Jules," Thrāix said in the warning tone of a parent with an angry toddler. "Don't even think what you're thinking, and I don't need any powers to know what that look in your stralen eyes means. Stop right there before you get us all killed."

He was right, and Jullien hated him for it.

Stepping back, he forced himself to calm down, then let out an evil laugh. "Fine, then. If I can't storm in there and kill them like the Andarion I am, let's do what we initially intended. . . . You two meet up with Jory, in private, and make sure everything's fine with his crew. I'm going off to screw with the bitch's head a bit. I'll meet you at the hangar later."

As Jullien started away, Thrāix caught his arm. "Be careful. She's not alone."

"I know, and I will. Believe me. I'm not giving her the satisfaction of putting me in the ground." Jullien lifted the cowl on his long black coat to conceal his features, and took a minute to calm his temper, before he went to one of the alley tables at the café's side. Once seated at the farthest table that was tucked beneath an awning shelter, he ordered a drink from the kiosk there.

While he waited for it to be served, he used the terminal to access the video feed so that he could spy on his grandmother and cousin with his powers.

What a peculiar and ironic day this had turned into. The gods had to be bored.

As a prince, he'd been the one who couldn't so much as jerk off without them spying on him. Back then, he'd never had a minute's peace. Either Merrell, Nyran, or Chrisen had made a point of being planted at his side every second of every day. Literally.

The only time he was spared their onerous company had been his stints in prison, under the tender care of Eriadne's wardens and personal thugs, who made sure that he had regretted every ounce of Anatole blood that flowed through his veins. The very thought of it all was enough to send him into a homicidal rage.

*Stop it!*

He needed a clear head so that he could pay attention to them. Not dwell on his past.

Irritated at himself for letting them into his mind, he fished his coins out for his drink. He forced his thoughts to remain here in the present, on them and only on what they were saying now.

Screw the past.

It'd definitely screwed him.

Inside the restaurant, Nyran sat at ease in Eriadne's presence, something Jullien had never been able to do. She'd always put him on edge. Made him nervous and twitchy to the point, he'd been more jittery than an ADD cat trying to cross rush hour traffic. There'd been a time in his childhood that whenever he heard her so much as whisper his name, he'd wet himself in terror of having to face her.

Tylie, too, for that matter. He could hear the clicking of that bitch's heels in the hallway outside his room, and his bladder would start leaking.

And his wife wondered why he never got nervous around his enemies. . . .

They were all pussies when compared to the venomous shrews who'd raised him with their bitter cocktail of murder, betrayal, insults, and hatred.

Enlarging the view from the café's internal surveillance on his kiosk, he watched as Eriadne sat back in her chair with complete decorum and grace. Ever refined. He had to admit that for such an old whore, she looked good. No human would have any idea she was over a hundred years old. She barely appeared a well-preserved fifty.

Still lean and voluptuous, she had a body most human women would kill for. Her long black hair was coiled in an elaborate style around her perfectly chiseled features, which barely held a single wrinkle anywhere on that smooth caramel skin. Of course, she never smiled, which gave credence to the old saying that resting bitch-face preserved beauty. It definitely had worked in her case.

She was ever a creature of elegant grace. Nyran, however, was still a foppish ass, who was hanging on her every word, with the sickening tenacity only an accomplished sycophant could master. As if she were too stupid to know better.

*Eriadne's a bitch, dumb-ass. She's not a fool.* And she never respected a suck-up. While she wouldn't hesitate to use them to her advantage when she could, she was just as quick to cut their throats once they were no longer useful to her.

When it came to dealing with her, whether in politics or life, one was always better off speaking with bold honesty than trying to mislead or couch the truth. That was the only trait she shared with Jullien's father.

"It's a shame we lost that little prick," she said as she daintily picked at her food. "Just when he could have actually been of use to us. . . . I swear, I think he died just to spite me. It's something that half-human bastard would have done."

"Indeed."

"Are you absolutely sure he's dead?"

Nyran shrugged. "There have been no transmissions from his chip. Given where I planted it, he'd have to be dead for it not to transmit. There's no way he could have found it or removed it. He's not *that* smart."

She narrowed her white gaze on Nyran. "Then have you made any more progress on our other mongrel infestation?"

"Almost. Unfortunately, that hybrid bastard is extremely paranoid and well trained. As is Zamir. I can't get near his bitch or their children. Between the Andarions, Triosans, Gourans, and Sentella, I have no viable access. It would take an act of war and a bombing run to get to them. The one shot we had, Jullien ruined before he died. They've now doubled the security and locked down the palace so that no civs are allowed in, at all, until after she's had this new litter of brats. It'd take us a year to get another operative inside."

"Start working on it."

"Will do, *mu tadara*." He took a bite of his steak. "I do have some good news, though. . . ."

She gave him a bored, nut-shriveling stare. "What? You want me to drag it out of you? Or reward you because you think you deserve something for managing some form of minor competency for once in your worthless, pathetic excuse of a life?"

Jullien took his drink from the waiter and tipped him as he choked on her vicious words. *Great Kadora, I have not missed being under that bitch's blistering tongue.*

*At all.*

Sadly, though, she was in a good mood. This was her better side while dealing with the family she actually liked. And it was far kinder than anything she'd ever said to him whenever he'd been forced to endure meals with her.

In retrospect, Jullien couldn't fathom how he'd ever managed to get a bite down his throat to become fat in the first place. But then, he knew. His eating disorder had taken place during midnight binges, when the staff was cleaning up and preparing for the morning, and everyone else was either asleep or off screwing whatever hapless creature had caught their fancy.

With a temporary reprieve from his family's blistering ridicule, he'd plowed through the day's leftovers, much to the dismayed horror of their head cook, who hadn't dared to stop him. Meanwhile, the rest of the staff had been even more terrified that his appetite would spread from the food to them, and that one of them would find themselves as his next course.

But he wasn't his family. He only voluntarily mauled pastries and pot roasts. Never the sanctity of another person's personal space or body.

Nyran mustered a pained smile for his fallen queen. "I finally found what you've wanted most."

"What? Your missing set of testicles? I do wish you'd find them soon, as I grow weary of having the only set in our entire family."

Wisely ignoring her causticity, Nyran cleared his throat as he rudely snapped his fingers and signaled one of their bodyguards to step forward with a large, ornate, inlaid wooden case. A human might mistake it for a musical instrument of some kind.

Jullien, however, knew that the handcrafted cherrywood case that shone like a gem in the dim light contained an Andarion Warsword. Unlike the battle swords and blasters other species carried, Andarion Warswords couldn't be bought in a store. They were sacred objects that had to be commissioned, and they cost as much as a legacy, because that was exactly what they were.

One didn't simply walk in and buy an Andarion Warsword. You earned it.

By blood, valor, or inheritance.

Through families, the swords, as with male wedding rings and lineage symbols, were the sacred property of the females, and it was their utmost duty to protect and watch over them. They were the sole owners and keepers of the swords and lineages, and only the family's matriarch could decide which male had earned the honor and right to carry it in his lifetime and represent their unified family as its public voice.

Her choice. She could remove it from the warrior who held it at any time. For any reason. And pass it to another male of her blood lineage she deemed more worthy.

More rarely, Warswords were given by the Andarion tadara or tadar as rewards for high honors and offices, or for acts of great valor. That was how most families had originally come into possession of theirs, and why they treasured them as family legacies. It was how the great War Hauks had earned theirs centuries ago, when their family had sacrificed their lives to keep their species safe from foreign invaders. And how Jullien's mother had earned hers—the day she'd killed her own brother to save her sister's life.

Then the last way to claim a Warsword was through right of combat. When one warrior defeated another in battle, it was his right to take the Warsword of the fallen. But it was a harsh thing to do. Because according to Yllam tradition, only those who were deemed worthy were allowed into the paradise lands of the gods to spend eternity in battle by Their glorious sides.

As such, Andarions, male and female, were to be buried in full battle armor with replica swords laid across their bodies and their hilts placed in their hands. To arrive on the other side without your armor or sword would condemn you instantly to Tophet. Therefore, the taking of a family's Warsword wasn't simply an act of victory. It was a way of humiliating your opponent and publicly saying you bore no respect for them or their family honor, and were damning them all to hell, for eternity.

Hence why they were originally named Warswords. To save their family honor and the soul of their loved ones, Andarions had fought entire wars over those weapons.

And Jullien winced in pain at the sight of the elegant, ancient sword. *Whose family have they slaughtered to extinction now . . . ?*

Nyran preened happily. "*Mu tadara,* I give you *y'anurikriega evest* Edon Samari."

Jullien gaped.

"What?" Her hand actually trembled as she reached for it.

Nyran wiped daintily at his lips. "I had to kill a few to get it, but it's definitely the right one. I made sure of it."

Gasping, she lifted the ancient weapon in her hands. With a loving touch Jullien had never seen her give a living being, she fondled the blade as if it were a lover come back from the grave to visit her. Several people near them gasped in dismay. A few of the smarter ones even ran for the door. But in true regal fashion, she ignored the crowd around her completely.

After all, *they* didn't matter. She was always the most important being in the universe. Everyone else was merely an insignificant tool, nuisance, or target.

How glad he was that he hadn't inherited her way of viewing others.

In response to the panicking diners, the café manager stepped forward to tell Eriadne to put her weapon away.

Without a word, she angled it at him. And pressed the tip against his throat.

He withdrew instantly.

Ah yes, *that* was his grandmother. Little did the man know, he'd barely escaped a near-death experience.

But it did piss her off enough that she got up and, cradling the War-sword, headed for the nearest exit while leaving Nyran behind to pay her bill.

Also vintage Eriadne.

As she and her entourage passed by Jullien's outdoor alley table, he rose and followed them at a discreet distance. This actually was working out even better than his original plan. He could use that sword to his advantage.

And he planned on using it to slice her treacherous head off.

Her guards escorted her several blocks away, to an elegant hotel that had seen better days. Even so, it still held a certain faded dignity to it. And it was a lot better than the squalor she'd forced Jullien to endure in his exile. While she would no doubt argue, she wasn't hurting at all in her fallen grace.

With his new powers, Jullien didn't have a difficult time slipping past the lax security guards—who were probably hoping someone would knife their charge and liberate them from her acerbic tongue—through the hotel, and into Eriadne's dimly lit suite of rooms.

It was as coldly sterile as the female who lived here. Nothing out of place.

Eriadne reverently knelt before the antique sofa and returned the sword to its case, but she didn't close it. Rather, she continued to trace the engraving of the hilt.

In that moment, Jullien would kill to know her thoughts. If she remembered his grandfather . . .

Was she even capable of regret?

With that question came a violent flashback of when he was seven . . . to the day he'd told her that he wanted to leave Andaria and live with his father.

Jullien had been in the palace courtyard, clutching one of Nykyrian's action figures—which he'd found lurking in his own closet, where his brother must have dropped it during a play session—and trying his best not to cry over it. Andarion tahrs didn't cry. They held their emotions in. Their heads high. They never let anyone know when they suffered.

But the pain inside him was more than he could bear at his young age. He missed his brother so much. Every single minute of every single day.

Instead of getting easier, every day without Nyk was harder. More miserable. Longer and more grueling.

And he was bitterly alone. Haunted with a soul-deep sorrow he dared not express to anyone. Because their own grandmother had murdered the better part of them.

His breathing ragged, he didn't know what to do. He had no one he dared confide in. No one to even talk to.

"Why did you leave me, brother?" he'd whispered to the doll, wanting to hate Nykyrian for abandoning him to this life. They were twins. They weren't supposed to be separated. Not for anything.

And on that fateful day when Nykyrian had headed off to school, Jullien had begged his brother not to go without him.

Nyk had laughed in his face. *"I don't want to stay here. Study harder and stop being so stupid, Julie, and maybe you'll get out one day, too."*

"What are you doing!"

Jullien had gasped at the sound of his mother's furious growl. Eyes wide, he turned to see her descending on him like some vengeful *kybbyk* out for his blood. He'd forgotten that her room, like his, looked out onto the courtyard. Mostly because she never left her room.

Her face flushed by anger, she snatched the toy from his hand. "This isn't yours!"

"I know."

Tears had streamed down her face as she looked from the toy to him and rage contorted her beautiful features. "Is this why you killed my baby? You wanted his things?"

Horrified at the accusation, Jullien had gasped. "W-wha——? No! How could you think that?"

Hysteria had overtaken her then as she grabbed him and started slapping and hitting him. "It is, isn't it? Admit it! You killed him because you wanted to replace him. You wanted to be heir! You're just like the rest of them! Selfish! Ruthless! Monster! You have no feelings for anyone but yourself!"

Covering his head, Jullien had been too stunned to answer. He'd tried to escape her wrath, but in spite of her madness, she was a fully trained, decorated warrior and he was just a frightened boy.

By the time Tylie had finally pulled his mother off him to calm her, his lip had been busted and his nose bleeding.

His entire body shaking, Jullien pushed himself to his feet and wiped at his nose with the back of his hand.

Tylie had sneered at him. "What did you do?"

Gaping, he'd stared dumbfounded at the question as his mother showed Tylie the toy and sobbed about Nykyrian.

"He killed my baby!"

"I know, Cairie. Shhh. It'll be all right."

Jullien had felt his own tears stinging his eyes as he watched Tylie hand his mother off to her nurse for care. When he went to get the toy from his aunt, Tylie had shoved him away.

"This belongs to your mother. Not *you*!"

Unshed tears choked him. "It's mine!" His mother had a room full of things Nykyrian had left behind for her to hold on to, but that toy was all he had left of his brother. It alone had been something they'd played with together.

Desperate to keep one precious memento for himself, he'd reached for it.

Tylie had slapped him for the effort. "You selfish little brat! I hope someday someone takes something from you that you love and gives you exactly what you deserve!" And with that, she'd stormed off.

"But it's mine," Jullien had whispered as his tears finally came in a violent burst of sobs. He just wanted *one* thing of his brother's to hold in comfort.

Just one.

He'd rather have Nykyrian. He'd give anything, his own life, his soul—anything of his worthlessness—if he could have Nykyrian back for one heartbeat. But the gods were mean and uncaring.

Like everyone else, they'd abandoned him, too. And he hated them. He would always hate them for what they'd taken. So he cried like he'd never cried before.

"What is this?"

Jullien had opened his eyes to see his grandmother standing over him.

She curled her lip. "Are you *weeping*? Like a girl?"

Suddenly, he'd had enough of them all. He hated this place. Hated his mother and his aunt. This courtyard. That palace.

Most of all, he hated the bitch glaring down at him like he was gar-bage.

Sniffing, he stood to boldly face her. "I'm not living here anymore. I'm calling my father to come get me."

That was what Jullien could have sworn he'd said. But apparently, the Andarion words Eriadne heard were more akin to telling her that her dress made her ass look fat, and they had the same effect as pissing in his grandfather's pool on the man's birthday.

Because the severe ass-beating they'd resulted in had taught him to never, *ever* cry again.

Most importantly, he'd learned not to tell his grandmother that he had any intention of leaving Andaria to live with his father.

And with those bitter memories, and the sight of her in front of him now, came the full weight of his animosity for her. All the years of ha-tred and of her blistering, unrelenting scorn and humiliations.

Of his wanting her dead and gone.

It was time.

Before Jullien even realized what he was doing or what he intended, he silently opened his coil knife and was moving straight for Eriadne's throat, with the full intention of slicing through it.

But just as he would have reached her, the door of the next room opened.

That wasn't what saved her life.

Normally, he would have killed his grandmother and whoever came through it, without reservation.

Had it been *anyone* else, he wouldn't have hesitated.

Yet as he heard his mother call out for her own matarra, he froze in-stantly. Unaware of the fact that he stood barely three feet from her, Eriadne rose and rushed to the other room to greet her daughter.

"So . . . you actually came, *mu tina*."

Cairistiona let out a tired sigh. "I told you I would. Did you doubt me?"

Eriadne glared at the guards around his mother. Guards that included the ever-beautiful Galene Batur and a garrison of males who kept his mother well protected from the former tadara. "Where's your sister?"

"Tylie isn't as forgiving."

Eriadne rolled her eyes. "I just wanted to see my girls. Neither of you will take my calls."

Cairistiona exchanged a bitterly amused smirk with Galene. "You have to forgive me, Matarra. I'm a little busy these days. I'm sure you can understand and appreciate the extent of my duties."

While Jullien listened to them, he moved toward the Warsword that had been wielded in battle by a grandfather he'd never known existed. Had it not been for two rare genetic defects, he'd have never known about his grandmother's indiscretion. It would have been a secret his grandmother would have taken to her grave.

Like all such weapons, the ancient Warsword was a thing of absolute beauty and grace. Perfectly balanced for war. The guard fanned outward like ornate, spiked dragon wings from the center dragon head over the elaborately cut out, etched, and engraved blade and fuller. The worn leather grip was sewn with gold thread that led up to the pommel, which had been shaped like the *Kadorai Sojara*—"Kadora's Rose." It was carefully cradled in and protected by the claws of a dragon.

A chill went down his spine as he felt an instant connection to that sword. It was as if something in his very blood remembered it, and his mind flashed on the image of a blond, battle-worn male clutching it in his hands. Yet even though he was badly bruised and bleeding, his pale eyes were charged by raw determination, and they held the image of lightning flashing in the sky.

Jullien knew instinctively that it wasn't Edon he saw in his mind, but rather Altaris Samari. Edon's father. The Samari who'd been born on the battlefield while his mother fought against Eriadne's.

And when Jullien touched the hilt, the dark red stone that made up the *Kadorai Sojara* on the pommel illuminated, making it appear as if the sword itself came alive. How strange that it hadn't reacted to Eriadne's or Nyran's touch at all. It was as if the sword knew it was in the hands of a Samari now.

And it welcomed him.

Unlike the women in the adjoining parlor, who were still talking, unaware of his presence. As they'd always done him. They gave him no thought whatsoever.

They never had.

A painful ache choked him as that reality slapped him. Gripping the cold, metal Warsword to his chest, he crept to the door to watch them. They sat as if no evil had ever taken place in their family. As if all were right in the Andarion Empire. Even Galene held her composure as she stood behind his mother's chair, ever her loyal protector. Since she was the prime commander of their military forces, she didn't have to be here for this. Her rank was too high for such a lowly task.

Yet her friendship with his mother was absolute, and had been for as far back as he could remember.

Speaking of memory . . . this was the only time he'd seen his mother sober in his whole lifetime. She sounded so . . .

*Normal.* Intelligent. Even humorous. For once, he saw a grand, elegant tadara, and not the hate-filled creature who had cursed and condemned him every time he neared her.

As did Galene. Neither sounded like the monsters he'd painted them in his mind. Like the cold-blooded reptiles he remembered from his nightmares.

Had he known nothing of their past with him, and met them on the street, he would actually like them, and they could easily be friends. . . .

The thought screwed with his head.

Badly.

*If everyone you meet is the asshole. Maybe the asshole's you.*

Jullien stared down at the glowing sword in his hand and the knife he still held in his other. *I was going to cut the throat of my own grandmother.* A female who sat there cordially conversing with her daughter . . .

No, they weren't the monsters.

*I am.*

And before he could gather his thoughts and collect himself, the light came on in the room.

Eriadne gasped as she came through a side door, and stared straight at him.

# CHAPTER 29

Her face turning pale, Eriadne swallowed hard. "Edon?"

Hissing, Jullien expelled a burst of flames at her. Turning, he clutched his grandfather's sword and ran for the window, then ducked out before she could call for reinforcements. He used his grappling hook to quickly descend to the street below and vanish into the crowd. But with every step he took that separated them, he cursed himself. One, that he had missed another chance to kill her.

Two, that he was every bit the animal they'd accused him of being.

Not since the night Nyk had thrown him over that table had he seen himself so clearly. *You destroy everything you touch. You are nothing but a rabid lorina that needs to be put down . . .*

They were all right. He was an Anatole. He could bleach his hair. Breathe fire. Lie all he wanted. But when all was said and done, he couldn't hide the truth. His roots would always come back. Blood was blood, and it never changed. The curse of his family would forever be his to bear.

*What have I done?*

He'd ruined a beautiful female. Caused strife in her family. Tainted her with the stench of generations of psychotic animals, who'd devoured their own.

*We are chromosomally damaged. Genetically wrong.*

And he had no idea how to fix any of this. His heart pounding, Jullien looked down at his wedding ring.

*I promised not to hurt you, Shara.* Yet he hurt everyone he was around. Sooner or later. There was something deeply rooted inside him that was suicidal and nuclear. It was a daily struggle to keep it leashed.

It'd always been disastrous those times when it escaped his tight control. For everyone near him. He'd always been self-destructive. A complete and utter prick.

*I need clarity.*

Jullien glanced down at the Warsword, and in that moment, he caught a vivid image of Edon Samari. Of this sword being ripped from his dying hands by Eriadne's sister before she used it to finish Edon off.

The legacy of his family was that of blood and violence. Brutality. Hatred. Jealousy. Cold-blooded treachery. He couldn't take that home to Ushara. Maybe if their daughters were raised without him, they would be like Nykyrian, and be spared the Anatole curse. His brother, alone, had escaped it. He was the only one of them who wasn't broken and mentally damaged. Perhaps that was why. Nyk hadn't been around any of them during his formative years.

He'd grown up around humans.

And that was what Jullien wanted for his girls. He wanted them to be like Jay and Ana. Close and tight. Inseperable. The way twins were supposed to be. Not to hate each other and be eternally divided like he and his brother were. To have one of them despise the very air the other breathed.

To swear out a death warrant for them.

"I have to leave you." It was the only hope his girls had for a life worth living. Before either he, or his blood, or his birth family did irreparable harm to them. It was just a matter of time. He knew that now. Whatever it took, he had to secure them.

Now and forever.

*Please, Shara, forgive me, and understand.*


Jullien came awake with a start as his ship's alarm screeched to notify him that another ship had invaded his perimeter.

When he went to move, his head throbbed from a vicious hangover. Cursing the pain, he stumbled half-dressed to the bridge to see what new "fun" he was facing. Honestly, he figured at most a cargo ship passing through.

It wasn't.

Stunned, he stared at the readings. *Am I still flagged? That can't be right. . . .*

"What the Tophet?" He actually thumped the screen to see if it was malfunctioning.

Nothing changed. There were six heavily armed ships coming straight at him. All were locked on his position.

They weren't League. Was it his cousins? Surely they weren't *that* stupid or suicidal.

Then again . . .

His sight blurry, he slid into the captain's chair and was just about to initiate some awesomely aggressive maneuvers when he heard a deep sultry voice call out to him.

"Jules? I know that's you. If you start those engines and flee me again, I swear to the gods, I will find you and unleash my full Andarion wrath on your ass with such venom that you will physically feel the pain of every single nanosecond of worry you've given me."

"Yeah!" Davel said. "And I'll help . . . with a lot of backup! Which I have, as every one of my sisters is here with me, and they all want their turn at you! Fear us!"

Jullien actually smiled at the lunatic threat. His hand lingered on the controls. A part of him was tempted to run, consquences be damned. It would be the best thing to do.

For all of them.

But he couldn't.

The last four months had almost killed him—and that wasn't counting the assassins and other suicidal runs he'd made. It was the excruciating loneliness of not having Shara by his side. Of watching over her and not speaking to her.

Honestly? He'd rather be dead than live without her another day.

Unable to stand it, Jullien was still sitting in the chair with his hand on the controls when Ushara entered the bridge. The look on her face was one she only wore when Vas failed to take out the trash or Jullien forgot to reset logs.

*I'm in so much trouble. . . .*

Ushara hesitated as she saw Jullien for the first time in months. She was pissed, relieved, happy, and hurt—all at once. The little snot had skillfully evaded every single member of her family.

Even Trajen and Thrāix. With a stubbornness that could only come from an Anatole, he'd refused to answer any of their calls. Not even Vas or Nadya had been able to get through to him. The only reason she'd known he was still alive was his band, which would send his heartbeat to her whenever she buzzed for it, and she continued to get care packages that showed he continued to monitor her through the system he'd installed.

The aggravating beast had even finished off the nursery for their daughters with everything she'd wanted, right down to the tiniest detail, such as the baby socks she'd picked out and the twin mobiles. Thus letting her know that he was keeping extremely close tabs on them, while ignoring them completely.

Would he ever stop being such a frustrating dichotomy?

"Not one call?" she whispered.

He refused to look at her. Instead, he kept his gaze locked stubbornly on the control panel in front of him like some sullen child.

Even though she was furious and hurt enough that she wanted to shoot him, her heart broke at the wretched sight of his neglected condition. Honestly, she'd never seen him like this. Not even when he'd been homeless and destitute. His hair was shaggy and unkempt, as were his whiskers. Shirtless and barefoot. His pants were barely fastened around his hips—and their loose fit said he hadn't been eating. He reeked of excessive alcohol consumption.

Gah, his hair even stood up on end, as if he'd had a bad scare or electrical shock. It would be comical were her heart not broken by the sight of his obvious anguish.

When he continued not to speak, she closed the distance between them, wondering if he'd get up and run.

Slow and easy, so as not to cause him to bolt, she reached out to touch his hair so that she could smooth it down. He drew a ragged breath the moment she touched his scalp. Finally, he clutched her hand in his and kissed her knuckles as if they were sacred.

His eyes filled with shame, he met her gaze. "Zēritui."

"If you're sorry, why did you leave?"

His gaze fell to her belly, which was now enormous. Anguish furrowed his brow as he placed his hands there. "We are cursed." Tears swam in his tired eyes. "I don't want our daughters to know the horrors of my lineage. I want them to grow up like you. With love, and without fear. Safe and protected, where they're free to laugh and to play. To know nothing of my bloodline."

"They need their father."

He shook his head. "I don't deserve them. Or you. I only want you to be happy and safe."

"Jullien—"

"No, Shara," he breathed. "You don't understand. I was *there*. Sword in hand to kill my grandmother. Without hesitation or remorse. Who does that?"

"Someone pushed to the brink of madness by her cruelty and threats."

"It doesn't make it right."

She smoothed down the furrows of his brow. "Then let it go."

"What?"

"Walk away. They think you're dead. You're listed as dead, and they have no way to prove otherwise. They've not come after us since I told Eriadne that you'd been killed. It's time for you to stop walking in two worlds. . . . Jullien eton Anatole is gone—put him in the grave and leave him there. Nail his coffin shut."

She gently balled her hand in his hair and bent down until her nose almost touched his. "You are my husband. That's all you need be. Jules Dagger Samari. Father of my children. Let the rest drift away and be gone. Forever."

Ushara gestured at the screen and the ships that surrounded his. "*That's* your family now. Not the ones who threw you away." She enlarged the images on the monitor. "Look at them, Jules. We've all been worried sick about you. I know you're not used to caring about anyone or having anyone care about you, but *we* do. Even Jory and Chayden have been relentless in this search for you. Because we *love* you. We all care about you, even when you don't. You can trust in that. I swear it to you. Now, tell me the truth. Are you ready to come home or do we leave you here to wallow in this hell you've built around yourself?"

Jullien swallowed hard as happiness and pain mixed inside him. He hadn't meant to hurt her or anyone else. Nor had he wanted to stress her during the pregnancy. Honestly, he'd been trying not to burden her with his problems or psychosis. He'd wanted to spare her everything.

And this had seemed the most rational way of dealing with it all.

To withdraw and be alone. It was what he'd always done. What he'd always known.

But when everything was stripped away, there was one thing he couldn't deny.

He didn't want to be alone in the darkness anymore.

"I want to come home."

Ushara didn't realize that she'd been fearing his answer until that moment when her breath left her in a rush. And if she had any doubt about his commitment to her, it dissipated as her gaze dropped to his bare chest and she saw something else that was different about her husband.

Scowling, she stepped closer to touch the center of his chest, where his grandmother had once tried to carve out his heart. Over that scar now lay a new, large tattoo.

Tears welled in her eyes. Andarions didn't mark themselves, especially not their princes. Yet there for all to see, Jullien had placed the Andarion symbols of eternal love wrapped around a black Kadoran rose that held her name and those of her son and their daughters.

He must have placed it there not long after he'd first run from her.

Splaying her hand over it, she met his gaze. "Should I ask?"

He covered her hand with his. "Nothing to ask. I merely made visible to the world the truth that I know in my heart. I will always be yours. No one else would ever have me."

Ushara scoffed at his self-deprecating sweetness. "That's not true." She pulled him into her arms and held him for a long minute before she stepped back to hail the others. "I've got him. Unira, take command of my ship. I'll stay on board with Jules, and we'll follow the rest of you in." She turned toward him. "Start the engines, and let me go make you something to eat."

As she stepped away, he caught her hand and pulled her to a stop. A blush crept over his face. "Um . . . you really don't want to go to the galley or the cargo bay. You definitely don't want to open any of the cooling units or freezer."

She scowled at him. "What? Why?"

Jullien hesitated as he tried to think of the best way to tell her what he'd been up to the last few months. But there honestly wasn't an easy way to let her know he'd gone crazy and, well . . . "I . . . uh . . . found my cousin Varan, and a few others who got in the way of my search for Nyran and my grandmother."

"Yeah?" Then she went stock-still as she finally understood. "Oh my God! Are you telling me you have bodies on board this ship?"

Sheepishly, he rubbed at his neck. "Well, not Varan's. I turned him in a while back. But some of the others are worth a lot of creds. Anyway, I was on my way to make a drop later today from my latest hunt."

Ushara was horrified, but she forced herself not to show it. Only because she knew that whatever he'd done to them had been fully justified. While he was a bit unstable, he never went on those kinds of attacks without incredible motivation. And never unwarranted. If he had bodies on board, they'd tried to kill him first.

"Okay, *sozibe*." She kissed his cheek, then returned to hail Unira. "*Scythian Nights*? Remain in holding and prepare for me to board with my husband."

Unira came on immediately. "Is everything all right?"

She stepped aside so that Unira could see him. "Jules, say hi to your very worried mother."

He screwed his face up like a little boy who had forgotten to brush his teeth. "Hi, Mum."

Unira growled at him. "Are you all right?" she repeated.

"Yeah, and I'm really sorry about what I did. I didn't mean to hurt or anger you or Thrāix. Is he going to kill me?"

With his arms crossed over his chest and wearing an expression of absolute murder, Thrāix stepped into the frame. "He might. Depends on if Trajen beats me to it. . . . Actually, there's a long list of folks here who want to kick your ass."

"There usually is." Jullien's tone was even drier than the Oksanan desert.

Ushara cleared her throat. "But I get first dibs on beating him."

At least that was her thought until he gave her a look so adorable that it completely erased every last bit of her anger. Which then infuriated her at herself. How could she love him so much and still want to kill him? She'd never understand the complicated emotions this male put her through.

Yet the one thing she couldn't deny . . . "I've missed you so much."

He gathered her in his arms, and she laughed at the fact that they no longer went around her enormous body.

"Go ahead," she laughed. "You can say it, and I won't be angry. I'm the size of a shuttle craft."

A playful, taunting grin spread across his face. "I think you're the most beautiful *tara* ever born. And my girls had better be treating you with proper respect." He pressed his cheek against her belly, where the girls were frolicking. It was as if they already knew he was their paka, and they wanted to play.

Brushing her hand through his tangled hair, she smiled down at him. "They do the same thing with Vas. Every time they hear his voice, your beans start jumping."

He rose to his feet and started to kiss her.

Ushara quickly ducked and moved away. "I love you dearly. I do. But, baby, you have to take a shower."

With a fierce grimace, he scratched at his beard. "Yeah, I probably smell like some of the things that are decaying in my freezer storage."

Wrinkling her nose, she nodded. "And a little marinated, too."

"I prefer the term well preserved."

"Hmm . . ." She narrowed her gaze on him. "And how much have you had to drink?"

"I don't know. I haven't been sober since the last day I talked to you."

"Oh, that's good. I find it so comforting whenever I leave you alone. Like handing a grenade to a toddler."

"Yeah, I know." He led her toward the airlock. "But at least I didn't piss in your pool on your birthday."

She laughed even though she didn't want to. "What am I going to do with you?"

"If you were smart? Throw me out the airlock." On the way to her ship, he grabbed a jacket from the floor to shrug over his bare torso.

She arched a brow at the mess and his rumpled clothes. "What? Your housekeeper quit, too?"

Again, he grimaced at her. "You're in a sassy mood."

Straightening his jacket and the collar, she harumphed. "You better be glad it's just sassy and not slappy." She led him through the airlock and to her ship, where both Thrāix and Trajen waited.

Trajen curled his lip the instant Jullien stepped on board. "Well, hell. I was going to kill him, but he smells like someone beat me to it a few years ago."

Thrāix laughed. "Yes, he does. Make sure no one breathes fire or holds any kind of open flame near him. Otherwise, he's likely to combust."

Unira tsked at them. "Stop it. Both of you. He's not that . . ." Her voice trailed off into an impressive gasp as she got a bit closer and realized that Jullien was indeed *that* bad. So she changed her argument. "You'll hurt his feelings."

Trajen grunted. "I stand by my earlier assertion that with that degree of stench, he's already dead and thus can't be offended by anything I say."

Thrāix nodded his agreement. "I'm going with that and to the fact there must be a funeral, 'cause he's making my eyes water, and it's not from happiness. I'm definitely grieving over the loss of my olfactory senses."

Ushara gaped at them. "Oh, dear Eri! You both are so evil. Stop! You're going to make him run off again."

Jullien snorted at them. "It's fine, Shara. I deserve it, and you're all correct. I need a shower, shave—"

"Fumigation," Trajen muttered.

"Detox and decontamination." Thrāix frowned at Trajen. "You think it's safe for Ushara to be standing that close to him in her delicate condition?"

"Honestly? I'm not sure it's safe for *us* to be standing this close to him."

Groaning out loud, Ushara pulled Jullien past his critics. "Ignore them and their meanness."

"You think *we're* being mean?" Trajen called after her. "Just wait until Davel and your sisters get ahold of him!"

She rolled her eyes at them and kept going with Jullien. "Sorry about that."

"It's fine. I've missed their disgruntled asses, too. Though, at the moment, I'm not sure why."

After leading him to the head in her quarters, she started the shower for him. "Other than slaughtering your family and pickling your internal organs . . . what else have you been up to?"

"Spying on you and Vas, mostly. I hate that new chair you bought for our bedroom, by the way."

She pulled his jacket off. "Get used to it. It's comfortable."

"I hate it. I didn't even know you could buy fabric that hideously bright a shade of pink . . . vomit."

She made a face at him. "Well, you weren't there to protest when I bought it, so you have to tolerate it in silence. Besides, it'll be comfy for breast-feeding."

At the mention of that last term, his gaze dropped to the aforementioned region of her body and darkened in a way that was all too familiar to her. She smiled up at him. "After you bathe."

He whimpered in protest. "You're killing me."

"You're the one who stayed away. I hope you're in agony."

Grumbling under his breath about her cruelty, Jullien peeled his pants off and stepped inside the shower. Ushara handed him soap and a razor through the door. But she didn't leave the room. Rather, she opened the door enough that she could watch him bathe and continue their conversation. Something that made him rock hard.

It was a cruel torture his Ger Tarra had devised to get back at him, and it was working.

She handed him a toothbrush. "Well, at least now I know where all those exorbitant creds came from that appeared suddenly in our accounts. I thought they were a banking error."

He brushed his teeth before he answered her. "I acted as your muscle dump and had them wire the creds to you whenever I claimed the bounties for my family and their friends. Otherwise, they'd have run my ID and prints for it." He handed her the toothbrush. "And that wouldn't have worked out well for me, since I'm supposed to be dead."

She gaped as she took it. "How can I claim them? I don't have a tracer's or assassin's license."

"You do now."

She went bug-eyed. "Pardon?"

He stepped back to wet and lather his hair. "Relax. It's through the Andarion Nizari Virgyl. One thing I know how to do is forge the Tophet out of our official paperwork." He paused in the middle of soaping his chest. "Although . . . is it really a forgery? I mean, I *was* tahrs. I technically could still be considered a tiziran . . . and my mother's the tadara. Tylie and Galene are the ones who normally sign off on those licenses, and if I weren't in exile, I could legally do it, too. So it might actually be legitimate, when you think about it. We could at least make a strong argument for its legality."

Scoffing, she stepped away to return his toothbrush to the stand. "How about we don't find out?"

"Yeah, with my luck . . ."

"They'll hang us both."

Jullien was going to respond to that, but when he turned around and opened his eyes, he saw Ushara peeling off her clothes. He could barely breathe as she stepped into the shower with him. "I thought I was too disgusting for you?"

"You *were*." She kissed his lips. "But you smell much better now." She took the cloth from his hand and finished bathing him with an excruciatingly slow thoroughness.

Jullien's head spun at the sensation of her hands sliding over his skin, of them delving into every part of his body as she set him on fire with her touch. Especially when she took extra-gentle care and time to stroke and cup his sac. Unable to stand it, he gently pinned her to the shower wall to kiss her.

Ushara growled at how good her husband tasted and felt in her arms. And at his raw hunger. This was what she'd missed most. The feeling of being needed and of belonging. Of knowing that to him, she was one of the most important things in the universe. No one held her the way he did.

As if she were the air he needed to breathe in order to live.

Until he pulled back suddenly and left her breathless and wanting.

Panting, he nipped at her chin and gave her the look of a starving beggar eyeing a banquet. "I don't want to be selfish and hurt you or the babies."

His thoughtfulness and the sincere fear she saw in his stralen eyes brought a lump to her throat. This was why she loved him so. For all his bluster and irritable ways, he always tried to put her and their children first. No matter his own needs or wants.

Even when he'd run, he'd done it in an effort to protect them, not out of his own selfishness or neglect. "You won't."

He scowled fiercely. "Are you sure? I can wait . . . trust me on that. While I don't enjoy it, I have the control of a Demurrist hermitic saint."

Laughing, she arched a brow at him. "Do you think I'd take a chance on harming them or you?"

"No. I know you wouldn't." His eyes darkened with inner turmoil. "I just don't want to hurt you, Shara."

"You only hurt me when you leave me."

He brushed his thumb down her lips. "Then I will never leave you again."

She smiled at him. "I'm going to hold you to that promise."

Jullien was about to turn the water off when she slowly sank to her knees in front of him. Mesmerized, he couldn't move as she took him into her mouth and made him see stars with her exquisite torture. His head spun from the pleasure of it. Unable to believe what a lucky bastard he was, he sank his hand in the wet strands of her hair while her hands stroked him in sync with her tongue.

Emotions tore through him as he surrendered himself to her. How a female so precious could have any tenderness for something as worthless as him, he'd never understand. The last thing he'd wanted was to leave her or hurt her.

*I'm no good for you, Shara.* He knew it for everything he wasn't worth.

Thank the gods she couldn't see it. And on the heels of that thought, he came in a blinding wave that left him weak and panting, and at her complete and utter mercy as she continued to tease his body until she'd wrung every last bit of pleasure from him.

With the sweetest smile, she stared up into his eyes. "Better?"

He traced the line of her jaw as he marveled at her beauty, and the miracle that had brought her into his life. "Yeah." He helped her to her feet. "But I'm not done with you." After turning the water off, he gently dried her, then led her to the bunk, only to discover it was a little too small for the two of them.

Growling, he whimpered in disappointed misery. Had she not been pregnant, he would have been a bit more creative and inventive somewhere else, but he didn't want to stress her body or risk injuring the babies.

She actually laughed at his pain as he slid off the bunk to stare down at her with a stern pout. "I wasn't married at the time I bought the ship, so I didn't really think about this aspect of the sleeping arrangements. Sorry."

"Fine, but when we get home . . ." He raked a hungry glower over her naked body.

"I'm all yours."

He kissed her cheek before he helped her off the narrow bunk and handed her a clean set of clothes. When he started for his old set, Ushara stopped him.

"You have fresh gear in the closet. Please, for the love of the gods, use it."

Arching his brow, he smirked at her. "You were that certain of success?"

"Yes. One way or another, I was coming home with you."

He laughed as he opened the closet to see that she wasn't joking. She had a full Tavali-sanctioned wardrobe in there for him. "Glad I didn't fight you."

"You would have lost. Painfully."

Yeah. He would have definitely, judging by this amount of determination.

As soon as they were dressed, Ushara's link buzzed. She answered it to find Trajen on the other end. "Hi, boss."

"Hi. Is your lesser half with you?"

"Right here." She handed the link to Jullien.

He turned the speaker on while he finished dressing. "What is it?"

"We want to make sure we have an accurate—and I use this word rather loosely, 'cause let's face it, they're not all here—head count. Sixteen bodies? Is that what you have in storage?"

Jullien turned bashful again as he glanced uncomfortably at her, then mumbled, "Um . . . eighteen, total."

"Oh, *eighteen*," Trajen said with mock happiness. "Hear that, Thray? And where, pray tell, might these extra bodies be stashed? Dare I ask?"

Jullien bit his lip. "They kind of slipped and fell into a bad situation. Check out the two yellow buckets in the freezer. But you might not want to open them, 'specially if you've eaten recently."

"Oh, okay, then. Thanks for the warning. Appreciate it, little buddy." Trajen's voice dripped with sarcasm. "And just for the record, Jules. Eighteen isn't a mission. It's the making of a serial killer."

"Hey, now. I didn't start this shit. I was only looking for my cousin and yaya. They're the ones who brought friends to the party. I tried to reason with them, and explained the future consequences of their unreasonable actions should they pursue conflict with me. They thought I was a *cocúpün* tiziran. I merely educated them on the fact that I was not."

"Ah, well, lesson learned. Filed under *Ew*—and next time you tell me not to look in a bucket, I will definitely listen." Trajen choked and coughed. Then cleared his throat. "And nice Warsword, by the way. I don't even want to know how you came into *its* possession. We'll handle it with the respect it deserves and make sure it's properly taken to your house. I have to go vomit now." He cut the transmission.

Jullien handed the link back to Ushara.

"Eighteen bodies?"

He shrugged. "Trust me, Shara. They were scum who deserved what they got, and worse. Besides, the girls and Vas need a college fund. My family owes them that much, and I sleep better knowing there are eighteen less psychos after you and them."

"Eighteen?" she repeated as the full horror of that number circled back around her mind. "Is that the total for all of them, or just the most recent conflict?"

"Recent."

She covered her face as her head reeled. "How many did you—?"

"Does it really matter? Most were Anatoles, and the rest served under them. Need I remind you what you and your family said to me the first time we met? You weren't wrong about us."

"Well-taken point." She moved to hug him about his lean waist. "You're right . . . you're right." She frowned as she stared up at him. "Are you okay? They were your family."

Jullien drew a ragged breath before he nodded. "Not all, but yeah. Sadly, I have no remorse. Anymore than they'd have had they killed me. Which is why I ran like I did. I realized it's not normal to feel like this. To be able to compartmentalize killing my own blood the way I do. I'm so broken."

Ushara placed her hand to his chest where his tattoo held their names above his heart as a permanent homage of his faith and love. "You're not like them, Jules. And you're not broken."

"Definitely chipped."

She laughed before she kissed him. "I'll give you *cracked*. But we can glue that back together. Besides, you're no worse than your brother, Nykyrian. I daresay, as a League command assassin, he's killed a lot more for a lot less reason."

As Jullien opened his mouth to respond, her link went off again. He growled. "I forgot how annoying that thing was."

Sighing, she answered it to find Chayden on the other end. "Yes, we got him finally. Why?" With a stern frown, she turned the speaker on. "Can you repeat that for Jules?"

"Hey, Dagger, I'm neck deep in some irritating family drama, and I just had a most *fascinating* conversation with a friend in The Sentella in the middle of it."

Dread filled him at where this was going. "Yeah?"

"He was asking me all kinds of questions about *your* wife, and if I had any information on someone who was going buck-wild on the Andarion royal family that was in exile. Seems a bunch of them have gone missing lately."

Jullien definitely didn't like where this conversation was headed. "What did you tell him?"

"I don't know nothing about any missing Andarion royals. I'm Tavali. And Tavili backs Tavili. Jewels, alcohol, and cheap women's all I know. Snitches get stitches. But I wanted you to know what I know, which isn't much, I grant you."

Jullien snorted at his odd friend. "Who in The Sentella was it?"

"Running mate of Nyran Venik, which is why I wanted you to know about it. Dumbass didn't know I knew he knew Nyran. But Psycho Bunny knows all and sees all. I just don't let others know I know, you know? Except for a few. You being among those few."

"Thanks, Chay."

"Anytime. And I'm still locked over here, helping my sister deal with her husband and the nuclear fallout of being disinherited. But if you guys need anything, don't hesitate to call, or if I hear anything else, I'll let you know."

Ushara scowled. "Your sister? Mack?"

"No. Not Mack. I actually have a real sister of my own. Full-blooded. It's a long story. At any rate, she needs me right now, and sadly for her, I'm about all she's got. So I'm here for her. But I will be there for you, should y'all need me. Holler at yo' bunny."

She smiled at his silliness. "Okay, Bunny, appreciate it."

"Later, Andarions."

Her smile faded as she saw the expression on Jullien's face. "What's wrong?"

"Nyran. He's still untouchable. As is my grandmother. After all *this,* I still couldn't get near them."

"Jules . . . what did we discuss?"

"Let it go."

"And what are you going to do?"

Jullien hesitated. He wanted to agree with her, he did. But deep inside, he had a feeling that this was far from over and that so long as they lived, his family was going to keep coming for him and for Ushara.

Even if he was dead.

After all, what good would it do for him to let go if they didn't? Because the one thing his family had taught him at a very early age— sometimes dead just wasn't dead enough.

# CHAPTER 30

Over the next few weeks, Jullien settled back in to the Gorturnum Cyperian StarStation with a shaky peace as they prepared for the imminent arrival of their daughters. After a stern "snubbing" that had lasted about half an hour and a lot of threatening should he ever leave again, Ushara's sisters had welcomed him back into the fold and forgiven him for leaving, as had her parents.

Vasili had been the most difficult one to face. Unlike Nadya, who had no real concept of time, he did. And the hurt in his eyes had been searing as Jullien went into his room to see him on his return.

At first, Vas had refused to meet his gaze.

"Vas, you know it had nothing to do with you, right?"

"Didn't feel like that."

Jullien had sat beside him on the floor and watched while he played his game. "I know. But can I confide in you?"

Vas had paused his game to look up at him without comment. But the accusation in those pale eyes had been searing and had gutted Jullien to the core of his soul.

"Adults don't know what they're doing any more than kids do most of the time. We get scared and make mistakes, too. Sometimes bad ones. In this case, I had predators after me that I had to thin out to make sure they didn't find you or your mother. It's why I couldn't contact you. I didn't want them to use it to find you and leave another surprise for you in your backpack."

Vasili scowled at him. "Truth?"

Jullien opened his shirt to show Vasili the tattoo that rested over his heart, where the boy's name was permanently inked on his flesh. "What do you think?"

"I think that hurt. Probably a lot."

Jullien laughed. "Not as much as not being here with you." He gave the boy a sheepish stare. "Am I forgiven?"

Vas smiled shyly and nodded. "I missed you, Paka."

"Missed you, too."

Ushara stepped back into the shadows as she watched Jullien pick up the other controller so that he and Vasili could play a round of the game that Jullien had sent while he was gone. Relief filled her that they appeared to be okay. Vasili had been so upset that she'd feared a permanent rift might have developed. Yet within a few minutes, he was laughing with Jullien as if nothing had ever been wrong.

Relieved beyond belief, she went to the nursery to check on the linens that had been delivered—one of the many things Jullien had taken care of for her. Even though he'd been gone, he single-handedly hired contractors to redesign the spare room off theirs into an amazing fantasy nursery unlike anything she could have imagined. She didn't even want to know what it'd cost. The soft pale pink, blue, and gray colors were soothing for their Andarion eyes, and the materials he'd chosen reminded her of walking into a cloud.

Each crib had a custom crown above it that held a sweeping fabric waterfall that cradled the crib to protect it and shield the babies from a stray draft. Somehow, he'd found a smaller version of the antique chandelier that hung in her bedroom for theirs and matching wall sconces. But one of her favorite pieces, aside from the antique white cribs, was the fabric ruffles on the bottom that fanned out in a luxurious waste of soft silk. His exquisite eye for such details was incredible.

Then again, for all his bluster, Jullien was an artist with the soul of a poet. When left alone, he could be the gentlest of beings. And this nursery was a window to that part of him.

Case in point, he'd made sure while they worked on the nursery for the girls to redo Vasili's room so that their son wouldn't feel left out. His bedroom was now designed to look like the interior of his favorite video game, right down to a fake stairway that vanished into the ceiling.

Jullien had even bought matching gaming chairs with surround sound that vibrated in sync to Vas's console. The poor boy was quickly becoming terribly spoiled.

And she loved every minute of it.

While she put the linens away, her link rang.

It was Trajen.

"Hey, boss."

"How's it going?"

Knowing Jullien had supersonic hearing, she pulled the door closed before answering. "Fine, I think. How about on your end?"

Trajen snorted. "Your little psycho husband went up against some pretty damn impressive and powerful players during his walkabout. No wonder Chayden called to warn us. Jules single-handedly wiped out his grandmother's personal wetwork team. He got all but three of them."

"Seriously?"

"Yeah. Her entire pet Nizari squad that she'd personally picked and licensed." Trajen's tone was one of awe, and that impressed her. She'd never heard anyone inspire that from him before. "Thrāix said that Jullien's managed to fully integrate into his ship, and we still haven't figured out how he managed to do *that* on his own either. So keep an eye on him. Make sure that he's really okay. We don't know if what Thrāix did had any lingering effects, or not."

There was an odd note in his voice. "What do you mean?"

"I don't mean that he's dangerous, Shara. Calm down. We're worried that he might have hurt himself. Done some kind of internal damage he may not even be aware of yet. You know him better than we do. He's not one to let anyone know if he's been injured. Just keep an eye out and let us know if he has any sign of illness."

"Tell Grandma I'm fine."

She jumped at the sound of Jullien in the room behind her. "Oh my God! Make some sound when you move!"

"Sorry. Been hunting assassins. Stealth is a hard habit to break."

Trajen laughed in her ear. "I'll leave you to him. Remember what I said. Make sure he hasn't burned out any of his three remaining brain cells."

She turned her link off and slid it into her pocket. "He's just worried about you."

"I know. I'm worried about me, too." He crossed the distance between them.

"So where did your Warsword come from?"

"My grandmother. It was in her hotel room. I'd planned to kill her with it, but it didn't quite work out."

Ushara's jaw went slack at the implication. "It's the Anatole sword?"

"No." He put the linens up in the top of the closet for her. "My mother has that one. It's kept in a vault under the palace. I've never even seen it, except in photos and official portraits. They only bring it out for coronations."

Which he'd never attended, since he'd been in exile when his mother had been crowned tadara. Though his tone was emotionless, that had to burn and hurt.

"This Warsword belonged to Edon Samari."

Okay, she gaped again and even more so at *that* bombshell. "For real? Are you sure?"

"Yeah. It's why I took it. I was going to return it to Matarra at temple, since it's rightfully hers. I couldn't stand the thought of it being in Anatole hands." His features paled as soon as he finished his sentence. "She's standing behind me, isn't she?"

Biting back a smile, Ushara nodded. "She just came in."

Jullien turned slightly to find Unira in the doorway, standing with tears in her eyes.

"You found my family Warsword?"

"Stole it more than found it, but yes."

Shaking her head at his dry tone, she tsked lovingly at him. "You can't steal what rightfully belongs to you, *m'tana*."

He didn't respond to that. Rather, he excused himself to leave the room.

Ushara let out a heartfelt sigh. "His humility makes me want to cry for him."

Unira nodded. "I can't believe he found the Samari *Anurikriega*. It's been missing for decades."

"What happened to it?"

"The stories, if you believe them, say that Faran eton Anatole challenged Edon in a test of arms and defeated him, then took possession of the sword as punishment against our family. We assumed he destroyed it for spite."

Jullien snorted as he returned to the nursery. "It wasn't a fair contest. Faran murdered him in cold blood. He would have never possessed the skills to take Edon down in a fair fight. Edon had been raised on a battlefield. Faran had never been in a real fight, not even a Ring match."

Unira frowned. "Didn't he defeat Dannon Hauk in a Ring match to take Eriadne's pledge from the War Hauk family?"

"Again, not a fair match. He drugged Dannon before the fight. It's why

Eriadne hates the War Hauk lineage to this day. She was in love with Dannon, at least as much as she could be. And it was one of his family who took the bribe to drug him—she holds that act against all the Hauks. They tried to placate her wrath by offering up Ferral Hauk as a pledge to my mother, and you know how that turned out." He looked first to Unira, then Ushara.

Ferral Hauk had allowed himself to be seduced by another Anatole cousin the night before he was to be formally pledged to Cairistiona. Needless to say, Cairistiona found out and refused him, then ended up sleeping with Jullien's father and conceiving Jullien and Nykyrian a few years later.

Ushara winced. "You know, you almost have to feel sorry for Eriadne. Every time she fell in love, she had to watch her beloved die."

Jullien screwed his face up into a painful grimace. "You can if you want, but I reserve the judgment that she's incapable of any real emotion. You have to remember, this is a bitch so cold that when she was a young female, she had a rival's aging process sped up so that her rival died of old age in her mid-twenties."

Ushara sputtered. "Why would she do that?"

"She overheard one of the courtiers make the comment that she was prettier than Eriadne." He held his hand up. "I swear it's the truth. She is *that* merciless." Then he turned to Unira and gave her the case in his hands. "For you, Matarra."

Unira opened it so that she could see the ornate hilt of the Samari Warsword. Tears glistened in her eyes. "It's as beautiful as I knew it'd be." And when she touched the grip, it lit up the same way it'd done when Jullien touched it. She gasped and laughed.

Ushara moved forward. "That's incredible. I've never seen one do that before."

Unira let go and the light went out.

When Ushara touched it, it remained dormant. She scowled. As did Unira.

Jullien smiled at them. "It appears that it only lights up in the hands of a Samari." He touched it and showed them that it glowed under his grip as well.

"Amazing," Ushara breathed.

"Agreed." Jullien released it to Unira. "Anyway, I'm glad I was able to bring it home to you, Matarra."

Wiping at her eyes, she closed the case, then held it out to him. "And I bestow it on you and your Ger Tarra, my precious boy. As the last Samari son, it's only right that you should carry it now. You've more than earned the rights to it."

"Unira—"

"No arguments," she said, cutting off his protest. "You are the last of our bloodline. Closer to it than even I am." She took Ushara's hands and placed the Warsword in them. "I'm entrusting our precious Fyreblood legacy to you, daughter, as the new Ger Tarra of our lineage. While I may be older, I'm not the one who will be carrying our future generations. So long as the gods allow, I will be here for both of you, but I gladly cede my matriarchal status as the Samari Ger Tarra to you, Ushara Samari."

Jullien swallowed hard at what she was giving them both. To be entrusted as the male who carried the family Warsword . . . There was no higher honor for any male in their society. To be the designated matriarch, especially when you weren't a blood daughter, was even more sacred and coveted. She was entrusting them with the care and keeping of her entire family legacy.

No. With the entire Samari family legacy and history.

"I will never bring dishonor to your lineage, Matarra."

Unira smiled. "*Our* lineage," she reminded him. "And I know. I'm very proud to have you as my son." She kissed his cheek. "Now, if you two will excuse me . . . I'm actually here to see to the younger Samari of the home. He and I had a date tonight."

Alone with Ushara, Jullien set the sword case down and grinned roguishly at her. "Ger Tarra Samari."

Smiling up at him, she nipped at his chin, sending chills all over him. "So, are you excited about the babies?"

"Mostly scared shitless."

She laughed. "At least you're honest."

He rubbed noses with her before he pulled back to scrutinize the nursery. "Would you be opposed to my painting a mural in here for our girls?"

"You can do anything you want."

He snorted. "You might want to reconsider that. . . . I made some notes while I was gone." Pulling out his link, he turned it on to show her sketches he'd made.

Ushara gasped at the different layouts he'd done for the girls' room. Not just as a nursery, but for several stages as they grew older.

He'd even done some for Vasili's room.

"These are incredible. Have you shown Vas?"

"Not yet. I wanted to make sure it was all right with you first."

"Absolutely. Though I think that double-layered castle bunk bed for the girls has to wait until they're quite a few years older."

"Okay, but I would like to do the mural. And the best part? The dragon's eyes light up with the switch."

She laughed at his giddy excitement. "That might scare them, you know. They will be little girls."

"Yeah, but they're *our* little girls. It'll take more than glowing eyes to scare them."

Unira stuck her head in the room. "Is it all right if Vasili and I go out for dessert? We'll only be gone about an hour, maybe two?"

Ushara smiled at her kindness, knowing exactly what she was doing. "Yes—and thank you, Matarra."

"No problem. I'll text you before we head back."

As they left, Ushara leaned the sword case against the wall. "We have an hour, my lord . . . whatever should we do?"

He was already unbuttoning her shirt as he gave her a warm, wicked grin. "I'm sure I can find something warm and delicious to get into while they're gone."


Six weeks later, Jullien had awakened with a bad feeling deep in his gullet, and it stayed with him all day long. "Are you sure there's nothing on the long-range scanners?"

Unira shook her head. "Nothing."

He glanced over to Davel, who was seated in the captain's chair.

Davel gave him a hostile grimace. "Ask me again, Dagger, and so help me gods, I will shoot you."

Gallatin laughed, then coughed to cover the sound.

Jullien held his hands up and backed off. Honestly, he would have felt better had Thrāix or Trajen come along for this mission, but it was just a short run that Davel had needed him for.

So here he was. . . .

Feeling unsettled. Something was wrong—he knew it. And it wasn't just because he'd taken out two of Nyran's Porturnum spies a week ago.

His link buzzed.

Jullien's scowl deepened as he saw his mother-in-law's frequency listed on it. Katira almost never called him. "Matarra? Is something wrong?"

"Ushara's in labor."

Davel cursed as Jullien unconsciously brought their ship to a screeching halt with his mental powers and reversed the engines. "What the hell, *drey?*"

Blinking, Jullien separated his thoughts from the ship and released the control back to Davel. "Sorry. I have to get home. I need a fighter."

Davel went pale. "Ushara?"

He nodded. "She's in labor."

"She's not due yet."

"I know. It's why I need the fighter." Jullien turned his link up so that Katira could speak to her son. "She's in labor right now. They just admitted her."

Davel reversed course on his own and called down to his engineer. "Boost the drives. Get us back to base as fast as possible. Burn us out if you have to."


With Davel one step behind him, Jullien met Trajen in the hospital waiting room, which was packed with Ushara's family and a terrified Vasili. He hugged his son reassuringly before he faced Trajen and Thrāix. "Where is she?"

"In the back. They won't let me through." Trajen took him to the nurses' station while Vas remained in the waiting room with his grandfather and great-grandfathers. The Trisani glowered at the head nurse. "This is Ushara's husband. Will you let *him* back there to see her?"

The sour look on her face said that she and Trajen must have been having a few choice rounds since Ushara's admittance. "Follow me," she said coldly.

Jullien was shaking as they went down the sterile hallway. He'd always hated hospitals. They brought back too many bad memories of his childhood.

Too many bad memories of his adulthood, for that matter. Nothing good ever happened to him in these places.

The nurse took him into a room and made him scrub down and change into a surgical cap and gown before she showed him into the delivery room, where Ushara was screaming and crying out in agony. Horror filled him as he saw her, and for a full minute, he couldn't move.

Or breathe.

*What have I done to her?*

Katira let out a relieved breath when she finally saw Jullien in the doorway. "Look, Shara! He made it like he promised!"

Panting from her labor pains, she glanced over, then smiled. "Jules!" She held her hand out to him.

Completely dazed, he stumbled forward to take her hand into his.

Katira laughed as he remained by her daughter's side. "No matter how much we drill them, they always forget what they're supposed to do."

Jullien paled as Ushara cried out again from a contraction. "Isn't she supposed to have something for the pain?"

Ushara tightened her grip on his hand. "It's okay, Jules."

"This is not okay." He glared at the doctor. "Can't you do something?"

The doctor gave him a droll stare. "We're doing everything we can to deliver your daughters."

Katira actually felt bad for the stricken expression on Jullien's face. "It's all good, *m'tana*. Everything's going as it's supposed to. Your daughters and wife are fine. Trust me. I wouldn't be so calm if *my* baby were in harm's way."

But as the hours passed, she could tell it was taking a hard toll on him. More so than even on Ushara. While he stood strong and helped her, there was a deep inner storm in his eyes that Katira didn't understand.

And it didn't abate until the doctor handed the first baby to her so that she could show the baby to Jullien and Ushara while they worked on prepping to deliver the next.

"What are we naming our firstborn daughter?" she asked Ushara.

Breathing through her contraction, Ushara inclined her head to Jullien. "Vladmira for the eldest?"

He nodded at the name, which had belonged to the first matriarch of his Samari Fyreblood clan.

"Vladmira," Katira repeated as she handed the infant off to the nurse to be inspected, recorded, and bathed.

Ten minutes later, Ushara let out a final cry as Vladmira's sister joined them. She fell back to hug Jullien as she burst into joyous tears.

The doctor smiled in satisfaction. "Would you like to cut the cord?" she asked him.

Jullien looked terrified as he shook his head. "Are you out of your *minsid* mind? I'm not the one with medical training. Last thing I want is to risk my incompetence harming them."

"Very well. What are we to name this one?" She handed the baby off to Ushara, who cried even harder as she cradled her daughter for the first time.

"My precious beauties look just like their paka." Holding the baby close, Ushara brushed at her daughter's thick mound of dark hair. "We shall name this little aнremia, Viveka, for the first matriarch of the Altaan Fyrebloods." She passed her to her mother for her approval on the name, then took Jullien's hand. "Are you all right, my darkheart?"

He nodded slowly before he pressed her open palm to his cheek. "I am so unworthy of you and your devotion."

"That's not true."

But his eyes denied her words.

Her mother held Viveka toward Jullien. "Would you like to hold your daughter?"

He paled as if the mere thought terrified him. "She's too tiny and fragile. I might harm her."

Ushara rubbed his hand, then explained his fright to her mother. "Jules has never seen a newborn before, Matarra."

She arched a brow at him. "Never?"

He stared in awe of the tiny baby in his mother-in-law's hands. "Just Davel's son."

Her mother gaped. "No wonder you're terrified. Maksim was twice their size at birth and a month old before you met him the first time. Is that really the only infant you've ever seen?"

He nodded.

She tsked lovingly at him. "You are in for a very eye-opening experience, *m'tana.*"

"That he is," the doctor agreed. "Now, let us get the babies registered and inspected, then we can release them to your care. My understanding is that there is a significant group outside, anxiously awaiting word about their safe arrival."

Katira laughed. "That there is. I'll go tell them and give you two a minute to catch your breath."

Ushara waited until she was alone with Jullien before she spoke again. An air of abject sorrow clung to him that she couldn't fathom. "What's wrong?"

He glanced around to make sure no one was within earshot before he spoke. "I swear I won't ever touch you again."

"What?" she gasped.

Sincerity burned deep in his red eyes. "I never meant to hurt you like this, Shara. I'm so sorry. I had no idea it would be so hard on you. No wonder my mother hates me so."

Cupping his face in her hands, she pulled him in to kiss him. "It's okay, precious. They're not my first foray into motherhood. I knew what I was getting into, and I wanted them. And I want more from you."

He paled even more. "Why?"

She laughed at his earnest question. "Because I love my husband and I love my children. Wait until you hold them. You'll see what I mean. And when you hear them call you Paka the first time . . . you will be lost forever to them."

Tears gathered in his eyes as he buried his face in the crook of her neck and held her. "I love you."

He was still holding her like that a few minutes later, when the nurses returned with their daughters.

"You ready to hold them?" Ushara asked, rubbing his back.

Pulling the cap from his hair, he sat up and nodded.

She smiled at his gentle hesitancy when the nurse carefully laid Vladmira in his arms.

His breathing ragged, he bit his lip as he studied his sleeping daughter. "She's all right?"

The nurse smiled approvingly at his eager question. "Indeed. She has all her fingers and toes. They both are perfectly healthy. A little underweight, but that's to be expected with twins."

Jullien lifted her so that he could place a kiss on her forehead. "My little Mira. No male shall ever come near you. Or my Viv. That I promise you both." He tilted his head to look over at Ushara and the baby she held.

Ushara tsked at him. "I have an equal say in that, you know."

He screwed his face up at her. "Like I would ever trust you in that department? Look who you chose for their father. Obviously, you lack all judgment when it comes to picking males of good moral character."

The nurse laughed. "Admiral, we do need one more thing before we can allow visitors. The babies' surname. How do you want it registered?"

Jullien held his breath. It was something they hadn't really discussed. Andarion culture was caste based, and the parents always chose the lineage of the higher-ranked parent for their children to use so that they would have the best social and political advantages in life.

What sickened him was that, by all rights, their daughters were tizirahi of Andaria and Triosa. They should be Anatoles on Andaria and Triosans on his father's planet—as Nyk's children were. But because of his own foul actions and hateful words to his parents, they were forever denied their legitimate and noble birthrights.

He had no one else to blame for that. His selfishness and stupidity had cost his daughters much in way of an advantage and future prospects. Never had he hated himself more than he did right then.

Yet there was no accusation or censure in Ushara's gaze as she smiled at him. "They are of the True Fyreblood Samari."

The nurse made a note. "Their father?"

"Jules Dagger vestewi Pavakahiri Samari."

The nurse's eyes widened at the name. "Son of the high priestess?"

"He is indeed my son." Unira came into the room with a bright smile and her arms loaded with two giant stuffed lorinas as she stepped around the nurse. "And I'm here to bless my precious granddaughters. Let me see my Mira and Viv!" She set the toys down next to the bed.

"This is Mira," Jullien said as he handed his daughter to her. "Shara has Viv."

Unira cooed proudly at her bundle. "You are going to be the most spoiled little girls ever born! Yes, you are! Both of you will be rotten to your precious cores. So I proclaim. You didn't see how fast your paka got here to be with you and your matarra, but I did."

Laughing, the nurse excused herself to go finish filling out the forms.

Ushara also laughed while Unira carried on. Then she met her husband's gaze and sobered. "I'm sorry that I broke my promise. I told you I wouldn't go into labor while you were away, and then what did I do the very hour you took off?"

Pausing, Unira looked up. "He knew it, too. From the moment he woke this morning, he nagged us that something wasn't right."

Ushara gaped at Jullien. "Did you?"

He shrugged as he sat on the bed by her side. "I had a strange premonition."

And before she could ask him anything else about that, the door opened to show Vasili and Trajen entering.

Vas hesitated until Ushara held her hand out to him. "Come here, baby. Meet your sisters."

He scowled as he looked back and forth between them. "How can I tell them apart?"

Jullien grinned. "For now, they have name bracelets. We might ought to keep those on for a bit."

She rolled her eyes at them. "They'll be different enough, all too soon, just like your aunts. It won't be long before you'll never confuse them again. I promise."

Trajen paused as he looked down at Mira. "They're so little. I don't think I've ever seen any *this* small before."

Unira handed Mira to him before he could stop her.

His expression horrified, he stared down at the baby as she opened her eyes to look up at him. Then she nuzzled against his arm and sighed contentedly as she clutched at his shirt.

If Ushara lived a thousand years, she'd never forget the look on Trajen's face. *That* was love in its purest form.

He swallowed hard, then glanced to her and Jullien. "Congratulations."

Jullien met his gaze and then spoke in private to him. *No, thank you, Tray. I wouldn't be here without you. Damn sure wouldn't have my family. I owe you everything, my brother.*

Trajen didn't respond. Rather, he moved to stare down at Viv and compare the two girls. "They are so amazing." When he returned Mira to Unira, he paused by her side. He indicated Jullien with a tilt of his chin. "Watch him."

"Why?"

"He's about to lose every last bit of his shit."

Ushara scowled at him. "What are you talking about?"

Trajen sighed heavily. "Jules? Look at me."

He did. "What?"

"There are nine hundred people ready to descend into this room. All of them will take a blast for your daughters, your wife, and Vas. I want you to keep repeating that over and over in your head until you actually believe it. Okay?"

Rolling his eyes, Jullien scoffed at Trajen's insanity. "I'm fine."

Trajen scratched his brow, then leaned over to hug Ushara. As he did so, he projected his thoughts into her head. *Call me when he goes nuts.*

She had no idea what he meant until five days later, after they were all home.

From the instant they left the hospital, Jullien refused to sleep. He barely ate. She'd never seen anything like it.

Worse, he refused to put the twins down. He would barely let go of them long enough for her to feed them. As soon as she finished, he'd cradle them back to his chest as if daring anyone to come near his daughters for any reason.

The only good to come out of it was that she didn't have to change their nappies. He was so neurotic about letting go that he took care of it without complaint or hesitation.

Even now, it was the middle of the night. Instead of resting in their bed, he had himself wedged on the nursery floor so that he couldn't move or accidentally roll should he doze, with the twins sleeping on his chest while he watched old movies.

Ushara knelt beside him. "Honey? What are you doing?"

"Nothing."

Tilting her head, she arched a doubting brow.

He sighed heavily before he spoke again. "Losing all my shit."

"Want to talk about it?"

"Not really."

"Then I'm going to call Trajen."

"Tattletale," he said sullenly.

She knelt back by his side. "If you don't want me to, then let me in and tell me what's going on."

He took a deep breath and turned the monitor off before he met her gaze. "They're defenseless, Shara. I just keep thinking about all the shit that was done to me and my brother. All the mean shit I did to others . . . I'm scared that the gods are going to punish me by hurting them, or you, or Vas. I don't want them hurt. How can I let them venture into this universe, knowing what's out there. What others are capable of?"

"You think I don't know it's scary? That I don't have nightmares, too?

That's how we met, Jullien. Remember? *You* saved my baby for me after he'd been abducted by slavers. And *I* never forget that. Every night when I go to tuck Vasili in, I know that I have you to thank for the fact that he's safe in his bed. You will never know what a hero that made you in my eyes."

Jullien looked down at the girls on his chest as they slept in peaceful ignorance of the violent universe that had never spared him a single nightmare. "I'm beginning to." He didn't move as Ushara pulled Viv off his chest so that she could cradle her against her shoulder.

"You can't keep living like this. You've got to eat and sleep, or you're not going to be around for them when they're grown."

He brushed his hand over Mira's dark hair before he touched her tiny hand. Even in sleep, she clutched at his finger. "Thank you, Shara."

"For what?"

His red gaze burned into hers. "For not recoiling from my daughters, and for suckling them."

Those words choked her. "Jules—"

"My mother refused to feed me when I was an infant. I was only seven the first time Merrell told me that. It was on my birthday, and I was indulging a bit too much with the cake. Merrell, being his usual asshole self, said it was no wonder I ate so much, since my mother had almost starved me to death when I was born because she refused to feed me. I didn't believe him. Not until I pulled my medical records and saw it for myself."

Ushara's heart sank. "What?"

He nodded glumly. "It was all true. They'd left me to fend alone for so long that it was one of the cleaning staff who'd finally realized I was unconscious in my crib and not sleeping. And only because she was changing my sheets and I didn't wake or move."

She choked on a sob. "Jullien . . ."

Tears glistened in his eyes as he met her gaze. "I keep looking at the girls and thinking that if they look like me and I was hated so much . . . what will become of them? They're Ixurian, too."

"No one will hurt them. I won't let them, and neither will you. You've seen my family. They love and adore them. Nothing will change that."

But even as she spoke those words, Jullien couldn't quite believe her. While her family had been accepting so far, would they remain so once the girls were walking and speaking?

And there was still the matter of her family members who continued their hostilities over his presence here. Kirill and such.

That rift had never mended.

*What have I done?*

He'd made himself more vulnerable than he'd ever been. Instead of
tightening and protecting what he loved, he'd created a greater liabil-
ity. Every time a Porturnum ship landed or came near their base, they
were running a gamble.

And sooner or later, their luck would run out and Nyran would have
him.

Worse, the bastard might claim the life of one of his daughters, Vasili,
or Ushara.

Suddenly, her link sounded with its command tone. Jullien frowned.
That was never a good sound to hear in the middle of the night. But at
least he knew no harm had come to any of her brothers or sisters. They
were all in port tonight.

She handed Viv back to him before she left to answer it. He was just
starting to calm down a bit when he heard her gasp of alarm.

Worried, he got up and placed his daughters in their cribs and went
to check on her. In their bedroom, she stood frozen, with tears glistening in her pale eyes. "Shara?"

Wincing, she set her link down. "It was Gavin's ship. They were hit
tonight."

"Are they okay?"

A single tear fell down her cheek as she shook her head. "They're
gone. All of them. Marshal. Daryn. Letia . . . every member."

His stomach shrank at the news. While Gavin had sided with his
brother Kirill, Jullien still had liked the male. Had it not been for him
and his crew, he'd have died on Steradore.

Crossing the floor, he drew her into his arms. "I'm so sorry. What
happened?"

"They think he was hit by either Mavericks or a crew of Dread Reckoning."

Jullien started to deny it, but stopped himself. Ushara was intelligent enough to know bullshit when she heard it, and there was no need
in hurting her any worse right now. Like The Tavali, The Mavericks were
a Vergyl of outlaw freighters and pirates who'd banded together to protect each other. And while the DR were more hostile and rogue, they

didn't prey on Tavali any more than a Maverick crew would. It would mean open war for them to do so, and they'd had a long-standing history of mutual respect and truce between their groups. They relied on each other's goodwill to keep flying and to shelter each other from The League and others who would do them harm.

No, this was something else, and the Trisani powers inside him said the source was much closer to home. It reeked of something Nyran would do to cause turmoil and mistrust. The best way to overtake an enemy was to divide from within. To turn them against each other and get them going at one another's throats.

A family at war with each other could never stand against an external enemy. It was what had finally brought his grandmother down and allowed him to hand Merrell and Chrisen over to the Baturs.

Worse, he knew that this would put a wedge between him and Ushara. More than that, it would drive a deeper rift between her family.

And even deeper inside, he knew this was just the beginning of the end. His grandmother was getting ready to go to war, and she wouldn't rest until she took them down.

Once and for all.

# CHAPTER 31

Ushara took a moment to savor what had to be one of the happiest events of her life. On this, one of the most sacred Andarion holidays—the celebration of the Day of Our Daughters, they'd given their infant girls their exordiom during temple.

By her side, dressed in his red Demurrist jacket and finery, with the Samari crest painted on his face, Jullien had stood before all, so incredibly proud and thrilled. And he'd finally been given a completely untainted memory of pure familial bliss.

Although, it'd almost been ruined when Unira forgot and, out of habit, asked for his male relatives to stand with him for the ritual paternal prayer. Suddenly stricken, Jules had glanced about nervously and opened his mouth to remind her that he had no family. But before he could, Trajen and Thrāix emerged from the congregation to stand by his side—along with Vasili, Davel, Jory, Chayden, Axl, Sparn, and her father and grandfathers.

Never had she loved her family so deeply or been more touched as they spared him the open embarrassment of standing alone at the altar, and returned the pride to his bashful stralen eyes. The grateful relief on Jullien's face over their unexpected loyalty, and the public declaration that they had finally accepted him fully into their lineage, made her cry even harder than the birth of their girls.

And even though they weren't Demurrists, Jullien had named Trajen as Mira's godfather and Thrāix as Viv's. She'd chosen her sisters Oxana and Jay for their respective godmothers.

Now they were home, with her entire family horde packed into her condo, which suddenly felt extremely tiny.

Trajen, Chayden, Jory, and Thrāix were laughing in the corner with her brothers and father while Jullien and Vas had taken the girls to the nursery for their naps.

At this point, Ushara had opened so many presents for the girls that her head was reeling and she was drowning in frilly wrapping paper. She was still laughing when another present suddenly manifested in her face. Rolling her eyes at what she assumed was one of her exuberant sisters, she started to take her family to task until she looked up to see that it was Dimitri.

Her laughter died instantly. The eldest of their family, he was also the most unforgiving and steadfast when it came to keeping with the old ways. Ever since the fallout with her and Kirill's branch of the family over Jullien, Dimitri had remained solidly aligned with her cousins and uncle against her. He'd avoided coming home or being around any of them.

And since Gavin's funeral, he'd been relentless about Jullien and his desire for Jullien to leave.

Now silence rang out through the entire room as everyone waited to see what her exceptionally large brother would say and do.

Clearing his throat gruffly, Dimitri tucked his chin to his chest while he awkwardly held the present in his hands out for her. "Sorry I was late. I did my best to get here in time for the ceremony, but we ran into some League trouble on the way home."

Stunned, she took his present. "Thank you, Misha."

He covered her hand with his and locked gazes with her. "Just so you know, I'm still not happy with your choice, but your daughters are my blood. I will kill or die for them and for you, *kisa*. . . . Your husband, however, remains on his own."

She bit back a laugh at his surly tone, which was so similar to Jullien's that the two of them should be best friends and not ever at odds. "Got it."

Inclining his head, he kissed her on the cheek. "So where are these adorable girls Madina has raved about for the last month? And please tell my wife that I was here so she'll put me back into our house system and give me access again. I'm sick and tired of being banned from my own home."

Their mother laughed out loud as she hugged him. "My poor Misha. Did you go by there first?"

"I tried. And was still locked out. None of my passcodes work."

Pouting in sympathetic pain, she ruffled his short white hair. "No worries. Madina and Adyn and Adi were here for a little while, then they went to Madina's mother's for the holiday celebrations there. I'm sure she'll answer your text if you try it. If not, your son or daughter will no doubt let you sleep at their place until their mother forgives you for being ridiculously stubborn."

Snickering under her breath, Ushara didn't comment on that as she unwrapped the hand-carved dolls he'd made. "Misha! These are beautiful! Thank you."

He inclined his head to her once more. "Since they were always Adyn's favorite when she was a girl, I thought I'd start the tradition with your daughters. I used to make one every year for her on the anniversary of her birth. She still has hers on a shelf in her home."

Sincerely touched by his thoughtful handmade gift, she set them aside and hugged him. Then she took him down the hall to the nursery, where Jullien sat in her garishly pink rocking chair, holding one of the girls while Vas was on the floor, working on his school assignment.

Jullien had the sleeping baby cradled to his shoulder with one hand as he leaned over the arm of the chair to help Vas. Their heads were almost level as they deciphered the chemistry and sat so similarly that from this angle, they appeared to be natural father and son. It was so genuinely sweet that for a full minute, she couldn't breathe.

And it still amazed her how often the sight of Jullien's rugged masculinity and unexpected tenderness caught her off guard and set her heart racing. No matter how much they were together, she still had the rawest hunger for him. There was something about him that was so incredibly sexy and compelling.

So undeniably precious.

The tender sight wasn't lost on Dimitri, who hesitated until Jullien glanced up and saw them. He straightened instantly. "Was I gone too long?"

Ushara shook her head at his question. While Jullien got along with her family, their exuberant boisterousness often overwhelmed his introverted nature, especially when they were all together for celebrations. As such, he had a tendency to quietly withdraw for a small time-out until he could regroup and face the swell of joyful, earsplitting cacophony again. Normally, he'd only be gone for ten- or fifteen-minute intervals. Unless he lost track of time, then it could be a lot longer.

"You're fine. My brother wanted to see the babies." She led him into the room. "Jullien, this is Dimitri."

At the mention of his name, Vasili turned around and jumped up to launch himself at Dimitri, who'd been standing behind him, out of his sight. "Basha Misha! Ah, Paka, I'm glad you finally get to meet him! He's the only one who can touch your scores on VR shooters."

Ushara held her breath at the sudden tension in the room as Jullien and Dimitri stared at each other in silent mutual scorn. Even Vas's enthusiasm died in the middle of his hug. He glanced to her with a concerned frown.

Trying to alleviate it, she looked at the occupied crib to figure out which twin was which. "Jullien's holding Viv. Mira's sleeping. Would you like to see Mira first?"

Before Dimitri could answer, her mother called for her.

Ushara hesitated. It seemed like a bad idea to leave them alone. However, her mother was being insistent. "I'll be right back."

Jullien didn't speak as Ushara left and Vas followed after her to get something to drink. Alone with Dimitri, he refused to take his gaze off him. He'd already made that mistake once.

And paid dearly for it.

"You haven't told her?" Dimitri whispered.

Jullien shifted his sleeping daughter in his arms. Now, he fully understood the reason Dimitri had avoided meeting him after all this time, and why the coward hadn't come near his family since Jullien's return.

Dimitri was the one who'd brought the Ladorian slaver to Kirill's ship to buy him from their crew.

Honestly, he still wanted to kill the bastard over it. But Ushara loved her older brother, so . . . "What happened is between us. All that knowledge would do is bring pain to your sister."

Dimitri at least had the good grace to look ashamed. "You've really never told her what happened?"

"Not a tattletale bitch. All she knows is what she saw. I won't hurt her by telling her anything else, and I'll beat the utter shit out of you if you do."

"I don't understand why you'd protect me."

"I'm not. It's Ushara and your family I'm protecting. None of them need to know what a treacherous asshole you really are."

Dimitri sighed. "For what it's worth, I'm sorry. I thought I was doing the right thing for my family." He glanced to the babies, then to Vasili's homework, which was still scattered about on the floor. "My wife has gleefully instructed me on the error of my ways where you're concerned." Completely abashed, he held his hands out for the baby. "May I?"

Jullien carefully handed Viv to her uncle, whose features softened instantly as he adjusted her in his massive arms.

Dimitri tucked the blanket around her. "It's been a long time since my daughter was this size. Enjoy every minute of it, Ixurian. It passes faster than a blink of your eye."

"So your mother keeps telling me." Jullien moved to check on Mira, who continued to sleep in blissful ignorance.

Dimitri paused to study the fairy tale mural Jullien had painted on their nursery wall. "Wow. Who painted that for them?"

"Jullien did." Trajen and Thrāix came into the room so that Trajen could eyeball the two of them. He focused his attention mostly on Jullien. "You good here?"

"I'm fine. No entrails currently on the walls, nor are they forthcoming. I don't want to scar my daughters the first month they're alive. But during their second . . . all bets are off."

Ignoring his sarcasm, Trajen cut a gimlet stare to Dimitri that said he knew what had happened between them even though Jullien had never told him. "Good. Wanted to let you know that I'm locking down the base. There's been another attack on an Altaan crew."

Dimitri froze. "Who?"

"Kirill's. We just got the call. The whole ship went up in flames, and Klavdii's blaming Jules."

"What!"

Trajen held his hand up at Jullien's outburst. "Relax. I know you didn't do it. You haven't left your daughters or Ushara alone since the girls were born. We all know that. But Klav's in pain and not listening to reason right now. He just lost two daughters and two sons in less than a month for reasons no one can make sense of. He wants someone's balls, and yours are within easy reach."

Dimitri winced. "I'm going to find my children and ground them."

Trajen nodded in sympathy. "From here on out, no one but Gort gets in or out of this base. No foreign crew or other Tavali Nation is allowed to step foot in our bays without my express approval or invitation."

Dimitri scowled at that. "Why?"

"To protect your sister and nieces. I'm not taking any chances on them. Or anyone else in our Nation. I'm tired of speaking at funerals."

Jullien went cold. "Has there been a specific threat against Ushara?"

"Not per se, but it's suspicious that they've only hit Altaan crews— the two crews that you were recorded to have flown on, no less. You still have five months to go until you're up for your citizenship hazard. As soon as you pass, I'm fast-tracking you to captain, based on merit and previous service."

Dimitri gaped. "Seriously?"

"Seriously. His Canting's already been designed and approved."

That only angered Dimitri more. "What the hell is that? He gets captain, first thing? *With* Canting?"

"And *ship*," Trajen added in an antagonistic tone.

Dimitri made a sound of total disgust.

Thrāix tsked at him. "Don't be hating, precious. You haven't seen his Canting." He let out an evil, villainous snicker.

Jullien cringed in dread. "Oh dear gods, what have you jackals done to abuse my dignity now?"

Pulling out his link, Thrāix turned it on and skimmed through his photos until he held one up for Jullien to view. "Here you go, princess."

Jullien sighed in irritation as Dimitri burst into laughter.

"Okay, I'm not jealous anymore. Cockroach Canting for a cockroach. Completely fitting. I approve wholeheartedly."

Jullien glared at his brother-in-law. "Yeah, go ahead and laugh, asshole. We're all big and brave, till you realize that cockroach has wings and can fly."

Dimitri sobered at the same time Thrāix and Trajen laughed.

"Hence my choice of your Canting," Trajen said with a smirk. "I thought it apropos. And I knew if anyone could appreciate the ironic humor behind it, it would be *you,* Dagger Ixur. Bug up the ass of all your enemies."

"And friends," Thrāix added.

Jullien snorted.

"So when's your test?" Dimitri asked, changing the subject.

Trajen answered for him. "Day after his temple wedding ceremony."

Dimitri arched a brow as he placed Viv in her crib. "Really?"

"Yeah. Ushara didn't want me busted and bruised until after we had the formal wedding."

While Jullien wanted to be a full Tavali citizen, he wasn't looking forward to the cock hazard, which required him to take on three of their strongest Tavali warriors—chosen by their administer of hazard—in order to prove that he could defend himself and the Gorturnum Nation in battle. Like an Andarion Ring match, the cock hazard was a free-for-all where all three warriors would do their best to tear him to shreds and keep him out of their Nation. He could lose to one of them. But if he lost to two, it was over, and he'd have to wait a year to apply again for citizenship.

If he passed and was admitted to the Nation, he'd have to undergo an annual anniversary hazard to maintain his citizenship, but that would never be as difficult as the initial one. The anniversary hazards were single matches against a regular citizen who was also up for their anniversary hazard. Lasting for half an hour, those didn't require a winner. Only that you showed the AOH that you were both still physically fit for hand-to-hand combat and could hold your own in a fight. Of course, you had to last the entire half an hour, or you could have your citizenship suspended or lose rank.

When it came to maintaining their members, The Tavali didn't play. They took their oaths and combat very seriously.

Frowning at Jullien, Dimitri indicated the twins. "Didn't you two postpone your wedding a bit too long?"

Jullien held his hands up in surrender. "I had nothing to do with it. Your mother and yaya planned it all."

"It's massive in size and scope. You'd think the tadara of Andaria was getting married." Trajen made a sound of supreme annoyance. "Hence the excessive planning time, and another reason I'm locking down the base. I don't want anyone around to know what's going on here with two of my primary soldiers and family. There's too much unrest right now."

Thrāix nodded in agreement. "We have bitter days ahead, my Tavali. *Styrian*'s coming."

Jullien was impressed that Thrāix knew that old Andarion phrase, given how little interaction he seemed to have with the other Andarions in the station. And the extremely dire meaning of it, because no Andarion used that phrase lightly. It basically meant to sac up and prepare for the bloodiest of wars.

Hell was coming, and with it, an army of its fiercest demons.

\* \* \*

While the next few months flew by, and his daughters and Vas grew as quickly as everyone had warned him they would, Jullien learned exactly what Thrāix and Trajen had meant as The League and Sentella tensions heated up, and The Tavali got caught between them.

Worse, the Andarions were being dragged into the thick of their mess as Cairistiona sided with Nykyrian in every bad decision he made against The League and its prime commander, Kyr Zemin. His brother was letting his old personal League grudges with Zemin, and that of Darling Cruel and Kyr, get him and his Sentella into all kinds of wrong situations. And there was nothing Jullien could do to spare his brother his grotesque stupidity.

*They overthrew me for this?*

It was adding insult to injury. Because there was no way Jullien would have allowed the Andarions and Triosans to be dragged into the thick of the political tensions and mess that Nyk dove into willingly to back his friends.

Meanwhile, Eriadne and Nyran continued to make strikes against both his mother and Nykyrian as they sought any weakness they could exploit to their advantage and try to overthrow them. Since neither Nyk nor his mother knew them as well as Jullien did, they were helpless against them. And again, were being hammered by their combined forces.

It was a dangerous game Jullien played as he tried to do as Ushara had asked, and stay out of it, and at the same time, he kept waiting for them to find out he was still alive. Either his brother or his grandmother, as both sides would kill him over his past mistakes.

There were times when he swore he could feel the clock running out on them all.

And it wasn't just that his girls were getting bigger every day, and Vasili was turning into an adult before their very eyes. Everywhere they flew, there was civil unrest as The League grew bolder, and The Sentella more defiant against its power. Mostly because his brother was a reactionary idiot, in Jullien's opinion. But then, he wasn't exactly known for his calm, rational decisions either.

Perhaps he and Nyk were more alike than either wanted to admit.

Intergalactic war was inevitable. Jullien could feel it with every innate political chromosome he possessed. Ushara was feeling the burden of her position, which locked her into the base while Jullien flew missions under her command that took him deep into Porturnum and Sentella territory. Each hated the separation, but they had no choice.

They were Tavali. The only thing that kept Jullien remotely sane was the tech that allowed them to talk and be together, no matter where his duties took him.

And the knowledge that Thrāix was staying closer to the Gorturnum base, rather than returning to his isolated home, where a prolonged war would trap him with no supplies or allies. In fact, he'd moved into the condo next door to theirs after Lev decided he could no longer stand living that close to them.

And every time Jullien saw one of Kirill's or Gavin's siblings, parents, widows, or children, guilt stole more of his soul. He couldn't help feeling responsible for their deaths. It ate at him constantly.

Which heightened his fear for Ushara and their own children at home, and her fear for Jullien and his crew whenever they left for a job. Poor Thrāix would often get caught between Jullien and Ushara as she ordered him to fly with Jullien as part of his crew, and Jullien ordered him to stay at the base and watch over his family.

To which Thrāix would inevitably cock a brow and remind them, "Really, Andarions? You do know that I'm not Tavali, and I don't answer to either of you? So a little *please, Thrāix* will go a long way in swaying my opinion. As will Tondarion Fire or Jullien's ale cake. Now, who's buying my loyalty first?"

Together, Thrāix and Jullien kept an eye on Bastien and ran supplies to him on Oksana whenever they could. But those runs were sadly few and far between, as they required him to venture deep into enemy territory and risk running into his brother's forces.

If only Jullien could find a doctor with the ability to remove Bastien's tag, or a way to block his as easily as he'd managed to do his own. Though he'd had a few leads, he had yet to locate a surgeon whose skill-set he trusted enough not to kill or maim Bastien.

As a precaution to keep his family as safe as possible, Jullien remained blond and wore the clear contacts, which really screwed everyone up when they saw them with his fangs. Since there was only one Fyreblood family that carried the stralen gene and the Samaris had been virtually extinct for decades, no one—Andarion or otherwise—was used to seeing a blond, red-eyed Andarion.

The reactions of those who first noted his fangs and put them together with his eyes were hysterical. Most were nervous or dumbstruck. A few openly rude and insulting. The rest ran as if they'd met their devil incarnate. Especially since Jullien had dispensed of his former names entirely, and only Samari or Dagger Ixur marked any of his gear or official forms. People and Andarions acted as if he really were *the* Dagger Ixur summoned from the bowels of Tophet to take their souls.

His grandmother and her cronies believed him to be Edon Samari's ghost, haunting her from the grave. Something he used to his advantage whenever he could. It was nice to be the one doing the mind-fucking for once, and not receiving it.

For that matter, with the exception of their immediate family, along with Zellen, Thrāix, Trajen, and Jupiter, no one remembered Jullien had ever borne another name. Not even Chayden knew of his real birth name. As far as the universe was concerned or knew, Jullien had always been Jules Dagger Ixur Samari, son of Unira Samari. Fyreblood Andarion and Tavali pirate. Husband of Ushara Altaan Samari, and Trajen's active field admiral.

He now wore nothing other than Tavali battlegear at all times, and kept his grandfather's Warsword strapped across his back whenever he acted in any official capacity. With an outlaw swagger and predator's glare, there was no trace whatsoever of the royal Andarion tiziran he'd once been.

Jullien eton Anatole was officially dead and buried.

If he'd had any doubts about that fact, they were adequately laid to rest when he, Thrāix, Mary, and Oxana flew a humanitarian mission into Caronese territory through a League blockade, at Ryn Cruel's behest. They'd landed a few hours ago in the main hangar bay of the capital city to offload supplies for Darling's people, who were being hammered by The League.

Apparently, Darling had gone into some kind of suicidal rampage against The League and the CDS—the representatives of the Caronese people who hated Darling and resented the fact that though his uncle had been an unreasonable tyrant, Darling had murdered him in cold blood so that he could ascend the throne.

Personally, Jullien was glad that Darling had finally stood up to the brutal bastard who'd rivaled Eriadne for cruelty. While Darling was still a child, Arturo Cruel had killed Darling's father so that he could wrongfully seize power, and then Arturo had spent the next eighteen years terrorizing the entire Caronese royal family to the point that Darling had been left with no choice except to put Arturo out of all their miseries before he sent Darling and his siblings to their graves.

Sadly, The League didn't agree and had placed the Caronese Empire under martial law. Darling's people were in an uproar as The League arrested their delegates without trial and bombed the shit out of them. Anyone who could bypass League cruisers with supplies for the Caronese was being paid premium prices to bring them in, and while Ushara didn't like the fact Jullien was doing this, she couldn't argue the creds it was worth.

Nor the fact that her sisters were going to make the run with or without him. And they were much safer with Jullien and Thrāix flying cover for them than they were flying solo or with Davel or Axl as their point.

Yet that being said, he was more than ready to go home. He hadn't seen Ushara, Vas, or his girls in almost three weeks. At least, nowhere other than on his link feed. And every minute they were here, he ran the risk of being recognized by one of his brother's Sentella members or the Andarions who were swarming all around them so thick, he couldn't sneeze without contaminating eight of them. He'd had no idea when they landed just how many of his brother's people would be in this place. But they were crawling all over the bay, giving him hives.

It was why he'd kept his Tavali mask securely in place. Unfortunately, he had to lower it and expose his face to speak with the hangar staff. Otherwise, they might mistake him for one of the bandits who kept stealing their supplies and shoot him on sight.

"How much longer?" he asked the worker who was making notes about his cargo for payment.

"We're almost done. Then we have the *Fire Kiss* to unload, and you'll be free to go."

Cursing in frustrated aggravation, Jullien headed toward Mary's ship while he texted her to let her know they had yet to even start unloading her hold. Three steps later, he collided with someone else who was rushing through the bay.

"Sorry," he mumbled as he dropped his link, then froze as he met the disgruntled gaze of his twin brother, Nykyrian.

Too late, he remembered his face was still exposed.

Staring him dead in the eyes, Nykyrian cleared his throat gruffly. "It's all right. I wasn't paying attention, either. Sorry about that." He leaned over to pick up his own link, which he'd dropped when they collided. He grabbed Jullien's and handed it to him, but not before he glanced down to see the lock screen that held a photo of Vasili and the twins. "Cute kids. Yours?"

"Yeah. . . . Thanks."

"Hey, Nyk?"

Jullien held his breath as Dancer Hauk came running over to them. While his brother had never spent much time around him, that wasn't true of Dancer.

Yet like Nyk before him, Dancer looked Jullien straight in the eyes, and there was no recognition at all. Inclining his head to Jullien as an acknowledgment and to excuse them, he pulled Nyk back a step. "We have a huge problem. Have you seen the news? We have to get to Darling. Immediately."

They ran off without so much as a backward glance.

*"Titana ræl,"* Jullien breathed. Neither one had known him. Not even a *hint* of recognition had darkened their gazes. Now, *that* was screwed up.

All of a sudden, activity picked up in the bay. Fighters began launching. Alarms sounded.

Jullien ran to Mary's ship and ascended the ramp to find her inside with Ana and Thrāix. "Hey, what's going on?"

"The League just reported that they've killed Darling Cruel's fiancée during their interrogation. It's why the Caronese are scrambling. They're expecting renewed League attacks."

Jullien winced in sympathetic pain. "We need to get out of here, then."

Mary gasped indignantly. "What about my cargo and payment?"

"Can't spend cred if you're dead. Let's cut our losses and go."

Thrāix nodded. "Yeah, I agree with Admiral Paranoia."

Jullien used his powers to turn her ship on. "Get your launch codes. I want both of you out and headed home immediately."

"Gah, I hate it when you do that. It's unnerving." Mary shivered and scowled at him. "I thought you weren't supposed to be able to do that to any ship but your own?"

Jullien passed an amused smirk to Thrāix. They had no idea why Jullien could do that when no one else had ever developed the ability before.

Chalk it up to screwy hybrid genes.

Oxana hesitated by Jullien's side. "What about you?"

"I'll be in your shadows, the whole way. We need to get out before The League locks this entire sector down." He nudged her forward. "Go! Your kids need you home."

"Ouch! Unfair." But Oxana listened and did as he said while Mary went through her prelaunch checks.

Thrāix and Jullien left her bridge to head for their ships. But as Jullien crossed the bay, he overheard some of the Caronese and other Tavali talking about a counterstrike Darling and The Sentella were planning.

Slowing down, he faltered.

Thrāix glared at him in a way that said he knew exactly what Jullien was thinking. "Are you crazy?"

"Yeah, I am," Jullien said with a laugh. "Has there ever been any doubt?"

Thrāix shook his head. "Don't do it. Don't even *think* about it. Your wife will kill you."

"Why? It's a *full* pardon. You heard them."

"Only for Caronese territory."

Jullien shook his head in denial. "Their allies will respect it, too. You know they will." And their allies included Andaria and Triosa. As well as Exeter and Gouran . . . and others. More than that, it was a large chunk of the shipping routes, territories, and sectors that the Gorturnum flew through and controlled.

If Jullien flew with the Caronese strike team as a Tavali, he could get at least part of The League warrant off his back in those systems and empires.

*A full pardon.*

Thrāix cursed at him. "Dagger . . ."

But Jullien wasn't listening to his warnings. "Are you speaking to me as a Tris with precog, or a worried friend?"

"I'm speaking as your wingman whose CO is your wife. She'll denut us both if you do this."

Jullien cupped Thrāix's ear in his hand and grinned at him. "It's only my balls on the chopping block. Get my sisters home. I have to do this, Thrāix. C'mon, it's the only way I'll ever have any kind of pardon. You know that. Some protection's better than none."

"And if someone recognizes you as who you used to be?"

"I have to take this chance."

Thrāix shoved him back. "You're an idiot. But Chay and Jory will be in the fighting. I'll have them cover you."

"Thanks."

"Thank me by not getting hurt." Thrāix growled low in his throat. "Remember, my balls are in your hand."

Laughing, Jullien screwed his face up. "Don't say shit like that in public. Folks'll get the wrong idea about us."

That only encouraged Thrāix to worsen it by giving him a light kiss before he headed for his ship. Had anyone else done that, Jullien would have gutted them.

But Thrāix was Thrāix.

Unique unto himself. And Jullien treasured their friendship, weird though it could be. Amused and irritated by his friend, he turned to catch one of the staff sneering at him.

Arching his brow in confrontation, Jullien unholstered his blaster, intending to shoot at him. But as he went to pull the trigger, someone lifted his arm up and tickled his armpit.

Jullien started to punch his attacker until he saw Jory laughing in his face. "*Idydrian!* What are you doing?"

"Saving you from your own stupidity, boyo. You can't go around shooting up the Caronese. Remember, you'll blow your pardon before you even get it."

He holstered his blaster. Maybe, but it might have been worth it. "Where's Psycho Bunny?"

"Already in flight. He's riding point for Precious Cargo and is at the head of all this with me sister to his right. I'll take you in as me wingman. You fueled?"

"Not yet." Jullien glanced over to check their progress. "They should be about done, though."

"Good. Our job's to keep Mack safe in battle for Ryn."

"Babysitting? Really?"

"Yeah, piss-poor waste of me talents. But what can I do? Besides, the way she flies and fights, we'll see more than our fair share of action. Mack won't be holding back."

That was true.

And with that thought, Jullien headed for the *Pet Hate* and made ready to launch. The battle plan was that Darling and The Sentella would lead them in. They were to hang back until Darling and Dancer could blow them an opening. Once The Sentella had the prison's shields down and control of The League's defenses, The Tavali were to get as many of the Caronese political prisoners as they could out of there and to safety.

Jullien's specific assignment was to provide air cover support for the transports and Sentella.

By the time he was grouped and in position with his Tavali team, his link started buzzing. His gut tightened automatically as he recognized Ushara's tone.

*I am in serious trouble now.*

But he knew better than to ignore her call. With a deep breath and prayer for divine mercy, he answered it. "Hey, *munatara.* How's my—?"

"Don't you even take that tone with me. My sisters have already ratted you out. What are you thinking?"

*That your sisters might keep a secret, for once.* He should have known better. "It's a full pardon, *mia.*"

"Dagger . . ."

"You know I need to do this. Trust me."

She turned on the video feed to show him an image of her holding Viv while Mira played beside them on the floor of their condo with Vasili. "I do trust you."

"Paka!" Both twins started laughing and slapping at the link to say hi to him the instant they saw his face.

Their happiness choked him. "Hey, my girls. Paka loves you."

They blew him sloppy kisses before they ran off, giggling.

Vasili inclined his head to him. "Hey, Paka. Stay safe. We miss you." Then he ran after his sisters, pretending to be a beast out to scare them. They shrieked and laughed in the background as they sought to escape their big brother.

He growled at Ushara, who was wearing a way-too-tight top that she knew drove him to distraction, and if he were home, would have him dragging her off to their bedroom. "You're playing dirty, *kimu.*"

"I use what I have."

He stared at her beautiful face, which was marred only by a worried frown. For him. "I'm not going to leave you or them. I'll be home soon and in your arms."

"You better."

His alarms started going off to warn him they were about to be under fire.

Tears welled in Ushara's eyes as she cut the transmission so that he could focus on his battle.

With a ragged breath, Jullien pulled his headset on and put his head in the battle as he followed Mack and Jory straight into the worst of the fighting. Yeah, it was thick. Most of The Sentella forces were already in the prison.

The Tavali ships stayed back to cover the Sentella as they landed, taking out as many of the exterior ion cannons and ground-to-air weapons as they could.

Since Jullien was left solo after Jory went to render aid to another pilot, he flew over to drop a missile. When he came up over the side, two fighters were waiting for him. He banked hard and rolled away, clearing them.

That should and would have brought him to safety, had a piece of another ship not come flying out of nowhere to hit one of his rear stabilizers and wedge in it. The impact sent him careening sideways.

His control panel lit up as the alarms sounded to warn him—as if he couldn't tell he was spiraling through space with no control. Even if he'd been asleep, the impact would have thrown him from his bunk and slammed him into a wall.

He tried to hold it steady, but his control panel went completely dark. "Jupiter?"

"I see you, Dagger. Headed your way."

Yet it was too late. If Jullien didn't set her down, he was going to lose the ship.

Maybe his life.

Jullien had no choice. Using his powers alone, he took control and did his best to limp the ship toward the prison grounds for a hot emergency landing. Just as his nose started bleeding from the strain of flying, Jory caught him with his tractor beam and helped to set her down not far from Chayden's ship. Jullien wiped at the sweat on his forehead and blood on his nose.

Dizzy, he could feel with his powers the shrapnel that was lodged in the panel. It wouldn't take long to get it cleared.

Unfortunately, he wouldn't be able to do it while they were taking fire on the ground. They needed to get the League prison under control and the soldiers off their backs.

Switching to a hardsuit, he geared up and went to help evacuate the prisoners.

He grabbed a rifle and tested his mic before he called out to the only Tavali he personally knew on the ground. "Psycho Bunny? Holler at your Gort *drey*. Dagger's on the ground to lend a hand. Where you at, boy?"

Chayden laughed over the headset. "Hey! Dagger, head down the left corridor from the main entrance. Got a party for you. Could use your expertise. Bring it, Andarion. I want some fire to rain down on these assholes."

Jullien headed to his location, then snorted as he saw them. *Shit.* . . . What the Bunny had failed to mention was that he, Ryn, his half-brother Drake Cruel, and the Sentella commander Jayne Erixour were all pinned down by League soldiers.

Luckily, Jullien came in *behind* the League forces and shot grenades into their positions. He dislodged them and opened fire so that Chayden and the others could get out and head toward safety.

Chayden paused by his side and grabbed extra ammo from Jullien's pack. "Thanks. I owe you. I ran out completely while we were trapped."

"It's all good."

They jogged back to where the bulk of their team was moving Caronese prisoners into transports.

Jullien took a younger kid from one of the Sentella soldiers, and half carried him on board one of The Sentella ships before he doubled back to help evacuate more from inside the prison.

As he neared Chayden, who was with more Tavali, he heard a strange popping, static sound. Concerned, Jullien slowed down.

Suddenly, the walls around them illuminated to show Kyr Zemin's furious face as he took inventory of the utter destruction The Sentella had wrought on his facility. He demanded they return the prisoners to their cells and leave the prison.

Immediately.

Jullien laughed as he joined Chayden's group. "Yeah, that always works. Enemies cooperate so well. Just for the hell of it. You know. If you ask politely enough."

Laughing, Chayden recharged his blaster while Darling told Zemin as much, in far ruder terms.

Fain and Ryn moved to stand near them.

"What are the odds that Darling is about to do something stupid?" Fain said under his breath to Ryn while Jullien took care to stay covered in Tavali gear so that neither recognized him for who he really was. He double-checked that even his voice was masked.

Chayden snorted. "I'll take odds on radically stupid."

"Put me down for nuclear-level idiocy," Jullien said in a low tone. "I've never known Cruel to hold his temper long in a situation like this."

A heartbeat later, as if on cue, Darling ripped his helmet off, exposing his face . . . which was a blatant act of war, since he was the ruler of Caron and he'd just led an attack on a League facility.

Zemin arched a daring brow at Darling. "So you're declaring war on us, then."

But Darling wasn't intimidated at all. "Interesting concept. I would say that *you* declared it on us when you marched your army into our empire and destroyed our property, and kidnapped our citizens. And now we're answering it. No one seizes my people. I don't care who you are."

"We were invited in by your own council, who wanted *you* removed from power."

"Were you?" Darling asked with a hint of hysterical laughter in his voice. "That's not what I heard. In fact, I have the entire CDS, who will swear they never asked for you to intervene. That you took it upon yourself to attack us without provocation."

"You have no idea what you're unleashing right now, *verikon*."

Jullien winced at *that* particular insult.

Which Darling answered with a worse one. "And neither do you, *ciratile*. You ever try this shit again with me and mine, and I will rape and plunder the village, and burn the motherfucker to the ground. . . ."

Jullien let out a low whistle at something he knew Kyr wouldn't take well.

Darling looked around at the bodies on the floor. "And as you've seen here today, there ain't nothing you bitches can do to stop me. Talk is cheap. Pain is free. And I'm peddling the shit out of it. So you come on and get some."

Jullien turned toward Chayden. "Pay up, Bunny. Nuclear stupid, for the win."

Chayden held an expression that said he'd just sprouted an Andarion-sized ulcer.

But all kidding aside, Jullien wasn't as lighthearted as he pretended. This was serious. While he might have his pardon out of this, The Sentella had just officially declared war on The League.

With Tavali help.

There was no going back now. Darling's dumbass temper had just pulled their entire universe into a bitter, nasty war. All the major empires would now be split. . . .

Those who still supported The League.

Those who backed The Sentella.

Jullien had no idea who would win it, if they would even survive it, but one thing was certain.

Nothing would ever be the same again.

# CHAPTER 32

The war is on."

Ushara froze as Jullien came into the command center, where she was having lunch with Trajen and the girls.

Unaware of what the word meant that their father had just used, the twins ran to him, laughing and shouting out, "Paka!" at the top of their shrill lungs.

Smiling in spite of the knot in his gut over what had happened on Caron, Jullien scooped them up and hugged them close, wishing to the gods he could put them under lock and key for the rest of eternity. This was what scared him most about Darling's stupidity. They would have to pay a price for it. Their children were the ones who would bear the worst brunt of their bad decisions.

Trajen exchanged a frown with Ushara.

"What war?" Trajen asked, seeking clarification.

Jullien carried the girls with him to sit in a chair before he turned on the monitor, and directed it to an Andarion news channel. "The Sentella has declared war on The League."

"What?" Ushara gasped. "When did this happen?"

"While we were helping Cruel liberate his fiancée from League custody. He and Zemin got into it, and . . . well, I would give you his exact spiel, but we have young ears in the room. The edited version is Darling, as emperor, declared war on The League, with the backing of Andaria, Exeter, and according to Ryn Dane, us."

"Paka?" Mira asked. "What's *war* mean?"

"It's a bad fight, *tura*." Jullien sighed as he smoothed the hair back from her forehead and kissed it. "I had no idea when I told Saf where they were keeping Zarya that he'd tell Cruel where she was. He was supposed to give that intel to my brother for a rescue, not her idiot SO."

Ushara gaped. "What?"

"I wanted him to pass the information on Zarya's location to Nyk. Not Cruel. Darling's never had his head on straight. . . . Did you know he once blew up Nyk's favorite fighter while running away from home? He's lucky he survived that. Nyk loves his ship the way I love mine."

"Who's Nyk, Paka?" Mira asked.

"My twin brother."

She gasped and looked at her sister. "Paka's gots a twin like us!"

"There's two Pakas!" Viv gasped, wide-eyed. "We's gots two pakas!"

Laughing, Jullien picked up Viv and kissed her cheek. "No, baby. You only have one paka. Please don't tell anyone else that you have two pakas or they'll give your mother strange looks. My twin brother is your ba-sha, like Trajen is."

Viv settled down into his lap and started tracing the lines of the IN-DURARI tattoo on his inner forearm with her fingertip. For some reason, it'd always fascinated her. Thankfully, she was now old enough that she no longer tried to bite into it. There had been a time or two when she was first cutting her fangs that she'd actually drawn blood.

Jullien met Trajen's gaze and sighed. "So, boss, we are now at war with The League . . . according to our ambassador."

"Does Dane have the authority to do that?" Ushara asked. "Doesn't he have to consult the UTC before he makes a declaration of this magnitude?"

Trajen gave her a droll stare. "Sure. But since his mother is the one we all answer to . . ." He glanced back to Jullien. "Not that it would matter. Venik would side with The Sentella just for the profiteering opportunities. And Exeter will do whatever Syn and Caillen say. If Exeter's in it, Chayden's in it. If Chayden's in it, Hinto and the Septurnum are in it. And Hermione Dane will always back whatever Darling does, since she thinks of him as her own. That leaves us as the solo Tavali Nation standing."

Which was never a good position to be in.

Ushara groaned out loud. She tugged a protesting Viv into her lap and held her close. "Tell me that you at least got your pardon out of this nightmare?"

Jullien pulled it up on his link and handed it to her. "That I did. I'm officially safe to fly through Sentella-held space for the rest of my life. Provided I don't prey on any of their cargo or people. If they win this fiasco, I'm home free."

Trajen let out a bitter laugh. "They'd all shit their pants if they knew who they'd really handed this pardon to."

"Yes, they would. Much as I almost did when I had to take it out of my father's secretary's hands to get it, while my father was standing over him."

Ushara's eyes widened. "What? For real?"

He nodded. "They broke us into groups by our surnames. "Lucky me, the *S*'s were being handled by the Triosans."

Mira gasped at his words. "Did you see the bad Andarions there, Paka? Did they try and hurt you?"

"I saw some." He widened his eyes and tickled her until she squealed and laughed. "But I was bigger and meaner."

Mira made a large O with her mouth.

Ushara continued to hold Viv.

Jullien didn't miss the panic in her gaze or the tenseness in her grip. And with that, he turned to face Trajen. "Did you get my transfer request?"

Trajen glanced to Ushara. "I did, and I noticed that you bypassed my VA to make it." He tsked at him. "You still haven't learned the proper chain of command, *drey*."

"What request?" The panic seeped into her voice. "What dumb idea are you contemplating now?"

Trajen laughed. "I'm so glad you phrased it that way. . . . Your husband wants to take a rank reduction to start making regular runs again."

"What!" She glared at him. "Why?"

Growling at both of them, Jullien adjusted Mira in his lap and handed Ushara his link. "Did you see *this*?"

She ground her teeth as she read the file. "Of course I did. I already chewed my father out for going behind my back and filing the forms for Vas. He came home yesterday, after withdrawing from his classes without consulting us, thinking I was going to put him on a crew. He's now swabbing out latrines for Sheila as punishment."

Amused at the thought, Jullien glanced to Trajen before he returned his link to his pocket and spoke to Ushara. "Your father wasn't wrong. It's been over a year since Vas graduated. We can't keep him from flying. It's in his blood."

That only seemed to piss her off more. "I wanted him at university . . . like his paka. It won't hurt him to get a degree first."

"But he's not me, Shar. He wants to be Tavali, not a professor or a politician. We have to give him credit. He spent a year at university like we asked, but he hates it. He's young and anxious to prove himself. Just like his mother was at his age."

"Don't you dare throw logic at me. You'll be sleeping on your ship tonight." Tears welled in her eyes as she tightened her grip on Viv to the point their daughter began protesting it. "I can't assign him to a crew. Especially not now!" There was a note of hysteria in her voice.

"I know, *mia*," Jullien said calmly, though he felt the same way she did. "It's why I requested the reduction. As you said, especially now that we're at war. I'll take him on as my crew, with Thrāix. You know we're not going to put him in harm's way. We would die before we let any harm come to him."

Trajen got up. "Hey, girls? Want to visit Basha Trajen's treasure room? See what new toys I have for you?"

They both shrieked in excited happiness as they scrambled from their parents' laps toward him.

He looked at Jullien, then Ushara. "You two work this out. I will do whatever you want about the ranks and assignments. Personally, I like Jules where he is. But Vas comes first. Send over whatever paperwork I have to authorize. I'll watch the twins until you two fight it out."

Trajen picked them up. Mira immediately hugged him and put her head down on his shoulder, where she smiled and flashed her little fangs. Trajen's features softened as the dark shadows of his past flitted across his eyes, leaving them haunted and filled with grief. "And don't worry about the war. The other Nations can fight if they want. We're sitting it out, officially. I won't stop any of our crews from making a profit from it, but I have no intention of putting our family on the line for them. I've seen enough war in my lifetime. I want no more of it."

Grateful for his position and words, Ushara squeezed her eyes shut until they were alone, so that she wouldn't cry. Clearing her throat, she locked gazes with Jullien. "Trajen told me earlier that you've only been running rescue the last few months for him? Not carrying cargo?"

"Yeah. It's what I'd keep doing with Vasili. That way he'll have his training and hours, but won't risk jail or fighting."

Getting up, she moved to sit in his lap. "You would really take a rank reduction?"

"For you and Vasili? Of course. Without hesitation."

She shook her head, amazed by him as she straddled his waist. Her darkheart was ever the most precious thing in her life. Always looking after them. "Then I'll assign him to your crew."

"And I will guard him for you."

Ushara cupped his whiskered cheek and stared into those beautiful stralen eyes. "I was so mad at you for staying behind to fight."

"I know."

She tugged at his bleached hair, missing his darker locks. "I always thought I'd be happier in a command position. I didn't want to be like my parents . . . dragging my kids along on missions. Or leaving them behind with their grandparents while my husband and I ran our own crew. I was so thrilled when Trajen made me his VA."

"I sense a *but* coming."

"But," she said with a sad smile. "I feel like I don't have your back. Like I'm leaving you unprotected."

He took her hand into his and led it to his cheek—the ultimate Ixurian expression of love and affection. "No, *mu tura*. I've been alone the whole of my life. Cast out by everyone, *except* you. Whether you're with me or on the other side of the universe, I can feel your protection. You are my Darling light. Ever guiding me home and keeping me straight."

Her heart pounding, she smiled at him while she traced his lips. "I hate being apart from you, for even a heartbeat."

"As do I." Jullien sucked his breath in as she reached down to stroke him. "Shara—"

"Hmmm?"

He forgot his protest the instant her cool fingers swept against his hard cock. Burying his hand in her soft hair, he kissed her.

Desperate to be inside her, he carefully stood with her in his arms and set her on her desk. As he pulled away from her lips, she stared up at him from beneath her lashes. That heated look, with her swollen lips, ragged breathing, and tousled hair always set him on fire.

Jullien fumbled with her pants until she laughed.

"Having trouble, *keramon*?"

He growled in his throat. "I swear half the time you choose clothes based on how much frustration they're going to cause me later."

Laughing, she nipped at his chin as she reached down to open her pants and slide them down so that he had access to her. "Better?"

Jullien couldn't speak while she slowly undid her top. Dipping his head to take her breast into his mouth, he slid inside her body.

Ushara cried out in pleasure and wrapped her legs around his hips. She reached under his shirt and dug her nails against the flesh of his back in the most exquisite way. It sent chills over his entire body as he thrust against her.

She hooked her heels behind his back and pulled him in even deeper. "*Kimi ti, mi ixur.*"

"*Iki, tu, hæfre.*"

She sank her fangs into his neck an instant before she came in his arms.

Jullien savored every shudder of her body against his as he waited for her finish. Only when she was completely sated did he join her.

Her eyes glowing with warmth and love, she placed her well-manicured hand that held her wedding ring against the tattoo in the center of his chest, over his heart. No one before her had ever looked at him the way she did.

Without scorn or hatred.

Without judgment.

With total acceptance.

She traced the petals of the rose with her fingernail, leaving a trail of goose bumps on his chest. "I wish I could keep you inside me forever."

Cupping her breast, he smiled down at her. "You're always inside me. There's not an instant of the day when I don't carry you in my heart."

Ushara bit back a sob at his tender words. "What's bothering you? And don't say *nothing*. I know you better."

With a ragged breath, he withdrew from her and pulled his pants up to fasten them. "Guilt."

Terrified of what he might have done while away, she paused as she righted her uniform. She tried not to jump to any conclusions, but her mind was running rampant with all manner of horrors. "Over what?"

He toyed with a lock of her hair. "I fucked up, Shara. And it's getting harder to live with it."

"What did you do?" She was really struggling to keep the anger from her tone. If it involved another female, she was going to kill them both.

Grief and pain marred his brow before he answered. "You know what I did. What I deprived my daughters of . . . and you and Vas. All of you should be living in a palace, with servants to fetch for you. I saw Annalise and Drake Cruel while I was on Caron. And it pains me that I can't wrap my children up in finery, or you in jewels." He picked her hand up so that he could brush his thumb over her small wedding bands. "I still haven't been able to save up enough to buy you a decent ring."

Relieved that was all it was, she took his hand into hers and held it tight. "I don't need a bigger ring. And the girls want for nothing. Trust me. You and Trajen have spoiled them rotten. I can't imagine them having more. As for Vasili, he's never cared about things. If he did, he'd stay in school and study hard to make more money. Instead, he wants to be with you, flying at warp speed. It's all he's wanted since the day he insisted we not leave you behind on Sterador."

"I still feel like I've deprived all of you."

"Of what? *Your* childhood?"

"Yeah, that sucked. But the palace and grounds were nice. Having your ass kissed in stores and restaurants was even nicer."

She laughed at his quirky grin. Kissing his lips, she cupped his face in her hand. "*You* have deprived them of nothing. Your parents made that decision. And they're the ones who've lost in this, much more than you have. They walked away from a wonderful son with a caring heart that they chose not to see. By turning their backs on you, they'll never know the beauty of our daughters or Vas. Never see what an incredible father and husband you are. So what if we don't live in a massive, cold palace? Instead, we have my crazy family, who piles in daily and intrudes at all hours of the day and night. I'd rather laugh with my sisters and brothers, and listen to the raucous play of our children with their cousins."

"You're right. I would much rather be here with all of you. There's nothing I would take for one single memory of our family."

And still that sadness remained behind his eyes, that tugged at her heart. She knew he loved them. But she also knew that it had to hurt to be so rejected by his birth family. To stand so close to them and to see them, and not be a part of their world.

As she fastened her top, she caught him staring at the news on the monitor. It was an interview with his mother, who sat in her office, surrounded by the official Andarion royal family portraits—none of which included Jullien. His brother's picture was there, as were those of his aunt, her partner, and Jullien's sister-in-law with his niece and nephews. Even Eriadne and his evil cousins who'd done him so wrong were on the wall.

But not a single image of him.

Yeah, *that* had to burn.

Taking his hand, she leaned against his shoulder.

He looked down and gave her a gentle smile. "I know. Let it go."

"She's your mother, Jules. That's a little different."

Jullien didn't comment on that. He couldn't, because Ushara was right. Unlike his grandmother's cruelty, his mother's abandonment had always burned like a fire inside him. It'd left a hole that nothing healed.

*What is so wrong with me that neither of my parents could love me? Could even tolerate being in a room with me?*

What disgusted him most was that even at his current age, he still had a childish urge to do something to get their attention. To act out and force them to deal with him . . . Which sadly, was what had brought him to this place in his life. He'd pushed them too far.

But there was nothing he could do about it now. It was ancient history.

Forcing himself not to think about it, he shook himself mentally. "I should head home and tell Vasili he's now my cock. That should ruin his day and make me feel better."

She laughed. "I would say you're wrong, but I have a feeling he wanted to get a little independence."

"Oh, I know he did. It's why I can't wait to hear the sounds of his screaming in agony." He winked at her. "I'll pick up the girls and see you at dinner."

"Okay. Love you."

"You, too."

Ushara watched as he left with that sexy swagger that never failed to make her want to take a bite of his shapely rump. Wishing she knew some way to make him feel better, she turned up the sound and listened to her mother-in-law.

"Andaria will stand with the Caronese. We don't condone any military organization that invades our nation without invitation or provocation, and holds our citizens as prisoners without due process. It was an

Andarion who first founded The League to protect our worlds. It would be remiss of me as tadara if I didn't help to protect the innocent now."

Ushara ground her teeth and turned it off. "Protect the innocent?" she snarled.

Yeah, nice talk from the same queen who'd abandoned her son into the hands of animals to fend for himself, first as a child. And then as an adult.

No . . . worse than animals. Cairistiona allowed a kill warrant to stand on his life.

Grimacing, Ushara couldn't even bear to think on it. "You better hope I never meet you, Tadara." If she did, she'd most likely shoot her on sight.


Jullien pushed open the door to Vasili's room and allowed the twins to run in on their brother and swarm him while he was playing his game against his cousins online. At seventeen, Vasili was a far cry from the defiant little boy Jullien had saved. He now looked more like a full-grown Andarion than the child who'd won his heart.

Worse? Vas was almost eye level with him these days, and getting taller and more muscular every day. Yet even so, whenever he looked at him, Jullien still saw the shy boy he'd taught to shave. The one who'd been so timid the first time he asked a female out. The same child who used to sneak past his yaya and work with him in the hangar bay after school.

But it was a struggle sometimes to find that boy inside the adult who was trying so hard to break free from their protection, and claim his own place in an extremely dangerous universe that Jullien knew would have no mercy on him. Especially when that adult was surly and lippy, and not as mindful of his mother's more tender feelings as Jullien felt he should be.

"Hey!" Vas shouted in true annoyance as the twins jumped on him. "I'm busy here!"

"Can I help?" Mira tried to grab the controller from his hands.

"I want to play!" Viv was attempting to climb up her brother's leg.

"Mum!" Vas shouted. "Can you get your spiders to quit trying to scale up my body? I'm not a tree!" Growling, he picked Mira up and set her gently on the bed. Then he did the same with Viv.

Thinking it was a game, they laughed and scrambled down to go after him again.

"Mum!" Vas repeated as he tried to extricate himself from their cloying grasps.

"Not your matarra." Jullien entered the room fully.

Vasili immediately forgot about the game as he realized he might be in trouble for withdrawing from school. "Um . . ." He looked around nervously before he picked up Mira to hold in front of his body and use as a shield. He held her out toward Jullien. "They've grown a lot this last month, haven't they?"

Crossing his arms over his chest, Jullien ignored the question. "Want to explain to me about school?"

Vas set his giggling sister down and sighed while he turned the game off. "I didn't fit in there."

"Why didn't you call me before you withdrew?"

"I didn't think you'd take my side."

Jullien tsked at him. "This isn't about sides, Vas. Your mom and I only want what's best for you."

"I know." Vas sighed. "So did you reinstate me for classes?"

"No. You're an adult. On Andaria, we'd be planning your unification by now. And while I respect that your mother still wants you in nappies, I know we have to give you the right to decide your future, even when we don't agree with it." Jullien grabbed the bag he'd left out in the hallway and set it down next to Vas's feet. "The rest of your gear will be delivered tomorrow."

Vas gaped as he realized it was a Tavali soft battlesuit and boots. "Is this for real? You're not messing with me?"

"Not messing with you."

Grabbing a twin from the floor, Vas squeezed his sister tight and kissed her cheek. "Look, Mira!" He pulled the sleeve out that bore his Gorturnum cock badge. "I'm a Tavali-in-training!"

"Is that good?"

"It's awesome!"

"Yah!" She threw her arms out and waved them for him.

Jullien laughed as Vas set her down so that she and Viv could chew on Vas's controllers.

"So what ship am I assigned to? Who's my captain?"

*Pet Hate."* Jullien gave that a few minutes to seep in before Vas screwed his face up and groaned out loud.

"Seriously?"

Jullien arched his brow. "You really want to be hazed and see your parents jailed for ripping the spine out of another Tavali?"

Turning slightly green, Vas let go of the sleeve. "Oh, I hadn't thought about that."

"We have. Trust me. This is much easier. On us all. And if you really want the hazing, Thrāix and I can make you wash out toilets with your toothbrush. I'm more than willing to find a few noxious chores for you." He cut a meaningful gaze down to the girls.

Vas laughed. "Mmm, think I'll pass on that."

Jullien grinned at him. "Thought you might." Glad that Vas was acclimating to the idea, he herded the twins toward the door.

"Paka?"

He paused to glance back at his son. "Yeah?"

"Are you mad at me?"

"That you want to grow up and become Tavali? No. I'm hurt that you felt like you couldn't talk to us before you pulled out of school. We've never given you a reason to not trust us. And I know you're not a coward."

Vas hung his head. "You're right. I'm not a coward. I was afraid you'd talk me into staying. And then I'd keep being miserable."

"Was it really *that* bad?"

Vas sat on the floor of his room as the girls ran by in the hallway behind Jullien, screaming and laughing in play. He snorted at the sight of them. Sobering, he met Jullien's gaze. "Have you ever felt like you didn't really belong somewhere? Like you were going through the motions and doing what you were supposed to, but something inside you was dying a little every day because it wasn't where you should be, and you knew it?" He raked his hand through his hair. "You probably have no idea what I mean."

"No, *tana*, I get it. In a way you can't imagine. University was one of the few places where I felt like I belonged and was accepted. At least sometimes. While I was still isolated from the other students, who didn't know what to make of my security detail or the fact that I was tahrs, my primary professors were delighted that I had an interest in their subjects. Granted, a few were only trying to suck up, thinking that I'd endow them after graduation, but a handful of them had a real interest in helping me advance my studies. I treasured them for the fact that they spoke to me like I was normal and made me feel welcome in their classes. I'm sorry you didn't have the same experience."

"Yeah. It was so weird. While I didn't have a problem keeping up, it was like they knew I wasn't one of them. No matter what I tried, they cut me out and wouldn't include me."

"Their loss."

"Thanks for understanding."

Jullien inclined his head to him. "You know, Vas, we don't have to agree with your decisions to support them. The gods know your mother supports my stupid ideas all the time while grinding her teeth."

Vas laughed. "I have seen her do that."

"Yeah. It's what being a family is. No matter what you do, right or wrong, we will always be here for you. . . . Though, we hope you always do right. And we will always catch you when you stumble and fall."

Vas got up and hugged him. "Love you, Paka."

"You, too. Now, let me go see what the girls are into. I don't like it when they're quiet. It's usually a bad sign."

Vas nodded in agreement. "Yeah. Last time that happened, I found them flushing Mum's makeup down the toilet."

"Oh dear gods . . ."

Luckily, this time Jullien found them asleep, curled together on the floor of their room. He smiled at the sight of them, then carefully carried them to bed and tucked them in to rest. They were so precious to him. No matter what they did or how much trouble they found, he couldn't bring himself to hurt them. He'd only yelled at them once when they were about to get hurt, and when they'd burst into tears, it'd crushed him so badly that he hadn't raised his voice to them since. Never once had he thought about lifting a hand to harm them.

Which made him wonder how his own parents could have hated him so vehemently. What had been so wrong with him, so defective, that he'd never been able to make them feel this in their hearts when they looked at him? Was it because he was a hybrid? Had that kept them from seeing him as theirs?

Or was it something more?

"Are you all right?"

He turned at the sound of Ushara's voice and offered her a smile. "Just admiring how much they favor their mother. And thinking how lucky I am."

"Glad to hear it. I've been thinking about something, too."

"Why does that tone of voice make my sphincter clench?"

She laughed at him. "Premonition?"

"Yeah, I think I'm about to make that diamond for you."

Laughing even harder, she shook her head. "It's not that bad. I wanted to talk to you about adding to our family."

"We're getting that puppy Mira wanted?"

"I'm being serious, Jules."

"So was I."

Snorting at his humor, she wrapped her arms around his waist and held him. "We could get a puppy, if you want, but I was thinking of going off birth control."

The humor died in his eyes. "Shara—"

She pressed her fingers against his lips to silence his protest. "I know what you're going to say, but I want more little Juleses running loose."

"Why? They already outnumber us. Dear gods, what if we have more twins? The horror of that alone is enough to make *me* want to be neutered. And I'm not the one who'd have to go through pregnancy and labor."

She laughed again. "You're so silly. Besides, I know better. I see the way your eyes light up the instant you come home and rush after them. You love every minute of it."

He glanced over at the bed, to the scribbles on the wall where Mira and Viv had left their marks. Ushara had wanted to paint over it, but he'd wanted it preserved. The girls had been so proud of their "art" that he'd put a frame around it to keep it safe.

Tilting her head, she tugged at his whiskers. "I don't mind the pregnancy or the birthing, Jules. But I don't want to force more on you if you're not ready."

"I will defer to your wishes, *mu turu*. But be warned, I might kill your husband during your labor for his part in putting you through it again."

# CHAPTER 33

Ushara turned the news off in her office and had to force herself not to throw the remote at the monitor. She was so angry, she was shaking. Furious, she gathered her things to go home.

Thrāix opened her door without being announced and froze as he took note of her mood. "Bad day?"

She paused to glare at him. "No. Awesome. Here to make it even better?"

"Depends. Your blaster fully charged?"

"Would you like me to drain it in your direction?"

"Oooh," Thrāix said, laughing, "you are in a foul mood. So glad I'm not Jules tonight." He tilted his head as if listening to her thoughts. Which only pissed her off more. "Ah . . . I get your anger now. And you're right . . . this will gut the shit out of him when he hears it."

Ushara blinked back the tears that drowned her anger beneath a wave of pain. She gestured at the blank monitor, where Cairistiona's face had been just a few minutes ago. "How could that bitch adopt someone else when she already has a son who would give *anything* to come home and have her accept him? After all he did to protect her and keep her safe while she lay in a drugged stupor for years, leaving him to fend for himself? Letting them hurt him! She turned her back on Jules and then adopts a stranger? What the hell? It's not right!"

Thrāix sighed heavily. "Life never is, Shara. Of all creatures, you know that. So does Dagger. I don't know what his mother's thinking, or why she did what she did. Then or now. Maybe it had something to do with the newest development with the war."

That took her anger down a notch as she frowned at him. "What newest development?"

"Did you not hear about the Phrixians?"

She straightened. "No. What about them?"

"They joined the Alliance today."

Her jaw dropped at that stunner. Kyr Zemin, the League prime commander, was the eldest son of the Phrixian emperor. Had he not left the royal family to join their ranks, he would have been heir to their empire. But for reasons no one outside their family knew, Kyr had abdicated his standing to his younger brother to become an assassin decades ago. To her knowledge, the emperor had been fine with Kyr's decision. Proud, in fact, given that the Phrixians were an insanely martial race that made the Andarions look like pacifists in comparison.

The emperor had always gotten along with his son and backed Kyr in all things.

Until now.

"What happened?"

Thrāix shrugged. "Apparently, some falling out over the youngest Phrixian prince, Safir Jari. Zemin busted his League assassin's rank without process and was holding him in a League prison and torturing him. Once word reached the emperor, the Phrixians broke Jari out, denounced Zemin for it, and have now joined the Alliance against The League."

She gaped. "What about Maris Sulle?" He was another of the Phrixian princes who'd been disinherited by the emperor—much like Jullien with his mother. They'd even issued a kill warrant for Sulle.

"All is forgiven, and all warrants canceled. Whatever Zemin did to Jari was far more egregious than the sin Sulle committed that got him disinherited."

Ushara let out a low whistle. "Politics. How they reek."

"Tell me about it. They cost me everything. Even my homeworld."

She cringed at his barely audible words as she realized how insensitive she'd been with her offhand comment. While politics might irritate her, they'd left Thrāix a homeless orphan. She might hate Eriadne and the Andarions for what they'd done to her kind, but it was nothing compared to what had been done to the Trisani. "Sorry."

"It's fine."

No, it wasn't. They both knew that. No one could lose everything that he and Trajen had lost and be okay with it. She couldn't imagine how they must feel to be without a race or any kind of national identity. To have nothing left of their once-proud people.

Like Jullien. To be alone and isolated from everything and everyone they'd ever known. To have no one and nothing to rely on, except themselves and their own bitter, raw determination and resolve to not lie down and let the universe defeat them.

She couldn't imagine trying to rebuild her life the way they'd been forced to. It was why she held them in such esteem and regard. They were warriors in the truest sense of the word, and she admired them for it.

Ushara smiled as she joined him in the hallway. "So what can I do for you?"

Thrāix hesitated.

She arched her brow at his sudden awkwardness as he stepped outside so that she could seal and lock her office to leave. How unlike him. He was always so cocksure and in charge. "Is something wrong?"

"No . . . and sort of." He rubbed at the back of his neck. "I kind of need your help, Admiral."

Admiral? Oh, now she was terrified as she adjusted her briefcase. "Um, okay. What's going on?"

He let out an elongated breath, but before he could speak, his link went off with a strange, upbeat frolicky tone that was extremely out of character for the somber, handsome Trisani. Oddly enough, it sounded a lot like her sister Mary's favorite song. Blushing, he pulled it from his pocket to check it. "Can you please give me one second? It's important."

"Sure."

She watched as he stepped away, toward Zellen's empty desk, to speak in private.

"Yeah, I'm here." He glanced back at her as he listened to his caller. Long and lean, he held a peculiar air about him that reminded her of Vasili whenever he was afraid of getting into trouble for something.

Or Jullien in the early days of their relationship whenever he was cautious that he'd done something to upset her or make her angry. Strange, she'd forgotten about that since Jullien had grown so comfortable with her now that she very rarely saw this side of his personality. It was so weird to see another male exhibit it around her, especially one she wasn't related to who held the extreme powers that Thrāix commanded so effortlessly.

Ushara was even more curious now. And her curiosity tripled as a slow blush crept over his chiseled, handsome features.

"I don't know if that's a good idea." He sputtered for several seconds before he finally let out an exasperated growl. "Fine . . . Okay. Hold on." Sheepishly, he headed back to Ushara and held the link out toward her. "It's for you."

Yeah, this was even more peculiar. She took it and held it to her ear. "Admiral Samari. May I help—?"

"Oh, like I don't know who you are. Really?"

Her eyes widened at the familiar voice. "Mary?"

"Yeah, it's me. Of course it's me. Like you don't know your sister when you hear her . . . And yeah, you're confused and by now my sugar-honey is probably glowing in the dark, so tell him that you're okay with him being my nummy treat so he doesn't die of embarrassment, okay?"

Now Ushara was sputtering as badly as Thrāix had been doing a moment ago when he spoke to Mary.

Was she hearing that correctly? Or was she hallucinating? "B-b-beg your pardon?"

Mary let out an aggravated sigh before she spoke to Ushara like a parent with a child she was trying not to strangle. "Tell Thrāix that you have no problem with us being together, as in a united couple. That our parents are not going to flip out because he's not a Fyreblood, and that you'll be there tonight when we tell them that I'm pregnant and that we're planning on a unification ceremony in a few weeks."

Her jaw fell wide open and hung there.

No. It locked there. She couldn't close her mouth for anything. She couldn't think. Couldn't move. She was stunned catatonic.

All Ushara could do was stare in shock at Thrāix, whose face was now bloodred.

Had she *really* heard that?

*Pregnant?* Mary? Her flibbertigibbet baby sister?

*With Thrāix?*

*No wonder he bought the condo next door. That* was why he'd been in such a hurry to get it when Lev moved out. Suddenly, a lot of odd things made sense. Things she'd noticed, but dismissed. Like how he always volunteered to run point for Mary every time she headed out, even though he wasn't Tavali . . .

He swallowed hard. "Admiral? Are you all right?"

No. Not even a little bit. Quite honestly, she'd stripped a gasket in her mind while trying to wrap her head around this whole unfathomable scenario.

Mary was sleeping with Thrāix.

*This must be how everyone felt when they found out about me and Jullien.* She finally understood their shock. Not that she objected to Thrāix. Far from it.

He was wonderful. A truly great guy whom she adored. She'd just had no idea that he and Mary were . . .

Anything. Never mind doing *that* together while naked. The two of them were *so* different. In *every* way. She couldn't imagine the two of them having a conversation, never mind an actual relationship.

Mary was all silly and fluff. And Thrāix was anything but.

"Shara?"

She blinked at Mary's voice. "Yeah, I'm here. I . . . I . . . What do you need me to do exactly?"

"Can you take Thrāix to the house for dinner? I wanted to do it, but I'm going to be late getting in. I'll be there as soon as I can. Just keep him calm for me—he's really nervous about this. You're the only one who knows besides me and him. I wanted him to see that the family will be fine about it. He's convinced Paka's going to geld him with a knife. Smile and tell him no one's going to gut him over it. Love you!" Mary cut the transmission without warning or preamble.

Flabbergasted, Ushara handed the link back to Thrāix, who looked positively green and sick.

He gave her a wan smile.

"Well," she said, stretching the word out. "They'll be a lot more welcoming to you than they were to Jullien."

"Not very comforting. As I recall, they almost killed him . . . twice, and sold him into slavery."

"See. *You* have nothing to worry about."

Sighing, he slid the link into his pocket and turned even greener. "How bad will it be? Really?"

"Depends. Are you willing to convert?"

"Already started." He pulled his sleeve back to show that he was wearing an Initiate's bracelet, which was given to those who had no background in any Andarion religion. Because Jullien had been raised in another branch of their basic faith, his conversion had been a little different and a lot quicker, as Jullien had intimate knowledge of their rituals, services, holidays, and gods.

Thrāix, on the other hand, would have to learn everything from the beginning. "Since I know how important temple and religion are to Mary and your family, I volunteered as soon as Mary told me she was expecting, and she agreed to marry me." He shrugged his sleeve down. "I lost faith in my gods a long time ago. Maybe yours will be kinder to me."

"Oh." She waved her hand and blew out air dismissively. "See, you've got nothing to worry about," she repeated. "That would be their biggest concern about your marriage, and you're already taking care of it. No, they won't be jumping through hoops. But it's Mary. We know she's never done anything the traditional way."

She led him from her office out toward the street. "Do you love her?"

"I'm Trisani," he said simply as he held the door for her.

She hesitated at his answer. "Not sure what that means."

He followed after her. "We don't have casual sex, Ushara. Ever. As much as we hear internal thoughts just standing next to someone, you don't want to know how much more we know about them when we're that intimately connected to them. There's a reason why Trajen and I are solitary creatures. And we damn sure don't share domiciles with someone voluntarily. That takes a special level of commitment and torture you can only appreciate if you're one of us." He quirked a charming grin. "Especially when you're involved with someone as spirited and open as Mary. Your sister holds nothing back, and can be quite overwhelming."

Ushara laughed at his tactful description. Mary was definitely an acquired taste. "Very true. So how long have you two been seeing each other?"

"Our son's due about two months after yours."

She stumbled. Thrāix caught her and set her back on her feet. "We just found out it was a boy two days ago."

"I know."

And that was the eerie part about being with a Trisani. Ushara was barely showing *her* pregnancy, and they were only now medically able to determine the gender of her baby, yet Thrāix already knew the gender of his child and most likely the exact day their son would be born.

Which made her wonder something. "Did you know the first time you met Mary that you'd be involved with her?"

"It doesn't quite work that way."

"What do you mean?"

"We have a degree of control over our destinies. So while I knew it was possible, I tried to behave."

"Meaning?"

"Your sister is a hard female to deny, especially when she sets her mind to something. She's the real reason I stayed here instead of returning to my base when war broke out. I wanted to make sure I was close by should she need me. And I didn't want her flying to my base to track me down." There was no missing the way his voice softened when he spoke of Mary. Or the way his eyes sparked.

He did love her.

Grateful that Mary had finally found someone who could appreciate her peculiar charms, Ushara opened the door to her condo. The twins rushed her and Thrāix with an excited scream that all but pierced her eardrums.

Jullien laughed at them. "So much for trying to get their shoes on them."

Thrāix swung Mira up over his shoulder and held her upside down while she laughed and kicked. "I think we can get some shoes on this one. If we hurry."

Ushara caught his gaze behind Jullien's back. *Does he know?* she mouthed.

"Do I know what?" Jullien asked without looking at her.

Ushara gaped at his hidden talents. "How do you do that?"

"Lived in a palace with enemies plotting against me. I can literally see through walls." He scowled at her. "What are you two up to?"

Thrāix tickled Mira before he used his powers to put her shoes on her feet. "He only knows because he walked in on us once."

Jullien grimaced. "Oh, crap. She found out about her sister?"

Ushara gasped as she glared her husband. "You knew and never told me?"

"Mary swore me to secrecy."

Gasping again, she popped him on the bottom.

Mira sucked her breath in sharply as she looked at her sister. "Mama spanked Paka!"

"Yes, I did. He kept a big secret from me."

Jullien rubbed at his posterior. "What's the big deal?"

"The big deal is that my sister is now pregnant."

Freezing, Jullien arched a brow at Thrāix. "Hell of a kiss, huh?"

Thrāix rolled his eyes. "Yes, my powers are *that* extreme. I can impregnate with my lips alone. Fear me."

Mira tugged at her father's sleeve. "What's *impregnate* mean, Paka?"

He brushed her hair back from her face. "Lyra Mary is having a baby like Mama."

Viv clapped her hands together. "We're having two babies?"

"Kind of," Ushara explained. "Mary and I will have our boys close together. They'll almost be twins like you and Mira."

Mira clapped her hands together. "So Basha Thrāix will be our real basha?"

Jullien nodded. "Yes."

Both twins ran and hugged him.

"Till your graspa turns him into your lyra."

Ushara snorted at Jullien's sarcasm, which confused them. "Stop!"

"I don't know," Thrāix said as he hugged the girls. "He's probably not too far off the mark."

After they herded the girls out the door to head to her parents', Ushara saw that Jullien had been watching the news as he turned the monitor off and locked the condo. . . . Which meant he'd most likely seen the report about his mother and her newest additions to the Andarion royal family.

Sobering, she allowed Thrāix to walk ahead with the girls, toward her parents' house. "You okay?"

He shrugged his jacket on. "Fine."

"Jules . . ."

He settled it on sideways as he always did, but she fixed it for him while they walked. "Really, Shara. I'm good. Yes, it hurt at first when I heard it. But my cousins and I were the main reason Fain Hauk was Outcast from his lineage. So I'm good with my mother taking him in. It feels right. I'm actually glad she did it. He deserves to have a family again."

"Okay. If you're sure?"

"Really. I swear." He tucked his scarf around the scars on his neck and put his red glasses on.

Deciding to believe him, she had just set it from her mind when they entered her parents' house and her link buzzed. It was the base comptroller.

Weird. They almost never called her.

She answered it while Jullien and Thrāix took the girls to Nadya and her sister's to play and say hi to Oxana.

At first, she didn't understand what they were telling her. It was hard to hear over the boisterousness of her family. "What? Can you repeat that?"

When she did, Ushara felt the room tilt.

"I said, Admiral, that a rogue group hit the convoy that was headed in. Right now, we're not showing any survivors. What do you want us to do?"

Ushara dropped the link as her stomach pitched hard and she stumbled against the wall.

Jullien turned toward her at the same time Thrāix went pale. No doubt from having heard her thoughts.

Numb, she swallowed before she told her parents and family what they'd just told her. "Mary and Ryna's convoy was hit. . . ."

# CHAPTER 34

Jullien and Ushara flew out on the *Pet Hate,* while Thrāix headed up the *Vengeance* with Zellen and Unira on board. Trajen and Davel ran point behind them on their own ships. Because they were emotionally overwrought and worthless in that condition, the rest of the Altaans had been left behind, including Vasili.

"How you doing over there, Thrāix?" Jullien asked as they went to investigate what had happened to the convoy.

"I'm not burying another wife and child." His tone was deadpan.

"Wife? What?" Davel's voice broke through the static. "Child? Did I hear that right? Who did Thrāix marry?"

"We'll talk about that later," Trajen said, cutting Davel off mid-tantrum.

As they neared Mary's last known coordinates, Jullien took Ushara's hand in his. What he saw made him sick to his stomach for her as his own grief and anger choked him. He loved Mary and Ryna, too. Since the early days of their marriage, her sisters had been welcoming and warm to him, especially Mary.

*Damn it!*

*How could this have happened?*

There was twisted wreckage all over this sector. Tears glistened in Ushara's eyes as she saw the remnants of her sisters' ships and the remains of a brutal, nasty fight. Her family had fought hard.

It just hadn't been enough.

Gutted, Jullien struggled to keep his emotions in check for Ushara. And he knew she was doing the same. How she managed to hold it together, he had no idea. This had to be tearing her apart. Yet she maintained her composure like a champ.

No, she held herself like the military commander she was.

Never had he respected her more. Though, to be honest, he wouldn't have faulted her for losing it under these circumstances.

Clearing his throat, he went over the readings, wanting the lifeblood of whoever was responsible.

"This wasn't a League hit." The League didn't leave a charred mess like this. They were clinical and precise. Had they gone after the convoy, they'd have left a team of sweepers who'd have removed all the debris to keep anyone else from running into it—or from seeing this as a warning that they were patrolling this sector. Plus, they'd have teams still in the vicinity, waiting for accomplices to show so they could arrest them.

Which Jullien and the others had been prepared to fight and evade.

But there were no League ships here. Not patrols or scouts.

Ushara glared at the damage that had been wrought. "This looks like Mavericks. They're the only ones I know who would leave behind this kind of destruction as a sign of pride that they were here. But I've never known them to hit us before."

Neither had Jullien. Because the Mavericks were another pirate group, like The Tavali, they had an understanding that they'd leave each other's ships and crews alone. Otherwise, it invited a nasty retaliation that could quickly escalate to open warfare.

It just wasn't done. It'd never been done in the history of their worlds. The Mavericks might unite with The Tavali to prey on The League or other governments. But they *never* went after each other.

Jullien opened the channel. "Are you guys picking up anything?"

"No." Trajen's voice was cold. Empty.

When Thrāix didn't answer, Jullien scowled at Ushara. "Sparda? You there?"

"I want blood, Andarion. No one's getting out of this alive." Thrāix's ship went off their scanners as he shot out of their range.

"Ah shit," Jullien breathed. "Tray, can you trace him?"

"No. You?"

"No, but I got a bad feeling I know where he's going. Follow me." Jullien used his powers to fly into the last sector he wanted to venture.

Ushara turned to stare at him as she saw their new heading. "Solaras? Why are we going there?"

"I guess I'm feeling suicidal," he answered sarcastically.

The only places worse for him were the Arcadian and Tryga Systems—the two ruled by his parents, where he was exiled. What made Solaras more dangerous for him was the small fact that it was controlled by The Sentella and Porturnum.

More precisely, it was where Nyran and Eriadne were currently shacked up, along with the majority of those who wanted Jullien most dead. If he had an enemy who lived to gut him, they seemed drawn to this particular sector.

So naturally, it was where Thrāix decided to have his nervous breakdown.

*Effing figures. So much for my pardon.*

His stomach knotted with dread and grief, Jullien led them to Barataria—the heart of Maverick-controlled territory.

While the Porturnum ruled a portion of the sector, the Mavericks dominated the majority of it. For that matter, the entire system was known for its spirited lawlessness. As well as the fact that no matter how hard The League tried, they couldn't quite bring it under heel. There was just something about the beings who called this area home, that they wouldn't be tamed. No matter how heavily patrolled or how many centuries went by, the Solaras System remained one of the raunchiest and deadliest in the Nine Worlds.

And the Mavericks were some of the worst of the worst. While The Tavali had a tight Code of conduct they swore to and a set of rigid laws that oversaw them, the Mavericks went by a more arbitrary cluster of nebulous guidelines they sometimes followed. Their basic law was, *Take whatever isn't nailed down, and if you aren't strong enough to keep it, then you don't deserve to have it.*

Eriadne would have made a perfect Maverick queen.

For that matter, some claimed that Cyprian and Wynne Proux, the Maverick leaders, were actually part Andarion. Since no one who ever met them had lived long enough to report back to authorities, or anyone else, anything about either of them, that was sheer speculation.

During the early days of his exile, Jullien had once ventured into their so-called *pravins* or territory while seeking refuge from his grandmother's wrath. He'd even made it into their main headquarters.

It hadn't gone well.

*Gah, I hope they don't have a long memory.*

Of course, he'd changed a lot physically since then. Hopefully, no one would recall the event.

And speaking of . . .

By the time they arrived in that old headquarters on the megastation known as Barataria, Thrāix had already landed hot and made a stellar announcement of his Trisani powers. Half the main Maverick landing bay had gone up in flames. Crews were still trying to put it out.

But that wasn't the most concerning part. What kept Jullien immobile in his ship was the sight of Thrāix and what had to be about half the members of the Maverick forces in a heated standoff. Neither side could move without detonating the rest of the station.

Jullien sat in the captain's chair, eyeing Thrāix with a mixture of awe, amusement, and horror. "Well," he drawled slowly to Ushara. "Could be worse."

She arched a brow. "How do you figure?"

"We could have Chayden or Jory in the mix. Or better yet, Caillen Dagan."

"Sure . . . let's be optimistic. Any idea how to fix this?"

"Not really. But let me try something catastrophically stupid."

Crossing her arms over her chest, she didn't appear the least bit pleased with him. "*Catastrophically?* Oh, I like that word coming out of the mouth of my babies' daddy. Any final words you wish me to convey to your children?"

"That I hope they inherit their mother's intelligence."

Laughing, she sighed heavily. "Okay, then."

When Jullien stood to leave the flight deck after telling the others over the link to hold their positions, Ushara moved to block his way. The concern in her pale eyes tightened his stomach.

"Please be careful. Remember, if anything happens to you, Davel will be the most prevalent male role model for your son."

He screwed his face up. "That hits below the belt." Unbuckling his holster, he kissed her gently and laid it in her hands. "Anything goes wrong, you blast out of here. Don't worry about me."

"Nothing better go wrong, Jules. 'Cause I'm not leaving here without you. I will follow you straight down to Tophet and back. No compromises on your safety. I will have the cannons trained on them. One word, and I will open fire."

With a deep growl at her for her stubbornness, and grateful to the gods for her, he lowered the ramp and headed from the ship, into the fray.

As soon as he came down the ramp, half the blasters and rifles took aim at his head.

Oh yeah, *that* was not comforting.

*Bet that guy who was so looking forward to coming back as a prince in his next life and got reincarnated as me is feeling seriously gipped right about now.*

Jullien held his hands up and out. "Hey now, I left my blasters on board my ship. Let's not get hostile, folks. No one sneeze or make any sudden moves, okay? I don't want to lose a body part I might need later."

"Declare yourself!"

"Uncommonly stupid for being here unarmed. Ridiculously loyal, though, to my friend you have pinned down. So . . . what say we talk this out for a minute, shall we?"

Someone backed their hammer.

"No, you don't want to do that." Jullien kept his tone calm and low. "The minute you open fire, we're all taking a free ride to Tophet. While my buddy and I are pretty sure we'll be partying with our gods tonight, are all of you ready for that final journey? I know some of you have got to be atheists, right? Y'all don't want it *all* to end."

Thrāix glared at him. "Stay out of this. I want the ones who attacked the *Fire Kiss*. I'm not leaving without them. The rest of you can walk away. Otherwise, we can all go to hell together."

"That's great for you, brother, but I got things I want to live for." Jullien glanced around at the others, scanning them for the one who seemed to be in charge.

Like The Tavali, The Mavericks were heavily painted for war and wearing body armor. Most had on blast helmets that kept their faces shielded.

Jullien moved slowly through them, sizing them up. Since he was unarmed and walking in front of their group, they didn't stop him. "What about the rest of you? Want to give my buddy what he wants? I know there's no real code between Mavericks for this kind of thing. You can kill us both, but it won't stop more Tavali coming for vengeance. You took two daughters of the Altaans tonight. You might as well have fucked over Tavali Snitch herself. They won't take this lightly."

That seemed to unsettle them.

A nervous ripple went through their ranks. But it didn't have the desired result. They weren't turning on each other. Nor was he catching a guilty vibe from anyone.

Suddenly, Jullien paused in front of a leaner Maverick. Yeah, this was what he was looking for. Even though she was obviously pregnant, she stood a little more cocksure. Clutched her rifle with confidence, and at the same time she seemed to have her attention on other things, too.

The others gave her more space. A respectful distance.

She was their leader. He knew it. That "in charge" aura bled from her pores.

Quicker than anyone could react, he used his telekinesis to snatch her rifle and angled it at her head. "This is war. And we can settle it or go nuclear. Your choice."

She gasped as the others scrambled to protect her. But as expected, they didn't dare shoot him and risk him squeezing the trigger out of reflex and killing her.

"Hold positions!" That was a fierce, deeply concerned male voice.

Jullien narrowed his gaze on the female in front of him. "Wynne Proux, I presume?"

She didn't respond.

He dug the tip of the rifle into the bottom of her shiny black blast helmet. "You can remove your helmet or I'll remove it for you."

With a fierce curse, she pulled the helmet off, exposing a wealth of coarse, wavy black hair, pale eyes, and caramel skin that said she was indeed Andarion. Young and beautiful. Curling her full red lips, she glared at him. "You bastard! How did you know?"

Jullien quirked a smile at her. "There's no way to miss a female in charge. You stood out in the crowd."

"And you're Andarion. You know what my husband will do to you for this."

"I'm stralen. You killed the beloved little sister of my pregnant wife. You're lucky you're still breathing."

That instantly took the fire out of her eyes. "We didn't do it."

"Liar!" Thrāix stepped toward them, but Jullien held his hand up to stop him.

"She's not lying, Thrāix. Calm down and use your powers." Jullien's had already detected it.

Something else was going on here. It was off. He just wasn't sure what it was.

Lowering the rifle, he tilted his head as he tried to figure it out. "What exactly happened?"

Wynne lifted her chin as she raked a sneer over him and Thrāix. "Before or after you attacked *us*?"

"*We* haven't attacked you."

She curled her lip at his arm patch. "Gorturnum Tavali? You've been attacking us for weeks now. Without letup."

"No. We haven't. As their field admiral, I'm giving you my word on that. None of our people have been near your *pravins*."

A much larger Maverick moved through the group. This would no doubt be her husband. A few inches shorter than Jullien, he paused by his side and removed his helmet. "How do we know we can trust what you say?"

Unlike his wife, the man wasn't Andarion at all. He was some human race. With black hair and brown eyes. Muscular and even in height with his wife, he seemed familiar, but Jullien couldn't place him. His long hair was laced with feathers and he had a black stripe painted horizontally across his face, beneath his eyes and over the bridge of his nose.

Jullien shrugged. "You don't know. But I give you my word."

"Word of a Tavali." Cyprian Proux spat on the ground at Jullien's feet.

He forced himself not to react to that. "I could be insulting and insulted, if I wanted. Or we can act like adults and put forth a bit of faith. If we had been attacking you in the past, why would we have only brought four ships here? Don't you think I'd have unleashed a tidal wave of hell against you for what you've done today? Think about it. You're in the trifecta of getting screwed by Tavali. The Ports are behind you with a massive station that is less than two hours away. My best friends are Seps, who we could rally to be here in no time. And we could call out to the Wasturnums, many of whom routinely travel this sector. And we would have brought fleets in to retaliate. Yet we didn't. We came alone to investigate so as not to cause a war."

"He has a point, Cy."

"Yeah, and it's not just the one on the top of my head."

Cyprian narrowed his eyes on Thrāix, then Jullien. "I know it's your Tavali that's been hitting us."

"Then give us information, and I promise you their heads. If it's Tavali, *I* will stop them myself and deliver them to you. Personally. With my initials branded on their ass cheeks."

Cyprian cocked his head to study Jullien's features. "Do I know you?"

Jullien cringed as he tried not to remember the disaster that was his last visit to this base. "Nah. I just have one of those faces."

He didn't quite buy that, but luckily he let the matter drop. His gaze went back to Thrāix. "We didn't attack your woman. Look around. We were hit hard with a blind strike a week ago. We don't have a battleship capable of assault right now. It's the only reason the four of you got in here today. A week ago, we'd have owned your asses."

As he explained that and total recognition as to who and what Cyprian really was dawned on him, a *really* crappy feeling went through Jullien.

*Shit, this is bad, bad, bad. . . .*

He tapped his earlink. "Trajen? Davel? Start your engines and get ready to launch. Open your ramps and take on as many of the Mavericks as you can hold."

Jullien looked at Thrāix. "This is a fucking setup and we just ran right into it."

Wynne and Cyprian scowled at him.

Cursing, he met Cyprian's gaze. "You're Abenbi's son, aren't you?"

"How'd you know that?"

"*Titana ræl.*" Jullien stepped back. "Nyran set this up to get the Probekeins to wipe us out. We've got to move now!"

Alarms began screeching.

Cyprian cursed. "Sound the evacuations!"

"Come with me. You and your wife. Do you have any other kids?"

"No, this is our first."

Jullien turned to Thrāix. "Do you trust me?"

He nodded.

"Then let's get out of here, and we'll get to the bottom of this. For now, grab as many of them as you can."

Thrāix inclined his head to him, then rushed to his ship. Jullien led Wynne and Cyprian onto his ship, where Ushara waited with an arch stare, but didn't say anything other than a quick greeting as she fired the engines and did a prelaunch.

They boarded more of Cyprian's people as fast as they could. But not before they were hailed by the crew of those approaching.

Using his powers, Jullien masked their frequency so that it appeared to be the station answering the incoming call. He inclined his head to Cyprian.

He answered it. "This is Barataria. Go."

"Barataria, this is Dagger Ixur, acting field admiral of the Gortunum Nation. I'm here to demand your surrender to our authority. Failure to do so will result in your utter destruction."

"On whose authority?"

"Trajen Thaumarturgus."

Jullien turned in his chair to stare at Cyprian. "In my defense, I'm not the minsid *acting* anything. I *am* the field admiral."

Ushara snorted. "Actually, you took a rank reduction, if you recall. You're technically not a field admiral at all, at the moment. You're just a commander, *keramon*."

"The vice admiral would be correct," Trajen said over the line. "And as the HAP of the Gorturnum Nation, I would like to know who the fuck this is posing as my FA, because I know the voice of my Dagger, and you, asshole, are not my active right hand. If you were, you'd know Ixur isn't his last name, it's his call sign, and that his mother is on board my ship with me. Now, who the hell are you?"

They answered with a volley of fire.

"Ah now, that's just rude," Trajen said. "Tavali? Let's teach these bitches some manners."

Thrāix banked left and went after them.

Jullien hesitated. "Hey, boss man? I'm toting two pieces of very precious cargo on board. Permission to pull back a bit?"

"Granted. Stay low."

"*Pakti.*"

Ushara gave him a droll stare. One that was duplicated by Wynne.

Jullien was completely unabashed. "Don't be hating on me, *mu tarir*. And need I remind you, Shara, both parents for our children are currently on board this ship. We go down, think about who'll be left raising our girls. Do you really want *that*?"

He had a most valid point. "You need to slow way down, precious. No need to take any unnecessary risks. *At all*."

"Yeah. I just knew that would reorient your way of thinking."

Cyprian moved to stand behind Jullien. "Thank you, Tavalian. I owe you, and I won't forget that you saved my wife and daughter."

"No problem. When's the baby due?"

"End of Edrinius. Yours?"

"First week of Samonius."

"Just a few weeks apart, then."

Jullien nodded. "As was Thrāix's. His son was due at the end of the year."

Cyprian winced in sympathy. "I swear on the life of my unborn daughter that we had nothing to do with that strike that took his woman." He looked at Ushara. "I know you think that we have no code, but we do value our children and those of others. We don't prey on innocents."

"I believe you." Ushara turned her attention back to the monitors. "Jules?"

"I see it." He banked to the left as a group of fighters came after them. "Strap down, everyone. We have incoming."

Cyprian headed for the guns, but Ushara stopped him. "Jullien has it. Believe me. You'll only interfere."

He moved to sit by his wife.

Jullien locked to his ship and let his mind sync with her perfectly. He heard both the silence of space and the roar of her engines.

Most of all, he heard the heartbeat of his wife and child. And he did his damnedest not to let that distract him.

This was when the Trisani part was annoying as hell. He'd made peace with most of what had been done to him. With the process that had allowed him to merge with his ship and opened his mind to the much larger universe and to the minds and bodies of others. And with the prospect of death. There had been a time when he courted Eternal Night as his mistress and closest companion.

Had desired her, point of fact.

Until Ushara came into his life.

Now that he shared a higher connection to his wife, she was a live wire in his mind that sucked when he needed to focus. It was like having an exposed nerve ending strung across an elephant farm . . . near their watering hole at bath time.

More ships dropped in on them. Not just fighters. Cruisers and attack squads.

"What the hell?" Jullien skidded to the side of his control panel and twisted as he watched Thrāix going in hard for a group of them. "Hey, *Coracinus Anima*? What you doing? There's no need in you going *Psycho Bunny* on us. Stay with me."

Thrāix didn't answer.

Jullien cursed silently as he saw more ships closing in and he real-

ized what Thrāix intended. "Buddy, listen to me. I know you're hurting, and I know that hunger in you to die and to take them with you.
I've been there. We all have. But you're my brother, Thrāix, and family's
something I don't have a lot of. Don't make me watch you die. You hear
me? We will get through this. And we will find the exact ones who hurt
Mary and make them pay for it in the worst way imaginable. Together.
C'mon. Don't do this. I need you in this fight. And remember, you're
not on that ship alone."

Thrāix let out a guttural cry that came from deep inside his soul.
Splintering and soul-wrenching, he rolled away and fell in behind Trajen.

Ushara bit back her tears as she watched Jullien calmly handle himself and face their attackers during the worst circumstances, all the while
dealing with Thrāix and keeping him under control. His ability to handle
and push people never failed to impress her.

Of course, he normally pushed them over the edge and past the point
of homicide. But when he chose to be diplomatic and caring . . .

There were few better at it. Even while facing death. He always kept
his wits intact and emotions under an iron restraint that amazed her. It
was why he was the only one she trusted to fly and train Vasili for his
citizenship.

Jullien was an exceptional commander. And it was a shame his parents had failed to see what an incredible leader he would have made. That
they never gave him a chance to take his place in history. For all of Nykyrian's abilities, Jullien would have been a valuable asset to his brother
and his races. It was a shame his parents had deprived the brothers and
their empires of Jullien's extraodianary abilities.

It broke her heart for him. But it made her glad that he was part of
their Nation. Most of all, she was grateful that five years ago, Trajen had
seen in Jullien the potential no one else had. It said a lot for her boss.

Five years . . .

In some ways, it seemed like yesterday—and in others, a blip. So
much had changed.

If they weren't in battle, she'd hug her sexy beast. Actually, she'd
like to do a little bit more than that. A slow smile curved her lips as a
very naughty thought went through her head while she watched him maneuvering.

The one thing about carrying a son over being pregnant with her
daughters . . .

She had an elevated libido.

"Shara?"

"Yes?"

Jullien glanced at her, over his shoulder. "You've really got to stop thinking about what you're thinking right now. 'Cause you're really distracting me at a time when I need to be focused on what I'm doing."

Heat exploded over her face, especially when the others turned to look at her. "Sorry."

Cyprian arched a curious brow.

Ushara quickly looked away.

But they remained quiet while Jullien fought off their attackers. When the fighting picked up, Ushara moved to take over communications for him.

She'd done it so seamlessly that Jullien hadn't realized it until the fighting was over and he collided with her. Frowning, he cupped her chin in his palm.

*You are such a part of me.* He sent the thought to her.

She blushed before she kissed him.

As soon as it was safe, they returned to base to regroup. Cyprian, Wynne, Trajen, and Jullien went to the conference room while Ushara led Thrāix and Davel to her parents. Unira and Zellen took over the temporary relief aid for the rest of the Mavericks, with the help of Sheila and several other Tavali.

Trajen shook his head as soon as they were secure. "So, someone is posing as us to set us against each other. . . ."

Cyprian crossed his arms over his chest. "Had I not been with you, Tavalian, I wouldn't have believed it."

"Do you think it's The League?" Wynne asked. "They've been after us for a while now."

Jullien sighed as he considered that. He met Cyprian's gaze. "Your father doesn't have a lot of friends there, that's for sure. However, I don't think The League would risk alienating an ally right now. Especially not one as powerful as the Probekeins, given that the Gourans are part of the Alliance. It'd be political suicide. Like it or not, the Probes are the Arhana System. You lose them, you lose Paradise City, Starken, and too many other resources The League needs right now for their team. If anything, I'd think Kyr would be kissing your asses to keep your father deliriously happy, and firmly attached to his hip."

Cyprian sighed. "Then who?"

"I have my suspicions, but I want confirmation before I say. Can you give me time to investigate it?"

He nodded. "Right now, I just want to see to what remains of my people."

His eyes sympathetic, Trajen stood. "I've got transports headed in that'll take you to your father's territory, or wherever you want to go. As well as volunteers to protect you until you're back on your feet."

"I won't forget this. While we've never really been allies before, that changes after this." Cyprian held his hand out to Trajen. "You ever need us, say the word. We're there. So long as I have shelter and food, you have shelter and food." For a Maverick, that was the highest testament of friendship.

"Thank you." Trajen shook his hand.

Cyprian turned to Jullien. "And you . . . you saved us." His gaze went to his wife. "From this day forward, you are family. You ever get tired of your Canting, call me. You'd make a fine Maverick."

"Hey now," Trajen groused. "Poaching one of my best while I'm standing here? Really?"

"Would you rather I poach him behind your back?"

"Rather you not poach him at all."

Jullien laughed. "No worries. The new wears off me real quick. Which is why I have to stay with Tray. He knows what an asshole I am."

Cyprian snorted as Trajen opened the door and had Ushara's receptionist escort them back to the bay, where the rest of their people were awaiting transports.

When Jullien started to leave, Trajen stopped him and closed the door. "Do you really think it's Nyran?"

"Worse. I think it's Braxen Venik."

"Explain."

"Something Nyran and Varan said when all this started." Jullien turned on the wall monitor and pulled up the star chart for Venik's territory. The Ports were based in the same system as the Andarions. "I'm thinking Venik and my grandmother are working together to overthrow my mother and brother, and to come after *you*."

"Jules . . ."

"Yeah, I know. I'm accusing a HAP of treason. It's why I didn't say anything. I need evidence."

"Yes, you do. *Hard* evidence, or it's your ass. And there won't be anything I can do to save it."

"Trust me, I know. But think about it. Who else would impersonate you and me? Why bother? And to what end?" Jullien walked to the maps. "Unless they broke us *and* the Mavericks." He marked it on the monitor. "Then they'd control the largest shipping routes in all the Nine Worlds. Everyone would cow to them. They'd be invincible. Forget Justicale Cruel. They'd be *the* shit."

Trajen narrowed his eyes on Jullien's notes. "They don't know I'm Trisani."

"No. Nor do they know about Thrāix."

"And they think you're dead."

Jullien nodded slowly. "Yeah, but they have some doubts."

"Because you won't keep your damn fool head down."

Crossing his arms over his chest, he screwed his face up. "I'm a little stubborn. But anyway, I think it's why Nyran's been so bold. If his father's leading this . . ."

"Makes sense." Trajen looked back at the monitor. "Too much, actually. Ven's always been in it for the profit, and for himself."

"Yeah. He's an entitled bastard."

"You know why, don't you?"

Jullien shook his head.

"C'mon, Jules. You're more intuitive than that. You know how assholes think. Especially entitled ones. What motivates them. Why do you think he's got the issues he has?"

Scowling, he ran over in his mind what little he knew about the pirate bastard. "He's a hybrid. That screws with you, in and of itself."

"And . . ."

Jullien felt really stupid as he drew a total blank. "I got nothing."

"Here, let me make this easy on you. His father was Serus of the Warring Blood Clan Venik."

Gaping, Jullien stared at Trajen as he finally saw the point with crystal clarity. "You're shitting me."

Trajen shook his head.

Yeah, that was a name he knew well. Serus had been disowned by his mother when he broke pledge with his Andarion fiancée and married a human. But that wasn't the most shocking part. The shocking part was why Jullien knew their names.

Serus had been a distant cousin of his.

More to the point, Serus's mother had been born Alya of the Warring Blood Clan of *Hauk*.

Which made Braxen Venik the second cousin of Fain Hauk. And put him firmly in the ranks of the single most prestigious military family on all of Andaria, and gave him royal blood.

*Shkyte ykel.*

"By that lovely expression on your face, I'm going to assume you got the relationship bingo." Trajen leaned down until he was eye level with him. "And now I'll screw you one better. His wife, Malys, is the cousin of Chayden Aniwaya's mother."

"What?"

"Yeah. Chayden's mother is the Qill queen, Sarra Denarii. Malys's mother is her aunt, Shea Denarii. That's why Brax has entitlement issues and believes himself royalty."

Because he technically was.

"*Titana ræl.*"

Trajen nodded. "Yeah. You put four egomaniacs with serious entitlement issues together, and what do you get?"

"Fun times for the rest of us."

Trajen nodded slowly. "But it's all speculation."

Jullien ground his teeth as his emotions churned and his anger rose. "You know we're not going to be able to stay out of this war."

His stare turned brittle. "Your son is seventeen. The day I declare it, he'll be among the first to strap a blaster to his hips and sign on. Think long and hard before you drag me to that fence. Unlike you, I've been on a front line. Ask Bastien or Thrāix about the nightmares you carry for the rest of your life. You think you had fun in prison as a prince? It's a birthday party compared to time spent as a POW when your parents are the commanders for the enemy, and they think you have information they can leverage. Or they can use you to get to them. And you don't want to know what happens when your government falls to someone not related to you."

"I do know. And I know what it's like to take a life when you're too young to cope with the guilt of it. And I also know what they'll do to us if we don't stop them."

Closing his eyes, Trajen ground his teeth. "I hate war, Jules. Everything to do with it."

SHERRILYN KENYON

"And it takes two to make peace. When one side is determined for war, you have no choice but to fight back. If we don't fight now, they'll take Vasili anyway. I'd rather he have a chance for survival, than die on his knees, begging." Jullien clapped him on his back as tears and grief choked him. "Now if you'll excuse me, I have to go help my wife and her family bury their daughters."

Trajen flinched. "They're going to blame you for this."

"I know that, too. But I'm not a coward. And maybe it is my fault. Petran said it in the beginning, and it's true—the history of my family is written in blood. Perhaps that's the real Anatole curse. Rather than carry a genetic defect, ours is that our bodies aren't diseased so much as our souls."

Trajen watched as Jullien left him alone in the room with memories and premonitions he wished he could purge from his brain. He didn't know which ones were worse.

Things that had already happened he couldn't change.

Or the ones to come he couldn't stop.

# CHAPTER 35

Jullien stood beside Ushara as she laid the small farewell bouquets in her sisters' memorial capsules. Unlike the funerals he'd grown up with, the Demurrists believed in celebrating the lives of the departed—in remembering only the good about them. They saw death as a new beginning where there was no pain or worries—where the departed soul was able to be reborn with a clean slate into a better life.

It was only sad for those who were left behind, who had to live on without them.

Honestly, he felt like shit.

This was all because of Eriadne and Nyran. But for him and his family, Mary and Ryna would still be here, laughing and dancing among their sisters and brothers.

"Don't." Trajen put his hand on Jullien's shoulder as Ushara went to hug her mother.

"What?"

"Blame yourself for this."

Jullien looked at Thrāix, who sat across from them, holding a sleeping Mira. "How can I not?"

"If you weren't here, Jules, Vasili wouldn't be either. Neither would those twin girls or Thrāix. And you don't want to know what would have happened to your eldest son. But I think you have a good idea what the slavers would have used him for."

He winced involuntarily. "Why does it have to be a trade-off?"

"I don't know, but you saved a lot of lives two days ago. Cyprian sent a message saying that they're temporarily settled with his father. They're still doing their own inquest, and they're sending over their second-in-command in a few days to help us with our investigation. He also wanted me to tell you that he and Wynne are planning on naming their daughter Julia Thrāixia in honor of you and Thrāix, for saving them."

"That's not creepy at all."

Viv came running up to him to tug at his sleeve. "Paka," she whispered. "Vivie gots to go bathroom!"

Smiling at her, he picked her up. "Okay, *nýba.*" He inclined his head to Trajen. "Small bladders wait for no one."

As quickly and quietly as he could, Jullien took her out the side door to the temple restrooms so that she could attend her needs.

Once she was finished, he helped her wash her hands in the sink.

In her temple clothes, Viv stood on the edge of the steel counter and stared at their reflection in the mirror. She moved her face back and forth.

Jullien assumed she was looking at her face paint and comparing it to his, especially since she pulled his glasses off to see his features more clearly.

Until she spoke. "We look like you, Paka, don't we?"

"But you're much prettier."

She frowned. "Why are our eyes green? Everybody else's are white. But yours. Yours are red. Why is that?"

Using his powers, he returned his to their non-stralen color. "Mine were the color of yours until I met your matarra."

She gasped as she looked from the mirror to his face. Turning, Viv touched his cheek to examine his eyes more closely. "Your eyes change color, Paka?"

"It's called stralen. Some Andarion males can do it."

"Why?"

"It means that we really love our families. That we will die to protect them."

Tears welled in her eyes before she burst into tears. "We don't want you to die like Lyra Mary and Lyra Ryna, Paka!"

"Shh, *nýba.*" He pulled her into his arms and held her. "Don't get upset. I'm not going anywhere. I'm right here. I'll be here for a long, long time."

"Okay." She sniffed and wiped her nose with the back of her chubby hand. Then she pouted again and turned to look in the mirror. "So why we gots dark hair when nobody else does?"

"Mine's really dark, too. I make it blond to blend in. But when I don't bleach it out, it looks just like yours."

She put her arms around his neck and pressed her cheek to his so that she could stare at their combined reflection in the mirror. "So Vivie and Mirie look just like their paka?"

"Yes. But prettier, like their matarra."

"Will the new baby look like us, too?"

"I don't know. He might. But he could look like Vasili. Either way, we'll love him."

Frowning, she turned back to face him and pulled at his hair as if trying to make it grow.

He grinned at her frustration. "What are you doing?" he asked with a hint of laughter in his voice.

"Will you make your hair dark again so that you'll look like us?"

"Would that make you happy?"

She nodded vigorously. "Then we won't be the only ones with dark hair and fangs."

"Okay, but I can't do it the same way I do my eyes. I'll have to darken it at home later tonight." Putting his glasses back on, he carried her outside and stopped as he saw a group of Wasturnum who didn't belong on their base. Trajen hadn't allowed any other Tavali Nation to dock here in years, so how they'd been granted landing permission, he had no idea. But someone's ass was going to be raw later over this.

Hating the fact that it was hard to look intimidating while holding an adorable toddler, who'd left smudged lip prints on his cheek from her kisses, Jullien approached them with his sternest frown. "Can I help you?"

"We need to see the VA."

"She's paying her respects at a funeral right now. You'll understand that I have no intention of disturbing her. However, I'm the FA. And you are?"

"Ambassador Ryn Dane. I'm here on official business. These are my adjutants. Utran Belakane and Zosia Viga."

Jullien steeled himself to show no emotion whatsoever. Especially since he'd gone to school with Utran Belakane and knew that little bastard intimately.

And this was definitely *not* him.

Not to mention the short dark-haired shithead pretending to be Ryn was most decidedly not the smooth-talking, debonaire Caronese prince who would casually rip the throat out of this impostor and smile while he did it. As for the female, she might be Zosia Viga—he had no idea who that was, but given that the others were lying, he'd lay odds she was, too.

The real question was why they were here masquerading as the Tavali ambassador and his running mates.

And how the hell had they breached Trajen's security to get this close to Jullien's family?

Until he knew, he wasn't going to give them any personal details about himself, or anything else. In fact, he planned to get them as far away from his family as he could.

As fast as possible.

"Pleased to meet you. If you'll give me one second . . ." He carried Viv to the temple door. *"Mia?"* he said gently so as not to alarm his daughter. "Find Mummy, okay? I need you to stay with her while I talk to these nice people. Can you do that for me?"

"Okay, Paka."

Jullien set her on her feet and watched as she ran down the aisle, straight to Ushara. He didn't move until he was sure she was in her mother's arms and he visually checked that Mira was still asleep with Thrāix. Vasili sat with his grandparents. Unira was at the altar, giving her eulogy. Trajen sat with Davel, Dimitri, Jay, Ana, and Axl, surrounded by their children.

Assured of their safety, he turned back to face the others, and used his powers to seal the temple doors behind him so that no one could get in to harm them. Likewise, he ran a check with his powers to make sure no one else had made an unauthorized landing. "Where were we?"

"Official Tavali business." The Ryn impostor moved closer. "Any chance we could talk to the HAP?"

"None whatsoever." Jullien gestured toward the main offices, and fell into his role of casual field admiral.

One of the many his grandmother had taught him early in life—how to handle the most terrifying situation as if it were a routine walk down the hall. To let no one ever see him panic or sweat. He could control his heart rate and facial expressions better than any spy or actor. "If you'd like to follow me, I can show you to a conference room where we can be more comfortable, and you can tell me what this is about."

"Ah, yes. I'm part of a special coalition that Nykyrian Quiakides has put together. Have you ever met the man?"

"No." Jullien folded his hands behind his back and allowed the impostor to give him more information so that he could see what the male actually knew, and what he didn't. "You?"

"Many times. He's quite the tactful politician. A real chip off his father."

Yeah, not even a little. Other than their physical genetic similarities, his brother and father were polar extremes in every way. His father would grind his teeth and suffer his worst enemy for an interminable tea, then invite him back for dinner and allow him to screw his wife and daughter in his bed—all to keep the peace in his kingdom.

As a former top League assassin, Nyk's philosophy was, *Kill them all and let the gods sort them out.* And that was just for inhaling his air space at the wrong time of day.

His father believed everyone had a right to be heard, no matter what thought was in their head—unless you happened to be his son named Jullien. Then every thought in your mind was trivial, ill-conceived, and drug-induced.

Nyk believed the wise spoke when they had something to say, an idiot when they had to say something. And if you were an idiot, you'd best keep your opinion to yourself.

Especially if you were his brother named Jullien.

Hmmm, they did have more in common than Jullien remembered.

Pushing that thought aside, he scanned the bay as they walked through it to make sure there were no other ships docked without clearance. As far as he could tell, these three were the only ones on the station who didn't belong here.

And there was only one unfamiliar ship in the bay. Regular class. Unremarkable.

Jullien opened the doors that led to the offices above, and allowed them to enter first so that he could keep an eye on them. "Met the emperor, have you?"

"Yes. Triosan's very stern, but fair. As you know, we're all coming together to form an alliance against The League."

"We've heard some rumors." He gestured toward the stairs on his left.

"It's more than rumors. My mother's expecting full cooperation from all the Nations. I'm here to get access codes for Nykyrian and his Sentella forces."

Jullien arched his brow at that. "You don't say?"

"Yes. We thought it best that I come in person, as it would be more secure than trying to transmit them."

Jullien swiped his card for his office door, then stood back for them to go inside ahead of him. "Very true. So what codes do you need?"

"We'll expect the overrides so that we can command your Hadean Corpsmen as we need them. As well as any Stitches you have. And we need to know where your ships, people, and bases are so that we don't accidentally trip over each other or put your people in the line of fire. We want to protect all Tavali resources."

Sounded more like they intended to raid them.

Jullien gestured for them to be seated. While the Ryn impostor continued to talk, the other two were much more attentive to the station details. Especially the woman. She was carefully making mental notes of everything they passed.

"I take it you're doing this with all the Nations?" he asked their leader.

"Of course."

"Even Venik?"

The impostor nodded. "He was first."

Jullien arched a brow at that. "He didn't balk?"

"No. Not at all."

"Fascinating."

The Ryn impostor walked around and slowly examined the artwork Viv and Mira had drawn that decorated Jullien's office walls. "You just have the two daughters?"

Tucking his hands into the pockets of his red jacket, he shrugged. "Well . . . we never really know, do we?"

"Pardon?"

Jullien decided to play repugnant nonchalance to its full extent. He wasn't about to voluntarily give them anything they could use against him. Rule two he'd learned at home—*never let anyone know what you care about, and it couldn't be used against you, especially if it was sentient and could bleed.* "You know what they say—*Mama's baby. Daddy's maybe.*"

As planned, that caught the bastard completely off-guard. "You doubt your wife's fidelity?"

"I doubt everyone's fidelity." Using his telekinesis, Jullien quietly tucked the photograph of Ushara and the kids under the papers on his desk before they saw it. If they didn't know his wife was the VA, he sure wasn't going to tell them. He also locked the door. "Is it just the three of you here today?"

"It is."

"And that was your ship in the bay?"

"Yes. We'll need it refueled before we leave. I'm sure you won't have a problem charging the UTC for it."

Jullien stroked his whiskers. "No. No problem there, but I do have one question, Ambassador."

"That is?"

"What happened to the *Cruel Victory*?"

The impostor scowled. "The *Cruel Victory*?"

"Yeah, you know . . . the ship your mother gave you when you became a captain. It's the only ship Ryn Cruel has ever flown. And he's never flown without his full crew, which is more than just his stryper and head HC."

Jullien drew his blasters at the same time they did. "Yeah," he said slowly as he held a blaster in both hands. One pointed at the woman and her accomplice and the other at *Ryn*. "I'm *that* fast. Now, who are you? Really?"

"I told you who we are. And I will have your ass for this."

"Yeah, I don't think so. I've known Ryn since the day I attended his coronation on Caron while he was still in nappies."

Then Jullien heard the subtle sound.

A trip wire.

Too late, he realized they weren't Tavali. They were tiradors—suicide bombers. And they were here to destroy them all.

# CHAPTER 36

Ushara felt the rumbles of an explosion rock through the station. Everyone stood while they looked around for the source.

The color drained from Trajen's face as he started past her.

"What is it?" she asked him.

He didn't answer.

By that alone, she knew it was bad. Ushara handed Viv off to her mother before she followed Trajen. Vasili was right behind her, with Thrāix and Davel. "Where's Jules?"

Like Trajen, Thrāix didn't answer.

Vas shrugged. "I don't know. He took Viv to the bathroom, last I saw."

Trajen stopped at the temple doors and turned back to face her. "You need to stay here with your family. Last thing you need is to inhale dangerous fumes in your condition."

But she knew that look on his face. "What happened?"

"Vas . . . keep your mom and sisters here. I'm depending on you."

True panic dimmed her sight. Trajen *never* kept things from her. Not unless he was trying to protect her, and there was only one thing she could think that he'd protect her from at a time like this.

Jullien's death.

Her breathing ragged, she grabbed his arm. "Trajen, don't treat me like this. Tell me what's going on!"

Thrāix met her gaze over his shoulder. "Jullien just saved our lives. Now we're going to try and save his." And with that, he vanished.

His dark eyes haunted, Trajen swallowed hard. "Yeah. Stay here and wait for us."

Oh like hell! If Jullien was in trouble, she was going to help, too.

Ushara turned toward her parents. "Matarra! Take the kids. I need to suit up." Without waiting on anyone or stopping for anything, she headed for the lockers in the bay where she kept her hardsuits stored.

As soon as she entered the hangar and saw the damage to the upstairs area where their offices were located, she stumbled and almost fell. Charred and blackened, it looked as if the Koriłon had unleashed a *kybyk* from Tophet to come after them. Streaks of white cut through the darkness in patterns that honestly reminded her of claw marks. It really did look as if the gates of Tophet had been thrown open.

What had happened?

Blinking back tears of fear for Jullien, she ran to the lockers and pulled out her gear. She had to find him.

A shadow fell over her as she dressed.

It was Jay and Oxana. With a grim nod, her sisters grabbed their own suits and quickly dressed alongside her. Once they were sealed in, they headed up to where the fire crews and rescue were resealing the area, after searching for bodies and survivors.

From what she overheard them saying, it appeared someone had sealed off the upper corridor before the explosion, protecting the station's precious environmental control and life support system, and mitigating the blast radius, thus curtailing the damage that the bomb could have done.

Her office, Trajen's, and Jullien's were on the other side of the sealed area. It appeared nothing much, if anything, remained of them.

She saw the HC captain pulling his crew back.

Ushara headed for him. "What's the final damage?"

He removed his helmet before he answered. "Since command was off today for your sisters' memorial, it appears no one was up here. So we're thinking no casualties. At least none we can find. We're not sure what caused the explosion or how this section got sealed off. Whoever did it saved our asses, though. Had it not been sealed, it would have taken out the major CES and caused a cascade failure of the temperature and pressure for the entire station."

It must have been Jullien. Which begged one question . . . "Have you seen High Admiral Thaumarturgus?"

"No, ma'am."

Suddenly, a body slammed against the sealed door behind the captain and, because there was no atmosphere on that side of the door, exploded.

Jay screamed.

Ushara stared in wide-eyed horror as the HC around them scrambled in an attempt to reclaim the remains.

*What did I tell you about not being here!* She flinched at the sound of Trajen's angry voice in her head.

"Like I'm listening to you when my husband's in danger! Where is he?"

*Shara . . .* Jullien's voice was so weak, pain-filled, and unsteady that it wrenched a sob from her. *You need to be with the girls.*

"Jules—"

*I won't break your heart. . . . Ana, take her and go.*

Ushara glanced around for them. All she saw were the HC and her sisters. It didn't make sense. "Where are you? What don't you want me to see?"

Jay let out a sharp gasp. When Ushara went to turn around to see what had her alarmed, her sister grabbed her and shook her head harshly. "We need to go."

Oxana's eyes widened. "Yes, we do. Now!"

Ushara felt sick to her stomach. "What is it!" she demanded as hysteria threatened to overwhelm her.

Her sisters flanked her, and each took an arm. "Think of that unborn baby and walk with us. Now!"

Ushara's hysteria mounted. For them to act like this, it had to be bad. "What happened to him? Why won't you tell me?"

"He's hurt," Oxana said slowly.

"How bad?"

"Bad. But Trajen and Thrāix have him," Jay said with an uncharacteristic calmness. "They're bringing him in right now. So breathe and let them do their jobs."

"Jullien?" she sobbed as she started to turn around.

Jay wouldn't let her. "Shara, look at me and focus. There's nothing you can do but get in the way. None of us are medical. He needs emergency care, okay?"

She nodded, knowing Jay was right. "I'll meet you at the hospital, Jules. Please be okay. I love you."

*Kimi asyado, mu sojara.*

Ushara cringed at the agony and strain she heard in his voice. She felt it as if it were her own. Praying that he'd be fine, she followed her sisters.

By the time they reached the hospital, her entire family was there, waiting for them.

Vasili was pale and shaken, and not speaking a word to anyone. He merely held on to Mira, and for once didn't lose patience with her as she asked him a million questions and climbed all over him.

Viv came running up to Ushara. "Did them strangers hurt Paka, Mama?"

"What strangers?"

"The strangers who took Paka away after I wents to the potty. Paka said for me to go to you. He said that he needed to talk to them. That they were nice people. Did the nice people hurt my paka, Mama? Were they the mean Andarions who don't like my paka or us? Is that why Paka's not here?"

"I don't know, precious. I don't know what happened."

"Me and Mira will beat them up if they hurt Paka, Mama. We will. No one will hurt our paka."

Her father came over. "Viv? Can I hold you for a little while?"

"Okay." She held her arms up for him to pick her up.

Grateful for his support, Ushara drew a ragged breath as her father wiped at the tears on her cheek.

"He'll be fine, baby. You married a good male. He's not about to leave you or your children."

She squeezed her father's hand. He'd come a long way from wanting Jullien's head on a platter. Over the years, he'd finally learned to love and accept her husband as one of them. Of course, the birth of the girls had helped a lot, especially once he saw how caring and protective Jullien was with them. How much time Jules spent with the girls and Vas.

The love and support he never failed to give her, personally.

Some of her father's feelings had been comprised with the deaths of her cousins, and now her sisters. Both her parents had been rather reserved and cool toward him lately, to the point they hadn't even spoken to him or looked his way over the last two days. So it warmed her heart to see that they hadn't returned to all-out hating her husband again.

"Shara?"

She looked up at Trajen's call to see him motioning her toward a room.

Her mother and sisters came to stand at her back as she joined him. "How's he doing?"

"Jules wants to see you, but we need you to stay completely calm. Remember, he's really weak right now. He used all his powers to seal the offices off and protect the station. Had he not acted fast and segre-gated our intruders, there's no telling how this would have played out. He took the brunt of the explosion to dampen it. Thrāix and I have done what we can with our powers, but he's going to need surgery and im-plants."

Her stomach churned at that last word and what it meant. "Implants?"

"He lost an arm."

Ushara would have crumpled had Oxana not caught her.

Trajen took her from her sister and held her against his side. "You okay?"

She nodded. "Yeah. Is that what all of you were trying to keep me from seeing?"

"Mostly. He was also burned and looked pretty raw when we pulled him in. None of us, including Jules, wanted you to see him like that. You didn't need the nightmare of it."

"Can I see him now?"

Trajen practically carried her inside the room, to the bed where Jul-lien lay motionless.

Horrified by his condition, Ushara choked on a sob. Bandages cov-ered his head and torso, but the ones that made her ache most were over where his right arm should have been. The entire right side of his face was covered and most of his left. Pain welled up inside her.

How could they have done this to him?

"We healed as much of him as we could. But there's some of it we couldn't touch yet. Thrāix and I have to rest for a bit, and we'll do more later tonight."

"Thank you both." Ushara stepped forward to touch Jullien's left hand. The moment she did, he wrapped his fingers around hers.

*Hi, munatara.*

Sobbing, she leaned over to kiss his hand. "What happened?"

*Tiradors. They came in pretending to be Ryn Dane, and wanting our passcodes. I'm not sure who hired them. There was a bomb on their ship, too, but I caught that one before detonation. I just wish I'd caught the ones on them, personally.*

"Oh, Jules . . . why didn't you tell us they were here?"

*You were where I wanted all of you. Safe.*

"I could choke you."

*Why? I saved my wedding ring.*

She scowled at his strange, unrelated comment. "What?"

He shook her hand. *After I grabbed the bomb, I realized that I was holding it in my left hand. Luckily, I had time to change it before it went off.*

She groaned at his humor. "Really? *That's* your main concern?"

*Hey now, don't mock. Had I not switched hands before detonation, I would have lost both the ring and my tattoo. That would have been a tragedy.*

Rolling her eyes at his facetious humor, she couldn't believe he'd try to make light of this. "You could have lost your life!"

*Nah, my life is holding my hand right now. Besides, I'm too contentious to die. Told you when we met, eton Anatoles are hard to kill.*

How could he find *any* humor in this?

But then suddenly she knew. He was doing it for her. To keep her mind off how bad this was for him. How much pain he had to be in. It was why she loved him so much.

"When you get better, I'm going to kill you."

*Looking forward to it. Especially if you do it in your temple chorus outfit.*

Yet in spite of his gentle teasing, she could tell he was weak and needed to rest. Leaning over him, she kissed his cheek. "I love you, *keramon*. Thank you for not breaking my heart."

*I am ever your nightmare, mu tura.*

She caressed his arm. "I'll stay here, beside you, and let you rest."

*Shara?*

"Yes?"

*I don't want the girls to see me like this. But I know Mira can't sleep until I read to her. I don't know how we're going to manage that tonight.*

Trajen pressed his thumb against his temple. "Let me and Thrāix rest, and we'll get the bandage off your head by dinner. That'll have you talking again for Mira by bedtime. You won't even have scars. We can cover the right side of your body with a thick blanket so as not to scare her."

*Thanks, Tray.*

*For everything.*

He touched Jullien's arm. "No, problem, little brother. I'm the one who owes you. I was upset over Mary and Ryna, and let my guard lax today. We damn near lost the station. I still don't know how. But I'm going to find out."

Ushara swallowed hard as she sniffed back the tears that burned her throat. "Promise me one thing, Tray."

"Sure."

"When you find out who was behind this, I want them."

Trajen arched his brow at her. "Pardon?"

Ushara met his gaze without flinching. "You heard me, boss. I want them. Intact. At my feet so I can gut them with my bare hands. No one does this to my husband and gets away with it."

"How's it feel?" Trajen asked.

Jullien flexed his cybernetic arm and grimaced. "A little timing delay, but not bad." Something sharp stuck in his shoulder. "Ow!" He jerked to see Thrāix grinning at him while holding a small needle.

"The nerve endings work."

"Really?" Jullien snapped. "How about I shove that prick up *your* ass?"

"I don't even want to know what I just walked in on."

Rubbing his abused shoulder, Jullien snorted at Ushara's shocked tone. "Thrāix acting like a two-year-old."

Thrāix had the nerve to hold his hands up as if he were innocent. "I'm not the one threatening assault. I just wanted to test your implants. Make sure they work properly."

Yeah, right. He didn't believe that for single instant. Jullien sneered at his lie while Ushara took his new arm in her hands to examine it.

She ran her hands over his shoulder and down to his wrist, palm, and fingers, leaving a trail of chills in her wake that sent an electrical charge straight to his groin. Now, *that* was the way to test his implant. And it brought other, much more sensual ideas to his mind for testing it, too.

Ushara smiled sweetly at him. "It looks and feels so natural."

"It's supposed to." Trajen jerked his chin at spare pieces they'd left on the counter. "We're not sure that we put it together right, though."

Jullien laughed at the expression on her face at Trajen's joke.

She froze in horror. "Not comforting, guys." She met Jullien's gaze. "Did you help them?"

"Little bit." He made a fist and tested the dexterity of his fingers by running them through her hair. "It's actually amazing how quickly it grafted and healed."

Thrāix nodded. "I've never seen anyone take to an implant so fast. You're a freak, Andarion."

Ushara wrapped her arms around his waist and hugged him. "No, you're not. You're wonderful."

Grateful she was completely blind to his multitude of faults, Jullien savored the warmth of her touch, but he didn't miss the pain that flitted across Thrāix's eyes. It'd only been six weeks since Mary's memorial.

For that, he was as eager for vengeance and payback as Thrāix.

But they still had one giant obstacle who stood in their way, and he was currently eyeballing him as if he were inside his head and reading his thoughts.

Jullien didn't flinch under the weight of Trajen's probing stare. "We're being pitted against each other. This is classic Eriadne."

"We still have no proof." Trajen sighed. "We've gone over every atom of that ship. It was wiped clean. All you know is someone posed as you with the Mavericks, and then came here posing as Ryn."

*Not just someone. Tiradors. Hired professionals who specialize in toppling governments and starting wars.* They weren't just anyone off the street.

But Jullien blocked that thought and didn't say it out loud, since it would only start the fight with Trajen that they'd been arguing for weeks now. "I know, and I've been thinking. . . ."

Ushara arched her brow. "That tone of voice terrifies me whenever you use it."

"Really?" Trajen said dryly. "It usually precedes something that pisses *me* off."

Ignoring Trajen, Jullien cradled her hand in his and kissed her knuckles reassuringly. Ever since Thrāix and Trajen saved him, Ushara had shadowed him worse than she did Vasili. It was as if she was terrified of letting him out of her sight for fear of losing him.

While flattering, he could barely go to the bathroom alone at this point. Half the time, he emerged to find her waiting for him just outside the door. She was beginning to make him even more paranoid than normal.

"It scares me, too, Shara. But . . . they're able to pit us against each other because we're remaining separate. If we unite with The Sentella and the other Tavali Nations, they can't use us against each other so easily. We'll know what we're all doing."

Trajen scoffed irritably. "We unite, and they will know *you're* alive and with us. Are you ready for that?"

"I don't care about them or me. I care about this station and all of you." Jullien jerked his chin toward Thrāix and Ushara. "I don't want to lose anymore family."

Trajen let out a disgusted sigh. "I'll consider it. But I think it's a profoundly bad idea. So does Thrāix."

"And me," Ushara chimed in.

Thrāix snorted at Trajen's evoking his name without his consent. "Excuse me? Thrāix hasn't spoken on this matter."

"Yes, you did. You just didn't know it."

"Oh, okay. How could I be so stupid?"

"Exactly. Stand there. Look cute and be my yes-man. That's your job. Be my unified whole against Jullien."

"I'll be a yes-man, maybe. But I'm not going to be your hole of any kind."

Ushara sighed. "Sometimes when I'm around the three of you, I feel like I'm at home, refereeing my children." She handed Jullien his shirt. "No wonder you're so good at it."

"Yeah. Lot of practice, especially when you throw your brothers into the mix. And don't get me started on Chay and Jory."

Ushara's stomach sank as her gaze fell to the new scars that had been added from the explosion. To the ones that had torn through the tattoo over Jullien's heart. Before she could think better of it, she ran her fingers over the jagged edges of the rose.

Jullien pressed her hand flat against his flesh and held her palm so that she could feel the deep steady beating of his heart. *"Hæfre tygara ixur, mu sojara."*

*Forever your darkheart, my rose.*

Those tender words choked her. "Please remember that the next time you decide to cuddle an IED, I would rather you not."

"Yeah," Trajen agreed. "You're a little hard to put back together again. I think you ran out of your nine lives about fourteen of them ago."

"Gah," Jullien groaned, "the way you and Thrāix bitch and moan, you'd think you're the ones who lost the arm. Bite it, already."

Suddenly, Ushara's link went off. Scowling, she pulled it out. Then she frowned even more as she saw who was hailing her. "It's a Porturnum frequency."

Trajen curled his lip. "What could they possibly want?"

Jullien fastened his shirt while she answered it.

"Are you solo?" Ushara listened for several seconds. "All right. North Bay. We'll pull you in. Come out unarmed." She hung up.

"What's going on?" Thrāix asked.

"The captain claims she has cargo for us. Something extremely valuable they salvaged. But she wouldn't elaborate or identify herself. She only said that she couldn't stay. She has to dump it and go."

Jullien scowled at the vagueness of those words. "Anyone else getting an ulcer from this?"

Trajen raised his hand.

Thrāix snorted. "Mine went up in flames six weeks ago. I got nothing left inside me now but raw fury and indifference."

Rubbing his back to comfort him, Ushara led them from the clinic, down to the bay, where they waited until the *Black Widow* landed. She turned toward Jullien with an amused smirk. "Well, I know who the captain is now."

Yeah, so did he and every male there.

The ship was so named because it was owned and operated by Braxen Venik's insanely attractive daughters, and any male who tried to get into their *business* ended up MIA. The only males who were ever allowed on that ship were Venik's two eldest sons, Stanis and Payne, who were better known by the call signs Stain and Pain, as that was all they left of any male dumb enough to try and talk to their sisters.

But as the ramp lowered, it didn't appear that either of the boys were aboard, since they normally were the first off the ship to scout for any wandering penises that might venture too close.

Rather Circe Venik, the captain herself, came out.

Tall and lithe, she held the same incredible build as her Qill mother, Malys. But she had her father's silvery-white Andarion eyes, and rumor claimed his "calmer" demeanor. A male was with her, yet he was younger than Pain or Stain.

Kareem Venik, if Ushara didn't miss her guess. Circe's younger brother. Between them was a third person, who was cloaked so that no trace of gender or species could be detected. Yet there was something about the figure that seemed oddly familiar to her.

Circe paused at the bottom of the ramp and waited for them to join her. When she spoke, she kept her voice low so that no one could overhear her. "Do not betray us or show any sign of what we're doing until after we're gone. Understood?"

"Okay." Baffled, Ushara glanced to Thrāix, Trajen, and Jullien.

"Kareem and I wanted no part of this. Don't blame my father. He's over a barrel, and they're screwing him badly. You've got to do something."

Ushara scowled at her. "I don't understand."

Circe met Jullien's gaze. "I left a message for you with our delivery. Do with it what you will. We have to go."

Kareem handed the hooded figure to Thrāix, then the two of them quickly rushed up the ramp and closed it.

Stunned and confused, Ushara had no idea what to think about it. But there was something going on with Thrāix, who had gone stark white and completely silent.

Before she could ask if he was all right, he literally ran with the hooded figure toward the lockers.

Totally confounded, Ushara followed with Jullien and Trajen.

When they arrived, they found Thrāix locked in an embrace so flagrantly hot and intense, she was surprised clothes weren't flying off both bodies.

But the breathless laugh that rang out sent a chill down her spine. "Mary?"

With her arms wrapped tightly around the Trisani, her sister peeped at her over Thrāix's muscular shoulder. "Hey!"

Tears welled in her eyes as she stared in utter disbelief. No . . . "You're alive?"

Mary nodded, reaching for her.

Ushara ran to embrace her, but Thrāix wouldn't release his own grip on Mary. Not for anything. He was latched on to her with a jealousy that was as annoying as it was sweet. "I don't understand."

"I was captured and taken prisoner when they attacked our convoy." "Ryna?"

She shook her head as a tear fled down her cheek. "They took a direct hit, without warning. There were no survivors on her ship. We got out on escape pods. Barely. I don't know where my crew is. I'm hoping they made it to some outposts or colonies. I don't know how they knew which pod was mine. But they homed right in on me and nabbed me."

"They?"

"Nyran and Eriadne."

Jullien cursed. "I knew it." He glared at Trajen.

"They still think you're dead, though," Mary said to Jullien. "And that Ushara is trying to get revenge on them by sending the Samari family to prey on their ships and supplies, and interfere with their plans."

Ushara gaped. "You're kidding?"

Mary shook her head. "They're wanting to split the Tavali Nations and are working to divide us and have us at each other's throats so that we'll be easy to take down and destroy."

"And your message?" Trajen asked.

"They're planning something against Jullien's mother. But I don't know what or when. I only know it's major and soon."

Thrāix swung her up in his arms, and cradled her against his chest like a beloved child. "Now, if you don't mind, I'm taking my girl home and never letting her out of my sight again."

"Before you go . . ." Ushara glanced down. "The baby?"

Thrāix smiled. "Sphinx is fine. I can feel him."

"Thank the gods."

Tugging on his sleeve, Mary made Thrāix turn around and allow her to hug her sister.

Ushara locked her arms around her as tears and love choked her. "I've missed you so much!"

"Me, too. I wasn't sure I'd ever see home again."

Thrāix hesitated. "Can you give us an hour before you tell the rest of the family she's back?"

Smiling, Ushara nodded. "Of course." She glanced to Jullien. "Believe me, I more than understand." She pulled the hood up over Mary's head and made sure to conceal her features before she kissed both their cheeks and sent them on their way.

Jullien moved to wrap his arms around her shoulders and placed his cheek against hers. It was a possessive hold that he only used whenever he was having a panic attack over his fear of losing her or the children, and needed to ground himself with the reassurance that she was fine. While they had been extremely commonplace in the beginning of their marriage, they'd lessened severely over the years to the point that she'd almost forgotten about them.

But she heard his ragged breathing in her ear and felt the tenseness in his body. Stroking his forearm, she laid her hand against his whiskered cheek and let her fingers play at the edges of his once-again dark hair. For their daughters, who didn't want to be the lone Ixurianir on the station, he'd returned to the midnight locks that she'd fallen in love with.

Suddenly, Jullien's link rang.

Ushara started at the sound. Unlike hers, his seldom went off. The only ones who ever called him were her, Trajen, Vas, or Thrāix. And since she knew it couldn't be any of them . . .

Jullien pulled the link out and checked the ID, then scowled. "Bas? You in trouble?"

Bas? Unfamiliar with the name, she turned as Jullien stepped away from her to listen to the caller.

"Hang on a sec." Jullien lowered his link to speak to Trajen. "Permission to land a *gadelyng* fighter in the North Bay?"

*Gadelyng* was the Tavali slang for a friendly noncitizen who usually had military training of some kind.

"You trust him?"

"With my life." He cut a meaningful glance to Ushara that warmed her and let Trajen know that he'd considered the ramifications of letting the pilot land.

"Then I trust you. Go ahead."

"Thanks." Jullien returned to the link. "I'm sending the clearance now. Disarm your weapons systems and leave your blasters on board." He laughed. "Nah, I trust you, *drey*. Besides, I know what a deadly bastard you are barehanded. It's to keep anyone else from getting twitchy and taking a shot at you, which would just piss you off and cull our Nation. See you in a few." He tucked the link in his pocket.

Ushara arched a brow. "Bas?"

"Bastien Cabarro. My Kirovarian cousin."

She exchanged a confused stare with Trajen. "I thought he was Ravin?"

"He is. I don't know how he got off Oksana. Or what's going on. But I do trust him. If he's here, there has to be a good reason for it. He wouldn't endanger us for anything."

Trajen snorted. "And for that reason, I've got to meet a man who inspires trust in your pathetically paranoid ass."

Snorting, Jullien fell quiet as he led them to the hangar, where Bastien was already landing.

In a Sentella Alliance fighter, of all things.

That was unexpected. Even more unexpected was the sight of him emerging from the cockpit in a Sentella flight suit and light Armstitch jacket. What the hell? This was not the unkempt refugee Jullien had been taking supplies to over the last few years.

This was the highly trained, cocksure Gyron Force officer who'd been fast-tracking his way up their ranks to one day replace his uncle as their commander general. The one no one messed with unless they wanted a free trip to a medical center.

At least until Bas cracked that familiar, charming grin and pulled Jullien in for a brotherly hug. Then he was just his boyhood cousin who used to drive his older siblings to attempted murder, and his parents into seeking priests for an exorcism of whatever demon had possessed their youngest, most irreverent and fearless child.

Jullien laughed when he saw that Bastien had kept his long brown hair and wore it pulled back into a messy ponytail. "What is this?" He tugged playfully at it.

Bastien shrugged. "A reminder that I'm no longer civilized, and I have no intention of ever again playing by anyone's rule book."

"I understand. And I take it by your presence here that you're no longer tagged?"

"No. Syn Wade pulled it out of me. Finally."

And that shocked him most of all. Just how tight was his cousin to his brother and The Sentella? "Really?"

Bastien clapped him on the arm. "Really long story short, they ended up on Oksana with The League hot on their ass, and I got caught in the cross fire. After a lot of bruising and damage, and a couple of near-fatal catastrophes, it ended well for me." His gaze went to Ushara.

Jullien stepped back to introduce them. "My much better half, Ushara. Shara, my cousin Bastien."

"*Imprä turu, Ger Tarra Samari.*"

She gaped at Bastien's formal Andarion greeting and bow. "You speak Andarion?"

Straightening, Bastien winked at Jullien. "Not really. Just a few words here and there that Julie taught me when we were kids."

"Impressive, nonetheless." Ushara gestured to Trajen. "And this is Trajen."

Bastien held his hand out. "Pleasure to meet you."

"And you . . . Highness."

Bastien shivered. "Please, don't. I was never all that into the pomp and ceremony, anyway. It's just Bastien or Bas. Asshole, if you really must."

"Ah God, there are two of you in this universe," Trajen muttered, glancing to Jullien as he shook Bastien's hand. "So what brings you here?"

"To beg a favor from my favorite cousin, which I know I shouldn't.

But . . ." He flashed another grin at Jullien. "Dancer Hauk blew up my base without warning."

Jullien gaped at that unexpected disclosure. "Pardon?"

Nodding, he snorted. "The whole bloody damn thing. I got nothing left. Not even my porn collection. And I need that database I shared with you, if you don't mind."

"You're going after Barnabas?"

"Hell yeah. He killed my family. Be damned if I'm going to let him sit on my father's throne in peace. I don't care who rules, just so long as it's not him or any bastard he spawned."

Jullien dropped his gaze to the Alliance patches on Bastien's sleeve. "The Sentella helping you?"

"They offered me a position with them. I'm not interested in that. All I took was the clothes and ship, which I intend to pay back. My mistress is Vengeance, and she's the only one I'm cuddling up to for now."

Jullien definitely understood that sentiment. "I'll get you a copy of the database. Is there anything else you need?"

"No. Just the files on the family. Once I have those dossiers, I'll be out of your hair. Sorry I dropped in unannounced." His gaze went to Ushara's stomach. "Congrats, by that way. I didn't realize you had another one on the way. Is Vasili excited or afraid of having more spiders he has to hide his things from?"

Ushara gaped. "You know Vas?"

"He's made a few stops with his father on my rock to drop off food and ammo."

She tsked at Jullien. "Someone's been keeping secret missions from me."

"Only to protect Bastien. I didn't want any logs of that particular landing stop, or anyone wondering why we kept going to the desert for no apparent reason. Just in case."

"Makes sense." She smiled at Bastien. "Why don't you stay for dinner, then? Meet the girls and say hi to Vasili? I'm sure he'd love to see you."

He looked to Jullien. "I don't want to intrude."

"Just don't flush my head down the toilet, and we're good."

Bastien burst out laughing. "Gah! You think you had it bad? I was the one who lived with her. *And* Quin. Plus, she ended up as my wingman. How the hell I survived my childhood without being drowned, I do not know. Can you imagine how much better a human I'd be if I hadn't suffered severe oxygen dep and brain trauma as a child?"

Trajen laughed. "I see now why you like him." He held his hand out to Bastien. "It was a pleasure to meet you, Bas. I've got a lot of things I need to take care of, so I'm heading out, but I'll make sure and clear you for any future visits you want to make here. Consider yourself welcome anytime. I know Jules would appreciate having some family around who doesn't want to hang him or screw him over."

By the grateful expression on Bastien's face as he thanked him, Ushara was pretty sure Jullien wasn't the only one, and that Trajen knew it.

While Bastien and Jullien headed for the condo, she walked with Trajen toward their makeshift offices.

Trajen slid a knowing gaze toward her. "Yes, he's fine, Shara. He bears no malice toward Jules at all. If he did, I wouldn't have granted him safe passage here."

She snorted as she realized why Trajen had shaken Bastien's hand— he'd been testing him. "Okay, boss. Thank you for allaying my fears."

He inclined his head to her. "No problem. And I meant what I said. It'll be good for Jules to have some blood family with him. And for Bastien, as well. Now, put your mind at ease. You know I'd never let harm come to you."

But there was something he wasn't telling her about the two of them, and she knew it. She could always tell whenever Trajen withheld information. Luckily, she trusted him and she knew when not to push him. He was terribly stubborn, like Jullien, and wouldn't answer until he was good and ready.

It was so irritating.

So she headed home to start dinner and to get to know this man that Jules had only mentioned in passing.

As the hours went by, she had to admit that Trajen was right. Bastien was extremely likable and charming. Like Jullien in the early days of their relationship, he had a deep sadness that haunted his dark hazel eyes. And a biting sarcasm that kept them all entertained and laughing.

The girls took to him immediately. Although, they were perplexed at first.

Mira had rudely pulled at his lips. "But if you're Paka's family, why don't you gots fangs, too?"

"And black hair?" Viv had chimed in. "Don't all Ixurianir have black hair?" She'd slapped her hands to her face. "I'm so confuzzled."

Laughing, Jules had picked her up and kissed her cheek. "My paka's human, and he's the older brother of Bastien's mother, who is also human. So a lot of folks on Andaria, and in some other places, don't consider me Andarion."

Bastien nodded. "Yeah, and I'm completely human. Sadly, I have no Andarion blood in my veins at all."

Mira sighed heavily before she patted Bastien's cheek in sympathy. "I am very sad for you. But we loves you anyway, *kyzi*. Even though you gots no fangs."

"Thank you, Mira. I deeply appreciate that." He ruffled her hair and flashed a handsome grin at Ushara. "They are precious. I can't believe anything so sweet came from Julie's surly, irritable hide."

Jullien snorted. "Thanks a lot."

"Well, you have to admit, you were never *this* cute." He tickled Mira until she squealed and jumped from his arms to run to her brother for protection.

"Neither were you."

"True. I was too busy being the baby brat. A job I relished quite seriously." He took the ale from Jullien's hand and lifted it for a swig. "You remember that god-awful summer camp when Barnabas was trying to make us run the obstacle course?"

"Remember? Hell, my dignity's still on that wall, pinned next to my left testicle."

Bastien laughed as he turned toward Ushara, who was stunned by Jullien's description. "My uncle's a total scabbing prick. I loved my dad, but he had some weird parenting techniques, which included occasional weekend maneuvers, and summers every year spent at Camp Hernia for a full six-week program of survival training. And poor Julie got roped in one year when you were what? Thirteen?"

"Fourteen. I was supposed to have been on my Andarion Endurance."

"Endurance?" Bastien scowled.

He took a drink of ale, then explained the term for Bastien. "It's an Andarion coming-of-age ceremony where an elder of the family takes a younger one on a quest to teach them how to survive on their own. The youngster goes out a kid and supposedly returns as a capable adult, ready to take their place in Andarion society."

"Ah. Then how'd you end up on Kirovar for it?"

"Because I was half human and fat, none of my Andarion relatives wanted the embarrassment of being seen with me when I failed the family quest. So my aunt shuffled me off to my father, who promptly sent me to yours, who then shunted me to your uncle. Fun times."

Bastien shook his head. "Indeed."

Ushara ground her teeth as she sliced vegetables, wishing it were the throat of her in-laws under the blade. She couldn't imagine how bad Jullien must have felt as a child to be tossed around like that by his insensitive family.

But Jullien didn't seem to care as he winked at her and Vas, who was suddenly interested in the story. "So there we were. The hottest summer in Kirovarian history, on maneuvers with these massively heavy backpacks Barnabas had loaded with heat-absorbing rocks, where it was eight hundred degrees in the shade. Not that there was any shade to be found on that course, mind you."

"He's not exaggerating. It was so hot, it melted my granola bar."

Vas scowled. "How do you melt a granola bar?"

"Exactly!" Bastien said with a laugh. "I swear the heels of my boots melted off."

"Yeah, and unlike Bas and his siblings, I was overweight, with atrophied muscles from a period of—" He paused as he glanced to Vasili. "—confinement, and I wasn't used to their atmosphere. At all. It's a lot thinner than what we have on Andaria, with different gravity and allergens. So I'm disoriented, choking and wheezing, and doubled over, puking."

Screwing his face up, Bastien nodded. "Not a pretty sight. My brother and sister are yelling at poor Julie because my uncle's threatening to make us run extra laps if he doesn't get back on the course and finish it. And I give him credit, he's on his hands and knees, trying his damnedest to push himself to his feet. Hell, he's even crawling in an effort to get to the end. I'd never seen anyone so determined to get up in my life, but it's just not happening. He's choking and sweating so badly that I'm expecting Julie to die any minute."

"So," Jullien says, interrupting him. "In true Bastien form—and keeping in mind that he's only seven at the time—he yanks off his helmet, throws his backpack down, and lies on the ground, using the helmet for a pillow, and says to them, and I quote verbatim, *Later, bitches. I'm done for the day. Y'all can carry me home or call for a lift. Either way, I ain't moving from here. My ass is too precious for this abuse."*

Ushara gasped at the image of Bastien doing that. "How did *that* go over?"

Bastien snorted. "Like sacrificing a fluffy kitten on a high holiday. My uncle set my precious ass on fire. But it got the attention off poor Julie."

"Yeah, but you bought yourself a world of hurt that day."

Bastien shrugged nonchalantly. "You weren't there when my mother saw the ass bruises after we got home. I promise you, what he did to me pales in comparison to her reaction on him when she saw them. But for my father's lightning-quick reflexes, I'd be shy a few cousins. I actually owe *you*. Because of that particular fun adventure, I didn't have to go back to summer camp until I was a teenager. And I went with bodyguards my mother had ordered to shoot my uncle if he, or anyone else, so much as raised an eyebrow to me." He grinned at Ushara. "As I said, my ass was quite precious."

Jullien laughed. "Your mother was something else. Until Shara, I'd never seen anyone so protective of her young. I'm amazed she ever allowed you to join the military."

"Again, you missed the fireworks. Holy Jacob . . . she actually tried to shoot *me* to get me out of it."

"I would say bullshit, but knowing your mother . . . it sounds about right."

Ushara gaped. "Seriously?"

Nodding, Bastien sobered as grief returned to his eyes. "Yeah, my mother loved us. We definitely lucked out when it came to parents. They didn't deserve what Barnabas did to them, and I won't rest until I make this right."

Jullien reached for a handful of the carrots she'd cubed. "You going after the throne?"

Bastien glanced over to where the twins were playing on the floor. "I don't know. I was never supposed to be ruler. . . . Third born. It should *never* have come to me. I was supposed to be the fun-loving playboy of the family, who screwed up and gave the others something scandalous to talk about at cocktail parties." Swallowing, he locked gazes with Jullien. "How did you handle the guilt when everyone thought Nyk was dead?"

"Didn't. Like you said, I never wanted the throne. But after a few years, when I realized that my mother wasn't going to sober up and have more children, and that my father had no intention of remarrying or fathering another heir, I threw myself into school to learn as much about politics, history, and diplomacy as I could. Not because I cared. Just felt like I owed it to my brother's memory to be the ruler I thought he'd have been."

Bastien sighed. "Never thought of it that way."

"That's because you were supposed to be the playboy. I was the spare."

He laughed and clapped Jullien on the back before they carried dinner to the table. Ushara remained mostly quiet as she listened to their bantering and stories. It was strange to see her husband with someone he'd known since childhood, that he was comfortable around.

And the more she listened, the more she loved Bastien. He was a little odd, but he had a generous heart. It was a shame that Jullien hadn't been allowed to spend more time at Bastien's home when he was young. From what she gathered, their visits had been preciously few.

After dinner, Bas helped her clean up while Jullien put the girls to bed and Vasili went to play online with his cousins. "Ushara?"

She paused at the serious note in Bastien's voice. "Yes?"

"Thank you."

"I'm not quite sure what you're thanking me for, but you're welcome."

He put away the glasses before he gave her a hard stare. "You give me hope, and that's something I haven't had in a long time."

She sealed the last of their leftovers into a tub and put them away. "What do you mean?"

"Unlike Jullien, I had a great childhood. The kind every kid ought to have. It's why I never understood how Aros could be so nice to us and then such a douche to his own son. I still don't really understand what crawled up his ass and grew there. Julie wasn't a bad kid. Just a lonely one who grew up intimately acquainted with a treacherous side of others that I was blissfully unaware of. I grew up in a world that if someone, even my uncle, did me harm, it was only because they cared about me and were trying to teach me a valuable life lesson and that it was for my own good."

"You were naïve."

"Blessedly so. Sheltered, even though I didn't know it. So when it all came crashing down on me, and those I thought were my family and friends turned out to be backbiting enemies . . . I lost all faith. In everything.

But this—" He gestured at the pictures of their family on the wall. "It helps more than you'll ever know. It restores some of the faith I'd lost. I'm glad you saw in Julie what I've always known."

She smiled at him. "I can't imagine my life any other way." Rubbing his arm, she motioned for him to follow her down the hall to the girls' room, where she cracked the door open so that he could see their bedtime ritual.

On top of the covers, Jullien lay on the queen-sized bed the girls shared with his ankles crossed, propped against a stack of stuffed animals. The twins were tucked under each of his arms, beneath the covers, and draped on his chest while he read to them.

His deep voice brought a smile to her lips and made the girls giggle. "And then the lorina tackled her sister and went *rawr*!" With a guttural sound effect, he grabbed Mira and tickled her until she squealed, then he turned and did the same to Viv.

"Jules," she said chidingly, "you're supposed to be putting them down, not winding them up."

Eyes wide, he gasped at the girls. "You got me into trouble again with mama."

They giggled and snuggled deeper into his side as he returned to reading the story.

Ushara headed back toward the living room.

Bastien lingered a moment longer before he rejoined her. "That's what I mean, Ushara. I wish you could see what a miracle *that* is." He gestured toward the hall with his thumb. "Julie didn't learn that from his parents. I've never known him to be so open and happy as he's been since he found you."

Embarrassed, she cleared her throat and changed the subject. "So you were with his brother before you came here?"

"Yeah."

"What's he like?"

Bastien shrugged. "I barely know Nykyrian, really. He was assumed dead my whole childhood. I was twenty-six when he returned and was reinstated as heir."

Anger darkened her vision. "And you didn't help Jullien when they threw him out?"

"I tried. Believe me. But you have to remember that it was only three months after Jullien was disinherited that my entire family was slaughtered and I was convicted for it and sentenced to being a Ravin. In retrospect, my father did him a favor. Had Julie been on Kirovar, he'd have been murdered, too."

She sucked her breath in sharply. "I didn't realize that happened so close together."

Bastien nodded. "So no, I never had a chance to get to know Nyk. At all. Not until a few weeks ago, when they showed up on Oksana. He seems decent enough. But I don't have the war stories with him that I share with Julie. Nyk never had to suffer through one of our grandfather's interminable parties."

She laughed. "So I've heard."

"I'll bet you have. To the day he died, my brother Quin counted Julie among his heroes for having the nerve to do that."

"Are we back to the pool pissing?"

Bastien turned at Jullien's question. "I could always count on you to make things interesting."

Jullien rolled his eyes. "Let's not go there." He pulled his jacket out of the closet. "I have the files you need stored on my ship. You want to stay here or come with me?"

"As much as I enjoy your wife's company, I'll come with you and give her a break from my boorishness."

"You're anything but a chore to put up with. And you're welcome here anytime."

"Thank you, Ger Tarra." Bastien took a minute to say good-bye to Vasili, who actually hugged him. It was obvious by the way Bastien held him that it meant a lot to the Kirovarian prince. "Take care, sport."

"You, too."

Ushara watched them leave, her heart light as she whispered a prayer for Bastien's protection. It meant a lot to her that Jullien had someone in his family who treated him with regard. If anyone deserved success, it was definitely Bas. She wished him all the luck in the universe and hoped that everything worked out for him.

She checked on the girls, who were sound asleep, then went to take a long bath and relax.

Two hours later, Jullien still hadn't returned. Concerned, she tried his link.

He didn't answer.

Which only worried her more. Her heart racing, she called Trajen.

She expected him to be at home, but instead he was in the middle of what sounded like a cheering crowd. "Trajen?"

"Uh . . . hey. Yeah?"

"I'm looking for Jules. Have you seen him?"

"Mmmm . . . can I plead LASI?"

Law Against Self-incrimination? That didn't sound promising. "What's going on?"

"Not sure I should answer that. You won't like it."

Oh yeah, not promising at all. In fact, her anger rose at those words. "Trajen!"

"We're in the east gym. That's all I'm saying. . . . Ow! Shit! That's going to leave a mark!"

Cutting off the transmission, she rushed to Vas's room, where it took a second to get his attention off the game and on to her. "I'm going out for a few minutes. Do you mind watching your sisters until I get back?"

Vas looked up from the game console. "They're asleep, right?"

"Yes."

"Okay. Just leave the doors open so I can hear them if they get up." He pulled his headset completely off his shoulders and set it on the floor, then switched the sound to the speakers so that he could listen for the twins.

Her boy was ever responsible.

Ushara closed the distance between them to kiss his cheek. "Thank you, *m'tana*. You're a wonderful brother. And you do me proud."

He scowled at her as if she were feverish. "You okay?"

"Not sure yet." And with that, she headed off for the gym to see what was going on.

The minute she arrived and saw the giant, cheering crowd that had gathered around two maniac fighters, her jaw went slack. Both Jullien and Bastien had stripped down to their waists and were now attempting to kill each other inside a training ring. At least that was what it appeared at first, until she realized they were both laughing and urging the other one to hit harder.

Gaping even wider, she moved to Trajen's side. "What is this?"

"Did you know Jules could fight like that?"

Not really. She watched as he ran at Bastien, wrapped around him in an impressive hold, and brought him down like a toppled tree. Bastien twisted and flipped, expertly escaping the hold. When he went to

pin Jullien, Jullien lifted his legs to catch him around the neck and un-
balance him enough that Jullien could roll out of his grasp and twist,
then flip to his feet.

Yeah, it was impressive.

"I knew he had to be good to survive the Ladorian hell we found him
in. But no . . . I've never seen him actually take on anyone this skilled
before. Like *that*." And Bastien *was* talented. If she didn't know better,
she'd swear he was an Andarion Ring fighter. He had moves she'd never
seen anywhere outside of their sport.

And the gods knew Jullien had *never* been this rough while training
with her or Vasili. Honestly, she hadn't realized just how much he'd held
back in their matches until now. No wonder he'd torn through her cousins so easily.

Trajen shook his head as he watched, and the crowd cheered even
louder. "Like you, I had no idea when I sparred with Jullien that he was
pulling back." He sucked his breath in as Jullien landed a staggering punch
on Bastien that Bastien returned with an equal amount of force. "I will
*never* spar with that bastard again, lest he have some kind of psychotic
episode and decide to hit me like that."

"Could you stop them, please?"

Trajen snorted at her. "I don't want to get in the middle of *that*. Are
you out of your mind?"

She glared at him before she headed toward the two combatants. On
the side of the ring, she stood with her hands on her hips.

Jullien started for Bastien, then glanced at her. The minute their gazes
met, he skidded to a stop. Until Bastien approached with another attack.
How he saw Bastien, she had no idea. But he whipped around, grabbed
him, and slammed him to the mat, then kissed his cheek. "We have to
stop now." He jerked his chin toward her.

Bastien looked over and laughed. "Ah crap. Now I'm the one who
got you into trouble with your female."

Grinning roguishly, Jullien got up and offered Bastien his hand to help
him to his feet. Both of them were bruised, sweating and bleeding. Yet
neither seemed to care. They actually appeared elated. How? She had
*no* idea.

Males . . . she'd never understand them.

Ushara shook her head. "Really? This is how you wanted to say good-
bye to each other?"

Jullien rubbed sheepishly at his neck while Bastien went for towels. "We were just going to practice a bit. Then we got a little carried away."

"A *little*?" She glanced to the blood all over the mat, which looked as if someone had been murdered there and their body dragged away to be hidden.

Trajen joined them. "I'm impressed with you both."

Bastien handed a towel to Jullien before he wiped at the sweat and blood on his stomach, where he still bore his League Ravin mark. "Yeah, I had no idea Julie could do all that. I'd love to see him and Fain Hauk go at it. Julie's the only one I've ever fought who could drag my ass around a mat as much as Fain did."

"War Hauk Fain?" Jullien scowled.

"Yeah. I used to train with him when he lived on Kirovar."

Jullien wiped his face. "I had no idea you knew him."

"Small universe, right? I figured you two probably knew each other, since he and his brother went to your school when you were kids, but given how Anatoles feel about War Hauks, and War Hauks feel about Anatoles, and the long-standing feud between your lineages, I knew to never, *ever* mention to him or his brother that we were related or knew each other in *any* capacity. Andarions are a *highly* territorial and volatile species."

"Good call. They'd have killed you."

"Exactly." Bastien wiped at his face and shoulders. "Sorry about this, Ushara. Please don't harm my cousin. It was all my fault."

"Hardly. I'm the one who started it."

When they began to argue over blame, Ushara stopped them. "It's fine." She gently wiped at the blood on Jullien's lip. "I'm glad that your arm's working so well. But you shouldn't be stressing it so soon."

"I wasn't using it too much. I don't have precise control over it yet, and I didn't want to kill him."

Ushara sighed in bitter amusement. "So, Bas, since it's now so late, are you staying until morning?"

"Nah, I was going to head on, especially after I got Julie into trouble. Don't want to risk wearing out any more of my welcome."

Jullien dried his hair. "Where are you headed?"

"Starken. Then I'm after Barnabas."

Ushara cringed at the thought. "Alone?"

He nodded. "I don't have anyone else I trust, really. Don't want a stranger at my back. Not about to drag Julie or Fain into this. So if I fall, it's only on my ass. And there's no one to really grieve over it."

Ushara wrinkled her nose at him. "Why don't you hit the showers before you leave?"

"What? You saying I stink?"

Trajen snorted. "Well, you did just spend two hours beating the utter hell out of my field admiral. You both smell like something rotted and died. How Ushara can stand being this close to either of you while pregnant, I have no idea."

"Fine. I can take a hint." Bastien headed for the locker room.

As soon as he was gone, Ushara dug out her link.

Jullien scowled at her. "What are you doing?"

"Hailing someone. Obviously."

Jullien met Trajen's gaze. A cold feeling went through his gut at her unexpected vague answer. He was usually the evasive ass, not her. "Who?"

She ignored his question. "Hey, this is Admiral Samari. I know you requested reassignment yesterday and that we were meeting about it tomorrow. Believe it or not, something interesting came up tonight. It's an outside mission. For Kirovar, but it's something I think you might be interested in." She paused to listen. "Yeah. You want to meet us in the North Bay in a few minutes?" A smiled curved her lips. "Great. I'll see you then."

Trajen growled low in his throat. "Do you know what you're doing?"

"Yes."

Completely confounded as his powers failed him, Jullien turned toward Trajen. "Could someone clue *me* in?"

Ushara tucked her link away. "Jay has grounded herself for a few months. She wants to spend more time with her kids, and let her husband do the runs. So her crew requested temporary reassignments."

"Okay . . ."

"I'm thinking one of them would make a perfect point for Bastien."

While Jullien appreciated the thought, he knew that wouldn't play well with his cousin. Bas was even more paranoid than he was. And with good reason. Once you'd been through the kind of betrayal they'd suffered, it tended to stay with you.

"Shara . . . Bas isn't going to put someone at his back he doesn't know."

"Yeah, but she has Gyron Force training. He has to respect that."

It wouldn't matter. In fact, that could be worse. If they knew each other, it could even anger Bas.

Jullien pulled his shirt on and groaned out loud. "Trajen, tell her what a bad idea this is. For all we know, they could be enemies."

"I don't think so," Ushara insisted. "She left Kirovar and joined The Tavali because of the overthrow."

"What was her rank?"

"Major."

Trajen crossed his arms over his chest. "Let them meet. See if they get along."

He made it sound easy, but Jullien knew better. He also knew better than to argue with the two of them. They invariably won. Trajen because he wouldn't give in. Ushara because she fought dirty.

Jullien tossed the towel in a bin. "Fine. I don't want him to do this alone anyway."

By the time Bastien was finished and they were in the bay, Jullien was having doubts about saying good-bye. He had a bad feeling in his gut that something catastrophic was going to happen to Bastien. That they wouldn't see each other again.

"You sure you want to do this? You know you're welcome to stay."

Bastien clapped him on the back. "And you make it tempting. But I have to do this. I owe it to my family."

"I understand. If you need anything else . . ."

Bastien cast a playful grin at Ushara. "Really appreciate it, but I won't take you from your family. They need you more than I do." He held his hand out to Jullien. "You take care, *drey*."

"And you."

He inclined his head to Ushara, then shook Trajen's hand.

Suddenly, a shrill voice cut through the bay. "Bastien Cabarro . . . you lousy, worthless piece of human shit!"

The color fled from Bastien's cheeks as he stepped away from Trajen and they turned to see the Hadean Corps officer from Jay's crew. At average height for a human woman, she barely came up to Jullien's waist and the middle of Bastien's chest.

Dressed black on black, she had that familiar military swagger that was ingrained in any Gyron Force officer. And she stalked Bastien like she fully intended to gut him.

With a rusted-out can opener.

Bastien didn't move or speak. He just stood there, gaping at the slender auburn-haired Tavali.

She stopped in front of him, hands on hips. "Have you *nothing* to say to me?"

"I thought you were dead?"

Sneering at his answer, she grabbed his jacket and jerked him forward. Instead of hitting him, as Jullien had expected, she gave him a kiss that really should have been reserved for the bedroom.

Wide-eyed, Ushara glanced at Trajen, then Jullien. "I think they know each other."

With a stifled smile, Jullien ran his thumb over his bottom lip. "Uh, yeah, I'm going to bet on that, too. Either that, or the greetings on Kirovar have vastly improved since the last time I visited."

Bastien finally came up for air, but the grin on his face said that he might be staying a little bit longer on the station than he'd anticipated.

Until she kneed him in the groin. Hard. "That's for marrying my sister, you feckless bastard."

Hissing in pain, Bastien limped away from her, clutching at his groin. He glared at her and cursed. "You broke up with *me*! Remember?"

Unrepentant, she curled her lip. "I wanted some time to think about where we were heading. That wasn't an invitation for you to go bang my sister five minutes later."

He sneered at her. "I didn't just go *bang your sister*. And it damn sure was more than five minutes later." Straightening, he tried to level his breathing. "She asked *me* out. Then I asked *you* and *you* said *you* didn't care what, and I directly quote, or *who* I did."

"I. *Lied*," she snapped between gritted teeth. "Holy Jake! You were my wingman. You were supposed to be able to read my expressions and know me better than that!"

Bastien held his hands up. "Not Trisani, Ember. Don't read minds. You told me you wanted us to be friends, and your sister said you only went out with me because you didn't want to turn me down and hurt my feelings, since we were partners and I was a prince. How was I to know?"

Raking him with a glare, she made a sound of supreme disgust. "Gah! You were always so dense!" She turned toward Ushara. "Is he my assignment?"

"Uh . . ." She glanced about nervously. "Yes? But I'm going to assume you want to pass on it."

Ember narrowed her gaze on Bastien. "You going after your uncle?"

"Of course."

"Then I'm in."

Bastien snorted. "Uh, yeah, no. I don't think so. Especially not after *this*." He gestured toward his abused groin. "I don't need the cold-cocking. Trust me. Life's done it enough."

"Don't even, Cabarro. You won't last ten seconds without us in this fight. You want vengeance. So do we."

"Us?"

"Riot Squad. We all got left for dead."

Ushara glanced between them. "Riot Squad?"

"Special tactical unit of Gyron Force," Bastien explained. "Commanded by her mother." He returned his attention to Ember. "Did all of you make it out?"

She shook her head. "You're not the only one who lost that day."

"I'm sorry."

"Yeah, well, we all got wounds to lick. So am I in? Or you running suicide?"

Bastien picked up the bag she'd dropped by his feet and slung it over his back. "Don't drag your ass, Wildstar. I won't tolerate slack."

"I don't want to hear it, GG. I outrank you."

"GG?" Jullien asked Ember.

"Ghost Gadget. So named for the way he always found the right tool whenever we needed to blow something up in battle. Or could repair anything mechanical or electrical that broke down."

Ushara passed an amused smile to Jullien. "Like you."

Jullien didn't comment. "And Wildstar?"

"Based off my last name. Wyldestarrin."

"Yeah. Not even," Bastien scoffed. "So dubbed for her temperament and the fact that during training, she set fire to a fellow classmate's airbee when she caught him cheating on her."

"Something *you* should have kept in mind. Huh?"

"I didn't cheat on you. *You* broke up with me. How many times do I have to repeat that?"

"Asshole!" Shaking her head, she rolled her eyes. "I take it yours is the Sentella fighter?"

"Yes. Are we going to fight the whole way?"

"Probably."

"Oh dear gods . . ."

Jullien draped his arm around Ushara as they watched them leave. "I'm not sure how I feel about this. Tray?"

Trajen sighed heavily. "If they don't kill each other, they might work it out."

"The *might* in that sentence makes my sphincter clench."

Laughing, Trajen clapped Jullien on the back. "Good night, kids."

Ushara bit her lip as the bay quieted down with Bastien's launch. "I'm so sorry. I thought Ember would help."

"It's fine. You had no way of knowing they had history."

"Did you know?"

He shook his head. "I was at his wedding, but I only barely remember his wife, or the event as a whole. Was rather high at the time."

"Do I want to know?"

Jullien screwed his face up. "Probably not. It wasn't one of my better days."

Suddenly, Ushara's link went off. Pulling it out, she checked it to see a text from her family. A smile curved her lips as she saw them at Mary's. "Thrāix finally let my sister up for air." She held it for Jullien to see a photo of them all celebrating. "Shall we join them?"

"Absolutely. But first . . ." He wrapped his arms around her, beneath her breasts and above her distended belly, and held her for several minutes.

She could feel his erection against her hip, but he didn't do anything more than sway with her while his warm breath caressed her neck. "You all right?"

"Fine." He placed his hand to her stomach, where their son was currently turning flips. "He's really active."

"I know. He's been using my bladder for a trampoline for the last half hour."

He let out a low laugh near her ear that sent chills over her. "I still can't believe you're willing to go through labor again. You are out of your mind."

She ran her hand down his artificial arm. He hadn't said a single word about any of the operations he'd gone through over the last few weeks, or the pain of losing it. Nothing about the grafts that had failed and succeeded or the therapies he'd had to endure while relearning the simplest tasks, such as fastening his clothes or picking up a spoon. Holding a glass. Or learning to hold the girls with one arm because he feared harming them when he wasn't sure how to adequately control the pressure and grips of the artificial limb, and didn't trust it with them.

Never a complaint. He'd merely ground his teeth and rose to the challenge with an unfailing courage that still staggered her.

Compared to childbirth . . .

*That* was over in only a few hours. He was still having pain and undergoing physical therapy from his injuries.

"And if someone threw an IED at one of us, would you jump on top of it again?"

"Of course."

"What's the difference? At least at the end of my few hours of finite pain, I have an adorable baby to cuddle and hold."

She felt his smile against her cheek. "Never thought of it that way."

"Now, can you relax about childbirth?"

He laughed. "I don't like seeing you in pain."

"And you think I enjoy seeing you in pieces? Literally?" She leaned her head to the side so that she could look him in the eye. "Have you *any* idea how it felt to walk into that room and see you in the bed after the explosion?"

He visibly cringed. "I'm sorry."

"Not so sorry you wouldn't do it again."

He released a heavy sigh. "You married an inconsiderate, contentious asshole. You knew that. I came into this marriage with a disclaimer." Wrinkling his nose at her, he stepped back and held his arms out. "What did you expect?"

Growling at him, she lunged to playfully pop at his rear.

He sidestepped her with a laugh and shuffled away while she chased after him. "You're pretty spry for a shuttle craft."

"What?" she gasped, and chased him toward the edge of the bay, where Davel's ship was docked. "You did not go there!"

"Oh yeah, I did. After that crack you made this morning about my age when I groaned getting out bed?" He dodged her hand and twisted away. "I promise you, it's the mileage on my chassis more than the years."

"Uh-huh, sure it is. You keep believing those lies you tell yourself." She grabbed his shirt and tickled him.

Jullien surrendered, laughing. Cupping her face, he kissed her and breathed her in, grateful to the gods that she was part of his life.

"You two, again? I swear . . ."

He laughed as Sheila walked past them, grumbling. Pulling back, he nibbled at Ushara's cheek, watching Sheila head toward her office. Until his gaze went toward Davel's most recent acquisition. And an idea struck him. "Hey . . . have you ever been inside a Gondarion luxury cruiser?"

Ushara gave him a suspicious stare. "I know that look in those stralen eyes. That's *not* what you're thinking."

He flashed a wicked grin at her. "Ever had sex in a Gondarion luxury cruiser?"

She rolled her eyes at him. "The answer to both questions is no, I haven't."

He lifted her hand to nibble playfully at her fingertips. "Would you like to?"

"My family's waiting."

"Fifteen minutes."

"You *never* take fifteen minutes."

He snorted. "Not true."

She laughed as she reconsidered that. "You rarely take fifteen minutes, and you haven't been on a run in months. Besides, you're all sweaty."

He kissed and licked at her palm. "I'd get all sweaty by the time I finished, anyway. You've never complained about that before. Besides, you always say you like the way I smell when I sweat." He nuzzled her neck.

Ushara sucked her breath in as chills spread through her body. She was trying so hard to be good and resist him. But he was making it exceptionally difficult. And he was right. She loved the way he smelled. There was something about the scent of his skin that was irresistible to her, especially whenever she was pregnant. She just wanted to bury her face in the crook of his neck and inhale his scent all night long. Her favorite thing was to lie in his arms and breathe him in. He was intoxicating.

And before she knew what she was doing, she followed him as he broke into the access panel and got on board faster than most who had the actual codes for it. "Should I even ask how a prince learned to do that?"

"You've seen my arrest records. I used to boost the Overseer's personal shuttles for joyrides as a kid anytime I got near them."

"Why?"

He shrugged. "Was trying to stay away from home for awhile. Kept hoping if I did it enough, the Gondarions would keep me in their lockup. Or call my father rather than my grandmother."

"Did it ever work?"

"Sadly, no. Since my father wasn't my legal guardian, his secretary refused to put the calls through regarding my arrests. They shunted the calls back to Andaria. And if by some mirable, I ever got through to my father, he refused to bail me out."

Ushara didn't miss the sadness that always darkened his eyes whenever they spoke about his past. While he'd come a long way with putting it to rest and letting it all go, there was still a part of his heart they owned. A part she couldn't quite chisel free from their cruel grasp, no matter how hard she tried. And it pained her deep inside to see the lasting damage it did to his soul.

Taking her hand, he led her inside the cruiser. *Luxury* was definitely the word for it.

She let out a low whistle at the incredibly opulent interior. No expense had been spared. "Is that gold on the ceiling?"

Jullien smiled. "Yeah. And on the trim and in the paint. It's why it glistens like that."

"Do I want to know the cost of this?"

"Probably not."

She stopped to run her hand over the gold veining in the titanium walls. "Did you take this for granted?"

"I'm not sure I know what you're asking."

"The wealth. What was it like to have all the credits you could possibly dream of, and not have to think twice about spending them?"

"Truth?"

She nodded.

"I was so worried about someone sliding a dagger in my back, poisoning my food, or setting an explosion for me that I never really enjoyed any of it. I'd have much rather been worried about debt than death." He opened a panel to expose a bar. A wide smile curved his lips. "Remember the first night you took me home? The alcohol I mentioned that would leave your panties on the floor?" Wagging his eyebrows, he pulled a bottle from the shelf.

She laughed at his eager playfulness. "My brother will expect payment for that, you know."

"Your brother has no idea how much this is worth . . . unless *you* tell him. Besides, he owes me."

"For what?"

"I fell on a friggin' bomb for him and his kids. Lost an arm."

She laughed even harder as he poured a glass. "You're so bad."

"Yeah, but you love that about me."

" 'Deed I do."

He handed the glass to her.

She shook her head. "You know I can't drink that while pregnant."

"One tiny sip won't hurt him. Believe me. I should have been born pickled. You have to taste it."

"One sip." She dipped her finger in and lifted it to her lips, then almost moaned out loud at how good it was. "Oh my . . ."

Jullien smiled knowingly. "Told you."

"I've never tasted anything so sublime."

"I have. Better even."

"I can't imagine anything better." She dipped her finger in again for one more tiny sample. "What in the universe could top this?"

Jullien leaned down to capture her lips with his. "The taste of *you*."

Those words melted her heart. "You were wrong, my darkest heart. It's not the wine that leaves my head in the clouds. It's ever you."

Jullien set his glass down on the shelf behind her before he pulled the hem of her skirt up. Ushara's heart raced as his ragged breath burned against her throat. She fumbled with his battlesuit, hating how hard it was to open. She despised anything that ever came between them.

Sinking her hands into his thick hair, she reclaimed his lips while he ran his hands over her breasts and his tongue tormented her ear with a sensual rhythm that left her breathless and hot.

He sucked his breath in sharply the moment she cupped him. She adored the sounds he made whenever she held him like this. And especially the tender, sweet way he looked at her. As if she was his reason for being alive.

Smiling, she touched his lips. "Love you."

He took her hand and led it to his cheek. Closing his eyes, he held it there. "Love you so much more." Then he lifted her up in that effortless way that made her feel so dainty and slid inside her.

Ushara groaned out loud as he filled her completely. She wrapped her arms around his shoulders and held him close as he slowly thrust against her hips. In spite of his earlier words, he was taking his time with her. There was no hurry to him at all as he savored each and every stroke.

Jullien nibbled at Ushara's chin as he watched the pleasure play across her face. There was nothing he enjoyed more than watching her when he was inside her. She was the only one who'd ever fully accepted him. Not once had she recoiled from his scars. Not even before they'd reattached his arm.

She'd stood by his side in a way no one ever had. In a way he'd never thought possible. He'd never known the kind of friendship, loyalty, and love she'd given him. Never imagined having a lover like her. Someone he could tease and laugh with, but never with mean-spirited barbs that left his soul bleeding and his heart scarred.

He had no right to the life she'd given him, and he knew it. It was why he couldn't shake the feeling that something was going to happen to take him away from her.

Something bad.

Happy endings didn't come to eton Anatoles. And they damn sure didn't come to creatures who'd lived a life like his.

Ushara's laughter filled his ears an instant before she came in his arms. Cupping her face, he smiled down at her as he watched the ecstasy play across her features. Patiently, he waited for her to finish, and then he joined her with one last fierce stroke where he buried himself deep inside her body and growled from the ferocity of his release.

Not just from that, but from the intensity of what he felt for her. The depth of his love and the need to protect her and their children. To make sure they remained safe, no matter what hell came to the rest of the universe.

He tightened his arms around her. "I have to say, that was much better than any dream I ever carried about it."

Tilting her head, she frowned up at him. "Are you telling me you've never done this before?"

"Never. Just a fantasy I've always had. Thank you for indulging me." He took the wine and downed it in one gulp.

"Hey!"

He gave her an unrepentant smile. "You're not supposed to have any in your condition."

She pouted.

Laughing at her misery, he opened the cabinet. "There are three bottles in there. I'll confiscate one more and pay Davel for the two. The second one I'll save, and we'll use it to celebrate the birth of our son after you wean him."

She smiled at his generous thoughtfulness. "Davel will forgive you, then . . . and so will I."

With an adorable grin, Jullien straightened his clothes, then bent over to retrieve her panties from the floor. He knelt dutifully in front of her and helped her dress, but not without lifting her skirt to place a lingering kiss to her stomach. She smiled down at him as his whiskers tickled her skin.

He splayed his hand beside her navel, where Vidarr rested. "Is he sleeping?"

The baby moved away as if he'd heard him.

She brushed her hand through his hair. "Not now."

Kissing her stomach again, Jullien lowered her skirt into place and rose to his feet. "Sorry."

"No, you're not," she teased.

The gleam in his eyes agreed with her as he poured himself another glass of wine, and he recorked the bottle for later.

Ushara couldn't resist exploring the ship a bit more. "This is quite decadent, isn't it?"

"Very much so."

"Who do you think owned it?"

"Let's take a look." He paused by a panel and turned it on.

She watched in quiet amazement as he quickly navigated the alien system that appeared to be written in gibberish. "What language is that? Can you read it?"

"Yeah. It's Gondarion. Vertan syntax with a Darish alphabet."

She didn't even understand what he was talking about. "How do you know that?"

"You married a freak." He scowled and snorted. "But apparently, not as big a freak as the Gondarion senator who owned it. He has quite the collection of porn." He stepped back and covered the screen with his hand. "Oh dear gods . . . I just went blind. Remind me to call my mother later tonight. I definitely need to confess my sins."

She laughed.

Until he uncovered the screen, flipped away from it, and the humor fled his features.

"What is it?"

Jullien didn't comment as his scowl deepened while he read whatever had his attention.

"Jules?"

"This is bad."

"What?"

"It's an attack plan, Shara. A confidential e-mail sent to the senator from Kyr, updating him on League actions against Andaria to bring them back into line and on The Sentella to crush them."

She gasped. "On what?"

"A Sentella base and two heavily populated Andarion outposts."

"Do we have time to warn them?"

Jullien clicked through the code. "It's encrypted. This is going to take me a while. You go on to your sister, and I'll work on it."

"Are you sure?"

"Yeah, I'll be fine."

"Okay. But I'm sending Sheila in here to watch over you."

He smiled at her. "Still don't trust me alone, huh? Fine. I would complain, except your worry is justified." He gave her a quick kiss and kept working, while his brain spun even faster. The last thing he wanted was to panic anyone.

Yet if he was reading this correctly . . .

Kyr was about to unleash holy hell on the entire Ichidian universe and all of them were going to feel that psycho's fury.

Especially those of them who flew outside traditional nations. And that was all Tavali.

*Shit.*

# CHAPTER 37

Jullien pushed open the door to Trajen's study to find his friend sitting in front of an old Trisani altar. The sight of him there caught him completely off-guard. "So you're not as anti-religion as you pretend."

Trajen sighed. "Let's keep this embarrassing little secret between us."

"You shouldn't be embarrassed."

Trajen blew out his prayer candle. "We're not here to talk about my secret religious habits."

"I can come back. I didn't mean to interrupt your Vespers."

Trajen made a sound of extreme irritation. "How much of my culture did you study, boy? Shit . . . I swear you know more about it than Thrāix, and he was raised in it."

"You really want to be impressed? Ask me about the Caronese, Phrixians, or Gourish. . . . Or Hyshians, for that matter. I spent way too much time in the repositories."

Trajen harumphed. "Out of curiosity, how many languages are you fluent in?"

"Counting gibberish and the twin speak of my girls?"

"Sure. Why not?"

"I don't know. About sixty-seven, roughly . . . with varying dialects."

"H-o-l-y shit. And neither of your parents ever had a clue?"

Jullien shrugged nonchalantly. "They never really spoke to me in any known language."

Trajen shook his head as he continued to tuck away his altar pieces in the ornate polished case that blended in seamlessly with the rest of his antique furniture. If you didn't know what it was, you'd never guess he had an altar on the premises. "Anyway, why are you in my home, annoying me?"

"I just spoke to my cousin, Bastien. And I'm here to revisit a sore topic."

Trajen released a foul curse that probably undid every bit of his evening prayers. "Let's go through the last three to four dozen of these we've had, shall we? I'm going to ask why. You're going to say that you think it's for everyone's good. I'm going to snort. You're going to say something smart-ass and piss me off. Is that it, roughly?"

"Basically. With a slight variation."

"And that is?"

"I tried to warn them about the last attack, and because we remain so isolated from the other Nations and I couldn't lay ears to Chayden or Jory"—and because of his history with Ryn and Darling, he hadn't dared attempt to contact Ryn or Mack—"no one took it seriously. They lost over three hundred people and had almost a thousand wounded. You know how hard we tried to mobilize Alliance forces. This time, The League's going after Hermione Dane and intending to bring her down and plant Ryn's bones on top of her grave. More than that, did you know Ryn was married?"

Trajen rose to his feet. "What? When?"

"Mack Hinto." Jullien crossed his arms over his chest. "Last night, Jory called to tell me that Mack just learned days ago that she's carrying the magic Dane heir who will one day unite three of the four branches of Tavali. 'Cause everyone knows that you might as well be Hermione's other blood-born son. How do you think Venik will react when this news hits him? More to the point, what do you think Nyran and Malys will do when they find out the Portnums are about to be a stand-alone Nation, subjugated to the whims of the Fetchyn who inherits that Tavali seat of power? 'Cause the next generation of Tavali HAPs will most likely all be related by blood."

Trajen gaped. "Why did Jory call you?"

"In the event Mack has to go into hiding with the pregnancy, he wanted to know if they could bring her here. I told him we'd be fine with it. Said you had plenty of room in your house for her."

"Excuse me? You said what?"

Jullien laughed. "Relax, Yaya. I offered her the spare suite in the new place we're buying. But I do like the panic in your eyes just now at the thought of you having to share space. Nice." He approached the altar, where Trajen had an extremely old and ragged copy of the Book of Harmony resting on top of it. It was obviously a family heirloom that he must have salvaged from the destruction of his homeworld—which said a lot, given how unsentimental Trajen was.

His gaze went to the mantel, where a small handful of photos were lined up. Trajen's sister with Thrāix. Ryn Dane as a child with his mother. Varys Dane, Hermione's brother who'd been killed years ago, standing with a teenaged Hermione. Ushara holding an infant Vasili at his exordiom. And the rarest of all—Trajen at the first birthday party for the twins, where they stood on each side of him, kissing his cheeks.

The surly bastard was actually smiling in that one. For whatever reason, Trajen loved Jullien's girls as much as he and Ushara did. And they and Vas were what had made this decision so hard for Jullien. Why he hadn't come to it lightly. But why he felt it had to be done.

"Like it or not, Tray, we have to choose a side to fight on, especially after I saw the hatred the League prime commander has for Tavali. I assume you want to go down protecting the Danes, and now the Hintos since they're married to them."

"And what about you?"

"My loyalty is here. To you and my family."

"No, it isn't. You're divided."

"Not divided at all. My first priority is, and will always be, Ushara. Then you."

"And your brother?"

Jullien looked away. "That's guilt. Plain and simple. Not loyalty."

"I'm proud you recognize that."

"I have no delusions where my birth family's concerned. I've never lied to myself about who and what I am or what I feel."

Trajen looked to the photos. "Family is a complicated thing, Jules. Careful where it leads you."

"I know. But no one will take me from my wife or children."

Nodding, Trajen fell quiet for several minutes while he considered the request.

Finally, he spoke. "You win. I'll do this for you. But only because *you've* asked it. You know how I feel about fighting in a political war. And I trust you alone to lead us. When you've had enough and you're done with them, we're out."

"I'll let Jory know we're in." Jullien inclined his head to him and started to withdraw.

"Hey, Jules?"

He paused to look back.

"Thank you."

That earnest gratitude confused him. "For what?"

"You think that I saved you by letting you stay here and earn rank. But the truth is, we both were given a shot out of a dark place. And Thrāix, too. He and I had died, we just hadn't found our tombs yet. Or maybe had. At any rate, we owe you as much as you think you owe us . . . maybe more. Just so you know."

Jullien grimaced. "So what? Are we going to kiss now? Gah, just don't fondle me in my marital bed again. I'm still having nightmares that Ushara's going to find out and geld us both."

Trajen laughed. "Get your cantankerous Andarion ass out of here."

"I'm going," Jullien said with a laugh of his own.

Still smiling, he left Trajen's house and headed for Ushara's office to let her know that they were now officially part of the Alliance against The League.

He'd just headed that way when his link buzzed. Assuming it was the babysitter telling him to come home and help with the twins, who were probably climbing up the walls again, he tapped his ear. "Admiral Samari."

"Hey, Dagger, this is Kareem Venik. Are you where you can talk free and clear?"

"Yeah. What's going on?"

Static answered him for a minute before Kareem dropped his voice two octaves. "Look, I got some intel, and I don't know what to do with it."

"What do you mean?"

"I overheard something I wasn't supposed to, and I'm not sure it's important, but given how it was said, and who said it, I'm certain it was. That being said, if anyone finds out I know it, or that I breathed a word to someone else . . . let's just say I need some real discretion."

"Okay."

"Anyway. It was something about the *skyva* being plowed down and replanted for the *lyfera* to return from the ashes."

His mind raced at what Kareem was saying. The *lyfera* was the mythological creature that decorated the Anatole family Warsword and coat of arms. A winged dragon, it was believed to burst open the womb of its parent, which it then consumed until nothing was left of its mother but ashes. Thereby, the child *lyfera* absorbed and took its first nourishment and life from its mother's essence and knowledge. Of course, family tradition said that it symbolized the fact that a new tadar or tadara couldn't ascend the throne until the death of their parent, after they stood over the funeral pyre to take their inheritance.

*Skyva* was the Andarion word for a Warsword's scabbard or for the main palace in Eris that "held" the royal family.

A bad feeling went through Jullien. . . .

"I'm sorry, Kareem. Could you repeat that?"

"The *skyva* is going to be plowed down and replanted for the *lyfera* to return from the ashes. . . . Does that make sense to you?"

His heart pounded as he checked the date on his link.

Six days.

*Oh shit.*

"Yeah, Kareem. It makes sense. Thanks for telling me. I need to go." He cut the transmission.

*Six days . . .*

His breathing ragged, he ran to Ushara's office as fast as he could. As soon as he flew past Zellen's desk, Zellen gasped but didn't say anything.

Jullien hit the release for Ushara's door and didn't speak until it closed behind him.

She swallowed and set her drink aside, then scowled at his eagerness. "Rare look for you. Holy terror? Haven't seen it on your face since you thought Mira had fallen and skinned her knee. What's wrong?"

"My grandmother's going to bomb the Andarion palace in six days."

Ushara froze as those words hung between them. "Trajen tell you this?"

"Kareem Venik overheard it."

"From?"

"I'm assuming Nyran."

"But you don't know . . . so it could be a trap."

"It's not. Shara, I know it's going to happen. Six days. That's Eriadne's birthday. And it's not just that. It's the way the message was coded. . . . *Mia,* you've just got to trust me on this. I know it's solid."

"Okay, so we tell them."

"You know they won't believe us."

Stubbornly, she shook her head. "They can fortify themselves. They have an army."

He raked his hand through his hair. "It didn't work last time. Shara, you know it's not that simple. I know the players involved and how they do these things. . . . She's going to kill my brother's family while he's away and can't protect them. Even if he believed us and turned around right now, he couldn't get back before her fleet would reach them."

Jullien ground his teeth at the cruelty of what his grandmother intended to do to her own blood kin. "It's a blow to him that he'll never recover from. And she knows it. This will destroy his life and his soul. Do you understand? I heard from Jory just last night that Nyk's on his way to the Ports, and he's having to fly dark so that The League won't pick up their transmissions. He thinks his wife and kids are safe with my idiot mother. His youngest daughter's what? Seven, eight months old now? The rest aren't much older. Kiara's a *minsid* moron. She's not you. She has no idea how to fight or survive, never mind protect those kids. They won't see this coming. If we call, they'll hang up on us like they did last time, and do nothing. They'll all be dead in less than a week."

"So what do you suggest?"

Jullien's brain whirled as he considered how to deal with this. "I have to kill Eriadne."

"Great plan. Little shy on details. As I recall, you've been trying to do that for years now. Hasn't really worked out."

He gave her a peeved glare. "Fine. Take the kids and do what we planned last night before I got Trajen to agree to cooperate with The Alliance. You head on to the Ports for the meeting with Jory and the Danes. I'll get Nyk's wife and kids and meet you there, with them in tow."

"What about your mother?"

"I don't give a *minsid* shit what happens to her. She's on her own. Like you said, she's got an army. My only concern is protecting my brother—after what I personally did to him, I owe him that much. I've done him enough harm. I will not let that bitch gut him this way. Not when I can stop it."

"You're just getting Kiara and the children?"

"Swear it. In and out. Small strike force. Walk in the park. Then we're headed straight for you, and everyone's happy."

"Okay. But only because there are babies involved. And I want you to take Thrāix with you, in case something weird happens."

"Yeah, that's not going to happen. You can't pry him off Mary. He hasn't come up for air since her return."

"He will go with you. Mary will see to it."

He laughed. "In that case, I believe you. She's the only one who could make him. But damn, Shara, he's going to be an irritable, unmanageable ass the whole trip. Why would you do that to me?"

She gave him a gimlet glare. "Because I love you, and you will *not* get hurt. You hear me?"

"Yes, Mistress Tormentor. I will *not* get hurt." He spoke in the tone of a mindless android.

"I mean it, Jules."

He winked at her. "So do I. I want all of you safe and protected, too. No chances."

She released a voice that said he was being ridiculous. "You know me better. Besides, I'm not the one who finds trouble in every shadow I cross. I swear I know where the girls get it." She rubbed her stomach. "May the gods have mercy on us all if this poor boy has one tenth of your proclivity for danger."

He kissed her cheek. "He won't."

"Better not. Otherwise, I'm beating you every time *he* gets into something he should have left alone."

"Me?"

"*You,* since it's obviously something genetically wrong with *your* bloodline."

"Oh yeah," Jullien said in a tone saturated with sarcasm, " 'cause *your* brothers *never* do *any*thing wrong. Your gene pool is *so* perfect." He choked and scoffed. "As I recall, when you picked me up in jail, I was handcuffed to one of your brothers."

"You're not helping yourself out of the dog house," she called after him.

As usual, he paid her no heed.

Ushara watched as Jullien left her office with a devilish grin that made her a lot hotter than it should, given her level of agitation at him. Anyone else would be grounded for that cocky swagger and the fact they'd pissed her off and ruined her mood.

Why she found his insolence adorable and charming, she had no idea. There was something innately affable about him whenever he chose to let that side of his personality out.

Sadly, he kept it hidden most of the time behind a wall of impenetrable suspicion. It was a shame, really. That kind of charisma was so rare. And with it, he could have been one of the most influential rulers in history.

Instead, he was content to be Trajen's eyes and ears on their fleet. Her heavy hand and enforcer whenever she needed it. While she was grateful that the gods had given him to her to have as her own, his wasted potential bothered her at times. The injustice of it.

But what truly made her ache was the shadow in the back of his eyes that never left. Even at his happiest, it forever lurked there, and nothing banished it completely. Like the real Dagger Ixur of their mythology, it was as if his family had splintered his heart and kept a part of it with them. A part that wouldn't allow him to live in peace.

Over the years, she'd done everything she could to make him forget them. To bring him home to her and their children.

Yet that other missing piece forever called him back to Andaria. Back to the cruelty that had birthed him.

He always denied it. And still she saw it clearly, even when he did his best to hide all traces.

Her greatest hope was that one day he'd wake up and think of them no more. That the light would shine again fully and that the missing piece would return so that his eyes would glow with a soul restored.

*You're a dreamer.*

*That* restoration of her own heart, she owed solely to Jullien. Chaz had crushed that part of her soul. He'd made her a pragmatic military commander. Jullien had taught her magic again. He'd returned her sense of whimsy.

So yes, she now believed in dreams once more.

And one day, she was going to exorcize those demons from her husband's heart.

Worried, and dreading the thought of what lay ahead, Jullien carried the twins on board their mother's ship, with Vasili trailing behind him. The boy had been complaining every step of the way here, until his voice rang like a cacophonous symphony in his ears.

"I don't understand why I have to fly with Mum. Why can't I come with you? I'm assigned to the *Pet Hate*. I'm your crew, Paka."

Jullien sighed. "I know, Vas. But I need you to guard your mom and sisters for me. I can't be in two places at once. So I have to depend on you for this."

Vasili rolled his eyes in typical teenage exasperation. Probably because he knew Jullien was lying and this was as much about keeping Vasili out of danger as it was keeping Ushara and the girls safe.

Mira snorted. "Vasi don't like that answer, Paka."

"Yeah, I know." He kissed her cheek. "And I need you two to be on your very best behavior for your matarra and Vasili. No making your brother crazy. Okay?"

"Okay."

He turned to her sister. "Viv?"

"Okies, Paka. No crazy." She stuck her tongue out to roll it around her mouth, then in and out, and her eyes around and around in a way that made him choke on his laughter.

Clearing his throat to conceal it, he forced himself to appear stern. "Good girls. Now, give me a kiss." He squeezed them and savored their embrace for a moment before he reluctantly let go.

He stood to face his irritated teenaged son. "Yes, it sucks. But . . ."

Vas sighed in resignation. "I'll miss you. Be safe."

"You, too." He hugged him. "Don't kill your sisters."

"I won't."

"And no locking them in a closet."

"That's too many restrictions. Now you're just being mean."

Jullien laughed at Vas's devilish grin. Ruffling his hair, he left him and went to say good-bye to Ushara. She was with Zellen and Unira. "Stay safe. Fly outside their tracking."

"And you."

Jullien took her hand in his and kissed her knuckles before he gently kissed her lips. He placed his hands around her stomach so that he could feel Vidar frolicking. "He feels like he's ready to lend a hand."

"Indeed. He might get out and push."

Shaking his head, he snorted at her humor. "Don't you dare have him without me."

"Trust me, I won't. I live too much to torture you."

Jullien kissed her one more time before he hugged Unira and inclined his head to Zellen. "Take care."

"And you, *m'tana*." Unira kissed his cheek.

With a heavy heart and his stomach knotted from the pain of being separated from them, Jullien waited until they'd launched before he went to the *Pet Hate*. As a safeguard against his shitty luck, they were flying this mission in two ships . . . just in case they had mechanical trouble of any kind. His and Davel's.

He tapped his link. "Dagger to Krunch. You ready for launch?"

"I'm with you, *drey*. All the way to Tophet and back."

"Let's hope it doesn't come to that. With any luck, we'll be back in a couple of days. No sweat. No drama."

Thrāix started the engines while Jullien closed the ramp. But as he swept his gaze over the bay and he saw Sheila smiling while she waved a friendly good-bye at him, a weird sense of foreboding went through him as he returned her gesture.

Trying to shrug it off, he headed for the flight deck to take his seat and head them to Andaria.


"I still don't understand why we don't use the pass for us to land in the main hangar bay," Davel groused. "This is a long effing walk."

Letting out an irritated sigh, Jullien passed a droll stare to Thrāix. "Whose bright idea was it to bring him?"

Thrāix growled low in his throat. As Jullien predicted, he'd been a surly asshole the entire time, due to his involuntary separation from his wife. "His."

"Then why's he bitching?"

"Apparently, he has a death wish."

"Just checking." Jullien glared at his brother-in-law over his shoulder. "But if he doesn't stop, I'm going to put a bark collar on him."

Gallatin covered her laugh with a cough. Axl wasn't so kind—he laughed until Davel shoved him.

Skipping to Jullien's side, Axl grabbed his arm. "Protect me, big brother!"

With a snort, Jullien playfully wrapped a light choke hold around him. "I'll keep you safe, little one. You've always been my favorite, anyway."

"Och," Davel mocked. "That's just rude. Holidays are coming up. I will remember this when it's time for you two jackals to want to hide out from the screaming family horde. No male cave privileges for you. Me and Thrāix, we *dreys*. We going to be laughing our asses off at you two and your communal misery."

"Yeah, yeah," Jullien said with a laugh. "If being surrounded by family who loves me during a holiday week is torture, then chain me to the wall." He sobered as they neared the palace grounds.

This was going to be interesting. . . .

Pulling his Tavali mask and helmet over his face, he let Thrāix take the lead. The last thing they could afford was for anyone here to recognize him in any way. If they did, they'd automatically assume he was working for his grandmother, and they'd all be arrested.

Rather, the game plan was that they'd tell Kiara they had orders from The Sentella to evacuate her and her children to Nyk's Arcadian base, which was on the outer reaches of this galaxy. Once they had her off the planet, they'd take her to the Porturnum StarStation and turn her and the kids over to his brother.

Simple.

She couldn't check with Nyk, as he was en route and flying through League-controlled space at the moment, with his high command. No one else would have knowledge of Nyk's orders to move his family—paranoid bastard would never leave something like that as public record.

If she wanted to talk to Tavali, they had that covered with their people, who would back their story.

Just a few more minutes, they'd be out of here. Kiara would never know Jullien was Jullien, and they would all sleep in peace tonight.

Thrāix approached the guard station and exposed his face. Like Jullien, he held the bearing of nobility and military command. It bled from every gesture and pore, and the guards knew it. They snapped to attention immediately.

"Commander?" The head guard moved forward to address them. "What's this about?"

Thrāix pulled out his orders. "Sorry to bother you so late, *Dryht*. As you can see, we have orders from His Highness to secure his family. We have reason to believe that a threat is imminent."

"Why didn't he send Sentella?"

Thrāix arched a condemning brow. "I'm a commander. My place isn't to question direct orders when they're given to me. It's to carry them out. I guess the Andarion military ranks follow a different protocol."

"Forgive me." He stepped back and buzzed them in, then motioned for a unit of guards to escort them to the palace entrance.

As they walked into his former home, through the front door and down the elegant main marble hallway, Jullien let them take lead and pulled point. He scanned every shadow they passed for any signs of his grandmother's attack. So far, it appeared their luck was holding and they'd beaten her forces here.

But as they turned down the family wing and he passed the door to his old room, he wasn't quite prepared for the unexpected blow it gave him, especially since that the door was slightly ajar, allowing him to see that it'd been completely redecorated for Nykyrian's oldest daughter. Not that he begrudged Thia having his room. He couldn't care less about that.

What stung was the memory of how his mother had treated Nyk's room for all the years his brother had been gone. No one had ever been allowed to enter it. To touch a single item that had belonged to Nyk. Not even to clean it. It had been sealed off as a holy shrine. If anyone so much as touched the doorknob, his mother would demand they be beaten for it.

He still had scars from the one and only time he'd made the mistake of venturing into it—one night a month after the funeral, when he'd gone in there seeking solace. All he'd done was lie on the bed and hold his brother's stuffed animal because he missed Nykyrian and wanted to feel his presence again.

His mother had reacted as if he'd devoured a living infant.

Obviously *his* room and personal effects weren't so important to her. She'd probably had a bonfire after Tylie drove him out at blasterpoint.

*Don't think about it.*

The guardsmen knocked on Kiara's door.

Her secretary answered a few seconds later with a stern frown.

"Sorry to disturb you, but we need to speak to Her Highness. We have an urgent message from the tahrs."

"I shall get her." She opened the door to admit them to the receiving room that was reserved for special dignitaries and visiting friends and family. This had been Tylie's room back in the day. . . .

His breathing ragged, Jullien hovered in the doorway while the others stood, waiting.

With her dark auburn hair braided, Kiara came out in a thick blue robe. A former dancer, she had perfect posture and the most delicate of features. Damn, he'd forgotten how tiny and frail she was. A gust of wind could snap her in two.

Confused, she glanced around their small group. "Is something wrong?"

Thrāix smiled warmly. "No, Your Highness. We're Tavali, and we've been sent to take you and your children to a secured Sentella base for Commander Quiakides. Just a precaution. But we need to hurry. Time is critical."

"What about the others?"

Thrāix scowled. "What others?"

"Shahara, Zarya, Ture, Desideria, and their kids. And Darling and Aros. Not to mention Kasen. They're all here, too."

Jullien let out a fetid curse. "That's why they're hitting it. Minsid hell! They're taking out the whole high command in one blow tonight."

Thrāix nodded in agreement. "We've got to get them out of here. Now!"

The guards turned on them.

Thrāix and Jullien used their powers to disarm them.

"Don't," Jullien snarled as he started to slap the guard nearest him. "We're not your enemies." He stepped closer to Kiara. "Highness, I know you don't know us, and that you can't get ahold of your husband to verify what we're saying, but you have to trust us. We are here to protect you. No deceit. No lies. Your safety and that of your children is all that matters to us. We need you to gather up every member of The Sentella's family under this roof so that we can evacuate all of you to a Sentella-held safe zone immediately. The League is en route, and they're coming for all of you."

"I believe you." She turned to her secretary. "Gather my children to the hall outside the tadara's room. Hurry! Don't dress them. Just grab a coat and go." She took Jullien's arm and pulled him after her. "Follow me, and we'll wake the others."

Something that wasn't too difficult until they got to Darling Cruel. First, they interrupted him in the middle of a very private moment with his wife, which pissed him off to no end, and almost blinded their entire group, as none of them, with the possible exception of Gallatin, wanted to see that much of the man's bare arse.

Or other naked body parts.

Second, the Sentella high commander and Caronese emperor wasn't used to taking orders from anyone except Jullien's brother.

Maybe Ryn.

Neither of whom was currently here. So, holding a sheet around his waist, Darling glared angrily at them and refused to cooperate. "I haven't heard any of this. What attack? Who's your source?"

Even more irritable by nature than Darling, Thrāix barked orders that said, *Hey, I'm in charge. Fuck off*! "We have the intel. It's legit. We need to go. Now. I'm not getting caught in this shit because you're an idiot." He gestured at Darling's groin. "Cover *that* and join us, or we're leaving you to fend for yourself. We came to secure the princess and her children for Commander Quiakides. Those are my orders that I'm standing on. Rest of you . . . collateral damage, as far as I'm concerned. Come or go. I don't give a flying shit."

Jullien released a tired sigh. "Yeah, you never worked in an embassy."

He turned that exasperated glare to Jullien. "No *scytel*, *drey*. Son of the vice-praetor. Draconarion decurion. Our unofficial motto was, Behave. Begone. Or be killed. I don't like my authority challenged. Even by *you*."

Jullien held his hands up. "I know better, *frater meus. Pax tecum.* No shooting the Dagger. Lower your hostility." He turned toward Darling. "Majesty . . . worst case, you lost some sleep for nothing. You wake up in your Sentella base. Everyone's grumpy but healthy. But if our intel is right, you, your son, and wife are about to be in the middle of a war zone and air strike. Is this really where you want them when it starts?"

He pulled his blaster out and offered it to Darling, grip first, showing him that it had a full charge. "We're on your side, Majesty. My Tavali father is Trajen Dane Thaumarturgus. I'm not about to let any son of Hermione's be harmed. And Trajen would cut my throat himself if I spilled one drop of Dane blood."

Darling inclined his head and pushed the blaster back toward Jullien. "*That* I believe. Especially since you said his name correctly and without stumbling over it. Only someone who knows him intimately can do that. Where are we meeting?"

"Hallway."

"Be there in two minutes."

As they headed out the door, Thrāix paused and listened.

Jullien knew that look. One heartbeat later, he felt it, too. "They're here."

Thrāix met his gaze. "We don't have time to clear the palace. They'll hit us before he can make it to the gate. We'll be in the open if we run for it."

"Get everyone to the queen's bedroom. Now! In her closet there's a doorway to an underground prison. It's reinforced enough, it should withstand the impact." He sent a mental image of its location to Thrāix. "Go!"

While he went ahead, Jullien ran back to check on Kiara, who had yet to leave her room.

"Highness?" he called from the doorway. "We have to go."

Distraught and frenzied, she searched the room violently. "I can't find Zarina's woobie. She can't sleep without it. I put her to bed with it and now it's gone!"

Damn. As the parent of two stubborn toddlers, he well understood that. There was nothing in the universe more unreasonable than a petulant child at bedtime.

Just when Jullien thought it couldn't get worse, his father walked in, holding a sleeping Zarina. "I looked all through the nursery. I didn't see it in there, either."

His father's unexpected presence slammed into him like a sledgehammer to his stones.

For a full minute, Jullien couldn't breathe. He couldn't move. He hadn't seen his father since the night Nykyrian had held him against the wall at Camry's and threatened to blow his brains out. His father had just stood there, saying nothing. Had Nyk pulled the trigger, his father wouldn't have done anything to stop it.

Aros probably would have applauded, then cursed Jullien's corpse for daring to make an inconsiderate mess for the staff to clean up.

Worse, Jullien remembered the sight of his father turning his back and walking away to callously leave him in the care of strangers after he'd choked him to death.

He'd never once in the whole of Jullien's life held him with the care he was now using to cradle Kiara's daughter.

The whistling sound of a missile drop in the distance finally shook him out of his stupor.

"What does her woobie look like?" he asked Kiara.

"It's a fox blanket."

Shots sounded outside in the palace yard. Lights from blasters lit up the windows. His father went stark white and almost dropped the baby as Zarina woke up and let out a foul, terrified scream.

Cursing him, Jullien took Zarina and handed her to her mother, then pushed his father toward the queen's bedroom. "To the tadara's chamber!"

He pulled his armor-plated jacket off and wrapped it around Kiara's shoulders before he gently and carefully tucked his niece against his chest with his cyber-arm. It was stronger and would protect her from a blast.

As they headed for the door, he saw the woobie on the floor, under Zarina's basinet by the window where it must have fallen out when they picked her up.

Using his telekinesis, Jullien held his hand out and snatched it from the floor at the same time League assassins came in through the windows next to it.

Kiara screamed again.

"Run!" he shouted, tucking the blanket around Zarina and using his body to shield her and her mother from the assassins. As they hurried toward his mother's bedroom, he opened fire on their pursuers.

With Zarina still in his custody, he sent Kiara ahead, then ran to divert the League soldiers away from her to buy her enough time to get to safety. He turned and skidded in the hallway on his knees with the baby tucked against his shoulder. Right now, he sincerely missed Ushara. She'd be fighting with him and reloading. Not falling apart and screaming until his ears bled from the shrill sound of her useless hysteria.

Or stopping continuously to check and see where they were.

Why did Kiara keep stopping?

He jerked a grenade from his belt and tossed it, then grabbed Kiara's elbow as he caught up to her and pulled her into the bedroom, where Thrāix waited at the door to finally offer some cover fire.

"Is everyone in?" Jullien passed the baby to his brother-in-law.

"Waiting on you," Thrāix said irritably. He took Kiara and the baby to the closet. "C'mon!"

After they left, Jullien hung back a moment to lock and block the door against their enemies.

As he stepped away from the door, it blew open, sending shrapnel all over him. Because he'd given his jacket to Kiara, he had nothing to protect him from it. Pain racked his entire body, while he stumbled for the closet at the same time more missiles fell closer to the palace. Glass shattered and rained down from the windows. The ground shook, knocking him from his feet.

Jullien hit the floor hard, and then it and the entire palace began to literally disintegrate around him. His ears buzzed.

*Fight, damn it, you worthless piece of shit! Get up and run!*

Just before him, within a few steps, he could see the door to the base-ment hell his grandmother's guards used to drag him to against his will. Hear her cruel laughter echoing as she promised him he'd regret what-ever he'd done to earn his stay there.

But his body wasn't listening as he crawled over falling rubble and burning debris toward safety.

Then he heard it.

Utter destruction as a League squadron broke through their armada and unleashed a massive bombing run on his mother's race. The entire building blew apart around him and on him.

Everything turned black.

# CHAPTER 38

His ears ringing from the last explosion, which had knocked everyone to the ground and sent pieces of the metal ceiling crashing down around them, Thrāix handed the squalling baby to her terrified mother, then stepped back to do a head count to make sure no one was trapped by the scattered debris of the partially collapsed tunnel he'd just run down.

The number of folks crammed into the decrepit, musty room stunned him. Damn, there were a lot more here than they'd planned on. This wasn't just Kiara and her kids. It looked like half the royal families of all the Nine Worlds.

*What the hell did you get us into, Jules?*

The tadara was in a corner with the Triosan emperor and two other noble Andarion females he didn't recognize. All four looked a bit put out to be here, but weren't saying much. Doing her best to soothe her unsettled brood, Kiara was on the floor with her six kids, all of whom were crying or complaining, especially the eldest daughter, who sat with the two oldest boys. And the rest of the men and women, and kids, were in a similar state, asking a multitude of questions he didn't care to answer.

Their only casualty appeared to be Shahara's mecha bodyguard who'd saved her and her son by pushing them out of the way when the tunnel had collapsed a moment ago. While they'd escaped without injuries, the walls had fallen on top of the mecha, crushing his android body and reducing him to worthless scrap.

As they continued to whine about their situation, Thrāix blocked their thoughts and their strident voices and cries.

His mission had been to preserve Jullien's sister-in-law and her children. Now it was to get them all out of here, alive and intact.

Davel coughed and wheezed as more debris fell from the ceiling. But so far, true to Jullien's prediction, the room they were in was holding and not collapsing. It was amazingly sound given what had just struck the palace.

"Lot more of us than we planned for, eh?" Davel brushed the dust from his Tavali flightsuit.

"Yeah."

Davel wiped at the smear on his chin. "We're going to have to commandeer at least one more ship for an evac. There's no way we'll all fit on what we brought."

"Yes, Dav," Thrāix said, his tone weighted with sarcasm. "I'm aware of that. I *can* count. We were taught basic math on Trisa, too."

Dimitri sneered at the large group. "Who the hell are all these bodies, anyway? Push to shove, do we have to save them?"

Davel shrugged at his brother's question. "Where's Dagger? This was all his brilliant planning . . . which is why it no doubt went to Tophet."

A cold chill went down Thrāix's spine as he realized that the only ones missing were from *their* group.

Jullien, Axl, and Gallatin.

He tapped his earlink. "Dagger? Life check. Where are you?"

Static answered him.

He met Davel's scared gaze as his own stomach cramped with sudden fear. "Dagger?" he tried again. "Piss me off, Andarion. C'mon, buddy. You better fucking answer me. I mean it! You drag my fat ass from my wife, you better not die—or I'll kill you."

Davel took up the irrational panic. "Talk to me, my brothers. Where are you? Don't you thin the paltry number of males in our family. I need every one of us at the table on temple day. Don't you dare leave us alone with your widows and our sisters!"

After an agonizing delay, Axl finally answered with heavy breathing that sounded like he was carrying an impossible weight. "Dagger's been hit. Bad."

Davel froze. "Did he say Dagger was hit?"

Thrāix nodded.

"Bad," Dimitri added as he headed for the collapsed tunnel to see if he could render aid. He started moving larger pieces aside to clear the path.

"No!" Davel glared at Thrāix, who went to help Dimitri. "Dagger ain't hit." Davel frantically shoved debris aside. "Dagger can't be hit. Dagger, don't you go down on us."

Thrāix decided to ignore those words, which Jullien would definitely have groaned aloud over if he were alert enough to hear them.

Suddenly, Axl and Gallatin stumbled through the remains, dragging Jullien's bleeding, inert body between them. They, too, were soaked in his blood.

"No, no, no!" Davel breathed as he and Dimitri moved forward to take Jullien from their shoulders and help lay him down on the floor. Dimitri stepped back immediately to allow Thrāix to tend him.

Davel stayed next to his side, complaining. "Damn it, Jules! Don't you dare die! Don't you make me make that call! Mom and Paka will kill me! They like you better, boy."

Ignoring him, Thrāix did his best to examine the bleeding wounds. "What the hell happened? Where's his flak jacket?"

"He gave it to me."

Thrāix cursed at Kiara's soft voice. "'Course he did. Damn it, Jullien! You're such an asshole!" He rolled him to his side to see the blaster wounds on his back, where someone had shot him, and the horrifying amount of damage he'd taken from the explosion that had shredded the skin there.

He let out a fierce groan of agonized pain. "My name isn't *Damn-It-Jullien,* you know? I'm really tired of everyone calling me that all the time."

Grateful to the gods, Thrāix released an irritated laugh as he heard Jullien's pain-filled, surly voice. "No, but it should have been. And Asshole should be your surname. You sure that's not what Anatole means in Andarion? They almost sound the same."

"Ha. Ha." Jullien unstrapped the blast helmet from his head.

Thrāix helped him remove it. Blood leaked from his ear and nose. "I think you broke your head, Andarion. Probably got brain damage."

"Like anyone could ever tell the difference." Jullien wiped at the blood.

Thrāix held his hand out for Jullien to take so that he could use his powers to heal him.

But Jullien hesitated. "Not too much. I'm too weak to carry your gargantuan ass. You fall down, I'm leaving you behind. Just get rid of the pain, and I'll manage till we get to base."

"You sure?"

He nodded. "We can't afford for both of us to pass out. One of us has to have some form of brain activity. And at present, the gods know that's definitely *not* me."

"All right. Hang on."

Jullien took a deep breath and braced himself for the unholy hell of Thrāix healing some of his blast wounds.

He hissed as soon as it began. *Son of a bitch, it hurt!* But after a few seconds, it loosened enough to where he could at least breathe without wanting to die.

Completely.

Thrāix was a little paler as he helped him sit up. However, the moment he was upright, two blast shots flew so close to his face that he felt the burn of them on his skin.

"What the hell?"

Axl, Davel, Dimitri, and Gallatin drew their blasters and pinned them on Shahara, Darling, Kelsei, and Tylie, who had their weapons drawn and aimed for Jullien's head. The six Andarion guards with them also drew weapons.

"Who shot at me?" Jullien demanded.

"The redhead." Davel switched his blaster from stun to kill with his thumb. "Want us to finish her?"

"No!" Jullien wiped at the blood on his cheek that Shahara had drawn. Pissed off, he glared at her. Then looked at his parents, who just stood there while ten of their party held weapons aimed to kill him.

Not a single word of protest.

Their son who had just saved them all from annihilation.

Why was he even surprised?

Thrāix shook his head with a sad sigh. "I'm so sorry for you, little brother."

Yeah, so was he. He'd spent his whole life having to explain away his family and why they didn't give a shit about him. Honestly, he was tired of it.

Darling glared at Jullien. "You weaselly bastard! What are you planning to do? Hand us over to Eriadne?"

"Sure," Jullien said, his voice carrying the full weight of his disgust and sarcasm. "'Cause given the hatred and Thrill-Kill warrant and grudge she has on me, she's *so* concerned about the lot of *you*." He passed a droll stare to Thrāix. "Take them to temple?"

"Sell it, little brother. Let's make Mama Samari proud."

They threw their hands out and used their powers to disarm all ten of them at once—and plant them on their asses.

Jullien turned toward his true family—the ones who actually loved and supported him. "Put it away. We have actual enemies we need to worry about, and right now, we have to figure out if we still have a way home." He clapped Davel on the shoulder, then hugged Axl, Dimitri, and Gallatin. "Thank you for digging me out and not leaving me behind."

Axl raked him with a disbelieving stare. "And face my sister without you? What kind of stupid do you think I am?"

Gallatin snorted. "You've heard her threaten me. Multiple times. Shara scares the snot out of me. Her last words were that I better not return without you. Pretty sure she meant it."

Thrāix narrowed his gaze on Darling as the emperor pushed himself to his feet. "You better be damn glad Trajen isn't here. Hermione's son or not, your brains would have been splintered the instant you took aim in his brother's direction. I suggest you keep a respectful distance and remember that. In this room, we value *his* life and loyalty. Not yours."

Darling curled his lip. "Then you're an idiot. Have you any idea what kind of snake you've put at your back?"

"You know nothing of our brother. None of you do. So if you don't mind, sit down, shut up, and let us regroup." Thrāix moved to stand by Jullien. "Is there a way out of here?"

"Yes, but I don't know if we can make it. I'm pretty sure the whole palace just came down on top of me. We need some eyes on the surface and a line out while we can to let our family know we're alive." Grimacing as pain cut through his entire body again, Jullien took a deep breath. He glanced around their decayed quarters. "The warden used to have an office down here, where he had communications and a monitor. We might be able to use that."

"Where?"

"This way." As Jullien headed for it, his mother and father finally stepped forward to address him.

Biting her lip, Cairistiona stared at him as if he were a stranger she was meeting for the first time.

Then again, that was exactly what he was.

"It really is you after all these years, isn't it?" The fact she had to ask that . . .

He gave her a flat, emotionless stare, then lifted it to meet his father's contemptuous gaze, which still judged him as inadequate and lacking.

There was a time he'd have agreed with his father that he was less than whole. Lacking in a family that loved him. Lacking in decency and intelligence. A heartless bastard who held a blackened soul filled only with resentment and hatred.

But that was a different creature, a lifetime ago. A different time and place.

And when Jullien spoke, it was the simple truth that he finally, unequivocally believed and accepted. "Jullien eton Anatole is dead."

He glanced over his shoulder at Davel and returned to their much more pressing discussion. "The guards also kept spare weapons and ammunitions near a cafeteria in back. We might be able to find some spare ammo. Maybe even some rations that haven't expired. And medical supplies."

Kelsei finally spoke. "What is this place?"

Tylie nodded. "Yeah. How did you know this was here? I've never seen it before. Cairie? Have you?"

"No, and it was concealed in my closet. I had no idea there was a hidden door that opened into anything. It's terrifying, actually, to think someone could have accessed my room and I'd have never known it." She looked back at Jullien. "Did my mother show this to you?"

A sudden wave of fury blinded Jullien at her question, and ignorance of something they both should have known about. Had either of them taken five minutes out of their self-absorbed, useless days to remove their heads from their asses, they'd have seen what their mother was doing to others right under their stuck-up noses.

Not just to him, but to dozens of other innocents.

His breathing turned ragged. "You want to know what this is? Fine." He walked backward toward a cell door that was covered by years of neglect, cobwebs, and rust. Grimacing against both his mental and physical pain, he used his bloody sleeve and fist to rub the filth off the nameplate and room number so that it could be read: TAHRS JUNKIE ASSWIPE.

He pulled out his blaster and shot the hinges off the steel door, then kicked it in so that it showed the tiny cell that doubled as an *interrogation* and *education* room. His blood still stained the wall and filthy thin mattress on the rusted, narrow steel bed. "While you lay upstairs in your drugged stupor under Galene's tender loving care, Matarra, with your guards to watch over and protect *you* from harm in your opulent luxury, this was where I was brutalized during my youth. Every time you ran to your mother, Tylie, and told her stories about how sorry I was as an Androkyn, or how I embarrassed you and Andaria, this was where I was sent to be reeducated and punished. When *you,* Father, refused to come get me or demanded that I go to rehab over the drugs my family was injecting in me against my will, this was where I usually ended up. Thank you all for my happy childhood memories. *Really.* They've only been surpassed by the diligent love and care you've given me these last few years after you exiled me and allowed the Thrill-Kill warrant on my life to stand uncontested and every assassin in the Nine Worlds to hunt me to the corners of the universe, where I've had absolutely no amnesty or haven whatsoever."

Jullien didn't bother to look inside the room. He knew every fucking inch of the cell where he'd once used his clawed nails to carve his name over and over into the walls. After a while, he'd grown bored with that and had started carving INDURARI to remind himself to hold on, that his days in that cell couldn't last forever. Sooner or later, he'd outlive the bitch holding him in captivity.

That had been the only thing that had allowed him to survive his childhood in this hell.

Putting it out of his mind, he went down the hall to the warden's office to look for a way to contact Ushara and the others to let them know they hadn't died in the bombing.

Luckily, the rusted-out door was unlocked and still capable of opening.

Thrāix followed him inside the spartan office. "You okay?"

"You know the answer. Not like you can't read my mind." Not that it wasn't really obvious, given the way he was slamming objects around like a two-year-old while he searched for something they could use.

He was deeply hurt and pissed.

Mostly pissed that he was allowing his birth family to continue to hurt him. He didn't want those people back inside his head. He'd spent too many years purging them, and it wasn't fair that they were here and dredging this shit up again. All he'd wanted to do was even a score he felt he needed to by saving Nyk's kids and wife, and get out before anything reopened old mental damage.

Too late now.

*No good deed goes unpunished.*

He should have known the gods would screw him over somehow. They always did.

With a grimace at the filthy desk, Jullien pulled the scarf from around his neck and used it to clean off the decades of dust and decay. Sitting in the chair, he let out a frustrated breath before he began working on the communications equipment. Given how many years it'd been left sitting up, unused, it actually didn't look too bad. "I think we can get this back online. It's older than shit, but—"

"You're a *minsid* genius. I have all faith in you."

"Feeling pretty stupid right now for getting everyone into this. You were right. I shouldn't have come. Damn sure shouldn't have dragged the rest of you from your families. I don't know what I was thinking."

"You were thinking about your brother . . . like you always do."

"Yeah, but I should have been thinking about my brothers who have stood at my back and not the one who doesn't give a shit about me. Blood doesn't always make family."

"True, but it's hard to break that bond. Like it or not, so long as they're alive, there's always a part of you tied to them by those genes. It's hard to let it go."

"Yeah, but maybe it's time I finally did."

Darling swallowed hard as he took in the prison cell that had clearly been reserved for Jullien. He wasn't sure what part of it sickened him more. Having been kept in a similar situation on Caron before he'd found the courage to rise up and kill his uncle over it, he felt for Jullien more than he would have ever thought possible.

Meanwhile, they'd all thought Jullien the spoiled, pampered Andarion heir. Of all people, Darling should have known that you couldn't tell what was really happening in someone's life or home by simply looking at them. He'd spent years living complicated lies and keeping silent secrets from even his closest friends.

And you damn sure couldn't tell what was in someone's heart or head. How could they have misjudged Jullien so badly? He felt like shit over it.

He met Shahara's haunted gaze as she saw the busted drawers of barbaric torture devices and restraints they'd used on Jullien. "Did you know about any of this?"

She shook her head. "I hauled him in for warrants a few times. Now that I think back on it, I should have suspected something was up. He was always getting into trouble away from home, and then trying to bribe me to keep him in lockup on Gondara and not transfer him back to Andaria. I stupidly thought it was because he didn't want to be embarrassed by their media."

Cairistiona picked up the bloodstained pillow that chronicled her child's silent nightmares. She wouldn't even look at the restraints. "There's no blanket in here?"

Darling shook his head.

A tear fell down Aros's cheek as he ran his hand over the gouged-out marks in the wall where Jullien had chronicled his name and days, trying to stay sane. The depth of them told just how frustrated and angry the boy had been. "All the times he begged to come stay with me because he didn't want to be here, and I coldly turned him down. . . . Told him to suck it up and act like a man."

Tylie let out a bitter, angry laugh. "You? You don't want to know the cruel things I've said to him. How many times I blamed him for Nykyrian being gone and for Cairie's condition. I had no idea he was in this kind of pain. He never said anything."

"We didn't listen," Cairie whispered. "He was acting out, trying to get our attention. And we ignored him, utterly." She swallowed hard as she met her sister's gaze. "And I have a bad feeling that he was the mysterious *War Hauk* who saved us from those assassins when Kiara was pregnant with the twins."

Tylie winced. "Had he been coming out from down here that day . . . it makes sense. Dear gods, Cairie. What have we done to him?"

Sick to his stomach, Darling left the cell to find that Jullien had returned. He was outside in the larger area with Kiara and her twin sons, who'd been crying nonstop with their two older brothers since they'd been awakened and rushed to flee with their nurse and big sister.

Jullien smiled patiently at the dark-haired twins, who were dressed in matching footed pajamas. "You're what? Four?"

With his curly hair tousled around his head, Taryn nodded and sniffed.

"I have twin daughters who are almost the same exact age you are. Want to see them?"

Sniffing, too, and rubbing his eyes, Tiernan sat forward. "You do?"

"I do." Jullien pulled his link out and turned it on. "They're named Mira and Viv."

Tiernan gasped. "They look like us!"

"I know, right? What's your name?"

"I'm Tiernan, and this is my brother Taryn."

"Taryn? That's the name of my Mira's favorite doll."

Taryn finally stopped crying. "It is?"

"Yeah, she's holding him in her picture. See?"

Taryn smiled at the picture.

"And you know what else? My girls and my son are what we Tavali call Fetchyns. Have you ever heard that term?"

They, and their brothers Adron and Jayce, who'd crawled closer to listen, shook their heads.

"Fetchyns are young honorary Tavali. And I'm a field admiral, which means that I'm the third highest-ranking member of my Nation. And your aunt Ushara and uncle Trajen are the vice admiral and high admiral of the Gorturnum Nation. That means they're my bosses. And that gives me the authority to swear you in as Fetchyn Tavalians, so I can make *you* pirates, too. Would you like that?"

They sucked their breaths in excitedly.

"Really?" Taryn clapped his hands together. "I can be a *pirate*?"

"Yes, you can. But . . . here's the thing. Pirates don't cry. And you'll have to stay strong to watch over your mother, brothers, and sisters. You think you can do that?"

Taryn glanced to Shahara's son, Devyn, who was still upset that his mecha unit had been smashed when a wall came down on it, and then to his brothers. "Yes! Dev? You want to be a Tavali Fetchyn, too?"

Devyn shook his head. "No, I'm a Dagan smuggler. We don't play with Tavali."

Jullien laughed. "Well . . . sometimes you do. We've been known to fly with the Dagans quite a few times, right, Kasen?"

"He's right," his aunt concurred. "We do rely on them sometimes.

They can be really important to us on our missions. And they've saved our hides a few times—like tonight."

Jullien turned back to his nephews. "So are you in?"

"We're in!" they shouted in unison.

"Okay." Jullien held his hand out. "Put your hands on mine. And repeat after me. . . . Tavali is an honor that comes with obligation. Hem me never."

The boys repeated it.

"United in purpose. United by bond. Forever Tavali." Jullien waited until they'd responded with those words. "Very good, my Fetchyns. It's my solemn honor to welcome you in as official Tavali youth citizens." He pulled the patches from his sleeves and pinned one to Taryn's shirt first. "This is my personal Canting that only I have so that all The Tavali know when they see it who I am and what Nation I belong to. When you wear it, they will all know that you are my Fetchyn and that if they dare touch you or harm you in any way, they will have to answer to me."

Davel snorted. "Yeah, and there ain't nobody who wants to be on the bad side of Dagger's temper. Ever. Believe you me. Your uncle makes the baddest of bad flinch."

Taryn scowled at Jullien's flag. "It looks like a bug."

Jullien grinned. "Yeah, it kind of does. Tells you what my boss thinks of me most days." He winked at his nephew. "I'm just a big old bug up his butt, irritating him."

They burst out laughing.

Jullien ruffled Taryn's hair. "My call sign is Dagger Ixur. But you, I dub Demonax."

"Demonax?"

Jullien nodded. "He was the son of Nemesis, and one of the fiercest of the Kadurr. Fearless in battle." Next, he pinned his Canting to Tiernan. "And you I shall call Daktyloi."

He screwed his face up. "Daktyloi? Why? Is he the twin of cool-sounding name?"

"No. Daktyloi was the first armed warrior created by the gods to guard their infant son from their enemies who wanted to eat him. His job was to create a frenzied dance with his shield and sword whenever the baby cried so as to drown the sounds out and keep him hidden. And to fight to the death to protect the baby should he be found."

Tiernan's whole face lit up as Jullien pinned the patch to his nightshirt. "Thank you for giving me my own! Nobody ever does that. Sometimes I think I'm just Taryn's spare part."

"You're very welcome. And I know what you mean. I felt the same way when I was a kid, with your paka. It's hard to be the younger twin. And my Viv complains about that with her older sister. So we always make sure she knows that she's not." He turned to Jayce, who appeared around six years old.

"Can I just have the patch 'cause it's cool? I'm going to grow up and be an assassin like my dad was."

"You're not going to grow up and be an assassin," Kiara said sharply. "I don't know why you keep saying that. It is *never* going to happen."

Laughing, Jullien motioned for Davel to give up his patches for the kids. "Sure."

When he went to give one to Adron, who was about two years older, the boy leaned in to whisper, "Same here. I'm going to be an assassin, too."

"Gotcha." Jullien pinned it to his arm.

But it was Taryn who was the most infatuated with his patch. He ran over to Ture and his infant son. "Look, Uncle Ture! Will you let Terek be on my crew when he's big?"

"I don't know, Terry. I'd rather he stay in my kitchen with me and be a chef. But if it's what he wants . . . sure."

Of course, for now, all Terek could do was teethe on the patch.

Kiara met Jullien's gaze. "Thank you for calming them down, and giving them something else to focus on."

"No problem."

She jerked her chin toward his link. "May I see your daughters?"

Jullien hesitated. He wasn't sure why, other than Kiara had never been particularly interested in anything other than putting as much space as she could between them—as quickly as possible. And this was as personal to him as showing someone the most naked part of his body or soul. Mainly because his family was the part of him that left him vulnerable and weak. They were the key to his utter destruction.

But they were also his greatest strength and the only thing in life he took pride in. In a lifetime marked with wrong decisions and mistakes, they were the only thing he'd ever done right.

So he glanced at the photo and smiled at their beautiful faces before he held it out to her. It was a picture of them with Ushara and Vasili from a few weeks ago.

Kiara looked down and gasped as if she'd half expected him to have been lying about having a family. "Your wife's currently pregnant?"

He nodded.

"And the boy in the photograph?"

"Our son, Vasili."

"They're beautiful, Jullien."

"Thank you." He slid the link into his pocket, then stood. "We have some communications up. The good news is . . . we're alive."

"But your palace is gravel."

He grimaced at his best friend. "Thank you, Thrāix. Way to spread sunshine over the landscape."

Completely unabashed, Thrāix shrugged. "I did not want to be here. Let's not lose sight of that one fact. I was drafted into this against my common sense and better judgment."

Jullien cleared his throat. "Everyone in this room has officially been declared dead."

They collectively gasped.

Jullien quickly tried to reassure all of them. "That's actually good news. Because you're *not* dead."

"Yet."

"Thrāix!" Jullien snapped. "Act like a Tris. They're not going to die."

"Unless I shoot them."

"You, go stand in a corner until I finish." He gave him a droll stare, unsure what had gotten into him. While Thrāix was never the most optimistic to have around, he wasn't normally quite this cantankerous. "Anyway . . . we need to contact Nyk and the Alliance, and let them know our status before Nyk and The Sentella do something profoundly stupid to retaliate in their grief. And yes, Desideria, that was directed primarily at your husband."

Kasen cleared her throat. "Hey! I take exception with that. Caillen is also *my* brother."

"And mine," Shahara added.

"I wouldn't claim that moron," Davel said under his breath.

Jullien agreed, but didn't comment on that. Instead, he spoke to his Tavali group so that they would understand the dynamics and importance of the people in the room with them. "Desideria's brother is also *our* family member and friend, Psycho Bunny. And we don't need Chayden on a suicide run. We have enough trouble with him when his head's on straight. Ture's husband and the father of his baby is Maris Xans-Sulle, the Phrixian prince."

Dimitri let out a low whistle. "Well, that explains why The League made this attack. What the hell were all you idiots thinking by being together in one place?"

"That we were in a palace with an army," Darling said dryly.

"And how did that work for you, punkin'?" Thrāix answered in an equally sarcastic tone. "Ever want to be schooled on the history of *that* stupidity, talk to my boy, Dr. Dagger, here." He jerked his chin to Jullien. "You should read his dissertations on the fall of the Trisani Empire and the rise and fall of your own ancestor Justicale Cruel. While y'all might not think much of what you raised, Jules has one of the keenest political minds ever born."

"Anyway," Jullien said again, trying to keep them on the topic at hand. "We have a narrow window to get a message out before it will be detected by Eriadne or The League. Thrāix? I need you to toss your shirt to me, real fast, so I can make a video to send to Shara, and she won't see me bloody and panic. I don't want to throw her into labor. We'll let them know we're alive, and then we'll work on getting out of here."

Thrāix pulled his shirt off.

Because he'd been married to Ushara for so long and she had never really reacted to his body, and her mother and Trajen had been treating his wounds for the last few years, Jullien had forgotten just how badly scarred he was.

Until he exposed his torso.

"Holy mother of the gods." His mother covered her mouth with her hand.

Tylie retched while his father stared at him in absolute horror.

Sighing from the hurt and shame, Jullien exchanged shirts with Thrāix.

His mother approached him with her eyes mirroring her sickened horror, but Jullien didn't want to see it. He stepped away from her to tuck his shirt in.

"What caused all that?"

He glanced at her. "You're my mother. Of all beings, *you* should know."

"I didn't mark you Outcast."

"Sure you did, Matarra," he said in a flat, emotionless tone. "The day you allowed your priests to refuse my exordiom, and then when you removed me from the royal family and had my name stricken from the Anatole lineage, and a kill warrant issued for my life. Is that not the very definition of Outcast?"

With those words spoken, he put his helmet on and handed his link to Thrāix to record.

Thrāix gave him an arch stare. "Helmet? Really?"

"Bite it and hit record." Jullien patted his pockets. "No, wait!" Then he remembered Thrāix wasn't really Tavali and didn't have patches on his gear, so he was fine. Ushara wouldn't realize he had on someone else's clothes. "Never mind. We're good."

"You sure?"

"Yeah. Let's do this."

But the minute he started to speak, he realized that Thrāix had been right. The helmet was a stupid idea. Not that he was ever going to admit that to the Tris.

He'd been thinking to keep his identity a secret from Nyk. But that wasn't going to work. His brother would have to know who Jullien was in order to cooperate with Shara and Trajen. Otherwise, he'd go off half-cocked and get himself killed.

Shit.

Fine. Whatever. He pulled the skull-decorated blast helmet from his head to expose his thick black hair and whiskered face. *Gods, I hope I don't have any blood on my skin.* Shara would die if she thought he'd been hurt in any way.

He should have checked. But it was too late.

Clearing his throat, he made sure to keep his eyes green so that no one in the Alliance would learn his secret. Or worse, his enemies might discover it and use it against them.

"Greetings, brother. I know I'm the last creature you want to see right now, but I had to let you know that everyone's safe, and that I'm sorry I couldn't forewarn you about The League attack on the palace. By the time I found out what Nyran and Eriadne had planned, there wasn't enough time to call you or Matarra, and I wasn't sure either of you'd even believe me. I didn't know who else to trust. So I did the only thing I knew to do. I came myself to secure them."

Jullien took his link from Thrāix and panned it around to show his brother and the rest of The Sentella that their families were fine and un-scathed, and in no danger whatsoever. Hopefully, that would be enough for them to not go after The Tavali or The League, or do anything else radically stupid.

Kind of asking a lot, but they had to trust in a miracle for this.

First, Jullien went to their parents, who stood together beside Tylie and her partner, Kelsei.

His mother smiled at the camera. "*Mi tana,* breathe easy. Jullien literally pulled us out minutes before everything went up in flames. We owe him our lives. I love you. Have no fear for us."

Aros inclined his head. "She's right. We're all fine." Their father stepped back to show Nyk's kids, who were complaining about the toys that had been left behind, and Thia, who grumbled about a broken nail and not having a hairbrush. She was extremely distraught he dared film her in such a state.

Jullien smiled at something Ushara's nieces would have done as well. He could just imagine Nadya's reaction over it.

Exhausted from it all, Shahara and Zarya were now both napping on the floor, with their children nestled beside them while Ture changed Terek's nappy as the baby gnawed on his fist.

Looking up, Ture smiled and waved. "I'm all right, Mare-bear. T, too. We just want you to be safe." He held the freshly dressed Terek up to wave. "We love you."

Darling paused in the middle of whatever he was working on. "Yeah, Nyk, I don't trust your brother, either. He's a bloody, traitorous bastard. We know it. But . . . he has given us one hell of a tactical advantage. The League thinks we're dead and that you're rattled and reactionary. So long as they think we're dead, they're not coming after us, and you can focus on kicking their asses with a clear head and single-minded objective. Use this to the best advantage possible, and don't let either of my brothers do *any*thing stupid while I'm gone. I know I'm asking a lot, but I'd like to still have an empire when I get out of here." He cut his gaze back to Jullien. "And if *your* brother gets frisky, don't worry. I will end him. Shahara will help. She already took two shots at him."

Even more agitated at them, Jullien handed his link back to Thrāix so that he could hold it while he addressed his brother. "Anyway, Nykyrian, I know you have absolutely no reason to trust me. And I know you're fighting with one hand tied behind your back so long as you're worried about whether or not I'm going to betray you when you least expect it. So as an act of good faith, to let you know that I understand that I hold in my hands everything in this universe you treasure, I've placed in your hands my very heart and soul. The very means by which to destroy me. And with you being a former League assassin, I know you won't hesitate to do so if I fuck this up. . . . I have your wife and family in my custody. So I have sent to you *my* wife, daughters, and sons. Please protect them. . . . I can't live without them, brother. They are all I have in this world. All that means anything to me. You are the only one I would ever trust them with."

Jullien paused as fear finally overtook him and he realized how much he had on the line.

Everything.

Tears choked him. "Shara, I love you, *munatara a la frah.* I'll be home as soon as I can. Don't you dare have Vidarri without me. And don't let Vasili fight without my brother winging him. I swear I'll loosen the noose on him soon, but he's not as skilled a fighter as he thinks he is, and I don't want to bury our son. He's just not ready to fight in this war. Kiss the girls for me, and tell Mira to be brave for her paka." He nodded at Thrāix, who turned the link off and handed it to him.

Drawing a ragged breath, Jullien quickly sent the recording to Ushara with a note letting her know he was safe and that he would not break her heart. She was going to be stuck with him for the rest of her life.

Yeah, he was just that cruel.

He swallowed against the tears that gathered in his throat to choke him.

Thrāix clapped him gently on the back. "Just breathe, little brother. You've been in worse predicaments. We both have."

He snorted. "Not helping." With a deep breath, he forced himself to focus on their immediate needs. Something hard to do, since Zarina kept fussing and crying.

Kiara couldn't seem to quiet her. And the gods forbid his mother should step in to aid with her granddaughter.

After a few minutes of them attempting a discussion over it and failing due to the distraction, Jullien went to Kiara.

"I'm sorry. I fed her, but she gets horrible colic. It's just her age, I'm told."

"It's not her age. Androkyn are a bit different from humans." He held his hands out for the baby. "May I?"

Nodding, she handed him her daughter.

Jullien tsked at his niece and spoke to her in his baby voice that always made Mira laugh whenever he used it. "What you doing, *bytazifm?* You trying to make Matarra lose her sanity?"

Kiara frowned at him. *"Bytazifm?"*

"Andarion word for *tender bit* or *morsel*." Jullien placed her so that she rested against his forearm. To keep her from squirming out and falling, he held her to his chest while he gently massaged her left side with two fingers until she finally belched and settled down to chew on his fingers. She instantly stopped crying.

Gaping, Kiara stared at him as if he'd just worked a miracle. "What did you do?"

"Our stomachs aren't quite in the same place as a human's. So when you attempt to burp an Andarion baby as you would a human, it doesn't work as well. We do better on our bellies."

"Hey, Dagger!"

Kiara reached for her daughter, but he was already across the room with Zarina. Sitting back, she tilted her head as she watched Jullien for a few minutes.

Desideria scooted next to her. "I know there's some kind of bad history with Jullien and Nykyrian, but he doesn't seem so horrible to me."

Kiara shook her head. "Yeah . . . I was never around him all that much. He creeped me out when I was younger."

"Why?"

"Well, he was gigantic, for one thing. I mean, he's still huge—don't get me wrong. But he was probably a good hundred and seventy pounds heavier, so he took up a lot of room, and it was extremely intimidating. Plus, he seemed to have a crush on me. Whenever he came around, he was all the time trying to ask me out or invite me to perform in his empires in a way that left me terrified I'd find myself locked up someplace like this, where no one would ever see me again. And then there was the small matter that he was always surrounded with an entourage that bled cruelty. You looked at them, and it was like watching a pack of snakes slithering by. Not to mention, he wore these weird red glasses and was *so* condescending and snotty to everyone he spoke to."

"He wasn't condescending. That's his defense mechanism whenever others are assholes to him first. I've never known him to pull that trigger without prior provocation."

She jumped at the deep voice of the one Jullien called Thrāix beside them. Dang, he moved as silently as her assassin husband.

He held two small bottled waters for them. "As for the glasses, he had to have them to be able to see. He still has to wear them in certain lighting conditions, or he gets vicious headaches."

"You don't know. You weren't there."

"I'm Trisani. Trust me, I can see your memories more clearly than you can because my view isn't clouded by your emotional reference point. And you're right. They were a pack of snakes around him, and he'd have sold his soul to break free from those bastards. Unfortunately, every time he tried, he was thrown back to them because none of you ever gave him a chance to escape."

Desideria scowled at Jullien. "What's he doing? Oh my God! I would kill to have Caillen do that without complaint!"

Turning his head to see what she was talking about, Thrāix laughed while Jullien changed Zarina's nappy without even pausing in his discussion with Davel and Darling. "He carries his own daughters around so much, he doesn't think anything about it. Mira's practically a symbiotic life-form who's permanently attached to her father's hip. And before them, his nieces used him as their own private jungle gym. Nadya basically claimed his shoulders and lap the first day they met and only grudgingly ceded them when his daughters were born. She still uses his shoulders to perch on for parades." He headed back to Jullien.

Kiara sat there, stunned. Even more so when a few minutes later, Adron, Jayce, and Taryn nudged their way into the planning group.

Aros started to send them off, but Jullien pulled Taryn to sit on his knee while Davel allowed Adron to sit on his and Thrāix took Jayce. It was obvious these Tavali thought nothing of having children around them as they discussed politics and battle strategy. They even took time to patiently answer the boys' questions and explain things to them.

Once Zarina was asleep and snuggled against Jullien's chest while he attempted to awkwardly draw out their plans, Kiara went over to to retrieve her youngest child. "May I?" she teased.

He looked up in confusion. "What?" Then it must have dawned on him that he still had her daughter. "Oh!" Blushing, he gently held Zarina out to her. "Sorry."

"I'm surprised you didn't yelp when she bit into your hand earlier. In fact, you barely reacted, and I know she caught some flesh with her fangs."

He shrugged nonchalantly. "My daughters do it all the time. Pretty sure the only teething ring Viv used was my fingers, knuckles, and thumb. Besides, it's my cyber-arm. The nerve endings aren't as sharp in it."

Kiara's jaw went slack. "You lost an arm?"

All of them grew silent at her question, especially his parents.

Grimacing as if the question embarrassed him, Jullien sighed. "What can I say? I'm an annoying asshole. No one likes me. Some really don't like me and try to kill me off."

"Can I see it?" Taryn asked.

"Taryn," Kiara growled at her son. "That's rude. We don't ask things like that."

"It's fine." Jullien rolled his sleeve back and allowed his nephew to examine it.

Taryn oohed and ahhed. "You can't tell."

Jullien rubbed at his shoulder. "You can, where they attached it. There's a lot of scarring. But you're right. Down on the arm itself, it looks natural. It's just a little darker than my normal skin."

His mother swallowed hard as she stared at him. "How did you lose it?"

"Doing something very few others would have," Dimitri said simply. "Threw himself on top of an IED that would have taken out our entire station and probably killed all our families had he not been willing to commit suicide rather than see his loved ones go up in the blast and aftershock."

Jullien scoffed. "Yeah, right. You would have done the same."

Davel laughed hard. "Uh, no. I don't think I could ever knowingly launch myself on top of a bomb. Gal?"

She shook her head.

Dimitri agreed with them. "He's right, Ixurian. You're a fool if you think that inclination comes naturally to others. We tend to run away, not toward explosions. Only *you're* that big an idiot."

"Oh. I just assume everyone's as stupid as I am. Anyway—" Jullien pointed back to the map. "If that tunnel is still holding, we should be able to reach the ships."

His mother scowled. "You keep acting like we need to run. My forces—"

"Will follow whoever wears the crown and holds the Anatole Warsword." He swept an annoyed glare over her. "That's not you. By now, it will be Eriadne, who most likely dug the Warsword out before she looked for survivors. She won't hesitate to reinstate herself and proclaim you dead."

"But if I'm alive—"

"You will be slaughtered before you can speak, and there's not enough of us to prevent that from happening. Dear gods, Matarra! Look around you. Look at this place. Do you think I learned nothing of how your mother thinks or operates? Believe me, her cruelty is seared into the fiber of my soul. I know that bitch like the back of my hand."

Standing up, Jullien placed Taryn on his feet so he could face his mother. "Do you think I put myself to the hazard the whole of my childhood to protect you to see you killed now? For once, use your head!"

She scowled at him. "What are you talking about? What hazard?"

Thrāix moved forward. "Tell her, Jules."

He laughed bitterly. "She won't believe me. And it doesn't matter." He glanced around at the children. "Our time is growing short. We have to move. By now Eriadne and the others will be gathering here for a press conference to reestablish her power. There should be enough chaos that we can forge documents for launch. But if we delay much longer, WAR will reunite and everyone's guard will go up."

Tylie sneered at him. "What do you know about WAR?"

Thrāix started for her, but Jullien caught him. "Let it go. You have a wife and a baby to get home to. Think of Mary and Sphinx. Your son will need his father. You don't want Trajen teaching him his powers, do you?"

"That's a low blow, Andarion."

"But an effective one." Jullien winked at him. "Let's wake our sleeping members and see if we can get this plan into motion."

"Uncle Jullien?"

He turned at Taryn's insistent tugging on his sleeve. "What is it, *luden*?"

"As your Fetchyn, can I be your point?"

Cupping his cheek, he smiled down at him. "I would be honored for you to be my wingman. You can march between me and Uncle Thrāix."

Taryn frowned. "Is he really my uncle?" He turned to Thrāix. "Are you really my uncle? Or are you like Uncle Darling?"

"I'm married to the sister of Dagger's wife . . . so to an Andarion, yes, that makes us *calduracyn,* with me your basha, and my children your *kyzir*." He looked at Jullien. "Did I get that right?"

He nodded. "You can be taught. Who knew?"

As the adults assembled, Jullien went to Thia. "How old are you, *sozibe*?"

"Nineteen."

"Can you handle a blaster?"

Her face lit up. "Yes! My father trained me, but he seldom lets me near them."

"Well, I'm not your father." Jullien handed her one of their spare holsters that contained a set of blasters. "Anyone comes near you you don't know, you lay them in the ground. Got it?"

"Excuse me?" Kiara shot to her feet. "We don't teach my daughter to kill things! She's—"

"Old enough to die and be raped. Or worse, sold into slavery." Jullien put Thia's hand on the grip. "Shoot to kill. Do not wound. Those are the same orders I give my son anytime he flies under my Canting."

Thia gaped. "You take your son out with you when you fly?"

"Of course. He's a member of my crew."

"Only reason Vas isn't here is that Jules didn't want him in the crossfire should something go wrong." Davel looked at Axl and laughed. "*We* should have heeded that fear, eh?"

"Speak for yourself, Krunch. *Mi cépandrey.*"

Davel shoved at his little brother. "Worthless suck-up. It's why you were always Mom's favorite."

"Nah, that's 'cause I'm the cutest." Axl playfully slapped at Davel, whose eyes flared.

Recognizing that battle sign, Jullien stepped between them. "And I'm about to cull the family if you two don't stop and act your age. Axl, to the back. Davel, go visit your stryper."

Jullien took a moment to wrap his armored jacket around Kiara and Zarina again.

She frowned at him. "Why are you risking your life for us?"

"Because I'm really sorry about what I did to you with Aksel. And I know this doesn't make up for it. That nothing ever will. If I don't make it back, tell Nyk that in spite of everything I said and did when we were in school, I do love him. I was just too fucked up mentally to know what to do to get us out of the situations we were in. Every time I moved, I ended up back here in this shit-hole."

Pausing, he ground his teeth. "I wish to the gods I'd done things differently, especially where you were concerned." He locked gazes with her so that she could see his sincerity. "I swear on the lives of my children that I had no idea Aksel would hurt you. He promised me he wouldn't. A part of me thought he might be lying, but honestly, I figured he'd be too afraid of your father to do any real harm to you personally. He said that once he had Nyk, he'd release you to your father, and I took him at his word. I was just so mad and hurt that night, and it wasn't even at Nyk. Or you. I should have never taken my anger out on you two. I only hope that I can get you home to him and that maybe this'll even our score."

"Why did you betray us?" his mother asked.

Jullien stepped back as those words slapped him like a physical blow. "*I* betrayed *you?*"

"Yes, you did. You handed Kiara over to your brother's worst enemy, and then you helped your grandmother escape our justice. Did you not think we'd find out what you did? *Haevoc Ichi?*"

Stunned and pissed, he stumbled back with a bitter laugh. "*Haevoc Ichi?* You really think *that* was my code name?" He looked to his father, then to his mother. "I have no idea where my intelligence comes from, but thank the gods, I didn't inherit either of yours."

And with that, he stormed to the front to lead them out of the vörgäte.

Thrāix moved to stand beside Aros and Cairistiona. "Jullien's alias was, and is, Dagger Ixur. He worked with WAR to get you and your sister to his father to keep you safe during the political overthrow he helped put in place. It was his intel and codes that were used to bring Eriadne to justice and capture her on the Porturnum base station. Something that has put him in jeopardy with The Tavali to this day. You know *nothing* of your son."

He started past them, then turned back. "And for the record, *Haevoc Ichi* was Chrisen Anatole. It was also his call sign, if you'd bother to check your own military database. *Ichi* was the unit he flew in. Kind of how Talyn Batur is *Viper Ichi.*"

When he moved to leave, Cairistiona pulled him to a stop. "Do you know why he kidnapped Kiara?"

Thrāix glanced to where Jullien had already vanished. He knew he should keep his mouth closed, but there was no need in it. The time for the truth had come. He met Darling Cruel's curious frown before he answered. "After he'd risked his life——" He gestured at the underground prison they stood in. "And you can see he was well versed in what real torture at your mother's hands meant for him, and after he'd done everything he could to protect *you,* including pit himself against your mother to keep you alive, he overheard that oh-so-pleasant conversation you had with your sister in the embassy."

"What conversation?"

Thrāix snorted bitterly. "How could you forget laughing and joking about throwing your own son in prison after you disinherited him?" He turned to Tylie. "And what was it you said? You wanted a ringside view as the convicts had their way with his spoiled ass? Only you doubted any of them would touch him because he was so repugnant?"

Darling sucked his breath in sharply as both his mother and aunt went stark white.

"He heard us?" Cairistiona

"Yeah. He heard you. Now that you see his extensive experience with an Andarion prison, I think you can understand why he went a little crazy that his own mother intended to put him in one permanently. And with even more psychotic, pissed-off felons. He also knew from personal experience just how wrong your theory was where he was concerned, Tylie. You didn't have to bribe inmates with pardons to attack him. Brutalizing a hand-cuffed royal eton Anatole was what they lived for."

Thrāix met Aros's gaze. "And just so *you* know, that last time your son called to ask for temporary asylum on a Triosan outpost and you had your secretary answer because you were too much of a coward to tell Jullien you'd personally denied his request for landing privileges? He was bleeding from a near fatal knife wound, where his own grandmother had almost carved his heart from his chest because she found out that he'd been the one who put his mother in power. That was why Eriadne swore out the Thrill-Kill warrant on his life. You know, the same warrant none of you could be bothered to fight against because of Nykyrian's precious feelings you didn't want to step on. And no, Jules doesn't know that dirty little secret. I would never hurt my brother by telling him the truth. He doesn't need to know what assholes you really are."

Darling followed after Thrāix as he left them behind to fend for themselves. "Hey, Thrāix, isn't it?"

He slowed down to scowl at him. And before Darling could speak, he answered the unspoken question. "Jules doesn't want anything from The Sentella or Nykyrian, Majesty. Nor does he want to be reinstated to the royal families that kicked him out. Once we return you to his brother, he will go back to being a forgotten ghost in your collective memories."

Thrāix glanced over Darling's shoulder to glare at Jullien's parents. "He has long since stopped using any semblance of the names he was born with. As far as he's concerned, his one true mother is Unira Samari, and he belongs to the Altaan family. He even carries the Samari Warsword. He's neither Andarion nor Triosan. He is Tavali. And unlike you, we love and respect him."

As they came to the end of the underground shaft, Jullien motioned them to silence. There were sirens and media all around. Soldiers were patrolling in thick numbers.

When his mother started forward, Jullien grabbed her arm and pointed to the site where the palace had stood. Flying over its remains was a League flag.

Eyes wide with fury, he shook his head *no* at her.

And as they crept forward, they overheard the reports of Eriadne proclaiming herself tadara and retaking the throne. Of her denouncing anyone who stood against her.

Just as Jullien had predicted, no one had risen to put her down. The Andarions had followed along with dutiful submission. Andarion caste order ruled all. Since Eriadne held the Anatole family Warsword, she was deemed the rightful heir.

For now.

If they were to try and stop her, it wouldn't go well for them.

When they finally reached the bay where they'd left their ships, Jullien pulled them to a stop and projected his thoughts to his men. *Thrāix, come with me. Dimitri, keep everyone else hidden.*

His heart pounding with the hope that no one would recognize him and tear their plan apart, Jullien crossed to the *Pet Hate.*

"Halt!"

Arching his brow in regal irritation, he turned an arrogant grimace at the technician. "There a problem?"

"This your ship?"

"Yeah. Captain Samari. I was supposed to pick up some cargo, but with everything that's happened, I was told to forget it. No one wants to flash paperwork bearing the seal of the former . . . well, you know."

The technician nodded. "Tell me about it." He looked at Thrāix. "What about you?"

"I own the other piece of shit docked beside it. We really needed this shipment."

"You got your former clearance codes?"

Jullien held them out.

He ran them, then nodded. "All right. I'll let the comptroller know to give you clearance."

"Grateful, brother." But as they lowered the ramp on the *Pet Hate,* Jullien went cold. *Thrāix, to your right. That's Kyr Zemin's ship. If he's screening this bay . . .*

"We're going to have to blast our way out."

Jullien nodded. This was all about to get really bloody.

# CHAPTER 39

Once they had the cargo bay doors open and ready, Jullien and Thrāix returned to the group. "All right, we stick to the plan. We're one ship short, so we get the most important ones out on the two we have. I'll stay behind and commandeer a ship once you leave and head out with the guards and nurses."

Thrāix choked on his grief as he saw the same future Jullien did. "We can make room for one more."

"You won't achieve escape velocity with my additional weight, and you know it. On either ship. Andarions weigh too much. And my huge, fat ass has always been a problem."

"Jules—"

"Don't. I got all of you into this. I should be the one who stays behind. Besides, it has to be. They'll need my clearance codes to get them through Tavali-held space." He hugged Thrāix. "Tell my girls and Vas that I love them. And Ushara that I won't break her heart. She shouldn't worry about me."

Thrāix fisted his hand in Jullien's hair. *"Unus ex meis intimis. Animae plusquam dimidium meae." Friend whom I dearly love. My second self.*

*"Et tu—" And you.* "I'll distract anyone who comes after you and make sure you get out safely."

Darling paused in front of Jullien and handed him his holster. As Jullien took it, Darling's gaze dropped down to the blood that had started dripping again from Jullien's earlier wounds, and saturating his clothes. The emperor didn't comment on that as he explained his gift. "The blasters are custom, with a larger-than-expected blast range and longer charges. The grenades have a better range, too. I designed them for maximum damage."

"Thanks."

"No," Darling said earnestly. "Thank *you*. I won't forget what you've done. Sorry for being an ass earlier."

"It's okay. Asshole's my natural state of being."

Smiling and clapping him on the shoulder, Darling headed up the ramp with his wife and infant son.

As Kiara started to leave with her children, Taryn ran to Jullien and grabbed his leg. "I want to stay with Basha Dagger! I can help fight off the bad guys!"

Jullien reached down and picked him up to hug him. "Nothing would please me more, Terry. But you have to go with your matarra and little sister to protect them. It's what Tavalian do. We protect our families at all costs. Even when they annoy us." Kissing his head, he set him down and taught him a Tavali salute.

Thrāix picked Taryn up and carried him inside the *Pet Hate* while Jullien stayed outside with the Andarion guards to cover them. "This is your uncle's prized ship that belonged to his mother."

"My yaya?"

"No. A different mother. But you'll like the ship. She's an antique." Once inside, Thrāix set Taryn down in a chair next to his twin and belted him in.

"How does this ship work?" Darling asked as Thrāix joined him on the flight deck. "I haven't touched anything yet, but it's already started doing preflight checks."

Thrāix ignored the question to speak to the ship. "Jules, let go of your baby. We've got it."

"She's a little buggy on the initial sequence. Don't set her down and try to restart her without contacting my matarra first. She's the only other pilot who can start her. I'll take you out as far as I can."

Darling gaped. "Is that Jullien?"

Thrāix nodded as he strapped himself in and assumed the captain's chair. "Anything else I need to know to pilot her, Yaya?"

"Don't scratch my paint or you will piss me off. Remember, this will one day go to my younger son."

"Don't you think Vidar deserves something better than this old piece of *scytel*?"

"Ah, you're just jealous Sphinx isn't going to listen to you."

"Now you're just being mean."

"Contentious to the end."

Thrāix fell silent as he heard Jullien's parents talking to him before they came on board, and he felt the pain in his friend's broken heart.

Jullien steeled himself as he faced his mother, father, and aunt. "You need to get on board. They're waiting to launch. You're endangering everyone by delaying."

"Thank you for coming." His mother moved to touch his face.

Unwilling to forgive them and not wanting to feel her touch now, Jullien stepped back, out of her reach. He watched as Dimitri and Davel secured the ramp on Davel's ship.

Meanwhile, his father stayed planted in front of him. "You never planned for us to know it was you who came here to warn us, did you?"

"No. Now, can you *please* get on board?" He glanced past them to see if anyone was noticing that they had yet to lock down their ramp. The delay was nerve-racking. Especially since Davel was now launching.

"Jullien . . ."

He glared at his mother. "What is there left to say? Really? We had decades together, and all we did was shit all over each other. There's nothing left between us. I wish you well, but our destinies were never that of a single path."

*"Jules!"*

Flinching at the sound of Thrāix's sharp warning in his head, he looked past them to see the security guards headed their way. "We've got company. Get on board. Now!" He practically shoved them up the ramp and used his powers to seal them in.

Sirens rang out.

"They're locking the bay down." Thrāix cursed. "Closing blast shields even as I speak."

Jullien snorted. "No, they're not." Using his powers, he bypassed the hangar's security codes and pulled his blaster out. He opened fire on their pursuers and drew the guards after him, away from their ship.

With a deep breath, Jullien ran and concentrated on launching the ship, and getting his family through the League patrols and out of Andarion airspace as quickly as possible.

It worked.

It also gave him a throbbing migraine that doubled as a brain tumor level of hell, complete with nosebleed and double vision. The pain left him nauseated. Only sheer determination kept him on his feet and mobile.

He held it together admirably and kept The League and the Andarions off them without much of a problem.

Just as the ship made the upper atmosphere and he surrendered control of the *Pet Hate* over to Thrāix to pilot home, he turned to face his mother's guards and Kiara's nurse, who'd all somehow managed to keep up with his mad dash through the hangar and out to the streets and alley, off to the side of the south bay, where he'd gone to hide from their pursuers.

He dodged a group of League soldiers who were outside, looking for them, and hid in a ventilation tube. "Okay, there are two more Tavali ships docked here. We can—"

"I have a better idea," his mother's head guard said with a slight smile. "The others made it safely out of here, correct?"

"Yeah. They've hit hyperspace and aren't being tracked."

"Good." He pulled a blaster out and shot Jullien at point-blank range, then fired two more rounds. One into Jullien's thigh and the other into his hip. "We turn you in. Get the reward. Then meet up with *Yara Maràstràda* and tell her you didn't make it out."

Switching from kill to stun, he unloaded his full charge into Jullien's body.


Thrāix let out a vicious battle cry of rage as he felt the betrayal against Jullien. The worst part about being Trisani? Seeing a future you couldn't alter. Knowing how sorry certain individuals were and not being able to stop them. He hated every effing minute of it. He always had.

"What the hell?" Dimitri shouted over their intercom. "What's going on over there?"

It took Thrāix a moment to bite back his temper so that he could answer in a reasonable tone. Telling them wouldn't stop anything. Damage was already done. If they turned back, they'd all be taken and Jullien would kill him for getting the others captured. "Nothing."

The lie was bitter on his tongue. But he refused to shit on his brother's sacrifice. They'd learn the truth soon enough.

And it took everything he had not to rise up and slap both of Jullien's parents. How he was going to face Ushara again, he had no idea.

"Excuse me?"

He glanced over to the tall, blond, eldest daughter of Nykyrian's. Like Kiara, she was extremely thin and absolutely beautiful. Delicately featured. "Yeah?"

"I don't mean to bug you, but . . ." She screwed her face up. "something's bothering me, and I feel like I need to tell someone 'cause I think it might be important."

"Okay . . ."

She let out an elongated breath. "My uncle gave me something right before we left."

That got his full attention. Thrāix turned toward Thia. "Gave you *what*?"

Thia pulled out an antique ruby signet ring from her pocket and held it up for him to see. "He said that this belonged to the eldest child of each generation of the ruling Andarion family, and that he wanted me to have it." She glanced over her shoulder at her grandmother. "He told me to keep it away from you, though, Yaya."

Cairistiona paled. "Is that the royal signet ring? I didn't even know he had it."

Tylie turned green. "I thought Matarra had buried it with Eadvard."

Thrāix cursed under his breath. "Well, that explains why he keeps handing it off."

The tadara scowled. "What do you mean?"

He gave her a droll stare. "You two have spent his whole life accusing him of being Eadvard reborn or the Koriłon incarnate—as if he had any choice in his looks. He knew you'd freak out to see it on him, and that your mother would cut his finger off to get it back if she found it on his body."

Thrāix rubbed his head. "Do me a favor, Thia. Don't let his wife see it. Jules sold it to buy parts for her sister's ship. You don't want me to tell you how he got it back or why. Suffice it to say, not something Ushara needs to be reminded about right now, and that memory will not be of benefit to any of you. I swear, that damned ring is cursed. And so's Jules."

Cairistiona scowled at him. "What's that supposed to mean?"

Thrāix turned to Darling. "Handing the ship to you for a minute."

He rose and went to Jullien's birth parents. "Our mission was strictly to protect Nykyrian's innocent wife and children. We didn't know anyone else would be in that *minsid* palace. Other than you, Tadara, and your sister. But you weren't the priority. Jules figured you had an army, you could fend for yourselves. Fight it out with your mother as you'd left him to do when he was just a kid. Imagine our surprise when we got there and realized we didn't have enough space to evacuate you all."

She at least had the decency to slink down in her seat.

His father wasn't so smart. "Had he stayed apprised of the news, he'd have known. Not like it was a secret."

"Be that as it may, he knew something neither the fucking news nor all your intel agencies combined had ever discovered, didn't he? For that matter, had *you* listened to him about the Bromese base when he tried to warn you months ago, over thirteen hundred families would have been spared that fun-filled nightmare. And we could have just made a call to you about tonight's impending doom, instead of coming here ourselves. And rather than saying *thank you* for leaving your families who love you and for risking your lives, you shot at him and dragged your asses like anchors that slowed down our escape, every step of the way. Ever occur to you that had you all cooperated, we might have all gotten out before the palace went down?" Disgusted, Thrāix retook his seat and checked their settings.

Darling cleared his throat. "This really Jullien's ship?"

"Yes. He's owned her for years."

"Then I take it the soundtracks are for his kids?" He pressed a link on the panel, and a childish voice began singing a goofy Andarion alphabet song.

In spite of his fury, Thrāix burst out laughing. "Yeah, Mira made him add that one so that he and Vas wouldn't miss her while they were out on missions. Whenever she calls, she makes them sing it with her over the link. Drives her brother crazy."

Darling snorted. "And Jullien actually sings it with her?"

"Oh yeah." Thrāix pulled up a link to show a log feed of Jullien doing it. He was even clapping in sync to it, and dancing with the puppets.

Darling gaped, then laughed so hard, he almost fell out of his chair.

"Hey now," Thrāix chided. "The boy loves his girls. There's nothing he won't do to make them happy."

Kiara moved to stand by his side so that she could watch the feed. "Is that his son with him?"

"Yeah."

Darling continued to scowl as he went through the playlists. "And the extremely religious stuff in here?"

"Unira's. She's a high priestess."

"And she's part of his crew?"

"Yes."

"I've never heard any of these." Darling cued one of the songs.

Cairistiona bristled as soon as it played. "She's a Demurrist?"

Thrāix glanced at her over his shoulder. "You might want to take that snotty tone down a notch. We're all Demurrists, and you're headed into a base that's predominately filled with them. Not to mention, Jules is one, too."

"Since when?"

"Since he married Ushara."

Cairistiona scowled. "And that was when?"

Shaking his head, Thrāix gave Darling a droll, gaping stare. "Am I the only one who thinks it's pathetic that the female who gave the child life has no idea of the most basic information about him?"

Cairistiona growled at him. "It's not my fault he cut us out."

"Not *your* fault? Ah, I see. I guess that was someone other than your very own sister, who ran him off when he came to see you and apologize, and told him that he would never be welcomed in your home again. And that he wasn't entitled to anything, including his own clothes and link, which she confiscated from him so that he couldn't even call any of you?"

Cairistiona turned to Tylie, who paled. "You did *what*?"

"I'm sorry. I was so angry at him after what he did to Nyk and Kiara. And I didn't want you hurt any worse. I was only trying to protect *you*."

"You threw my son out and didn't tell me?"

Tylie swallowed. "You were upset and staying with Nykyrian. We'd just gotten him home, and you were barely finding your stride as tadara. I didn't want to do anything to upset you."

Thrāix gave her no reprieve from her own culpability. "Don't blame Tylie. Didn't you ever find it odd that your son never bothered to pack a bag? Make a withdrawal? Grab his toothbrush?"

"Jullien was always petulant. I just assumed it was another way to strike out at me and make me worry about him."

Fury darkened his gaze as he turned to stare at both of Jullien's parents. Unable to comprehend her selfish stupidity, he gaped for a full minute before he could speak again. "Oh, okay. He was punishing *you*. 'Cause it's all about you, Majesty, I see. Tell you what . . . this is what Jules looked like when he met Ushara." Thrāix turned on the main monitor to show the images of Jullien rescuing Vasili on Steradore. "Yeah. He was *definitely* punishing *you*. Wish my enemies were that fucking considerate. . . . And let me give you a little advice. Tread easy around his wife. She's not Kiara. Ushara is trained to kill. Has a hair-trigger on her temper, even more so while she's pregnant, and unlike you, is highly protective of Jules. She loves him more than her life. When she finds out that he's been captured because of *you*, there's no telling what she's going to do. In fact, Nyk might be inheriting that throne a lot sooner than he thought."

Jullien came awake to a vicious pain in his skull, and a worse one in his leg and chest. Blinking slowly to try to clear his blurred vision, he found himself facedown on the floor of a filthy, overcrowded cell.

"Look who's finally coming to. Welcome back to Tophet, royal prick."

Someone kicked him hard in the ribs.

Jullien cursed as he tasted blood and bile.

Someone else stomped his arm and back, while another kicked his head.

"Stop it! Let the boy alone!"

"Let him alone? He and his kind are why we're in here." The speaker spat on him. "Anatole filth!"

"I say we hang the royal bastard!"

Dazed from the pain, Jullien forced himself to stand before they pummeled or stomped him to death on the ground. But it was hard. He stood in the middle of the crowd on shaky legs, especially the one he'd been shot in. That one really protested his weight.

He struggled to stay conscious as a male grabbed him from behind and another from the front. He kicked the one in front first, knocking him into the arms of another, then turned and backhanded the other. That male staggered away.

More rushed him from all directions.

Reacting on pure animal instinct, Jullien ducked the next blow, caught the male's arm and punched his throat, then head-butted him, causing him to stumble away. He caught the next attacker by his throat and snapped his neck.

Then they were on him like a pack of wild dogs. Fists, claws, fangs. They used whatever they could to bring him down as quickly and painfully as possible.

He shoved his attackers away as best he could, but the sheer number of them was overwhelming. He stumbled sideways, trying to escape them. Which caused his shirt to rip and temporarily bind his arms as he tried to free himself from their cloying grasps. Twisting, he pulled his arms out and moved to defend.

With a collective, audible gasp, they drifted away to gape at him.

Weak and bleeding, Jullien fell to one knee. Determined to see this through, he ground his teeth and forced his wounded body to stand again. By the gods, he wouldn't die on the ground. He would go out like a Samari.

On his feet. Fighting.

A shadow approached from behind.

Jullien turned, ready to strike with everything he had. Only it wasn't another attacker. It was an older nobleman.

Saren ezul Terronova. One of his grandmother's former advisors.

And the leader of WAR—Warriors Against Royalty. Back when his grandmother was tadara, it had been a resistance group that attempted to overthrow her.

With Jullien's help, they'd finally succeeded.

Jullien had once made weekly reports to this male. A male who now stared in total shock and dismay at the tattoo on his forearm.

"No," Saren breathed raggedly. "You can't be the one. It's just not possible. Is it?" He took Jullien's arm and brushed his hand over the War Hauk symbol. "*You* are Dagger Ixur?"

Jullien nodded weakly. "You were my main point-of-contact, even though my handler was technically Kerell eton Zeki."

"What's that mean?" one of the others asked.

Saren stared at the males around him. "It means that I will personally gut the next one who lays a claw or gives so much as a dirty look to this boy." He pulled his jacket off and wrapped it around Jullien's shoulders. "Find me something to bind his wounds with."

Jullien scoffed at his offer. "There's no need to waste valuable supplies on me. Eriadne won't let me live long enough for it to matter."

As if on cue, the doors of their cell slid open to admit a circle of guards. With trilassos, they collared Jullien and dragged him from the cell.

Laughing, Jullien grabbed the long pole and used it to ram the first guard into the wall. Then he whipped it around to trip the second, but before he could go after more, they opened fire on him with their service blasters.

Still Jullien tried to reach them before his nervous system gave out.

Relentless bastards stunned him to the ground. His breathing ragged, he coughed and wheezed in an effort to get air into either set of his lungs. Unfortunately, that cost him, as it drained his powers down to nothing. The pain was so great, he no longer had enough power to even disguise his eyes.

Saren gasped at the red color and stepped back. "You're stralen? How?"

"Sucks to be a mutant," Jullien choked. "Genes do all kinds of unexpected things." He had no power left in him at all.

"Little Julie . . . you uncooperative bastard. And here we all thought you dead. You have the most inconvenient timing."

Still choking, he glanced up at Nyran and laughed. "I strive to be the bug in your ass, *kyzi*. Your own personal hemorrhoid."

"You succeed. Now you can either come with me quietly or I'll have my brothers open fire on your entire family." Nyran turned the pad in his hands around so that Jullien could see a live feed at the Port StarStation.

Jullien went cold at the sight of Ushara and his daughters, who were blissfully playing, unaware that the Veniks were watching them through their station cameras. "You hurt them—"

"Save the threat for someone who gives a shit." He jerked his chin at his guards. "Cuff him and bring him."

Saren met his gaze. "You're not alone."

Jullien would appreciate the sentiment more if he wasn't about to die a horrible death at the hands of his grandmother. Unfortunately, the majority of doorways in life were designed to be walked through solo.

Death was the biggest of all. It was the one trip that everyone took alone.

And he wasn't a coward.

After the guards had him secured, they dragged him down the hall, to his grandmother's makeshift throne room. Oh yeah, fun times. He well remembered this. Brought back some thrilling childhood trauma he could have waited a lifetime to remember.

When Jullien refused to kneel before her, they kicked his wounded leg. Still, he remained standing, even though it was killing him.

Yeah, he was just *that* minsid stubborn.

Eriadne's nostrils flared as she glared at him. "Ever defiant, aren't you?"

He gave her a pleasant smile. "Hello, Yaya."

She backhanded him.

Damn, for an old bitch, her strength hadn't faded, at all. Nonchalantly licking the blood from his lips, he stood up slowly and acted as if she'd kissed him. He even flipped his hair back into place. Nothing pissed her off more than for him to act like her cruelty didn't faze him.

He knew *exactly* how to push her buttons.

And so he appeared completely bored. He even yawned.

Which caused her to shriek in fury. "You worthless, piece-of-shit bastard! I gave you everything, and how did you repay me?"

"With the same, exact treachery I learned at your cold, decrepit hands. Hard to be kind when I suckled venom from the withered tit of the ancient bitch of all evil, herself."

Shrieking again, she moved in to stab him.

But Jullien wasn't through with his surprises. He took a deep breath and used everything Ushara had taught him to pool the Samari blood inside.

As soon as they were close enough, he unleashed the hottest fire he'd ever spewed before.

Nyran screamed in agony as he stepped back and dropped to the floor to roll around in an effort to put out the flames.

Eriadne was harder to pin.

With a combination of his telekinesis and his cyber arm, Jullien broke the cuffs and gave chase to her as she fled the room. Her guards came for him, but he fought them off. His only goal was to finish this, once and for all.

He couldn't leave her alive. Not this time.

One of them had to die.

As they opened fire on him, he hit the ground and skidded on his knees, turning so that he could return their volley with his fyrebreath.

At the end of the corridor, he rolled for cover into another nearby hall-way.

Nyran continued to scream, letting him know the bastard wasn't dead yet.

"Come on, Eriadne," he called out for her. "You wanted a piece of my flesh. Come get some."

"I should have killed you when you were born!"

"Probably. Would have saved us both a lot of trouble."

"I would have made you the greatest tadar Andaria has ever known!"

Jullien snorted. "I'd have rather you just left me alone, bitch. But I do have to thank you for one gift." He turned the corner to find her hiding there. "The ability to move and function while I'm in excruciating pain."

Her eyes widened as she realized he was about to spew fire all over her.

Just as he opened his mouth to release it, someone wrapped a wire-collar around his neck and jerked him off his feet. Wheezing, and kicking as hard as he could, he tried desperately to pull it off, but couldn't.

"You want me to kill him, *Maràstràda?*" her guard asked as he put his foot on the center of Jullien's chest.

"Yes! There's no one left alive who matters enough to make his living worth our headache. Kill the bastard, and send his bloody heart back to his whore."

# CHAPTER 40

Thrāix felt sick as he came off the ship to meet Unira and the Altaans with no Jullien. The only thing that made him feel remotely better was the sight of Mary's happy face as she ran to him. He grabbed her into a fierce hug and let her warmth soothe the guilt and fear in his tattered soul.

She alone comforted him.

Petran scowled at the royalty they had in tow, but didn't really comment on their presence. "Did Dagger divert to meet up with Ushara?"

Sick to his stomach, Thrāix tightened his hold on Mary. Damn, this was the last thing he wanted to do, and it was a lot harder than he'd anticipated. In spite of their gruffness, Petran and Vidarri both loved and respected Jullien. They'd already lost too many members of their family in this war.

He hated bringing more bad news home to them.

But delaying it would only make it worse.

So he drew a deep breath and braced himself for the fallout. "Jules was captured during our escape."

Katira gasped and covered her heart with her hands. "What?"

"You let them take my son?" Unira gave each of Jullien's parents in turn a shaming glare. "What happened?"

"*Your* son?" Cairistiona arched a haughty brow. "I beg your pardon?"

Unira refused to be intimidated even by the tadara of Andaria. "Beg pardon all you want, Ixurian. You are the one Andarion I will *never* give it to. Not after what you've done to my child. How dare you abandon him yet again! What kind of mother leaves her child behind to seek her own safety? You're not worthy of motherhood. How could you be so cold?"

"Where's Basha Dagger?" Nadya came running with her sisters up to Thrāix, Axl, Dimitri, and Davel. "You can't let him get hurt! Go get him back! Now!"

Jay and Oxana stepped forward. "We can have a strike team assembled immediately."

Thrāix flinched. "We don't know where he is. Or where to begin looking."

"What do you mean, you don't know?" Katira stalked toward them. "Track him."

Thrāix pulled Jullien's link out of his coat. "Little bastard dropped it in my pocket while he said good-bye. I didn't discover it until after we'd launched. He must have done it to keep the Andarions from using it to locate his family."

Katira choked on a sob. "I can't bury another child. And I refuse to watch Ushara go through the pain of losing her heart. This will kill her!"

His old eyes steeled by determination, Vidarri scratched at his chin. "Rally every member of this Nation and Jupiter and Chayden. This is Dagger we're talking about. We will find him if we have to bomb that damn planet and her effing Ixurian race into oblivion! No one will take our Dagger from us! No one! Damn them all to Tophet!"

Darling stepped forward. "You have the full backing of my army. I have no intention of leaving him stranded after what he did for us. The Sentella, too. Tell me what you need, and I'll have it assembled immediately."

Vidarri clapped him on the arm so hard, Darling actually staggered sideways. "Good man, you. Come, Majesty. We've much to do to get our Dagger back."

Ushara knew the instant she landed at her Cyperian base station that something wasn't right. The bay was too active, and everyone appeared to be upset and out of sorts. Short-tempered. Even Sheila was more cross than usual.

More than that, there was a strange mood in the air. A deep sense of foreboding. She watched as The Sentella and The Andarions she'd brought with her from the Port StarStation disembarked from their ships. They seemed as skittish as she did.

Until a herd of unknown children came rushing forward with happy cries.

"Daddy!"

"Mama!"

"Dada!"

Suddenly, the whole place exploded with activity as Nykyrian's, Caillen's, Darling's, Syn's, and Maris's families ran into the hangar bay to greet them.

Ushara was completely overwhelmed by the sheer number of them, especially since they merged with the already large number of Sentella family she'd been escorting.

It was truly impressive.

Dancer Hauk's daughter Kalea ran from her father's arms to embrace a little blond boy named Jayce while Dancer's other son, Darice greeted Nykyrian's eldest daughter.

Seeking her own family in the mix, Ushara scowled. Darice walked past her with Fain Hauk's son and daughter, War and Vega, to introduce them to the rest of The Sentella's children. Apparently, Fain Hauk's brood had never met their cousins before.

Before long, they were mixing like old friends.

Ushara wasn't sharing their happiness. In fact, she became more worried as each second went by and she saw nothing of Jullien or his crew.

Determined to kick his rear section for this undue stress, she headed to Darling Cruel. He was the only one currently here she knew on sight who had been with them. "Where's Jullien?"

That sobered his happy group instantly.

Vasili came to stand at her back while Trajen picked up Mira and held Viv's hand. And that alone told her this wasn't going to be something she wanted to hear.

She glanced at him, but he refused to meet her gaze. Suddenly, Cairistiona approached her.

*Bad timing, bitch.* Because all she wanted right now was to punch the tadara for all she'd done to Jullien. And if he'd been hurt while rescuing her . . .

"It's an honor to meet you, daughter. You are as beautiful as Jullien said you were."

*Like* that *matters? What is wrong with her?*

Ushara swallowed hard. "Where is he?" she growled, fighting every part of her being so that she didn't jump an old Andarion in front of her children and start beating on her like a Ring fighter.

The tadara bit her lip as tears welled in her eyes.

"He's here . . . right?" Ushara looked past them. "Jullien! This isn't funny!" she snarled. "Show yourself! I mean it!" Approaching her slowly, Aros cleared his throat. He tried to speak, but he couldn't.

It was Nykyrian's wife, Kiara, who took Ushara's hand. "He distracted our pursuers so that we could get safely away. He said to tell you not to worry. That he wouldn't break your heart."

*I'm going to kill him! Beat him until he bleeds!*

Aros finally found his voice. But he didn't speak to her. Only to his son. The one he'd chosen over Jullien, who he'd thrown once more to the dogs.

The one he'd left to die.

"He saved Kiara's and Zarina's lives, Nykyrian. And mine. None of us would be here without him."

*And how did you repay him? You abandoned him! Again!* Ushara's vision clouded as those words lodged themselves in her throat. She glanced to her son and daughters. Only they kept her calm on the outside. Otherwise, she'd have already blasted every person in front of her.

Starting with her wretched in-laws.

His eyes telegraphing anger, Nykyrian kissed Kiara's hand as he stepped back. "Ready my fighter!" he announced to the nearest ground crew member.

Kiara visibly cringed at those words, but she didn't try to stop him.

Dancer's blond, human wife, Sumi, who was almost as far along with her pregnancy as Ushara, turned to face her Andarion husband. "I know . . ." She kissed him. "Do *not* get hurt. If you do, I'm naming your son something awful in your absence."

He laughed.

Shahara handed her sleeping son to Ture and kissed his cheek. "We'll be back."

Syn kissed his son's head before he took Shahara's hand and headed after Nykyrian and Dancer.

Maris Xans-Sulle hesitated at the tormented look on Ture's face. "I'm sorry, baby. I have to go."

Ture nodded. "I know. Be careful what you wish for. I wanted a soldier.

I should have said I wanted an artist. Just remember, it's really hard to get blood out of your uniform."

Maris kissed him, then Shahara's young son, Devyn, and his own son, Terek. "I'll be home soon. I promise."

"I know you will. Otherwise, I'll send Zarya after you, and you won't like that."

The Caronese empress, Zarya, kissed Maris's cheek before he left. She held Darling's hand when he started to leave, keeping him by her side for a moment longer. "I hate for you to fight without me."

"I know. You're the better shot, but you haven't been cleared for battle yet. And you're still nursing. If I could feed Cezar in your stead, I'd let you go, but I think our son would be seriously pissed at us both if I tried to suckle him."

"You're not funny."

With one last kiss, Darling left them to join his brethren. Desideria growled in equal frustration at her brother and then her husband. "It's not fair!"

Caillen Dagan kissed her and then his daughter and infant son. "Don't worry. Shahara will nag me to death before I ever get hurt. She still thinks I'm five years old."

Chayden gave his sister, Desideria, a light hug. "I know, sis. Guard your man-meat from harm. Don't worry. If anyone kills Caillen, I want the honors."

Ushara almost laughed at something that Jullien would have said about the male himself.

Before he left, Chayden came over and gave her a light kiss. "Don't worry, we'll bring the Dagger home."

A large mountain of a Qill male signed to her something Ushara couldn't translate. Then he ran after the others.

"I love all of you!" Desideria called after them. "Come back soon!"

Another human male, Hadrian, began protesting, but Jayne Erixour forced him to stay with their kids so that she could leave with the others to find Jullien.

A tall blond male who reminded her of a paler version of Trajen stepped forward to hug Hadrian. "Don't worry, little brother, I've got her back for you. Nothing's getting through me."

Only then did Hadrian relent. Scooping his son up, he held him and watched as Nero and Jayne walked off and left him with his daughters and son.

Fain started after them, but Galene stopped him. "Not without me, Hauk."

He looked at the others who stood around them. "You have a base to set up, Commander. You're needed here."

Galene turned to their son, Talyn, who was also the second-in-command for the Alliance forces. "Commander Batur? Take the camp and make sure everyone is safe and accounted for. You're OOD until my return."

Defiance blazed in his stralen eyes, but Talyn didn't argue. "Yes, ma'am."

Safir Jari clapped him on the shoulder. "Don't worry, Talyn. I'll keep her safe. Besides, your father isn't about to let anyone get near her." He hugged Ture and kissed his nephew Terek before he led Fain and Galene toward the others to mount a rescue for Jullien.

Talyn appeared sick to his stomach as he watched them launch. His wife, Felicia, took his hand in hers while Vega, War, and the rest of the kids played in their blissful ignorance of what was going on around them. How Ushara envied them that innocence.

Talyn turned to issue orders, then stopped. "Admiral?"

Ushara blinked before she met his gaze. "Yes?"

"We are guests in your home. And——"

"No," she said, cutting him off. Swallowing hard, she looked around at the ones who'd been left behind. And in particular at the innocent children who had no idea how harsh the world could be. A sob wedged in her throat as she realized that all of Nykyrian's sons wore Tavali badges.

Jullien's and Davel's personal arms.

There was only one male who would have the authority to claim them as Fetchyn, and pin them with that Canting. One male whose wishes she would uphold even while cursing him for doing this to her. Because with those badges on those tiny arms, she knew what Jullien was saying, not just to her, but to all their brethren.

She met Talyn's handsome gaze. "You are not guests. You're our family."

And it was time for her children to meet the part of their father's blood family that wasn't responsible for this disaster. The part that he'd risked his life to protect.

She took her daughters' hands from Trajen and led them to Nykyrian's twin sons so that she could introduce them.

The two sets of twins, who were only months apart in age, were amazed by each other. At first, they frowned and stared at each other as if trying to understand why they favored so strongly, but within a few seconds, they were old friends. Even Adron and Jayce embraced them.

Grateful they were getting along, Ushara took command so that she could show the newcomers where to bunk for their extended stay here. She'd already called ahead and had the facilities manager prepare them condos and apartments.

As she led them from the bay, Jayne's son Sway came running up for Talyn to carry. Even though he was impeccably dressed in his Andarion battle uniform, Talyn perched the boy on his shoulders, just as Jullien would have done Nadya or one of their other nephews or nieces. "Your base is *very* different from the Ports'. Much more family oriented."

"It is. The Tavali was founded on family, honor, and Code. And we were the first among the Nations. It's said that in the steel of our walls, you can feel the Snitches still watching over us, wishing us all well."

As they entered the main housing district, Ushara met Zellen, who handed over a duty tablet. "These are the accommodations we have. Since you know your team and their requirements, I leave the final housing assignments up to you, Commander Batur. This is my adjutant, Zellen. He will note who is assigned where for you, and make sure everyone has clearance and access to their new housing."

"Admiral?" Talyn called as she started away. "Is there anything I can do for you?"

She was touched that he'd asked. Fain and Galene had a wonderful son. "No, thank you. Please see that you're all settled, and if you need anything, just let me or my staff know, and we'll take care of it immediately."

And with that, she ushered her babies to their grandparents' home. Or at least tried.

The girls began a high-pitched symphony of whining. "Can't our cousins come with us? I want to play with a real Taryn doll!"

Ushara laughed, then turned toward Kiara. "Do you mind if your boys go to my parents' for a while?"

"Honestly, I'd really appreciate the break. Is that wrong to admit?"

Ushara glanced down at the baby in her arms. "She's what? About seven months old?"

"Very good. She is."

"Then you probably haven't slept in nine." Ushara glanced to the brood of scrapping boys. "Or more. It's fine. They'll be at my parents'. I'll text you their address and number so that you can check on them."

"Bless you!"

Vasili stepped forward to help her wrangle the six smaller children toward his grandparents.

"Are you our cousin, too?" the eldest boy asked Vasili.

"I am. My name's Vas. And you are?"

"Adron! This is my brother Jayce. You look more like us than your dad does." He frowned at the girls. "So you only have sisters?"

He grinned at Ushara. "I'll have a brother any day now."

"Poor you!"

Vasili laughed. "It's not so bad. I love my sisters so long as they're not climbing all over me like I'm a piece of furniture."

"So you're the one who flies with Basha Jullien?"

He paused as a very attractive young blond woman drew near. "Um, yeah."

She held her hand out to him. "I'm your cousin, Thia. How much to have your father give mine lessons on how to loosen the noose?"

Vas scoffed at her. "What are you talking about? My noose is double-knotted around my throat. You get kidnapped once in your life, and your parents never, ever forget it."

"Oh my God! You, too? It's awful!"

Ushara shook her head as the two of them wandered off to continue their discussion on the horrors of having parents who loved them.

Her stomach burning, she rubbed against her son, who was turning somersaults inside her. It was as if he knew something had happened to his father.

Unable to stand it, she surrendered the children to her parents, who were waiting outside for their arrival, then made her way to the command center, where she could sit and monitor communications.

One way or another, Jullien would get word to her. She knew it. His band was still transmitting a heartbeat. So long as she could feel that, she wouldn't panic. Yes, his heart was racing most of the time, but he might be running or in hiding.

Her Dagger Ixur was good at survival. Better than anyone. If there was any way for him to pull through, he'd find it.

Determined to believe that, she turned her link on and scrolled to the last message he'd sent her. The one that had come over with his video.

*Don't panic. You knew something would go wrong. It's me, after all. Ever a thorn in the ass of Coreła—please don't rat me out to my matarra for posting that. She said if I didn't stop saying such things, she'd wash out my mouth and break my texting fingers. I love you, Shara. You know I won't break your heart.*

*Ever your Jules.*

She choked on a sob.

"Matarra?"

Turning, she saw Vasili, who must have entered the room while she had been reading. She pressed her hand to her lips and forced her tears into submission. "Yes, baby?"

He knelt down beside her chair like he used to do when he was a boy. "Paka won't leave us. He's the strongest fighter in all the Nine Worlds. Better than even the Iron Hammer."

She laughed at his choice of champions. "You know Commander Batur is the Iron Hammer, right?"

He gaped. "Really?"

She nodded. "You can ask him about it. Or his nephews."

"His nephews?"

"The two Andarion officers who are attached to his hip? Gavarian and Brach ezul Terronova."

"I didn't know that. So they're from Felicia's family?"

"Her older brother is their paka."

"Ah. Does Paka know them?"

"He does. But he and Talyn aren't on the best of terms." No sooner had she spoken those words than Talyn entered the room.

He paused just inside the door and looked about as if impressed with their facilities.

Ushara's acting adjutant immediately stiffened as she took in Talyn's dark, handsome features. Like most of them, her adjutant was gun-shy of the Ixurianir who had taken up temporary residence with them.

She smiled at the Fyreblood female. "Relax, Captain. Commander Batur and the others here are at peace with us."

Only then did she return to sit in her chair.

Releasing Vas's hand, Ushara returned to her monitoring. "What brings you here, Commander?"

"The same as you. I wanted to hear them and make sure you weren't left alone. After all, as you said, you're my family."

Those words touched her almost as much as Vasili's had. She'd been right. While Talyn had issues with Jullien, he was still a decent Andarion male who had compassion for others.

With a grateful smile, she indicated the chair by her side. "There's really nothing to hear right now. They're flying dark through League space."

Relaxed and yet very commanding in his uniform, Talyn sat down by her side. "Then it's going to be a long night." He took her hand and squeezed it comfortingly. "But we will see it through together."

No sooner had he spoken those words than the tadara, Sumi, Felicia, and Aros came through the door to stand vigil with them.

Within the hour, the room was filled to capacity. Even Trajen came to sit in a corner, wordlessly observing them all while they waited for news.

The look on his face said that he knew more than he was relaying to her. Ushara wasn't sure why he was keeping it to himself. It actually terrified her. Especially after she learned that Thrāix and Dimitri had been gone for days in search of Jullien's whereabouts and had yet to find a single clue as to his location.

Unable to stand it, she got up to walk for a bit and check on the girls. They should be asleep, but she wanted to make sure. Mira had been beside herself since they'd lost contact with Jullien. He was her woobie. She didn't sleep well unless her father held her and read to her until she collapsed in his arms.

Jullien never complained or minded. No matter how long it took for the twins to fall asleep. Whenever he was forced by missions to be gone, he'd call in and read over their link while Ushara held them in his stead.

Choking, she twisted her wedding band and waited for it to send over his heartbeat.

"Ushara?"

Involuntarily, she let out a sound of supreme disgust as the tadara called out to her. With a deep breath for patience, she turned. "Yes, *Maràstràda?*"

Cairistiona scowled at her. "I'm your matarra. Surely, you can dispense with such formalities?"

She had to bite back what she really wanted to say. "My husband was disowned by you, *Maràstràda*. Turned out to be tortured and dismembered in the streets after he'd saved your life. Forgive me if I'm not in a benevolent mood where you're concerned."

"I didn't know about any of that."

Ushara gaped at her. "What? You never once bothered to read the warrant your own mother swore out on his life?"

"No. My advisors told me it was for treason against the crown. I assumed they meant me. Honestly, I was too upset to read it myself. I didn't want to see a public record of my own child turning on me."

"So you and his father decided to make a public record of turning on him? You're right. That's so much better."

"We didn't know," she insisted.

"I don't care. You had one job . . . to protect the child you brought into this world."

Cairistiona glared at her. "It's not that simple."

"It *is* that simple. I've seen the photos of his childhood, *Maràstràda*. Jules never speaks of the cruelty you personally did to him. He actually defends you to this day. His father, not so much, but *you* . . . you, he still defends. So tell me honestly, did you ever once *hold* him when he cried? Nurse him when he was sick?"

"He wasn't . . ." Her voice trailed off as if seeking a lie.

"What? Lovable? That's what he says when he defends you. He was an asshole, unworthy of your respect. Do you know that his first words to me after our daughters were born were that he finally understood why you hated him so much? It took forever to get him back in my bed after that. He was so traumatized by my labor that he couldn't understand how I could still love my children when his own mother had never loved him for the pain he gave her on his arrival."

"I never meant to hurt him. You have no idea what it's like to have to look someone in the eye who bears the face of your brother who tried to kill you."

"No, you're right. I don't have that. But I do have a son who is the spitting image of a father who tried to kill us all."

Cairistiona sucked her breath in sharply. "What?"

"Vasili. His father was a traitor to this Nation. No one knows that I know. I've kept it from my child and everyone else, because I would *never* see Vasili hurt for something his father did. I think my son might know the truth of his father. And it's why he didn't speak until the day Jules saved him and gave him back to me. Why Vas has chosen to forsake his father's name in favor of Jules's."

"Who wouldn't want to be the son of an eton Anatole?"

"Jules, for one," Ushara said coldly. "Check his records, *Maràstràda*. He dropped your family name a long time ago for Jules Dagger Samari." She looked past her shoulder as Aros joined them. "He wants nothing from either of you. Not even the names you gave him when he was born."

"Mama?"

She turned at the sound of the twins calling to her to find her parents walking with them toward her.

"Are you okay, Shara?" her mother asked.

"I'm fine." Wiping at her cheeks, she knelt to hug her babies. "How are my girls?"

"I want Paka!" Mira whined. "Why won't he answer my call, Mama?"

"He can't, *mia*. You know if he could, he'd answer it in a heartbeat."

Her lip quivering, Viv looked up at Cairistiona. "Are you the bad Andarions who hurt my paka? He always said that you'd come for him and that we had to watch for you so that you didn't hurt us, too."

"No," Cairistiona said, her voice breaking. "I'm your yaya."

Mira slapped her hand against her forehead. "We gots three yayas? I'm so confuzzled."

Ushara laughed at her drama. "I can play Paka's video for you."

"Not the same." Viv's lips quivered as tears welled in her eyes. "He doesn't talk to us in the video. I want to talk to Paka."

"I know, *sozibu*. So do I." Her link began to buzz. For an instant, she hoped it was Jullien.

But as she pulled it out, she saw it was Thrāix. Hoping for a miracle, she answered it. "Hey? Did you find him?"

"No. Sorry. Are you still getting his heartbeat?"

"Yes. Why?"

"Don't panic. We're picking up a lot of bizarre activity on Andaria that we can't understand."

"Define *bizarre activity*."

"That's just it. We can't."

Terrified, Ushara pressed her ring.

This time, no heartbeat returned.

"No . . . no."

"Shara?"

Her head light, she looked at her parents and Jullien's, then at the girls.

She pressed for his heartbeat and waited.

Again, there was no response.

Unable to tell her girls that their father was dead, she collapsed.

# CHAPTER 41

D on't take this wrong, but I seriously hope Jules is dead."

Ushara gasped at Thrāix's harsh, deadpan words. "Pardon?"

He raked a grimace over her extremely pregnant body as she continued to arm herself. " 'Cause if he's not, he's going to kill every last one of us for letting you do this."

Scoffing, she fastened the blaster harness over her shoulders with the help of a tiny green alien named Morra Deathblade, who'd come in with The Sentella to help them make this rescue run. Sadly, because of her distended belly, Ushara couldn't carry a traditional holster. For that matter, she could barely get the shoulder one to fit comfortably. But for sheer determination and Morra's ingenuity, she'd have been unarmed. The tiny green Phrixian was amazing when it came to knowing her weapons.

Ushara checked the charge levels, then slid the blasters into place.

Morra hissed at Saf, then left the room to prep her ship.

Ignoring her hostility, which had been nonstop since Saf's arrival, Saf Jari inclined his head to Ushara in approval. Tall and handsome with black hair and dark, intelligent eyes that missed no detail about anything, he reminded her a lot of Jullien. They even favored enough physically that they could almost pass as relatives. "I love going into battle with an Andarion female."

She arched a brow at the former League assassin. It was a very peculiar comment coming from the mouth of a Phrixian warrior. As an extremely misogynistic race, they kept their females under strict lock and key—which was why Morra was so hostile to him. She was Schvardan, and apparently more than just the green skin differentiated her species from Saf's Naglfari Phrixian race.

Only Saf's brother Maris was immune from Morra's hatred of

Naglfari males. And only because Morra loved and respected him, and had dubbed Maris an honorary Schvardan.

Supposedly, to protect them from all threats, the Naglfari females were banned from any dangerous activity, including military service. From what Ushara had been told, they weren't even allowed to leave their homes to visit a friend or family member without a male escort. And he *must* be her husband, father, brother, or son, or another *very* close blood relation. Any female found without an escort could be arrested.

So Saf's comment was highly unusual for his upbringing. "Why's that?" she asked him.

"Aside from the fact that you're some of the best trained soldiers I've ever had the honor of serving with, your females are voraciously protective of their team, and especially their males. I know you're not going to let anything get through you. And if it comes down to it, you'll go out fighting with everything you have. I respect your warrior's code." He handed her his rifle. "Watch the kick on it. It's a Phrixian weapon, stronger than anything you've ever shot before. Think of it like a handheld ion cannon."

Saf took a second to show her how to properly hold and fire it. "Just make sure you have it anchored at your shoulder when you shoot, or it'll break your collarbone."

"Thank you."

"*Lützu.*"

She arched her brow, amazed at his intellect. "You speak Andarion?"

"A few basic words and phrases. Nothing too impressive." He winked at her.

Ushara watched while Saf armed himself from their locker. It was odd to be walking into a fray with him. When they'd been on the Port StarStation, she was highly suspicious of the Naglfari male as she noted his quiet, subversive ways.

Like Jullien, he kept secrets and was extremely wary and watchful. Lethally reserved around everyone.

But the moment he came here with the others and realized that Jullien was Dagger Ixur, his entire demeanor had drastically changed. He'd looked from her to Darling and let out an ironic laugh. "You know who Dagger Ixur is, right?"

Darling had shaken his head. "Should I?"

"He's the one who gave me the League intel we used to locate Zarya when she was being held by Kyr."

Gaping, Darling had stared at him for a moment as those words sank in. "You're shitting me?"

"No. I have no idea how he got what I couldn't access, but we'd have never found her without him. No one could bypass Kyr's security. You know that. Yet, somehow, Dagger busted through it and gave it to me. More than that, he's the one who had the layout and codes for the prison, and the guard rotation schedules."

Darling scowled at Ushara. "Why would he help me after the shit I've said to him in the past?"

"I told you. Jules carries a lot of guilt about what he did to his brother and Dancer when they were in school. To what he allowed his cousins to do to Talyn Batur. And he knows how much you mean to them, and to Hermione, who's important to Trajen. In spite of what you think you know about him, he has a very tender heart and generous spirit. Every time his grandmother goes after one of your families, or anyone you care about, he feels honor-bound to stop her and protect them for you."

She looked at them both before she also told them another fact about her husband. "You do know that after he got that intel for you, he was in that rescue battle with all of you, too, as one of the Tavali fighters?"

"Bullshit!" Darling's emphatic contradiction offended her.

Determined to serve him a giant piece of humble pie, she pulled up Jullien's pardon and shoved the link in his face. "This is the pardon you authorized for all Tavali who participated that day, is it not?"

It was a race as to whose jaw had fallen faster—Darling's, Aros's, or Nykyrian's.

Crossing his arms over his chest, Saf had nodded. "I remember seeing him in the footage of that fight when Kyr made me review it with him afterward. Dagger Ixur has that distinctive bug Canting, and he was one of the few Gorturnum in the battle. You can't miss it. That's why I assumed he must have been working with Sentella to get the intel we used to free Zarya and Ture."

Darling took her link to study it more closely. "He fought beside us and never said a word." He handed it to Nykyrian. "There were a lot of Tavali in that fight. But I don't remember him specifically. 'Course, I was a bit distracted by other things that day."

Nykyrian appeared sick as he passed her link to his father. "Why didn't he say something?"

"You would have shot him without hesitation or question," Ushara had said simply.

Their father had winced as he returned her link. "I was at the station when they handed him his pardon. He'd have been right there, in front of me, and I didn't even recognize him. He must have been covered the whole time for *me* not to recognize my own son, but I don't remember seeing a Tavali who was shielded."

"He would have had white-blond hair then. With a full beard and stralen eyes. A pierced left ear."

"Stralen?" Nykyrian asked.

She nodded.

"Shit." He looked at Darling. "I remember him in our group. We bumped into each other. . . . I even commented on it at the time, because it was so unusual. When I asked his lineage, he told me Samari, so I didn't make the connection. I took him as a Fyreblood and let it go so as not to draw attention to him from the Ixurian Andarions." He cursed under his breath. "I can't believe that was my own twin and that I spoke to him, and didn't know it."

Her thoughts returning to the present, Ushara paused while preparing for the next battle as she remembered the expression on their faces as they came to grips with the number of things Jullien had done for them that they'd never known about. It was only topped by the one on his mother's face after Ushara had turned Jullien's chips over to her that he'd recovered from Andaria, and his mother had viewed them. The ones that proved to all just who and what Dagger Ixur really was, and why Eriadne and his cousins wanted him dead so badly.

For weeks now, they'd pooled their resources as tightly as they could to find him.

But it was Saf and Fain, working together, who'd finally come through for her. As she'd first suspected when they evacuated Venik's Porturnum base, Saf was still talking to his brother, Kyr. Yet not for the reasons she'd feared.

In spite of everything that had happened between them, Saf still loved his brother and wanted Kyr to surrender. He was playing double agent in an effort to try and capture Kyr rather than slaughter him as the other Sentella members wanted.

Just as he'd been unable to turn on Maris at the whims of his family, Saf couldn't bring himself to turn on Kyr and execute him. He wanted the League prime commander deposed, but kept alive.

He was loyal to his own detriment.

And that was something she could respect. Something Saf had in common with the male she loved most.

With that thought foremost in her mind, she reached for Jullien's Samari Warsword.

"What are you doing?" Nykyrian asked the moment he saw her with it.

"Jules made two oaths to me. The first that he'd never break my heart, and the second was that this couldn't end and he wouldn't be able to rest in peace until he drove his grandfather's sword through the heart of the bitch who'd betrayed you all, and mounted her head on the flag post of the Andarion palace. This fight began the day Eriadne declared war on the Pavakahir and drove us from our native soil. It won't end until a Samari son takes his vengeance for his *velir*."

"*Velir?*" Chayden asked.

Nykyrian answered for her. "The Andarion word for *people*. But since Andarions aren't people, they refuse to use a human term for their group."

Chayden grinned at her. "I can respect that. So what word do you use for *nation?*"

"Same as *empire. Insara.*"

"*Insara,*" Chayden repeated. "Ah, that makes sense."

Jory snorted as he finished arming himself. "How? And in what possible way does that make sense?"

"*Tadara* and *Tadar* for *empress* and *emperor*? *Insara* for *empire*. That would make *ara* the root for *territory,* correct?"

Nykyrian gaped at Chayden. "Indeed. I'm impressed. Most don't catch that."

"*Pakti.* Although . . ." Chayden scowled at Ushara. "It does beg one question about the root of tara, Ger Tarra, and Matarra. Also *territory?*" He asked that as if afraid of offending her.

Nykyrian laughed. "From the Andarion *Hygitir evest Marvikriegir*—a barbaric time in our history. Yes. Back when we viewed our females as our territory, or property." He passed an amused look to Ushara. "They have since taught us better."

"Yes, we have." She smiled. "Now, let's pray Saf's information is correct and that Jules is still alive and being moved later today." She refused to believe what his ring said. He wasn't dead. He couldn't be. The gods wouldn't do that to her again. "It's time to bring my husband home. And to keep the promise I made to him."

Ryn Dane frowned at her. "What promise?"

"That unlike his parents, I would *never* turn my back on him and leave him in the hands of his enemies to suffer. No matter where he was or how difficult the task, I would find him and I would bring him home."

Fain buckled his holster around his thigh. "If anyone had ever, *ever* told me that I'd be flying out for the benefit of Jullien eton Anatole, I'd have punched them in the throat. Never mind the fact that I had to beat down half my Tavali Nation to get the information on his whereabouts. I've never known so many to keep a secret this tight before. And I thought I had a lot of folks who hated *me*. . . . Damn. No one wanted to see an Anatole go free."

Ryn sighed. "I wish Fain were joking about the body count. Are any of the Veniks still talking to you?"

"Kareem. Maybe Circe. I'm waiting for Brax to go after my Canting over the damage I've wrought."

His expression deadly earnest, Ryn clapped him on the back. "We won't let that happen."

"No, we won't," Ushara promised him. "You and Saf need anything, ever—just say the word." And with that, she led them for their ships.

It was time to bring Jullien home.


Weak and in more pain than he'd ever been in before, Jullien pulled himself up by his trembling arms into the rickety desk chair. He glanced behind him at the crushed and bleeding bodies he'd left in his wake.

Eriadne had broken her final pact. Instead of holding him and torturing him for her amusement, she should have killed him while she had the chance.

Just as he should have killed her that night in her bedroom when he was a boy.

Missed opportunities.

But no more. Blinking his eyes, he tried to clear them so that he could operate the communications equipment in front of him. He had to warn The Tavali and Sentella to stay away from here.

It was a trap.

And just as he turned it on, someone snatched him from behind and jerked him out of his slumber, back into reality.

*Damn it!*

It'd been another dream.

Not real.

Jullien woke up to find himself still in his filthy cell, facedown on the harsh white tile floor. Still bound in chains, with his hands behind his back, and muzzled, wearing only his ragged and torn pants.

Eriadne stood over him, tsking as she gave him a petulant smirk. "Having a nightmare, little Julie? You were always a pussy that way."

He sneered at her, not that she could see it for the muzzle he wore. The nightmares didn't come to him during his sleep. Those had been solely reserved for his waking hours.

Glaring at her, he wished he had the ability to curse her and tell her what he thought. But the muzzle and neuroinhibitor around his throat kept him from breathing fire or speaking a single sound. He couldn't even use his telepathy to push his thoughts to her. She'd made sure he was as helpless as he'd been all those years ago when he was a boy in her tender, loving care in the *vörgäte*.

She let out a tired sigh. "How so very disappointing. No one cares about you at all. Here, I thought surely one of those bastards would come to save you. But alas, not a one has shown in all this time. How utterly pathetic you are. Every bit as worthless and unwanted as you've been since the moment my daughter shat you out and refused you her tit to suckle. We should have left you to wither and die in your crib."

Eriadne stepped back and gestured for the guards. "Take him. There's no need to delay his execution another minute."

Saddest part?

Jullien knew she was right. That must have been the source of his dream. His mind was trying to come up with a solid reason as to why no one had come for him. He wanted it to be his fault.

Not theirs.

It was easier to accept it if he were to blame because he'd told them to stay away, than to deal with the trauma that they, like his parents, had just gone on with their daily routine as if he didn't matter. Cleaned out his room, given away all his belongings, and forgotten he was ever a part of their lives.

Just like his parents had done once Nykyrian returned. They hadn't even had the decency to tell him themselves that he'd been locked out of their lives.

Locked out of his home.

Banished and forgotten.

So much for Ushara's promises that she would always find him. That, no matter what, they would track him down and bring him home.

The bitter reality shattered his heart as he lost hope of ever seeing her again. Of ever hearing the voices of his daughters or son.

*I just wanted to matter to someone.*

*One sentient being.*

But that only happened in fantasies. And for others who were born worthy.

Not for contentious assholes no one gave a shit about, who'd fucked up their lives. From beginning to end.

*Face it, Jules. You used up all your chances. It was a wasted try. There was never any real hope for you.*

Closing his eyes, Jullien fought against the despair that overwhelmed him. To be fair, he'd told Ushara to stay out of this fight. He'd even destroyed his wedding ring to keep her safe from Eriadne's clutches so that his enemies couldn't use it to find her.

*It's what you wanted.*

Still, it stung.

After Eriadne had dragged him out of WAR's reach and deep inside her new hiding hole so that no one would be able to help him or stop her from torturing him, it had become obvious that he wasn't going to be rescued—that his grandmother intended to keep him hidden in her lair until she'd had her fill of fun—Jullien had thought the kindest move would be to let his wife think it was over, rather than to drag it out indefinitely. The worst was always the not knowing.

Hope was a cruel, vicious bitch. Better to stop it and let Ushara move on than to delay the inevitable.

Now . . .

He just wished he could see her one last time. Touch her white-blond hair and smell its fresh, apple scent. Hear her laughter in his ear as he held her.

Wincing, he tried to stand and walk as they literally dragged him from his cell, down the narrow hall, to a waiting transport. They roughly shoved him inside and slammed the doors before they headed off to take him to a new location.

Their tactics surprised him. He'd assumed they'd kill him in his cell with no one to witness the deed and bury his body in an unmarked grave somewhere.

Apparently, Eriadne had something else in mind.

Strange . . . she seldom wanted an audience for her crimes. But as they reached their destination, opened the doors, and jerked him out so that he saw the public display and waiting crowd, complete with full media coverage from all Nine Worlds, he fully understood his grand-mother's final act of cruelty.

Eriadne wasn't allowing him to die as one of her hated political en-emies or rivals, or a warrior, or even a tiziran.

She was giving him the death of a traitor on the same spot where she thought she'd murdered his mother.

His throat would be cut over a basin, and he'd be left to bleed out in public for everyone to witness his last choking breaths. No priest to pray over his corpse. No chance for his soul to find peace, whatsoever.

Not that any Yllam priest would give him last or burial rights anyway, since he bore a Demurrist emblem on his chest. They'd even refused to bring him prayer beads while Eriadne held him in his cell.

Even his prayer band Nadya had made for his birthday had been vin-dictively cut from his wrist and burned.

*Just breathe. A few minutes more, and this whole damn miserable life will fi-nally be over.*

Swallowing hard, Jullien conjured an image of Ushara with his girls and son. That was the only comfort he wanted, and it was the one thing they couldn't take from him.

His guards led him up the stairs of a makeshift platform that had been placed over the ruins of the palace, and shoved him down on his knees in front of the basin. When Jullien started to fight, they quickly used the chains to secure his arms to the basin's stand, and pulled him for-ward so that he was forced to lean over it at an awkward angle.

If only he wasn't wearing the damn inhibitor, he'd be able to free himself and beat them all down. . . .

The huge executioner came forward to hold his head down by his hair while the crowd cheered and chanted for his slow, painful death.

His grandmother's senior advisor cleared his throat, then read the charges against him for the reporters and crowd. "Jullien eton Anatole, for crimes and treason against Andaria, her tadara and rādix, your own blood lineage and family, for betraying your sacred duties and honor, and turning against all you have known, you have been stripped of your titles and are condemned to die. May the gods take no mercy upon you or your rotten soul."

He inclined his head to the executioner, who cupped Jullien's muzzled chin in his gloved hand.

At peace with his violent death, Jullien waited to feel the bite of the blade against his throat. He held perfectly still, refusing to give anyone the satisfaction of seeing him cower or beg.

He expected the executioner to be rough. So when the male caressed his cheek with a loving touch, then sliced him, he was stunned.

Doubly stunned when a minute went by and he was still alive and coherent.

*What the hell?*

Scowling, he looked up at the hooded figure to stare into a pair of beautiful, familiar silvery-white eyes. Not to mention, that wasn't an overweight belly he'd felt against his shoulder.

Rather a very pregnant one.

*Ushara!*

Her eyes filled with warmth and love, she smiled down at him. "I told you I'd never leave you alone again. You're not the only one who keeps your promises, Jules Samari."

It took him another minute to realize she'd sliced through his muzzle and not his flesh. And that she wasn't here alone. Trajen and Thrāix used their powers to free his hands and snap the neuroinhibitor from his neck.

With a strength he'd never known, he rose to his feet and pulled her against him. *"Urtui æbre gevyly frag, mu sojara."*

She placed her hand over his heart and smiled up at him. *"Hæfre m'ixuri."* Forever my darkheart.

Tears gathered in his eyes until she pressed something cold and metallic into his palm.

His grandfather's Warsword.

"It's time to finish this." Ushara pulled her blasters out and opened fire on his enemies to cover him. "Your grandmother's on my right. Trajen and Thrāix have cleared you a path to her seat. She's all yours, baby. Get her!"

He hesitated to leave her side, until he saw that she wasn't alone. Nyk, Dancer, Chayden, Fain, Ryn, Darling, Syn, Jayne, Saf, Maris, Galene, Shahara, Nero, Talyn, Caillen, Davel, and Jory were there to cover her for him.

Nykyrian inclined his head. "We've got Ushara for you, little brother. Nothing's getting through us."

More grateful than mere words could ever express, Jullien saluted him before he turned and cut through the guards who came forward to block his path. Like an unstoppable storm, he tore a swath through them, with one single goal. . . .

This time, no one would stop the Dagger Ixur from fulfilling his dark quest and ending the Andarion kakistocracy forever.

Shrieking in outrage, Eriadne opened fire as soon as she realized his intent. She ran for cover.

Twirling his sword around his body, Jullien used his powers to deflect her blasts. He spewed his fyrebreath and ripped open everyone who came at him. Most shrank back immediately, realizing they were no match for a pissed-off Samari hybrid with fyre and telekinesis.

A few braver souls engaged him for their tadara, and they died valiantly for that effort.

When he finally caught up to Eriadne, she was in the marble hallway of the senate building, which stood next door to where the palace had been. Her bracelet had caught in the giant tapestry that hung in the foyer. Though how she'd managed *that*, Jullien couldn't imagine.

Desperately, she was trying to free herself. "We can make a deal, Jullien. It's not too late for you to return to your place as my tahrs."

He laughed bitterly. "I would ask if you were insane, but I already know the answer. I told you when I was a child what I would do to you if you ever went for my matarra again. Twice, I allowed you to live. Now—"

She snapped her hand free. Too late he realized that she hadn't been caught in the tapestry. She'd been using it to unwind the bracelet from her wrist.

And that wasn't a bracelet. It was a sling bow with a poisoned dart.

One she shot straight into his bare chest. "You didn't really think Faran or my sister killed Edon Samari, did you?" she sneered at him as he staggered back in pain. "While he was a bold bastard and she a heinous bitch, even they lacked the balls to take out one of my lovers without my permission."

Gasping, Jullien pulled the dart from of his heart and dropped it to the floor.

She laughed at his pain and shoved him back another step. Then she had the stupidity to keep talking, instead of running. "I should have killed your mother the moment I birthed her, too. I kept hoping one of you wouldn't be a disappointment. No matter. I—"

Jullien cut her words off with one final stroke of Edon Samari's Warsword. "Fuck you, bitch," he snarled over her headless corpse. "I am the blood of Edon Samari and an eton Anatole. No damn whore is going to kill me and live. I'll see your worthless ass in Tophet. Make sure to save me a place by your side so I can torture you for eternity."

Grabbing his grisly war trophy from the floor by the hair his grandmother had been so proud of, Jullien had one last promise to fulfill before the Koriłon came to take his rotten soul to the gods for its final Rekkynynge.

Ushara withdrew from the fighting as Nykyrian finally quelled the crowd and brought it under control. While they might hate Jullien, the Andarions loved *him*. And no one wanted his grandmother back in power.

No one.

It didn't take Nykyrian long to get them to turn against the foreign League soldiers who'd been assigned there. The speed with which the trained army dropped weapons and fled was actually comical.

Even faster was how quickly the Andarion armada retook an oath of allegiance to Nykyrian even without his having the Anatole family Warsword in his possession.

Ushara scanned the crowd. "Where's Jullien?"

Thrāix grimaced. "I'm not sure you want that answer."

Trajen sucked his breath in sharply between his teeth. "Yeah . . . we might want to face you in another direction."

"What?" She glanced up to follow their line of sight, then wished she hadn't. "Oh dear gods. Is that . . . a *head*?"

Nykyrian laughed as he saw it. "Damn. That's *so* cold." His laughter faded as he took note of the other objects Jullien had left behind on the flagpole. "Not sure exactly what my brother is trying to say by that flag order. Should I be upset . . . or concerned?"

"What do you mean?" Ushara asked.

He screwed his face up. "He put his flag above mine."

Trajen slid an evil smirk to Nykyrian. "Technically, he put *my* flag over yours. That's the Gorturnum National flag. Not Jules's personal Canting, which he could have done, as he has his own. For that matter, it's not even the UTC flag."

Ushara nodded. "Yeah, so I wouldn't take it personally, *Alteske*. I think all it means is that he values our branch of The Tavali over The Sentella and Andaria."

But a tattered Alliance flag now flew once more above them all.

She headed for that flagpole as fast as she could, knowing Jullien would be coming from that direction.

Jullien met her halfway through the crowd. The instant she saw him, she knew something was wrong. There was a paleness to his features that wasn't normal. His skin held a grayish cast to it as he dragged two swords by his side.

"Jules?"

He was shivering and sweating. "She poisoned me."

"No!"

"It's okay. You're safe now. They can't touch you."

"No, it's not okay! Jullien, don't you do this to me. You fight. You hear me!"

He nodded weakly, then fell to his hands and knees. Ushara sank down by his side.

Thrāix and Trajen rushed to them.

"Boy," Trajen said between gritted teeth as he saw Jullien's state of near unconsciousness. "You get yourself into more shit."

Thrāix snorted his agreement. "He's going to hate us."

"He'll get over it." Trajen gently moved her aside so that he could kneel on one side of Jullien while Thrāix knelt on the other.

Together, they used their powers to siphon the poison from his system and heal him. But judging from the way Jullien writhed and groaned, it must have been excruciating. He cursed them worse than she'd cursed him while she was in labor.

When he was finally healed, Jullien hissed at Thrāix and actually slapped his hand away.

Scowling, Thrāix popped him back. "You are such an irritable asshole."

Jullien smirked. "Contentious from my first breath to my last."

With a laugh, Thrāix helped him back to his feet while Trajen shrugged his jacket off and gave it to Jullien to put on. Then, Thrāix handed him the sheath for the Samari Warsword so that Jullien could strap it over his back.

As soon as he was dressed, Jullien grabbed Ushara and kissed her. Until he realized his brother was staring at them.

He pulled back. "What did I screw up now?"

Nykyrian snorted as he met Darling's gaze, then Dancer's and Fain's. "He really is a contrary asshole." He held his hand out to Jullien. "Thank you. I owe you my life, little brother."

Jullien shook his head. "No, *drey*." He met Ushara's gaze and smiled at her. "I owe you mine." Only then did he take Nyk's hand and allow him to pull him in for a brief hug.

"So where does this leave us?" Nykyrian asked with a frown.

Jullien looked around at The Sentella and in particular the War Hauk family. Shame darkened his eyes, especially when he met Talyn's red gaze. "Familiar strangers. I know there's no reparation for what I've done. Against any of you. Or for what I've taken. *Sorry* will never cover the scars I gouged out of your souls. Believe me, I know and understand the hatred I earned. We are what we've always been . . . dysfunctional."

"Maybe in time . . ."

He scoffed at his brother's kindness. "We're not saints, Nyk. We're warriors. Means I don't have to like you to fight to the death for you. If you ever need extra firepower, I'm always one unanswered call away."

Nyk laughed. "Ditto."

With a bashful grin, Jullien scratched his chin with his thumb. "Ah hell, who knows? Maybe someday our kids can grow up to be friends. I think that's the best any of us can hope for. In the meantime, just pretend I died that night in the restaurant. You really owe me nothing. You already put me through a wall and kicked my ass. That's all I deserve and what I earned."

Nykyrian had the decency to look embarrassed. "Are you really happy?"

"More than I have a right to be." Jullien cradled Ushara's hand in his. "It took me a while, and a lot of well-earned ass-beatings, but what I finally had to learn was that happiness isn't something someone gives you, and it isn't something you find or buy. It's something you make.

Something you sometimes have to work hard for. It comes from within, not without."

He kissed Ushara's palm. "And by the gods, having earned it now and being lucky enough to finally have it in my life, I'll be fucking damned if I ever let anyone take it from me again."

Nyk inclined his head to them. "All right, I shall leave you to it. But I am going to reconfirm the report that Jullien eton Anatole is dead and make damn sure that the Kill-Warrant is canceled. For good, this time. And I will file a death certificate for that name—just to be safe. The Sentella will purge your prints and DNA from all records and databases, and I will personally make sure that your accounts and holdings are transferred by way of inheritance to Jullien's maternal cousin, Dagger Samari."

"Why would you do that?"

"Because they're yours by right of birth. You and your children, and wife should have what you're entitled to. And when you and your children are ready, if they want to join Andarion society, I'll make sure they enter as full tizirani and tizirahie. Same for Triosa. It's only fair. The Anatoles put us both through hell. Besides, you need every cred you can lay hands to for therapy. Trust me, I know."

Snorting, Jullien used his powers to retrieve the second Warsword from the ground where he'd dropped it. He handed it to his brother.

Nyk scowled at it.

"It's yours. I took it from Eriadne's body. Make sure your mother returns it to the Anatole family vault once you rebuild the palace. And don't worry, it's not the one I took her head with." He gestured at the Samari Warsword that was now strapped across his back, over Trajen's jacket. "I used mine for that honor."

Ushara's breath caught as it dawned on her that this was the first time he didn't claim Cairistiona as his own mother.

His brother hesitated at the realization that this was the Anatole family Warsword. "You could have seized the throne of Andaria with this."

"Never wanted your throne, *drey*. Damn sure don't want the drama or nightmare that comes with it." He draped his arm over Ushara and held her close. "I have everything I need right here."

Nykyrian hugged them both. "I wish you both well, and all the blessings of the gods."

"You, too, brother. You, too."

As Nyk walked away, Dancer came up to Jullien. For several long seconds, they stood without speaking.

"You really tried to save me when the pod crashed that day in school?"

"Check the hospital records, Dancer. I was admitted an hour after you were. Chrisen and Merrell overdosed me out of fear that I would tell on them. My grandmother told your parents it was from the injuries I sustained from the crash, but the hospital records show the truth. Plus I have the scars where they held me in place. I didn't want you hurt. They wanted Fain punished and under control. You were just their unfortunate victim that day. And for that, I'm eternally sorry."

"Why didn't you tell me?"

"You were a kid. Same as me. What would you have done? Your mother wasn't about to cross my grandmother. Endine would have cut Fain's throat herself, *and* yours to curry royal favor. And you wouldn't have believed me back then, anyway. We were both children against a vindictive tadara and your bitch of a mother. There was nothing to be done."

Fain let out a tired breath as he joined them. "I've hated you for so long that it pains me to admit how right you are."

Jullien looked past him to his son Talyn. "You've got much better reasons to hate me, Hauk."

He stiffened as Talyn and his mother drew near and waited for the famed Ring fighter to knock his head off. It was what he fully deserved for what they'd done to the kid.

Instead, Talyn glanced to Ushara, then back to Jullien. "You're in luck, asshole. As a former lack-Vest, I've never been in the position that I could afford to hold on to grudges. Besides, I'd be dead right now had you not sent Ushara and Trajen to the Port StarStation. As much as I'd like to hate you for that little stint in prison I had, I keep thinking back to Trajen pulling that wall off me and my paka." He held his hand out to Jullien. "Thank you for that."

Still, Jullien hesitated. "You're not going to sucker-punch me, now, are you?"

"If I wanted to kill you, I'd just shoot you. Be easier than risking a hand injury on your hard head."

Laughing, Jullien took his hand.

"But . . . I have to say this. I do hate you for another reason."

Jullien arched a brow as he searched his mind. For the life of him, he couldn't think of anything else Talyn could possibly hold against him. "That is?"

"Cutting the bitch's head off. I wanted that kill. Damn you for it."

He laughed. "It's all right. I wanted Merrell and Chrisen, and you got those honors. Any idea how much I hated you for *that*?"

Talyn snorted. "You didn't miss much. One pissed on me. The other barfed."

Jullien rolled his eyes. "Yeah, that sounds like the cousins I knew and loathed so well."

Ushara stiffened as Galene stepped forward, and she waited to see what the female would do. As an Andarion mother, she well understood Galene's animosity for Jullien. However, she wasn't about to allow Galene to harm her husband.

Not for any reason.

If she so much as scowled at him, they were about to throw-down.

Jullien's grip tightened on her hand, but other than that, he gave no indication of his reservation.

Finally, Galene spoke. "I never once considered how cruel it was for you to see Talyn being held so often and loved on by your mother while we banned you from her presence. I keep thinking back to how many times I found you lurking in the shadows outside her door, day and night. And I'd yell at you for it. My only thought was how upset Cairie would be to find you there, and how hard she'd be to calm down, thinking you were Eadvard come to harm her. Not once did I consider the fact that you were just a child needing someone's lap to sit on, too. And that you were only there, trying to seek some modicum of affection from anyone you could find. And instead of kindness, all you found was more insults and cruelty. I'm sorry, Jullien."

Jullien glanced to Talyn. "That doesn't excuse what I let happen to Talyn, when I knew better. Worse, I kept his whereabouts from you and hid what they'd done. I'm damned for that one act alone, and I know it. It's why I made sure WAR approved him for admission to their group after Jayne freed him from Onoria, and I saw the way Eriadne and Chrisen intended to keep going for his throat. I knew WAR would protect him from their treachery. But don't worry. I won't darken your doorways ever again and remind you of what I did."

Galene smiled at him. "I don't know, Jullien. Had you not darkened our doorway, both Fain *and* Talyn would be dead now. Thank you for saving their lives." She stepped forward and kissed his cheek.

"Aw!" Chayden said as he sidled up to Jullien's side. "Can I kiss your cheek, too?"

Jullien scoffed and shoved him back. "Something is so profoundly wrong with you." He glanced around. "Where have you and Jory been, anyway?"

"Do not ask questions you do not want answered, my brother. Remember, ninety percent of survival in this life is plausible deniability. Especially when you're as high-ranking in the command food chain as *you* are."

"Now you're scaring me."

"Good." Chayden flashed a devilish grin.

Nykyrian gave the orders for everyone to pack up and head back to the Cyperian base.

Ushara took Jullien's hand. "Ready to go home?"

That question brought a lump to his throat as he handed her his Samari Warsword. "More than you'll ever know."

"Thrāix Sparda?"

As they headed for their ships to return, Thrāix cut an irritated grimace to Trajen at the sound of the familiar voice that belonged to the very person they'd both been avoiding this entire adventure.

Steeling his emotions, and in particular his anger, he turned to face Nero Scalera—Trajen's older brother, who was one of Nykyrian's best friends and a member of The Sentella.

Bastard hadn't changed much since the day they'd fled the Chillers hunting them. Just looked more like their mother.

More like Julia.

A lot older and more haunted.

Same dark blond hair. Same steel-blue eyes that could sear a soul to its bitter core. Eyes that were shaped and colored identically to Darling Cruel's—the only thing that marked Darling as their first cousin.

And it was those eyes that made it hardest of all for Thrāix to look at Nero, as they reminded him of everything that had been brutally ripped from him.

Nero's breathing turned ragged. "I thought you were dead."

Thrāix shrugged. "We endured."

"We?"

"He married Julia," Trajen said dryly.

Nero gaped. "When?"

"Before she was murdered." Thrāix's tone was frigid.

Without a word, Trajen continued on to the ships, leaving Thrāix with Nero. *Thanks, asshole.*

Nero let out a tired sigh. "You hate me as much as my brother does?"

"Don't take it personally. I hate every minsid body. You're really not special."

Nero laughed at his surly tone. "Did anyone else survive?"

"Not that we know."

Nero winced. "Why didn't my brother come to me after he escaped?"

"Same reason I lived alone for decades. In order to survive our hell, we were forced to go Thaumarturgus. You don't *ever* want to know what that cost us. The price we continue to pay for it. There's a reason our powers don't drain like yours. Why we can do things you and Hadrian can't imagine, including gift powers to others. Tray lives in constant anguish, Nero. Mental and physical. You can't even begin to fathom it."

Nero choked on his own pain, which swelled inside him over those words. That pain reached out to Thrāix as he realized just how much the man wanted his family whole.

Damn it.

Nero wasn't an enemy. Like it or not, he was family, and that was something the Scaleras were frightfully short on. And as much as Trajen wanted to deny he was one of them, his connection to their blood was what had him protecting Darling, even when he didn't want to. And since he was related to Darling's mother and not his father, Trajen might not share blood with the Danes, but he still protected them because they were dear to Darling.

"I love my brothers, Thrāix, and I loved Julia. I would have given my life for hers. And I would still give it for Trajen. Is there anything I can do to help him?"

"Can you leave your ship docked here?"

"Yes."

"Follow me."

Nero scowled. "What are we doing?"

"Something that is going to seriously wreck Trajen's day. Probably get my ass kicked. But since we rescued Jules, we're in luck. We have the one Andarion on board his ship who can back Trajen down. So let's go have some fun at his expense, I say."

Kyr Zemin, the prime commander of The League, went cold as he watched the latest report from Andaria. And he saw the images coming through.

Especially the one of Eriadne's head hanging from a flagpole that currently contained an Alliance flag with a Tavali, Sentella, and Andarion one below it.

And a League flag that bore an obscenity along with the name of one former Andarion prince he intended to hunt down and skewer.

His breathing ragged, he saw red. And it wasn't just the uniform he was wearing. Picking up his link, he called his second-in-command.

"How the hell did we lose Andaria?" he growled without preamble.

"The Sentella, sir. They came in without warning. They were led by the former tahrs himself."

"And no one picked up anything? Like, say, an entire fucking Sentella attack fleet flying through our airspace?"

"No, sir."

"Useless!" Kyr cut the transmission as his anger roiled through every part of his being.

Choking on it, he pulled out the single photograph he had of his wife and daughter. His one and only tie to them.

It was so old and tattered—like his withered heart and soul.

Even now, he could hear the sounds of Nisa screaming in his ear as she was murdered, calling out to him on his link to help her.

But he'd been on the other side of the galaxy on a bullshit assignment. Too far away to get to her or do anything other than die inside as they ravaged her. Agony tore him apart as he relived that day.

His beautiful daughter would be grown now. Every time he passed by a girl the age she would be had she lived, who bore any feature similar to her or her mother, he imagined her as his own. Imagined what it would be like to have her call him *Dad* and to greet him with a happy, loving smile.

It was all he'd ever wanted in his life. He'd given up everything to be with Nisa. His royal titles. His throne.

His father's love.

None of that had mattered.

Only her.

And after she was gone, all he'd wanted was the throat of the bastards who had taken his precious Nisa and Risald from him.

Nykyrian Quiakides had denied him that justice.

"Nemesis, my *minsid* ass!" he growled. That rancid bastard didn't believe in justice for victims. If he did, he'd have stood down and given Kyr what he needed to sleep at night. Nykyrian would have allowed him the satisfaction of ripping the heart from the one who'd gutted him. Instead, Nykyrian took the kill for his own selfish reasons.

And instead of killing Kyr when he could have and ending his fucking misery, once and for all, Nykyrian had taken his eye and left him here in this eternal hell.

For those sins, he wouldn't rest until he stood over Nykyrian's grave.

The Sentella may have won the battle today, but the war was far from over.

And Kyr still had one of their own he commanded. One not even Saf knew about. His little brother had no idea what he was playing with. Saf thought himself clever, but he was nothing more than a tenderhearted tool Kyr manipulated.

Before all was said and done, he would teach them the price of crossing The League. His family, and especially that hybrid bastard who had started this the day he failed to mind his place as a simple League assassin.


"Wow," Nykyrian said slowly as he came off the ramp to a sadly lackluster greeting of a large group that actually pouted to see his arrival. "Good thing my ego's solid or this would hurt my feelings."

Kiara laughed as she approached him with Zarina in her arms and kissed his lips. "Don't feel bad. They've been doing that to every ship that lands. They're waiting for your brother to arrive."

Dancer snorted irritably as he saw the huge group with banners, balloons, and flowers. "Damn. I need a better press agent."

Pausing at his side, Fain draped his arm around his brother's shoulders. "Hang the bitch's head from a flagpole, and we'll throw you a welcome party next time."

Kiara made a face. "Did he really? I mean, I saw the pictures, but I was hoping they were faked."

Nykyrian grimaced in a similar fashion. "Yeah . . . no, they weren't faked. They were quite real. Jullien definitely had some leftover childhood trauma he needed to get out of his system." He flashed an exaggerated smile at her. "Been there."

Laughing, Syn and Shahara joined them as they disembarked from one of the other ships. "*Drey,* we all have, especially with *your* grandmother."

While waiting on everyone to return, they went to stand with Nykyrian's parents and aunt, and their own families, who were slightly segregated from the Gorturnum and Fyrebloods. Not because The Sentella had a problem with them. Just that the Gorts were an extremely mistrustful group.

And they seemed to have a lot of problems with Nykyrian's parents and aunt, which made Nykyrian rather nervous.

Nykyrian held Tiernan while he watched Jullien's daughters running around in a game of chase with their older brother, Taryn, Thia, and other cousins. "You didn't want to play with them?"

Tiernan pouted. "I did, but Mama was afraid I'd get hurt and made me stop."

He glanced over to Kiara.

"His heart rate was too high."

Nykyrian grimaced at something that always concerned them, and made them even more protective of their youngest son than they were of the others.

Tiernan's congenital heart defect. "Sorry, bug."

"Me, too, Daddy."

Finally, Trajen's ship began docking. The adult Tavali quickly rounded up the kids to a safe distance from the docking equipment and ship's engines and ramps. Nykyrian had to smile at the expert way they wrangled them in. It was obvious they had a lot of practice doing it.

And when Jullien came down the ramp, it sounded like a rock star was in the bay. Nykyrian had never heard such a cacophony of joyous screams or seen so many rush forward in greeting in his life.

When his parents started to join the crowd, he stopped them.

His mother scowled at him. "What are you doing?"

"We're not his family, Matarra."

"I'm his mother."

Nykyrian jerked his chin toward Unira, who was embracing Jullien with tears streaming down her face. She clutched at his shoulders and held on to him in a way he knew his own mother had never done with Jullien. That was someone who only wanted the best for her child and who never wanted to let him out of her arms.

"Not anymore. Trust me. If you have any love for him at all, the kindest thing you can do is let him go with your blessings. Don't try to tether his heart to our broken past. He's right. We've all hurt each other too much. Maybe in time we can reunite as friends. But for now, he's where he belongs. Look at how much they love and accept him. *That's* what he needs to heal. Don't taint this moment for him."

His father swallowed hard. "What made you so wise?"

"It's not wisdom. Some of it's self-preservation. While I like the new Jullien, I haven't forgotten or forgiven the old one. One day, I might have a bad flashback or psychotic episode that ends with his bloody demise. The farther he stays away from me, the less likely he is to be within my striking distance should that happen. . . . I am, after all, a fully trained League assassin."

Jullien's eyes watered as he held his little girls against his chest and they bounced with giddy laughter. He never wanted to let them go again. Love and relief overwhelmed him so much that he couldn't speak. He'd never expected a homecoming like this. It looked like half the base was here to greet him.

Nadya stood at his back, hugging him with her sisters and cousins. Even little Taryn was here with his Dagger Ixur Canting still pinned to his sleeve.

One by one, Jullien hugged and kissed each child there.

As he rose to his feet, Sheila shook her head at him. "You are ever our bane, Shithead. What are we to do with you?"

"No idea."

As if on cue, Anders, the XO of the Hadean Corps who'd arrested Jullien and Davel for fighting back in his early days here, walked up nonchalantly and clapped Jullien on the biceps. "Glad to have you back, Admiral," he said dryly. "Glad to have you back."

The instant he walked off, Ushara burst out laughing.

Jullien scowled at her. "What?"

Pointing at his arm, she fanned herself as she continued to laugh.

Thrāix took one look at it and also laughed, along with Mary. "You've been officially marked now, boy. IRIS."

Jullien looked down and groaned at the sight of the red, black, and gold Tavali Special Forces patch that was reserved for their lunatic brigade they sent out on the most dangerous runs through the deadliest sectors. These were the kind of pilots who made Psycho Bunny and Jupiter appear timid in comparison. Two inverted pyramids, split with a divided skull and flanked with lightning bolts and wings, and topped by a rising sun and an explosion over the IRIS acronym, which stood for *I Require Intense Supervision*.

Trajen also held such a patch from his non-HAP days.

Yeah. Jullien would be offended, if it weren't true.

Ushara sighed. "I guess this means that the day will never come when I can leave you alone and you won't find trouble?"

"Nope. Face it, my love. You're stuck with me."

Ushara would have it no other way.

And as they left the bay, surrounded by loving family, to head for their home, and the party her parents had prepared for his arrival, and Jullien didn't ask about his brother or birth parents, she realized something. . . .

After all these years and all this time, the phantom pain that had lingered behind his stralen eyes was no longer there.

Since the day his grandmother had attempted to kill his brother, Jullien had felt that he'd stolen Nykyrian's life away from him and done his brother irreparable harm. Now that he'd saved Nykyrian's wife and children that Nykyrian needed most to be happy, and returned them to his brother's side, Jullien finally felt that he'd evened the score.

That he could now live in peace, free from the family that had anchored him in misery. Free from the guilt that had flogged him relentlessly.

His ghosts haunted him no more.

# EPILOGUE

Unira smiled as she handed Jullien his infant son. Ever dutiful in their roles, Vasili and Trajen stood by his side for the exordiom.

"What name is he to carry?" Unira asked.

Jullien hesitated. That had been a hard decision for him. Andarion custom dictated that mothers and grandmothers choose the names of daughters, and that fathers chose the names of their sons so as to honor *their* fathers and those they admired. There was no way in Tophet he was going to name his son for his birth father.

And both Gavin and Dimitri carried Petran's name already. However, after much consideration, there was only one name he wanted for what might be the only son he would ever be blessed enough to name. . . .

"Trajen Vidarri."

Ushara's grandfather smiled proudly. Trajen's eyes widened as if he was shocked by the choice.

"And the name he will use?"

"Vidarri."

Unira hesitated before she finished his exordiom—which concerned him. Had he broken some kind of Demurrist custom out of ignorance?

Even Ushara was looking at him strangely as she took the baby from his hands and cuddled him to her shoulder. While they had agreed on the name, they had also decided that Trajen would be his daily name, even though they'd been calling him Vidar between them. But now that it was time to make it permanent, Jullien preferred the Vidarri they'd been using over Trajen. Besides, it would be less confusing.

Why would that be a problem?

It wasn't until temple ended that he found out the answer.

Ushara let out a tired breath. "Vidarri Samari? Really? Was it your goal to have him beaten up in school?"

Jullien slapped his forehead as he realized what he'd unintentionally done to his poor child. "*Shkyte!* I didn't even think of that. In my mind, I always referred to him has Vidar."

"It's all right. I forgive you." She kissed his cheek. "However, your son probably won't. . . . *Ever,*" she breathed teasingly.

But as they entered the banquet hall, Jullien drew up short to find Nykyrian and his family, along with their parents and the entire Sentella High Command there.

Nykyrian handed him an ale. "You didn't really think we'd miss your son's exordiom, did you?"

"I had no idea you knew about it."

Ushara grinned. "I invited them. I hope you don't mind."

"Not at all. Thank you."

Fain and Dancer laughed as they looked at Nykyrian and Jullien standing together.

"You know," Dancer said to his brother. "This is the one thing I never thought I'd live to see . . . the two of you in one room without bloodshed. Damn, we're getting old."

Nykyrian snorted. "I'm not what's aging you." He inclined his head toward Hauk's daughter, who was dancing with Nyk's son Jayce.

"Lea-lea!" Dancer snapped before he went to separate them.

Fain laughed even harder. "Those two are going to get married one day."

"Gah, I hope so. It's the only thing that'll keep that boy out of The League."

Jullien scowled at his brother. "Why do you say that?"

"It's all he talks about. Him and Adron. They terrify me with it."

Jullien narrowed his eyes as he remembered a verse in the *Book of Harmony.* "*Careful what seeds you plant. For the most bitter harvest is the one you could have prevented.*"

Nykyrian lifted his brow. "What's that?"

"An old Trisani saying. . . . Speaking of, has anyone heard from Bastien lately?"

Nyk shook his head. "Not since he went after his family."

Jullien had expected to hear *something* by now. But as each day passed with no word, he began to fear the worst.

"How can you possibly be sad today?" Ushara placed Vidarri in Jullien's hands.

He smiled instantly. "Not sad at all. Just worried about Bastien."

"Shara!" Mary and Ana cried in unison. "Presents!"

She sighed heavily. "Please put him down for his nap for me?"

"Absolutely." He kissed her cheek, then tucked Vidarri against his chest to sleep.

Nykyrian frowned at him. "Is that *down*?"

Trajen snorted as he joined them. "For him, it is. I think the girls were . . . what? Three before you let them sleep in their own beds without supervision?"

"About that age."

An instant later, an alarm went off.

Vidarri woke up as everyone realized The League was attacking one of the Gorturnum's bases.

Ushara rushed to take Vidarri from Jullien. "Stay out of trouble."

"I'll do my best."

She screwed her face up, then looked to Thrāix. "Keep him out of trouble."

"How did I get to be *his* keeper?"

Ushara turned her gaze toward Mary, who then looked at her husband.

Mary kissed him. "Keep Jules out of trouble, Thrāix."

"Yes, ma'am," he said dutifully. Then he glared at Jullien. "I hate you."

With a sad countenance, Vasili sighed as he met Jullien near the door. "I know, Paka. Stay and watch my sisters."

Jullien fisted his hand in his son's white-blond hair and pulled him in for a hug. Then he made the hardest decision of his life.

"Grab your gear."

Vasili gasped. "What?"

"Are you not part of my crew?"

"Yeah . . . I mean, yes, sir!"

"Then grab your gear and haul your ass. We have a battle waiting."

He took off like a jackrabbit.

Tears filled Ushara's eyes as fear wedged in her heart. But she knew Jullien was right. They couldn't hold Vasili at home forever. He was old enough, and it was better he learn under someone who loved him than a callous captain who wouldn't lay his life down to protect him.

This was how life was meant to be. It was scary at times, but you had to trust in the ones you loved to see you through the madness of it.

Jullien winked at her. "Don't worry, Shara. I won't break your heart. You are my Darling star, and no matter how dark the night or how perilous my journey, your divine light alone will always guide me home."